WITHIN A
BUDDING GROVE

WITHIN A
BUDDING GROVE

Marcel Proust

TRANSLATED
FROM THE FRENCH BY
C. K. Scott Moncrieff

Vintage Books
A DIVISION OF RANDOM HOUSE
NEW YORK

TRANSLATOR'S DEDICATION

To

K. S. S.

THAT men in armour may be born
    With serpents' teeth the field is sown;
Rains mould, winds bend, suns gild the corn
    Too quickly ripe, too early mown.

I scan the quivering heads, behold
    The features, catch the whispered breath
Of friends long garnered in the cold
    Unopening granaries of death,

Whose names in solemn cadence ring
    Across my slow oblivious page.
Their friendship was a finer thing
    Than fame, or wealth, or honoured age,

And—while you live and I—shall last
    Its tale of seasons with us yet
Who cherish, in the undying past,
    The men we never can forget.

Bad Kissingen,   C. K. S. M.
    July 31, 1923.

CONTENTS

Part I

Part II

WITHIN A
BUDDING GROVE

PART I

MADAME SWANN AT HOME

My mother, when it was a question of our having M. de Norpois to dinner for the first time, having expressed her regret that Professor Cottard was away from home, and that she herself had quite ceased to see anything of Swann, since either of these might have helped to entertain the old Ambassador, my father replied that so eminent a guest, so distinguished a man of science as Cottard could never be out of place at a dinner-table, but that Swann, with his ostentation, his habit of crying aloud from the house-tops the name of everyone that he knew, however slightly, was an impossible vulgarian whom the Marquis de Norpois would be sure to dismiss as—to use his own epithet—a 'pestilent' fellow. Now, this attitude on my father's part may be felt to require a few words of explanation, inasmuch as some of us, no doubt, remember a Cottard of distinct mediocrity and a Swann by whom modesty and discretion, in all his social relations, were carried to the utmost refinement of delicacy. But in his case, what had happened was that, to the original 'young Swann' and also to the Swann of the Jockey Club, our old friend had added a fresh personality (which was not to be his last), that of Odette's husband. Adapting to the humble ambitions of that lady the instinct, the desire, the industry which he had always had, he had laboriously constructed for himself, a long way beneath the old, a new position more appropriate to the companion who was to share it with him. In this he shewed himself another man. Since (while he continued to go, by himself, to the houses of his own friends, on whom he did not care to inflict Odette unless they had expressly asked that she should be introduced to them) it was a new life that he had begun to lead, in common with his wife, among a new set of people, it was quite intelligible that, in order to estimate the importance of these new friends and thereby the pleasure, the self-esteem that were to be derived from entertaining them, he should have made use, as a standard of comparison, not of the brilliant society in which he himself had moved before his marriage but of the earlier environment of Odette. And yet, even when one knew that it was with unfashionable officials and their faded wives, the wallflowers of ministerial ball-rooms, that he was now anxious

3

to associate, it was still astonishing to hear him, who in the old days, and even still, would so gracefully refrain from mentioning an invitation to Twickenham or to Marlborough House, proclaim with quite unnecessary emphasis that the wife of some Assistant Under-Secretary for Something had returned Mme. Swann's call. It will perhaps be objected here that what this really implied was that the simplicity of the fashionable Swann had been nothing more than a supreme refinement of vanity, and that, like certain other Israelites, my parents' old friend had contrived to illustrate in turn all the stages through which his race had passed, from the crudest and coarsest form of snobbishness up to the highest pitch of good manners. But the chief reason—and one which is applicable to humanity as a whole—was that our virtues themselves are not free and floating qualities over which we retain a permanent control and power of disposal; they come to be so closely linked in our minds with the actions in conjunction with which we make it our duty to practise them, that, if we are suddenly called upon to perform some action of a different order, it takes us by surprise, and without our supposing for a moment that it might involve the bringing of those very same virtues into play. Swann, in his intense consciousness of his new social surroundings, and in the pride with which he referred to them, was like those great artists—modest or generous by nature—who, if at the end of their career they take to cooking or to gardening, display a childlike gratification at the compliments that are paid to their dishes or their borders, and will not listen to any of the criticism which they heard unmoved when it was applied to their real achievements; or who, after giving away a canvas, cannot conceal their annoyance if they lose a couple of francs at dominoes.

As for Professor Cottard, we shall meet him again and can study him at our leisure, much later in the course of our story, with the 'Mistress,' Mme. Verdurin, in her country house La Raspelière. For the present, the following observations must suffice; first of all, in the case of Swann the alteration might indeed be surprising, since it had been accomplished and yet was not suspected by me when I used to see Gilberte's father in the Champs-Elysées, where, moreover, as he never spoke to me, he could not very well have made any display of his political relations. It is true that, if he had done so, I might not at once have discerned his vanity, for the idea that one has long held of a person is apt to stop one's eyes and ears; my mother, for three whole years, had no more noticed the salve with which one of her nieces used to paint her lips than if it had been wholly and invisibly dissolved in some clear liquid; until one day a streak too much, or possibly something else, brought about the phenomenon known as super-saturation; all the paint that had hitherto passed unperceived was now crystallised, and my mother, in the face of this sudden riot of colour, declared, in the best Combray manner, that it was a perfect scandal, and almost severed relations with her niece. With Cottard, on the contrary, the epoch in which we have seen him assisting at the first introduction of Swann to the Verdurins was now buried in the past; whereas honours, offices and titles come with the passage of years; moreover, a man may be illiterate, and make stupid puns, and yet have a special gift, which no amount of general culture can replace—such as the gift of a great strategist or physician. And so it was not merely as an obscure practitioner, who had attained in course of time to European celebrity, that the rest of his profession regarded Cottard. The most intelligent of the younger doctors used to assert—for a year or two, that is to say, for fashions, being themselves begotten of the desire for change, are quick to change also—that if they themselves ever fell ill Cottard was the only one of the leading men to whom they would entrust their lives. No doubt they preferred, socially, to meet certain others who were better read, more artistic, with whom they could discuss Nietzsche and Wagner. When there was a musical party at Mme. Cottard's, on the evenings when she entertained—in the hope that it might one day make him Dean of the Faculty—the colleagues and pupils of her husband, he, instead of listening, preferred to play cards in another room. Yet everybody praised the quickness, the penetration, the unerring confidence with which, at a glance, he could diagnose disease. Thirdly, in considering the general impression which Professor Cottard must have made on a man like my father, we must bear in mind that the character which a man exhibits in the latter half of his life is not always, even if it is often his original character developed or withered, attenuated or enlarged; it is sometimes the exact opposite, like a garment that has been turned. Except from the Verdurins, who were infatuated with him, Cottard's hesitating manner, his excessive timidity and affability had, in his young days, called down upon him endless taunts and sneers. What charitable friend counselled that glacial air? The importance of his professional standing made it all the more easy to adopt. Wherever he went, save at the Verdurins', where he instinctively became himself again, he would assume a repellent coldness, remain silent as long as possible, be peremptory when he was obliged to speak, and not forget to say the most cutting things. He had every opportunity of rehearsing this new attitude before his patients, who, seeing him for the first time, were not in a position to make comparisons, and would have been greatly surprised to learn that he was not at all a rude man by nature. Complete impassivity was what he strove to attain, and even while visiting his hospital wards, when he allowed himself to utter one of those puns which left everyone, from the house physician to the junior student, helpless with laughter, he would always make it without moving a muscle of his face, while even that was no longer recognisable now that he had shaved off his beard and moustache.

But who, the reader has been asking, was the Marquis de Norpois? Well, he had been Minister Plenipotentiary before the War, and was actually an Ambassador on the Sixteenth of May; in spite of which, and to the general astonishment, he had since been several times chosen to represent France on Extraordinary Missions,—even as Controller of the Public Debt in Egypt, where, thanks to his great capability as a financier, he had rendered important services—by Radical Cabinets under which a reactionary of the middle classes would have declined to serve, and in whose eyes M. de Norpois, in view of his past, his connexions and his opinions, ought presumably to have been suspect. But these advanced Ministers seemed to consider that, in making such an appointment, they were shewing how broad their own minds were, when the supreme interests of France were at stake, were raising themselves above the general run of politicians, were meriting, from the *Journal des Débats* itself, the title of 'Statesmen,' and were reaping direct advantage from the weight that attaches to an aristocratic name and the dramatic interest always aroused by an unexpected appointment. And they knew also that they could reap these advantages by making an appeal to M. de Norpois, without having to fear any want of political loyalty on his part, a fault against which his noble birth not only need not put them on their guard but offered a positive guarantee. And in this calculation the Government of the Republic were not mistaken. In the first place, because an aristocrat of a certain type, brought up from his cradle to regard his name as an integral part of himself of which no accident can deprive him (an asset of whose value his peers, or persons of even higher rank, can form a fairly exact estimate), knows that he can dispense with the efforts (since they can in no way enhance his position) in which, without any appreciable result, so many public men of the middle class spend themselves,—to profess only the 'right' opinions, to frequent only the 'sound' people. Anxious, on the other hand, to increase his own importance in the eyes of the princely or ducal families which take immediate precedence of his own, he knows that he can do so by giving his name that complement which hitherto it has lacked, which will give it priority over other names heraldically its equals: such as political power, a literary or an artistic reputation, or a large fortune. And so what he saves by avoiding the society of the ineffective country squires, after whom all the professional families run helter-skelter, but of his intimacy with whom, were he to profess it, a prince would think nothing, he will lavish on the politicians who (free-masons, or worse, though they be) can advance him in Diplomacy or 'back' him in an election, and on the artists or scientists whose patronage can help him to 'arrive' in those departments in which they excel, on everyone, in fact, who is in a position to confer a fresh distinction or to 'bring off' a rich marriage.

But in the character of M. de Norpois there was this predominant feature, that, in the course of a long career of diplomacy, he had become imbued with that negative, methodical, conservative spirit, called 'governmental,' which is common to all Governments and, under every Government, particularly inspires its Foreign Office. He had imbibed, during that career, an aversion, a dread, a contempt for the methods of procedure, more or less revolutionary and in any event quite incorrect, which are those of an Opposition. Save in the case of a few illiterates—high or low, it makes no matter—by whom no difference in quality is perceptible, what attracts men one to another is not a common point of view but a consanguinity of spirit. An Academician of the kind of Legouvé, and therefore an upholder of the classics, would applaud Maxime Ducamp's or Mezière's eulogy of Victor Hugo with more fervour than that of Boileau by Claudel. A common Nationalism suffices to endear Barrès to his electors, who scarcely distinguish between him and M. Georges Berry, but does not endear him to those of his brother Academicians who, with a similar outlook on politics but a different type of mind, will prefer to him even such open adversaries as M. Ribot and M. Deschanel, with whom, in turn, the most loyal Monarchists feel themselves more closely allied than with Maurras or Léon Daudet, although these also are living in the hope of a glorious Restoration. Miserly in the use of words, not only from a professional scruple of prudence and reserve, but because words themselves have more value, present more subtleties of definition to men whose efforts, protracted over a decade, to bring two countries to an understanding, are condensed, translated—in a speech or in a protocol—into a single adjective, colourless in all appearance, but to them pregnant with a world of meaning, M. de Norpois was considered very stiff, at the Commission, where he sat next to my father, whom everyone else congratulated on the astonishing way in which the old Ambassador unbent to him. My father was himself more astonished than anyone. For not being, as a rule, very affable, his company was little sought outside his own intimate circle, a limitation which he used modestly and frankly to avow. He realised that these overtures were an outcome, in the diplomat, of that point of view which everyone adopts for himself in making his choice of friends, from which all a man's intellectual qualities, his refinement, his affection are a far less potent recommendation of him, when at the same time he bores or irritates one, than are the mere straightforwardness and good-humour of another man whom most people would regard as frivolous or even fatuous. "De Norpois has asked me to dinner again; it's quite extraordinary; everyone on the Commission is amazed, as he never has any personal relations with any of us. I am sure he's going to tell me something thrilling, again, about the 'Seventy war." My father knew that M. de Norpois had warned, had perhaps been alone in warning the Emperor of the growing strength and bellicose designs of Prussia, and that Bismarck rated his intelligence most highly. Only the other day, at the Opera, during the gala performance given for King Theodosius, the newspapers had all drawn attention to the long conversation which that Monarch had held with M. de Norpois. "I must ask him whether the King's visit had any real significance," my father went on, for he was keenly interested in foreign politics. "I know old Norpois keeps very close as a rule, but when he's with me he opens out quite charmingly."

As for my mother, perhaps the Ambassador had not the type of mind towards which she felt herself most attracted. I should add that his conversation furnished so exhaustive a glossary of the superannuated forms of speech peculiar to a certain profession, class and period—a period which, for that profession and that class, might be said not to have altogether passed away—that I sometimes regret that I have not kept any literal record simply of the things that I have heard him say. I should thus have obtained an effect of old-fashioned courtesy by the same process and at as little expense as that actor at the Palais-Royal who, when asked where on earth he managed to find his astounding hats, answered, "I do not find my hats. I keep them." In a word, I suppose that my mother considered M. de Norpois a trifle 'out-of-date,' which was by no means a fault in her eyes, so far as manners were concerned, but attracted her less in the region—not, in this instance, of ideas, for those of M. de Norpois were extremely modern—but of idiom. She felt, however, that she was paying a delicate compliment to her husband when she spoke admiringly of the diplomat who had shewn so remarkable a predilection for him. By confirming in my father's mind the good opinion that he already had of M. de Norpois, and so inducing him to form a good opinion of himself also, she knew that she was carrying out that one of her wifely duties which consisted in making life pleasant and comfortable for her husband, just as when she saw to it that his dinner was perfectly cooked and served in silence. And as she was incapable of deceiving my father, she compelled herself to admire the old Ambassador, so as to be able to praise him with sincerity. Incidentally she could naturally, and did, appreciate his kindness, his somewhat antiquated courtesy (so ceremonious that when, as he was walking along the street, his tall figure rigidly erect, he caught sight of my mother driving past, before raising his hat to her he would fling away the cigar that he had just lighted); his conversation, so elaborately circumspect, in which he referred as seldom as possible to himself and always considered what might interest the person to whom he was speaking; his promptness in answering a letter, which was so astonishing that whenever my father, just after posting one himself to M. de Norpois, saw his handwriting upon an envelope, his first thought was always one of annoyance that their letters must, unfortunately, have crossed in the post; which, one was led to suppose, bestowed upon him the special and luxurious privilege of extraordinary deliveries and collections at all hours of the day and night. My mother marvelled at his being so punctilious although so busy, so friendly although so much in demand, never realising that 'although,' with such people, is invariably an unrecognised 'because,' and that (just as old men are always wonderful for their age, and kings extraordinarily simple, and country cousins astonishingly well-informed) it was the same system of habits that enabled M. de Norpois to undertake so many duties and to be so methodical in answering letters, to go everywhere and to be so friendly when he came to us. Moreover she made the mistake which everyone makes who is unduly modest; she rated everything that concerned herself below, and consequently outside the range of, other people's duties and engagements. The letter which it seemed to her so meritorious in my father's friend to have written us promptly, since in the course of the day he must have had ever so many letters to write, she excepted from that great number of letters, of which actually it was a unit; in the same way she did not consider that dining with us was, for M. de Norpois, merely one of the innumerable activities of his social life; she never guessed that the Ambassador had trained himself, long ago, to look upon dining-out as one of his diplomatic functions, and to display, at table, an inveterate charm which it would have been too much to have expected him specially to discard when he came to dine with us.

The evening on which M. de Norpois first appeared at our table, in a year when I still went to play in the Champs-Elysées, has remained fixed in my memory because the afternoon of the same day was that upon which I at last went to hear Berma, at a *matinée*, in *Phèdre*, and also because in talking to M. de Norpois I realised suddenly, and in a new and different way, how completely the feelings aroused in me by all that concerned Gilberte Swann and her parents differed from any that the same family could inspire in anyone else.

It was no doubt the sight of the depression in which I was plunged by the approach of the New Year holidays, in which, as she herself had informed me, I was to see nothing of Gilberte, that prompted my mother one day, in the hope of distracting my mind, to suggest, "If you are still so anxious to hear Berma, I think that your father would allow you perhaps to go; your grandmother can take you."

But it was because M. de Norpois had told him that he ought to let me hear Berma, that it was an experience for a young man to remember in later life, that my father, who had hitherto been so resolutely opposed to my going and wasting my time, with the added risk of my falling ill again, on what he used to shock my grandmother by calling 'futilities,' was now not far from regarding this manner of spending an afternoon as included, in some vague way, in the list of precious formulae for success in a brilliant career. My grandmother, who, in renouncing on my behalf the profit which, according to her, I should have derived from hearing Berma, had made a considerable sacrifice in the interests of my health, was surprised to find that this last had become of no account at a mere word from M. de Norpois. Reposing the unconquerable hopes of her rationalist spirit in the strict course of fresh air and early hours which had been prescribed for me, she now deplored, as something disastrous, this infringement that I was to make of my rules, and in a tone of despair protested, "How easily led you are!" to my father, who replied angrily "What! So it's you that are not for letting him go, now. That is really too much, after your telling us all day and every day that it would be so good for him."

M. de Norpois had also brought about a change in my father's plans in a matter of far greater importance to myself. My father had always meant me to become a diplomat, and I could not endure the thought that, even if I did have to stay for some years, first, at the Ministry, I should run the risk of being sent, later on, as Ambassador, to capitals in which no Gilberte dwelt. I should have preferred to return to the literary career that I had planned for myself, and had been abandoned, years before, in my wanderings along the Guermantes way. But my father had steadily opposed my devoting myself to literature, which he regarded as vastly inferior to diplomacy, refusing even to dignify it with the title of career, until the day when M. de Norpois, who had little love for the more recent generations of diplomatic agents, assured him that it was quite possible, by writing, to attract as much attention, to receive as much consideration, to exercise as much influence, and at the same time to preserve more independence than in the Embassies.

"Well, well, I should never have believed it. Old Norpois doesn't at all disapprove of your idea of taking up writing," my father had reported. And as he had a certain amount of influence himself, he imagined that there was nothing that could not be 'arranged,' no problem for which a

happy solution might not be found in the conversation of people who
'counted.' "I shall bring him back to dinner, one of these days, from the
Commission. You must talk to him a little, and let him see what he thinks
of you. Write something good that you can shew him; he is an intimate
friend of the editor of the *Deux-Mondes;* he will get you in there; he will
arrange it all, the cunning old fox; and, upon my soul, he seems to think
that diplomacy, nowadays—— !"

My happiness in the prospect of not being separated from Gilberte
made me desirous, but not capable, of writing something good which could
be shewn to M. de Norpois. After a few laboured pages, weariness made
the pen drop from my fingers; I cried with anger at the thought that I
should never have any talent, that I was not 'gifted,' that I could not
even take advantage of the chance that M. de Norpois's coming visit was
to offer me of spending the rest of my life in Paris. The recollection that
I was to be taken to hear Berma alone distracted me from my grief. But
just as I did not wish to see any storms except on those coasts where they
raged with most violence, so I should not have cared to hear the great
actress except in one of those classic parts in which Swann had told me
that she touched the sublime. For when it is in the hope of making a priceless discovery that we desire to receive certain impressions from nature or
from works of art, we have certain scruples about allowing our soul to
gather, instead of these, other, inferior, impressions, which are liable to
make us form a false estimate of the value of Beauty. Berma in *Andromaque,* in *Les Caprices de Marianne,* in *Phèdre,* was one of those
famous spectacles which my imagination had so long desired. I should
enjoy the same rapture as on the day when in a gondola I glided to the
foot of the Titian of the Frari or the Carpaccios of San Giorgio dei Schia-
voni, were I ever to hear Berma repeat the lines beginning,

"On dit qu'un prompt départ vous éloigne de nous, Seigneur,——"

I was familiar with them from the simple reproduction in black and white
which was given of them upon the printed page; but my heart beat
furiously at the thought—as of the realisation of a long-planned voyage—
that I should at length behold them, bathed and brought to life in the
atmosphere and sunshine of the voice of gold. A Carpaccio in Venice,
Berma in *Phèdre,* masterpieces of pictorial or dramatic art which the
glamour, the dignity attaching to them made so living to me, that is to
say so indivisible, that if I had been taken to see Carpaccios in one of the
galleries of the Louvre, or Berma in some piece of which I had never heard,
I should not have experienced the same delicious amazement at finding
myself at length, with wide-open eyes, before the unique and inconceivable object of so many thousand dreams. Then, while I waited, expecting
to derive from Berma's playing the revelation of certain aspects of nobility
and tragic grief, it would seem to me that whatever greatness, whatever
truth there might be in her playing must be enhanced if the actress imposed
it upon a work of real value, instead of what would, after all, be but em-
broidering a pattern of truth and beauty upon a commonplace and vulgar
web.

Finally, if I went to hear Berma in a new piece, it would not be easy for me to judge of her art, of her diction, since I should not be able to differentiate between a text which was not already familiar and what she added to it by her intonations and gestures, an addition which would seem to me to be embodied in the play itself; whereas the old plays, the classics which I knew by heart, presented themselves to me as vast and empty walls, reserved and made ready for my inspection, on which I should be able to appreciate without restriction the devices by which Berma would cover them, as with frescoes, with the perpetually fresh treasures of her inspiration. Unfortunately, for some years now, since she had retired from the great theatres, to make the fortune of one on the boulevards where she was the 'star,' she had ceased to appear in classic parts; and in vain did I scan the hoardings; they never advertised any but the newest pieces, written specially for her by authors in fashion at the moment. When, one morning, as I stood searching the column of announcements to find the afternoon performances for the week of the New Year holidays, I saw there for the first time—at the foot of the bill, after some probably insignificant curtain-raiser, whose title was opaque to me because it had latent in it all the details of an action of which I was ignorant—two acts of *Phèdre* with Mme. Berma, and, on the following afternoons, *Le Demi-Monde, Les Caprices de Marianne*, names which, like that of *Phèdre*, were for me transparent, filled with light only, so familiar were those works to me, illuminated to their very depths by the revealing smile of art. They seemed to me to invest with a fresh nobility Mme. Berma herself when I read in the newspapers, after the programme of these performances, that it was she who had decided to shew herself once more to the public in some of her early creations. She was conscious, then, that certain stage-parts have an interest which survives the novelty of their first production or the success of a revival; she regarded them, when interpreted by herself, as museum pieces which it might be instructive to set before the eyes of the generation which had admired her in them long ago, or of that which had never yet seen her in them. In thus advertising, in the middle of a column of plays intended only to while away an evening, this *Phèdre*, a title no longer than any of the rest, nor set in different type, she added something indescribable, as though a hostess, introducing you, before you all go in to dinner, to her other guests, were to mention, casually, amid the string of names which are the names of guests and nothing more, and without any change of tone:—"M. Anatole France."

The doctor who was attending me—the same who had forbidden me to travel—advised my parents not to let me go to the theatre; I should only be ill again afterwards, perhaps for weeks, and should in the long run derive more pain than pleasure from the experience. The fear of this might have availed to stop me, if what I had anticipated from such a spectacle had been only a pleasure for which a subsequent pain could so compensate as to cancel it. But what I demanded from this performance—just as from the visit to Balbec, the visit to Venice for which I had so intensely longed—was something quite different from pleasure; a series of verities pertaining to a world more real than that in which I lived, which,

once acquired, could never be taken from me again by any of the trivial
incidents—even though it were the cause of bodily suffering—of my
otiose existence. At best, the pleasure which I was to feel during the performance appeared to me as the perhaps inevitable form of the perception of these truths; and I hoped only that the illness which had been
forecast for me would not begin until the play was finished, so that my
pleasure should not be in any way compromised or spoiled. I implored my
parents, who, after the doctor's visit, were no longer inclined to let me go
to *Phèdre*. I repeated, all day long, to myself, the speech beginning,

"On dit qu'un prompt départ vous éloigne de nous,——"

seeking out every intonation that could be put into it, so as to be able
better to measure my surprise at the way which Berma would have found
of uttering the lines. Concealed, like the Holy of Holies, beneath the veil
that screened her from my gaze, behind which I invested her, every
moment, with a fresh aspect, according to which of the words of Bergotte—in the pamphlet that Gilberte had found for me—was passing
through my mind; "plastic nobility," "Christian austerity" or "Jansenist
pallor," "Princess of Troezen and of Cleves" or "Mycenean drama,"
"Delphic symbol," "Solar myth"; that divine Beauty, whom Berma's acting was to reveal to me, night and day, upon an altar perpetually illumined,
sat enthroned in the sanctuary of my mind, my mind for which not itself
but my stern, my fickle parents were to decide whether or not it was to
enshrine, and for all time, the perfections of the Deity unveiled, in the
same spot where was now her invisible form. And with my eyes fixed upon
that inconceivable image, I strove from morning to night to overcome the
barriers which my family were putting in my way. But when those had
at last fallen, when my mother—albeit this *matinée* was actually to coincide with the meeting of the Commission from which my father had promised to bring M. de Norpois home to dinner—had said to me, "Very
well, we don't wish you to be unhappy;—if you think that you will enjoy
it so very much, you must go; that's all;" when this day of theatre-going,
hitherto forbidden and unattainable, depended now only upon myself,
then for the first time, being no longer troubled by the wish that it might
cease to be impossible, I asked myself if it were desirable, if there were
not other reasons than my parents' prohibition which should make me
abandon my design. In the first place, whereas I had been detesting them
for their cruelty, their consent made them now so dear to me that the
thought of causing them pain stabbed me also with a pain through which
the purpose of life shewed itself as the pursuit not of truth but of loving-
kindness, and life itself seemed good or evil only as my parents were happy
or sad. "I would rather not go, if it hurts you," I told my mother, who,
on the contrary, strove hard to expel from my mind any lurking fear that
she might regret my going, since that, she said, would spoil the pleasure
that I should otherwise derive from *Phèdre*, and it was the thought of my
pleasure that had induced my father and her to reverse their earlier decision. But then this sort of obligation to find a pleasure in the performance seemed to me very burdensome. Besides, if I returned home ill,

should I be well again in time to be able to go to the Champs-Elysées as soon as the holidays were over and Gilberte returned? Against all these arguments I set, so as to decide which course I should take, the idea, invisible there behind its veil, of the perfections of Berma. I cast into one pan of the scales "Making Mamma unhappy," "risking not being able to go on the Champs-Elysées," and the other, "Jansenist pallor," "Solar myth," until the words themselves grew dark and clouded in my mind's vision, ceased to say anything to me, lost all their force; and gradually my hesitations became so painful that if I had now decided upon the theatre it would have been only that I might bring them to an end, and be delivered from them once and for all. It would have been to fix a term to my sufferings, and no longer in the expectation of an intellectual bene-diction, yielding to the attractions of perfection, that I would let myself be taken, not now to the Wise Goddess, but to the stern, implacable Divinity, featureless and unnamed, who had been secretly substituted for her behind the veil. But suddenly everything was altered. My desire to go and hear Berma received a fresh stimulus which enabled me to await the coming of the *matinée* with impatience and with joy; having gone to take up, in front of the column on which the playbills were, my daily sta-tion, as excruciating, of late, as that of a stylite saint, I had seen there, still moist and wrinkled, the complete bill of *Phèdre,* which had just been pasted up for the first time (and on which, I must confess, the rest of the cast furnished no additional attraction which could help me to decide). But it gave to one of the points between which my indecision wavered a form at once more concrete and—inasmuch as the bill was dated not from the day on which I read it but from that on which the performance would take place, and from the very hour at which the curtain would rise—almost imminent, well on the way, already, to its realisation, so that I jumped for joy before the column at the thought that on that day, and at that hour precisely, I should be sitting there in my place, ready to hear the voice of Berma; and for fear lest my parents might not now be in time to secure two good seats for my grandmother and myself, I raced back to the house, whipped on by the magic words which had now taken the place, in my mind, of "Jansenist pallor" and "Solar myth";—"Ladies will not be admitted to the stalls in hats. The doors will be closed at two o'clock."

Alas! that first *matinée* was to prove a bitter disappointment. My father offered to drop my grandmother and me at the theatre, on his way to the Commission. Before leaving the house he said to my mother: "See that you have a good dinner for us to-night; you remember, I'm bringing de Norpois back with me." My mother had not forgotten. And all that day, and overnight, Françoise, rejoicing in the opportunity to devote herself to that art of the kitchen,—of which she was indeed a past-master, stimu-lated, moreover, by the prospect of having a new guest to feed, the con-sciousness that she would have to compose, by methods known to her alone, a dish of beef in jelly,—had been living in the effervescence of crea-tion; since she attached the utmost importance to the intrinsic quality of the materials which were to enter into the fabric of her work, she had gone herself to the Halles to procure the best cuts of rump-steak, shin of beef, calves'-feet, as Michelangelo passed eight months in the mountains of Carrara choosing the most perfect blocks of marble for the monument of Julius II—Françoise expended on these comings and goings so much ardour that Mamma, at the sight of her flaming cheeks, was alarmed lest our old servant should make herself ill with overwork, like the sculptor of the Tombs of the Medici in the quarries of Pietrasanta. And overnight Françoise had sent to be cooked in the baker's oven, shielded with bread-crumbs, like a block of pink marble packed in sawdust, what she called a "Nev'-York ham." Believing the language to be less rich than it actually was in words, and her own ears less trustworthy, the first time that she heard anyone mention York ham she had thought, no doubt,—feeling it to be hardly conceivable that the dictionary could be so prodigal as to include at once a 'York' and a 'New York'—that she had misheard what was said, and that the ham was really called by the name already familiar to her. And so, ever since, the word York was preceded in her ears, or before her eyes when she read it in an advertisement, by the affix 'New' which she pronounced 'Nev'.' And it was with the most perfect faith that she would say to her kitchen-maid: "Go and fetch me a ham from Olida's. Madame told me especially to get a Nev'-York." On that par-ticular day, if Françoise was consumed by the burning certainty of crea-tive genius, my lot was the cruel anxiety of the seeker after truth. No doubt, so long as I had not yet heard Berma speak, I still felt some pleas-ure. I felt it in the little square that lay in front of the theatre, in which, in two hours' time, the bare boughs of the chestnut trees would gleam with a metallic lustre as the lighted gas-lamps shewed up every detail of their structure; before the attendants in the box-office, the selection of whom, their promotion, all their destiny depended upon the great artist—for she alone held power in the theatre, where ephemeral managers followed one after the other in an obscure succession—who took our tickets without even glancing at us, so preoccupied were they with their anxiety lest any of Mme. Berma's instructions had not been duly transmitted to the new members of the staff, lest it was not clearly, everywhere, understood that the hired applause must never sound for her, that the windows must all be kept open so long as she was not on the stage, and every door closed tight, the moment that she appeared; that a bowl of hot water must be concealed somewhere close to her, to make the dust settle: and, for that matter, at any moment now her carriage, drawn by a pair of horses with flowing manes, would be stopping outside the theatre, she would alight from it muffled in furs, and, crossly acknowledging everyone's salute, would send one of her attendants to find out whether a stage box had been kept for her friends, what the temperature was 'in front,' who were in the other boxes, if the programme sellers were looking smart; theatre and public being to her no more than a second, an outermost cloak which she would put on, and the medium, the more or less 'good' conductor through which her talent would have to pass. I was happy, too, in the theatre itself; since I had made the discovery that—in contradiction of the picture so long entertained by my childish imagination—there was but one stage for everybody, I had supposed that I should be prevented from seeing it properly by the presence of the other spectators, as one is when in the thick of a crowd; now I registered the fact that, on the contrary, thanks to an arrangement which is, so to speak, symbolical of all spectatorship, everyone feels himself to be the centre of the theatre; which explained to me why, when Françoise had been sent once to see some melodrama from the top gallery, she had assured us on her return that her seat had been the best in the house, and that instead of finding herself too far from the stage she had been positively frightened by the mysterious and living proximity of the curtain. My pleasure increased further when I began to distinguish behind the said lowered curtain such confused rappings as one hears through the shell of an egg before the chicken emerges, sounds which speedily grew louder and suddenly, from that world which, impenetrable by our eyes, yet scrutinised us with its own, addressed themselves, and to us indubitably, in the imperious form of three consecutive hammer-blows as moving as any signals from the planet Mars. And—once this curtain had risen,—when on the stage a writing-table and a fireplace, in no way out of the ordinary, had indicated that the persons who were about to enter would be, not actors come to recite, as I had seen them once and heard them at an evening party, but real people, just living their lives at home, on whom I was thus able to spy without their seeing me—my pleasure still endured; it was broken by a momentary uneasiness; just as I was straining my ears in readiness before the piece began, two men entered the theatre from the side of the stage, who must have been very angry with each other, for they were talking so loud that in the auditorium, where there were at least a thousand people, we could hear every word, whereas in quite a small *café* one is obliged to call the waiter and ask what it is that two men, who appear to be quarrelling, are saying; but at that moment, while I sat astonished to find that the audience was listening to them without protest, drowned as it was in a universal silence upon which broke, presently, a laugh here and there, I understood that these insolent fellows were the actors and that the short piece known as the 'curtain-raiser' had now begun. It was followed by an interval so long that the audience, who had returned to their places, grew impatient and began to stamp their feet. I was terrified at this; for just as in the report of a criminal trial, when I read that some noble-minded person was coming, against his own interests, to testify on behalf of an innocent prisoner, I was always afraid that they would not be nice enough to him, would not shew enough gratitude, would not recompense him lavishly, and that he, in disgust, would then range himself on the side of injustice; so now attributing to genius, in this respect, the same qualities as to virtue, I was afraid lest Berma, annoyed by the bad behaviour of so ill-bred an audience—in which, on the other hand, I should have liked her to recognise, with satisfaction, a few celebrities to whose judgment she would be bound to attach importance—should express her discontent and disdain by acting badly. And I gazed appealingly round me at these stamping brutes who were about to shatter, in their insensate rage, the rare and fragile impression which I had come to seek. The last moments of my pleasure were during the opening scenes of *Phèdre*. The heroine herself does not appear in these first scenes of the second act; and yet, as soon as the curtain rose, and another curtain, of red velvet this time, was parted in the middle (a curtain which was used to halve the depth of the stage in all the plays in which the 'star' appeared), an actress entered from the back who had the face and voice which, I had been told, were those of Berma. The cast must therefore have been changed; all the trouble that I had taken in studying the part of the wife of Theseus was wasted. But a second actress now responded to the first. I must, then, have been mistaken in supposing that the first was Berma, for the second even more closely resembled her, and, more than the other, had her diction. Both of them, moreover, enriched their parts with noble gestures—which I could vividly distinguish, and could appreciate in their relation to the text, while they raised and let fall the lovely folds of their tunics—and also with skilful changes of tone, now passionate, now ironical, which made me realise the significance of lines that I had read to myself at home without paying sufficient attention to what they really meant. But all of a sudden, in the cleft of the red curtain that veiled her sanctuary, as in a frame, appeared a woman, and simultaneously with the fear that seized me, far more vexing than Berma's fear could be, lest someone should upset her by opening a window, or drown one of her lines by rustling a programme, or annoy her by applauding the others and by not applauding her enough;—in my own fashion, still more absolute than Berma's, of considering from that moment theatre, audience, play and my own body only as an acoustic medium of no importance, save in the degree to which it was favourable to the inflexions of that voice,—I realised that the two actresses whom I had been for some minutes admiring bore not the least resemblance to her whom I had come to hear. But at the same time all my pleasure had ceased; in vain might I strain towards Berma's eyes, ears, mind, so as not to let one morsel escape me of the reasons which she would furnish for my admiring her, I did not succeed in gathering a single one. I could not even, as I could with her companions, distinguish in her diction and in her playing intelligent intonations, beautiful gestures. I listened to her as though I were reading *Phèdre*, or as though Phaedra herself had at that moment uttered the words that I was hearing, without its appearing that Berma's talent had added anything at all to them. I could have wished, so as to be able to explore them fully, so as to attempt to discover what it was in them that was beautiful, to arrest, to immobilise for a time before my senses every intonation of the artist's voice, every expression of her features; at least I did attempt, by dint of my mental agility in having, before a line came, my attention ready and tuned to catch it, not to waste upon preparations any morsel of the precious time that each word, each gesture occupied, and, thanks to the intensity of my observation, to manage to penetrate as far into them as if I had had whole hours to spend upon them, by myself. But how short their duration was! Scarcely had a sound been received by my ear than it was displaced there by another. In one scene, where Berma stands motionless for a moment, her arm raised to the level of a face bathed, by some piece of stagecraft, in a greenish light, before a back-cloth painted to represent the sea, the whole house broke out in applause; but already the actress had moved, and the picture that I should have liked to study existed no longer. I told my grandmother that I could not see very well; she handed me her glasses. Only, when one believes in the reality of a thing, making it visible by artificial means is not quite the same as feeling that it is close at hand. I thought now that it was no longer Berma at whom I was looking, but her image in a magnifying glass. I put the glasses down, but then possibly the image that my eye received of her, diminished by distance, was no more exact; which of the two Bermas was the real? As for her speech to Hippolyte, I had counted enormously upon that, since, to judge by the ingenious significance which her companions were disclosing to me at every moment in less beautiful parts, she would certainly render it with intonations more surprising than any which, when reading the play at home, I had contrived to imagine; but she did not attain to the heights which Œnone or Aricie would naturally have reached, she planed down into a uniform flow of melody the whole of a passage in which there were mingled together contradictions so striking that the least intelligent of tragic actresses, even the pupils of an academy, could not have missed their effect; besides which, she ran through the speech so rapidly that it was only when she had come to the last line that my mind became aware of the deliberate monotony which she had imposed on it throughout.

Then, at last, a sense of admiration did possess me, provoked by the frenzied applause of the audience. I mingled my own with theirs, endeavouring to prolong the general sound so that Berma, in her gratitude, should surpass herself, and I be certain of having heard her on one of her great days. A curious thing, by the way, was that the moment when this storm of public enthusiasm broke loose was, as I afterwards learned, that in which Berma reveals one of her richest treasures. It would appear that certain transcendent realities emit all around them a radiance to which the crowd is sensitive. So it is that when any great event occurs, when on a distant frontier an army is in jeopardy, or defeated, or victorious, the vague and conflicting reports which we receive, from which an educated man can derive little enlightenment, stimulate in the crowd an emotion by which that man is surprised, and in which, once expert criticism has informed him of the actual military situation, he recognises the popular perception of that 'aura' which surrounds momentous happenings, and which may be visible hundreds of miles away. One learns of a victory either after the war is over, or at once, from the hilarious joy of one's hall porter. One discovers the touch of genius in Berma's acting a week after one has heard her, in the criticism of some review, or else on the spot, from the thundering acclamation of the stalls. But this immediate recognition by the crowd was mingled with a hundred others, all quite erroneous; the applause came, most often, at wrong moments, apart from the fact that it was mechanically produced by the effect of the applause that had gone before, just as in a storm, once the sea is sufficiently disturbed, it will continue to swell, even after the wind has begun to subside. No matter; the more I applauded, the better, it seemed to me, did Berma act. "I say," came from a woman sitting near me, of no great social pretensions, "she fairly gives it you, she does; you'd think she'd do herself an injury, the way she runs about. I call that acting, don't you?" And happy to find these reasons for Berma's superiority, though not without a suspicion that they no more accounted for it than would for that of the Gioconda or of Benvenuto's Perseus a peasant's gaping "That's a good bit of work. It's all gold, look! Fine, ain't it?", I greedily imbibed the strong wine of this popular enthusiasm. I felt, all the same, when the curtain had fallen for the last time, disappointed that the pleasure for which I had so longed had been no greater, but at the same time I felt the need to prolong it, not to depart for ever, when I left the theatre, from this strange life of the stage which had, for a few hours, been my own, from which I should be tearing myself away, as though I were going into exile, when I returned to my own home, had I not hoped there to learn a great deal more about Berma from her admirer, to whom I was indebted already for the permission to go to *Phèdre*, M. de Norpois. I was introduced to him before dinner by my father, who summoned me into his study for the purpose. As I entered, the Ambassador rose, held out his hand, bowed his tall figure and fixed his blue eyes attentively on my face. As the foreign visitors who used to be presented to him, in the days when he still represented France abroad, were all more or less (even the famous singers) persons of note, with regard to whom he could tell, when he met them, that he would be able to say, later on, when he heard their names mentioned in Paris or in Petersburg, that he remembered perfectly the evening he had spent with them at Munich or Sofia, he had formed the habit of impressing upon them, by his affability, the pleasure with which he was making their acquaintance; but in addition to this, being convinced that in the life of European capitals, in contact at once with all the interesting personalities that passed through them and with the manners and customs of the native populations, one acquired a deeper insight than could be gained from books into the intellectual movement throughout Europe, he would exercise upon each newcomer his keen power of observation, so as to decide at once with what manner of man he had to deal. The Government had not for some time now entrusted to him a post abroad, but still, as soon as anyone was introduced to him, his eyes, as though they had not yet been informed of their master's retirement, began their fruitful observation, while by his whole attitude he endeavoured to convey that the stranger's name was not unknown to him. And so, all the time, while he spoke to me kindly and with the air of importance of a man who is conscious of the vastness of his own experience, he never ceased to examine me with a sagacious curiosity, and to his own profit, as though I had been some exotic custom, some historic and instructive building or some 'star' upon his course. And in this way he gave proof at once, in his attitude towards me, of the majestic benevolence of the sage Mentor and of the zealous curiosity of the young Anacharsis.

He offered me absolutely no opening to the *Revue des Deux-Mondes,* but put a number of questions to me on what I had been doing and reading; asked what were my own inclinations, which I heard thus spoken of for the first time as though it might be a quite reasonable thing to obey their promptings, whereas hitherto I had always supposed it to be my duty to

suppress them. Since they attracted me towards Literature, he did not dissuade me from that course; on the contrary, he spoke of it with deference,
as of some venerable personage whose select circle, in Rome or at Dresden,
one remembers with pleasure, and regrets only that one's multifarious
duties in life enable one to revisit it so seldom. He appeared to be envying
me, with an almost jovial smile, the delightful hours which, more fortunate
than himself and more free, I should be able to spend with such a Mistress.
But the very terms that he employed shewed me Literature as something
entirely different from the image that I had formed of it at Combray, and
I realised that I had been doubly right in abandoning my intention. Until
now, I had reckoned only that I had not the 'gift' for writing; now
M. de Norpois took from me the ambition also. I wanted to express to him
what had been my dreams; trembling with emotion, I was painfully appre-
hensive that all the words which I could utter would not be the sincerest
possible equivalent of what I had felt, what I had never yet attempted
to formulate; that is to say that my words had no clear significance. Perhaps by a professional habit, perhaps by virtue of the calm that is acquired
by every important personage whose advice is commonly sought, and who,
knowing that he will keep the control of the conversation in his own hands,
allows the other party to fret, to struggle, to take his time; perhaps also
to emphasize the dignity of his head (Greek, according to himself, despite
his sweeping whiskers), M. de Norpois, while anything was being explained to him, would preserve a facial immobility as absolute as if you
had been addressing some ancient and unhearing bust in a museum. Until
suddenly, falling upon you like an auctioneer's hammer, or a Delphic
oracle, the Ambassador's voice, as he replied to you, would be all the more
impressive, in that nothing in his face had allowed you to guess what sort
of impression you had made on him, or what opinion he was about to
express.

"Precisely;" he suddenly began, as though the case were now heard and
judged, and after allowing me to writhe in increasing helplessness beneath
those motionless eyes which never for an instant left my face. "There is
the case of the son of one of my friends, which, *mutatis mutandis*, is very
much like yours." He adopted in speaking of our common tendency the
same reassuring tone as if it had been a tendency not to literature but to
rheumatics, and he had wished to assure me that it would not necessarily
prove fatal. "He too has chosen to leave the Quai d'Orsay, although the
way had been paved for him there by his father, and without caring what
people might say, he has settled down to write. And certainly, he's had no
reason to regret it. He published two years ago—of course, he's much
older than you, you understand—a book dealing with the Sense of the
Infinite on the Western Shore of Victoria Nyanza, and this year he has
brought out a little thing, not so important as the other, but very brightly,
in places perhaps almost too pointedly written, on the Repeating Rifle in
the Bulgarian Army; and these have put him quite in a class by himself.
He's gone pretty far already, and he's not the sort of man to stop half way;
I happen to know that (without any suggestion, of course, of his standing
for election) his name has been mentioned several times, in conversation,

and not at all unfavourably, at the Academy of Moral Sciences. And so, one can't say yet, of course, that he has reached the pinnacle of fame, still he has made his way, by sheer industry, to a very fine position indeed, and success—which doesn't always come only to agitators and mischief-makers and men who make trouble which is usually more than they are prepared to take—success has crowned his efforts."

My father, seeing me already, in a few years' time, an Academician, was tasting a contentment which M. de Norpois raised to the supreme pitch when, after a momentary hesitation in which he appeared to be calculating the possible consequences of so rash an act, he handed me his card and said: "Why not go and see him yourself? Tell him I sent you. He may be able to give you some good advice," plunging me by his words into as painful a state of anxiety as if he had told me that, next morning, I was to embark as cabin-boy on board a sailing ship, and to go round the world.

My Aunt Léonie had bequeathed to me, together with all sorts of other things and much of her furniture, with which it was difficult to know what to do, almost all her unsettled estate—revealing thus after her death an affection for me which I had hardly suspected in her lifetime. My father, who was trustee of this estate until I came of age, now consulted M. de Norpois with regard to several of the investments. He recommended certain stocks bearing a low rate of interest, which he considered particularly sound, notably English consols and Russian four per cents. "With absolutely first class securities such as those," said M. de Norpois, "even if your income from them is nothing very great, you may be certain of never losing any of your capital." My father then told him, roughly, what else he had bought. M. de Norpois gave a just perceptible smile of congratulation; like all capitalists, he regarded wealth as an enviable thing, but thought it more delicate to compliment people upon their possessions only by a half-indicated sign of intelligent sympathy; on the other hand, as he was himself immensely rich, he felt that he shewed his good taste by seeming to regard as considerable the meagre revenues of his friends, with a happy and comforting resilience to the superiority of his own. He made amends for this by congratulating my father, without hesitation, on the "composition" of his list of investments, selected "with so sure, so delicate, so fine a taste." You would have supposed, to hear him, that he attributed to the relative values of investments, and even to investments themselves, something akin to aesthetic merit. Of one, comparatively recent and still little known, which my father mentioned, M. de Norpois, like the people who have always read the books of which, you imagine, you yourself alone have ever heard, said at once, "Ah, yes, I used to amuse myself for some time with watching it in the papers; it was quite interesting," with the retrospective smile of a regular subscriber who has read the latest novel already, in monthly instalments, in his magazine. "It would not be at all a bad idea to apply for some of this new issue. It is distinctly attractive; they are offering it at a most tempting discount." But when he came to some of the older investments, my father, who could not remember their exact names, which it was easy to confuse with others of the same kind, opened a drawer and shewed the securities themselves to the Ambassador. The sight of them enchanted me. They were ornamented with cathedral spires and allegorical figures, like the old, romantic editions that I had pored over as a child. All the products of one period have something in common; the artists who illustrate the poetry of their generation are the same artists who are employed by the big financial houses. And nothing reminds me so much of the monthly parts of *Notre-Dame de Paris,* and of various books by Gérard de Nerval, that used to hang outside the grocer's door at Combray, than does, in its rectangular and flowery border, supported by recumbent river-gods, a 'personal share' in the Water Company.

The contempt which my father had for my kind of intelligence was so far tempered by his natural affection for me that, in practice, his attitude towards anything that I might do was one of blind indulgence. And so he had no qualm about telling me to fetch a little 'prose poem' which I had made up, years before, at Combray, while coming home from a walk. I had written it down in a state of exaltation which must, I felt certain, infect everyone who read it. But it was not destined to captivate M. de Norpois, for he handed it back to me without a word.

My mother, who had the most profound respect for all my father's occupations, came in now, timidly, to ask whether dinner might be served. She was afraid to interrupt a conversation in which she herself could have no part. And indeed my father was continually reminding the Marquis of some useful suggestion which they had decided to make at the next meeting of the Commission; speaking in the peculiar tone always adopted, when in a strange environment by a pair of colleagues—as exclusive, in this respect, as two young men from the same college—whose professional routine has furnished them with a common fund of memories to which the others present have no access, and to which they are unwilling to refer before an audience.

But the absolute control over his facial muscles to which M. de Norpois had attained allowed him to listen without seeming to hear a word. At last my father became uneasy. "I had thought," he ventured, after an endless preamble, "of asking the advice of the Commission . . ." Then from the face of the noble virtuoso, who had been sitting inert as a player in an orchestra sits until the moment comes for him to begin his part, were uttered, with an even delivery, on a sharp note, and as though they were no more than the completion (but scored for a different voice) of the phrase that my father had begun, the words: "of which you will not hesitate, of course, to call a meeting; more especially as the present members are all known to you personally, and there may be a change any day." This was not in itself a very remarkable ending. But the immobility that had preceded it made it detach itself with the crystal clarity, the almost malicious unexpectedness of those phrases in which the piano, silent until then, 'takes up,' at a given moment, the violoncello to which one has just been listening, in a Mozart concerto.

"Well, did you enjoy your *matinée?*" asked my father, as we moved to the dining-room; meaning me to 'shew off,' and with the idea that my enthusiasm would give M. de Norpois a good opinion of me. "He has just been to hear Berma. You remember, we were talking about it the other day," he went on, turning towards the diplomat, in the same tone of retro-spective, technical, mysterious allusiveness as if he had been referring to a meeting of the Commission.

"You must have been enchanted, especially if you had never heard her before. Your father was alarmed at the effect that the little jaunt might have upon your health, which is none too good, I am told, none too robust. But I soon set his mind at rest. Theatres to-day are not what they were even twenty years ago. You have more or less comfortable seats now, and a certain amount of ventilation, although we have still a long way to go before we come up to Germany or England, which in that respect as in many others are immeasurably ahead of us. I have never seen Mme. Berma in *Phèdre,* but I have always heard that she is excellent in the part. You were charmed with her, of course?"

M. de Norpois, a man a thousand times more intelligent than myself, must know that hidden truth which I had failed to extract from Berma's playing; he knew, and would reveal it to me; in answering his question I would implore him to let me know in what that truth consisted; and he would tell me, and so justify me in the longing that I had felt to see and hear the actress. I had only a moment, I must make what use I could of it and bring my cross-examination to bear upon the essential points. But what were they? Fastening my whole attention upon my own so confused impressions, with no thought of making M. de Norpois admire me, but only that of learning from him the truth that I had still to discover, I made no attempt to substitute ready-made phrases for the words that failed me— I stood there stammering, until finally, in the hope of provoking him into declaring what there was in Berma that was admirable, I confessed that I had been disappointed.

"What's that?" cried my father, annoyed at the bad impression which this admission of my failure to appreciate the performance must make on M. de Norpois, "What on earth do you mean; you didn't enjoy it? Why, your grandmother has been telling us that you sat there hanging on every word that Berma uttered, with your eyes starting out of your head; that everyone else in the theatre seemed quite bored, beside you."

"Oh, yes, I was listening as hard as I could, trying to find out what it was that was supposed to be so wonderful about her. Of course, she's frightfully good, and all that . . ."

"If she is 'frightfully good,' what more do you want?"

"One of the things that have undoubtedly contributed to the success of Mme. Berma," resumed M. de Norpois, turning with elaborate courtesy towards my mother, so as not to let her be left out of the conversation, and in conscientious fulfilment of his duty of politeness to the lady of the house, "is the perfect taste that she shews in selecting her parts; thus she can always be assured of success, and success of the right sort. She hardly ever appears in anything trivial. Look how she has thrown herself into the part of Phèdre. And then, she brings the same good taste to the choice of her costumes, and to her acting. In spite of her frequent and lucrative tours in England and America, the vulgarity—I will not say of John Bull; that would be unjust, at any rate to the England of the Victorian era—but of Uncle Sam has not infected her. No loud colours, no rant. And then that admirable voice, which has been of such service to her, with which she plays so delightfully—I should almost be tempted to describe it as a musical instrument!"

My interest in Berma's acting had continued to grow ever since the fall of the curtain, because it was then no longer compressed within the limits of reality; but I felt the need to find explanations for it; moreover it had been fixed with the same intensity, while Berma was on the stage, upon everything that she offered, in the indivisibility of a living whole, to my eyes and ears; there was nothing separate or distinct; it welcomed, accordingly, the discovery of a reasonable cause in these tributes paid to the simplicity, to the good taste of the actress, it attracted them to itself by its power of absorption, seized hold of them, as the optimism of a drunken man seizes hold of the actions of his neighbour, in each of which he finds an excuse for emotion. "He is right!" I told myself. "What a charming voice, what an absence of shrillness, what simple costumes, what intelligence to have chosen *Phèdre*. No; I have not been disappointed!"

The cold beef, spiced with carrots, made its appearance, couched by the Michelangelo of our kitchen upon enormous crystals of jelly, like transparent blocks of quartz.

"You have a chef of the first order, Madame," said M. de Norpois, "and that is no small matter. I myself, who have had, when abroad, to maintain a certain style in housekeeping, I know how difficult it often is to find a perfect master-cook. But this is a positive banquet that you have set before us!"

And indeed Françoise, in the excitement of her ambition to make a success, for so distinguished a guest, of a dinner the preparation of which had been obstructed by difficulties worthy of her powers, had given herself such trouble as she no longer took when we were alone, and had recaptured her incomparable Combray manner.

"That is a thing you can't get in a chophouse,—in the best of them, I mean; a spiced beef in which the jelly does not taste of glue and the beef has caught the flavour of the carrots; it is admirable! Allow me to come again," he went on, making a sign to shew that he wanted more of the jelly. "I should be interested to see how your Vatel managed a dish of quite a different kind; I should like, for instance, to see him tackle a *bœuf Stroganoff*."

M. de Norpois, so as to add his own contribution to the gaiety of the repast, entertained us with a number of the stories with which he was in the habit of regaling his colleagues in "the career," quoting now some ludicrous sentence uttered by a politician, an old offender, whose sentences were always long and packed with incoherent images, now some monumental epigram of a diplomat, sparkling with attic salt. But, to tell the truth, the criterion which for him set apart these two kinds of phrase in no way resembled that which I was in the habit of applying to literature. Most of the finer shades escaped me; the words which he repeated with derision seemed to me not to differ very greatly from those which he found remarkable. He belonged to the class of men who, had we come to discuss the books that I liked, would have said: "So you understand that, do you? I must confess that I do not understand, I am not initiated;" but I could have matched his attitude, for I did not grasp the wit or folly, the eloquence or pomposity which he found in a statement or a speech, and the absence of any perceptible reason for one's being badly and the other's well expressed made that sort of literature seem more mysterious, more obscure to me than any other. I could distinguish only that to repeat what everybody else was thinking was, in politics, the mark not of an inferior but of a superior mind. When M. de Norpois made use of certain expressions which were 'common form' in the newspapers, and uttered them with emphasis, one felt that they became an official pronouncement by the mere fact of his having employed them, and a pronouncement which would provoke a string of comment.

My mother was counting greatly upon the pineapple and truffle salad. But the Ambassador, after fastening for a moment on the confection the penetrating gaze of a trained observer, ate it with the inscrutable discretion of a diplomat, and without disclosing to us what he thought of it. My mother insisted upon his taking some more, which he did, but saying only, in place of the compliment for which she was hoping: "I obey, Madame, for I can see that it is, on your part, a positive ukase!"

"We saw in the 'papers that you had a long talk with King Theodosius," my father ventured.

"Why, yes; the King, who has a wonderful memory for faces, was kind enough to remember, when he noticed me in the stalls, that I had had the honour to meet him on several occasions at the Court of Bavaria, at a time when he had never dreamed of his oriental throne—to which, as you know, he was summoned by a European Congress, and indeed had grave doubts about accepting the invitation, regarding that particular sovereignty as unworthy of his race, the noblest, heraldically speaking, in the whole of Europe. An aide-de-camp came down to bid me pay my respects to his Majesty, whose command I hastened, naturally, to obey."

"And I trust, you are satisfied with the results of his visit?"

"Enchanted! One was justified in feeling some apprehension as to the manner in which a Sovereign who is still so young would handle a situation requiring tact, particularly at this highly delicate juncture. For my own part, I reposed entire confidence in the King's political sense. But I must confess that he far surpassed my expectations. The speech that he made at the Elysée, which, according to information that has come to me from a most authoritative source, was composed, from beginning to end, by himself, was fully deserving of the interest that it has aroused in all quarters. It was simply masterly; a trifle daring, I quite admit, but with an audacity which, after all, has been fully justified by the event. Traditional diplomacy is all very well in its way, but in practice it has made his country and ours live in an hermetically sealed atmosphere in which it was no longer possible to breathe. Very well! There is one method of letting in fresh air, obviously not one of the methods which one could officially recommend, but one which King Theodosius might allow himself to adopt —and that is to break the windows. Which he accordingly did, with a spontaneous good humour that delighted everybody, and also with an aptness in his choice of words in which one could at once detect the race of scholarly princes from whom he is descended through his mother. There can be no question that when he spoke of the 'affinities' that bound his country to France, the expression, rarely as it may occur in the vocabulary of the Chancelleries, was a singularly happy one. You see that literary ability is no drawback, even in diplomacy, even upon a throne," he went on, turning for a moment to myself. "The community of interests had long been apparent, I quite admit, and the relations of the two Powers were excellent. Still, it needed putting into words. The word was what we were all waiting for, it was chosen with marvellous aptitude; you have seen the effect it had. For my part, I must confess I applauded openly."

"Your friend M. de Vaugoubert will be pleased, after preparing for the agreement all these years."

"All the more so that his Majesty, who is quite incorrigible, really, in some ways, had taken care to spring it on him as a surprise. And it did come as a complete surprise, incidentally, to everyone concerned, beginning with the Foreign Minister himself, who—I have heard—did not find it at all to his liking. It appears that someone spoke to him about it and that he replied, pretty sharply, and loud enough to be overheard by the people on either side of them: 'I have been neither consulted nor informed!' indicating clearly by that that he declined to accept any responsibility for the consequences. I must own that the incident has given rise to a great deal of comment, and I should not go so far as to deny," he went on with a malicious smile, "that certain of my colleagues, for whom the supreme law appears to be that of inertia, may have been shaken from their habitual repose. As for Vaugoubert, you are aware that he has been bitterly attacked for his policy of bringing that country into closer relations with France, which must have been more than ordinarily painful to him, he is so sensitive, such an exquisite nature. I can amply testify to that, since, for all that he is considerably my junior, I have had many dealings with him, we are friends of long standing and I know him intimately. Besides, who could help knowing him? His is a heart of crystal. Indeed, that is the one fault that there is to be found with him; it is not necessary for the heart of a diplomat to be as transparent as all that. Still, that does not prevent their talking of sending him to Rome, which would be a fine rise for him, but a pretty big plum to swallow. Between ourselves, I fancy that Vaugoubert, utterly devoid of ambition as he is, would be very well pleased, and would by no means ask for that cup to pass from him. For all we know, he may do wonders down there; he is the chosen candidate of the Consulta, and for my part I can see him very well placed, with his artistic leanings, in the setting of the Farnese Palace and the Caracci Gallery. At least you would suppose that it was impossible for any one to hate him; but there is a whole camarilla collected round King Theodosius which is more or less held in fief by the Wilhelmstrasse, whose inspiration its members dutifully absorb, and these men have done everything in their power to checkmate him. Not only has Vaugoubert had to face these backstairs intrigues, he has had to endure also the insults of a gang of hireling pamphleteers who later on, being like every subsidised journalist the most arrant cowards, have been the first to cry quits, but in the interval had not shrunk from hurling at our Representative the most fatuous accusations that the wit of irresponsible fools could invent. For a month and more Vaugoubert's enemies had been dancing round him, howling for his scalp," M. de Norpois detached this word with sharp emphasis. "But forewarned is forearmed; as for their insults, he spurned them with his foot!" he went on with even more determination, and with so fierce a glare in his eye that for a moment we forgot our food. "In the words of a fine Arab proverb, 'The dogs may bark; the caravan goes on!' "

After launching this quotation M. de Norpois paused and examined our faces, to see what effect it had had upon us. Its effect was great, the proverb being familiar to us already. It had taken the place, that year, among people who 'really counted,' of "He who sows the wind shall reap the whirlwind," which was sorely in need of a rest, not having the perennial freshness of "Working for the King of Prussia." For the culture of these eminent men was an alternate, if not a tripartite and triennial culture. Of course, the use of quotations such as these, with which M. de Norpois excelled in jewelling his articles in the *Revue,* was in no way essential to their appearing solid and well-informed. Even without the ornament which the quotations supplied, it sufficed that M. de Norpois should write at a given point (as he never failed to write): "The Court of St. James's was not the last to be sensible of the peril," or "Feeling ran high on the Singers' Bridge, which with anxious eyes was following the selfish but skilful policy of the Dual Monarchy," or "A cry of alarm sounded from Montecitorio," or yet again, "That everlasting double-dealing which is so characteristic of the Ballplatz." By these expressions the profane reader had at once recognised and had paid deference to the diplomat *de carrière.* But what had made people say that he was something more than that, that he was endowed with a superior culture, had been his careful use of quotations, the perfect example of which, at that date, was still: "Give me a good policy and I will give you good finances, *to quote the favourite words of Baron Louis*": for we had not yet imported from the Far East: "Victory is on the side that can hold out a quarter of an hour longer than the other, *as the Japanese say.*" This reputation for immense literary gifts, combined with a positive genius for intrigue which he kept concealed beneath a mask of indifference, had secured the election of M. de Norpois to the Académie des Sciences Morales. And there were some who even thought that he would not be out of place in the Académie Française, on the famous day when, wishing to indicate that it was only by drawing the Russian Alliance closer that we could hope to arrive at an understanding with Great Britain, he had not hesitated to write: "Be it clearly understood in the Quai d'Orsay, be it taught henceforward in all the manuals of geography, which appear to be incomplete in this respect, be his certificate of graduation remorselessly withheld from every candidate who has not learned to say, 'If all roads lead to Rome, nevertheless the way from Paris to London runs of necessity through St. Petersburg.'"

"In short," M. de Norpois went on, addressing my father, "Vaugoubert has won himself considerable distinction from this affair, quite beyond anything on which he can have reckoned. He expected, you understand, a correctly worded speech (which, after the storm-clouds of recent years, would have been something to the good) but nothing more. Several persons who had the honour to be present have assured me that it is impossible, when one merely reads the speech, to form any conception of the effect that it produced when uttered—when articulated with marvellous clearness of diction by the King, who is a master of the art of public speaking and in that passage underlined every possible shade of meaning. I allowed myself, in this connexion, to listen to a little anecdote which brings into prominence once again that frank, boyish charm by which King Theodosius has won so many hearts. I am assured that, just as he uttered that word 'affinities,' which was, of course, the startling innovation of the speech, and one that, as you will see, will provoke discussion in the Chancellories for years to come, his Majesty, anticipating the delight of our Ambassador, who was to find in that word the seal, the crown set upon all his labours, on his dreams, one might almost say, and, in a word, his marshal's baton, made a half turn towards Vaugoubert and fixing upon him his arresting gaze, so characteristic of the Oettingens, fired at him that admirably chosen word 'affinities,' a positive treasure-trove, uttering it in a tone which made it plain to all his hearers that it was employed of set purpose and with full knowledge of the circumstances. It appears that Vaugoubert found some difficulty in mastering his emotion, and I must confess that, to a certain extent, I can well understand it. Indeed, a person who is entirely to be believed has told me, in confidence, that the King came up to Vaugoubert after the dinner, when His Majesty was holding an informal court, and was heard to say, 'Well, are you satisfied with your pupil, my dear Marquis?'

"One thing, however," M. de Norpois concluded, "is certain; and that is that a speech like that has done more than twenty years of negotiation towards bringing the two countries together, uniting their 'affinities,' to borrow the picturesque expression of Theodosius II. It is no more than a word, if you like, but look what success it has had, how the whole of the European press is repeating it, what interest it has aroused, what a new note it has struck. Besides it is distinctly in the young Sovereign's manner. I will not go so far as to say that he lights upon a diamond of that water every day. But it is very seldom that, in his prepared speeches, or better still in the impulsive flow of his conversation, he does not reveal his character—I was on the point of saying 'does not affix his signature'— by the use of some incisive word. I myself am quite free from any suspicion of partiality in this respect, for I am stoutly opposed to all innovations in terminology. Nine times out of ten they are most dangerous."

"Yes, I was thinking, only the other day, that the German Emperor's telegram could not be much to your liking," said my father.

M. de Norpois raised his eyes to heaven, as who should say, "Oh, that fellow!" before he replied: "In the first place, it is an act of ingratitude. It is more than a crime; it is a blunder, and one of a crassness which I can describe only as pyramidal! Indeed, unless some one puts a check on his activities, the man who has got rid of Bismarck is quite capable of repudiating by degrees the whole of the Bismarckian policy; after which it will be a leap in the dark."

"My husband tells me, sir, that you are perhaps going to take him to Spain one summer; that will be nice for him; I am so glad."

"Why, yes; it is an idea that greatly attracts me; I amuse myself, planning a tour. I should like to go there with you, my dear fellow. But what about you, Madame; have you decided yet how you are going to spend your holidays?"

"I shall perhaps go with my son to Balbec, but I am not certain."

"Oh, but Balbec is quite charming, I was down that way a few years ago. They are beginning to build some very pretty little villas there; I think you'll like the place. But may I ask what has made you choose Balbec?"

"My son is very anxious to visit some of the churches in that neighbourhood, and Balbec church in particular. I was a little afraid that the tiring journey there, and the discomfort of staying in the place might be too much for him. But I hear that they have just opened an excellent hotel, in which he will be able to get all the comfort that he requires."

"Indeed! I must make a note of that, for a certain person who will not turn up her nose at a comfortable hotel."

"The church at Balbec is very beautiful, sir, is it not?" I inquired, repressing my sorrow at learning that one of the attractions of Balbec consisted in its pretty little villas.

"No, it is not bad; but it cannot be compared for a moment with such positive jewels in stone as the Cathedrals of Rheims and Chartres, or with what is to my mind the pearl among them all, the Sainte-Chapelle here in Paris."

"But, surely, Balbec church is partly romanesque, is it not?"

"Why, yes, it is in the romanesque style, which is to say very cold and lifeless, with no hint in it anywhere of the grace, the fantasy of the later gothic builders, who worked their stone as if it had been so much lace. Balbec church is well worth a visit, if you are in those parts; it is decidedly quaint; on a wet day, when you have nothing better to do, you might look inside; you will see the tomb of Tourville."

"Tell me, were you at the Foreign Ministry dinner last night?" asked my father. "I couldn't go."

"No," M. de Norpois smiled, "I must confess that I renounced it for a party of a very different sort. I was dining with a lady whose name you may possibly have heard, the beautiful Mme. Swann." My mother checked an impulsive movement, for, being more rapid in perception than my father, she used to alarm herself on his account over things which only began to upset him a moment later. Anything unpleasant that might occur to him was discovered first by her, just as bad news from France is always known abroad sooner than among ourselves. But she was curious to know what sort of people the Swanns managed to entertain, and so inquired of M. de Norpois as to whom he had met there.

"Why, my dear lady, it is a house which (or so it struck me) is especially attractive to gentlemen. There were several married men there last night, but their wives were all, as it happened, unwell, and so had not come with them," replied the Ambassador with a mordancy sheathed in good-humour, casting on each of us a glance the gentleness and discretion of which appeared to be tempering while in reality they deftly intensified its malice.

"In all fairness," he went on, "I must add that women do go to the house, but women who belong rather—what shall I say—to the Republican world than to Swann's" (he pronounced it "Svann's") "circle. Still, you can never tell. Perhaps it will turn into a political or a literary salon some day. Anyhow, they appear to be quite happy as they are. Indeed, I feel that Swann advertises his happiness just a trifle too blatantly. He told us the names of all the people who had asked him and his wife out for the next week, people with whom there was no particular reason to be proud of being intimate, with a want of reserve, of taste, almost of tact which I was astonished to remark in so refined a man. He kept on repeating, 'We haven't a free evening!' as though that had been a thing to boast of, positively like a *parvenu*, and he is certainly not that. For Swann had always plenty of friends, women as well as men, and without seeming over-bold, without the least wish to appear indiscreet, I think I may safely say that not all of them, of course, nor even the majority of them, but one at least, who is a lady of the very highest rank, would perhaps not have shewn herself inexorably averse from the idea of entering upon relations with Mme. Şwann, in which case it is safe to assume that more than one sheep of the social flock would have followed her lead. But it seems that there has been no indication on Swann's part of any movement in that direction.

"What do I see? A Nesselrode pudding! As well! I declare, I shall need a course at Carlsbad after such a Lucullus-feast as this.

"Possibly Swann felt that there would be too much resistance to over-come. The marriage—so much is certain—was not well received. There has been some talk of his wife's having money, but that is all humbug. Anyhow, the whole affair has been looked upon with disfavour. And then, Swann has an aunt who is excessively rich and in an admirable position socially, married to a man who, financially speaking, is a power. Not only has she refused to meet Mme. Swann, she has actually started a campaign to force her friends and acquaintances to do the same. I do not mean to say that anyone who moves in a good circle in Paris has shewn any actual incivility to Mme. Swann. . . . No! A hundred times no! Quite apart from her husband's being eminently a man to take up the challenge. Anyhow, there is one curious thing about it, to see the immense importance that Swann, who knows so many and such exclusive people, attaches to a society of which the best that can be said is that it is extremely mixed. I myself, who knew him in the old days, must admit that I felt more aston-ished than amused at seeing a man so well-bred as he is, so much at home

in the best houses, effusively thanking the Chief Secretary to the Minister
of Posts for having come to them, and asking him whether Mme. Swann
might *take the liberty* of calling upon his wife. He must feel something of
an exile, don't you know; evidently, it's quite a different world. I don't
think, all the same, that Swann is unhappy. It is true that for some years
before the marriage she was always trying to blackmail him in a rather
disgraceful way; she would take the child away whenever Swann refused
her anything. Poor Swann, who is as unsophisticated as he is, for all that,
sharp, believed every time that the child's disappearance was a coincidence,
and declined to face the facts. Apart from that, she made such continual
scenes that everyone expected that, from the day she attained her object
and was safely married, nothing could possibly restrain her and that their
life would be a hell on earth. Instead of which, just the opposite has happened. People are inclined to laugh at the way in which Swann speaks of
his wife; it's become a standing joke. Of course, one could hardly expect
that, conscious, more or less of being a—(you remember Molière's line)
he would go and proclaim it *urbi et orbi;* still that does not prevent one
from finding a tendency in him to exaggerate when he declares that she
makes an excellent wife. And yet that is not so far from the truth as people
imagine. In her own way—which is not, perhaps, what all husbands would
prefer, but then, between you and me, I find it difficult to believe that
Swann, who has known her for ever so long and is far from being an utter
fool, did not know what to expect—there can be no denying that she
does seem to have a certain regard for him. I do not say that she is not
flighty, and Swann himself has no fault to find with her for that, if one
is to believe the charitable tongues which, as you may suppose, continue
to wag. But she is distinctly grateful to him for what he has done for her,
and, despite the fears that were everywhere expressed of the contrary,
her temper seems to have become angelic."

This alteration was perhaps not so extraordinary as M. de Norpois professed to find it. Odette had not believed that Swann would ever consent
to marry her; each time that she made the suggestive announcement that
some man about town had just married his mistress she had seen him
stiffen into a glacial silence, or at the most, if she were directly to challenge
him, asking: "Don't you think it very nice, a very fine thing that he has
done, for a woman who sacrificed all her youth to him?" had heard him
answer dryly: "But I don't say that there's anything wrong in it. Everyone does what he himself thinks right." She came very near, indeed,
to believing that (as he used to threaten in moments of anger) he was
going to leave her altogether, for she had heard it said, not long
since, by a woman sculptor, that "You cannot be surprised at anything
men do, they're such brutes," and impressed by the profundity of this
maxim of pessimism she had appropriated it for herself, and repeated it
on every possible occasion with an air of disappointment which seemed
to imply: "After all, it's not impossible in any way; it would be just my
luck." Meanwhile all the virtue had gone from the optimistic maxim which
had hitherto guided Odette through life: "You can do anything with
men when they're in love with you, they're such idiots!" a doctrine which

was expressed on her face by the same tremor of an eyelid that might have accompanied such words as: "Don't be frightened; he won't break anything." While she waited, Odette was tormented by the thought of what one of her friends, who had been married by a man who had not lived with her for nearly so long as Odette herself had lived with Swann, and had had no child by him, and who was now in a definitely respectable position, invited to the balls at the Elysée and so forth, must think of Swann's behaviour. A consultant more discerning than M. de Norpois would doubtless have been able to diagnose that it was this feeling of shame and humiliation that had embittered Odette, that the devilish characteristics which she displayed were no essential part of her, no irremediable evil, and so would easily have foretold what had indeed come to pass, namely that a new rule of life, the matrimonial, would put an end, with almost magic swiftness, to these painful incidents, of daily occurrence but in no sense organic. Practically everyone was surprised at the marriage, and this, in itself, is surprising. No doubt very few people understand the purely subjective nature of the phenomenon that we call love, or how it creates, so to speak, a fresh, a third, a supplementary person, distinct from the person whom the world knows by the same name, a person most of whose constituent elements are derived from ourself, the lover. And so there are very few who can regard as natural the enormous proportions that a creature comes to assume in our eyes who is not the same as the creature that they see. It would appear, none the less, that so far as Odette was concerned people might have taken into account the fact that if, indeed, she had never entirely understood Swann's mentality, at least she was acquainted with the titles, and with all the details of his studies, so much so that the name of Vermeer was as familiar to her as that of her own dressmaker; while as for Swann himself she knew intimately those traits of character of which the rest of the world must remain ignorant or merely laugh at them, and only a mistress or a sister may gain possession of the revealing, cherished image; and so strongly are we attached to such eccentricities, even to those of them which we are most anxious to correct, that it is because a woman comes in time to acquire an indulgent, an affectionately mocking familiarity, such as we ourselves have with them, or our relatives have, that amours of long standing have something of the sweetness and strength of family affection. The bonds that unite us to another creature receive their consecration when that creature adopts the same point of view as ourself in judging one of our imperfections. And among these special traits there were others, besides, which belonged as much to his intellect as to his character, which, all the same, because they had their roots in the latter, Odette had been able more easily to discern. She complained that when Swann turned author, when he published his essays, these characteristics were not to be found in them as they were in his letters, or in his conversation, where they abounded. She urged him to give them a more prominent place. She would have liked that because it was these things that she herself preferred in him, but since she preferred them because they were the things most typical of himself, she was perhaps not wrong in wishing that they might

be found in his writings. Perhaps also she thought that his work, if endowed with more vitality, so that it ultimately brought him success, might
enable her also to form what at the Verdurins' she had been taught to
value above everything else in the world—a salon.

Among the people to whom this sort of marriage appeared ridiculous,
people who in their own case would ask themselves, "What will M. de
Guermantes think, what will Bréauté say when I marry Mlle. de Montmorency?", among the people who cherished that sort of social ideal
would have figured, twenty years earlier, Swann himself, the Swann who
had taken endless pains to get himself elected to the Jockey Club, and had
reckoned at that time on making a brilliant marriage which, by con-
solidating his position, would have made him one of the most conspicuous
figures in Paris. Only, the visions which a marriage like that suggests
to the mind of the interested party need, like all visions, if they are not
to fade away and be altogether lost, to receive sustenance from without.
Your most ardent longing is to humiliate the man who has insulted you.
But if you never hear of him again, having removed to some other place,
your enemy will come to have no longer the slightest importance for
you. If one has lost sight for a score of years of all the people on whose
account one would have liked to be elected to the Jockey Club or the
Institute, the prospect of becoming a member of one or other of those
corporations will have ceased to tempt one. Now fully as much as retirement, ill-health or religious conversion, protracted relations with a woman
will substitute fresh visions for the old. There was not on Swann's part,
when he married Odette, any renunciation of his social ambitions, for from
these ambitions Odette had long ago, in the spiritual sense of the word,
detached him. Besides, had he not been so detached, his marriage would
have been all the more creditable. It is because they imply the sacrifice
of a more or less advantageous position to a purely private happiness that,
as a general rule, 'impossible' marriages are the happiest of all. (One
cannot very well include among the 'impossible' marriages those that
are made for money, there being no instance on record of a couple, of
whom the wife or even the husband has thus sold himself, who have not
sooner or later been admitted into society, if only by tradition, and on
the strength of so many precedents, and so as not to have two conflicting
standards.) Perhaps, on the other hand, the artistic, if not the perverse
side of Swann's nature would in any event have derived a certain amount
of pleasure from coupling with himself, in one of those crossings of species
such as Mendelians practise and mythology records, a creature of a different race, archduchess or prostitute, from contracting a royal alliance
or from marrying beneath him. There had been but one person in all the
world whose opinion he took into consideration whenever he thought of his
possible marriage with Odette; that was, and from no snobbish motive,
the Duchesse de Guermantes. With whom Odette, on the contrary, was
but little concerned, thinking only of those people whose position was
immediately above her own, rather than in so vague an empyrean. But
when Swann in his daydreams saw Odette as already his wife he invariably formed a picture of the moment in which he would take her—her,

and above all her daughter—to call upon the Princesse des Laumes (who was shortly, on the death of her father-in-law, to become Duchesse de Guermantes). He had no desire to introduce them anywhere else, but his heart would soften as he invented—uttering their actual words to himself—all the things that the Duchess would say of him to Odette, and Odette to the Duchess, the affection that she would shew for Gilberte, spoiling her, making him proud of his child. He enacted to himself the scene of this introduction with the same precision in each of its imaginary details that people shew when they consider how they would spend, supposing they were to win it, a lottery prize the amount of which they have arbitrarily determined. In so far as a mental picture which accompanies one of our resolutions may be said to be its motive, so it might be said that if Swann married Odette it was in order to present her and Gilberte, without anyone's else being present, without, if need be, anyone's else ever coming to know of it, to the Duchesse de Guermantes. We shall see how this sole social ambition that he had entertained for his wife and daughter was precisely that one the realisation of which proved to be forbidden him by a veto so absolute that Swann died in the belief that the Duchess would never possibly come to know them. We shall see also that, on the contrary, the Duchesse de Guermantes did associate with Odette and Gilberte after the death of Swann. And doubtless he would have been wiser —seeing that he could attach so much importance to so small a matter— not to have formed too dark a picture of the future, in this connexion, but to have consoled himself with the hope that the meeting of the ladies might indeed take place when he was no longer there to enjoy it. The laborious process of causation which sooner or later will bring about every possible effect, including (consequently) those which one had believed to be most nearly impossible, naturally slow at times, is rendered slower still by our impatience (which in seeking to accelerate only obstructs it) and by our very existence, and comes to fruition only when we have ceased to desire it—have ceased, possibly, to live. Was not Swann conscious of this from his own experience, had there not been already, in his life, as it were a prefiguration of what was to happen after his death, a posthumous happiness in this marriage with this Odette whom he had passionately loved— even if she had not been pleasing to him at first sight—whom he had married when he no longer loved her, when the creature that, in Swann, had so longed to live, had so despaired of living all its life in company with Odette, when that creature was extinct?

I began next to speak of the Comte de Paris, to ask whether he was not one of Swann's friends, for I was afraid lest the conversation should drift away from him. "Why, yes!" replied M. de Norpois, turning towards me and fixing upon my modest person the azure gaze in which floated, as in their vital element, his immense capacity for work and his power of assimilation. And "Upon my word," he added, once more addressing my father, "I do not think that I shall be overstepping the bounds of the respect which I have always professed for the Prince (although without, you understand, maintaining any personal relations with him, which would inevitably compromise my position, unofficial as that may be), if I tell you of a little episode which is not without point; no more than four years ago, at a small railway station in one of the countries of Central Europe, the Prince happened to set eyes on Mme. Swann. Naturally, none of his circle ventured to ask his Royal Highness what he thought of her. That would not have been seemly. But when her name came up by chance in conversation, by certain signs—imperceptible, if you like, but quite un-mistakable—the Prince appeared willing enough to let it be understood that his impression of her had, in a word, been far from unfavourable."

"But there could have been no possibility, surely, of her being presented to the Comte de Paris?" inquired my father.

"Well, we don't know; with Princes one never does know," replied M. de Norpois. "The most exalted, those who know best how to secure what is due to them, are as often as not the last to let themselves be embarrassed by the decrees of popular opinion, even by those for which there is most justification, especially when it is a question of their rewarding a personal attachment to themselves. Now it is certain that the Comte de Paris has always most graciously recognised the devotion of Swann, who is, for that matter, a man of character, in spite of it all."

"And what was your own impression, your Excellency? Do tell us!" my mother asked, from politeness as well as from curiosity.

All the energy of the old connoisseur broke through the habitual modera-tion of his speech as he answered: "Quite excellent!"

And knowing that the admission that a strong impression has been made on one by a woman takes its place, provided that one makes it in a playful tone, in a certain category of the art of conversation that is highly appreci-ated, he broke into a little laugh that lasted for several seconds, moistening the old diplomat's blue eyes and making his nostrils, with their network of tiny scarlet veins, quiver. "She is altogether charming!"

"Was there a writer of the name of Bergotte at this dinner, sir?" I asked timidly, still trying to keep the conversation to the subject of the Swanns.

"Yes, Bergotte was there," replied M. de Norpois, inclining his head courteously towards me, as though in his desire to be pleasant to my father he attached to everything connected with him a real importance, even to the questions of a boy of my age who was not accustomed to see such politeness shewn to him by persons of his. "Do you know him?" he went on, fastening on me that clear gaze, the penetration of which had won the praise of Bismarck.

"My son does not know him, but he admires his work immensely," my mother explained.

"Good heavens!" exclaimed M. de Norpois, inspiring me with doubts of my own intelligence far more serious than those that ordinarily dis-tracted me, when I saw that what I valued a thousand thousand times more than myself, what I regarded as the most exalted thing in the world, was for him at the very foot of the scale of admiration. "I do not share your son's point of view. Bergotte is what I call a flute-player: one must admit that he plays on it very agreeably, although with a great deal of mannerism, of affectation. But when all is said, it is no more than that, and that is nothing very great. Nowhere does one find in his enervated writings anything that could be called construction. No action—or very little—but above all no range. His books fail at the foundation, or rather they have no foundation at all. At a time like the present, when the ever-increasing complexity of life leaves one scarcely a moment for reading, when the map of Europe has undergone radical alterations, and is on the eve, very probably, of undergoing others more drastic still, when so many new and threatening problems are arising on every side, you will allow me to suggest that one is entitled to ask that a writer should be something else than a fine intellect which makes us forget, amid otiose and byzantine discussions of the merits of pure form, that we may be overwhelmed at any moment by a double tide of barbarians, those from without and those from within our borders. I am aware that this is a blasphemy against the sacrosanct school of what these gentlemen term 'Art for Art's sake,' but at this period of history there are tasks more urgent than the manipulation of words in a harmonious manner. Not that Bergotte's manner is not now and then quite attractive. I have no fault to find with that, but taken as a whole, it is all very precious, very thin, and has very little virility. I can now understand more easily, when I bear in mind your altogether excessive regard for Bergotte, the few lines that you shewed me just now, which it would have been unfair to you not to overlook, since you yourself told me, in all simplicity, that they were merely a childish scribbling." (I had, indeed, said so, but I did not think anything of the sort.) "For every sin there is forgiveness, and especially for the sins of youth. After all, others as well as yourself have such sins upon their conscience, and you are not the only one who has believed himself to be a poet in his day. But one can see in what you have shewn me the evil influence of Bergotte. You will not, of course, be surprised when I say that there was in it none of his good qualities, since he is a past-master in the art—incidentally quite superficial —of handling a certain style of which, at your age, you cannot have acquired even the rudiments. But already there is the same fault, that paradox of stringing together fine-sounding words and only afterwards troubling about what they mean. That is putting the cart before the horse, even in Bergotte's books. All those Chinese puzzles of form, all these deliquescent mandarin subtleties seem to me to be quite futile. Given a few fireworks, let off prettily enough by an author, and up goes the shout of genius. Works of genius are not so common as all that! Bergotte cannot place to his credit—does not carry in his baggage, if I may use the expression—a single novel that is at all lofty in its conception, any of those books which one keeps in a special corner of one's library. I do not discover one such in the whole of his work. But that does not exclude the fact that, with him, the work is infinitely superior to the author. Ah! there is a man who justifies the wit who insisted that one ought never to know an author except through his books. It would be impossible to imagine an individual who corresponded less to his—more pretentious, more pompous, less fitted for human society. Vulgar at some moments, at others talking like a book, and not even like one of his own, but like a boring book, which his, to do them justice, are not—such is your Bergotte. He has the most confused mind, alembicated, what our ancestors called a *diseur de phébus,* and he makes the things that he says even more unpleasant by the manner in which he says them. I forget for the moment whether it is Loménie or Sainte-Beuve who tells us that Vigny repelled people by the same eccentricity. But Bergotte has never given us a *Cinq-Mars*, or a *Cachet Rouge*, certain pages of which are regular anthology pieces."

Paralysed by what M. de Norpois had just said to me with regard to the fragment which I had submitted to him, and remembering at the same time the difficulties that I experienced when I attempted to write an essay or merely to devote myself to serious thought, I felt conscious once again of my intellectual nullity and that I was not born for a literary life. Doubtless in the old days at Combray certain impressions of a very humble order, or a few pages of Bergotte used to plunge me into a state of musing which had appeared to me to be of great value. But this state was what my poem in prose reflected; there could be no doubt that M. de Norpois had at once grasped and had seen through the fallacy of what I had discovered to be beautiful simply by a mirage that must be entirely false since the Ambassador had not been taken in by it. He had shewn me, on the other hand, what an infinitely unimportant place was mine when I was judged from outside, objectively, by the best-disposed and most intelligent of experts. I felt myself to be struck speechless, overwhelmed; and my mind, like a fluid which is without dimensions save those of the vessel that is provided for it, just as it had been expanded a moment ago so as to fill all the vast capacity of genius, contracted now, was entirely contained in the straitened mediocrity in which M. de Norpois had of a sudden enclosed and sealed it.

"Our first introduction—I speak of Bergotte and myself——" he resumed, turning to my father, "was somewhat beset with thorns (which is, after all, only another way of saying that it was not lacking in points). Bergotte—some years ago, now—paid a visit to Vienna while I was Ambassador there; he was presented to me by the Princess Metternich, came and wrote his name, and expected to be asked to the Embassy. Now, being in a foreign country as the Representative of France, to which he has after all done some honour by his writings, to a certain extent (let us say, to be quite accurate, to a very slight extent), I was prepared to set aside the unfavourable opinion that I hold of his private life. But he was not travelling alone, and he actually let it be understood that he was not to be invited without his companion. I trust that I am no more of a prude than most men, and, being a bachelor, I was perhaps in a position to throw open the doors of the Embassy a little wider than if I had been married and the father of a family. Nevertheless, I must admit that there are depths of degradation to which I should hesitate to descend, while these are rendered more repulsive still by the tone, not moral, merely—let us be quite frank and say moralising,—that Bergotte takes up in his books, where one finds nothing but perpetual and, between ourselves, somewhat wearisome analyses, torturing scruples, morbid remorse, and all for the merest peccadilloes, the most trivial naughtinesses (as one knows from one's own experience), while all the time he is shewing such an utter lack of conscience and so much cynicism in his private life. To cut a long story short, I evaded

the responsibility, the Princess returned to the charge, but without success.
So that I do not suppose that I appear exactly in the odour of sanctity
to the gentleman, and I am not sure how far he appreciated Swann's kindness in inviting him and myself on the same evening. Unless of course it
was he who asked for the invitation. One can never tell, for really he is
not normal. Indeed that is his sole excuse."

"And was Mme. Swann's daughter at the dinner?" I asked M. de Norpois, taking advantage, to put this question, of a moment in which, as we
all moved towards the drawing-room, I could more easily conceal my
emotion than would have been possible at table, where I was held fast in
the glare of the lamplight.

M. de Norpois appeared to be trying for a moment to remember; then:
"Yes, you mean a young person of fourteen or fifteen? Yes, of course, I
remember now that she was introduced to me before dinner as the daughter of our Amphitryon. I may tell you that I saw but little of her; she
retired to bed early. Or else she went out to see a friend—I forget. But I
can see that you are very intimate with the Swann household."

"I play with Mlle. Swann in the Champs-Elysées, and she is delightful."

"Oh! so that is it, is it? But I assure you, I thought her charming. I
must confess to you, however, that I do not believe that she will ever be
anything like her mother, if I may say as much without wounding you in
a vital spot."

"I prefer Mlle. Swann's face, but I admire her mother, too, enormously;
I go for walks in the Bois simply in the hope of seeing her pass."

"Ah! But I must tell them that; they will be highly flattered."

While he was uttering these words, and for a few seconds after he had
uttered them, M. de Norpois was still in the same position as anyone else
who, hearing me speak of Swann as an intelligent man, of his family as
respectable stockbrokers, of his house as a fine house, imagined that I
would speak just as readily of another man equally intelligent, of other
stockbrokers equally respectable, of another house equally fine; it was the
moment in which a sane man who is talking to a lunatic has not yet perceived that his companion is mad. M. de Norpois knew that there was
nothing unnatural in the pleasure which one derived from looking at pretty
women, that it was a social convention, when anyone spoke to you of a
pretty woman with any fervour, to pretend to think that he was in love
with her, and to promise to further his designs. But in saying that he would
speak of me to Gilberte and her mother (which would enable me, like an
Olympian deity who has taken on the fluidity of a breath of wind, or rather
the aspect of the old greybeard whose form Minerva borrows, to penetrate,
myself, unseen, into Mme. Swann's drawing-room, to attract her attention,
to occupy her thoughts, to arouse her gratitude for my admiration, to appear before her as the friend of an important person, to seem to her worthy
to be invited by her in the future and to enter into the intimate life of her
family), this important person who was going to make use, in my interests,
of the great influence which he must have with Mme. Swann inspired in
me suddenly an affection so compelling that I had difficulty in restraining
myself from kissing his gentle hands, white and crumpled, which looked

as though they had been left lying too long in water. I even sketched in
the air an outline of that impulsive movement, but this I supposed that
I alone had observed. For it is difficult for any of us to calculate exactly
on what scale his words or his gestures are apparent to others. Partly from
the fear of exaggerating our own importance, and also because we enlarge
to enormous proportions the field over which the impressions formed by
other people in the course of their lives are obliged to extend, we imagine
that the accessories of our speech and attitudes scarcely penetrate the consciousness, still less remain in the memory of those with whom we converse.
It is, we may suppose, to a prompting of this sort that criminals yield when
they 'touch up' the wording of a statement already made, thinking that
the new variant cannot be confronted with any existing version. But it is
quite possible that, even in what concerns the millennial existence of the
human race, the philosophy of the journalist, according to which everything
is destined to oblivion, is less true than a contrary philosophy which would
predict the conservation of everything. In the same newspaper in which
the moralist of the 'Paris column' says to us of an event, of a work of art,
all the more forcibly of a singer who has enjoyed her 'crowded hour':
"Who will remember this in ten years' time?" overleaf does not the report
of the Académie des Inscriptions speak often of a fact, in itself of smaller
importance, of a poem of little merit, which dates from the epoch of the
Pharaohs and is now known again in its entirety? Is it not, perhaps, just
the same in our brief life on earth? And yet, some years later, in a house
in which M. de Norpois, who was also calling there, had seemed to me the
most solid support that I could hope to find, because he was the friend of
my father, indulgent, inclined to wish us all well, and besides, by his profession and upbringing, trained to discretion, when, after the Ambassador
had gone, I was told that he had alluded to an evening long ago when he
had seen the moment in which I was just going to kiss his hands, not only
did I colour up to the roots of my hair but I was stupefied to learn how
different from all that I had believed were not only the manner in which
M. de Norpois spoke of me but also the constituents of his memory: this
tittle-tattle enlightened me as to the incalculable proportions of absence
and presence of mind, of recollection and forgetfulness which go to form
the human intelligence; and I was as marvellously surprised as on the day
on which I read for the first time, in one of Maspero's books, that we had
an exact list of the sportsmen whom Assurbanipal used to invite to his
hunts, a thousand years before the Birth of Christ.

"Oh, sir," I assured M. de Norpois, when he told me that he would inform Gilberte and her mother how much I admired them, "if you would
do that, if you would speak of me to Mme. Swann, my whole life would
not be long enough for me to prove my gratitude, and that life would be
all at your service. But I feel bound to point out to you that I do not know
Mme. Swann, and that I have never been introduced to her."

I had added these last words from a scruple of conscience, and so as not
to appear to be boasting of an acquaintance which I did not possess. But
while I was uttering them I felt that they were already superfluous, for
from the beginning of my speech of thanks, with its chilling ardour, I had

seen flitting across the face of the Ambassador an expression of hesitation
and dissatisfaction, and in his eyes that vertical, narrow, slanting look
(like, in the drawing of a solid body in perspective, the receding line of
one of its surfaces), that look which one addresses to the invisible audience
whom one has within oneself at the moment when one is saying something
that one's other audience, the person whom one has been addressing—myself, in this instance—is not meant to hear. I realised in a flash that these
phrases which I had pronounced, which, feeble as they were when measured against the flood of gratitude that was coursing through me, had
seemed to me bound to touch M. de Norpois and to confirm his decision
upon an intervention which would have given him so little trouble and me
so much joy, were perhaps (out of all those that could have been chosen,
with diabolical malice, by persons anxious to do me harm) the only ones
that could result in making him abandon his intention. Indeed, when he
heard me speak, just as at the moment when a stranger with whom we have
been exchanging—quite pleasantly—our impressions, which we might suppose to be similar to his, of the passers-by, whom we have agreed in regarding as vulgar, reveals suddenly the pathological abyss that divides him
from us by adding carelessly, as he runs his hand over his pocket: "What
a pity, I haven't got my revolver here; I could have picked off the lot!"
M. de Norpois, who knew that nothing was less costly or more easy than
to be commended to Mme. Swann and taken to her house, and saw that
to me, on the contrary, such favours bore so high a price and were consequently, no doubt, of great difficulty, thought that the desire, apparently
normal, which I had expressed must cloak some different thought, some
suspect intention, some pre-existent fault, on account of which, in the certainty of displeasing Mme. Swann, no one hitherto had been willing to
undertake the responsibility for conveying a message to her from me. And
I understood that this office was one which he would never discharge, that
he might see Mme. Swann daily, for years to come, without ever mentioning
my name. He did indeed ask her, a few days later, for some information
which I required, and charged my father to convey it to me. But he had
not thought it his duty to tell her at whose instance he was inquiring. So
she would never discover that I knew M. de Norpois and that I hoped so
greatly to be asked to her house; and this was perhaps a less misfortune
than I supposed. For the second of these discoveries would probably not
have added much to the efficacy, in any event uncertain, of the first. In
Odette the idea of her own life and of her home awakened no mysterious
disturbance; a person who knew her, who came to see her, did not seem
to her a fabulous creature such as he seemed to me who would have flung
a stone through Swann's windows if I could have written upon it that I
knew M. de Norpois; I was convinced that such a message, even when
transmitted in so brutal a fashion, would have done far more to exalt me
in the eyes of the lady of the house than it would have prejudiced her
against me. But even if I had been capable of understanding that the mis-
sion which M. de Norpois did not perform must have remained futile, nay,
more than that, might even have damaged my credit with the Swanns, I
should not have had the courage, had he shewn himself consenting, to

release the Ambassador from it, and to renounce the pleasure—however fatal its consequences might prove—of feeling that my name and my person were thus brought for a moment into Gilberte's presence, in her unknown life and home.

After M. de Norpois had gone my father cast an eye over the evening paper; I dreamed once more of Berma. The pleasure which I had found in listening to her required to be made complete, all the more because it had fallen far short of what I had promised myself; and so it at once assimilated everything that was capable of giving it nourishment, those merits, for instance, which M. de Norpois had admitted that Berma possessed, and which my mind had absorbed at one draught, like a dry lawn when water is poured on it. Then my father handed me the newspaper, pointing me out a paragraph which ran more or less as follows:—

The performance of *Phèdre*, given this afternoon before an enthusiastic audience, which included the foremost representatives of society and the arts, as well as the principal critics, was for Mme. Berma, who played the heroine, the occasion of a triumph as brilliant as any that she has known in the course of her phenomenal career. We shall discuss more fully in a later issue this performance, which is indeed an event in the history of the stage; for the present we need only add that the best qualified judges are unanimous in the pronouncement that such an interpretation sheds an entirely new light on the part of Phèdre, which is one of the finest and most studied of Racine's creations, and that it constitutes the purest and most exalted manifestation of dramatic art which it has been the privilege of our generation to witness.

Immediately my mind had conceived this new idea of "the purest and most exalted manifestation of dramatic art," it, the idea, sped to join the imperfect pleasure which I had felt in the theatre, added to it a little of what was lacking, and their combination formed something so exalting that I cried out within myself: "What a great artist!" It may doubtless be argued that I was not absolutely sincere. But let us bear in mind, rather, the numberless writers who, dissatisfied with the page which they have just written, if they read some eulogy of the genius of Chateaubriand, or evoke the spirit of some great artist whose equal they aspire to be, by humming to themselves, for instance, a phrase of Beethoven, the melancholy of which they compare with what they have been trying to express in prose, are so filled with that idea of genius that they add it to their own productions, when they think of them once again, see them no longer in the light in which at first they appeared, and, hazarding an act of faith in the value of their work, say to themselves: "After all!" without taking into account that, into the total which determines their ultimate satisfaction, they have introduced the memory of marvellous pages of Chateaubriand which they assimilate to their own, but of which, in cold fact, they are not the authors; let us bear in mind the numberless men who believe in the love of a mistress on the evidence only of her betrayals; all those, too, who are sustained by the alternative hopes, either of an incomprehensible survival of death, when they think, inconsolable husbands, of the wives whom they have lost but have not ceased to love, or, artists, of the posthumous glory which they may thus enjoy; or else the hope of complete extinction which comforts them when their thoughts turn to the misdeeds that otherwise they must expiate after death; let us bear in mind also the travellers who come home enraptured by the general beauty of a tour of which, from day to day, they have felt nothing but the tedious incidents; and let us then declare whether, in the communal life that is led by our ideas in the enclosure of our minds, there is a single one of those that make us most happy which has not first sought, a very parasite, and won from an alien but neighbouring idea the greater part of the strength that it originally lacked.

My mother appeared none too well pleased that my father no longer thought of 'the career' for myself. I fancy that, anxious before all things that a definite rule of life should discipline the eccentricity of my nervous system, what she regretted was not so much seeing me abandon diplomacy as the prospect of my devoting myself to literature. But "Let him alone!" my father protested; "the main thing is that a man should find pleasure in his work. He is no longer a child. He knows pretty well now what he likes, it is not at all probable that he will change, and he is quite capable of deciding for himself what will make him happy in life." That evening, as I waited for the time to arrive when, thanks to the freedom of choice which they allowed me, I should or should not begin to be happy in life, my father's words caused me great uneasiness. At all times his unexpected kindnesses had, when they were manifested, prompted in me so keen a desire to kiss, above where his beard began, his glowing cheeks, that if I did not yield to that desire, it was simply because I was afraid of annoying him. And on that day, as an author becomes alarmed when he sees the fruits of his own meditation, which do not appear to him to be of great value since he does not separate them from himself, oblige a publisher to choose a kind of paper, to employ a fount of type finer, perhaps, than they deserve, I asked myself whether my desire to write was of sufficient importance to justify my father in dispensing so much generosity. But apart from that, when he spoke of my inclinations as no longer liable to change, he awakened in me two terrible suspicions. The first was that (at a time when, every day, I regarded myself as standing upon the threshold of a life which was still intact and would not enter upon its course until the following morning) my existence was already begun, and that, furthermore, what was yet to follow would not differ to any extent from what had already elapsed. The second suspicion, which was nothing more, really, than a variant of the first, was that I was not situated somewhere outside the realm of Time, but was subject to its laws, just like the people in novels who, for that reason, used to plunge me in such depression when I read of their lives, down at Combray, in the fastness of my wicker sentry-box. In theory one is aware that the earth revolves, but in practice one does not perceive it, the ground upon which one treads seems not to move, and one can live undisturbed. So it is with Time in one's life. And to make its flight perceptible novelists are obliged, by wildly accelerating the beat of the pendulum, to transport the reader in a couple of minutes over ten, or twenty, or even thirty years. At the top of one page we have left a lover full of hope; at the foot of the next we meet him again, a bowed old man

of eighty, painfully dragging himself on his daily walk about the courtyard of an almshouse, scarcely replying to what is said to him, oblivious of
the past. In saying of me, "He is no longer a child," "His tastes will not
change now," and so forth, my father had suddenly made me apparent
to myself in my position in Time, and caused me the same kind of depression as if I had been, not yet the enfeebled old pensioner, but one of those
heroes of whom the author, in a tone of indifference which is particularly
galling, says to us at the end of a book: "He very seldom comes up now
from the country. He has finally decided to end his days there."

Meanwhile my father, so as to forestall any criticism that we might feel
tempted to make of our guest, said to my mother: "Upon my word, old
Norpois was rather 'typical,' as you call it, this evening, wasn't he? When
he said that it would not have been 'seemly' to ask the Comte de Paris a
question, I was quite afraid you would burst out laughing."

"Not at all!" answered my mother. "I was delighted to see a man of his
standing, and age too, keep that sort of simplicity, which is really a sign
of straightforwardness and good-breeding."

"I should think so, indeed! That does not prevent his having a shrewd
and discerning mind; I know him well, I see him at the Commission, remember, where he is very different from what he was here," exclaimed
my father, who was glad to see that Mamma appreciated M. de Norpois,
and anxious to persuade her that he was even superior to what she supposed, because a cordial nature exaggerates a friend's qualities with as
much pleasure as a mischievous one finds in depreciating them. "What
was it that he said, again—'With Princes one never does know.' . . . ?"

"Yes, that was it. I noticed it at the time; it was very neat. You can see
that he has a vast experience of life."

"The astonishing thing is that he should have been dining with the
Swanns, and that he seems to have found quite respectable people there,
officials even. How on earth can Mme. Swann have managed to catch
them?"

"Did you notice the malicious way he said: 'It is a house which is especially attractive to gentlemen!'?"

And each of them attempted to reproduce the manner in which M. de
Norpois had uttered these words, as they might have attempted to capture
some intonation of Bressant's voice or of Thiron's in *L'Aventurière* or in
the *Gendre de M. Poirier*. But of all his sayings there was none so keenly
relished as one was by Françoise, who, years afterwards, even, could not
'keep a straight face' if we reminded her that she had been qualified by
the Ambassador as 'a chef of the first order,' a compliment which my
mother had gone in person to transmit to her, as a War Minister publishes
the congratulations addressed to him by a visiting Sovereign after the
grand review. I, as it happened, had preceded my mother to the kitchen.
For I had extorted from Françoise, who though opposed to war was cruel,
that she would cause no undue suffering to the rabbit which she had to
kill, and I had had no report yet of its death. Françoise assured me that
it had passed away as peacefully as could be desired, and very swiftly. "I
have never seen a beast like it; it died without uttering a word; you would

have thought it was dumb." Being but little versed in the language of
beasts I suggested that the rabbit had not, perhaps, a cry like the chicken's.
"Just wait till you see," said Françoise, filled with contempt for my ignorance, "if rabbits don't cry every bit as much as chickens. Why, they
are far noisier." She received the compliments of M. de Norpois with the
proud simplicity, the joyful and (if but for the moment) intelligent expression of an artist when someone speaks to him of his art. My mother
had sent her when she first came to us to several of the big restaurants to
see how the cooking there was done. I had the same pleasure, that evening,
in hearing her dismiss the most famous of them as mere cookshops that I
had had long ago, when I learned with regard to theatrical artists that
the hierarchy of their merits did not at all correspond to that of their repu-
tations. "The Ambassador," my mother told her, "assured me that he
knows no place where he can get cold beef and *soufflés* as good as yours."
Françoise, with an air of modesty and of paying just homage to the truth,
agreed, but seemed not at all impressed by the title 'Ambassador'; she
said of M. de Norpois, with the friendliness due to a man who had taken
her for a chef: "He's a good old soul, like me." She had indeed hoped to
catch sight of him as he arrived, but knowing that Mamma hated their
standing about behind doors and in windows, and thinking that Mamma
would get to know from the other servants or from the porter that she
had been keeping watch (for Françoise saw everywhere nothing but
'jealousies' and 'tale-bearings,' which played the same grim and unending
part in her imagination as do for others of us the intrigues of the Jesuits
or the Jews), she had contented herself with a peep from the kitchen window, 'so as not to have words with Madame,' and beneath the momentary
aspect of M. de Norpois had 'thought it was Monsieur Legrand,' because
of what she called his 'agelity' and in spite of their having not a single
point in common. "Well," inquired my mother, "and how do you explain
that nobody else can make a jelly as well as you—when you choose?" "I
really couldn't say how that becomes about," replied Françoise, who had
established no very clear line of demarcation between the verb 'to come,'
in certain of its meanings at least, and the verb 'to become.' She was
speaking the truth, if not the whole truth, being scarcely more capable—
or desirous—of revealing the mystery which ensured the superiority of
her jellies or her creams than a leader of fashion the secrets of her toilet
or a great singer those of her song. Their explanations tell us little; it
was the same with the recipes furnished by our cook. "They do it in too
much of a hurry," she went on, alluding to the great restaurants, "and
then it's not all done together. You want the beef to become like a sponge,
then it will drink up all the juice to the last drop. Still, there was one of
those Cafés where I thought they did know a little bit about cooking. I
don't say it was altogether my jelly, but it was very nicely done, and the
soufflés had plenty of cream." "Do you mean Henry's?" asked my father
(who had now joined us), for he greatly enjoyed that restaurant in the
Place Gaillon where he went regularly to club dinners. "Oh, dear no!"
said Françoise, with a mildness which cloaked her profound contempt. "I
meant a little restaurant. At that Henry's it's all very good, sure enough,

but it's not a restaurant, it's more like a—soup-kitchen." "Weber's, then?" "Oh, no, sir, I meant a good restaurant. Weber's, that's in the Rue Royale; that's not a restaurant, it's a drinking-shop. I don't know that the food they give you there is even served. I think they don't have any table-cloths; they just shove it down in front of you like that, with a take it or leave it." "Ciro's?" "Oh! there I should say they have the cooking done by ladies of the world." ('World' meant for Françoise the under-world.) "Lord! They need that to fetch the boys in." We could see that, with all her air of simplicity, Françoise was for the celebrities of her profession a more disastrous 'comrade' than the most jealous, the most infatuated of actresses. We felt, all the same, that she had a proper feeling for her art and a respect for tradition; for she went on: "No, I mean a restaurant where they looked as if they kept a very good little family table. It's a place of some consequence, too. Plenty of custom there. Oh, they raked in the coppers there, all right." Françoise, being an economist, reckoned in coppers, where your plunger would reckon in gold. "Madame knows the place well enough, down there to the right along the main boulevards, a little way back." The restaurant of which she spoke with this blend of pride and good-humoured tolerance was, it turned out, the Café Anglais.

When New Year's Day came, I first of all paid a round of family visits with Mamma who, so as not to tire me, had planned them beforehand (with the aid of an itinerary drawn up by my father) according to districts rather than to degrees of kinship. But no sooner had we entered the drawing-room of the distant cousin whose claim to being visited first was that her house was at no distance from ours, than my mother was horrified to see standing there, his present of *marrons glacés* or *déguisés* in his hand, the bosom friend of the most sensitive of all my uncles, to whom he would at once go and report that we had not begun our round with him. And this uncle would certainly be hurt; he would have thought it quite natural that we should go from the Madeleine to the Jardin des Plantes, where he lived, before stopping at Saint-Augustin, on our way to the Rue de l'Ecole de Médecine.

Our visits ended (my grandmother had dispensed us from the duty of calling on her, since we were to dine there that evening), I ran all the way to the Champs-Elysées to give to our own special stall-keeper, with instructions to hand it over to the person who came to her several times a week from the Swanns to buy gingerbread, the letter which, on the day when my friend had caused me so much anxiety, I had decided to send her at the New Year, and in which I told her that our old friendship was vanishing with the old year, that I would forget, now, my old sorrows and disappointments, and that, from this first day of January, it was a new friendship that we were going to cement, one so solid that nothing could destroy it, so wonderful that I hoped that Gilberte would go out of her way to preserve it in all its beauty, and to warn me in time, as I promised to warn her, should either of us detect the least sign of a peril that might endanger it. On our way home Françoise made me stop at the corner of the Rue Royale, before an open-air stall from which she selected for her own stock of presents photographs of Pius IX and Raspail, while for myself I pur-

chased one of Berma. The innumerable admiration which that artist excited gave an air almost of poverty to this one face that she had to
respond with, unalterable and precarious as are the garments of people
who have not a 'change,' this face on which she must continually expose
to view only the tiny dimple upon her upper lip, the arch of her eyebrows,
a few other physical peculiarities always the same, which, when it came
to that, were at the mercy of a burn or a blow. This face, moreover, could
not in itself have seemed to me beautiful, but it gave me the idea, and consequently the desire to kiss it by reason of all the kisses that it must have
received, for which, from its page in the album, it seemed still to be appealing with that coquettishly tender gaze, that artificially ingenuous smile.
For our Berma must indeed have felt for many young men those longings
which she confessed under cover of the personality of Phaedra, longings
of which everything, even the glamour of her name which enhanced her
beauty and prolonged her youth, must render the gratification so easy to
her. Night was falling; I stopped before a column of playbills, on which
was posted that of the piece in which she was to appear on January 1.
A moist and gentle breeze was blowing. It was a time of day and year that
I knew; I suddenly felt a presentiment that New Year's Day was not a
day different from the rest, that it was not the first day of a new world, in
which, I might, by a chance that had never yet occurred, that was still
intact, make Gilberte's acquaintance afresh, as at the Creation of the
World, as though the past had no longer any existence, as though there
had been obliterated, with the indications which I might have preserved
for my future guidance, the disappointments which she had sometimes
brought me; a new world in which nothing should subsist from the old—
save one thing, my desire that Gilberte should love me. I realised that if my
heart hoped for such a reconstruction, round about it, of a universe that had
not satisfied it before, it was because my heart had not altered, and I told
myself that there was no reason why Gilberte's should have altered either;
I felt that this new friendship was the same, just as there is no boundary
ditch between their forerunners and those new years which our desire for
them, without being able to reach and so to modify them, invests, unknown to themselves, with distinctive names. I might dedicate this new
year, if I chose, to Gilberte, and as one bases a religious system upon the
blind laws of nature, endeavour to stamp New Year's Day with the particular image that I had formed of it; but in vain, I felt that it was not
aware that people called it New Year's Day, that it was passing in a wintry
dusk in a manner that was not novel to me; in the gentle breeze that
floated about the column of playbills I had recognised, I had felt reappear
the eternal, the universal substance, the familiar moisture, the unheeding
fluidity of the old days and years.

I returned to the house. I had spent the New Year's Day of old men,
who differ on that day from their juniors, not because people have ceased
to give them presents but because they themselves have ceased to believe
in the New Year. Presents I had indeed received, but not that present
which alone could bring me pleasure, namely a line from Gilberte. I was
young still, none the less, since I had been able to write her one, by means

of which I hoped, in telling her of my solitary dreams of love and longing, to arouse similar dreams in her. The sadness of men who have grown old lies in their no longer even thinking of writing such letters, the futility of which their experience has shewn.

After I was in bed, the noises of the street, unduly prolonged upon this festive evening, kept me awake. I thought of all the people who were ending the night in pleasure, of the lover, the troop, it might be, of debauchees who would be going to meet Berma at the stage-door after the play that I had seen announced for this evening. I was not even able, so as to calm the agitation which that idea engendered in me during my sleepless night, to assure myself that Berma was not, perhaps, thinking about love, since the lines that she was reciting, which she had long and carefully rehearsed, reminded her at every moment that love is an exquisite thing, as of course she already knew, and knew so well that she displayed its familiar pangs—only enriched with a new violence and an unsuspected sweetness—to her astonished audience; and yet each of them had felt those pangs himself. I lighted my candle again, to look once more upon her face. At the thought that it was, no doubt, at that very moment being caressed by those men whom I could not prevent from giving to Berma and receiving from her joys superhuman but vague, I felt an emotion more cruel than voluptuous, a longing that was aggravated presently by the sound of a horn, as one hears it on the nights of the Lenten carnival and often of other public holidays, which, because it then lacks all poetry, is more saddening, coming from a toy squeaker, than "at evening, in the depth of the woods." At that moment, a message from Gilberte would perhaps not have been what I wanted. Our desires cut across one another's paths, and in this confused existence it is but rarely that a piece of good fortune coincides with the desire that clamoured for it.

I continued to go to the Champs-Elysées on fine days, along streets whose stylish pink houses seemed to be washed (because exhibitions of water-colours were then at the height of fashion) in a lightly floating atmosphere. It would be untrue to say that in those days the palaces of Gabriel struck me as being of greater beauty, or even of another epoch than the adjoining houses. I found more style, and should have supposed more antiquity if not in the Palais de l'Industrie at any rate in the Trocadéro. Plunged in a restless sleep, my adolescence embodied in one uniform vision the whole of the quarter through which it might be strolling, and I had never dreamed that there could be an eighteenth century building in the Rue Royale, just as I should have been astonished to learn that the Porte-Saint-Martin and the Porte-Saint-Denis, those glories of the age of Louis XIV, were not contemporary with the most recently built tenements in the sordid regions that bore their names. Once only one of Gabriel's palaces made me stop for more than a moment; that was because, night having fallen, its columns, dematerialised by the moonlight, had the appearance of having been cut out in pasteboard, and by recalling to me a scene in the operetta *Orphée aux Enfers* gave me for the first time an impression of beauty.

Meanwhile Gilberte never came to the Champs-Elysées. And yet it was imperative that I should see her, for I could not so much as remember what she was like. The questing, anxious, exacting way that we have of looking at the person we love, our eagerness for the word which shall give us or take from us the hope of an appointment for the morrow, and, until that word is uttered, our alternative if not simultaneous imaginings of joy and of despair, all these make our observation, in the beloved object's presence, too tremulous to be able to carry away a clear impression of her. Perhaps, also, that activity of all the senses at once which endeavours to learn from the visible aspect alone what lies behind it is over-indulgent to the thousand forms, to the changing fragrance, to the movements of the living person whom as a rule, when we are not in love, we regard as fixed in one permanent position. Whereas the beloved model does not stay still; and our mental photographs of her are always blurred. I did not rightly know how Gilberte's features were composed, save in the heavenly moments when she disclosed them to me; I could remember nothing but her smile. And not being able to see again that beloved face, despite every effort that I might make to recapture it, I would be disgusted to find, outlined in my memory with a maddening precision of detail, the meaningless, emphatic faces of the man with the wooden horses and of the barley-sugar woman; just as those who have lost a dear friend whom they never see even while they are asleep, are exasperated at meeting incessantly in their dreams any number of insupportable creatures whom it is quite enough to have known in the waking world. In their inability to form any image of the object of their grief they are almost led to assert that they feel no grief. And I was not far from believing that, since I could not recall the features of Gilberte, I had forgotten Gilberte herself, and no longer loved her. At length she returned to play there almost every day, setting before me fresh pleasures to desire, to demand of her for the morrow, indeed making my love for her every day, in this sense, a new love. But an incident was to change once again, and abruptly, the manner in which, at about two o'clock every afternoon, the problem of my love confronted me. Had M. Swann intercepted the letter that I had written to his daughter, or was Gilberte merely confessing to me long after the event, and so that I should be more prudent in future, a state of things already long established? As I was telling her how greatly I admired her father and mother, she assumed that vague air, full of reticence and kept secrets, which she invariably wore when anyone spoke to her of what she was going to do, her walks, drives, visits—then suddenly expressed it with: "You know, they can't abide you!" and, slipping from me like the Undine that she was, burst out laughing. Often her laughter, out of harmony with her words, seemed, as music seems, to be tracing an invisible surface on another plane. M. and Mme. Swann did not require Gilberte to give up playing with me, but they would have been just as well pleased, she thought, if we had never begun. They did not look upon our relations with a kindly eye; they believed me to be a young person of low moral standard and imagined that my influence over their daughter must be evil. This type of unscrupulous young man whom the Swanns thought that I resembled, I pictured him to myself as detesting the parents of the girl he loved, flattering them to their faces but, when he was alone with her, making fun of them, urging her on to disobey them and, when once he had completed his conquest, not allowing them even to set eyes on her again. With these characteristics (though they are never those under which the basest of scoundrels recognises himself) how vehemently did my heart contrast the sentiments that did indeed animate it with regard to Swann, so passionate, on the contrary, that I never doubted that, were he to have the least suspicion of them, he must repent of his condemnation of me as of a judicial error. All that I felt about him I made bold to express to him in a long letter which I entrusted to Gilberte, with the request that she would deliver it. She consented. Alas! so he saw in me an even greater impostor than I had feared; those sentiments which I had supposed myself to be portraying, in sixteen pages, with such amplitude of truth, so he had suspected them; in short, the letter that I had written him, as ardent and as sincere as the words that I had uttered to M. de Norpois, met with no more success. Gilberte told me next day, after taking me aside behind a clump of laurels, along a little path by which we sat down on a couple of chairs, that as he read my letter, which she had now brought back to me, her father had shrugged his shoulders, with: "All this means nothing; it only goes to prove how right I was." I, who knew the purity of my intentions, the goodness of my soul, was furious that my words should not even have impinged upon the surface of Swann's ridiculous error. For it was an error; of that I had then no doubt. I felt that I had described with such accuracy certain irrefutable characteristics of my generous sentiments that, if Swann had not at once reconstructed these from my indications, had not come to ask my forgiveness and to admit that he had been mistaken, it must be because these noble sentiments he had never himself experienced, which would make him incapable of understanding the existence of them in other people.

Well, perhaps it was simply that Swann knew that generosity is often no more than the inner aspect which our egotistical feelings assume when we have not yet named and classified them. Perhaps he had recognised in the sympathy that I expressed for him simply an effect—and the strongest possible proof—of my love for Gilberte, by which, and not by any subordinate veneration of himself, my subsequent actions would be irresistibly controlled. I was unable to share his point of view, since I had not succeeded in abstracting my love from myself, in forcing it back into the common experience of humanity, and thus suffering, experimentally, its consequences; I was in despair. I was obliged to leave Gilberte for a moment; Françoise had called me. I must accompany her into a little pavilion covered in a green trellis, not unlike one of the disused toll-houses of old Paris, in which had recently been installed what in England they call a lavatory but in France, by an ill-informed piece of anglomania, 'water-closets.' The old, damp walls at the entrance, where I stood waiting for Françoise, emitted a chill and fusty smell which, relieving me at once of the anxieties that Swann's words, as reported by Gilberte, had just awakened in me, pervaded me with a pleasure not at all of the same character as other pleasures, which leave one more unstable than before, incapable of retaining them, of possessing them, but, on the contrary, with a consistent pleasure on which I could lean for support, delicious, soothing, rich with a truth that was lasting, unexplained and certain. I should have liked, as long ago in my walks along the Guermantes way, to endeavour to penetrate the charm of this impression which had seized hold of me, and, remaining there motionless, to interrogate this antiquated emanation which invited me not to enjoy the pleasure which it was offering me only as an 'extra,' but to descend into the underlying reality which it had not yet disclosed to me. But the tenant of the establishment, an elderly dame with painted cheeks and an auburn wig, was speaking to me. Françoise thought her 'very well-to-do indeed.' Her 'missy' had married what Françoise called 'a young man of family,' which meant that he differed more, in her eyes, from a workman than, in Saint-Simon's, a duke did from a man 'risen from the dregs of the people.' No doubt the tenant, before entering upon her tenancy, had met with reverses. But Françoise was positive that she was a 'marquise,' and belonged to the Saint-Ferréol family. This 'marquise' warned me not to stand outside in the cold, and even opened one of her doors for me, saying: "Won't you go inside for a minute? Look, here's a nice, clean one, and I shan't charge *you* anything." Perhaps she just made this offer in the spirit in which the young ladies at Gouache's, when we went in there to order something, used to offer me one of the sweets which they kept on the counter under glass bells, and which, alas, Mamma would never allow me to take; perhaps with less innocence, like an old florist whom Mamma used to have in to replenish her flower-stands, who rolled languishing eyes at me as she handed me a rose. In any event, if the 'marquise' had a weakness for little boys, when she threw open to them the hypogean doors of those cubicles of stone in which men crouch like sphinxes, she must have been moved to that generosity less by the hope of corrupting them than by the pleasure which all of us feel in displaying a needless prodigality to those whom we love, for I have never seen her with any other visitor except an old park-keeper.

A moment later I said good-bye to the 'marquise,' and went out accompanied by Françoise, whom I left to return to Gilberte. I caught sight of her at once, on a chair, behind the clump of laurels. She was there so as not to be seen by her friends: they were playing at hide-and-seek. I went and sat down by her side. She had on a flat cap which drooped forwards over her eyes, giving her the same 'underhand,' brooding, crafty look which I had remarked in her that first time at Combray. I asked her if there was not some way for me to have it out with her father, face to face. Gilberte said that she had suggested that to him, but that he had not thought it of any use. "Look," she went on, "don't go away without your letter; I must run along to the others, as they haven't caught me."

Had Swann appeared on the scene then before I had recovered it, this letter, by the sincerity of which I felt that he had been so unreasonable in not letting himself be convinced, perhaps he would have seen that it was he who had been in the right. For as I approached Gilberte, who, leaning back in her chair, told me to take the letter but did not hold it out to me, I felt myself so irresistibly attracted by her body that I said to her:

"Look! You try to stop me from getting it; we'll see which is the stronger."

She thrust it behind her back; I put my arms round her neck, raising the plaits of hair which she wore over her shoulders, either because she was still of an age for that or because her mother chose to make her look a child for a little longer so that she herself might still seem young; and we wrestled, locked together. I tried to pull her towards me, she resisted; her cheeks, inflamed by the effort, were as red and round as two cherries; she laughed as though I were tickling her; I held her gripped between my legs like a young tree which I was trying to climb; and, in the middle of my gymnastics, when I was already out of breath with the muscular exercise and the heat of the game, I felt, as it were a few drops of sweat wrung from me by the effort, my pleasure express itself in a form which I could not even pause for a moment to analyse; immediately I snatched the letter from her. Whereupon Gilberte said, good-naturedly:

"You know, if you like, we might go on wrestling for a little."

Perhaps she was dimly conscious that my game had had another object than that which I had avowed, but too dimly to have been able to see that I had attained it. And I, who was afraid that she had seen (and a slight recoil, as though of offended modesty which she made and checked a moment later made me think that my fear had not been unfounded), agreed to go on wrestling, lest she should suppose that I had indeed no other object than that, after which I wished only to sit quietly by her side.

On my way home I perceived, I suddenly recollected the impression, concealed from me until then, towards which, without letting me distinguish or recognise it, the cold, almost sooty smell of the trellised pavilion had borne me. It was that of my uncle Adolphe's little sitting-room at Combray, which had indeed exhaled the same odour of humidity. But I could not understand, and I postponed the attempt to discover why the recollection of so trivial an impression had given me so keen a happiness. It struck me, however, that I did indeed deserve the contempt of M. de Norpois; I had preferred, hitherto, to all other writers, one whom he styled a mere 'flute-player' and a positive rapture had been conveyed to me, not by any important idea, but by a mouldy smell.

For some time past, in certain households, the name of the Champs-Elysées, if a visitor mentioned it, would be greeted by the mother of the family with that air of contempt which mothers keep for a physician of established reputation whom they have (or so they make out) seen make too many false diagnoses to have any faith left in him; people insisted that these gardens were not good for children, that they knew of more than one sore throat, more than one case of measles and any number of feverish chills for which the Champs must be held responsible. Without venturing openly to doubt the maternal affection of Mamma, who continued to let me play there, several of her friends deplored her inability to see what was as plain as daylight.

Neurotic subjects are perhaps less addicted than any, despite the time-honoured phrase, to 'listening to their insides': they can hear so many things going on inside themselves, by which they realise later that they did wrong to let themselves be alarmed, that they end by paying no attention to any of them. Their nervous systems have so often cried out to them for help, as though from some serious malady, when it was merely because snow was coming, or because they had to change their rooms, that they have acquired the habit of paying no more heed to these warnings than a soldier who in the heat of battle perceives them so little that he is capable, although dying, of carrying on for some days still the life of a man in perfect health. One morning, bearing arranged within me all my regular disabilities, from whose constant, internal circulation I kept my mind turned as resolutely away as from the circulation of my blood, I had come running into the dining-room where my parents were already at table, and —having assured myself, as usual, that to feel cold may mean not that one ought to warm oneself but that, for instance, one has received a scolding, and not to feel hungry that it is going to rain, and not that one ought not to eat anything—had taken my place between them when, in the act of swallowing the first mouthful of a particularly tempting cutlet, a nausea, a giddiness stopped me, the feverish reaction of a malady that had already begun, the symptoms of which had been masked, retarded by the ice of my indifference, but which obstinately refused the nourishment that I was not in a fit state to absorb. Then, at the same moment, the thought that they would stop me from going out if they saw that I was unwell gave me, as the instinct of self-preservation gives a wounded man, the strength to crawl to my own room, where I found that I had a temperature of 104, and then to get ready to go to the Champs-Elysées. Through the languid and vulnerable shell which encased them, my eager thoughts were urging me towards, were clamouring for the soothing delight of a game of prisoner's base with Gilberte, and an hour later, barely able to keep on my feet, but happy in being by her side, I had still the strength to enjoy it.

Françoise, on our return, declared that I had been 'taken bad,' that I must have caught a 'hot and cold,' while the doctor, who was called in at once, declared that he 'preferred' the 'severity,' the 'virulence' of the rush of fever which accompanied my congestion of the lungs, and would be no more than 'a fire of straw,' to other forms, more 'insidious' and 'septic.' For some time now I had been liable to choking fits, and our doctor, braving the disapproval of my grandmother, who could see me already dying a drunkard's death, had recommended me to take, as well as the caffeine which had been prescribed to help me to breathe, beer, champagne or brandy when I felt an attack coming. These attacks would subside, he told me, in the 'euphoria' brought about by the alcohol. I was often obliged, so that my grandmother should allow them to give it to me, instead of dissembling, almost to make a display of my state of suffocation. On the other hand, as soon as I felt an attack coming, never being quite certain what proportions it would assume, I would grow distressed at the thought of my grandmother's anxiety, of which I was far more afraid than of my own sufferings. But at the same time my body, either because it was too weak to keep those sufferings secret, or because it feared lest, in their ignorance of the imminent disaster, people might demand of me some exertion which it would have found impossible or dangerous, gave me the need to warn my grandmother of my attacks with a punctiliousness into which I finally put a sort of physiological scruple. Did I perceive in myself a disturbing symptom which I had not previously observed, my body was in distress so long as I had not communicated it to my grandmother. Did she pretend to pay no attention, it made me insist. Sometimes I went too far; and that dear face, which was no longer able always to control its emotion as in the past, would allow an expression of pity to appear, a painful contraction. Then my heart was wrung by the sight of her grief; as if my kisses had had power to expel that grief, as if my affection could give my grandmother as much joy as my recovery, I flung myself into her arms. And its scruples being at the same time calmed by the certainty that she now knew the discomfort that I felt, my body offered no opposition to my reassuring her. I protested that this discomfort had been nothing, that I was in no sense to be pitied, that she might be quite sure that I was now happy; my body had wished to secure exactly the amount of pity that it deserved, and, provided that someone knew that it 'had a pain' in its right side, it could see no harm in my declaring that this pain was of no consequence and was not an obstacle to my happiness; for my body did not pride itself on its philosophy; that was outside its province. Almost every day during my convalescence I passed through these crises of suffocation. One evening, after my grandmother had left me comparatively well, she returned to my room very late and, seeing me struggling for breath, "Oh, my poor boy," she exclaimed, her face quivering with sympathy, "you are in dreadful pain." She left me at once; I heard the outer gate open, and in a little while she came back with some brandy which she had gone out to buy, since there was none in the house. Presently I began to feel better. My grandmother, who was rather flushed, seemed 'put out' about something, and her eyes had a look of weariness and dejection.

"I shall leave you alone now, and let you get the good of this improvement," she said, rising suddenly to go. I detained her, however, for a kiss, and could feel on her cold cheek something moist, but did not know whether it was the dampness of the night air through which she had just passed. Next day, she did not come to my room until the evening, having had, she told me, to go out. I considered that this shewed a surprising indifference to my welfare, and I had to restrain myself so as not to reproach her with it.

As my chokings had persisted long after any congestion remained that could account for them, my parents asked for a consultation with Professor Cottard. It is not enough that a physician who is called in to treat cases of this sort should be learned. Brought face to face with symptoms which may or may not be those of three or four different complaints, it is in the long run his instinct, his eye that must decide with which, despite the more or less similar appearance of them all, he has to deal. This mysterious gift does not imply any superiority in the other departments of the intellect, and a creature of the utmost vulgarity, who admires the worst pictures, the worst music, in whose mind there is nothing out of the common, may perfectly well possess it. In my case, what was physically evident might

equally well have been due to nervous spasms, to the first stages of tuberculosis, to asthma, to a toxi-alimentary dyspnoea with renal insufficiency,
to chronic bronchitis, or to a complex state into which more than one of
these factors entered. Now, nervous spasms required to be treated firmly,
and discouraged, tuberculosis with infinite care and with a 'feeding-up'
process which would have been bad for an arthritic condition such as
asthma, and might indeed have been dangerous in a case of toxi-alimentary
dyspnoea, this last calling for a strict diet which, in return, would be fatal
to a tuberculous patient. But Cottard's hesitations were brief and his
prescriptions imperious. "Purges; violent and drastic purges; milk for
some days, nothing but milk. No meat. No alcohol." My mother murmured that I needed, all the same, to be 'built up,' that my nerves were
already weak, that drenching me like a horse and restricting my diet
would make me worse. I could see in Cottard's eyes, as uneasy as though
he were afraid of missing a train, that he was asking himself whether he
had not allowed his natural good-humour to appear. He was trying to
think whether he had remembered to put on his mask of coldness, as one
looks for a mirror to see whether one has not forgotten to tie one's tie.
In his uncertainty, and, so as, whatever he had done, to put things right,
he replied brutally: "I am not in the habit of repeating my instructions.
Give me a pen. Now remember, milk! Later on, when we have got the
crises and the agrypnia by the throat, I should like you to take a little
clear soup, and then a little broth, but always with milk; *au lait*! You'll
enjoy that, since Spain is all the rage just now; *ollé, ollé*!" His pupils
knew this joke well, for he made it at the hospital whenever he had to put a
heart or liver case on a milk diet. "After that, you will gradually return to
your normal life. But whenever there is any coughing or choking—purges,
injections, bed, milk!" He listened with icy calm, and without uttering a
word, to my mother's final objections, and as he left us without having
condescended to explain the reasons for this course of treatment, my parents concluded that it had no bearing on my case, and would weaken me
to no purpose, and so they did not make me try it. Naturally they sought
to conceal their disobedience from the Professor, and to succeed in this
avoided all the houses in which he was likely to be found. Then, as my
health became worse, they decided to make me follow out Cottard's prescriptions to the letter; in three days my 'rattle' and cough had ceased, I
could breathe freely. Whereupon we realised that Cottard, while finding,
as he told us later on, that I was distinctly asthmatic, and still more inclined to 'imagine things,' had seen that what was really the matter with
me at the moment was intoxication, and that by loosening my liver and
washing out my kidneys he would get rid of the congestion of my bronchial
tubes and thus give me back my breath, my sleep and my strength. And
we realised that this imbecile was a clinical genius. At last I was able to get
up. But they spoke of not letting me go any more to the Champs-Elysées.
They said that it was because the air there was bad; but I felt sure that
this was only a pretext so that I should not see Mlle. Swann, and I forced
myself to repeat the name of Gilberte all the time, like the native tongue
which peoples in captivity endeavour to preserve among themselves so

as not to forget the land that they will never see again. Sometimes my mother would stroke my forehead with her hand, saying: "So little boys don't tell Mamma their troubles any more?" And Françoise used to come up to me every day with: "What a face, to be sure! If you could just see yourself! Anyone would think there was a corpse in the house." It is true that, if I had simply had a cold in the head, Françoise would have assumed the same funereal air. These lamentations pertained rather to her 'class' than to the state of my health. I could not at the time discover whether this pessimism was due to sorrow or to satisfaction. I decided provisionally that it was social and professional.

One day, after the postman had called, my mother laid a letter upon my bed. I opened it carelessly, since it could not bear the one signature that would have made me happy, the name of Gilberte, with whom I had no relations outside the Champs-Elysées. And lo, at the foot of the page, embossed with a silver seal representing a man's head in a helmet, and under him a scroll with the device *Per viam rectam*, beneath a letter written in a large and flowing hand, in which almost every word appeared to be underlined, simply because the crosses of the 't's' ran not across but over them, and so drew a line beneath the corresponding letters of the word above, it was indeed Gilberte's signature and nothing else that I saw. But because I knew that to be impossible upon a letter addressed to myself, the sight of it, unaccompanied by any belief in it, gave me no pleasure. For a moment it merely struck an impression of unreality on everything round about me. With lightning rapidity the impossible signature danced about my bed, the fireplace, the four walls. I saw everything sway, as one does when one falls from a horse, and I asked myself whether there was not an existence altogether different from the one I knew, in direct contradiction of it, but itself the true existence, which, being suddenly revealed to me, filled me with that hesitation which sculptors, in representing the Last Judgment, have given to the awakening dead who find themselves at the gates of the next world. "My dear Friend," said the letter, "I hear that you have been very ill and have given up going to the Champs-Elysées. I hardly ever go there either because there has been such an enormous lot of illness. But I'm having my friends to tea here every Monday and Friday. Mamma asks me to tell you that it will be a great pleasure to us all if you will come too, as soon as you are well again, and we can have some more nice talks here, just like the Champs-Elysées. Good-bye, dear friend; I hope that your parents will allow you to come to tea very often. With all my kindest regards. GILBERTE."

While I was reading these words, my nervous system was receiving, with admirable promptitude, the news that a piece of great good fortune had befallen me. But my mind, that is to say myself, and in fact the party principally concerned, was still in ignorance. Such good fortune, coming from Gilberte, was a thing of which I had never ceased to dream; a thing wholly in my mind, it was, as Leonardo says of painting, *cosa mentale*. Now, a sheet of paper covered with writing is not a thing that the mind assimilates at once. But as soon as I had finished reading the letter, I thought of it, it became an object of my dreams, became, it also, *cosa mentale*, and I loved it so much already that every few minutes I must read it, kiss it again. Then at last I was conscious of my happiness.

Life is strewn with these miracles, for which people who are in love can always hope. It is possible that this one had been artificially brought about by my mother who, seeing that for some time past I had lost all interest in life, may have suggested to Gilberte to write to me, just as, when I was little and went first to the sea-side, so as to give me some pleasure in bathing, which I detested because it took away my breath, she used secretly to hand to the man who was to 'dip' me marvellous boxes made of shells, and branches of coral, which I believed that I myself had discovered lying at the bottom of the sea. However, with every occurrence which, in our life and among its contrasted situations, bears any relation to love, it is best to make no attempt to understand it, since in so far as these are inexorable, as they are unlooked-for, they appear to be governed by magic rather than by rational laws. When a multi-millionaire—who for all his millions is quite a charming person—sent packing by a poor and unattractive woman with whom he has been living, calls to his aid, in his desperation, all the resources of wealth, and brings every worldly influence to bear without succeeding in making her take him back, it is wiser for him, in the face of the implacable obstinacy of his mistress, to suppose that Fate intends to crush him, and to make him die of an affection of the heart, than to seek any logical explanation. These obstacles, against which lovers have to contend, and which their imagination, over-excited by suffering, seeks in vain to analyse, are contained, as often as not, in some peculiar characteristic of the woman whom they cannot bring back to themselves, in her stupidity, in the influence acquired over her, the fears suggested to her by people whom the lover does not know, in the kind of pleasures which, at the moment, she is demanding of life, pleasures which neither her lover nor her lover's wealth can procure for her. In any event, the lover is scarcely in a position to discover the nature of these obstacles, which her womanly cunning hides from him and his own judgment, falsified by love, prevents him from estimating exactly. They may be compared with those tumours which the doctor succeeds in reducing, but without having traced them to their source. Like them these obstacles remain mysterious but are temporary. Only they last, as a rule, longer than love itself. And as that is not a disinterested passion, the lover who is no longer in love does not seek to know why the woman, neither rich nor virtuous, with whom he was in love refused obstinately for years to let him continue to keep her.

Now the same mystery which often veils from our eyes the reason for a catastrophe, when love is in question, envelops just as frequently the suddenness of certain happy solutions, such as had come to me with Gilberte's letter. Happy, or at least seemingly happy, for there are few solutions that can really be happy when we are dealing with a sentiment of such a kind that every satisfaction which we can bring to it does no more, as a rule, than dislodge some pain. And yet sometimes a respite is granted us, and we have for a little while the illusion that we are healed.

So far as concerns this letter, at the foot of which Françoise declined to recognise Gilberte's name, because the elaborate capital 'G' leaning against the undotted 'i' looked more like an 'A,' while the final syllable was indefinitely prolonged by a waving flourish, if we persist in looking for a rational explanation of the sudden reversal of her attitude towards me which it indicated, and which made me so radiantly happy, we may perhaps find that I was to some extent indebted for it to an incident which I should have supposed, on the contrary, to be calculated to ruin me for ever in the sight of the Swann family. A short while back, Bloch had come to see me at a time when Professor Cottard, whom, now that I was following his instructions, we were again calling in, happened to be in my room. As his examination of me was over, and he was sitting with me simply as a visitor because my parents had invited him to stay to dinner, Bloch was allowed to come in. While we were all talking, Bloch having mentioned that he had heard it said that Mme. Swann was very fond of me, by a lady with whom he had been dining the day before, who was herself very intimate with Mme. Swann, I should have liked to reply that he was most certainly mistaken, and to establish the fact (from the same scruple of conscience that had made me proclaim it to M. de Norpois, and for fear of Mme. Swann's taking me for a liar) that I did not know her and had never spoken to her. But I had not the courage to correct Bloch's mistake, because I could see quite well that it was deliberate, and that, if he invented something that Mme. Swann could not possibly have said, it was simply to let us know (what he considered flattering to himself, and was not true either) that he had been dining with one of that lady's friends. And so it fell out that, whereas M. de Norpois, on learning that I did not know but would very much like to know Mme. Swann, had taken great care to avoid speaking to her about me, Cottard, who was her doctor also, having gathered from what he had heard Bloch say that she knew me quite well and thought highly of me, concluded that to remark, when next he saw her, that I was a charming young fellow and a great friend of his could not be of the smallest use to me and would be of advantage to himself, two reasons which made him decide to speak of me to Odette whenever an opportunity arose.

Thus at length I found my way into that abode from which was wafted even on to the staircase the scent that Mme. Swann used, though it was embalmed far more sweetly still by the peculiar, disturbing charm that emanated from the life of Gilberte. The implacable porter, transformed into a benevolent Eumenid, adopted the custom, when I asked him if I might go upstairs, of indicating to me, by raising his cap with a propitious hand, that he gave ear to my prayer. Those windows which, seen from outside, used to interpose between me and the treasures within, which were not intended for me, a polished, distant and superficial stare, which seemed to me the very stare of the Swanns themselves, it fell to my lot, when in the warm weather I had spent a whole afternoon with Gilberte in her room, to open them myself, so as to let in a little air, and even to lean over the sill of one of them by her side, if it was her mother's 'at home' day, to watch the visitors arrive who would often, raising their heads as they stepped out of their carriages, greet me with a wave of the hand, taking me for some nephew of their hostess. At such moments Gilberte's plaits used to brush my cheek. They seemed to me, in the fineness of their grain, at once natural and supernatural, and in the strength of their constructed tracery, a matchless work of art, in the composition of which had been used the very grass of Paradise. To a section of them, even infinitely minute, what celestial herbary would I not have given as a reliquary. But since I never hoped to obtain an actual fragment of those plaits, if at least I had been able to have their photograph, how far more precious than one of a sheet of flowers traced by Vinci's pencil! To acquire one of these, I stooped—with friends of the Swanns, and even with photographers—to servilities which did not procure for me what I wanted, but tied me for life to a number of extremely tiresome people.

Gilberte's parents, who for so long had prevented me from seeing her, now—when I entered the dark hall in which hovered perpetually, more formidable and more to be desired than, at Versailles of old, the apparition of the King, the possibility of my encountering them, in which too, invariably, after butting into an enormous hat-stand with seven branches, like the Candlestick in Holy Writ, I would begin bowing confusedly before a footman, seated among the skirts of his long grey coat upon the woodbox, whom in the dim light I had mistaken for Mme. Swann—Gilberte's parents, if one of them happened to be passing at the moment of my arrival, so far from seeming annoyed would come and shake hands with a smile, and say:

"How d'e do?" (They both pronounced it in the same clipped way, which, you may well imagine, once I was back at home, I made an incessant and delightful practice of copying.) "Does Gilberte know you're here? She does? Then I'll leave you to her."

Better still, the tea-parties themselves to which Gilberte invited her friends, parties which for so long had seemed to me the most insurmountable of the barriers heaped up between her and myself, became now an opportunity for uniting us of which she would inform me in a few lines, written (because I was still a comparative stranger) upon sheets that were always different. One was adorned with a poodle embossed in blue, above a fantastic inscription in English with an exclamation mark after it; another was stamped with an anchor, or with the monogram G. S. preposterously elongated in a rectangle which ran from top to bottom of the page, or else with the name Gilberte, now traced across one corner in letters of gold which imitated my friend's signature and ended in a flourish, beneath an open umbrella printed in black, now enclosed in a monogram in the shape of a Chinaman's hat, which contained all the letters of the word in capitals without its being possible to make out a single one of them. At last, as the series of different writing-papers which Gilberte possessed, numerous as it might be, was not unlimited, after a certain number of weeks I saw reappear the sheet that bore (like the first letter she had written me) the motto *Per viam rectam,* and over it the man's head in a helmet, set in a medallion of tarnished silver. And each of them was chosen, on one day rather than another, by virtue of a certain ritual, as I then supposed, but more probably, as I now think, because she tried to remember which of them she had already used, so as never to send the same one twice to any of her correspondents, of those at least whom she took special pains to please, save at the longest possible intervals. As, on account of the different times of their lessons, some of the friends whom Gilberte used to invite to her parties were obliged to leave just as the rest were arriving, while I was still on the stairs I could hear escaping from the hall a murmur of voices which, such was the emotion aroused in me by the imposing ceremony in which I was to take part, long before I had reached the landing, broke all the bonds that still held me to my past life, so that I did not even remember that I was to take off my muffler as soon as I felt too hot, and to keep an eye on the clock so as not to be late in getting home. That staircase, besides, all of wood, as they were built about that time in certain houses, in keeping with that Henri II style which had for so long been Odette's ideal though she was shortly to lose interest in it, and furnished with a placard, to which there was no equivalent at home, on which one read the words: "NOTICE. The lift must not be taken downstairs," seemed to me a thing so marvellous that I told my parents that it was an ancient staircase brought from ever so far away by M. Swann. My regard for the truth was so great that I should not have hesitated to give them this information even if I had known it to be false, for it alone could enable them to feel for the dignity of the Swanns' staircase the same respect that I felt myself. It was just as, when one is talking to some ignorant person who cannot understand in what the genius of a great physician consists, it is as well not to admit that he does not know how to cure a cold in the head. But since I had no power of observation, since, as a general rule, I never knew either the name or the nature of things that were before my eyes, and could understand only that when they were connected with the Swanns they must be extraordinary, I was by no means certain that in notifying my parents of the artistic value and remote origin ot the staircase I was guilty of falsehood. It did not seem certain; but it must have seemed probable, for I felt myself turn very red when my father interrupted me with: "I know those houses; I have been in one; they are all alike; Swann just has several floors in one; it was Berlier built them all." He added that he had thought of taking a flat in one of them, but that he had changed his mind, finding that they were not conveniently arranged, and that the landings were too dark. So he said; but I felt instinctively that my mind must make the sacrifices necessary to the glory of the Swanns and to my own happiness, and by a stroke of internal authority, in spite of what I had just heard, I banished for ever from my memory, as a good Catholic banishes Renan's *Vie de Jésus,* the destroying thought that their house was just an ordinary flat in which we ourselves might have been living.

Meanwhile on those tea-party days, pulling myself up the staircase step by step, reason and memory already cast off like outer garments, and myself no more now than the sport of the basest reflexes, I would arrive in the zone in which the scent of Mme. Swann greeted my nostrils. I felt that I could already behold the majesty of the chocolate cake, encircled by plates heaped with little cakes, and by tiny napkins of grey damask with

figures on them, as required by convention but peculiar to the Swanns.
But this unalterable and governed whole seemed, like Kant's necessary
universe, to depend on a supreme act of free will. For when we were all
together in Gilberte's little sitting-room, suddenly she would look at the
clock and exclaim:

"I say! It's getting a long time since luncheon, and we aren't having
dinner till eight. I feel as if I could eat something. What do you say?"

And she would make us go into the dining-room, as sombre as the interior
of an Asiatic Temple painted by Rembrandt, in which an architectural
cake, as gracious and sociable as it was imposing, seemed to be enthroned
there in any event, in case the fancy seized Gilberte to discrown it of its
chocolate battlements and to hew down the steep brown slopes of its
ramparts, baked in the oven like the bastions of the palace of Darius.
Better still, in proceeding to the demolition of that Babylonitish pastry,
Gilberte did not consider only her own hunger; she inquired also after
mine, while she extracted for me from the crumbling monument a whole
glazed slab jewelled with scarlet fruits, in the oriental style. She asked me
even at what o'clock my parents were dining, as if I still knew, as if the
disturbance that governed me had allowed to persist the sensation of
satiety or of hunger, the notion of dinner or the picture of my family in
my empty memory and paralysed stomach. Alas, its paralysis was but
momentary. The cakes that I took without noticing them, a time would
come when I should have to digest them. But that time was still remote.
Meanwhile Gilberte was making 'my' tea. I went on drinking it indefinitely,
whereas a single cup would keep me awake for twenty-four hours. Which
explains why my mother used always to say: "What a nuisance it is; he
can never go to the Swanns' without coming home ill." But was I aware
even, when I was at the Swanns', that it was tea that I was drinking? Had
I known, I should have taken it just the same, for even supposing that I
had recovered for a moment the sense of the present, that would not have
restored to me the memory of the past or the apprehension of the future.
My imagination was incapable of reaching to the distant time in which I
might have the idea of going to bed, and the need to sleep.

Gilberte's girl friends were not all plunged in that state of intoxication
in which it is impossible to make up one's mind. Some of them refused tea!
Then Gilberte would say, using a phrase highly fashionable that year: "I
can see I'm not having much of a success with my tea!" And to destroy
more completely any idea of ceremony, she would disarrange the chairs
that were drawn up round the table, with: "We look just like a wedding
breakfast. Good lord, what fools servants are!"

She nibbled her cake, perched sideways upon a cross-legged seat placed
at an angle to the table. And then, just as though she could have had all
those cakes at her disposal without having first asked leave of her mother,
when Mme. Swann, whose 'day' coincided as a rule with Gilberte's tea-
parties, had shewn one of her visitors to the door, and came sweeping in,
a moment later, dressed sometimes in blue velvet, more often in a black
satin gown draped with white lace, she would say with an air of astonish-

ment: "I say, that looks good, what you've got there. It makes me quite hungry to see you all eating cake."

"But, Mamma, do! We invite you!" Gilberte would answer.

"Thank you, no, my precious; what would my visitors say? I've still got Mme. Trombert and Mme. Cottard and Mme. Bontemps; you know dear Mme. Bontemps never pays very short visits, and she has only just come. What would all those good people say if I never went back to them? If no one else calls, I'll come in again and have a chat with you (which will be far more amusing) after they've all gone. I really think I've earned a little rest; I have had forty-five different people to-day, and forty-two of them told me about Gérôme's picture! But you must come alone one of these days," she turned to me, "and take 'your' tea with Gilberte. She will make it for you just as you like it, as you have it in your own little 'studio,' " she went on, flying off to her visitors, as if it had been something as familiar to me as my own habits (such as the habit that I should have had of taking tea, had I ever taken it; as for my 'studio,' I was uncertain whether I had one or not) that I had come to seek in this mysterious world. "When can you come? To-morrow? We will make you 'toast' every bit as good as you get at Colombin's. No? You are horrid!"
—for, since she also had begun to form a salon, she had borrowed Mme. Verdurin's mannerisms, and notably her tone of petulant autocracy. 'Toast' being as incomprehensible to me as 'Colombin's,' this further promise could not add to my temptation. It will appear stranger still, now that everyone uses such expressions—and perhaps even at Combray they are creeping in—that I had not at first understood of whom Mme. Swann was speaking when I heard her sing the praises of our old 'nurse.' I did not know any English; I gathered, however, as she went on that the word was intended to denote Françoise. I who, in the Champs-Elysées, had been so terrified of the bad impression that she must make, I now learned from Mme. Swann that it was all the things that Gilberte had told them about my 'nurse' that had attracted her husband and her to me. "One feels that she is so devoted to you; she must be nice!" (At once my opinion of Françoise was diametrically changed. By the same token, to have a governess equipped with a waterproof and a feather in her hat no longer appeared quite so essential.) Finally I learned from some words which Mme. Swann let fall with regard to Mme. Blatin (whose good nature she recognised but dreaded her visits) that personal relations with that lady would have been of less value to me than I had supposed, and would not in any way have improved my standing with the Swanns.

If I had now begun to explore, with tremors of reverence and joy the faery domain which, against all probability, had opened to me its hitherto locked approaches, this was still only in my capacity as a friend of Gilberte. The kingdom into which I was received was itself contained within another, more mysterious still, in which Swann and his wife led their supernatural existence and towards which they made their way, after taking my hand in theirs, when they crossed the hall at the same moment as myself but in the other direction. But soon I was to penetrate also to the heart of the Sanctuary. For instance, Gilberte might be out when I called, but M. or Mme. Swann was at home. They would ask who had rung, and on being told that it was myself would send out to ask me to come in for a moment and talk to them, desiring me to use in one way or another, and with this or that object in view, my influence over their daughter. I reminded myself of that letter, so complete, so convincing, which I had written to Swann only the other day, and which he had not deigned even to acknowledge. I marvelled at the impotence of the mind, the reason and the heart to effect the least conversion, to solve a single one of those difficulties which, in the sequel, life, without one's so much as knowing what steps it has taken, so easily unravels. My new position as the friend of Gilberte, endowed with an excellent influence over her, entitling me now to enjoy the same favours as if, having had as a companion at some school where they had always put me at the head of my class the son of a king, I had owed to that accident the right of informal entry into the palace and to audiences in the throne-room, Swann, with an infinite benevolence and as though he were not over-burdened with glorious occupations, would make me go into his library and there let me for an hour on end respond in stammered monosyllables, timid silences broken by brief and incoherent bursts of courage, to utterances of which my emotion prevented me from understanding a single word; would shew me works of art and books which he thought likely to interest me, things as to which I had no doubt, before seeing them, that they infinitely surpassed in beauty anything that the Louvre possessed or the National Library, but at which I found it impossible to look. At such moments I should have been grateful to Swann's butler, had he demanded from me my watch, my tie-pin, my boots, and made me sign a deed acknowledging him as my heir: in the admirable words of a popular expression of which, as of the most famous epics, we do not know who was the author, although, like those epics, and with all deference to Wolff and his theory, it most certainly had an author, one of those inventive, modest souls such as we come across every year, who light upon such gems as 'putting a name to a face,' though their own names they never let us learn, I did not know what I was doing. All the greater was my astonishment, when my visit was prolonged, at finding to what a zero of realisation, to what an absence of happy ending those hours spent in the enchanted dwelling led me. But my disappointment arose neither from the inadequacy of the works of art that were shewn to me nor from the impossibility of fixing upon them my distracted gaze. For it was not the intrinsic beauty of the objects themselves that made it miraculous for me to be sitting in Swann's library, it was the attachment to those objects—which might have been the ugliest in the world —of the particular feeling, melancholy and voluptuous, which I had for so many years localised in that room and which still impregnated it; similarly the multitude of mirrors, of silver-backed brushes, of altars to Saint Anthony of Padua, carved and painted by the most eminent artists, her friends, counted for nothing in the feeling of my own unworthiness and of her regal benevolence which was aroused in me when Mme. Swann received me for a moment in her own room, in which three beautiful and impressive creatures, her principal and second and third maids, smilingly prepared for her the most marvellous toilets, and towards which, on the order conveyed to me by the footman in knee-breeches that Madame wished to say a few words to me, I would make my way along the tortuous path of a corridor all embalmed, far and near, by the precious essences which exhaled without ceasing from her dressing-room a fragrance exquisitely sweet.

When Mme. Swann had returned to her visitors, we could still hear her talking and laughing, for even with only two people in the room, and as though she had to cope with all the 'good friends' at once, she would raise her voice, ejaculate her words, as she had so often in the 'little clan' heard its 'Mistress' do, at the moments when she 'led the conversation.' The expressions which we have borrowed from other people being those which, for a time at least, we are fondest of using, Mme. Swann used to select at one time those which she had learned from distinguished people whom her husband had not managed to prevent her from getting to know (it was from them that she derived the mannerism which consists in suppressing the article or demonstrative pronoun, in French, before an adjective qualifying a person's name), at another time others more plebeian (such as "It's a mere nothing!" the favourite expression of one of her friends), and used to make room for them in all the stories which, by a habit formed among the 'little clan,' she loved to tell about people. She would follow these up automatically with, "I do love that story!" or "Do admit, it's a very *good* story!" which came to her, through her husband, from the Guermantes, whom she did not know.

Mme. Swann had left the dining-room, but her husband, who had just returned home, made his appearance among us in turn. "Do you know if your mother is alone, Gilberte?" "No, Papa, she has still some people." "What, still? At seven o'clock! It's appalling! The poor woman must be absolutely dead. It's odious." (At home I had always heard the first syllable of this word pronounced with a long 'o,' like 'ode,' but M. and Mme. Swann made it short, as in 'odd.') "Just think of it; ever since two o'clock this afternoon!" he went on, turning to me. "And Camille tells me that between four and five he let in at least a dozen people. Did I say a dozen? I believe he told me fourteen. No, a dozen; I don't remember. When I came home I had quite forgotten it was her 'day,' and when I saw all those carriages outside the door I thought there must be a wedding in the house. And just now, while I've been in the library for a minute, the bell has never stopped ringing; upon my word, it's given me quite a headache. And are there a lot of them in there still?" "No; only two." "Who are they, do you know?" "Mme. Cottard and Mme. Bontemps." "Oh! the wife of the Chief Secretary to the Minister of Posts." "I know her husband's a clerk in some Ministry or other, but I don't know what he does." Gilberte assumed a babyish manner.

"What's that? You silly child, you talk as if you were two years old. What do you mean; 'a clerk in some Ministry or other' indeed! He is nothing less than Chief Secretary, chief of the whole show, and what's more—what on earth am I thinking of? Upon my word, I'm getting as stupid as yourself; he is not the Chief Secretary, he's the Permanent Secretary."

"I don't know, I'm sure; does that mean a lot, being Permanent Secretary?" answered Gilberte, who never let slip an opportunity of displaying her own indifference to anything that gave her parents cause for vanity. (She may, of course, have considered that she only enhanced the brilliance of such an acquaintance by not seeming to attach any undue importance to it.)

"I should think it did 'mean a lot'!" exclaimed Swann, who preferred to this modesty, which might have left me in doubt, a more explicit mode of speech. "Why it means simply that he's the first man after the Minister. In fact, he's more important than the Minister, because it is he that does all the work. Besides, it appears that he has immense capacity, a man quite of the first rank, a most distinguished individual. He's an Officer of the Legion of Honour. A delightful man, he is, and very good-looking too."

(This man's wife, incidentally, had married him against everyone's wishes and advice because he was a 'charming creature.' He had, what may be sufficient to constitute a rare and delicate whole, a fair, silky beard, good features, a nasal voice, powerful lungs and a glass eye.)

"I may tell you," he added, turning again to me, "that I am greatly amused to see that lot serving in the present Government, because they are Bontemps of the Bontemps-Chenut family, typical old-fashioned middle-class people, reactionary, clerical, tremendously strait-laced. Your grandfather knew quite well—at least by name and by sight he must have known old Chenut, the father, who never tipped the cabmen more than a ha'penny, though he was a rich enough man for those days, and the Baron Bréau-Chenut. All their money went in the Union Générale smash—you're too young to remember that, of course—and, gad! they've had to get it back as best they could."

"He's the uncle of a little girl who used to come to my lessons, in a class a long way below mine, the famous 'Albertine.' She's certain to be dreadfully 'fast' when she's older, but just now she's the quaintest spectacle."

"She is amazing, this daughter of mine. She knows everyone."

"I don't know her. I only used to see her going about, and hear them calling 'Albertine' here, and 'Albertine' there. But I do know Mme. Bontemps, and I don't like her much either."

"You are quite wrong; she is charming, pretty, intelligent. In fact, she's quite clever. I shall go in and say how d'e do to her, and ask her if her husband thinks we're going to have war, and whether we can rely on King Theodosius. He's bound to know, don't you think, since he's in the counsels of the gods."

It was not thus that Swann used to talk in days gone by; but which of us cannot call to mind some royal princess of limited intelligence who let herself be carried off by a footman, and then, ten years later, tried to get back into society, and found that people were not very willing to call upon her; have we not found her spontaneously adopting the language of all the old bores, and, when we referred to some duchess who was at the height of fashion, heard her say: "She came to see me only yesterday," or "I live a very quiet life." So that it is superfluous to make a study of manners, since we can deduce them all from psychological laws.

The Swanns shared this eccentricity of people who have not many friends; a visit, an invitation, a mere friendly word from some one ever so little prominent were for them events to which they aspired to give full publicity. If bad luck would have it that the Verdurins were in London when Odette gave a rather smart dinner-party, arrangements were made by which some common friend was to 'cable' a report to them across the Channel. Even the complimentary letters and telegrams received by Odette the Swanns were incapable of keeping to themselves. They spoke of them to their friends, passed them from hand to hand. Thus the Swanns' drawing-room reminded one of a seaside hotel where telegrams containing the latest news are posted up on a board.

Still, people who had known the old Swann not merely outside society, as I had known him, but in society, in that Guermantes set which, with certain concessions to Highnesses and Duchesses, was almost infinitely exacting in the matter of wit and charm, from which banishment was sternly decreed for men of real eminence whom its members found boring or vulgar,—such people might have been astonished to observe that their old Swann had ceased to be not only discreet when he spoke of his acquaintance, but difficult when he was called upon to enlarge it. How was it that Mme. Bontemps, so common, so ill-natured, failed to exasperate him? How could he possibly describe her as attractive? The memory of the Guermantes set must, one would suppose, have prevented him; as a matter of fact it encouraged him. There was certainly among the Guermantes, as compared with the great majority of groups in society, taste, indeed a refined taste, but also a snobbishness from which there arose the possibility of a momentary interruption in the exercise of that taste. If it were a question of some one who was not indispensable to their circle, of a Minister for Foreign Affairs, a Republican and inclined to be pompous, or of an Academician who talked too much, their taste would be brought to bear heavily against him, Swann would condole with Mme. de Guermantes on having had to sit next to such people at dinner at one of the Embassies, and they would a thousand times rather have a man of fashion, that is to say a man of the Guermantes kind, good for nothing, but endowed with the wit of the Guermantes, some one who was 'of the same chapel' as themselves. Only, a Grand Duchess, a Princess of the Blood, should she dine often with Mme. de Guermantes, would soon find herself enrolled in that chapel also, without having any right to be there, without being at all so endowed. But with the simplicity of people in society, from the moment they had her in their houses they went out of their way to find her attractive, since they were unable to say that it was because she was attractive that they invited her. Swann, coming to the rescue of Mme. de Guermantes, would say to her after the Highness had gone: "After all, she's not such a bad woman; really, she has quite a sense of the comic. I don't suppose for a moment that she has mastered the *Critique of Pure Reason*; still, she is not unattractive." "Oh, I do so entirely agree with you!" the Duchess would respond. "Besides, she was a little frightened of us all; you will see that she can be charming." "She is certainly a great deal less devastating than Mme. X——" (the wife of the talkative Academician, and herself a remarkable woman) "who quotes twenty volumes at you." "Oh, but there isn't any comparison between them." The faculty of saying such things as these, and of saying them sincerely, Swann had acquired from the Duchess, and had never lost. He made use of it now with reference to the people who came to his house. He forced himself to distinguish, and to admire in them the qualities that every human being will display if we examine him with a prejudice in his favour, and not with the distaste of the nice-minded; he extolled the merits of Mme. Bontemps, as he had once extolled those of the Princesse de Parme, who must have been excluded from the Guermantes set if there had not been privileged terms of admission for certain Highnesses, and if, when they presented themselves for election, no consideration had indeed been paid except to wit and charm. We have seen already, moreover, that Swann had always an inclination (which he was now putting into practice, only in a more lasting fashion) to exchange his social position for another which, in certain circumstances, might suit him better. It is only people incapable of analysing, in their perception, what at first sight appears indivisible who believe that one's position is consolidated with one's person. One and the same man, taken at successive points in his life, will be found to breathe, at different stages on the social ladder, in atmospheres that do not of necessity become more and more refined; whenever, in any period of our existence, we form or re-form associations with a certain environment, and feel that we can move at ease in it and are made comfortable, we begin quite naturally to make ourselves fast to it by putting out roots and tendrils.

In so far as Mme. Bontemps was concerned, I believe also that Swann, in speaking of her with so much emphasis, was not sorry to think that my parents would hear that she had been to see his wife. To tell the truth, in our house the names of the people whom Mme. Swann was gradually getting to know pricked our curiosity more than they aroused our admiration. At the name of Mme. Trombert, my mother exclaimed: "Ah! That's a new recruit, and one who will bring in others." And as though she found a similarity between the somewhat summary, rapid and violent manner in which Mme. Swann acquired her friends, as it were by conquest, and a Colonial expedition, Mamma went on to observe: "Now that the Tromberts have surrendered, the neighbouring tribes will not be long in coming in." If she had passed Mme. Swann in the street, she would tell us when she came home: "I saw Mme. Swann in all her war-paint; she must have been embarking on some triumphant offensive against the Massachutoes, or the Cingalese, or the Tromberts." And so with all the new people whom I told her that I had seen in that somewhat composite and artificial society, to which they had often been brought with great difficulty and from widely different surroundings, Mamma would at once divine their origin, and, speaking of them as of trophies dearly bought, would say: "Brought back from an Expedition against the so-and-so!"

As for Mme. Cottard, my father was astonished that Mme. Swann could find anything to be gained by getting so utterly undistinguished a woman to come to her house, and said: "In spite of the Professor's position, I must say that I cannot understand it." Mamma, on the other hand, understood quite well; she knew that a great deal of the pleasure which a woman finds in entering a class of society different from that in which she has previously lived would be lacking if she had no means of keeping her old associates informed of those others, relatively more brilliant, with whom she has replaced them. Therefore, she requires an eye-witness who may be allowed to penetrate this new, delicious world (as a buzzing, browsing insect bores its way into a flower) and will then, as the course of her visits may carry her, spread abroad, or so at least one hopes, with the tidings, a latent germ of envy and of wonder. Mme. Cottard, who might have been created on purpose to fill this part, belonged to that special category in a visiting list which Mamma (who inherited certain facets of her father's turn of mind) used to call the 'Tell Sparta' people. Besides—apart from another reason which did not come to our knowledge until many years later—Mme. Swann, in inviting this good-natured, reserved and modest friend, had no need to fear lest she might be introducing into her drawing-room, on her brilliant 'days,' a traitor or a rival. She knew what a vast number of homely blossoms that busy worker, armed with her plume and card-case, could visit in a single afternoon. She knew the creature's power of dissemination, and, basing her calculations upon the law of probability, was led to believe that almost certainly some intimate of the Verdurins would be bound to hear, within two or three days, how the Governor of Paris had left cards upon her, or that M. Verdurin himself would be told how M. Le Hault de Pressagny, the President of the Horse Show, had taken them, Swann and herself, to the King Theodosius gala; she imagined the Verdurins as informed of these two events, both so flattering to herself and of these alone, because the particular materialisations in which we embody and pursue fame are but few in number, by the default of our own minds which are incapable of imagining at one time all the forms which, none the less, we hope—in a general way—that fame will not fail simultaneously to assume for our benefit.

Mme. Swann had, however, met with no success outside what was called the 'official world.' Smart women did not go to her house. It was not the presence there of Republican 'notables' that frightened them away. In the days of my early childhood, conservative society was to the last degree worldly, and no 'good' house would ever have opened its doors to a Republican. The people who lived in such an atmosphere imagined that the impossibility of ever inviting an 'opportunist'—still more, a 'horrid radical' —to their parties was something that would endure for ever, like oil-lamps and horse-drawn omnibuses. But, like a kaleidoscope which is every now and then given a turn, society arranges successively in different orders elements which one would have supposed to be immovable, and composes a fresh pattern. Before I had made my first Communion, ladies on the 'right side' in politics had had the stupefaction of meeting, while paying calls, a smart Jewess. These new arrangements of the kaleidoscope are produced by what a philosopher would call a 'change of criterion.' The

Dreyfus case brought about another, at a period rather later than that in which I began to go to Mme. Swann's, and the kaleidoscope scattered once again its little scraps of colour. Everything Jewish, even the smart lady herself, fell out of the pattern, and various obscure nationalities appeared in its place. The most brilliant drawing-room in Paris was that of a Prince who was an Austrian and ultra-Catholic. If instead of the Dreyfus case there had come a war with Germany, the base of the kaleidoscope would have been turned in the other direction, and its pattern reversed. The Jews having shewn, to the general astonishment, that they were patriots also, would have kept their position, and no one would have cared to go any more, or even to admit that he had ever gone to the Austrian Prince's. All this does not, however, prevent the people who move in it from imagining, whenever society is stationary for the moment, that no further change will occur, just as in spite of having witnessed the birth of the telephone they decline to believe in the aeroplane. Meanwhile the philosophers of journalism are at work, castigating the preceding epoch, and not only the kind of pleasures in which it indulged, which seem to them to be the last word in corruption, but even the work of its artists and philosophers, which have no longer the least value in their eyes, as though they were indissolubly linked to the successive moods of fashionable frivolity. The one thing that does not change is that at any and every time it appears that there have been 'great changes.' At the time when I went to Mme. Swann's the Dreyfus storm had not yet broken, and some of the more prominent Jews were extremely powerful. None more so than Sir Rufus Israels, whose wife, Lady Israels, was Swann's aunt. She had not herself any intimate acquaintance so distinguished as her nephew's, while he, since he did not care for her, had never much cultivated her society, although he was, so far as was known, her heir. But she was the only one of Swann's relatives who had any idea of his social position, the others having always remained in the state of ignorance, in that respect, which had long been our own. When, from a family circle, one of its members emigrates into 'high society'—which to him appears a feat without parallel until after the lapse of a decade he observes that it has been performed in other ways and for different reasons by more than one of the men whom he knew as boys—he draws round about himself a zone of shadow, a *terra incognita*, which is clearly visible in its minutest details to all those who inhabit it with him, but is darkest night and nothingness to those who may not penetrate it but touch its fringe without the least suspicion of its existence in their midst. There being no news agency to furnish Swann's lady cousins with intelligence of the people with whom he consorted, it was (before his appalling marriage, of course) with a smile of condescension that they would tell one another, over family dinner-tables, that they had spent a 'virtuous' Sunday in going to see 'cousin Charles,' whom (regarding him as a 'poor relation' who was inclined to envy their prosperity,) they used wittily to name, playing upon the title of Balzac's story, *Le Cousin Bête*. Lady Israels, however, was letter-perfect in the names and quality of the people who lavished upon Swann a friendship of which she was frankly jealous. Her husband's family, which almost equalled the Rothschilds in importance, had for several generations managed the affairs of the Orleans Princes. Lady Israels, being immensely rich, exercised a wide influence, and had employed it so as to ensure that no one whom she knew should be 'at home' to Odette. One only had disobeyed her, in secret, the Comtesse de Marsantes. And then, as ill luck would have it, Odette having gone to call upon Mme. de Marsantes, Lady Israels had entered the room almost at her heels. Mme. de Marsantes was on tenter-hooks. With the craven impotence of those who are at liberty to act as they choose, she did not address a single word to Odette, who thus found little encouragement to press further the invasion of a world which, moreover, was not at all that into which she would have liked to be welcomed. In this complete detachment of the Faubourg Saint-Germain, Odette continued to be regarded as the illiterate 'light woman,' utterly different from the respectable ladies, 'well up' in all the minutest points of genealogy, who endeavoured to quench by reading biographies and memoirs their thirst for the aristocratic relations with which real life had omitted to provide them. And Swann, for his part, continued no doubt to be the lover in whose eyes all these peculiarities of an old mistress would appear lovable or at least inoffensive, for I have often heard his wife profess what were really social heresies, without his attempting (whether from lingering affection for her, loss of regard for society or weariness of the effort to make her perfect) to correct them. It was perhaps also another form of the simplicity which for so long had misled us at Combray, and which now had the effect that, while he continued to know, on his own account at least, many highly distinguished people, he did not make a point, in conversation in his wife's drawing-room, of our seeming to feel that they were of the smallest importance. They had, indeed, less than ever for Swann, the centre of gravity of his life having been displaced. In any case, Odette's ignorance of social distinctions was so dense that if the name of the Princesse de Guermantes were mentioned in conversation after that of the Duchess, her cousin, "So those ones are Princes, are they?" she would exclaim; "Why, they've gone up a step." Were anyone to say "the Prince," in speaking of the Duc de Chartres, she would put him right with, "The Duke, you mean; he is Duc de Chartres, not Prince." As for the Duc d'Orléans, son of the Comte de Paris: "That's funny; the son is higher than the father!" she would remark, adding, for she was afflicted with anglomania, "Those *Royalties* are so dreadfully confusing!"—while to someone who asked her from what province the Guermantes family came she replied, "From the Aisne."

But, so far as Odette was concerned, Swann was quite blind, not merely to these deficiencies in her education but to the general mediocrity of her intelligence. More than that; whenever Odette repeated a silly story Swann would sit listening to his wife with a complacency, a merriment, almost an admiration into which some survival of his desire for her must have entered; while in the same conversation, anything subtle, anything deep even that he himself might say would be listened to by Odette with an habitual lack of interest, rather curtly, with impatience, and would at times be sharply contradicted. And we must conclude that this enslavement of refinement by vulgarity is the rule in many households, when we think, conversely, of all the superior women who yield to the blandishments of a boor, merciless in his censure of their most delicate utterances, while they go into ecstasies, with the infinite indulgence of love, over the feeblest of his witticisms. To return to the reasons which prevented Odette, at this period, from making her way into the Faubourg Saint-Germain, it must be observed that the latest turn of the social kaleidoscope had been actuated by a series of scandals. Women to whose houses one had been going with entire confidence had been discovered to be common prostitutes, if not British spies. One would, therefore, for some time to come expect people (so, at least, one supposed) to be, before anything else, in a sound position, regular, settled, accountable. Odette represented simply everything with which one had just severed relations, and was incidentally to renew them at once (for men, their natures not altering from day to day, seek in every new order a continuance of the old) but to renew them by seeking it under another form which would allow one to be innocently taken in, and to believe that it was no longer the same society as before the disaster. However, the scapegoats of that society and Odette were too closely alike. People who move in society are very short-sighted; at the moment in which they cease to have any relations with the Israelite ladies whom they have known, while they are asking themselves how they are to fill the gap thus made in their lives, they perceive, thrust into it as by the windfall of a night of storm, a new lady, an Israelite also; but by virtue of her novelty she is not associated in their minds with her predecessors, with what they are convinced that they must abjure. She does not ask that they shall respect her God. They take her up. There was no question of anti-semitism at the time when I used first to visit Odette. But she was like enough to it to remind people of what they wished, for a while, to avoid.

As for Swann himself, he was still a frequent visitor of several of his former acquaintance, who, of course, were all of the very highest rank. And yet when he spoke to us of the people whom he had just been to see I noticed that, among those whom he had known in the old days, the choice that he made was dictated by the same kind of taste, partly artistic, partly historic, that inspired him as a collector. And remarking that it was often some great lady or other of waning reputation, who interested him because she had been the mistress of Liszt or because one of Balzac's novels was dedicated to her grandmother (as he would purchase a drawing if Chateaubriand had written about it) I conceived a suspicion that we had, at Combray, replaced one error, that of regarding Swann as a mere stockbroker, who did not go into society, by another, when we supposed him to be one of the smartest men in Paris. To be a friend of the Comte de Paris meant nothing at all. Is not the world full of such 'friends of Princes,' who would not be received in any house that was at all 'exclusive'? Princes know themselves to be princes, and are not snobs; besides, they believe themselves to be so far above everything that is not of their blood royal that great nobles and 'business men' appear, in the depths beneath them, to be practically on a level.

But Swann went farther than this; not content with seeking in society, such as it was, when he fastened upon the names which, inscribed upon its roll by the past, were still to be read there, a simple artistic and literary pleasure, he indulged in the slightly vulgar diversion of arranging as it were social nosegays by grouping heterogeneous elements, bringing together people taken at hazard, here, there and everywhere. These experiments in the lighter side (or what was to Swann the lighter side) of sociology did not stimulate an identical reaction, with any regularity, that is to say, in each of his wife's friends. "I'm thinking of asking the Cottards to meet the Duchesse de Vendôme," he would laughingly say to Mme. Bontemps, in the appetised tone of an epicure who has thought of, and intends to try the substitution, in a sauce, of cayenne pepper for cloves. But this plan, which was, in fact, to appear quite humorous, in an archaic sense of the word, to the Cottards, had also the power of infuriating Mme. Bontemps. She herself had recently been presented by the Swanns to the Duchesse de Ven-dôme, and had found this as agreeable as it seemed to her natural. The thought of winning renown from it at the Cottards', when she related to them what had happened, had been by no means the least savoury ingredient of her pleasure. But like those persons recently decorated who, their investiture once accomplished, would like to see the fountain of honour turned off at the main, Mme. Bontemps would have preferred that, after herself, no one else in her own circle of friends should be made known to the Princess. She denounced (to herself, of course) the licentious taste of Swann who, in order to gratify a wretched aesthetic whim, was obliging her to scatter to the winds, at one swoop, all the dust that she would have thrown in the eyes of the Cottards when she told them about the Duchesse de Ven-dôme. How was she even to dare to announce to her husband that the Pro-fessor and his wife were in their turn to partake of this pleasure, of which she had boasted to him as though it were unique. And yet, if the Cottards could only be made to know that they were being invited not seriously but for the amusement of their host! It is true that the Bontemps had been in-vited for the same reason, but Swann, having acquired from the aristocracy that eternal 'Don Juan' spirit which, in treating with two women of no im-portance, makes each of them believe that it is she alone who is seriously loved, had spoken to Mme. Bontemps of the Duchesse de Vendôme as of a person whom it was clearly laid down that she must meet at dinner. "Yes, we're determined to have the Princess here with the Cottards," said Mme. Swann a few weeks later; "My husband thinks that we might get some-thing quite amusing out of that conjunction." For if she had retained from the 'little nucleus' certain habits dear to Mme. Verdurin, such as that of shouting things aloud so as to be heard by all the faithful, she made use, at the same time, of certain expressions, such as 'conjunction,' which were dear to the Guermantes circle, of which she thus felt unconsciously and at a distance, as the sea is swayed by the moon, the attraction, though without being drawn perceptibly closer to it. "Yes, the Cottards and the Duchesse de Vendôme. Don't you think that might be rather fun?" asked Swann. "I think they'll be exceedingly ill-assorted, and it can only lead to a lot of bother; people oughtn't to play with fire, is what I say!" snapped Mme. Bontemps, furious. She and her husband were, all the same, invited, as was the Prince d'Agrigente, to this dinner, which Mme. Bontemps and Cottard had each two alternative ways of describing, according to whom they were telling about it. To one set Mme. Bontemps for her part, and Cottard for his would say casually, when asked who else had been of the party: "Only the Prince d'Agrigente; it was all quite intimate." But there were others who might, alas, be better informed (once, indeed, some one had challenged Cottard with: "But weren't the Bontemps there too?" "Oh, I forgot them," Cottard had blushingly admitted to the tactless questioner whom he ever afterwards classified among slanderers and speakers of evil). For these the Bontemps and Cottards had each adopted, without any mutual arrangement, a version the framework of which was identical for both parties, their own names alone changing places. "Let me see;" Cottard would say, "there were our host and hostess, the Duc and Duchesse de Vendôme—" (with a satisfied smile) "Professor and Mme. Cottard, and, upon my soul, heaven only knows how they got there, for they were about as much in keeping as hairs in the soup, M. and Mme. Bontemps!" Mme. Bontemps would recite an exactly similar 'piece,' only it was M. and Mme. Bontemps who were named with a satisfied emphasis between the Duchesse de Vendôme and the Prince d'Agrigente, while the 'also ran,' whom finally she used to accuse of having invited themselves, and who completely spoiled the party, were the Cottards.

When he had been paying calls Swann would often come home with little time to spare before dinner. At that point in the evening, six o'clock, when in the old days he had felt so wretched, he no longer asked himself what Odette might be about, and was hardly at all concerned to hear that she had people still with her, or had gone out. He recalled at times that he had once, years ago, tried to read through its envelope a letter addressed by Odette to Forcheville. But this memory was not pleasing to him, and rather than plumb the depth of shame that he felt in it he preferred to indulge in a little grimace, twisting up the corners of his mouth and adding, if need be, a shake of the head which signified "What does it all matter?" In truth, he considered now that the hypothesis by which he had often been brought to a standstill in days gone by, according to which it was his jealous imagination alone that blackened what was in reality the innocent life of Odette—that this hypothesis (which after all was beneficent, since, so long as his amorous malady had lasted, it had diminished his sufferings by making them seem imaginary) was not the truth, that it was his jealousy that had seen things in the right light, and that if Odette had loved him better than he supposed, she had deceived him more as well. Formerly, while his sufferings were still keen, he had vowed that, as soon as he should have ceased to love Odette, and so to be afraid either of vexing her or of making her believe that he loved her more than he did, he would afford himself the satisfaction of elucidating with her, simply from his love of truth and as a historical point, whether or not she had had Forcheville in her room that day when he had rung her bell and rapped on her window without being let in, and she had written to Forcheville that it was an uncle of hers who had called. But this so interesting problem, of which he was waiting to attempt the solution only until his jealousy should have subsided, had precisely lost all interest in Swann's eyes when he had ceased to be jealous. Not immediately, however. He felt no other jealousy now with regard to Odette than what the memory of that day, that afternoon spent in knocking vainly at the little house in the Rue La Pérouse, had continued to excite in him; as though his jealousy, not dissimilar in that respect from those maladies which appear to have their seat, their centre of contagion less in certain persons than in certain places, in certain houses, had had for its object not so much Odette herself as that day, that hour in the irrevocable past when Swann had beaten at every entrance to her house in turn. You would have said that that day, that hour alone had caught and preserved a few last fragments of the amorous personality which had once been Swann's, and that there alone could he now recapture them. For a long time now it had made no matter to him that Odette had been false to him, and was false still. And yet he had continued for some years to seek out old servants of Odette, so strongly in him persisted the painful curiosity to know whether on that day, so long ago, at six o'clock, Odette had been in bed with Forcheville. Then that curiosity itself had disappeared, without, however, his abandoning his investigations. He continued the attempt to discover what no longer interested him, because his old ego though it had shrivelled to the extreme of decrepitude still acted mechanically, following the course of preoccupations so utterly abandoned that Swann could not now succeed even in forming an idea of that anguish—so compelling once that he had been unable to foresee his ever being delivered from it, that only the death of her whom he loved (death which, as will be shewn later on in this story, by a cruel example, in no way diminishes the sufferings caused by jealousy) seemed to him capable of making smooth the road, then insurmountably barred to him, of his life.

But to bring to light, some day, those passages in the life of Odette to which he owed his sufferings had not been Swann's only ambition; he had in reserve that also of wreaking vengeance for his sufferings when, being no longer in love with Odette, he should no longer be afraid of her; and the opportunity of gratifying this second ambition had just occurred, for Swann was in love with another woman, a woman who gave him—grounds for jealousy, no, but who did all the same make him jealous, because he was not capable, now, of altering his way of making love, and it was the way he had used with Odette that must serve him now for another. To make Swann's jealousy revive it was not essential that this woman should be unfaithful, it sufficed that for any reason she was separated from him, at a party for instance, where she was presumably enjoying herself. That was enough to reawaken in him the old anguish, that lamentable and inconsistent excrescence of his love, which held Swann ever at a distance from what she really was, like a yearning to attain the impossible (what this young woman really felt for him, the hidden longing that absorbed her days, the secret places of her heart), for between Swann and her whom he loved this anguish piled up an unyielding mass of already existing suspicions, having their cause in Odette, or in some other perhaps who had preceded Odette, allowing this now ageing lover to know his mistress of the moment only in the traditional and collective phantasm of the 'woman who made him jealous,' in which he had arbitrarily incarnated his new love. Often, however, Swann would charge his jealousy with the offence of making him believe in imaginary infidelities; but then he would remember that he had given Odette the benefit of the same argument and had in that been wrong. And so everything that the young woman whom he loved did in those hours when he was not with her appeared spoiled of its innocence in his eyes. But whereas at that other time he had made a vow that if ever he ceased to love her whom he did not then imagine to be his future wife, he would implacably exhibit to her an indifference that would at length be sincere, so as to avenge his pride that had so long been trampled upon by her—of those reprisals which he might now enforce without risk to himself (for what harm could it do him to be taken at his word and deprived of those intimate moments with Odette that had been so necessary to him once), of those reprisals he took no more thought; with his love had vanished the desire to shew that he was in love no longer. And he who, when he was suffering at the hands of Odette, would have looked forward so keenly to letting her see one day that he had fallen to a rival, now that he was in a position to do so took infinite precautions lest his wife should suspect the existence of this new love.

❧

It was not only in those tea-parties, on account of which I had formerly had the sorrow of seeing Gilberte leave me and go home earlier than usual, that I was henceforth to take part, but the engagements that she had with her mother, to go for a walk or to some afternoon party, which by preventing her from coming to the Champs-Elysées had deprived me of her, on those days when I loitered alone upon the lawn or stood before the wooden horses,—to these outings M. and Mme. Swann henceforth admitted me, I had a seat in their landau, and indeed it was me that they asked if I would rather go to the theatre, to a dancing lesson at the house of one of Gilberte's friends, to some social gathering given by friends of her parents (what Odette called 'a little meeting') or to visit the tombs at Saint-Denis.

On days when I was going anywhere with the Swanns I would arrive at the house in time for *déjeuner*, which Mme. Swann called 'le lunch'; as one was not expected before half-past twelve, while my parents in those days had their meal at a quarter past eleven, it was not until they had risen from the table that I made my way towards that sumptuous quarter, deserted enough at any hour, but more particularly just then, when everyone had gone indoors. Even on winter days of frost, if the weather held, tightening every few minutes the knot of a gorgeous necktie from Charvet's and looking to see that my varnished boots were not getting dirty, I would roam to and fro among the avenues, waiting until twenty-seven minutes past the hour. I could see from afar in the Swanns' little garden-plot the sunlight glittering like hoar frost from the bare-boughed trees. It is true that the garden boasted but a pair of them. The unusual hour presented the scene in a new light. Into these pleasures of nature (intensified by the suppression of habit and indeed by my physical hunger) the thrilling prospect of sitting down to luncheon with Mme. Swann was infused; it did not diminish them, but taking command of them trained them to its service; so that if, at this hour when ordinarily I did not perceive them, I seemed now to be discovering the fine weather, the cold, the wintry sunlight, it was all as a sort of preface to the creamed eggs, as a patina, a cool and coloured glaze applied to the decoration of that mystic chapel which was the habitation of Mme. Swann, and in the heart of which there were, by contrast, so much warmth, so many scents and flowers.

At half-past twelve I would finally make up my mind to enter that house which, like an immense Christmas stocking, seemed ready to bestow upon me supernatural delights. (The French name 'Noël' was, by the way, unknown to Mme. Swann and Gilberte, who had substituted for it the English 'Christmas,' and would speak of nothing but 'Christmas pudding,' what people had given them as 'Christmas presents' and of going away— the thought of which maddened me with grief—'for Christmas.' At home even, I should have thought it degrading to use the word 'Noël,' and always said 'Christmas,' which my father considered extremely silly.)

I encountered no one at first but a footman who after leading me through several large drawing-rooms shewed me into one that was quite small, empty, its windows beginning to dream already in the blue light of afternoon; I was left alone there in the company of orchids, roses and violets, which, like people who are kept waiting in a room beside you but do not know you, preserved a silence which their individuality as living things made all the more impressive, and received coldly the warmth of a glowing fire of coals, preciously displayed behind a screen of crystal, in a basin of white marble over which it spilled, now and again, its perilous rubies.

I had sat down, but I rose hurriedly on hearing the door opened; it was only another footman, and then a third, and the minute result that their vainly alarming entrances and exits achieved was to put a little more coal on the fire or water in the vases. They departed, I found myself alone, once that door was shut which Mme. Swann was surely soon going to open. Of a truth, I should have been less ill at ease in a magician's cave than in this little waiting-room where the fire appeared to me to be performing alchemical transmutations as in Klingsor's laboratory. Footsteps sounded afresh, I did not rise, it was sure to be just another footman; it was M. Swann. "What! All by yourself? What is one to do; that poor wife of mine has never been able to remember what time means! Ten minutes to one. She gets later every day. And you'll see, she will come sailing in without the least hurry, and imagine she's in heaps of time." And as he was still subject to neuritis, and as he was becoming a trifle ridiculous, the fact of possessing so unpunctual a wife, who came in so late from the Bois, forgot everything at her dressmaker's and was never in time for luncheon made Swann anxious for his digestion but flattered his self-esteem.

He shewed me his latest acquisitions and explained their interest to me,

but my emotion, added to the unfamiliarity of being still without food at
this hour, sweeping through my mind left it void, so that while able to
speak I was incapable of hearing. Anyhow, so far as the works of art in
Swann's possession were concerned, it was enough for me that they were
contained in his house, formed a part there of the delicious hour that preceded luncheon. The Gioconda herself might have appeared there without
giving me any more pleasure than one of Mme. Swann's indoor gowns, or
her scent bottles.

I continued to wait, alone or with Swann, and often with Gilberte,
come in to keep us company. The arrival of Mme. Swann, prepared for
me by all those majestic apparitions, must (so it seemed to me) be something truly immense. I strained my ears to catch the slightest sound. But
one never finds quite as high as one has been expecting a cathedral, a wave
in a storm, a dancer's leap in the air; after those liveried footmen, suggesting the chorus whose processional entry upon the stage leads up to
and at the same time diminishes the final appearance of the queen, Mme.
Swann, creeping furtively in, with a little otter-skin coat, her veil lowered
to cover a nose pink-tipped by the cold, did not fulfil the promises lavished,
while I had been waiting, upon my imagination.

But if she had stayed at home all morning, when she arrived in the
drawing-room she would be clad in a wrapper of *crêpe-de-Chine,* brightly
coloured, which seemed to me more exquisite than any of her dresses.

Sometimes the Swanns decided to remain in the house all afternoon,
and then, as we had had luncheon so late, very soon I must watch setting,
beyond the garden-wall, the sun of that day which had seemed to me bound
to be different from other days; then in vain might the servants bring in
lamps of every size and shape, burning each upon the consecrated altar
of a console, a card-table, a corner-cupboard, a bracket, as though for the
celebration of some strange and secret rite; nothing extraordinary trans-
pired in the conversation, and I went home disappointed, as one often is
in one's childhood after the midnight mass.

But my disappointment was scarcely more than mental. I was radiant
with happiness in this house where Gilberte, when she was still not with
us, was about to appear and would bestow on me in a moment, and for
hours to come, her speech, her smiling and attentive gaze, just as I had
caught it, that first time, at Combray. At the most I was a trifle jealous
when I saw her so often disappear into vast rooms above, reached by a
private staircase. Obliged myself to remain in the drawing-room, like a man
in love with an actress who is confined to his stall 'in front' and wonders
anxiously what is going on behind the scenes, in the green-room, I put to
Swann, with regard to this other part of the house questions artfully veiled,
but in a tone from which I could not quite succeed in banishing the note of
uneasiness. He explained to me that the place to which Gilberte had gone
was the linen-room, offered himself to shew it to me, and promised me that
whenever Gilberte had occasion to go there again he would insist upon
her taking me with her. By these last words and the relief which they
brought me Swann at once annihilated for me one of those terrifying interior
perspectives at the end of which a woman with whom we are in love ap-

pears so remote. At that moment I felt for him an affection which I believed to be deeper than my affection for Gilberte. For he, being the master over his daughter, was giving her to me, whereas she, she withheld herself now and then, I had not the same direct control over her as I had indirectly through Swann. Besides, it was she whom I loved and could not, therefore look upon without that disturbance, without that desire for something more which destroys in us, in the presence of one whom we love, the sensation of loving.

As a rule, however, we did not stay indoors, we went out. Sometimes, before going to dress, Mme. Swann would sit down at the piano. Her lovely hands, escaping from the pink, or white, or, often, vividly coloured sleeves of her *crêpe-de-Chine* wrapper, drooped over the keys with that same melancholy which was in her eyes but was not in her heart. It was on one of those days that she happened to play me the part of Vinteuil's sonata that contained the little phrase of which Swann had been so fond. But often one listens and hears nothing, if it is a piece of music at all complicated to which one is listening for the first time. And yet when, later on, this sonata had been played over to me two or three times I found that I knew it quite well. And so it is not wrong to speak of hearing a thing for the first time. If one had indeed, as one supposes, received no impression from the first hearing, the second, the third would be equally 'first hearings' and there would be no reason why one should understand it any better after the tenth. Probably what is wanting, the first time, is not comprehension but memory. For our memory, compared to the complexity of the impressions which it has to face while we are listening, is infinitesimal, as brief as the memory of a man who in his sleep thinks of a thousand things and at once forgets them, or as that of a man in his second childhood who cannot recall, a minute afterwards, what one has just been saying to him. Of these multiple impressions our memory is not capable of furnishing us with an immediate picture. But that picture gradually takes shape, and, with regard to works which we have heard more than once, we are like the schoolboy who has read several times over before going to sleep a lesson which he supposed himself not to know, and finds that he can repeat it by heart next morning. It was only that I had not, until then, heard a note of the sonata, whereas Swann and his wife could make out a distinct phrase that was as far beyond the range of my perception as a name which one endeavours to recall and in place of which one discovers only a void, a void from which, an hour later, when one is not thinking about them, will spring of their own accord, in one continuous flight, the syllables that one has solicited in vain. And not only does one not seize at once and retain an impression of works that are really great, but even in the content of any such work (as befell me in the case of Vinteuil's sonata) it is the least valuable parts that one at first perceives. Thus it was that I was mistaken not only in thinking that this work held nothing further in store for me (so that for a long time I made no effort to hear it again) from the moment in which Mme. Swann had played over to me its most famous passage; I was in this respect as stupid as people are who expect to feel no astonishment when they stand in Venice

before the front of Saint Mark's, because photography has already acquainted them with the outline of its domes. Far more than that, even
when I had heard the sonata played from beginning to end, it remained
almost wholly invisible to me, like a monument of which its distance or a
haze in the atmosphere allows us to catch but a faint and fragmentary
glimpse. Hence the depression inseparable from one's knowledge of such
works, as of everything that acquires reality in time. When the least obvious beauties of Vinteuil's sonata were revealed to me, already, borne
by the force of habit beyond the reach of my sensibility, those that I had
from the first distinguished and preferred in it were beginning to escape,
to avoid me. Since I was able only in successive moments to enjoy all the
pleasures that this sonata gave me, I never possessed it in its entirety: it
was like life itself. But, less disappointing than life is, great works of art
do not begin by giving us all their best. In Vinteuil's sonata the beauties
that one discovers at once are those also of which one most soon grows
tired, and for the same reason, no doubt, namely that they are less different from what one already knows. But when those first apparitions have
withdrawn, there is left for our enjoyment some passage which its composition, too new and strange to offer anything but confusion to our mind,
had made indistinguishable and so preserved intact; and this, which we
have been meeting every day and have not guessed it, which has thus
been held in reserve for us, which by the sheer force of its beauty has
become invisible and has remained unknown, this comes to us last of all.
But this also must be the last that we shall relinquish. And we shall love
it longer than the rest because we have taken longer to get to love it. The
time, moreover, that a person requires—as I required in the matter of this
sonata—to penetrate a work of any depth is merely an epitome, a symbol,
one might say, of the years, the centuries even that must elapse before
the public can begin to cherish a masterpiece that is really new. So that
the man of genius, to shelter himself from the ignorant contempt of the
world, may say to himself that, since one's contemporaries are incapable
of the necessary detachment, works written for posterity should be read
by posterity alone, like certain pictures which one cannot appreciate when
one stands too close to them. But, as it happens, any such cowardly precaution to avoid false judgments is doomed to failure; they are inevitable.
The reason for which a work of genius is not easily admired from the first
is that the man who has created it is extraordinary, that few other men
resemble him. It was Beethoven's Quartets themselves (the Twelfth, Thir-
teenth, Fourteenth and Fifteenth) that devoted half a century to forming, fashioning and enlarging a public for Beethoven's Quartets, marking
in this way, like every great work of art, an advance if not in artistic merit
at least in intellectual society, largely composed to-day of what was not
to be found when the work first appeared, that is to say of persons capable
of enjoying it. What artists call posterity is the posterity of the work of
art. It is essential that the work (leaving out of account, for brevity's
sake, the contingency that several men of genius may at the same time
be working along parallel lines to create a more instructed public in the
future, a public from which other men of genius shall reap the benefit)

shall create its own posterity. For if the work were held in reserve, were revealed only to posterity, that audience, for that particular work, would be not posterity but a group of contemporaries who were merely living half-a-century later in time. And so it is essential that the artist (and this is what Vinteuil had done), if he wishes his work to be free to follow its own course, shall launch it, wherever he may find sufficient depth, confidently outward bound towards the future. And yet this interval of time, the true perspective in which to behold a work of art, if leaving it out of account is the mistake made by bad judges, taking it into account is at times a dangerous precaution of the good. No doubt one can easily imagine, by an illusion similar to that which makes everything on the horizon appear equidistant, that all the revolutions which have hitherto occurred in painting or in music did at least shew respect for certain rules, whereas that which immediately confronts us, be it impressionism, a striving after discord, an exclusive use of the Chinese scale, cubism, futurism or what you will, differs outrageously from all that have occurred before. Simply because those that have occurred before we are apt to regard as a whole, forgetting that a long process of assimilation has melted them into a continuous substance, varied of course but, taking it as a whole, homogeneous, in which Hugo blends with Molière. Let us try to imagine the shocking incoherence that we should find, if we did not take into account the future, and the changes that it must bring about, in a horoscope of our own riper years, drawn and presented to us in our youth. Only horoscopes are not always accurate, and the necessity, when judging a work of art, of including the temporal factor in the sum total of its beauty introduces, to our way of thinking, something as hazardous, and consequently as barren of interest, as every prophecy the non-fulfilment of which will not at all imply any inadequacy on the prophet's part, for the power to summon possibilities into existence or to exclude them from it is not necessarily within the competence of genius; one may have had genius and yet not have believed in the future of railways or of flight, or, although a brilliant psychologist, in the infidelity of a mistress or of a friend whose treachery persons far less gifted would have foreseen.

If I did not understand the sonata, it enchanted me to hear Mme. Swann play. Her touch appeared to me (like her wrappers, like the scent of her staircase, her cloaks, her chrysanthemums) to form part of an individual and mysterious whole, in a world infinitely superior to that in which the mind is capable of analysing talent. "Attractive, isn't it, that Vinteuil sonata?" Swann asked me. "The moment when night is darkening among the trees, when the arpeggios of the violin call down a cooling dew upon the earth. You must admit that it is rather charming; it shews all the static side of moonlight, which is the essential part. It is not surprising that a course of radiant heat such as my wife is taking, should act on the muscles, since moonlight can prevent the leaves from stirring. That is what he expresses so well in that little phrase, the Bois de Boulogne plunged in a cataleptic trance. By the sea it is even more striking, because you have there the faint response of the waves, which, of course, you can hear quite distinctly, since nothing else dares to move. In Paris it is the other way; at the most, you may notice unfamiliar lights among the old buildings, the sky brightened as though by a colourless and harmless conflagration, that sort of vast variety show of which you get a hint here and there. But in Vinteuil's little phrase, and in the whole sonata for that matter, it is not like that; the scene is laid in the Bois; in the *gruppetto* you can distinctly hear a voice saying: 'I can almost see to read the paper!'" These words from Swann might have falsified, later on, my impression of the sonata, music being too little exclusive to inhibit absolutely what other people suggest that we should find in it. But I understood from other words which he let fall that this nocturnal foliage was simply that beneath whose shade in many a restaurant on the outskirts of Paris he had listened on many an evening to the little phrase. In place of the profound significance that he had so often sought in it, what it recalled now to Swann were the leafy boughs, arranged, wreathed, painted round about it (which it gave him the desire to see again because it seemed to him to be their inner, their hidden self, as it were their soul); was the whole of one spring season which he had not been able to enjoy before, not having had—feverish and moody as he then was—enough strength of body and mind for its enjoyment, which, as one puts by for an invalid the dainties that he has not been able to eat, it had kept in store for him. The charm that he had been made to feel by certain evenings in the Bois, a charm of which Vinteuil's sonata served to remind him, he could not have recaptured by questioning Odette, although she, as well as the little phrase, had been his companion there. But Odette had been merely his companion, by his side, not (as the phrase had been) within him, and so had seen nothing—nor would she, had she been a thousand times as comprehending, have seen anything of that vision which for no one among us (or at least I was long under the impression that this rule admitted no exception) can be made externally visible. "It is rather charming, don't you think," Swann continued, "that sound can give a reflection, like water, or glass. It is curious, too, that Vinteuil's phrase now shews me only the things to which I paid no attention then. Of my troubles, my loves of those days it recalls nothing, it has altered all my values." "Charles, I don't think that's very polite to me, what you're saying." "Not polite? Really, you women are superb! I was simply trying to explain to this young man that what the music shews—to me, at least—is not for a moment 'Free-will' or 'In Tune with the Infinite,' but shall we say old Verdurin in his frock coat in the palm-house at the Jardin d'Acclimatation. Hundreds of times, without my leaving this room, the little phrase has carried me off to dine with it at Armenonville. Gad, it is less boring, anyhow, than having to go there with Mme. de Cambremer." Mme. Swann laughed. "That is a lady who is supposed to have been violently in love with Charles," she explained, in the same tone in which, shortly before, when we were speaking of Vermeer of Delft, of whose existence I had been surprised to find her conscious, she had answered me with: "I ought to explain that M. Swann was very much taken up with that painter at the time he was courting me. Isn't that so, Charles dear?" "You're not to start saying things about Mme. de Cambremer!" Swann checked her, secretly flattered. "But I'm only repeating what I've been told. Besides, it seems that she's an extremely clever woman; I don't know her myself. I believe she's very pushing, which surprises me rather in a clever woman. But everyone says that she was quite mad about you; there's no harm in repeating that." Swann remained silent as a deaf-mute which was in a way a confirmation of what she had said, and a proof of his own fatuity. "Since what I'm playing reminds you of the Jardin d'Acclimatation," his wife went on, with a playful semblance of being offended, "we might take him there some day in the carriage, if it would amuse him. It's lovely there just now, and you can recapture your fond impressions! Which reminds me, talking of the Jardin d'Acclimatation, do you know, this young man thought that we were devotedly attached to a person whom I cut, as a matter of fact, whenever I possibly can, Mme. Blatin! I think it is rather crushing for us, that she should be taken for a friend of ours. Just fancy, dear Dr. Cottard, who never says a harsh word about anyone, declares that she's positively contagious." "A frightful woman! The one thing to be said for her is that she is exactly like Savonarola. She is the very image of that portrait of Savonarola, by Fra Bartolomeo." This mania which Swann had for finding likenesses to people in pictures was defensible, for even what we call individual expression is—as we so painfully discover when we are in love and would fain believe in the unique reality of the beloved— something diffused and general, which can be found existing at different periods. But if one had listened to Swann, the processions of the Kings of the East, already so anachronistic when Benozzo Gozzoli introduced in their midst various Medici, would have been even more so, since they would have included the portraits of a whole crowd of men, contemporaries not of Gozzoli but of Swann, subsequent, that is to say not only by fifteen centuries to the Nativity but by four more to the painter himself. There was not missing from those trains, according to Swann, a single living Parisian of any note, any more than there was from that act in one of Sardou's plays, in which, out of friendship for the author and for the leading lady, and also because it was the fashion, all the best known men in Paris, famous doctors, politicians, barristers, amused themselves, each on a different evening, by 'walking on.' "But what has she got to do with the Jardin d'Acclimatation?" "Everything!" "What? You don't suggest that she's got a sky-blue behind, like the monkeys?" "Charles, you really are too dreadful! I was thinking of what the Cingalese said to her. Do tell him, Charles; it really is a gem." "Oh, it's too silly. You know, Mme. Blatin loves asking people questions, in a tone which she thinks friendly, but which is really overpowering." "What our good friends on the Thames call 'patronising,' " interrupted Odette. "Exactly. Well, she went the other day to the Jardin d'Acclimatation, where they have some blackamoors— Cingalese, I think I heard my wife say; she is much 'better up' in ethnology than I am." "Now, Charles, you're not to make fun of poor me." "I've no intention of making fun, I assure you. Well, to continue, she went up to one of these black fellows with 'Good morning, nigger!' . . ." "Oh, it's too absurd!" "Anyhow, this classification seems to have displeased the black. 'Me nigger,' he shouted (quite furious, don't you know), to Mme.

Blatin, 'me nigger; you, old cow!' " "I do think that's so delightful! I adore that story. Do say it's a good one. Can't you see old Blatin standing there, and hearing him: 'Me nigger; you, old cow'?" I expressed an intense desire to go there and see these Cingalese, one of whom had called Mme. Blatin an old cow. They did not interest me in the least. But I reflected that in going to the Jardin d'Acclimatation, and again on our way home, we should pass along that Allée des Acacias in which I had loved so, once, to gaze on Mme. Swann, and that perhaps Coquelin's mulatto friend, to whom I had never managed to exhibit myself in the act of saluting her, would see me there, seated at her side, as the victoria swept by.

During those minutes in which Gilberte, having gone to 'get ready,' was not in the room with us, M. and Mme. Swann would take delight in revealing to me all the rare virtues of their child. And everything that I myself observed seemed to prove the truth of what they said. I remarked that, as her mother had told me, she had not only for her friends but for the servants, for the poor, the most delicate attentions carefully thought out, a desire to give pleasure, a fear of causing annoyance, translated into all sorts of trifling actions which must often have meant great inconvenience to her. She had done some 'work' for our stall-keeper in the Champs-Elysées, and went out in the snow to give it to her with her own hands, so as not to lose a day. "You have no idea how kind-hearted she is, she won't let it be seen," her father assured me. Young as she was, she appeared far more sensible already than her parents. When Swann boasted of his wife's grand friends Gilberte would turn away, and remain silent, but without any air of reproaching him, for it seemed inconceivable to her that her father could be subjected to the slightest criticism. One day, when I had spoken to her of Mlle. Vinteuil, she said to me:

"I shall never know her, for a very good reason, and that is that she was not nice to her father, by what one hears, she gave him a lot of trouble. You can't understand that any more than I, can you; I'm sure you could no more live without your papa than I could, which is quite natural after all. How can one ever forget a person one has loved all one's life?"

And once when she was making herself particularly endearing to Swann, as I mentioned this to her when he was out of the room:

"Yes, poor Papa, it is the anniversary of his father's death, just now. You can understand what he must be feeling; you do understand, don't you; you and I feel the same about things like that. So I just try to be a little less naughty than usual." "But he doesn't ever think you naughty. He thinks you're quite perfect." "Poor Papa, that's because he's far too good himself."

But her parents were not content with singing the praises of Gilberte— that same Gilberte, who, even, before I had set eyes on her, used to appear to me standing before a church, in a landscape of the Ile de France, and later, awakening in me not dreams now but memories, was embowered always in a hedge of pink hawthorn, in the little lane that I took when I was going the Méséglise way. Once when I had asked Mme. Swann (and had made an effort to assume the indifferent tone of a friend of the family, curious to know the preferences of a child), which among all her play-mates Gilberte liked the best, Mme. Swann replied: "But you ought to know a great deal better than I do. You are in her confidence, her great favourite, her 'chum,' as the English say."

It appears that in a coincidence as perfect as this was, when reality is folded over to cover the ideal of which we have so long been dreaming, it completely hides that ideal, absorbing it in itself, as when two geometrical figures that are congruent are made to coincide, so that there is but one, whereas we would rather, so as to give its full significance to our enjoyment, preserve for all those separate points of our desire, at the very moment in which we succeed in touching them, and so as to be quite certain that they are indeed themselves, the distinction of being intangible. And our thought cannot even reconstruct the old state so as to confront the new with it, for it has no longer a clear field: the acquaintance that we have made, the memory of those first, unhoped-for moments, the talk to which we have listened are there now to block the passage of our conscious-ness, and as they control the outlets of our memory far more than those of our imagination, they react more forcibly upon our past, which we are no longer able to visualise without taking them into account, than upon the form, still unshaped, of our future. I had been able to believe, year after year, that the right to visit Mme. Swann was a vague and fantastic privilege to which I should never attain; after I had spent a quarter of an hour in her drawing-room, it was the period in which I did not yet know her that was become fantastic and vague like a possibility which the reali-sation of an alternative possibility has made impossible. How was I ever to dream again of her dining-room as of an inconceivable place, when I could not make the least movement in my mind without crossing the path of that inextinguishable ray cast backwards to infinity, even into my own most distant past, by the lobster à l'Américaine which I had just been eating? And Swann must have observed in his own case a similar phe-nomenon; for this house in which he entertained me might be regarded as the place into which had flowed, to coincide and be lost in one another, not only the ideal dwelling that my imagination had constructed, but an-other still, that which his jealous love, as inventive as any fantasy of mine, had so often depicted to him, that dwelling common to Odette and himself which had appeared so inaccessible once, on evenings when Odette had taken him home with Forcheville to drink orangeade with her; and what had flowed in to be absorbed, for him, in the walls and furniture of the dining-room in which we now sat down to luncheon was that unhoped-for paradise in which, in the old days, he could not without a pang imagine that he would one day be saying to *their* butler those very words, "Is Madame ready yet?" which I now heard him utter with a touch of impa-tience mingled with self-satisfaction. No more than, probably, Swann himself could I succeed in knowing my own happiness, and when Gilberte once broke out: "Who would ever have said that the little girl you watched playing prisoners' base, without daring to speak to her, would one day be your greatest friend, and you would go to her house whenever you liked?" she spoke of a change the occurrence of which I could verify only by observing it from without, finding no trace of it within myself, for it was composed of two separate states on both of which I could not, without their ceasing to be distinct from one another, succeed in keeping my thoughts fixed at one and the same time.

And yet this house, because it had been so passionately desired by Swann, must have kept for him some of its attraction, if I was to judge by myself for whom it had not lost all its mystery. That singular charm in which I had for so long supposed the life of the Swanns to be bathed I had not completely exorcised from their house on making my own way into it; I had made it, that charm, recoil, overpowered as it must be by the sight of the stranger, the pariah that I had been, to whom now Mme. Swann pushed forward graciously for him to sit in it an armchair exquisite, hostile, scandalised; but all round me that charm, in my memory, I can still distinguish. Is it because, on those days on which M. and Mme. Swann invited me to luncheon, to go out afterwards with them and Gilberte, I imprinted with my gaze,—while I sat waiting for them there alone—on the carpet, the sofas, the tables, the screens, the pictures, the idea engraved upon my mind that Mme. Swann, or her husband, or Gilberte was about to enter the room? Is it because those objects have dwelt ever since in my memory side by side with the Swanns, and have gradually acquired something of their personal character? Is it because, knowing that the Swanns passed their existence among all those things, I made of all of them as it were emblems of the private lives, of those habits of the Swanns from which I had too long been excluded for them not to continue to appear strange to me, even when I was allowed the privilege of sharing in them? However it may be, always when I think of that drawing-room which Swann (not that the criticism implied on his part any intention to find fault with his wife's taste) found so incongruous—because, while it was still planned and carried out in the style, half conservatory, half studio, which had been that of the rooms in which he had first known Odette, she had, none the less, begun to replace in its medley a quantity of the Chinese ornaments, which she now felt to be rather gimcrack, a trifle dowdy, by a swarm of little chairs and stools and things upholstered in old Louis XIV silks; not to mention the works of art brought by Swann himself from his house on the Quai d'Orléans—it has kept in my memory, on the contrary, that composite, heterogeneous room, a cohesion, a unity, an individual charm never possessed even by the most complete, the least spoiled of such collections that the past has bequeathed to us, or the most modern, alive and stamped with the imprint of a living personality; for we alone can, by our belief that they have an existence of their own, give to certain of the things that we see a soul which they afterwards keep, which they develop in our minds. All the ideas that I had formed of the hours, different from those that exist for other men, passed by the Swanns in that house which was to their life what the body is to the soul, and must give expression to its singularity, all those ideas were rearranged, amalgamated—equally disturbing and indefinite throughout—in the arrangement of the furniture, the thickness of the carpets, the position of the windows, the ministrations of the servants. When, after luncheon, we went in the sunshine to drink our coffee in the great bay window of the drawing-room, while Mme. Swann was asking me how many lumps of sugar I took, it was not only the silk-covered stool which she pushed towards me that emitted, with the agonising charm that I had long ago felt—first among the pink hawthorn and then beside the clump of laurels—in the name of Gilberte, the hostility that her parents had shewn to me, which this little piece of furniture seemed to have so well understood, to have so completely shared that I felt myself unworthy, and found myself almost reluctant to set my feet on its defenceless cushion; a personality, a soul was latent there which linked it secretly to the light of two o'clock in the afternoon, so different from any other light, in the gulf in which there played about our feet its sparkling tide of gold out of which the bluish crags of sofas and vaporous carpet beaches emerged like enchanted islands; and there was nothing, even to the painting by Rubens hung above the chimney-piece, that was not endowed with the same quality and almost the same intensity of charm as the laced boots of M. Swann, and that hooded cape, the like of which I had so dearly longed to wear, whereas now Odette would beg her husband to go and put on another, so as to appear more smart, whenever I did them the honour of driving out with them. She too went away to change her dress—not heeding my protestations that no 'outdoor' clothes could be nearly so becoming as the marvellous garment of *crêpe-de-Chine* or silk, old rose, cherry-coloured, Tiepolo pink, white, mauve, green, red or yellow, plain or patterned, in which Mme. Swann had sat down to luncheon and which she was now going to take off. When I assured her that she ought to go out in that costume, she laughed, either in scorn of my ignorance or from delight in my compliment. She apologised for having so many wrappers, explaining that they were the only kind of dress in which she felt comfortable, and left us, to go and array herself in one of those regal toilets which imposed their majesty on all beholders, and yet among which I was sometimes summoned to decide which of them I preferred that she should put on.

In the Jardin d'Acclimatation, how proud I was when we had left the carriage to be walking by the side of Mme. Swann! While she strolled carelessly on, letting her cloak stream on the air behind her, I kept eyeing her with an admiring gaze to which she coquettishly responded in a lingering smile. And now, were we to meet one or other of Gilberte's friends, boy or girl, who saluted us from afar, I would in my turn be looked upon by them as one of those happy creatures whose lot I had envied, one of those friends of Gilberte who knew her family and had a share in that other part of her life, the part which was not spent in the Champs-Elysées.

Often upon the paths of the Bois or the Jardin we passed, we were greeted by some great lady who was Swann's friend, whom he perchance did not see, so that his wife must rally him with a "Charles! Don't you see Mme. de Montmorency?" And Swann, with that amicable smile, bred of a long and intimate friendship, bared his head, but with a slow sweeping gesture, with a grace peculiarly his own. Sometimes the lady would stop, glad of an opportunity to shew Mme. Swann a courtesy which would involve no tiresome consequences, by which they all knew that she would never seek to profit, so thoroughly had Swann trained her in reserve. She had none the less acquired all the manners of polite society, and however smart, however stately the lady might be, Mme. Swann was invariably a match for her; halting for a moment before the friend whom her husband had recognised and was addressing, she would introduce us, Gilberte and myself, with so much ease of manner, would remain so free, so tranquil in her exercise of courtesy, that it would have been hard to say, looking at them both, which of the two was the aristocrat. The day on which we went to inspect the Cingalese, on our way home we saw coming in our direction, and followed by two others who seemed to be acting as her escort, an elderly but still attractive woman cloaked in a dark mantle and capped with a little bonnet tied beneath her chin with a pair of ribbons. "Ah! Here is someone who will interest you!" said Swann. The old lady, who had come within a few yards of us, now smiled at us with a caressing sweetness. Swann doffed his hat. Mme. Swann swept to the ground in a curtsey and made as if to kiss the hand of the lady, who, standing there like a Winterhalter portrait, drew her up again and kissed her cheek. "There, there; will you put your hat on, you!" she scolded Swann in a thick and almost growling voice, speaking like an old and familiar friend. "I am going to present you to Her Imperial Highness," Mme. Swann whispered. Swann drew me aside for a moment while his wife talked of the weather and of the animals recently added to the Jardin d'Acclimatation, with the Princess. "That is the Princesse Mathilde," he told me; "you know who' I mean, the friend of Flaubert, Sainte-Beuve, Dumas. Just fancy, she's the niece of Napoleon I. She had offers of marriage from Napoleon III and the Emperor of Russia. Isn't that interesting? Talk to her a little. But I hope she won't keep us standing here for an hour! . . . I met Taine the other day," he went on, addressing the Princess, "and he told me that your Highness was vexed with him." "He's behaved like a perfect peeg!" she said gruffly, pronouncing the word *cochon* as though she referred to Joan of Arc's contemporary, Bishop Cauchon. "After his article on the Emperor I left my card on him with p. p. c. on it." I felt the surprise that one feels on opening the Correspondence of that Duchesse d'Orléans who was by birth a Princess Palatine. And indeed Princesse Mathilde, animated by sentiments so entirely French, expressed them with a straightforward bluntness that recalled the Germany of an older generation, and was inherited, doubtless, from her Württemberg mother. This somewhat rude and almost masculine frankness she softened, as soon as she began to smile, with an Italian languor. And the whole person was clothed in a dress so typically 'Second Empire' that—for all that the Princess wore it simply and solely, no doubt, from attachment to the fashions that she had loved when she was young—she seemed to have deliberately planned to avoid the slightest discrepancy in historic colour, and to be satisfying the expectations of those who looked to her to evoke the memory of another age. I whispered to Swann to ask her whether she had known Musset. "Very slightly, sir," was the answer, given in a tone which seemed to feign annoyance at the question, and of course it was by way of a joke that she called Swann

'Sir,' since they were intimate friends. "I had him to dine once. I had
invited him for seven o'clock. At half-past seven, as he had not appeared,
we sat down to dinner. He arrived at eight, bowed to me, took his seat,
never opened his lips, went off after dinner without letting me hear the
sound of his voice. Of course, he was dead drunk. That hardly encouraged me to make another attempt." We were standing a little way off,
Swann and I. "I hope this little audience is not going to last much longer,"
he muttered, "the soles of my feet are hurting. I cannot think why my
wife keeps on making conversation. When we get home it will be she that
complains of being tired, and she knows I simply cannot go on standing
like this." For Mme. Swann, who had had the news from Mme. Bontemps,
was in the course of telling the Princess that the Government, having at
last begun to realise the depth of its depravity, had decided to send her an
invitation to be present on the platform in a few days' time, when the Tsar
Nicholas was to visit the Invalides. But the Princess who, in spite of appearances, in spite of the character of her circle, which consisted mainly of
artists and literary people, had remained at heart and shewed herself, whenever she had to take action, the niece of Napoleon, replied: "Yes, Madame,
I received it this morning, and I sent it back to the Minister, who must
have had it by now. I told him that I had no need of an invitation to go
to the Invalides. If the Government desires my presence there, it will not
be on the platform, it will be in our vault, where the Emperor's tomb is.
I have no need of a card to admit me there. I have my keys. I go in and
out when I choose. The Government has only to let me know whether it
wishes me to be present or not. But if I do go to the Invalides, it will be
down below there or nowhere at all." At that moment we were saluted,
Mme. Swann and I, by a young man who greeted her without stopping,
and whom I was not aware that she knew; it was Bloch. I inquired about
him, and was told that he had been introduced to her by Mme. Bontemps,
and that he was employed in the Minister's secretariat, which was news
to me. Anyhow, she could not have seen him often—or perhaps she had
not cared to utter the name, hardly 'smart' enough for her liking, of
Bloch, for she told me that he was called M. Moreul. I assured her that
she was mistaken, that his name was Bloch. The Princess gathered up the
train that flowed out behind her, while Mme. Swann gazed at it with admiring eyes. "It is only a fur that the Emperor of Russia sent me," she
explained, "and as I have just been to see him I put it on, so as to shew
him that I'd managed to have it made up as a mantle." "I hear that Prince
Louis has joined the Russian Army; the Princess will be very sad at losing
him," went on Mme. Swann, not noticing her husband's signals of distress. "That was a fine thing to do. As I said to him, 'Just because there's
been a soldier, before, in the family, that's no reason!' " replied the
Princess, alluding with this abrupt simplicity to Napoleon the Great. But
Swann could hold out no longer. "Ma'am, it is I that am going to play the
Prince, and ask your permission to retire; but, you see, my wife has not
been so well, and I do not like her to stand still for any time." Mme.
Swann curtseyed again, and the Princess conferred upon us all a celestial
smile, which she seemed to have summoned out of the past, from among

the graces of her girlhood, from the evenings at Compiègne, a smile which glided, sweet and unbroken, over her hitherto so sullen face; then she went on her way, followed by the two ladies in waiting, who had confined themselves, in the manner of interpreters, of children's or invalids' nurses, to punctuating our conversation with insignificant sentences and superfluous explanations. "You should go and write your name in her book, one day this week," Mme. Swann counselled me. "One doesn't leave cards upon these 'Royalties,' as the English call them, but she will invite you to her house if you put your name down."

Sometimes in those last days of winter we would go, before proceeding on our expedition, into one of the small picture-shows that were being given at that time, where Swann, as a collector of mark, was greeted with special deference by the dealers in whose galleries they were held. And in that still wintry weather the old longing to set out for the South of France and Venice would be reawakened in me by those rooms in which a springtime, already well advanced, and a blazing sun cast violet shadows upon the roseate Alpilles and gave the intense transparency of emeralds to the Grand Canal. If the weather were inclement, we would go to a concert or a theatre, and afterwards to one of the fashionable tearooms. There, whenever Mme. Swann had anything to say to me which she did not wish the people at the next table, or even the waiters who brought our tea, to understand, she would say it in English, as though that had been a secret language known to our two selves alone. As it happened everyone in the place knew English—I only had not yet learned the language, and was obliged to say so to Mme. Swann in order that she might cease to make, on the people who were drinking tea or were serving us with it, remarks which I guessed to be uncomplimentary without either my understanding or the person referred to losing a single word.

Once, in the matter of an afternoon at the theatre, Gilberte gave me a great surprise. It was precisely the day of which she had spoken to me some time back, on which fell the anniversary of her grandfather's death. We were to go, she and I, with her governess, to hear selections from an opera, and Gilberte had dressed with a view to attending this performance, and wore the air of indifference with which she was in the habit of treating whatever we might be going to do, with the comment that it might be anything in the world, no matter what, provided that it amused me and had her parents' approval. Before luncheon, her mother drew us aside to tell us that her father was vexed at the thought of our going to a theatre on that day. This seemed to me only natural. Gilberte remained impassive, but grew pale with an anger which she was unable to conceal; still she uttered not a word. When M. Swann joined us his wife took him to the other end of the room and said something in his ear. He called Gilberte, and they went together into the next room. We could hear their raised voices. And yet I could not bring myself to believe that Gilberte, so submissive, so loving, so thoughtful, would resist her father's appeal, on such a day and for so trifling a matter. At length Swann reappeared with her, saying: "You heard what I said. Now you may do as you like."

Gilberte's features remained compressed in a frown throughout luncheon, after which we retired to her room. Then suddenly, without hesitating and as though she had never at any point hesitated over her course of action: "Two o'clock!" she exclaimed. "You know the concert begins at half past." And she told her governess to make haste.

"But," I reminded her, "won't your father be cross with you?"

"Not the least little bit!"

"Surely, he was afraid it would look odd, because of the anniversary."

"What difference can it make to me what people think? I think it's perfectly absurd to worry about other people in matters of sentiment. We feel things for ourselves, not for the public. Mademoiselle has very few pleasures; she's been looking forward to going to this concert. I am not going to deprive her of it just to satisfy public opinion."

"But, Gilberte," I protested, taking her by the arm, "it is not to satisfy public opinion, it is to please your father."

"You are not going to pass remarks upon my conduct, I hope," she said sharply, plucking her arm away.

⁂

A favour still more precious than their taking me with them to the Jardin d'Acclimatation, the Swanns did not exclude me even from their friendship with Bergotte, which had been at the root of the attraction that I had found in them when, before I had even seen Gilberte, I reflected that her intimacy with that godlike elder would have made her, for me, the most passionately enthralling of friends, had not the disdain that I was bound to inspire in her forbidden me to hope that she would ever take me, in his company, to visit the towns that he loved. And lo, one day, came an invitation from Mme. Swann to a big luncheon-party. I did not know who else were to be the guests. On my arrival I was disconcerted, as I crossed the hall, by an alarming incident. Mme. Swann seldom missed an opportunity of adopting any of those customs which pass as fashionable for a season, and then, failing to find support, are speedily abandoned (as, for instance, many years before, she had had her 'private hansom,' or now had, printed in English upon a card inviting you to luncheon, the words, 'To meet,' followed by the name of some more or less important personage). Often enough these usages implied nothing mysterious and required no initiation. Take, for instance, a minute innovation of those days, imported from England; Odette had made her husband have some visiting cards printed on which the name Charles Swann was preceded by 'Mr.'. After the first visit that I paid her, Mme. Swann had left at my door one of these 'pasteboards,' as she called them. No one had ever left a card on me before; I felt at once so much pride, emotion, gratitude that, scraping together all the money I possessed, I ordered a superb basket of camellias and had it sent to Mme. Swann. I implored my father to go and leave a card on her, but first, quickly, to have some printed on which his name should bear the prefix 'Mr.'. He vouchsafed neither of my prayers; I was in despair for some days, and then asked myself whether he might not after all have been right. But this use of 'Mr.,' if it meant nothing, was at least intel-

ligible. Not so with another that was revealed to me on the occasion of
this luncheon-party, but revealed without any indication of its purport.
At the moment when I was about to step from the hall into the drawing-
room the butler handed me a thin, oblong envelope upon which my name
was inscribed. In my surprise I thanked him; but I eyed the envelope with
misgivings. I no more knew what I was expected to do with it than a foreigner knows what to do with one of those little utensils that they lay by
his place at a Chinese banquet. I noticed that it was gummed down; I was
afraid of appearing indiscreet, were I to open it then and there; and so I
thrust it into my pocket with an air of knowing all about it. Mme. Swann
had written to me a few days before, asking me to come to luncheon with
'just a few people.' There were, however, sixteen of us, among whom I
never suspected for a moment that I was to find Bergotte. Mme. Swann,
who had already 'named' me, as she called it, to several of her guests, suddenly, after my name, in the same tone that she had used in uttering it
(in fact, as though we were merely two of the guests at her party, who
ought each to feel equally flattered on meeting the other), pronounced that
of the sweet Singer with the snowy locks. The name Bergotte made me
jump like the sound of a revolver fired at me point blank, but instinctively,
for appearance's sake, I bowed; there, straight in front of me, as by one
of those conjurers whom we see standing whole and unharmed, in their
frock coats, in the smoke of a pistol shot out of which a pigeon has just flut-
tered, my salute was returned by a young common little thick-set peering
person, with a red nose curled like a snail-shell and a black tuft on his chin.
I was cruelly disappointed, for what had just vanished in the dust of the
explosion was not only the feeble old man, of whom no vestige now remained; there was also the beauty of an immense work which I had contrived to enshrine in the frail and hallowed organism that I had constructed,
like a temple, expressly for itself, but for which no room was to be found
in the squat figure, packed tight with blood-vessels, bones, muscles, sinews,
of the little man with the snub nose and black beard who stood before me.
All the Bergotte whom I had slowly and delicately elaborated for myself,
drop by drop, like a stalactite, out of the transparent beauty of his books,
ceased (I could see at once) to be of any use, the moment I was obliged
to include in him the snail-shell nose and to utilise the little black beard;
just as we must reject as worthless the solution of a problem the terms
of which we have not read in full, having failed to observe that the total
must amount to a specified figure. The nose and beard were elements
similarly ineluctable, and all the more aggravating in that, while forcing
me to reconstruct entirely the personage of Bergotte, they seemed further
to imply, to produce, to secrete incessantly a certain quality of mind, alert
and self-satisfied, which was not in the picture, for such a mind had no
connexion whatever with the sort of intelligence that was diffused throughout those books, so intimately familiar to me, which were permeated by
a gentle and godlike wisdom. Starting from them, I should never have
arrived at that snail-shell nose; but starting from the nose, which did not
appear to be in the slightest degree ashamed of itself, but stood out alone
there like a grotesque ornament fastened on his face, I must proceed in

a diametrically opposite direction from the work of Bergotte, I must arrive, it would seem, at the mentality of a busy and preoccupied engineer, of the sort who when you accost him in the street thinks it correct to say: "Thanks, and you?" before you have actually inquired of them how they are, or else, if you assure them that you have been charmed to make their acquaintance, respond with an abbreviation which they imagine to be effective, intelligent and up-to-date, inasmuch as it avoids any waste of precious time on vain formalities: "Same here!" Names are, no doubt, but whimsical draughtsmen, giving us of people as well as of places sketches so little like the reality that we often experience a kind of stupor when we have before our eyes, in place of the imagined, the visible world (which, for that matter, is not the true world, our senses being little more endowed than our imagination with the art of portraiture, so little, indeed, that the final and approximately lifelike pictures which we manage to obtain of reality are at least as different from the visible world as that was from the imagined). But in Bergotte's case, my preconceived idea of him from his name troubled me far less than my familiarity with his work, to which I was obliged to attach, as to the cord of a balloon, the man with the little beard, without knowing whether it would still have the strength to raise him from the ground. It seemed quite clear, however, that it really was he who had written the books that I had so greatly enjoyed, for Mme. Swann having thought it incumbent upon her to tell him of my admiration for one of these, he shewed no surprise that she should have mentioned this to him rather than to any other of the party, nor did he seem to regard her action as due to a misapprehension, but, swelling out the frock coat which he had put on in honour of all these distinguished guests with a body distended in anticipation of the coming meal, while his mind was completely occupied by other, more real and more important considerations, it was only as at some finished episode in his early life, as though one had made an illusion to a costume of the Duc de Guise which he had worn, one season, at a fancy dress ball, that he smiled as he bore his mind back to the idea of his books; which at once began to fall in my estimation (dragging down with them the whole value of Beauty, of the world, of life itself), until they seemed to have been merely the casual amusement of a man with a little beard. I told myself that he must have taken great pains over them, but that, if he had lived upon an island surrounded by beds of pearl-oysters, he would instead have devoted himself to, and would have made a fortune out of, the pearling trade. His work no longer appeared to me so inevitable. And then I asked myself whether originality did indeed prove that great writers were gods, ruling each one over a kingdom that was his alone, or whether all that was not rather make-believe, whether the differences between one man's book and another's were not the result of their respective labours rather than the expression of a radical and essential difference between two contrasted personalities.

Meanwhile we had taken our places at the table. By the side of my plate I found a carnation, the stalk of which was wrapped in silver paper. It embarrassed me less than the envelope that had been handed to me in the hall, which, however, I had completely forgotten. This custom,

strange as it was to me, became more intelligible when I saw all the male
guests take up the similar carnations that were lying by their plates and
slip them into the buttonholes of their coats. I did as they had done, with
the air of spontaneity that a free-thinker assumes in church, who is not
familiar with the order of service but rises when everyone else rises and
kneels a moment after everyone else is on his knees. Another usage, equally
strange to me but less ephemeral, disquieted me more. On the other side of
my plate was a smaller plate, on which was heaped a blackish substance
which I did not then know to be caviare. I was ignorant of what was to
be done with it but firmly determined not to let it enter my mouth.

Bergotte was sitting not far from me and I could hear quite well everything that he said. I understood then the impression that M. de Norpois
had formed of him. He had indeed a peculiar 'organ'; there is nothing that
so much alters the material qualities of the voice as the presence of thought
behind what one is saying; the resonance of one's diphthongs, the energy
of one's labials are profoundly affected—in fact, one's whole way of
speaking. His seemed to me to differ entirely from his way of writing, and
even the things that he said from those with which he filled his books. But
the voice issues from behind a mask through which it is not powerful
enough to make us recognise, at first sight, a face which we have seen
uncovered in the speaker's literary style. At certain points in the conversation, when Bergotte, by force of habit, began to talk in a way which no
one but M. de Norpois would have thought affected or unpleasant, it was
a long time before I discovered an exact correspondence with the parts of
his books in which his form became so poetic and so musical. At those
points I could see in what he was saying a plastic beauty independent
of whatever his sentences might mean, and as human speech reflects the
human soul, though without expressing it as does literary style, Bergotte
appeared almost to be talking nonsense, intoning certain words and, if
he were secretly pursuing, beneath them, a single image, stringing them
together uninterruptedly on one continuous note, with a wearisome monotony. So that a pretentious, emphatic and monotonous opening was a sign
of the rare aesthetic value of what he was saying, and an effect, in his
conversation, of the same power which, in his books, produced that harmonious flow of imagery. I had had all the more difficulty in discovering
this at first since what he said at such moments, precisely because it was
the authentic utterance of Bergotte, had not the appearance of being
Bergotte's. It was an abundant crop of clearly defined ideas, not included
in that 'Bergotte manner' which so many story-tellers had appropriated
to themselves; and this dissimilarity was probably but another aspect—
made out with difficulty through the stream of conversation, as an eclipse
is seen through a smoked glass—of the fact that when one read a page of
Bergotte it was never just what would have been written by any of those
lifeless imitators who, nevertheless, in newspapers and in books, adorned
their prose with so many 'Bergottish' images and ideas. This difference
in style arose from the fact that what was meant by 'Bergottism' was,
first and foremost, a priceless element of truth hidden in the heart of everything, whence it was extracted by that great writer, by virtue of his genius,

and that this extraction, and not simply the perpetration of 'Bergottisms,' was my sweet Singer's aim in writing. Though, it must be added, he continued to perpetrate them in spite of himself, and because he was Bergotte, so that, in one sense, every fresh beauty in his work was the little drop of Bergotte buried at the heart of a thing which he had distilled from it. But if, for that reason, each of those beauties was related to all the rest, and had a 'family likeness,' yet each remained separate and individual, as was the act of discovery that had brought it to the light of day; new, and consequently different from what was called the Bergotte manner, which was a loose synthesis of all the 'Bergottisms' already invented and set forth by him in writing, with no indication by which men who lacked genius might forecast what would be his next discovery. So it is with all great writers, the beauty of their language is as incalculable as that of a woman whom we have never seen; it is creative, because it is applied to an external object of which, and not of their language or its beauty, they are thinking, to which they have not yet given expression. An author of memorials of our time, wishing to write without too obviously seeming to be writing like Saint-Simon, might, on occasion, give us the first line of his portrait of Villars: "He was a rather tall man, dark . . . with an alert, open, expressive physiognomy," but what law of determinism could bring him to the discovery of Saint-Simon's next line, which begins with "and, to tell the truth, a trifle mad"? The true variety is in this abundance of real and unexpected elements, in the branch loaded with blue flowers which thrusts itself forward, against all reason, from the spring hedgerow that seemed already overcharged with blossoms, whereas the purely formal imitation of variety (and one might advance the same argument for all the other qualities of style) is but a barren uniformity, that is to say the very antithesis of variety, and cannot, in the work of imitators, give the illusion or recall other examples of variety save to a reader who has not acquired the sense of it from the masters themselves.

And so—just as Bergotte's way of speaking would no doubt have been charming if he himself had been merely an amateur repeating imitations of Bergotte, whereas it was attached to the mind of Bergotte, at work and in action, by essential ties which the ear did not at once distinguish—so it was because Bergotte applied that mind with precision to the reality which pleased him that his language had in it something positive, something over-rich, disappointing those who expected to hear him speak only of the 'eternal torrent of forms,' and of the 'mystic thrills of beauty.' Moreover the quality, always rare and new, of what he wrote was expressed in his conversation by so subtle a manner of approaching a question, ignoring every aspect of it that was already familiar, that he appeared to be seizing hold of an unimportant detail, to be quite wrong about it, to be speaking in paradox, so that his ideas seemed as often as not to be in confusion, for each of us finds lucidity only in those ideas which are in the same state of confusion as his own. Besides, as all novelty depends upon the elimination, first, of the stereotyped attitude to which we have grown accustomed, and which has seemed to us to be reality itself, every new conversation, as well as all original painting and music, must always appear laboured and tedious. It is founded upon figures of speech with which we are not familiar, the speaker appears to us to be talking entirely in metaphors; and this wearies us, and gives us the impression of a want of truth. (After all, the old forms of speech must in their time have been images difficult to follow when the listener was not yet cognisant of the universe which they depicted. But he has long since decided that this must be the real universe, and so relies confidently upon it.) So when Bergotte—and his figures appear simple enough to-day—said of Cottard that he was a mannikin in a bottle, always trying to rise to the surface, and of Brichot that "to him even more than to Mme. Swann the arrangement of his hair was a matter for anxious deliberation, because, in his twofold preoccupation over his profile and his reputation, he had always to make sure that it was so brushed as to give him the air at once of a lion and of a philosopher," one immediately felt the strain, and sought a foothold upon something which one called more concrete, meaning by that more ordinary. These unintelligible words, issuing from the mask that I had before my eyes, it was indeed to the writer whom I admired that they must be attributed, and yet they could not have been inserted among his books, in the form of a puzzle set in a series of different puzzles, they occupied another plane and required a transposition by means of which, one day, when I was repeating to myself certain phrases that I had heard Bergotte use, I discovered in them the whole machinery of his literary style, the different elements of which I was able to recognise and to name in this spoken discourse which had struck me as being so different.

From a less immediate point of view the special way, a little too meticulous, too intense, that he had of pronouncing certain words, certain adjectives which were constantly recurring in his conversation, and which he never uttered without a certain emphasis, giving to each of their syllables a separate force and intoning the last syllable (as for instance the word *visage*, which he always used in preference to *figure*, and enriched with a number of superfluous v's and s's and g's, which seemed all to explode from his outstretched palm at such moments) corresponded exactly to the fine passages in which, in his prose, he brought those favourite words into the light, preceded by a sort of margin and composed in such a way in the metrical whole of the phrase that the reader was obliged, if he were not to make a false quantity, to give to each of them its full value. And yet one did not find in the speech of Bergotte a certain luminosity which in his books, as in those of some other writers, often modified in the written phrase the appearance of its words. This was doubtless because that light issues from so profound a depth that its rays do not penetrate to our spoken words in the hours in which, thrown open to others by the act of conversation, we are to a certain extent closed against ourselves. In this respect, there were more intonations, there was more accent in his books than in his talk; an accent independent of the beauty of style, which the author himself has possibly not perceived, for it is not separable from his most intimate personality. It was this accent which, at the moments when, in his books, Bergotte was entirely natural, gave a rhythm to the words—often at such times quite insignificant—that he wrote. This accent is not marked on the printed page, there is nothing there to indicate it, and yet it comes of its own accord to his phrases, one cannot pronounce them in any other way, it is what was most ephemeral and at the same time most profound in the writer, and it is what will bear witness to his true nature, what will say whether, despite all the austerity that he has expressed he was gentle, despite all his sensuality sentimental.

Certain peculiarities of elocution, faint traces of which were to be found in Bergotte's conversation, were not exclusively his own; for when, later on, I came to know his brothers and sisters, I found those peculiarities much more accentuated in their speech. There was something abrupt and harsh in the closing words of a light and spirited utterance, something faint and dying at the end of a sad one. Swann, who had known the Master as a boy, told me that in those days one used to hear on his lips, just as much as on his brothers' and sisters', those inflexions, almost a family type, shouts of violent merriment interspersed with murmurings of a long-drawn melancholy, and that in the room in which they all played together he used to perform his part, better than any of them, in their symphonies, alternately deafening and subdued. However characteristic it may be, the sound that escapes from human lips is fugitive and does not survive the speaker. But it was not so with the pronunciation of the Bergotte family. For if it is difficult ever to understand, even in the *Meistersinger*, how an artist can invent music by listening to the twittering of birds, yet Bergotte had transposed and fixed in his written language that manner of dwelling on words which repeat themselves in shouts of joy, or fall, drop by drop, in melancholy sighs. There are in his books just such closing phrases where the accumulated sounds are prolonged (as in the last chords of the overture of an opera which cannot come to an end, and repeats several times over its supreme cadence before the conductor finally lays down his baton), in which, later on, I was to find a musical equivalent for those phonetic 'brasses' of the Bergotte family. But in his own case, from the moment in which he transferred them to his books, he ceased instinctively to make use of them in his speech. From the day on which he had begun to write—all the more markedly, therefore, in the later years in which I first knew him—his voice had lost this orchestration for ever.

These young Bergottes—the future writer and his brothers and sisters —were doubtless in no way superior, far from it, to other young people, more refined, more intellectual than themselves, who found the Bergottes rather 'loud,' that is to say a trifle vulgar, irritating one by the witticisms which characterised the tone, at once pretentious and puerile, of their household. But genius, and even what is only great talent, springs less from seeds of intellect and social refinement superior to those of other people than from the faculty of transposing, and so transforming them. To heat a liquid over an electric lamp one requires to have not the strongest lamp possible, but one of which the current can cease to illuminate, can be diverted so as instead of light to give heat. To mount the skies it is not necessary to have the most powerful of motors, one must have a motor which, instead of continuing to run along the earth's surface, intersecting with a vertical line the horizontal which it began by follow-ing, is capable of converting its speed into ascending force. Similarly the men who produce works of genius are not those who live in the most delicate atmosphere, whose conversation is most brilliant or their culture broadest, but those who have had the power, ceasing in a moment to live only for themselves, to make use of their personality as of a mirror, in such a way that their life, however unimportant it may be socially, and even, in a sense, intellectually speaking, is reflected by it, genius consist-ing in the reflective power of the writer and not in the intrinsic quality of the scene reflected. The day on which young Bergotte succeeded in shewing to the world of his readers the tasteless household in which he had passed his childhood, and the not very amusing conversations be-tween himself and his brothers, on that day he climbed far above the friends of his family, more intellectual and more distinguished than him-self; they in their fine Rolls Royces might return home expressing due contempt for the vulgarity of the Bergottes; but he, with his modest engine which had at last left the ground, he soared above their heads.

But there were other characteristics of his elocution which it was not with the members of his family, but with certain contemporary writers, that he must share. Younger men, who were beginning to repudiate him as a master and disclaimed any intellectual affinity to him in themselves, displayed their affinity without knowing it when they made use of the same adverbs, the same prepositions that he incessantly repeated, when they constructed their sentences in the same way, spoke in the same quiescent, lingering tone, by a reaction from the eloquent, easy language of an earlier generation. Perhaps these young men—we shall come across some of whom this may be said—had never known Bergotte. But his way of thinking, inoculated into them, had led them to those alterations of syntax and of accent which bear a necessary relation to originality of mind. A relation which, incidentally, requires to be traced. Thus Bergotte, if he owed nothing to any man for his manner of writing, derived his manner of speaking from one of his early associates, a marvellous talker to whose ascendancy he had succumbed, whom he imitated, unconsciously, in his conversation, but who himself, being less gifted, had never written any really outstanding book. So that if one had been in quest of originality in speech, Bergotte must have been labelled a disciple, a writer at second-hand, whereas, influenced by his friend only so far as talk went, he had been original and creative in his writings. Doubtless again, so as to dis-tinguish himself from the previous generation, too fond as it had been of abstractions, of weighty commonplaces, when Bergotte wished to speak favourably of a book, what he would bring into prominence, what he would quote with approval would always be some scene that furnished the reader with an image, some picture that had no rational significance. "Ah, yes!" he would exclaim, "it is quite admirable! There is a little girl in an orange shawl. It is excellent!" or again, "Oh, yes, there is a passage in which there is a regiment marching along the street; yes, it is excellent!" As for style, he was not altogether of his time (though he remained quite exclusively of his race, abominating Tolstoy, George Eliot,

Ibsen and Dostoievsky), for the word that always came to his lips when he wished to praise the style of any writer was 'mild.' "Yes, you know I like Chateaubriand better in *Atala* than in *René*; he seems to me to be 'milder.' " He said the word like a doctor who, when his patient assures him that milk will give him indigestion, answers, "But, you know, it's very 'mild'." And it is true that there was in Bergotte's style a kind of harmony similar to that for which the ancients used to praise certain of their orators in terms which we now find it hard to understand, accustomed as we are to our own modern tongues in which effects of that kind are not sought.

He would say also, with a shy smile, of pages of his own for which some one had expressed admiration: "I think it is more or less true, more or less accurate; it may be of some value perhaps," but he would say this simply from modesty, as a woman to whom one has said that her dress, or her daughter, is charming replies, "It is comfortable," or "She is a good girl." But the constructive instinct was too deeply implanted in Bergotte for him not to be aware that the sole proof that he had built usefully and on the lines of truth lay in the pleasure that his work had given, to himself first of all and afterwards to his readers. Only many years later, when he no longer had any talent, whenever he wrote anything with which he was not satisfied, so as not to have to suppress it, as he ought to have done, so as to be able to publish it with a clear conscience he would repeat, but to himself this time: "After all, it is more or less accurate, it must be of some value to the country." So that the phrase murmured long ago among his admirers by the insincere voice of modesty came in the end to be whispered in the secrecy of his heart by the uneasy tongue of pride. And the same words which had served Bergotte as an unwanted excuse for the excellence of his earliest works became as it were an ineffective consolation to him for the hopeless mediocrity of the latest.

A kind of austerity of taste which he had, a kind of determination to write nothing of which he could not say that it was 'mild,' which had made people for so many years regard him as a sterile and precious artist, a chiseller of exquisite trifles, was on the contrary the secret of his strength, for habit forms the style of the writer just as much as the character of the man, and the author who has more than once been patient to attain, in the expression of his thoughts, to a certain kind of attractiveness, in so doing lays down unalterably the boundaries of his talent, just as if he yields too often to pleasure, to laziness, to the fear of being put to trouble, he will find himself describing in terms which no amount of revision can modify, the forms of his own vices and the limits of his virtue.

If, however, despite all the analogies which I was to perceive later on between the writer and the man, I had not at first sight, in Mme. Swann's drawing-room, believed that this could be Bergotte, the author of so many divine books, who stood before me, perhaps I was not altogether wrong, for he himself did not, in the strict sense of the word, 'believe' it either. He did not believe it because he shewed a great assiduity in the presence of fashionable people (and yet he was not a snob), of literary men and journalists who were vastly inferior to himself. Of course he had long since learned, from the suffrage of his readers, that he had genius, compared to which social position and official rank were as nothing. He had learned that he had genius, but he did not believe it because he continued to simulate deference towards mediocre writers in order to succeed, shortly, in becoming an Academician, whereas the Academy and the Faubourg Saint-Germain have no more to do with that part of the Eternal Mind which is the author of the works of Bergotte than with the law of causality or the idea of God. That also he knew, but as a kleptomaniac knows, without profiting by the knowledge, that it is wrong to steal. And the man with the little beard and snail-shell nose knew and used all the tricks of the gentleman who pockets your spoons, in his efforts to reach the coveted academic chair, or some duchess or other who could dispose of several votes at the election, but while on his way to them he would endeavour to make sure that no one who would consider the pursuit of such an object a vice in him should see what he was doing. He was only half-successful; one could hear, alternating with the speech of the true Bergotte, that of the other Bergotte, ambitious, utterly selfish, who thought it not worth his while to speak of any but his powerful, rich or noble friends, so as to enhance his own position, he who in his books, when he was really himself, had so well portrayed the charm, pure as a mountain spring, of poverty.

As for those other vices to which M. de Norpois had alluded, that almost incestuous love, which was made still worse, people said, by a want of delicacy in the matter of money, if they contradicted, in a shocking manner, the tendency of his latest novels, in which he shewed everywhere a regard for what was right and proper so painfully rigid that the most innocent pleasures of their heroes were poisoned by it, and that even the reader found himself turning their pages with a sense of acute discomfort, and asked himself whether it was possible to go on living even the quietest of lives, those vices did not at all prove, supposing that they were fairly imputed to Bergotte, that his literature was a lie and all his sensitiveness mere play-acting. Just as in pathology certain conditions similar in appearance are due, some to an excess, others to an insufficiency of tension, of secretion and so forth, so there may be vice arising from supersensitiveness just as much as from the lack of it. Perhaps it is only in really vicious lives that the moral problem can arise in all its disquieting strength. And of this problem the artist finds a solution in the terms not of his own personal life but of what is for him the true life, a general, a literary solution. As the great Doctors of the Church began often, without losing their virtue, by acquainting themselves with the sins of all mankind, out of which they extracted their own personal sanctity, so great artists often, while being thoroughly wicked, make use of their vices in order to arrive at a conception of the moral law that is binding upon us all. It is the vices (or merely the weaknesses and follies) of the circle in which they live, the meaningless conversation, the frivolous or shocking lives of their daughters, the infidelity of their wives, or their own misdeeds that writers have most often castigated in their books, without, however, thinking it necessary to alter their domestic economy or to improve the tone of their households. And this contrast had never before been so striking as it was in Bergotte's time, because, on the one hand, in proportion as society grew more corrupt, our notions of morality were increasingly exalted, while on the other hand the public were now told far more than they had ever hitherto known about the private lives of literary men; and on certain evenings in the theatre people would point out the author whom I had so greatly admired at Combray, sitting at the back of a box the mere composition of which seemed an oddly humorous, or perhaps keenly ironical commentary upon—a brazen-faced denial of—the thesis which he had just been maintaining in his latest book. Not that anything which this or that casual informant could tell me was of much use in helping me to settle the question of the goodness or wickedness of Bergotte. An intimate friend would furnish proofs of his hardheartedness; then a stranger would cite some instance (touching, since he had evidently wished it to remain hidden) of his real depth of feeling. He had behaved cruelly to his wife. But in a village inn, where he had gone to spend the night, he had stayed on to watch over a poor woman who had tried to drown herself, and when he was obliged to continue his journey had left a large sum of money with the landlord, so that he should not turn the poor creature out, but see that she got proper attention. Perhaps the more the great writer was developed in Bergotte at the expense of the little man with the beard, so much the more his own personal life was drowned in the flood of all the lives that he imagined, until he no longer felt himself obliged to perform certain practical duties, for which he had substituted the duty of imagining those other lives. But at the same time, because he imagined the feelings of others as completely as if they had been his own, whenever he was obliged, for any reason, to talk to some person who had been unfortunate (that is to say in a casual encounter) he would, in doing so, take up not his own personal standpoint but that of the sufferer himself, a standpoint in which he would have been horrified by the speech of those who continued to think of their own petty concerns in the presence of another's grief. With the result that he gave rise everywhere to justifiable rancour and to undying gratitude.

Above all, he was a man who in his heart of hearts loved nothing really except certain images and (like a miniature set in the floor of a casket) the composing and painting of them in words. For a trifle that some one had sent him, if that trifle gave him the opportunity of introducing one or two of these images, he would be prodigal in the expression of his gratitude, while shewing none whatever for an expensive present. And if he had had to plead before a tribunal, he would inevitably have chosen his words not for the effect that they might have on the judge but with an eye to certain images which the judge would certainly never have perceived.

That first day on which I met him with Gilberte's parents, I mentioned to Bergotte that I had recently been to hear Berma in *Phèdre*; and he told me that in the scene in which she stood with her arm raised to the level of her shoulder—one of those very scenes that had been greeted with such applause—she had managed to suggest with great nobility of art certain classical figures which, quite possibly, she had never even seen, a Hesperid carved in the same attitude upon a metope at Olympia, and also the beautiful primitive virgins on the Erechtheum.

"It may be sheer divination, and yet I fancy that she visits the museums. It would be interesting to 'establish' that." ('Establish' was one of those regular Bergotte expressions, and one which various young men who had never met him had caught from him, speaking like him by some sort of telepathic suggestion.)

"Do you mean the Cariatides?" asked Swann.

"No, no," said Bergotte, "except in the scene where she confesses her passion to Œnone, where she moves her hand exactly like Hegeso on the stele in the Ceramic, it is a far more primitive art that she revives. I was referring to the Korai of the old Erechtheum, and I admit that there is perhaps nothing quite so remote from the art of Racine, but there are so many things already in *Phèdre*, . . . that one more . . . Oh, and then, yes, she is really charming, that little sixth century Phaedra, the rigidity of the arm, the lock of hair 'frozen into marble,' yes, you know, it is wonderful of her to have discovered all that. There is a great deal more antiquity in it than in most of the books they are labelling 'antique' this year."

As Bergotte had in one of his volumes addressed a famous invocation to these archaic statues, the words that he was now uttering were quite intelligible to me and gave me a fresh reason for taking an interest in Berma's acting. I tried to picture her again in my mind, as she had looked in that scene in which I remembered that she had raised her arm to the level of her shoulder. And I said to myself, "There we have the Hesperid of Olympia; there we have the sister of those adorable suppliants on the Acropolis; there is indeed nobility in art!" But if these considerations were to enhance for me the beauty of Berma's gesture, Bergotte should have put them into my head before the performance. Then, while that attitude of the actress was actually existing in flesh and blood before my eyes, at that moment in which the thing that was happening had still the substance of reality, I might have tried to extract from it the idea of archaic sculpture. But of Berma in that scene all that I retained was a memory which was no longer liable to modification, slender as a picture which lacks that abundant perspective of the present tense where one is free to delve and can always discover something new, a picture to which one cannot retrospectively give a meaning that is not subject to verification and correction from without. At this point Mme. Swann joined in the conversation, asking me whether Gilberte had remembered to give me what Bergotte had written about *Phèdre,* and adding, "My daughter is such a scatter-brain!" Bergotte smiled modestly and protested that they were only a few pages, of no importance. "But it is perfectly charming, that little pamphlet, that little 'tract' of yours!" Mme. Swann assured him, to shew that she was a good hostess, to make the rest of us think that she had read Bergotte's essay, and also because she liked not merely to flatter Bergotte, but to make a selection for herself out of what he wrote, to control his writing. And it must be admitted that she did inspire him, though not in the way that she supposed. But when all is said there is, between what constituted

the smartness of Mme. Swann's drawing-room and a whole side of Bergotte's work, so close a correspondence that either of them might serve,
among elderly men to-day, as a commentary upon the other.

I let myself go in telling him what my impressions had been. Often
Bergotte disagreed, but he allowed me to go on talking. I told him that I
had liked the green light which was turned on when Phaedra raised her arm.
"Ah! The designer will be glad to hear that; he is a real artist. I shall
tell him you liked it, because he is very proud of that effect. I must say,
myself, that I do not care for it very much, it drowns everything in a sort
of aqueous vapour, little Phaedra standing there looks too like a branch
of coral on the floor of an aquarium. You will tell me, of course, that it
brings out the cosmic aspect of the play. That is quite true. All the same,
it would be more appropriate if the scene were laid in the Court of Neptune.
Oh yes, of course, I know the Vengeance of Neptune does come into the
play. I don't suggest for a moment that we should think only of Port-
Royal, but after all the story that Racine tells us is not the 'Loves of
the Sea-Urchins.' Still, it is what my friend wished to have, and it is very
well done, right or wrong, and it's really quite pretty when you come to
look at it. Yes, so you liked that, did you; you understood what it meant,
of course; we feel the same about it, don't we, really; it is a trifle un-
balanced, what he's done, you agree with me, but on the whole it is very
clever of him." And so, when Bergotte had to express an opinion which
was the opposite of my own, he in no way reduced me to silence, to
the impossibility of framing any reply, as M. de Norpois would have done.
This does not prove that Bergotte's opinions were of less value than the
Ambassador's; far from it. A powerful idea communicates some of its
strength to him who challenges it. Being itself a part of the riches of the
universal Mind, it makes its way into, grafts itself upon the mind of him
whom it is employed to refute, slips in among the ideas already there,
with the help of which, gaining a little ground, he completes and corrects
it; so that the final utterance is always to some extent the work of both
parties to a discussion. It is to ideas which are not, properly speaking,
ideas at all, to ideas which, founded upon nothing, can find no support,
no kindred spirit among the ideas of the adversary, that he, grappling with
something which is not there, can find no word to say in answer. The arguments of M. de Norpois (in the matter of art) were unanswerable simply
because they were without reality.

Since Bergotte did not sweep aside my objections, I confessed to him
that they had won the scorn of M. de Norpois. "But he's an old parrot!"
was the answer. "He keeps on pecking you because he imagines all the
time that you're a piece of cake, or a slice of cuttle-fish." "What's that?"
asked Swann. "Are you a friend of Norpois?" "He's as dull as a wet
Sunday," interrupted his wife, who had great faith in Bergotte's judgment,
and was no doubt afraid that M. de Norpois might have spoken ill of
her to us. "I tried to make him talk after dinner; I don't know if it's his
age or his indigestion, but I found him too sticky for words. I really
thought I should have to 'dope' him." "Yes, isn't he?" Bergotte chimed in.
"You see, he has to keep his mouth shut half the time so as not to use up

all the stock of inanities that hold his shirt-front down and his white waistcoat up." "I think that Bergotte and my wife are both very hard on him," came from Swann, who took the 'line,' in his own house, of a plain, sensible man. "I quite see that Norpois cannot interest you very much, but from another point of view," (for Swann made a hobby of collecting scraps of 'real life') "he is quite remarkable, quite a remarkable instance of a lover. When he was Secretary at Rome," he went on, after making sure that Gilberte could not hear him, "he had, here in Paris, a mistress with whom he was madly in love, and he found time to make the double journey every week, so as to see her for a couple of hours. She was, as it happens, a most intelligent woman, and is quite attractive to this day; she is a dowager now. And he has had any number of others since then. I'm sure I should have gone stark mad if the woman I was in love with lived in Paris and I was kept shut up in Rome. Nervous men ought always to love, as the lower orders say, 'beneath' them, so that their women have a material inducement to do what they tell them." As he spoke, Swann realised that I might be applying this maxim to himself and Odette, and as, even among superior beings, at the moment when you and they seem to be soaring together above the plane of life, their personal pride is still basely human, he was seized by a violent ill-will towards me. But this was made manifest only in the uneasiness of his glance. He said nothing more to me at the time. Not that this need surprise us. When Racine (according to a story the truth of which has been exploded, though the theme of it may be found recurring every day in Parisian life) made an illusion to Scarron in front of Louis XIV, the most powerful monarch on earth said nothing to the poet that evening. It was on the following day, only, that he fell.

But as a theory requires to be stated as a whole, Swann, after this momentary irritation, and after wiping his eyeglass, finished saying what was in his mind in these words, words which were to assume later on in my memory the importance of a prophetic warning, which I had not had the sense to take: "The danger of that kind of love, however, is that the woman's subjection calms the man's jealousy for a time but also makes it more exacting. After a little he will force his mistress to live like one of those prisoners whose cells they keep lighted day and night, to prevent their escaping. And that generally ends in trouble."

I reverted to M. de Norpois. "You must never trust him; he has the most wicked tongue!" said Mme. Swann in an accent which seemed to me to indicate that M. de Norpois had been 'saying things' about her, especially as Swann looked across at his wife with an air of rebuke, as though to stop her before she went too far.

Meanwhile Gilberte, who had been told to go and get ready for our drive, stayed to listen to the conversation, and hovered between her mother and her father, leaning affectionately against his shoulder. Nothing, at first sight, could be in greater contrast to Mme. Swann, who was dark, than this child with her red hair and golden skin. But after looking at them both for a moment one saw in Gilberte many of the features—for instance, the nose cut short with a sharp, unfaltering decision by the unseen sculptor whose chisel repeats its work upon successive generations—the expression, the movements of her mother; to take an illustration from another form of art, she made one think of a portrait that was not a good likeness of Mme. Swann, whom the painter, to carry out some whim of colouring, had posed in a partial disguise, dressed to go out to a party in Venetian 'character.' And as not merely was she wearing a fair wig, but every atom of a swarthier complexion had been discharged from her flesh which, stripped of its veil of brownness, seemed more naked, covered simply in rays of light shed by an internal sun, this 'make-up' was not just superficial but was incarnate in her; Gilberte had the appearance of embodying some fabulous animal or of having assumed a mythological disguise. This reddish skin was so exactly that of her father that nature seemed to have had, when Gilberte was being created, to solve the problem of how to reconstruct Mme. Swann piecemeal, without any material at her disposal save the skin of M. Swann. And nature had utilised this to perfection, like a master carver who makes a point of leaving the grain, the knots of his wood in evidence. On Gilberte's face, at the corner of a perfect reproduction of Odette's nose, the skin was raised so as to preserve intact the two beauty spots of M. Swann. It was a new variety of Mme. Swann that was thus obtained, growing there by her side like a white lilac-tree beside a purple. At the same time it did not do to imagine the boundary line between these two likenesses as definitely fixed. Now and then, when Gilberte smiled, one could distinguish the oval of her father's cheek upon her mother's face, as though some one had mixed them together to see what would result from the blend; this oval grew distinct, as an embryo grows into a living shape, it lengthened obliquely, expanded, and a moment later had disappeared. In Gilberte's eyes there was the frank and honest gaze of her father; this was how she had looked at me when she gave me the agate marble and said, "Keep it, to remind yourself of our friendship." But were one to put a question to Gilberte, to ask her what she had been doing, then one saw in those same eyes the embarrassment, the uncertainty, the prevarication, the misery that Odette used in the old days to shew, when Swann asked her where she had been and she gave him one of those lying answers which, in those days, drove the lover to despair and now made him abruptly change the conversation, as an incurious and prudent husband. Often in the Champs-Elysées I was disturbed by seeing this look on Gilberte's face. But as a rule my fears were unfounded. For in her, a purely physical survival of her mother, this look (if nothing else) had ceased to have any meaning. It was when she had been to her classes, when she must go home for some lesson, that Gilberte's pupils executed that movement which, in time past, in the eyes of Odette, had been caused by the fear of disclosing that she had, during the day, opened the door to one of her lovers, or was at that moment in a hurry to be at some trysting-place. So one could see the two natures of M. and Mme. Swann ebb and flow, encroaching alternately one upon the other in the body of this Mélusine.

It is, of course, common knowledge that a child takes after both its father and its mother. And yet the distribution of the merits and defects which it inherits is so oddly planned that, of two good qualities which seemed inseparable in one of the parents you will find but one in the child, and allied to that very fault in the other parent which seemed most irreconcilable with it. Indeed, the incarnation of a good moral quality in an incompatible physical blemish is often one of the laws of filial resemblance. Of two sisters, one will combine with the proud bearing of her father the mean little soul of her mother; the other, abundantly endowed with the paternal intelligence, will present it to the world in the aspect which her mother has made familiar; her mother's shapeless nose and scraggy bosom are become the bodily covering of talents which you had learned to distinguish beneath a superb presence. With the result that of each of the sisters one can say with equal justification that it is she who takes more after one or other of her parents. It is true that Gilberte was an only child, but there were, at the least, two Gilbertes. The two natures, her father's and her mother's, did more than just blend themselves in her; they disputed the possession of her—and yet one cannot exactly say that, which would let it be thought that a third Gilberte was in the meantime suffering by being the prey of the two others. Whereas Gilberte was alternately one and the other, and at any given moment no more than one of the two, that is to say incapable, when she was not being good, of suffering accordingly, the better Gilberte not being able at the time, on account of her momentary absence, to detect the other's lapse from virtue. And so the less good of the two was free to enjoy pleasures of an ignoble kind. When the other spoke to you from the heart of her father, she held broad views, you would have liked to engage with her upon a fine and beneficent enterprise; you told her so, but, just as your arrangements were being completed, her mother's heart would already have resumed its control; hers was the voice that answered; and you were disappointed and vexed—almost baffled, as in the face of a substitution of one person for another—by an unworthy thought, an insincere laugh, in which Gilberte saw no harm, for they sprang from what she herself at that moment was. Indeed, the disparity was at times so great between these two Gilbertes that you asked yourself, though without finding an answer, what on earth you could have said or done to her, last time, to find her now so different. When she herself had arranged to meet you somewhere, not only did she fail to appear, and offer no excuse afterwards, but, whatever the influence might have been that had made her change her mind, she shewed herself in so different a character when you did meet her that you might well have supposed that, taken in by a likeness such as forms the plot of the *Menaechmi,* you were now talking to some one not the person who had so politely expressed her desire to see you, had she not shewn signs of an ill-humour which revealed that she felt herself to be in the wrong, and wished to avoid the necessity of an explanation.

"Now then, run along and get ready; you're keeping us waiting," her mother reminded her.

"I'm so happy here with my little Papa; I want to stay just for a minute," replied Gilberte, burying her head beneath the arm of her father, who passed his fingers lovingly through her bright hair.

Swann was one of those men who, having lived for a long time amid the illusions of love, have seen the prosperity that they themselves brought to numberless women increase the happiness of those women without exciting in them any gratitude, any tenderness towards their benefactors; but in their child they believe that they can feel an affection which, being incarnate in their own name, will enable them to remain in the world after their death. When there should no longer be any Charles Swann, there would still be a Mlle. Swann, or a Mme. something-else, *née* Swann, who would continue to love the vanished father. Indeed, to love him too well, perhaps, Swann may have been thinking, for he acknowledged Gilberte's caress with a "Good girl!" in that tone, made tender by our apprehension, to which, when we think of the future, we are prompted by the too passionate affection of a creature who is destined to survive us. To conceal his emotion, he joined in our talk about Berma. He pointed out to me, but in a detached, a listless tone, as though he wished to remain to some extent unconcerned in what he was saying, with what intelligence, with what an astonishing fitness the actress said to Œnone, "You knew it!" He was right. That intonation at least had a value that was really intelligible, and might therefore have satisfied my desire to find incontestable reasons for admiring Berma. But it was by the very fact of its clarity that it did not at all content me. Her intonation was so ingenious, so definite in intention and in its meaning, that it seemed to exist by itself, so that any intelligent actress might have learned to use it. It was a fine idea; but whoever else should conceive it as fully must possess it equally. It remained to Berma's credit that she had discovered it, but is one entitled to use the word 'discover' when the object in question is something that would not be different if one had been given it, something that does not belong essentially to one's own nature seeing that some one else may afterwards reproduce it?

"Upon my soul, your presence among us does raise the tone of the conversation!" Swann observed to me, as though to excuse himself to Bergotte; for he had formed the habit, in the Guermantes set, of entertaining great artists as if they were just ordinary friends whom one seeks only to make eat the dishes that they like, play the games, or, in the country, indulge in whatever form of sport they please. "It seems to me that we're talking a great deal of art," he went on. "But it's so nice, I do love it!" said Mme. Swann, throwing me a look of gratitude, as well from good nature as because she had not abandoned her old aspirations towards a more intellectual form of conversation. After this it was to others of the party, and principally to Gilberte, that Bergotte addressed himself. I had told him everything that I felt with a freedom which had astonished me, and was due to the fact that, having acquired with him, years before (in the course of all those hours of solitary reading, in which he was to me merely the better part of myself), the habit of sincerity, of frankness, of confidence, I was less frightened by him than by a person with whom I should have been talking for the first time. And yet, for the same reason, I was greatly disturbed by the thought of the impression that I must have been making on him, the contempt that I had supposed he would feel for

my ideas dating not from that afternoon but from the already distant
time in which I had begun to read his books in our garden at Combray.
And yet I ought perhaps to have reminded myself that, since it was in
all sincerity, abandoning myself to the train of my thoughts, that I had
felt, on the one hand, so intensely in sympathy with the work of Bergotte
and on the other hand, in the theatre, a disappointment the reason of
which I did not know, those two instinctive movements which had both
carried me away could not be so very different from one another, but must
be obedient to the same laws; and that that mind of Bergotte which I had
loved in his books could not be anything entirely foreign and hostile to
my disappointment and to my inability to express it. For my intelligence
must be a uniform thing, perhaps indeed there exists but a single intelligence, in which everyone in the world participates, towards which each
of us from the position of his own separate body turns his eyes, as in a
theatre where, if everyone has his own separate seat, there is on the other
hand but a single stage. Of course, the ideas which I was tempted to seek
to disentangle were probably not those whose depths Bergotte usually
sounded in his books. But if it were one and the same intelligence which
we had, he and I, at our disposal, he must, when he heard me express those
ideas, be reminded of them, cherish them, smile upon them, keeping probably, in spite of what I supposed, before his mind's eye a whole world of
intelligence other than that an excerpt of which had passed into his books,
an excerpt upon which I had based my imagination of his whole
mental universe. Just as priests, having the widest experience of the
human heart, are best able to pardon the sins which they do not themselves commit, so genius, having the widest experience of the human intelligence, can best understand the ideas most directly in opposition to
those which form the foundation of its own writings. I ought to have
told myself all this (though, for that matter, it was none too consoling a
thought, for the benevolent condescension of great minds has as a corollary
the incomprehension and hostility of small; and one derives far less happiness from the friendliness of a great writer, which one finds expressed, failing a more intimate association, in his books, than suffering from the
hostility of a woman whom one did not choose for her intelligence but
cannot help loving). I ought to have told myself all this, but I did not;
I was convinced that I had appeared a fool to Bergotte, when Gilberte
whispered in my ear:

"You can't think how delighted I am, because you have made a conquest of my great friend Bergotte. He's been telling Mamma that he found
you extremely intelligent."

"Where are we going?" I asked her. "Oh, wherever you like; you know,
it's all the same to me." But since the incident that had occurred on the
anniversary of her grandfather's death I had begun to ask myself whether
Gilberte's character was not other than I had supposed, whether that
indifference to what was to be done, that wisdom, that calm, that gentle
and constant submission did not indeed conceal passionate longings which
her self-esteem would not allow to be visible and which she disclosed only
by her sudden resistance whenever by any chance they were frustrated.

As Bergotte lived in the same neighbourhood as my parents, we left the house together; in the carriage he spoke to me of my health. "Our friends were telling me that you had been ill. I am very sorry. And yet, after all, I am not too sorry, because I can see quite well that you are able to enjoy the pleasures of the mind, and they are probably what mean most to you, as to everyone who has known them."

Alas, what he was saying, how little, I felt, did it apply to myself, whom all reasoning, however exalted it might be, left cold, who was happy only in moments of pure idleness, when I was comfortable and well; I felt how purely material was everything that I desired in life, and how easily I could dispense with the intellect. As I made no distinction among my pleasures between those that came to me from different sources, of varying depth and permanence, I was thinking, when the moment came to answer him, that I should have liked an existence in which I was on intimate terms with the Duchesse de Guermantes, and often came across, as in the old toll-house in the Champs-Elysées, a chilly smell that would remind me of Combray. But in this ideal existence which I dared not confide to him the pleasures of the mind found no place.

"No, sir, the pleasures of the mind count for very little with me; it is not them that I seek after; indeed I don't even know that I have ever tasted them."

"You really think not?" he replied. "Well, it may be, no, wait a minute now, yes, after all that must be what you like best, I can see it now clearly, I am certain of it."

As certainly, he did not succeed in convincing me; and yet I was already feeling happier, less restricted. After what M. de Norpois had said to me, I had regarded my moments of dreaming, of enthusiasm, of self-confidence as purely subjective and barren of truth. But according to Bergotte, who appeared to understand my case, it seemed that it was quite the contrary, that the symptom I ought to disregard was, in fact, my doubts, my disgust with myself. Moreover, what he had said about M. de Norpois took most of the sting out of a sentence from which I had supposed that no appeal was possible.

"Are you being properly looked after?" Bergotte asked me. "Who is treating you?" I told him that I had seen, and should probably go on seeing, Cottard. "But that's not at all the sort of man you want!" he told me. "I know nothing about him as a doctor. But I've met him at Mme. Swann's. The man's an imbecile. Even supposing that that doesn't prevent his being a good doctor, which I hesitate to believe, it does prevent his being a good doctor for artists, for men of intelligence. People like you must have suitable doctors, I would almost go so far as to say treatment and medicines specially adapted to themselves. Cottard will bore you, and that alone will prevent his treatment from having any effect. Besides, the proper course of treatment cannot possibly be the same for you as for any Tom, Dick or Harry. Nine tenths of the ills from which intelligent people suffer spring from their intellect. They need at least a doctor who understands their disease. How do you expect that Cottard should be able to treat you; he has made allowances for the difficulty of digesting sauces, for gastric trouble, but he has made no allowance for the effect of reading Shakespeare. So that his calculations are inaccurate in your case, the balance is upset; you see, always the little bottle-imp bobbing up again. He will find that you have a dilated stomach; he has no need to examine you for it, since he has it already in his eye. You can see it there, reflected in his glasses." This manner of speaking tired me greatly; I said to myself, with the stupidity of common sense: "There is no more any dilated stomach reflected in Professor Cottard's glasses than there are inanities stored behind the white waistcoat of M. de Norpois." "I should recommend you, instead," went on Bergotte, "to consult Dr. du Boulbon, who is quite an intelligent man." "He is a great admirer of your books," I replied. I saw that Bergotte knew this, and I decided that kindred spirits soon come together, that one has few really 'unknown friends.' What Bergotte had said to me with respect to Cottard impressed me, while running contrary to everything that I myself believed. I was in no way disturbed by finding my doctor a bore; I expected of him that, thanks to an art the laws of which were beyond me, he should pronounce on the subject of my health an infallible oracle, after consultation of my entrails. And I did not at all require that, with the aid of an intellect, in which I easily outstripped him, he should seek to understand my intellect, which I pictured to myself merely as a means, of no importance in itself, of trying to attain to certain external verities. I doubted greatly whether intellectual people required a different form of hygiene from imbeciles, and I was quite prepared to submit myself to the latter kind. "I'll tell you who does need a good doctor, and that is our friend Swann," said Bergotte. And on my asking whether he was ill, "Well, don't you see, he's typical of the man who has married a whore, and has to swallow a hundred serpents every day, from women who refuse to meet his wife, or men who were there before him. You can see them in his mouth, writhing. Just look, any day you're there, at the way he lifts his eyebrows when he comes in, to see who's in the room." The malice with which Bergotte spoke thus to a stranger of the friends in whose house he had so long been received as a welcome guest was as new to me as the almost amorous tone which, in that house, he had constantly been adopting to speak to them. Certainly a person like my great-aunt, for instance, would have been incapable of treating any of us with that politeness which I had heard Bergotte lavishing upon Swann. Even to the people whom she liked, she enjoyed saying disagreeable things. But behind their backs she would never have uttered a word to which they might not have listened. There was nothing less like the social 'world' than our society at Combray. The Swanns' house marked a stage on the way towards it, towards its inconstant tide. If they had not yet reached the open sea, they were certainly in the lagoon. "This is all between ourselves," said Bergotte as he left me outside my own door. A few years later I should have answered: "I never repeat things." That is the ritual phrase of society, from which the slanderer always derives a false reassurance. It is what I should have said then and there to Bergotte, for one does not invent all one's speeches, especially when one is acting merely as a card in the social pack. But I did not yet know the formula. What my great-aunt, on the other hand, would have said on a similar occasion was: "If you don't wish it to be repeated, why do you say it?" That is the answer of the unsociable, of the quarrelsome. I was nothing of that sort: I bowed my head in silence.

Men of letters who were in my eyes persons of considerable importance had had to plot for years before they succeeded in forming with Bergotte relations which continued to the end to be but dimly literary, and never emerged beyond the four walls of his study, whereas I, I had now been installed among the friends of the great writer, at the first attempt and without any effort, like a man who, instead of standing outside in a crowd for hours in order to secure a bad seat in a theatre, is shewn in at once to the best, having entered by a door that is closed to the public. If Swann had thus opened such a door to me, it was doubtless because, just as a king finds himself naturally inviting his children's friends into the royal box, or on board the royal yacht, so Gilberte's parents received their daughter's friends among all the precious things that they had in their house, and the even more precious intimacies that were enshrined there. But at that time I thought, and perhaps was right in thinking, that this friendliness on Swann's part was aimed indirectly at my parents. I seemed to remember having heard once at Combray that he had suggested to them that, in view of my admiration for Bergotte, he should take me to dine with him, and that my parents had declined, saying that I was too young, and too easily excited to 'go out' yet. My parents, no doubt, represented to certain other people (precisely those who seemed to me the most marvellous) something quite different from what they were to me, so that, just as when the lady in pink had paid my father a tribute of which he had shewn himself so unworthy, I should have wished them to understand what an inestimable present I had just received, and to testify their gratitude to that generous and courteous Swann who had offered it to me, or to them rather, without seeming any more to be conscious of its value than is, in Luini's fresco, the charming Mage with the arched nose and fair hair, to whom, it appeared, Swann had at one time been thought to bear a striking resemblance.

Unfortunately, this favour that Swann had done me, which, as I entered the house, before I had even taken off my greatcoat, I reported to my parents, in the hope that it would awaken in their hearts an emotion equal to my own, and would determine them upon some immense and decisive act of politeness towards the Swanns, did not appear to be greatly appreciated by them. "Swann introduced you to Bergotte? An excellent friend for you, charming society!" cried my father, ironically. "It only wanted that!" Alas, when I had gone on to say that Bergotte was by no means inclined to admire M. de Norpois:

"I dare say!" retorted my father. "That simply proves that he's a foolish and evil-minded fellow. My poor boy, you never had much common sense, still, I'm sorry to see you fall among a set that will finish you off altogether."

Already the mere fact of my frequenting the Swanns had been far from delighting my parents. This introduction to Bergotte seemed to them a

fatal but natural consequence of an original mistake, namely their own
weakness in controlling me, which my grandfather would have called a
'want of circumspection.' I felt that I had only, in order to complete their
ill humour, to tell them that this perverse fellow who did not appreciate
M. de Norpois had found me extremely intelligent. For I had observed
that whenever my father decided that anyone, one of my school friends
for instance, was going astray—as I was at that moment—if that person
had the approval of somebody whom my father did not rate high, he
would see in this testimony the confirmation of his own stern judgment.
The evil merely seemed to him more pronounced. I could hear him already
exclaiming, "Of course, it all hangs together," an expression that terrified
me by the vagueness and vastness of the reforms the introduction of which
into my quiet life it seemed to threaten. But since, were I not to tell them
what Bergotte had said of me, even then nothing could efface the impression my parents had formed, that this should be made slightly worse
mattered little. Besides, they seemed to me so unfair, so completely mistaken, that not only had I not any hope, I had scarcely any desire to bring
them to a more equitable point of view. At the same time, feeling, as the
words came from my lips, how alarmed they would be by the thought
that I had found favour in the sight of a person who dismissed clever
men as fools and had earned the contempt of all decent people, praise
from whom, since it seemed to me a thing to be desired, would only encourage me in wrongdoing, it was in faltering tones and with a slightly
shamefaced air that, coming to the end of my story, I flung them the
bouquet of: "He told the Swanns that he had found me extremely intelligent." Just as a poisoned dog, in a field, rushes, without knowing why,
straight to the grass which is the precise antidote to the toxin that he
has swallowed, so I, without in the least suspecting it, had said the one
thing in the world that was capable of overcoming in my parents this
prejudice with respect to Bergotte, a prejudice which all the best reasons
that I could have urged, all the tributes that I could have paid him, must
have proved powerless to defeat. Instantly the situation changed.

"Oh! He said that he found you intelligent," repeated my mother. "I
am glad to hear that, because he is a man of talent."

"What! He said that, did he?" my father joined in. "I don't for a
moment deny his literary distinction, before which the whole world bows;
only it is a pity that he should lead that scarcely reputable existence to
which old Norpois made a guarded allusion, when he was here," he went
on, not seeing that against the sovran virtue of the magic words which I
had just repeated the depravity of Bergotte's morals was little more able
to contend than the falsity of his judgment.

"But, my dear," Mamma interrupted, "we've no proof that it's true.
People say all sorts of things. Besides M. de Norpois may have the most
perfect manners in the world, but he's not always very good-natured,
especially about people who are not exactly his sort."

"That's quite true; I've noticed it myself," my father admitted.

"And then, too, a great deal ought to be forgiven Bergotte, since he thinks well of my little son," Mamma went on, stroking my hair with her fingers and fastening upon me a long and pensive gaze.

My mother had not, indeed, awaited this verdict from Bergotte before telling me that I might ask Gilberte to tea whenever I had friends coming. But I dared not do so for two reasons. The first was that at Gilberte's there was never anything else to drink but tea. Whereas at home Mamma insisted on there being a pot of chocolate as well. I was afraid that Gilberte might regard this as 'common'; and so conceive a great contempt for us. The other reason was a formal difficulty, a question of procedure which I could never succeed in settling. When I arrived at Mme. Swann's she used to ask me: "And how is your mother?" I had made several overtures to Mamma to find out whether she would do the same when Gilberte came to us, a point which seemed to me more serious than, at the Court of Louis XIV, the use of 'Monseigneur.' But Mamma would not hear of it for a moment.

"Certainly not. I do not know Mme. Swann."

"But neither does she know you."

"I never said she did, but we are not obliged to behave in exactly the same way about everything. I shall find other ways of being civil to Gilberte than Mme. Swann has with you."

But I was unconvinced, and preferred not to invite Gilberte.

Leaving my parents, I went upstairs to change my clothes and on emptying my pockets came suddenly upon the envelope which the Swanns' butler had handed me before shewing me into the drawing-room. I was now alone. I opened it; inside was a card on which I was told the name of the lady whom I ought to have 'taken in' to luncheon.

It was about this period that Bloch overthrew my conception of the world and opened for me fresh possibilities of happiness (which, for that matter, were to change later on into possibilities of suffering), by assuring me that, in contradiction of all that I had believed at the time of my walks along the Méséglise way, women never asked for anything better than to make love. He added to this service a second, the value of which I was not to appreciate until much later; it was he who took me for the first time into a disorderly house. He had indeed told me that there were any number of pretty women whom one might enjoy. But I could see them only in a vague outline for which those houses were to enable me to substitute actual human features. So that if I owed to Bloch—for his 'good tidings' that beauty and the enjoyment of beauty were not inaccessible things, and that we have acted foolishly in renouncing them for all time—a debt of gratitude of the same kind that we owe to an optimistic physician or philosopher who has given us reason to hope for length of days in this world and not to be entirely cut off from it when we shall have passed beyond the veil, the houses of assignation which I began to frequent some years later—by furnishing me with specimens of beauty, by allowing me to add to the beauty of women that element which we are powerless to invent, which is something more than a mere summary of former beauties, that present indeed divine, the one present that we cannot bestow upon ourselves, before which faint and fail all the logical creations of our intellect, and which we

can seek from reality alone: an individual charm—deserved to be ranked
by me with those other benefactors more recent in origin but of comparable
utility (before finding which we used to imagine without any warmth the
seductive charms of Mantegna, of Wagner, of Siena, by studying other
painters, hearing other composers, visiting other cities): namely illustrated editions of the history of painting, symphonic concerts and hand-
books to 'Mediaeval Towns.' But the house to which Bloch led me (and
which he himself, for that matter, had long ceased to visit), was of too
humble a grade, its denizens were too inconspicuous and too little varied
to be able to satisfy my old or to stimulate new curiosities. The mistress of
this house knew none of the women with whom one asked her to negotiate,
and was always suggesting others whom one did not want. She boasted to
me of one in particular, one of whom, with a smile full of promise (as
though this had been a great rarity and a special treat) she would whisper:
"She is a Jewess! Doesn't that make you want to?" (That, by the way,
was probably why the girl's name was Rachel.) And with a silly and
affected excitement which, she hoped, would prove contagious, and which
ended in a hoarse gurgle, almost of sensual satisfaction: "Think of that,
my boy, a Jewess! Wouldn't that be lovely? Rrrr!" This Rachel, of whom
I caught a glimpse without her seeing me, was dark and not good looking,
but had an air of intelligence, and would pass the tip of her tongue over
her lips as she smiled, with a look of boundless impertinence, at the 'boys'
who were introduced to her and whom I could hear making conversation.
Her small and narrow face was framed in short curls of black hair, irregular
as though they were outlined in pen-strokes upon a wash-drawing in In-
dian ink. Every evening I promised the old woman who offered her to me
with a special insistence, boasting of her superior intelligence and her
education, that I would not fail to come some day on purpose to make the
acquaintance of Rachel, whom I had nicknamed "Rachel when from the
Lord." But the first evening I had heard her, as she was leaving the house,
say to the mistress: "That's settled then; I shall be free to-morrow, if you
have anyone you won't forget to send for me."

And these words had prevented me from recognising her as a person
because they had made me classify her at once in a general category of
women whose habit, common to all of them, was to come there in the
evening to see whether there might not be a louis or two to be earned. She
would simply vary her formula, saying indifferently: "If you want me" or
"If you want anybody."

The mistress, who was not familiar with Halévy's opera, did not know
why I always called the girl "Rachel when from the Lord." But failure to
understand a joke has never yet made anyone find it less amusing, and it
was always with a whole-hearted laugh that she would say to me:

"Then there's nothing doing to-night? When am I going to fix you up
with 'Rachel when from the Lord'? Why do you always say that, 'Rachel
when from the Lord'? Oh, that's very smart, that is. I'm going to make a
match of you two. You won't be sorry for it, you'll see."

Once I was just making up my mind, but she was 'in the press,' another
time in the hands of the hairdresser, an elderly gentleman who never did

anything for the women except pour oil on their loosened hair and then comb it. And I grew tired of waiting, even though several of the humbler frequenters of the place (working girls, they called themselves, but they always seemed to be out of work), had come to mix drinks for me and to hold long conversations to which, despite the gravity of the subjects discussed, the partial or total nudity of the speakers gave an attractive simplicity. I ceased moreover to go to this house because, anxious to present a token of my good-will to the woman who kept it and was in need of furniture, I had given her several pieces, notably a big sofa, which I had inherited from my aunt Léonie. I used never to see them, for want of space had prevented my parents from taking them in at home, and they were stored in a warehouse. But as soon as I discovered them again in the house where these women were putting them to their own uses, all the virtues that one had imbibed in the air of my aunt's room at Combray became apparent to me, tortured by the cruel contact to which I had abandoned them in their helplessness! Had I outraged the dead, I should not have suffered such remorse. I returned no more to visit their new mistress, for they seemed to me to be alive, and to be appealing to me, like those objects, apparently inanimate, in a Persian fairy-tale, in which are embodied human souls that are undergoing martyrdom and plead for deliverance. Besides, as our memory presents things to us, as a rule, not in their chronological sequence but as it were by a reflexion in which the order of the parts is reversed, I remembered only long afterwards that it was upon that same sofa that, many years before, I had tasted for the first time the sweets of love with one of my girl cousins, with whom I had not known where to go until she somewhat rashly suggested our taking advantage of a moment in which aunt Léonie had left her room.

A whole lot more of my aunt Léonie's things, and notably a magnificent set of old silver plate, I sold, in spite of my parents' warnings, so as to have more money to spend, and to be able to send more flowers to Mme. Swann who would greet me, after receiving an immense basket of orchids, with: "If I were your father, I should have you up before the magistrate for this." How was I to suppose that one day I might regret more than anything the loss of my silver plate, and rank certain other pleasures more highly than that (which would have shrunk perhaps into none at all) of bestowing favours upon Gilberte's parents. Similarly, it was with Gilberte in my mind, and so as not to be separated from her, that I had decided not to enter a career of diplomacy abroad. It is always thus, impelled by a state of mind which is destined not to last, that we make our irrevocable decisions. I could scarcely imagine that that strange substance which was housed in Gilberte, and from her permeated her parents and her home, leaving me indifferent to all things else, could be liberated from her, could migrate into another person. The same substance, unquestionable, and yet one that would have a wholly different effect on me. For a single malady goes through various evolutions, and a delicious poison can no longer be taken with the same impunity when, with the passing of the years, the heart's power of resistance has diminished.

My parents meanwhile would have liked to see the intelligence that

Bergotte had discerned in me made manifest in some remarkable achievement. When I still did not know the Swanns I thought that I was prevented from working by the state of agitation into which I was thrown by the impossibility of seeing Gilberte when I chose. But, now that their door stood open to me, scarcely had I sat down at my desk than I would rise and run to them. And after I had left them and was at home again, my isolation was only apparent, my mind was powerless to swim against the stream of words on which I had allowed myself mechanically to be borne for hours on end. Sitting alone, I continued to fashion remarks such as might have pleased or amused the Swanns, and to make this pastime more entertaining I myself took the parts of those absent players, I put to myself imagined questions, so chosen that my brilliant epigrams served merely as happy answers to them. Though conducted in silence, this exercise was none the less a conversation and not a meditation, my solitude a mental society in which it was not I myself but other imaginary speakers who controlled my choice of words, and in which I felt as I formulated, in place of the thoughts that I believed to be true, those that came easily to my mind, and involved no introspection from without, that kind of pleasure, entirely passive, which sitting still affords to anyone who is burdened with a sluggish digestion.

Had I been less firmly resolved upon setting myself definitely to work, I should perhaps have made an effort to begin at once. But since my resolution was explicit, since within twenty-four hours, in the empty frame of that long morrow in which everything was so well arranged because I myself had not yet entered it, my good intentions would be realised without difficulty, it was better not to select an evening on which I was ill-disposed for a beginning for which the following days were not, alas, to shew themselves any more propitious. But I was reasonable. It would have been puerile, on the part of one who had waited now for years, not to put up with a postponement of two or three days. Confident that by the day after next I should have written several pages, I said not a word more to my parents of my decision; I preferred to remain patient for a few hours and then to bring to a convinced and comforted grandmother a sample of work that was already under way. Unfortunately the morrow was not that vast, external day to which I in my fever had looked forward. When it drew to a close, my laziness and my painful struggle to overcome certain internal obstacles had simply lasted twenty-four hours longer. And at the end of several days, my plans not having matured, I had no longer the same hope that they would be realised at once, no longer the courage, therefore, to subordinate everything else to their realisation: I began again to keep late hours, having no longer, to oblige me to go to bed early on any evening, the certain hope of seeing my work begun next morning. I needed, before I could recover my creative energy, several days of relaxation, and the only time that my grandmother ventured, in a gentle and disillusioned tone, to frame the reproach: "Well, and that work of yours; aren't we even to speak of it now?" I resented her intrusion, convinced that in her inability to see that my mind was irrevocably made up, she had further and perhaps for a long time postponed the execution of my task, by the shock which her denial of justice to me had given my nerves, since until I had recovered from that shock I should not feel inclined to begin my work. She felt that her scepticism had charged blindly into my intention. She apologised, kissing me: "I am sorry; I shall not say anything again," and, so that I should not be discouraged, assured me that, from the day on which I should be quite well again, the work would come of its own accord from my superfluity of strength.

Besides, I said to myself, in spending all my time with the Swanns, am I not doing exactly what Bergotte does? To my parents it seemed almost as though, idle as I was, I was leading, since it was spent in the same drawing-room with a great writer, the life most favourable to the growth of talent. And yet the assumption that anyone can be dispensed from having to create that talent for himself, from within himself, and can acquire it from some one else, is as impossible as it would be to suppose that a man can keep himself in good health, in spite of neglecting all the rules of hygiene and of indulging in the worst excesses, merely by dining out often in the company of a physician. The person, by the way, who was most completely taken in by this illusion, which misled me as well as my parents, was Mme. Swann. When I explained to her that I was unable to come, that I must stay at home and work, she looked as though she were thinking that I made a great fuss about nothing, that there was something foolish as well as ostentatious in what I had said.

"But Bergotte is coming, isn't he? Do you mean that you don't think it good, what he writes? It will be better still, very soon," she went on, "for he is more pointed, he concentrates more in newspaper articles than in his books, where he is apt to spread out too much. I've arranged that in future he's to do the leading articles in the *Figaro*. He'll be distinctly the 'right man in the right place' there." And, finally, "Come! He will tell you, better than anyone, what you ought to do."

And so, just as one invites a gentleman ranker to meet his colonel, it was in the interests of my career, and as though masterpieces of literature arose out of 'getting to know' people, that she told me not to fail to come to dinner with her next day, to meet Bergotte.

And so there was not from the Swanns any more than from my parents, that is to say from those who, at different times, had seemed bound to place obstacles in my way, any further opposition to that pleasant existence in which I might see Gilberte as often as I chose, with enjoyment if not with peace of mind. There can be no peace of mind in love, since the advantage one has secured is never anything but a fresh starting-point for further desires. So long as I had not been free to go to her, having my eyes fixed upon that inaccessible goal of happiness, I could not so much as imagine the fresh grounds for anxiety that lay in wait for me there. Once the resistance of her parents was broken, and the problem solved at last, it began to set itself anew, and always in different terms. Each evening, on arriving home, I reminded myself that I had things to say to Gilberte of prime importance, things upon which our whole friendship hung, and these things were never the same. But at least I was happy, and no further menace arose to threaten my happiness. One was to appear, alas, from a quarter in which I had never detected any peril, namely from Gilberte and myself. And yet I ought to have been tormented by what, on the contrary, reassured me, by what I mistook for happiness. We are, when we love, in an abnormal state, capable of giving at once to an accident, the most simple to all appearance and one that may at any moment occur, a serious aspect which that accident by itself would not bear. What makes us so happy is the presence in our heart of an unstable element which we are perpetually arranging to keep in position, and of which we cease almost to be aware so long as it is not displaced. Actually, there is in love a permanent strain of suffering which happiness neutralises, makes conditional only, procrastinates, but which may at any moment become what it would long since have been had we not obtained what we were seeking, sheer agony.

On several occasions I felt that Gilberte was anxious to put off my visits. It is true that when I was at all anxious to see her I had only to get myself invited by her parents who were increasingly persuaded of my excellent influence over her. "Thanks to them," I used to think, "my love is running no risk; the moment I have them on my side, I can set my mind at rest; they have full authority over Gilberte." Until, alas, I detected certain signs of impatience which she allowed to escape her when her father made me come to the house, almost against her will, and asked myself whether what I had regarded as a protection for my happiness was not in fact the secret reason why that happiness could not endure.

The last time that I called to see Gilberte, it was raining; she had been asked to a dancing lesson in the house of some people whom she knew too slightly to be able to take me there with her. In view of the dampness of the air I had taken rather more caffeine than usual. Perhaps on account of the weather, or because she had some objection to the house in which this party was being given, Mme. Swann, as her daughter was leaving the room, called her back in the sharpest of tones: "Gilberte!" and pointed to me, to indicate that I had come there to see her and that she ought to stay with me. This 'Gilberte!' had been uttered, or shouted rather, with the best of intentions towards myself, but from the way in which Gilberte shrugged her shoulders as she took off her outdoor clothes I divined that her mother had unwittingly hastened the gradual evolution, which until then it had perhaps been possible to arrest, which was gradually drawing away from me my friend. "You don't need to go out dancing every day," Odette told her daughter, with a sagacity acquired, no doubt, in earlier days, from Swann. Then, becoming once more Odette, she began speaking to her daughter in English. At once it was as though a wall had sprung up to hide from me a part of the life of Gilberte, as though an evil genius had spirited my friend far away. In a language that we know, we have substituted for the opacity of sounds, the perspicuity of ideas. But a language which we do not know is a fortress sealed, within whose walls she whom we love is free to play us false, while we, standing without, desperately alert in our impotence, can see, can prevent nothing. So this conversation in English, at which, a month earlier, I should merely have smiled, interspersed with a few proper names in French which did not fail to accentuate, to give a point to my uneasiness, had, when conducted within a few feet of me by two motionless persons, the same degree of cruelty, left me as much abandoned and alone as the forcible abduction of my companion. At length Mme. Swann left us. That day, perhaps from resentment against myself, the unwilling cause of her not going out to enjoy herself, perhaps also because, guessing her to be angry with me, I was precautionally colder than usual with her, the face of Gilberte, divested of every sign of joy, bleak, bare, pillaged, seemed all afternoon to be devoting a melancholy regret to the pas-de-quatre in which my arrival had prevented her from going to take part, and to be defying every living creature, beginning with myself, to understand the subtle reasons that had determined in her a sentimental attachment to the boston. She confined herself to exchanging with me, now and again, on the weather, the increasing violence of the rain, the fastness of the clock, a conversation punctuated with silences and monosyllables, in which I lashed myself on, with a sort of desperate rage, to the destruction of those moments which we might have devoted to friendship and happiness. And on each of our remarks was stamped, as it were, a supreme harshness, by the paroxysm of their stupefying unimportance, which at the same time consoled me, for it prevented Gilberte from being taken in by the banality of my observations and the indifference of my tone. In vain was my polite: "I thought, the other day, that the clock was slow, if anything"; she evidently understood me to mean: "How tiresome you are being!" Obstinately as I might protract, over the whole length of that rain-sodden afternoon, the dull cloud of words through which no fitful ray shone, I knew that my coldness was not so unalterably fixed as I pretended, and that Gilberte must be fully aware that if, after already saying it to her three times, I had hazarded a fourth repetition of the statement that the evenings were drawing in, I should have had difficulty in restraining myself from bursting into tears. When she was like that, when no smile filled her eyes or unveiled her face, I cannot describe the devastating monotony that stamped her melancholy eyes and sullen features. Her face, grown almost livid, reminded me then of those dreary beaches where the sea, ebbing far out, wearies one with its faint shimmering, everywhere the same, fixed in an immutable and low horizon. At length, as I saw no sign in Gilberte of the happy change for which I had been waiting now for some hours, I told her that she was not being nice. "It is you that are not being nice," was her answer. "Oh, but surely——!" I asked myself what I could have done, and, finding no answer, put the question to her. "Naturally, you think yourself nice!" she said to me with a laugh, and went on laughing. Whereupon I felt all the anguish that there was for me in not being able to attain to that other, less perceptible, plane of her mind which her laughter indicated. It seemed, that laughter, to mean: "No, no, I'm not going to let myself be moved by anything that you say, I know you're madly in love with me, but that leaves me neither hot nor cold, for I don't care a rap for you." But I told myself that, after all, laughter was not a language so well defined that I could be certain of understanding what this laugh really meant. And Gilberte's words were affectionate. "But how am I not being nice?" I asked her. "Tell

me; I will do anything you want." "No; that wouldn't be any good. I
can't explain." For a moment I was afraid that she thought that I did not
love her, and this was for me a fresh agony, no less keen, but one that
required treatment by a different conversational method. "If you knew
how much you were hurting me you would tell me." But this pain which,
had she doubted my love for her, must have rejoiced her, seemed instead to
make her more angry. Then, realising my mistake, making up my mind to
pay no more attention to what she said, letting her (without bothering to
believe her) assure me: "I do love you, indeed I do; you will see one day,"
(that day on which the guilty are convinced that their innocence will be
made clear, and which, for some mysterious reason, never happens to be
the day on which their evidence is taken), I had the courage to make a
sudden resolution not to see her again, and without telling her of it yet
since she would not have believed me.

Grief that is caused one by a person with whom one is in love can be
bitter, even when it is interpolated among preoccupations, occupations,
pleasures in which that person is not directly involved and from which our
attention is diverted only now and again to return to it. But when such
a grief has its birth—as was now happening—at a moment when the happiness of seeing that person fills us to the exclusion of all else, the sharp
depression that then affects our spirits, sunny hitherto, sustained and
calm, lets loose in us a raging tempest against which we know not whether
we are capable of struggling to the end. The tempest that was blowing in
my heart was so violent that I made my way home baffled, battered, feeling that I could recover my breath only by retracing my steps, by returning,
upon whatever pretext, into Gilberte's presence. But she would have said
to herself: "Back again! Evidently I can go to any length with him; he
will come back every time, and the more wretched he is when he leaves
me the more docile he'll be." Besides, I was irresistibly drawn towards her
in thought, and those alternative orientations, that mad careering between
them of the compass-needle within me, persisted after I had reached home,
and expressed themselves in the mutually contradictory letters to Gilberte
which I began to draft.

I was about to pass through one of those difficult crises which we generally find that we have to face at various stages in life, and which, for all
that there has been no change in our character, in our nature (that nature
which itself creates our loves, and almost creates the women whom we love,
even to their faults), we do not face in the same way on each occasion,
that is to say at every age. At such moments our life is divided, and so to
speak distributed over a pair of scales, in two counterpoised pans which
between them contain it all. In one there is our desire not to displease, not
to appear too humble to the creature whom we love without managing to
understand her, but whom we find it more convenient at times to appear
almost to disregard, so that she shall not have that sense of her own indis-
pensability which may turn her from us; in the other scale there is a feeling
of pain—and one that is not localised and partial only—which cannot be
set at rest unless, abandoning every thought of pleasing the woman and
of making her believe that we can dispense with her, we go at once to find

her. When we withdraw from the pan in which our pride lies a small quantity of the will-power which we have weakly allowed to exhaust itself with increasing age, when we add to the pan that holds our suffering a physical pain which we have acquired and have let grow, then, instead of the courageous solution that would have carried the day at one-and-twenty, it is the other, grown too heavy and insufficiently balanced, that crushes us down at fifty. All the more because situations, while repeating themselves, tend to alter, and there is every likelihood that, in middle life or in old age, we shall have had the grim satisfaction of complicating our love by an intrusion of habit which adolescence, repressed by other demands upon it, less master of itself, has never known.

I had just written Gilberte a letter in which I allowed the tempest of my wrath to thunder, not however without throwing her the lifebuoy of a few words disposed as though by accident on the page, by clinging to which my friend might be brought to a reconciliation; a moment later, the wind having changed, they were phrases full of love that I addressed to her, chosen for the sweetness of certain forlorn expressions, those 'nevermores' so touching to those who pen them, so wearisome to her who will have to read them, whether she believe them to be false and translate 'nevermore' by 'this very evening, if you want me,' or believe them to be true and so to be breaking the news to her of one of those final separations which make so little difference to our lives when the other person is one with whom we are not in love. But since we are incapable, while we are in love, of acting as fit predecessors of the next persons whom we shall presently have become, and who will then be in love no longer, how are we to imagine the actual state of mind of a woman whom, even when we are conscious that we are of no account to her, we have perpetually represented in our musings as uttering, so as to lull us into a happy dream or to console us for a great sorrow, the same speeches that she would make if she loved us. When we come to examine the thoughts, the actions of a woman whom we love, we are as completely at a loss as must have been, face to face with the phenomena of nature, the world's first natural philosophers, before their science had been elaborated and had cast a ray of light over the unknown. Or, worse still, we are like a person in whose mind the law of causality barely exists, a person who would be incapable, therefore, of establishing any connexion between one phenomenon and another, to whose eyes the spectacle of the world would appear unstable as a dream. Of course I made efforts to emerge from this incoherence, to find reasons for things. I tried even to be 'objective' and, to that end, to bear well in mind the disproportion that existed between the importance which Gilberte had in my eyes and that, not only which I had in hers, but which she herself had in the eyes of other people, a disproportion which, had I failed to remark it, would have involved my mistaking mere friendliness on my friend's part for a passionate avowal, and a grotesque and debasing display on my own for the simple and graceful movement with which we are attracted towards a pretty face. But I was afraid also of falling into the contrary error, in which I should have seen in Gilberte's unpunctuality in keeping an appointment an irremediable hostility. I tried to discover between these two perspectives, equally distorting, a third which would enable me to see things as they really were; the calculations I was obliged to make with that object helped to take my mind off my sufferings; and whether in obedience to the laws of arithmetic or because I had made them give me the answer that I desired, I made up my mind that next day I would go to the Swanns', happy, but happy in the same way as people who, having long been tormented by the thought of a journey which they have not wished to make, go no farther than to the station and return home to unpack their boxes. And since, while one is hesitating, the bare idea of a possible resolution (unless one has rendered that idea sterile by deciding that one will make no resolution) develops, like a seed in the ground, the lineaments, every detail of the emotions that will be born from the performance of the action, I told myself that it had been quite absurd of me to be as much hurt by the suggestion that I should not see Gilberte again as if I had really been about to put that suggestion into practice, and that since, on the contrary, I was to end by returning to her side, I might have saved myself the expense of all those vain longings and painful acceptances. But this resumption of friendly relations lasted only so long as it took me to reach the Swanns'; not because their butler, who was really fond of me, told me that Gilberte had gone out (a statement the truth of which was confirmed, as it happened, the same evening, by people who had seen her somewhere), but because of the manner in which he said it. "Sir, the young lady is not at home; I can assure you, sir, that I am speaking the truth. If you wish to make any inquiries I can fetch the young lady's maid. You know very well, sir, that I would do everything in my power to oblige you, and that if the young lady was at home I would take you to her at once." These words being of the only kind that is really important, that is to say spontaneous, the kind that gives us a radiograph shewing the main points, at any rate, of the unimaginable reality which would be wholly concealed beneath a prepared speech, proved that in Gilberte's household there was an impression that I bothered her with my visits; and so, scarcely had the man uttered them before they had aroused in me a hatred of which I preferred to make him rather than Gilberte the victim; he drew upon his own head all the angry feelings that I might have had for my friend; freed from these complications, thanks to his words, my love subsisted alone; but his words had, at the same time, shewn me that I must cease for the present to attempt to see Gilberte. She would be certain to write to me, to apologise. In spite of which, I should not return at once to see her, so as to prove to her that I was capable of living without her. Besides, once I had received her letter, Gilberte's society was a thing with which I should be more easily able to dispense for a time, since I should be certain of finding her ready to receive me whenever I chose. All that I needed in order to support with less pain the burden of a voluntary separation was to feel that my heart was rid of the terrible uncertainty whether we were not irreconcilably sundered, whether she had not promised herself to another, left Paris, been taken away by force. The days that followed resembled the first week of that old New Year which I had had to spend alone, without Gilberte. But when that week had dragged to its end, then for one thing

my friend would be coming again to the Champs-Elysées, I should be seeing her as before; I had been sure of that; for another thing, I had known
with no less certainty that so long as the New Year holidays lasted it
would not be worth my while to go to the Champs-Elysées, which meant
that during that miserable week, which was already ancient history, I had
endured my wretchedness with a quiet mind because there was blended
in it neither fear nor hope. Now, on the other hand, it was the latter of
these which, almost as much as my fear of what might happen, rendered
intolerable the burden of my grief. Not having had any letter from Gilberte that evening, I had attributed this to her carelessness, to her other
occupations, I did not doubt that I should find something from her in the
morning's post. This I awaited, every day, with a beating heart which
subsided, leaving me utterly prostrate, when I had found in it only letters
from people who were not Gilberte, or else nothing at all, which was no
worse, the proofs of another's friendship making all the more cruel those
of her indifference. I transferred my hopes to the afternoon post. Even
between the times at which letters were delivered I dared not leave the
house, for she might be sending hers by a messenger. Then, the time coming at last when neither the postman nor a footman from the Swanns' could
possibly appear that night, I must procrastinate my hope of being set at
rest, and thus, because I believed that my sufferings were not destined to
last, I was obliged, so to speak, incessantly to renew them. My disappointment was perhaps the same, but instead of just uniformly prolonging, as
in the old days, an initial emotion, it began again several times daily,
starting each time with an emotion so frequently renewed that it ended—
it, so purely physical, so instantaneous a state—by becoming stabilised, so
consistently that the strain of waiting having hardly time to relax before a
fresh reason for waiting supervened, there was no longer a single minute
in the day in which I was not in that state of anxiety which it is so difficult to bear even for an hour. So my punishment was infinitely more cruel
than in those New Year holidays long ago, because this time there was in
me, instead of the acceptance, pure and simple, of that punishment, the
hope, at every moment, of seeing it come to an end. And yet at this state of
acceptance I ultimately arrived; then I understood that it must be final,
and I renounced Gilberte for ever, in the interests of my love itself and
because I hoped above all that she would not retain any contemptuous
memory of me. Indeed, from that moment, so that she should not be led
to suppose any sort of lover's spite on my part, when she made appoint-
ments for me to see her I used often to accept them and then, at the last
moment, write to her that I was prevented from coming, but with the
same protestations of my disappointment that I should have made to anyone whom I had not wished to see. These expressions of regret, which we
keep as a rule for people who do not matter, would do more, I imagined,
to persuade Gilberte of my indifference than would the tone of indifference
which we affect only to those whom we love. When, better than by mere
words, by a course of action indefinitely repeated, I should have proved to
her that I had no appetite for seeing her, perhaps she would discover once
again an appetite for seeing me. Alas! I was doomed to failure; to attempt,

by ceasing to see her, to reawaken in her that inclination to see me was to lose her for ever; first of all, because, when it began to revive, if I wished it to last I must not give way to it at once; besides, the most agonising hours would then have passed; it was at this very moment that she was indispensable to me, and I should have liked to be able to warn her that what presently she would have to assuage, by the act of seeing me again, would be a grief so far diminished as to be no longer (what a moment ago it would still have been), nor the thought of putting an end to it, a motive towards surrender, reconciliation, further meetings. And then again, later on, when I should at last be able safely to confess to Gilberte (so far would her liking for me have regained its strength) my liking for her, the latter, not having been able to resist the strain of so long a separation, would have ceased to exist; Gilberte would have become immaterial to me. I knew this, but I could not explain it to her; she would have assumed that if I was pretending that I should cease to love her if I remained for too long without seeing her, that was solely in order that she might summon me back to her at once. In the meantime, what made it easier for me to sentence myself to this separation was the fact that (in order to make it quite clear to her that despite my protestations to the contrary it was my own free will and not any conflicting engagement, not the state of my health that prevented me from seeing her), whenever I knew beforehand that Gilberte would not be in the house, was going out somewhere with a friend and would not be home for dinner, I went to see Mme. Swann who had once more become to me what she had been at the time when I had such difficulty in seeing her daughter and (on days when the latter was not coming to the Champs-Elysées) used to repair to the Allée des Acacias. In this way I should be hearing about Gilberte, and could be certain that she would in due course hear about me, and in terms which would shew her that I was not interested in her. And I found, as all those who suffer find, that my melancholy condition might have been worse. For being free at any time to enter the habitation in which Gilberte dwelt, I constantly reminded myself, for all that I was firmly resolved to make no use of that privilege, that if ever my pain grew too sharp there was a way of making it cease. I was not unhappy, save only from day to day. And even that is an exaggeration. How many times in an hour (but now without that anxious expectancy which had strained every nerve of me in the first weeks after our quarrel, before I had gone again to the Swanns') did I not repeat to myself the words of the letter which, one day soon, Gilberte would surely send, would perhaps even bring to me herself. The perpetual vision of that imagined happiness helped me to endure the desolation of my real happiness. With women who do not love us, as with the 'missing,' the knowledge that there is no hope left does not prevent our continuing to wait for news. We live on tenterhooks, starting at the slightest sound; the mother whose son has gone to sea on some perilous voyage of discovery sees him in imagination every moment, long after the fact of his having perished has been established, striding into the room, saved by a miracle and in the best of health. And this strain of waiting, according to the strength of her memory and the resistance of her bodily organs, either helps her on her journey through the years, at the end of which she will be able to endure the knowledge that her son is no more, to forget gradually and to survive his loss, or else it kills her.

On the other hand, my grief found consolation in the idea that my love must profit by it. Each visit that I paid to Mme. Swann without seeing Gilberte was a cruel punishment, but I felt that it correspondingly enhanced the idea that Gilberte had of me.

Besides, if I always took care, before going to see Mme. Swann, that there should be no risk of her daughter's appearing, that arose, it is true, from my determination to break with her, but no less perhaps from that hope of reconciliation which overlay my intention to renounce her (very few of such intentions are absolute, at least in a continuous form, in this human soul of ours, one of whose laws, confirmed by the unlooked-for wealth of illustration that memory supplies, is intermittence), and hid from me all that in it was unbearably cruel. As for that hope, I saw clearly how far it was chimerical. I was like a pauper who moistens his dry crust with fewer tears if he assures himself that, at any moment, a total stranger is perhaps going to leave him the whole of his fortune. We are all of us obliged, if we are to make reality endurable, to nurse a few little follies in ourselves. Now my hope remained more intact—while at the same time our separation became more effectual—if I refrained from meeting Gilberte. If I had found myself face to face with her in her mother's drawing-room, we might perhaps have uttered irrevocable words which would have rendered our breach final, killed my hope and, on the other hand, by creating a fresh anxiety, reawakened my love and made resignation harder.

Ever so long ago, before I had even thought of breaking with her daughter, Mme. Swann had said to me: "It is all very well your coming to see Gilberte; I should like you to come sometimes for my sake, not to my 'kettledrums,' which would bore you because there is such a crowd, but on the other days, when you will always find me at home if you come fairly late." So that I might be thought, when I came to see her, to be yielding only after a long resistance to a desire which she had expressed in the past. And very late in the afternoon, when it was quite dark, almost at the hour at which my parents would be sitting down to dinner, I would set out to pay Mme. Swann a visit, in the course of which I knew that I should not see Gilberte, and yet should be thinking only of her. In that quarter, then looked upon as remote, of a Paris darker than Paris is to-day, where even in the centre there was no electric light in the public thoroughfares and very little in private houses, the lamps of a drawing-room situated on the ground level, or but slightly raised above it, as were the rooms in which Mme. Swann generally received her visitors, were enough to lighten the street, and to make the passer-by raise his eyes, connecting with their glow, as with its apparent though hidden cause, the presence outside the door of a string of smart broughams. This passer-by was led to believe, not without a certain emotion, that a modification had been effected in this mysterious cause, when he saw one of the carriages begin to move; but it was merely a coachman who, afraid of his horses' catching cold, started them now and again on a brisk walk, all the more impressive because the rubber-tired wheels gave the sound of their hooves a background of silence from which it stood out more distinct and more explicit.

The 'winter-garden,' of which in those days the passer-by generally caught a glimpse, in whatever street he might be walking, if the drawing-room did not stand too high above the pavement, is to be seen to-day only in photogravures in the gift-books of P. J. Stahl, where, in contrast to the infrequent floral decorations of the Louis XVI drawing-rooms now in fashion—a single rose or a Japanese iris in a long-necked vase of crystal into which it would be impossible to squeeze a second—it seems, because of the profusion of indoor plants which people had then, and of the absolute want of style in their arrangement, as though it must have responded in the ladies whose houses it adorned to some living and delicious passion for botany rather than to any cold concern for lifeless decoration. It suggested to one, only on a larger scale, in the houses of those days, those tiny, portable hothouses laid out on New Year's morning beneath the lighted lamp—for the children were always too impatient to wait for daylight—among all the other New Year's presents but the loveliest of them all, consoling them with its real plants which they could tend as they grew for the bareness of the winter soil; and even more than those little houses themselves, those winter-gardens were like the hothouse that the children could see there at the same time, portrayed in a delightful book, another of their presents, and one which, for all that it was given not to them but to Mlle. Lili, the heroine of the story, enchanted them to such a pitch that even now, when they are almost old men and women, they ask themselves whether, in those fortunate years, winter was not the loveliest of the seasons. And inside there, beyond the winter-garden, through the various kinds of arborescence which from the street made the lighted window appear like the glass front of one of those children's playthings, pictured or real, the passer-by, drawing himself up on tiptoe, would generally observe a man in a frock coat, a gardenia or a carnation in his buttonhole, standing before a seated lady, both vaguely outlined, like two intaglios cut in a topaz, in the depths of the drawing-room atmosphere clouted by the samovar—then a recent importation—with steam which may very possibly be escaping from it still to-day, but to which, if it does, we are grown so accustomed now that no one notices it. Mme. Swann attached great importance to her 'tea'; she thought that she shewed her originality and expressed her charm when she said to a man, "You will find me at home any day, fairly late; come to tea!" so that she allowed a sweet and delicate smile to accompany the words which she pronounced with a fleeting trace of English accent, and which her listener duly noted, bowing solemnly in acceptance, as though the invitation had been something important and uncommon which commanded deference and required attention. There was another reason, apart from those given already, for the flowers' having more than a merely ornamental part in Mme. Swann's drawing-room, and this reason pertained not to the period, but, in some degree, to the former life of Odette. A great courtesan, such as she had been, lives largely for her lovers, that is to say at home, which means that she comes in time to live for her home. The things that one sees in the house of a 'respectable' woman, things which may of course appear to her also to be of importance, are those which are in any event of the utmost importance to the courtesan. The culminating point of her day is not the moment in which she dresses herself for all the world to see, but that in which she undresses herself for a man. She must be as smart in her wrapper, in her nightgown, as in her outdoor attire. Other women display their jewels, but as for her, she lives in the intimacy of her pearls. This kind of existence imposes on her as an obligation and ends by giving her a fondness for luxury which is secret, that is to say which comes near to being disinterested. Mme. Swann extended this to include her flowers. There was always beside her chair an immense bowl of crystal filled to the brim with Parma violets or with long white daisy-petals scattered upon the water, which seemed to be testifying, in the eyes of the arriving guest, to some favourite and interrupted occupation, such as the cup of tea which Mme. Swann would, for her own amusement, have been drinking there by herself; an occupation more intimate still and more mysterious, so much so that one felt oneself impelled to apologise on seeing the flowers exposed there by her side, as one would have apologised for looking at the title of the still open book which would have revealed to one what had just been read by—and so, perhaps, what was still in the mind of Odette. And unlike the book the flowers were living things; it was annoying, when one entered the room to pay Mme. Swann a visit, to discover that she was not alone, or if one came home with her not to find the room empty, so prominent a place in it, enigmatic and intimately associated with hours in the life of their mistress of which one knew nothing, did those flowers assume which had not been made ready for Odette's visitors but, as it were, forgotten there by her, had held and would hold with her again private conversations which one was afraid of disturbing, the secret of which one tried in vain to read, fastening one's eyes on the moist purple, the still liquid water-colour of the Parma violets. By the end of October Odette would begin to come home with the utmost punctuality for tea, which was still known, at that time, as 'five-o'clock tea,' having once heard it said, and being fond of repeating that if Mme. Verdurin had been able to form a salon it was because people were always certain of finding her at home at the same hour. She imagined that she herself had one also, of the same kind, but freer, *senza rigore* as she used to say. She saw herself figuring thus as a sort of Lespinasse, and believed that she had founded a rival salon by taking from the du Deffant of the little group several of her most attractive men, notably Swann himself, who had followed her in her secession and into her retirement, according·to a version for which one can understand that she had succeeded in gaining credit among her more recent friends, ignorant of what had passed, though without convincing herself. But certain favourite parts are played by us so often before the public and rehearsed so carefully when we are alone that we find it easier to refer to their fictitious testimony than to that of a reality which we have almost entirely forgotten. On days on which Mme. Swann had not left the house, one found her in a wrapper of *crêpe-de-Chine,* white as the first snows of winter, or, it might be, in one of those long pleated garments of *mousseline-de-soie,* which seemed nothing more than a shower of white or rosy petals, and would be regarded to-day as hardly suitable for winter, though quite wrongly. For these light fabrics and soft colours gave to a woman—in the stifling warmth of the drawing-rooms of those days, with their heavily curtained doors, rooms of which the most effective thing that the society novelists of the time could find to say was that they were 'exquisitely cushioned'—the same air of coolness that they gave to the roses which were able to stay in the room there by her side, despite the winter, in the glowing flesh tints of their nudity, as though it were already spring. By reason of the muffling of all sound in the carpets, and of the remoteness of her cosy retreat, the lady of the house, not being apprised of your entry as she is to-day, would continue to read almost until you were standing before her chair, which enhanced still further that sense of the romantic, that charm of a sort of secret discovery, which we find to-day in the memory of those gowns, already out of fashion even then, which Mme. Swann was perhaps alone in not having discarded, and which give us the feeling that the woman who wore them must have been the heroine of a novel because most of us have scarcely set eyes on them outside the pages of certain of Henry Gréville's tales. Odette had, at this time, in her drawing-room, when winter began, chrysanthemums of enormous size and a variety of colours such as Swann, in the old days, certainly never saw in her drawing-room in the Rue La Pérouse. My admiration for them—when I went to pay Mme. Swann one of those melancholy visits during which, prompted by my sorrow, I discovered in her all the mystical poetry of her character as the mother of that Gilberte to whom she would say on the morrow: "Your friend came to see me yesterday,"—sprang, no doubt, from my sense that, rose-pale like the Louis XIV silk that covered her chairs, snow-white like her *crêpe-de-Chine* wrapper, or of a metallic red like her samovar, they superimposed upon the decoration of the room another, a supplementary scheme of decoration, as rich, as delicate in its colouring, but one which was alive and would last for a few days only. But I was touched to find that these chrysanthemums appeared less ephemeral than, one might almost say, lasting, when I compared them with the tones, as pink, as coppery, which the setting sun so gorgeously displays amid the mists of a November afternoon, and which, after seeing them, before I had entered the house, fade from the sky, I found again inside, prolonged, transposed on to the flaming palette of the flowers. Like the fires caught and fixed by a great colourist from the impermanence of the atmosphere and the sun, so that they should enter and adorn a human dwelling, they invited me, those chrysanthemums, to put away all my sorrows and to taste with a greedy rapture during that 'tea-time' the too fleeting joys of November, of which they set ablaze all around me the intimate and mystical glory. Alas, it was not in the conversations to which I must listen that I could hope to attain to that glory; they had but little in common with it. Even with Mme. Cottard, and although it was growing late, Mme. Swann would assume her most caressing manner to say: "Oh, no, it's not late, really; you mustn't look at the clock; that's not the right time; it's stopped; you can't possibly have anything else to do now, why be in such a hurry?" as she pressed a final tartlet upon the Professor's wife, who was gripping her card-case in readiness for flight.

"One simply can't tear oneself away from this house!" observed Mme. Bontemps to Mme. Swann, while Mme. Cottard, in her astonishment at hearing her own thought put into words, exclaimed: "Why, that's just what I always say myself, what I tell my own little judge, in the court of conscience!" winning the applause of the gentlemen from the Jockey Club, who had been profuse in their salutations, as though confounded at such an honour's being done them, when Mme. Swann had introduced them to this common and by no means attractive little woman, who kept herself, when confronted with Odette's brilliant friends, in reserve, if not on what she herself called 'the defensive,' for she always used stately language to describe the simplest happenings. "I should never have suspected it," was Mme. Swann's comment, "three Wednesdays running you've played me false." "That's quite true, Odette; it's simply ages, it's an eternity since I saw you last. You see, I plead guilty; but I must tell you," she went on with a vague suggestion of outraged modesty, for although a doctor's wife she would never have dared to speak without periphrasis of rheumatism or of a chill on the kidneys, "that I have had a lot of little troubles. As we all have, I dare say. And besides that I've had a crisis among my masculine domestics. I'm sure, I'm no more imbued with a sense of my own authority than most ladies; still I've been obliged, just to make an example you know, to give my Vatel notice; I believe he was looking out anyhow for a more remunerative place. But his departure nearly brought about the resignation of my entire ministry. My own maid refused to stay in the house a moment longer; oh, we have had some Homeric scenes. However I held fast to the reins through thick and thin; the whole affair's been a perfect lesson, which won't be lost on me, I can tell you. I'm afraid I'm boring you with all these stories about servants, but you know as well as I do what a business it is when one is obliged to set about rearranging one's household.

"Aren't we to see anything of your delicious child?" she wound up. "No, my delicious child is dining with a friend," replied Mme. Swann, and then, turning to me: "I believe she's written to you, asking you to come and see her to-morrow. And your babies?" she went on to Mme. Cottard. I breathed a sigh of relief. These words by which Mme. Swann proved to me that I could see Gilberte whenever I chose gave me precisely the comfort which I had come to seek, and which at that time made my visits to Mme. Swann so necessary. "No, I'm afraid not; I shall write to her, anyhow, this evening. Gilberte and I never seem to see one another now," I added, pretending to attribute our separation to some mysterious agency, which gave me a further illusion of being in love, supported as well by the affectionate way in which I spoke of Gilberte and she of me. "You know, she's simply devoted to you," said Mme. Swann. "Really, you won't come to-morrow?" Suddenly my heart rose on wings; the thought had just struck me—"After all, why shouldn't I, since it's her own mother who suggests it?" But with the thought I fell back into my old depression.

I was afraid now lest, when she saw me again, Gilberte might think that my indifference of late had been feigned, and it seemed wiser to prolong our separation. During these asides Mme. Bontemps had been complaining of the insufferable dulness of politicians' wives, for she pretended to find everyone too deadly or too stupid for words, and to deplore her husband's official position. "Do you mean to say you can shake hands with fifty doctors' wives, like that, one after the other?" she exclaimed to Mme. Cottard, who, unlike her, was full of the kindest feelings for everybody and of determination to do her duty in every respect. "Ah! you're a law-abiding woman! You see, in my case, at the Ministry, don't you know, I simply have to keep it up, of course. It's too much for me, I can tell you; you know what those officials' wives are like, it's all I can do not to put my tongue out at them. And my niece Albertine is just like me. You really wouldn't believe the impudence that girl has. Last week, on my 'day,' I had the wife of the Under Secretary of State for Finance, who told us that she knew nothing at all about cooking. 'But surely, ma'am,' my niece chipped in with her most winning smile, 'you ought to know everything about it, after all the dishes your father had to wash.' " "Oh, I do love that story; I think it's simply exquisite!" cried Mme. Swann. "But certainly on the Doctor's consultation days you should make a point of being 'at home,' among your flowers and books and all your pretty things," she urged Mme. Cottard. "Straight out like that! Bang! Right in the face; bang! She made no bones about it, I can tell you! And she'd never said a word to me about it, the little wretch; she's as cunning as a monkey. You are lucky to be able to control yourself; I do envy people who can hide what is in their minds." "But I've no need to do that, Mme. Bontemps, I'm not so hard to please," Mme. Cottard gently expostulated. "For one thing, I'm not in such a privileged position," she went on, slightly raising her voice as was her custom, as though she were underlining the point of her remark, whenever she slipped into the conversation any of those delicate courtesies, those skilful flatteries which won her the admiration and assisted the career of her husband. "And besides I'm only too glad to do anything that can be of use to the Professor."

"But, my dear, it isn't what one's glad to do; it's what one is able to do! I expect you're not nervous. Do you know, whenever I see the War Minister's wife making faces, I start copying her at once. It's a dreadful thing to have a temperament like mine."

"To be sure, yes," said Mme. Cottard, "I've heard people say that she had a twitch; my husband knows someone else who occupies a very high position, and it's only natural, when gentlemen get talking together . . ."

"And then, don't you know, it's just the same with the Chief of the Registry; he's a hunchback. Whenever he comes to see me, before he's been in the room five minutes my fingers are itching to stroke his hump. My husband says I'll cost him his place. What if I do! A fig for the Ministry! Yes, a fig for the Ministry! I should like to have that printed as a motto on my notepaper. I can see I am shocking you; you're so frightfully proper, but I must say there's nothing amuses me like a little devilry now and then. Life would be dreadfully monotonous without it."

And she went on talking about the Ministry all the time, as though it had been Mount Olympus. To change the conversation, Mme. Swann turned to Mme. Cottard: "But you're looking very smart to-day. Redfern *fecit*?"

"No, you know, I always swear by Rauthnitz. Besides, it's only an old thing I've had done up." "Not really! It's charming!"

"Guess how much. . . . No, change the first figure!"

"You don't say so! Why, that's nothing; it's given away! Three times that at least, I should have said." "You see how history comes to be written," apostrophised the doctor's wife. And pointing to a neck-ribbon which had been a present from Mme. Swann: "Look, Odette! Do you recognise this?"

Through the gap between a pair of curtains a head peeped with ceremonious deference, making a playful pretence of being afraid of disturbing the party; it was Swann. "Odette, the Prince d'Agrigente is with me in the study. He wants to know if he may pay his respects to you. What am I to tell him?" "Why, that I shall be delighted," Odette would reply, secretly flattered, but without losing anything of the composure which came to her all the more easily since she had always, even in her 'fast' days, been accustomed to entertain men of fashion. Swann disappeared to deliver the message, and would presently return with the Prince, unless in the meantime Mme. Verdurin had arrived. When he married Odette Swann had insisted on her ceasing to frequent the little clan. (He had several good reasons for this stipulation, though, had he had none, he would have made it just the same in obedience to a law of ingratitude which admits no exception, and proves that every 'go-between' is either lacking in foresight or else singularly disinterested.) He had conceded only that Odette and Mme. Verdurin might exchange visits once a year, and even this seemed excessive to some of the 'faithful,' indignant at the insult offered to the 'Mistress' who for so many years had treated Odette and even Swann himself as the spoiled children of her house. For if it contained false brethren who 'failed' upon certain evenings in order that they might secretly accept an invitation from Odette, ready, in the event of discovery, with the excuse that they were anxious to meet Bergotte (although the Mistress assured them that he never went to the Swanns', and even if he did, had no vestige of talent, really—in spite of which she was making the most strenuous efforts, to quote one of her favourite expressions, to 'attract' him), the little group had its 'die-hards' also. And these, though ignorant of those conventional refinements which often dissuade people from the extreme attitude one would have liked to see them adopt in order to annoy some one else, would have wished Mme. Verdurin, but had never managed to prevail upon her, to sever all connection with Odette, and thus deprive Odette of the satisfaction of saying, with a mocking laugh: "We go to the Mistress's very seldom now, since the Schism. It was all very well while my husband was still a bachelor, but when one is married, you know, it isn't always so easy. . . . If you must know, M. Swann can't abide old Ma Verdurin, and he wouldn't much like the idea of my going there regularly, as I used to. And I, as a dutiful spouse, don't you see . . . ?"

Swann would accompany his wife to their annual evening there but would
take care not to be in the room when Mme. Verdurin came to call. And
so, if the 'Mistress' was in the drawing-room, the Prince d'Agrigente would
enter it alone. Alone, too, he was presented to her by Odette, who preferred
that Mme. Verdurin should be left in ignorance of the names of her humbler guests, and so might, seeing more than one strange face in the room,
be led to believe that she was mixing with the cream of the aristocracy,
a device which proved so far successful that Mme. Verdurin said to her
husband, that evening, with profound contempt: "Charming people, her
friends! I met all the fine flower of the Reaction!" Odette was living, with
respect to Mme. Verdurin, under a converse illusion. Not that the latter's
salon had ever begun, at that time, to develop into what we shall one day
see it to have become. Mme. Verdurin had not yet reached the period of
incubation in which one dispenses with one's big parties, where the few
brilliant specimens recently acquired would be lost in too numerous a
crowd, and prefers to wait until the generative force of the ten righteous
whom one has succeeded in attracting shall have multiplied those ten
seventyfold. As Odette was not to be long now in doing, Mme. Verdurin
did indeed entertain the idea of 'Society' as her final objective, but her
zone of attack was as yet so restricted, and moreover so remote from that
in which Odette had some chance of arriving at an identical goal, of breaking the line of defence, that the latter remained absolutely ignorant of the
strategic plans which the 'Mistress' was elaborating. And it was with the
most perfect sincerity that Odette, when anyone spoke to her of Mme.
Verdurin as a snob, would answer, laughing, "Oh, no, quite the opposite!
For one thing, she never gets a chance of being a snob; she doesn't know
anyone. And then, to do her justice, I must say that she seems quite pleased
not to know anyone. No, what she likes are her Wednesdays, and people
who talk well." And in her heart of hearts she envied Mme. Verdurin
(for all that she did not despair of having herself, in so eminent a school,
succeeded in acquiring them) those arts to which the 'Mistress' attached
such paramount importance, albeit they did but discriminate between
shades of the Non-existent, sculpture the void, and were, properly speaking, the Arts of Nonentity: to wit those, in the lady of a house, of knowing
how to 'bring people together,' how to 'group,' to 'draw out,' to 'keep in
the background,' to act as a 'connecting link.'

In any case, Mme. Swann's friends were impressed when they saw in
her house a lady of whom they were accustomed to think only as in her
own, in an inseparable setting of her guests, amid the whole of her little
group which they were astonished to behold thus suggested, summarised,
assembled, packed into a single armchair in the bodily form of the 'Mistress,' the hostess turned visitor, muffled in her cloak with its grebe trim-
ming, as shaggy as the white skins that carpeted that drawing-room
embowered in which Mme. Verdurin was a drawing-room in herself. The
more timid among the women thought it prudent to retire, and using the
plural, as people do when they mean to hint to the rest of the room that
it is wiser not to tire a convalescent who is out of bed for the first time:
"Odette," they murmured, "we are going to leave you." They envied Mme.

Cottard, whom the 'Mistress' called by her Christian name. "Can I drop you anywhere?" Mme. Verdurin asked her, unable to bear the thought that one of the faithful was going to remain behind instead of following her from the room. "Oh, but this lady has been so very kind as to say, she'll take me," replied Mme. Cottard, not wishing to appear to be forgetting, when approached by a more illustrious personage, that she had accepted the offer which Mme. Bontemps had made of driving her home behind her cockaded coachman. "I must say that I am always specially grateful to the friends who are so kind as to take me with them in their vehicles. It is a regular godsend to me, who have no Automedon." "Especially," broke in the 'Mistress,' who felt that she must say something, since she knew Mme. Bontemps slightly and had just invited her to her Wednesdays, "as at Mme. de Crécy's house you're not very near home. Oh, good gracious, I shall never get into the way of saying Mme. Swann!" It was a recognised pleasantry in the little clan, among those who were not overendowed with wit, to pretend that they could never grow used to saying 'Mme. Swann.' "I have been so accustomed to saying Mme. de Crécy that I nearly went wrong again!" Only Mme. Verdurin, when she spoke to Odette, was not content with the nearly, but went wrong on purpose. "Don't you feel afraid, Odette, living out in the wilds like this? I'm sure I shouldn't feel at all comfortable, coming home after dark. Besides, it's so damp. It can't be at all good for your husband's eczema. You haven't rats in the house, I hope!" "Oh, dear no. What a horrid idea!" "That's a good thing; I was told you had. I'm glad to know it's not true, because I have a perfect horror of the creatures, and I should never have come to see you again. Good-bye, my dear child, we shall meet again soon; you know what a pleasure it is to me to see you. You don't know how to put your chrysanthemums in water," she went on, as she prepared to leave the room, Mme. Swann having risen to escort her. "They are Japanese flowers; you must arrange them the same way as the Japanese." "I do not agree with Mme. Verdurin, although she is the Law and the Prophets to me in all things! There's no one like you, Odette, for finding such lovely chrysanthemums, or chrysanthema rather, for it seems that's what we ought to call them now," declared Mme. Cottard as soon as the 'Mistress' had shut the door behind her. "Dear Mme. Verdurin is not always very kind about other people's flowers," said Odette sweetly. "Whom do you go to, Odette," asked Mme. Cottard, to forestall any further criticism of the 'Mistress.' "Lemaître? I must confess, the other day in Lemaître's window I saw a huge, great pink bush which made me do something quite mad." But modesty forbade her to give any more precise details as to the price of the bush, and she said merely that the Professor, "and you know, he's not at all a quick-tempered man," had 'waved his sword in the air' and told her that she "didn't know what money meant." "No, no, I've no regular florist except Debac." "Nor have I," said Mme. Cottard, "but I confess that I am un-faithful to him now and then with Lachaume." "Oh, you forsake him for Lachaume, do you; I must tell Debac that," retorted Odette, always anxious to shew her wit, and to lead the conversation in her own house, where she felt more at her ease than in the little clan. "Besides, Lachaume is really becoming too dear; his prices are quite excessive, don't you know; I find his prices impossible!" she added, laughing.

Meanwhile Mme. Bontemps, who had been heard a hundred times to declare that nothing would induce her to go to the Verdurins', delighted at being asked to the famous Wednesdays, was planning in her own mind how she could manage to attend as many of them as possible. She was not aware that Mme. Verdurin liked people not to miss a single one; also she was one of those people whose company is but little sought, who, when a hostess invites them to a series of parties, do not accept and go to them without more ado, like those who know that it is always a pleasure to see them, whenever they have a moment to spare and feel inclined to go out; people of her type deny themselves it may be the first evening and the third, imagining that their absence will be noticed, and save themselves up for the second and fourth, unless it should happen that, having heard from a trustworthy source that the third is to be a particularly brilliant party, they reverse the original order, assuring their hostess that "most unfortunately, we had another engagement last week." So Mme. Bontemps was calculating how many Wednesdays there could still be left before Easter, and by what means she might manage to secure one extra, and yet not appear to be thrusting herself upon her hostess. She relied upon Mme. Cottard, whom she would have with her in the carriage going home, to give her a few hints. "Oh, Mme. Bontemps, I see you getting up to go; it is very bad of you to give the signal for flight like that! You owe me some compensation for not turning up last Thursday. . . . Come, sit down again, just for a minute. You can't possibly be going anywhere else before dinner. Really, you won't let yourself be tempted?" went on Mme. Swann, and, as she held out a plate of cakes, "You know, they're not at all bad, these little horrors. They don't look nice, but just taste one, I know you'll like it." "On the contrary, they look quite delicious," broke in Mme. Cottard. "In your house, Odette, one is never short of victuals. I have no need to ask to see the trade-mark; I know you get everything from Rebattet. I must say that I am more eclectic. For sweet biscuits and everything of that sort I repair, as often as not, to Bourbonneux. But I agree that they simply don't know what an ice means. Rebattet for everything iced, and syrups and sorbets; they're past masters. As my husband would say, they're the *ne plus ultra*." "Oh, but we just make these in the house. You won't, really?" "I shan't be able to eat a scrap of dinner," pleaded Mme. Bontemps, "but I will just sit down again for a moment; you know, I adore talking to a clever woman like you." "You will think me highly indiscreet, Odette, but I should so like to know what you thought of the hat Mme. Trombert had on. I know, of course, that big hats are the fashion just now. All the same, wasn't it just the least little bit exaggerated? And compared to the hat she came to see me in the other day, the one she had on just now was microscopic!" "Oh no, I am not at all clever," said Odette, thinking that this sounded well. "I am a perfect simpleton, I believe everything people say, and worry myself to death over the least thing." And she insinuated that she had, just at first, suffered terribly from the thought of having married a man like Swann, who had a separate life of his own and was unfaithful to her. Meanwhile the Prince d'Agrigente, having caught the words "I am not at all clever," thought it incumbent on him to protest; unfortunately he had not the knack of repartee. "Tut, tut, tut, tut!" cried Mme. Bontemps, "Not clever; you!" "That's just what I was saying to myself—'What do I hear?'," the Prince clutched at this straw, "My ears must have played me false!" "No, I assure you," went on Odette, "I am really just an ordinary woman, very easily shocked, full of prejudices, living in my own little groove and dreadfully ignorant." And then, in case he had any news of the Baron de Charlus, "Have you seen our dear Baronet?" she asked him. "You, ignorant!" cried Mme. Bontemps. "Then I wonder what you'd say of the official world, all those wives of Excellencies who can talk of nothing but their frocks. . . . Listen to this, my friend; not more than a week ago I happened to mention *Lohengrin* to the Education Minister's wife. She stared at me, and said *'Lohengrin?* Oh, yes, the new review at the Folies-Bergères. I hear it's a perfect scream!' What do you say to that, eh? You can't help yourself; when people say things like that it makes your blood boil. I could have struck her. Because I have a bit of a temper of my own. What do you say, sir;" she turned to me, "was I not right?" "Listen," said Mme. Cottard, "people can't help answering a little off the mark when they're asked a thing like that point blank, without any warning. I know something about it, because Mme. Verdurin also has a habit of putting a pistol to your head." "Speaking of Mme. Verdurin," Mme. Bontemps asked Mme. Cottard, "do you know who will be there on Wednesday? Oh, I've just remembered that we've accepted an invitation for next Wednesday. You wouldn't care to dine with us on Wednesday week? We could go on together to Mme. Verdurin's. I should never dare to go there by myself; I don't know why it is, that great lady always terrifies me." "I'll tell you what it is," replied Mme. Cottard, "what frightens you about Mme. Verdurin is her organ. But you see everyone can't have such a charming organ as Mme. Swann. Once you've found your tongue, as the 'Mistress' says, the ice will soon be broken. For she's a very easy person, really, to get on with. But I can quite understand what you feel; it's never pleasant to find oneself for the first time in a strange country." "Won't you dine with us, too?" said Mme. Bontemps to Mme. Swann. "After dinner we could all go to the Verdurins' together, 'do a Verdurin'; and even if it means that the 'Mistress' will stare me out of countenance and never ask me to the house again, once we are there we'll just sit by ourselves and have a quiet talk, I'm sure that's what I should like best." But this assertion can hardly have been quite truthful, for Mme. Bontemps went on to ask: "Who do you think will be there on Wednesday week? What will they be doing? There won't be too big a crowd, I hope!" "I certainly shan't be there," said Odette. "We shall just look in for a minute on the last Wednesday of all. If you don't mind waiting till then——" But Mme. Bontemps did not appear to be tempted by the proposal.

Granted that the intellectual distinction of a house and its smartness are generally in inverse rather than direct ratio, one must suppose, since Swann found Mme. Bontemps attractive, that any forfeiture of position

once accepted has the consequence of making us less particular with regard to the people among whom we have resigned ourselves to finding
entertainment, less particular with regard to their intelligence as to everything else about them. And if this be true, men, like nations, must see their
culture and even their language disappear with their independence. One
of the effects of this indulgence is to aggravate the tendency which after
a certain age we have towards finding pleasure in speeches that are a
homage to our own turn of mind, to our weaknesses, an encouragement
to us to yield to them; that is the age at which a great artist prefers to the
company of original minds that of pupils who have nothing in common
with him save the letter of his doctrine, who listen to him and offer in-
cense; at which a man or woman of mark, who is living entirely for love,
will find that the most intelligent person in a gathering is one perhaps of
no distinction, but one who has shewn by some utterance that he can understand and approve what is meant by an existence devoted to gallantry,
and has thus pleasantly excited the voluptuous instincts of the lover or
mistress; it was the age, too, at which Swann, in so far as he had become
the husband of Odette, enjoyed hearing Mme. Bontemps say how silly it
was to have nobody in one's house but duchesses (concluding from that,
quite the contrary of what he would have decided in the old days at the
Verdurins', that she was a good creature, extremely sensible and not at
all a snob) and telling her stories which made her 'die laughing' because
she had not heard them before, although she always 'saw the point' at
once, liked flattering her for his own amusement. "Then the Doctor is
not mad about flowers, like you?" Mme. Swann asked Mme. Cottard.
"Oh, well, you know, my husband is a sage; he practises moderation in all
things. Yet, I must admit, he has a passion." Her eye aflame with malice,
joy, curiosity, "And what is that, pray?" inquired Mme. Bontemps. Quite
simply Mme. Cottard answered her, "Reading." "Oh, that's a very restful
passion in a husband!" cried Mme. Bontemps suppressing an impish laugh.
"When the Doctor gets a book in his hands, you know!" "Well, that
needn't alarm you much . . ." "But it does, for his eyesight. I must go
now and look after him, Odette, and I shall come back on the very first
opportunity and knock at your door. Talking of eyesight, have you heard
that the new house Mme. Verdurin has just bought is to be lighted by
electricity? I didn't get that from my own little secret service, you know,
but from quite a different source; it was the electrician himself, Mildé,
who told me. You see, I quote my authorities! Even the bedrooms, he
says, are to have electric lamps with shades which will filter the light. It
is evidently a charming luxury, for those who can afford it. But it seems
that our contemporaries must absolutely have the newest thing if it's the
only one of its kind in the world. Just fancy, the sister-in-law of a friend
of mine has had the telephone installed in her house! She can order things
from her tradesmen without having to go out of doors! I confess that I've
made the most bare-faced stratagems to get permission to go there one
day, just to speak into the instrument. It's very tempting, but more in a
friend's house than at home. I don't think I should like to have the telephone in my establishment. Once the first excitement is over, it must be

a perfect racket going on all the time. Now, Odette, I must be off; you're not to keep Mme. Bontemps any longer, she's looking after me. I must absolutely tear myself away; you're making me behave in a nice way, I shall be getting home after my husband!"

And for myself also it was time to return home, before I had tasted those wintry delights of which the chrysanthemums had seemed to me to be the brilliant envelope. These pleasures had not appeared, and yet Mme. Swann did not look as though she expected anything more. She allowed the servants to carry away the tea-things, as who should say "Time, please, gentlemen!" And at last she did say to me: "Really, must you go? Very well; good-bye!" I felt that I might have stayed there without encountering those unknown pleasures, and that my unhappiness was not the cause of my having to forego them. Were they to be found, then, situated not upon that beaten track of hours which leads one always to the moment of departure, but rather upon some cross-road unknown to me along which I ought to have digressed? At least, the object of my visit had been attained; Gilberte would know that I had come to see her parents when she was not at home, and that I had, as Mme. Cottard had incessantly assured me, "made a complete conquest, first shot, of Mme. Verdurin," whom, she added, she had never seen 'make so much' of anyone. ("You and she must have hooked atoms.") She would know that I had spoken of her as was fitting, with affection, but that I had not that incapacity for living without our seeing one another which I believed to be at the root of the boredom that she had shewn at our last meetings. I had told Mme. Swann that I should not be able to see Gilberte again. I had said this as though I had finally decided not to see her any more. And the letter which I was going to send Gilberte would be framed on those lines. Only to myself, to fortify my courage, I proposed no more than a supreme and concentrated effort, lasting a few days only. I said to myself: "This is the last time that I shall refuse to meet her; I shall accept the next invitation." To make our separation less difficult to realise, I did not picture it to myself as final. But I knew very well that it would be.

The first of January was exceptionally painful to me that winter. So, no doubt, is everything that marks a date and an anniversary when we are unhappy. But if our unhappiness is due to the loss of some dear friend, our suffering consists merely in an unusually vivid comparison of the present with the past. There was added to this, in my case, the unexpressed hope that Gilberte, having intended to leave me to take the first steps towards a reconciliation, and discovering that I had not taken them, had been waiting only for the excuse of New Year's Day to write to me, saying: "What is the matter? I am madly in love with you; come, and let us explain things properly; I cannot live without seeing you." As the last days of the old year went by, such a letter began to seem probable. It was, perhaps, nothing of the sort, but to make us believe that such a thing is probable the desire, the need that we have for it suffices. The soldier is convinced that a certain interval of time, capable of being indefinitely prolonged, will be allowed him before the bullet finds him, the thief before he is taken, men in general before they have to die. That is the amulet which preserves people—and sometimes peoples—not from danger but from the fear of danger, in reality from the belief in danger, which in certain cases allows them to brave it without their actually needing to be brave. It is confidence of this sort, and with as little foundation, that sustains the lover who is counting upon a reconciliation, upon a letter. For me to cease to expect a letter it would have sufficed that I should have ceased to wish for one. However unimportant one may know that one is in the eyes of her whom one still loves, one attributes to her a series of thoughts (though their sum-total be indifference) the intention to express those thoughts, a complication of her inner life in which one is the constant object possibly of her antipathy but certainly of her attention. But to imagine what was going on in Gilberte's mind I should have required simply the power to anticipate on that New Year's Day what I should feel on the first day of any of the years to come, when the attention or the silence or the affection or the coldness of Gilberte would pass almost unnoticed by me and I should not dream, should not even be able to dream of seeking a solution of problems which would have ceased to perplex me. When we are in love, our love is too big a thing for us to be able altogether to contain it within us. It radiates towards the beloved object, finds in her a surface which arrests it, forcing it to return to its starting-point, and it is this shock of the repercussion of our own affection which we call the other's regard for ourselves, and which pleases us more then than on its outward journey because we do not recognise it as having originated in ourselves. New Year's Day rang out all its hours without there coming to me that letter from Gilberte. And as I received a few others containing greetings tardy or retarded by the overburdening of the mails at that season, on the third and fourth of January I hoped still, but my hope grew hourly more faint. Upon the days that followed I gazed through a mist of tears. This undoubtedly meant that, having been less sincere than I thought in my renunciation of Gilberte, I had kept the hope of a letter from her for the New Year. And seeing that hope exhausted before I had had time to shelter myself behind another, I suffered as would an invalid who had emptied his phial of morphia without having another within his reach. But perhaps also in my case—and these two explanations are not mutually exclusive, for a single feeling is often made up of contrary elements—the hope that I entertained of ultimately receiving a letter had brought to my mind's eye once again the image of Gilberte, had reawakened the emotions which the expectation of finding myself in her presence, the sight of her, her way of treating me had aroused in me before. The immediate possibility of a reconciliation had suppressed in me that faculty the immense importance of which we are apt to overlook: the faculty of resignation. Neurasthenics find it impossible to believe the friends who assure them that they will gradually recover their peace of mind if they will stay in bed and receive no letters, read no newspapers. They imagine that such a course will only exasperate their twitching nerves. And similarly lovers, who look upon it from their enclosure in a contrary state of mind, who have not begun yet to make trial of it, are unable to believe in the healing power of renunciation.

In consequence of the violence of my palpitations, my doses of caffeine were reduced; the palpitations ceased. Whereupon I asked myself whether it was not to some extent the drug that had been responsible for the anguish that I had felt when I came near to quarrelling with Gilberte, an anguish which I had attributed, on every recurrence of it, to the distressing prospect of never seeing my friend again or of running the risk of seeing her only when she was a prey to the same ill-humour. But if this medicine had been at the root of the sufferings which my imagination must in that case have interpreted wrongly (not that there would be anything extraordinary in that, seeing that, among lovers, the most acute mental suffering assumes often the physical identity of the woman with whom they are living), it had been, in that sense, like the philtre which, long after they have drunk of it, continues to bind Tristan to Isolde. For the physical improvement which the reduction of my caffeine effected almost at once did not arrest the evolution of that grief which my absorption of the toxin had perhaps—if it had not created it—at any rate contrived to render more acute.

Only, as the middle of the month of January approached, once my hopes of a letter on New Year's Day had been disappointed, once the additional disturbance that had come with their disappointment had grown calm, it was my old sorrow, that of 'before the holidays,' which began again. What was perhaps the most cruel thing about it was that I myself was its architect, unconscious, wilful, merciless and patient. The one thing that mattered, my relations with Gilberte, it was I who was labouring to make them impossible by gradually creating out of this prolonged separation from my friend, not indeed her indifference, but what would come to the same thing in the end, my own. It was to a slow and painful suicide of that part of me which was Gilberte's lover that I was goading myself with untiring energy, with a clear sense not only of what I was presently doing but of what must result from it in the future; I knew not only that after a certain time I should cease to love Gilberte, but also that she herself would regret it and that the attempts which she would then make to see me would be as vain as those that she was making now, no longer because I loved her too well but because I should certainly be in love with some other woman whom I should continue to desire, to wait for, through hours of which I should not dare to divert any particle of a second to Gilberte who would be nothing to me then. And no doubt at that very moment in which (since I was determined not to see her again, unless after a formal request for an explanation or a full confession of love on her part, neither of which was in the least degree likely to come to me now) I had already lost Gilberte, and loved her more than ever, and could feel all that she was to me better than in the previous year when, spending all my afternoons in her company, or as many as I chose, I believed that no peril threatened our friendship,—no doubt at that moment the idea that I should one day entertain identical feelings for another was odious to me, for that idea carried me away beyond the range of Gilberte, my love and my sufferings. My love, my sufferings in which through my tears I attempted to discern precisely what Gilberte was, and was obliged to recognise that they did not pertain exclusively to her but would, sooner or later, be some other woman's portion. So that—or such, at least, was my way of thinking then—we are always detached from our fellow-creatures; when a man loves one of them he feels that his love is not labelled with their two names, but may be born again in the future, may have been born already in the past for another and not for her. And in the time when he is not in love, if he makes up his mind philosophically as to what it is that is inconsistent in love, he will find that the love of which he can speak unmoved he did not, at the moment of speaking, feel, and therefore did not know, knowledge in these matters being intermittent and not outlasting the actual presence of the sentiment. That future in which I should not love Gilberte, which my sufferings helped me to divine although my imagination was not yet able to form a clear picture of it, certainly there would still have been time to warn Gilberte that it was gradually taking shape, that its coming was, if not imminent, at least inevitable, if she herself, Gilberte, did not come to my rescue and destroy in the germ my nascent indifference. How often was I not on the point of writing, or of going to Gilberte to tell her: "Take care. My mind is made up. What I am doing now is my supreme effort. I am seeing you now for the last time. Very soon I shall have ceased to love you." But to what end? By what authority should I have reproached Gilberte for an indifference which, not that I considered myself guilty on that count, I too manifested towards everything that was not herself? The last time! To me, that appeared as something of immense significance, because I was in love with Gilberte. On her it would doubtless have made just as much impression as those letters in which our friends ask whether they may pay us a visit before they finally leave the country, an offer which, like those made by tiresome women who are in love with us, we decline because we have pleasures of our own in prospect. The time which we have at our disposal every day is elastic; the passions that we feel expand it, those that we inspire contract it; and habit fills up what remains.

Besides, what good would it have done if I had spoken to Gilberte; she would not have understood me. We imagine always when we speak that it is our own ears, our own mind that are listening. My words would have come to her only in a distorted form, as though they had had to pass through the moving curtain of a waterfall before they reached my friend, unrecognisable, giving a foolish sound, having no longer any kind of meaning. The truth which one puts into one's words does not make a direct path for itself, is not supported by irresistible evidence. A considerable time must elapse before a truth of the same order can take shape in the words themselves. Then the political opponent who, despite all argument, every proof that he has advanced to damn the votary of the rival doctrine as a traitor, will himself have come to share the hated conviction by which he who once sought in vain to disseminate it is no longer bound. Then the masterpiece of literature which for the admirers who read it aloud seemed to make self-evident the proofs of its excellence, while to those who listened it presented only a senseless or commonplace image, will by these too be proclaimed a masterpiece, but too late for the author to learn of their discovery. Similarly in love the barriers, do what one may, cannot be broken down from without by him whom they maddeningly exclude; it is when he is no longer concerned with them that suddenly, as the result of an effort directed from elsewhere, accomplished within the heart of her who did not love him, those barriers which he has charged without success will fall to no advantage. If I had come to Gilberte to tell her of my future indifference and the means of preventing it, she would have assumed from my action that my love for her, the need that I had of her, were even greater than I had supposed, and her distaste for the sight of me would thereby have been increased. And incidentally it is quite true that it was that love for her which helped me, by means of the incongruous states of mind which it successively produced in me, to foresee, more clearly than she herself could, the end of that love. And yet some such warning I might perhaps have addressed, by letter or with my own lips, to Gilberte, after a long enough interval, which would render her, it is true, less indispensable to me, but would also have proved to her that she was not so indispensable. Unfortunately certain persons—of good or evil intent—spoke of me to her in a fashion which must have led her to think that they were doing so at my request. Whenever I thus learned that Cottard, my own mother, even M. de Norpois had by a few ill-chosen words rendered useless all the sacrifice that I had just been making, wasted all the advantage of my reserve by giving me, wrongly, the appearance of having emerged from it, I was doubly angry. In the first place I could no longer reckon from any date but the present my laborious and fruitful abstention which these tiresome people had, unknown to me, interrupted and so brought to nothing. And not only that; I should have less pleasure in seeing Gilberte, who would think of me now no longer as containing myself in dignified resignation, but as plotting in the dark for an interview which she had scorned to grant me. I cursed all the idle chatter of people who so often, without any intention of hurting us or of doing us a service, for no reason, for talking's sake, often because we ourselves have not been able to refrain from talking in their presence, and because they are indiscreet (as we ourselves are), do us, at a crucial moment, so much harm. It is true that in the grim operation performed for the eradication of our love they are far from playing a part equal to that played by two persons who are in the habit, from excess of good nature in one and of malice in the other, of undoing everything at the moment when everything is on the point of being settled. But against these two persons we bear no such grudge as against the inopportune Cottards of this world, for the latter of them is the person whom we love and the former is ourself.

Meanwhile, since on almost every occasion of my going to see her Mme. Swann would invite me to come to tea another day, with her daughter, and tell me to reply directly to her, I was constantly writing to Gilberte, and in this correspondence I did not choose the expressions which might, I felt, have won her over, sought only to carve out the easiest channel for the torrent of my tears. For, like desire, regret seeks not to be analysed but to be satisfied. When one begins to love, one spends one's time, not in getting to know what one's love really is, but in making it possible to meet

next day. When one abandons love one seeks not to know one's grief but
to offer to her who is causing it that expression of it which seems to one
the most moving. One says the things which one feels the need of saying,
and which the other will not understand, one speaks for oneself alone. I
wrote: "I had thought that it would not be possible. Alas, I see now that
it is not so difficult." I said also: "I shall probably not see you again;"
I said it while I continued to avoid shewing a coldness which she might
think affected, and the words, as I wrote them, made me weep because I
felt that they expressed not what I should have liked to believe but what
was probably going to happen. For at the next request for a meeting which
she would convey to me I should have again, as I had now, the courage
not to yield, and, what with one refusal and another, I should gradually
come to the moment when, by virtue of not having seen her again, I should
not wish to see her. I wept, but I found courage enough to sacrifice, I
tasted the sweets of sacrificing the happiness of being with her to the
probability of seeming attractive to her one day, a day when, alas, my
seeming attractive to her would be immaterial to me. Even the supposition, albeit so far from likely, that at this moment, as she had pretended
during the last visit that I had paid her, she loved me, that what I took
for the boredom which one feels in the company of a person of whom one
has grown tired had been due only to a jealous susceptibility, to a feint of
indifference analogous to my own, only rendered my decision less painful.
It seemed to me that in years to come, when we had forgotten one another,
when I should be able to look back and tell her that this letter which I
was now in course of writing had not been for one moment sincere, she
would answer, "What, you really did love me, did you? If you had only
known how I waited for that letter, how I hoped that you were coming to
see me, how I cried when I read it." The thought, while I was writing it,
immediately on my return from her mother's house, that I was perhaps
helping to bring about that very misunderstanding, that thought, by the
sadness in which it plunged me, by the pleasure of imagining that I was
loved by Gilberte, gave me the impulse to continue my letter.

If, at the moment of leaving Mme. Swann, when her tea-party ended,
I was thinking of what I was going to write to her daughter, Mme. Cottard, as she departed, had been filled with thoughts of a wholly different
order. On her little 'tour of inspection' she had not failed to congratulate
Mme. Swann on the new 'pieces,' the recent 'acquisitions' which caught
the eye in her drawing-room. She could see among them some, though only
a very few, of the things that Odette had had in the old days in the Rue
La Pérouse, for instance her animals carved in precious stones, her fetishes.

For since Mme. Swann had picked up from a friend whose opinion she
valued the word 'dowdy'—which had opened to her a new horizon because
it denoted precisely those things which a few years earlier she had considered 'smart'—all those things had, one after another, followed into
retirement the gilded trellis that had served as background to her chrysanthemums, innumerable boxes of sweets from Giroux's, and the coroneted
note-paper (not to mention the coins of gilt pasteboard littered about
on the mantelpieces, which, even before she had come to know Swann, a

man of taste had advised her to sacrifice). Moreover in the artistic disorder, the studio-like confusion of the rooms, whose walls were still painted
in sombre colours which made them as different as possible from the white-
enamelled drawing-rooms in which, a little later, you were to find Mme.
Swann installed, the Far East recoiled more and more before the invading
forces of the eighteenth century; and the cushions which, to make me
'comfortable,' Mme. Swann heaped up and buffeted into position behind
my back were sprinkled with Louis XV garlands and not, as of old, with
Chinese dragons. In the room in which she was usually to be found, and
of which she would say, "Yes, I like this room; I use it a great deal. I
couldn't live with a lot of horrid vulgar things swearing at me all the time;
this is where I do my work——" though she never stated precisely at
what she was working. Was it a picture? A book, perhaps, for the hobby
of writing was beginning to become common among women who liked to
'do something,' not to be quite useless. She was surrounded by Dresden
pieces (having a fancy for that sort of porcelain, which she would name
with an English accent, saying in any connexion: "How pretty that is;
it reminds me of Dresden flowers,"), and dreaded for them even more
than in the old days for her grotesque figures and her flower-pots the ignorant handling of her servants who must expiate, every now and then, the
anxiety that they had caused her by submitting to outbursts of rage at
which Swann, the most courteous and considerate of masters, looked on
without being shocked. Not that the clear perception of certain weaknesses in those whom we love in any way diminishes our affection for them;
rather that affection makes us find those weaknesses charming. Rarely
nowadays was it in one of those Japanese wrappers that Odette received
her familiars, but rather in the bright and billowing silk of a Watteau
gown whose flowering foam she made as though to caress where it covered
her bosom, and in which she immersed herself, looked solemn, splashed
and sported, with such an air of comfort, of a cool skin and long-drawn
breath, that she seemed to look on these garments not as something decorative, a mere setting for herself, but as necessary, in the same way as her
'tub' or her daily 'outing,' to satisfy the requirements of her style of beauty
and the niceties of hygiene. She used often to say that she would go without bread rather than give up 'art' and 'having nice things about her,'
and that the burning of the 'Gioconda' would distress her infinitely more
than the destruction, by the same element, of 'millions' of the people she
knew. Theories which seemed paradoxical to her friends, but made her
pass among them as a superior woman, and qualified her to receive a visit
once a week from the Belgian Minister, so that in the little world whose
sun she was everyone would have been greatly astonished to learn that
elsewhere—at the Verdurins', for instance—she was reckoned a fool. It
was this vivacity of expression that made Mme. Swann prefer men's society
to women's. But when she criticised the latter it was always from the
courtesan's standpoint, singling out the blemishes that might lower them
in the esteem of men, a lumpy figure, a bad complexion, inability to spell,
hairy legs, foul breath, pencilled eyebrows. But towards a woman who
had shewn her kindness or indulgence in the past she was more lenient,

especially if this woman were now in trouble. She would defend her warmly, saying: "People are not fair to her. I assure you, she's quite a nice woman really."

It was not only the furniture of Odette's drawing-room, it was Odette herself that Mme. Cottard and all those who had frequented the society of Mme. de Crécy would have found it difficult, if they had not seen her for some little time, to recognise. She seemed to be so much younger. No doubt this was partly because she had grown stouter, was in better condition, seemed at once calmer, more cool, more restful, and also because the new way in which she braided her hair gave more breadth to a face which was animated by an application of pink powder, and into which her eyes and profile, formerly too prominent, seemed now to have been reabsorbed. But another reason for this change lay in the fact that, having reached the turning-point of life, Odette had at length discovered, or invented, a physiognomy of her own, an unalterable 'character,' a 'style of beauty,' and on her incoherent features—which for so long, exposed to every hazard, every weakness of the flesh, borrowing for a moment, at the slightest fatigue, from the years to come, a sort of flickering shadow of anility, had furnished her, well or ill, according to how she was feeling, how she was looking, with a countenance dishevelled, inconstant, formless and attractive—had now set this fixed type, as it were an immortal youthfulness.

Swann had in his room, instead of the handsome photographs that were now taken of his wife, in all of which the same cryptic, victorious expression enabled one to recognise, in whatever dress and hat, her triumphant face and figure, a little old daguerreotype of her, quite plain, taken long before the appearance of this new type, so that the youth and beauty of Odette, which she had not yet discovered when it was taken, appeared to be missing from it. But it is probable that Swann, having remained constant, or having reverted to a different conception of her, enjoyed in the slender young woman with pensive eyes and tired features, caught in a pose between rest and motion, a more Botticellian charm. For he still liked to recognise in his wife one of Botticelli's figures. Odette, who on the other hand sought not to bring out but to make up for, to cover and conceal the points in herself that did not please her, what might perhaps to an artist express her 'character' but in her woman's eyes were merely blemishes, would not have that painter mentioned in her presence. Swann had a wonderful scarf of oriental silk, blue and pink, which he had bought because it was exactly that worn by Our Lady in the *Magnificat*. But Mme. Swann refused to wear it. Once only she allowed her husband to order her a dress covered all over with daisies, cornflowers, forget-me-nots and campanulas, like that of the Primavera. And sometimes in the evening, when she was tired, he would quietly draw my attention to the way in which she was giving, quite unconsciously, to her pensive hands the uncontrolled, almost distraught movement of the Virgin who dips her pen into the inkpot that the angel holds out to her, before writing upon the sacred page on which is already traced the word *'Magnificat.'* But he added, "Whatever you do, don't say anything about it to her; if she knew she was doing it, she would change her pose at once."

Save at these moments of involuntary relaxation, in which Swann es-
sayed to recapture the melancholy cadence of Botticelli, Odette seemed
now to be cut out in a single figure, wholly confined within a line which,
following the contours of the woman, had abandoned the winding paths,
the capricious re-entrants and salients, the radial points, the elaborate
dispersions of the fashions of former days, but also, where it was her
anatomy that went wrong by making unnecessary digressions within or
without the ideal circumference traced for it, was able to rectify, by a
bold stroke, the errors of nature, to make up, along a whole section of its
course, for the failure as well of the human as of the textile element. The
pads, the preposterous 'bustle' had disappeared, as well as those tailed
corsets which, projecting under the skirt and stiffened by rods of whale-
bone, had so long amplified Odette with an artificial stomach and had
given her the appearance of being composed of several incongruous pieces
which there was no individuality to bind together. The vertical fall of
fringes, the curve of trimmings had made way for the inflexion of a body
which made silk palpitate as a siren stirs the waves, gave to cambric a
human expression now that it had been liberated, like a creature that had
taken shape and drawn breath, from the long chaos and nebulous envelop-
ment of fashions at length dethroned. But Mme. Swann had chosen, had
contrived to preserve some vestiges of certain of these, in the very thick
of the more recent fashions that had supplanted them. When in the evening, finding myself unable to work and feeling certain that Gilberte had
gone to the theatre with friends, I paid a surprise visit to her parents, I
used often to find Mme. Swann in an elegant dishabille the skirt of which,
of one of those rich dark colours, blood-red or orange, which seemed always
as though they meant something very special, because they were no
longer the fashion, was crossed diagonally, though not concealed, by a
broad band of black lace which recalled the flounces of an earlier day.
When on a still chilly afternoon in Spring she had taken me (before my
rupture with her daughter) to the Jardin d'Acclimatation, under her coat,
which she opened or buttoned up according as the exercise made her feel
warm, the dog-toothed border of her blouse suggested a glimpse of the
lapel of some non-existent waistcoat such as she had been accustomed to
wear, some years earlier, when she had liked their edges to have the same
slight indentations; and her scarf—of that same 'Scotch tartan' to which
she had remained faithful, but whose tones she had so far softened, red
becoming pink and blue lilac, that one might almost have taken it for one
of those pigeon's-breast taffetas which were the latest novelty—was knot-
ted in such a way under her chin, without one's being able to make out
where it was fastened, that one could not help being reminded of those
bonnet-strings which were now no longer worn. She need only 'hold out'
like this for a little longer and young men attempting to understand her
theory of dress would say: "Mme. Swann is quite a period in herself, isn't
she?" As in a fine literary style which overlays with its different forms and
so strengthens a tradition which lies concealed among them, so in Mme.
Swann's attire those half-hinted memories of waistcoats or of ringlets,
sometimes a tendency, at once repressed, towards the 'all aboard,' or even

a distant and vague allusion to the 'chase me' kept alive beneath the concrete form the unfinished likeness of other, older forms which you would
not have succeeded, now, in making a tailor or a dressmaker reproduce,
but about which your thoughts incessantly hovered, and enwrapped Mme.
Swann in a cloak of nobility—perhaps because the sheer uselessness of
these fripperies made them seem meant to serve some more than utilitarian
purpose, perhaps because of the traces they preserved of vanished years,
or else because there was a sort of personality permeating this lady's
wardrobe, which gave to the most dissimilar of her costumes a distinct
family likeness. One felt that she did not dress simply for the comfort or
the adornment of her body; she was surrounded by her garments as by
the delicate and spiritualised machinery of a whole form of civilisation.

When Gilberte, who, as a rule, gave her tea-parties on the days when
her mother was 'at home,' had for some reason to go out, and I was therefore free to attend Mme. Swann's 'kettledrum,' I would find her dressed
in one of her lovely gowns, some of which were of taffeta, others of gros-
grain, or of velvet, or of *crêpe-de-Chine,* or satin or silk, gowns which, not
being loose like those that she generally wore in the house but buttoned
up tight as though she were just going out in them, gave to her stay-at-
home laziness on those afternoons something alert and energetic. And no
doubt the daring simplicity of their cut was singularly appropriate to her
figure and to her movements, which her sleeves appeared to be symbolising
in colours that varied from day to day: one would have said that there was
a sudden determination in the blue velvet, an easy-going good humour
in the white taffeta, and that a sort of supreme discretion full of dignity in
her way of holding out her arm had, in order to become visible, put on the
appearance, dazzling with the smile of one who had made great sacrifices,
of the black *crêpe-de-Chine.* But at the same time these animated gowns
took from the complication of their trimmings, none of which had any
practical value or served any conceivable purpose, something detached,
pensive, secret, in harmony with the melancholy which Mme. Swann
never failed to shew, at least in the shadows under her eyes and the drooping arches of her hands. Beneath the profusion of sapphire charms,
enamelled four-leaf clovers, silver medals, gold medallions, turquoise amu-
lets, ruby chains and topaz chestnuts there would be, on the dress itself,
some design carried out in colour which pursued across the surface of
an inserted panel a preconceived existence of its own, some row of little
satin buttons, which buttoned nothing and could not be unbuttoned, a
strip of braid that sought to please the eye with the minuteness, the discretion of a delicate reminder; and these, as well as the trinkets, had the
effect—for otherwise there would have been no possible justification of
their presence—of disclosing a secret intention, being a pledge of affection, keeping a secret, ministering to a superstition, commemorating a
recovery from sickness, a granted wish, a love affair or a 'philippine.' And
now and then in the blue velvet of the bodice a hint of 'slashes,' in the Henri
II style, in the gown of black satin a slight swelling which, if it was in
the sleeves, just below the shoulders, made one think of the 'leg of mutton'
sleeves of 1830, or if, on the other hand, it was beneath the skirt, with its

Louis XV paniers, gave the dress a just perceptible air of being 'fancy dress' and at all events, by insinuating beneath the life of the present day a vague reminiscence of the past, blended with the person of Mme. Swann the charm of certain heroines of history or romance. And if I were to draw her attention to this: "I don't play golf," she would answer, "like so many of my friends. So I should have no excuse for going about, as they do, in sweaters."

In the confusion of her drawing-room, on her way from shewing out one visitor, or with a plateful of cakes to 'tempt' another, Mme. Swann as she passed by me would take me aside for a moment: "I have special in-structions from Gilberte that you are to come to luncheon the day after to-morrow. As I wasn't sure of seeing you here, I was going to write to you if you hadn't come." I continued to resist. And this resistance was costing me steadily less and less, because, however much one may love the poison that is destroying one, when one has compulsorily to do without it, and has had to do without it for some time past, one cannot help attaching a certain value to the peace of mind which one had ceased to know, to the absence of emotion and suffering. If one is not altogether sincere in assur-ing oneself that one does not wish ever to see again her whom one loves, one would not be a whit more sincere in saying that one would like to see her. For no doubt one can endure her absence only when one promises oneself that it shall not be for long, and thinks of the day on which one shall see her again, but at the same time one feels how much less painful are those daily recurring dreams of a meeting immediate and incessantly postponed than would be an interview which might be followed by a spasm of jealousy, with the result that the news that one is shortly to see her whom one loves would cause a disturbance which would be none too pleas-ant. What one procrastinates now from day to day is no longer the end of the intolerable anxiety caused by separation, it is the dreaded renewal of emotions which can lead to nothing. How infinitely one prefers to any such interview the docile memory which one can supplement at one's pleasure with dreams, in which she who in reality does not love one seems, far from that, to be making protestations of her love for one, when one is by oneself; that memory which one can contrive, by blending gradually with it a portion of what one desires, to render as pleasing as one may choose, how infinitely one prefers it to the avoided interview in which one would have to deal with a creature to whom one could no longer dictate at one's pleasure the words that one would like to hear on her lips, but from whom one would meet with fresh coldness, unlooked-for violence. We know, all of us, when we no longer love, that forgetfulness, that even a vague memory do not cause us so much suffering as an ill-starred love. It was of such forgetfulness that in anticipation I preferred, without ac-knowledging it to myself, the reposeful tranquillity.

Moreover, whatever discomfort there may be in such a course of psy-chical detachment and isolation grows steadily less for another reason, namely that it weakens while it is in process of healing that fixed obses-sion which is a state of love. Mine was still strong enough for me to be able to count upon recapturing my old position in Gilberte's estimation, which in view of my deliberate abstention must, it seemed to me, be steadily increasing; in other words each of those calm and melancholy days on which I did not see her, coming one after the other without interruption, continuing too without prescription (unless some busy-body were to meddle in my affairs), was a day not lost but gained. Gained to no purpose, it might be, for presently they would be able to pronounce that I was healed. Resignation, modulating our habits, allows certain elements of our strength to be indefinitely increased. Those—so wretchedly inadequate—that I had had to support my grief, on the first evening of my rupture with Gilberte, had since multiplied to an incalculable power. Only, the tendency which everything that exists has to prolong its own existence is sometimes interrupted by sudden impulses to which we give way with all the fewer scruples over letting ourselves go since we know for how many days, for how many months even we have been able, and might still be able to abstain. And often it is when the purse in which we hoard our savings is nearly full that we undo and empty it, it is without waiting for the result of our medical treatment and when we have succeeded in growing accustomed to it that we abandon it. So, one day, when Mme. Swann was repeating her familiar statement of what a pleasure it would be to Gilberte to see me, thus putting the happiness of which I had now for so long been depriving myself, as it were within arm's length, I was stupefied by the realisation that it was still possible for me to enjoy that pleasure, and I could hardly wait until next day, when I had made up my mind to take Gilberte by surprise, in the evening, before dinner.

What helped me to remain patient throughout the long day that followed was another plan that I had made. From the moment in which everything was forgotten, in which I was reconciled to Gilberte, I no longer wished to visit her save as a lover. Every day she should receive from me the finest flowers that grew. And if Mme. Swann, albeit she had no right to be too severe a mother, should forbid my making a daily offering of flowers, I should find other gifts, more precious and less frequent. My parents did not give me enough money for me to be able to buy expensive things. I thought of a big bowl of old Chinese porcelain which had been left to me by aunt Léonie, and of which Mamma prophesied daily that Françoise would come running to her with an "Oh, it's all come to pieces!" and that that would be the end of it. Would it not be wiser, in that case, to part with it, to sell it so as to be able to give Gilberte all the pleasure I could. I felt sure that I could easily get a thousand francs for it. I had it tied up in paper; I had grown so used to it that I had ceased altogether to notice it; parting with it had at least the advantage of making me realise what it was like. I took it with me as I started for the Swanns', and, giving the driver their address, told him to go by the Champs-Elysées, at one end of which was the shop of a big dealer in oriental things, who knew my father. Greatly to my surprise he offered me there and then not one thousand but ten thousand francs for the bowl. I took the notes with rapture. Every day, for a whole year, I could smother Gilberte in roses and lilac. When I left the shop and got into my cab again the driver (naturally enough, since the Swanns lived out by the Bois) instead of taking the ordinary way began to drive me along the Avenue des Champs-Elysées. He had just passed the end of the Rue de Berri when, in the failing light, I thought I saw, close to the Swanns' house but going in the other direction, going away from it, Gilberte, who was walking slowly, though with a firm step, by the side of a young man with whom she was conversing, but whose face I could not distinguish. I stood up in the cab, meaning to tell the driver to stop; then hesitated. The strolling couple were already some way away, and the parallel lines which their leisurely progress was quietly drawing were on the verge of disappearing in the Elysian gloom. A moment later, I had reached Gilberte's door. I was received by Mme. Swann. "Oh! she will be sorry!" was my greeting, "I can't think why she isn't in. She came home just now from a lesson, complaining of the heat, and said she was going out for a little fresh air with another girl." "I fancy I passed her in the Avenue des Champs-Elysées." "Oh, I don't think it can have been. Anyhow, don't mention it to her father; he doesn't approve of her going out at this time of night. Must you go? Good-bye." I left her, told my driver to go home the same way, but found no trace of the two walking figures. Where had they been? What were they saying to one another in the darkness so confidentially?

I returned home, desperately clutching my windfall of ten thousand francs, which would have enabled me to arrange so many pleasant surprises for that Gilberte whom now I had made up my mind never to see again. No doubt my call at the dealer's had brought me happiness by allowing me to expect that in future, whenever I saw my friend, she would be pleased with me and grateful. But if I had not called there, if my cabman had not taken the Avenue des Champs-Elysées, I should not have seen Gilberte with that young man. Thus a single action may have two contradictory effects, and the misfortune that it engenders cancel the good fortune that it has already brought one. There had befallen me the opposite of what so frequently happens. We desire some pleasure, and the material means of obtaining it are lacking. "It is a mistake," Labruyère tells us, "to be in love without an ample fortune." There is nothing for it but to attempt a gradual elimination of our desire for that pleasure. In my case, however, the material means had been forthcoming, but at the same moment, if not by a logical effect, at any rate as a fortuitous consequence of that initial success, my pleasure had been snatched from me. As, for that matter, it seems as though it must always be. As a rule, however, not on the same evening on which we have acquired what makes it possible. Usually, we continue to struggle and to hope for a little longer. But the pleasure can never be realised. If we succeed in overcoming the force of circumstances, nature at once shifts the battle-ground, placing it within ourselves, and effects a gradual change in our heart until it desires something other than what it is going to obtain. And if this transposition has been so rapid that our heart has not had time to change, nature does not, on that account, despair of conquering us, in a manner more gradual, it is true, more subtle, but no less efficacious. It is then, at the last moment, that the possession of our happiness is wrested from us, or rather it is that very possession which nature, with diabolical cleverness, uses to

destroy our happiness. After failure in every quarter of the domain of life
and action, it is a final incapacity, the mental incapacity for happiness,
that nature creates in us. The phenomenon of happiness either fails to
appear, or at once gives way to the bitterest of reactions.

I put my ten thousand francs in a drawer. But they were no longer of
any use to me. I ran through them, as it happened, even sooner than if I
had sent flowers every day to Gilberte, for when evening came I was always too wretched to stay in the house and used to go and pour out my
sorrows upon the bosoms of women whom I did not love. As for seeking
to give any sort of pleasure to Gilberte, I no longer thought of that; to
visit her house again now could only have added to my sufferings. Even the
sight of Gilberte, which would have been so exquisite a pleasure only yesterday, would no longer have sufficed me. For I should have been miserable
all the time that I was not actually with her. That is how a woman, by
every fresh torture that she inflicts on us, increases, often quite unconsciously, her power over us and at the same time our demands upon her.
With each injury that she does us, she encircles us more and more completely, doubles our chains—but halves the strength of those which
hitherto we had thought adequate to bind her in order that we might retain
our own peace of mind. Only yesterday, had I not been afraid of annoying Gilberte, I should have been content to ask for no more than occasional
meetings, which now would no longer have contented me and for which I
should now have substituted quite different terms. For in this respect love
is not like war; after the battle is ended we renew the fight with keener
ardour, which we never cease to intensify the more thoroughly we are defeated, provided always that we are still in a position to give battle. This
was not my position with regard to Gilberte. Also I preferred, at first, not
to see her mother again. I continued, it is true, to assure myself that Gilberte did not love me, that I had known this for ever so long, that I could
see her again if I chose, and, if I did not choose, forget her in course of
time. But these ideas, like a remedy which has no effect upon certain complaints, had no power whatsoever to obliterate those two parallel lines
which I kept on seeing, traced by Gilberte and the young man as they
slowly disappeared along the Avenue des Champs-Elysées. This was a
fresh misfortune, which like the rest would gradually lose its force, a fresh
image which would one day present itself to my mind's eye completely
purged of every noxious element that it now contained, like those deadly
poisons which one can handle without danger, or like a crumb of dyna-
mite which one can use to light one's cigarette without fear of an explosion. Meanwhile there was in me another force which was striving with
all its might to overpower that unwholesome force which still shewed me,
without alteration, the figure of Gilberte walking in the dusk: to meet
and to break the shock of the renewed assaults of memory, I had, toiling
effectively on the other side, imagination. The former force did indeed
continue to shew me that couple walking in the Champs-Elysées, and
offered me other disagreeable pictures drawn from the past, as for instance
Gilberte shrugging her shoulders when her mother asked her to stay and
entertain me. But the other force, working upon the canvas of my hopes,

outlined a future far more attractively developed than this poor past which, after all, was so restricted. For one minute in which I saw Gilberte's sullen face, how many were there in which I planned to my own satisfaction all the steps that she was to take towards our reconciliation, perhaps even towards our betrothal. It is true that this force, which my imagination was concentrating upon the future, it was drawing, for all that, from the past. I was still in love with her whom, it is true, I believed that I detested. But whenever anyone told me that I was looking well, or was nicely dressed, I wished that she could have been there to see me. I was irritated by the desire that many people shewed about this time to ask me to their houses, and refused all their invitations. There was a scene at home because I did not accompany my father to an official dinner at which the Bontemps were to be present with their niece Albertine, a young girl still hardly more than a child. So it is that the different periods of our life overlap one another. We scornfully decline, because of one whom we love and who will some day be of so little account, to see another who is of no account to-day, with whom we shall be in love to-morrow, with whom we might, perhaps, had we consented to see her now, have fallen in love a little earlier and who would thus have put a term to our present sufferings, bringing others, it is true, in their place. Mine were steadily growing less. I had the surprise of discovering in my own heart one sentiment one day, another the next, generally inspired by some hope or some fear relative to Gilberte. To the Gilberte whom I kept within me. I ought to have reminded myself that the other, the real Gilberte, was perhaps entirely different from mine, knew nothing of the regrets that I ascribed to her, was thinking probably less about me, not merely than I was thinking about her but that I made her be thinking about me when I was closeted alone with my fictitious Gilberte, wondering what really were her feelings with regard to me and so imagining her attention as constantly directed towards myself.

During those periods in which our bitterness of spirit, though steadily diminishing, still persists, a distinction must be drawn between the bitterness which comes to us from our constantly thinking of the person herself and that which is revived by certain memories, some cutting speech, some word in a letter that we have had from her. The various forms which that bitterness can assume we shall examine when we come to deal with another and later love affair; for the present it must suffice to say that, of these two kinds, the former is infinitely the less cruel. That is because our conception of the person, since it dwells always within ourselves, is there adorned with the halo with which we are bound before long to invest her, and bears the marks if not of the frequent solace of hope, at any rate of the tranquillity of a permanent sorrow. (It must also be observed that the image of a person who makes us suffer counts for little if anything in those complications which aggravate the unhappiness of love, prolong it and prevent our recovery, just as in certain maladies the cause is insignificant beyond comparison with the fever which follows it and the time that must elapse before our convalescence.) But if the idea of the person whom we love catches and reflects a ray of light from a mind which is on the whole optimistic, it is not so with those special memories, those cutting words, that inimical letter (I received only one that could be so described from Gilberte); you would say that the person herself dwelt in those fragments, few and scattered as they were, and dwelt there multiplied to a power of which she falls ever so far short in the idea which we are accustomed to form of her as a whole. Because the letter has not—as the image of the beloved creature has—been contemplated by us in the melancholy calm of regret; we have read it, devoured it in the fearful anguish with which we were wrung by an unforeseen misfortune. Sorrows of this sort come to us in another way; from without; and it is along the road of the most cruel suffering that they have penetrated to our heart. The picture of our friend in our mind, which we believe to be old, original, authentic, has in reality been refashioned by her many times over. The cruel memory is not itself contemporary with the restored picture, it is of another age, it is one of the rare witnesses to a monstrous past. But inasmuch as this past continues to exist, save in ourselves, who have been pleased to substitute for it a miraculous age of gold, a paradise in which all mankind shall be reconciled, those memories, those letters carry us back to reality, and cannot but make us feel, by the sudden pang they give us, what a long way we have been borne from that reality by the baseless hopes engendered daily while we waited for something to happen. Not that the said reality is bound always to remain the same, though that does indeed happen at times. There are in our life any number of women whom we have never wished to see again, and who have quite naturally responded to our in no way calculated silence with a silence as profound. Only in their case as we never loved them, we have never counted the years spent apart from them, and this instance, which would invalidate our whole argument, we are inclined to forget when we are considering the healing effect of isolation, just as people who believe in presentiments forget all the occasions on which their own have not 'come true.'

But, after a time, absence may prove efficacious. The desire, the appetite for seeing us again may after all be reborn in the heart which at present contemns us. Only, we must allow time. Now the demands which we ourselves make upon time are no less exorbitant than those of a heart in process of changing. For one thing, time is the very thing that we are least willing to allow, for our own suffering is keen and we are anxious to see it brought to an end. And then, too, the interval of time which the other heart needs to effect its change our own heart will have spent in changing itself also, so that when the goal which we had set ourselves becomes attainable it will have ceased to count as a goal, or to seem worth attaining. This idea, however, that it will be attainable, that what, when it no longer spells any good fortune to us, we shall ultimately secure is not good fortune, this idea embodies a part, but a part only of the truth. Our good fortune accrues to us when we have grown indifferent to it. But the very fact of our indifference will have made us less exacting, and allow us in retrospect to feel convinced that we should have been in raptures over our good fortune had it come at a time when, very probably, it would have seemed to us miserably inadequate. People are not very hard to satisfy nor are they very good judges of matters in which they take no interest. The friendly overtures of a person whom we no longer love, overtures which strike us, in our indifference to her, as excessive, would perhaps have fallen a long way short of satisfying our love. Those tender speeches, that invitation or acceptance, we think only of the pleasure which they would have given us, and not of all those other speeches and meetings by which we should have wished to see them immediately followed, which we should, as likely as not, simply by our avidity for them, have precluded from ever happening. So that we can never be certain that the good fortune which comes to us too late, when we are no longer in love, is altogether the same as that good fortune the want of which made us, at one time, so unhappy. There is only one person who could decide that; our ego of those days; he is no longer with us, and were he to reappear, no doubt that would be quite enough to make our good fortune—whether identical or not—vanish.

Pending these posthumous fulfilments of a dream in which I should not, when the time came, be greatly interested, by dint of my having to invent, as in the days when I still hardly knew Gilberte, speeches, letters in which she implored my forgiveness, swore that she had never loved anyone but myself and besought me to marry her, a series of pleasant images incessantly renewed came by degrees to hold a larger place in my mind than the vision of Gilberte and the young man, which had nothing now to feed upon. At this point I should perhaps have resumed my visits to Mme. Swann but for a dream that came to me, in which one of my friends, who was not, however, one that I could identify, behaved with the utmost treachery towards me and appeared to believe that I had been treacherous to him. Abruptly awakened by the pain which this dream had given me, and finding that it persisted after I was awake, I turned my thoughts back to the dream, racked my brains to discover who could have been the friend whom I had seen in my sleep, the sound of whose name—a Spanish name—was no longer distinct in my ears. Combining Joseph's part with Pharaoh's, I set to work to interpret my dream. I knew that, when one is interpreting a dream, it is often a mistake to pay too much attention to the appearance of the people one saw in it, who may perhaps have been disguised or have exchanged faces, like those mutilated saints on the walls of cathedrals which ignorant archaeologists have restored, fitting the body of one to the head of another and confusing all their attributes and names. Those that people bear in a dream are apt to mislead us. The person with whom we are in love is to be recognised only by the intensity of the pain that we suffer. From mine I learned that, though transformed while I was asleep into a young man, the person whose recent betrayal still hurt me was Gilberte. I remembered then that, the last time I had seen her, on the day when her mother had forbidden her to go out to a dancing-lesson, she had, whether in sincerity or in make-believe, declined, laughing in a strange manner, to believe in the genuineness of my feeling for her. And by association this memory brought back to me another. Long before that, it had been Swann who would not believe in my sincerity, nor that I was a suitable friend for Gilberte. In vain had

I written to him, Gilberte had brought back my letter and had returned it to me with the same incomprehensible laugh. She had not returned it to me at once: I remembered now the whole of that scene behind the clump of laurels. As soon as one is unhappy one becomes moral. Gilberte's recent antipathy for me seemed to me a judgment delivered on me by life for my conduct that afternoon. Such judgments one imagines one can escape because one looks out for carriages when one is crossing the street, and avoids obvious dangers. But there are others that take effect within us. The accident comes from the side to which one has not been looking, from inside, from the heart. Gilberte's words: "If you like, we might go on wrestling," made me shudder. I imagined her behaving like that, at home perhaps, in the linen-room, with the young man whom I had seen escorting her along the Avenue des Champs-Elysées. And so, just as when, a little time back, I had believed myself to be calmly established in a state of happiness, it had been fatuous in me, now that I had abandoned all thought of happiness, to take for granted that at least I had grown and was going to remain calm. For, so long as our heart keeps enshrined with any permanence the image of another person, it is not only our happiness that may at any moment be destroyed; when that happiness has vanished, when we have suffered, and, later, when we have succeeded in lulling our sufferings to sleep, the thing then that is as elusive, as precarious as ever our happiness was, is our calm. Mine returned to me in the end, for the cloud which, lowering our resistance, tempering our desires, has penetrated, in the train of a dream, the enclosure of our mind, is bound, in course of time, to dissolve, permanence and stability being assured to nothing in this world, not even to grief. Besides, those whose suffering is due to love are, as we say of certain invalids, their own physicians. As consolation can come to them only from the person who is the cause of their grief, and as their grief is an emanation from that person, it is there, in their grief itself, that they must in the end find a remedy: which it will disclose to them at a given moment, for as long as they turn it over in their minds this grief will continue to shew them fresh aspects of the loved, the regretted creature, at one moment so intensely hateful that one has no longer the slightest desire to see her, since before finding enjoyment in her company one would have first to make her suffer, at another so pleasant that the pleasantness in which one has invested her one adds to her own stock of good qualities and finds in it a fresh reason for hope. But even although the anguish that had reawakened in me did at length grow calm, I no longer wished—except just occasionally—to visit Mme. Swann. In the first place because, among those who love and have been forsaken, the state of incessant—even if unconfessed—expectancy in which they live undergoes a spontaneous transformation, and, while to all appearance unchanged, substitutes for its original elements others that are precisely the opposite. The first were the consequences of—a reaction from—the painful incidents which had upset us. The tension of waiting for what is yet to come is mingled with fear, all the more since we desire at such moments, should no message come to us from her whom we love, to act for ourselves, and are none too confident of the success of a step which, once we have taken it, we may find it impossible to follow up. But presently, without our having noticed any change, this tension, which still endures, is sustained, we discover, no longer by our recollection of the past but by anticipation of an imaginary future. From that moment it is almost pleasant. Besides, the first state, by continuing for some time, has accustomed us to living in expectation. The suffering that we felt during those last meetings survives in us still, but is already lulled to sleep. We are in no haste to arouse it, especially as we do not see very clearly what to ask for now. The possession of a little more of the woman whom we love would only make more essential to us the part that we did not yet possess, which is bound to remain, whatever happens, since our requirements are begotten of our satisfactions, an irreducible quantity.

Another, final reason came later on to reinforce this, and to make me discontinue altogether my visits to Mme. Swann. This reason, slow in revealing itself, was not that I had now forgotten Gilberte but that I must make every effort to forget her as speedily as possible. No doubt, now that the keen edge of my suffering was dulled, my visits to Mme. Swann had become once again, for what sorrow remained in me, the sedative and distraction which had been so precious to me at first. But what made the sedative efficacious made the distraction impossible, namely that with these visits the memory of Gilberte was intimately blended. The distraction would be of no avail to me unless it was employed to combat a sentiment which the presence of Gilberte no longer nourished, thoughts, interests, passions in which Gilberte should have no part. These states of consciousness, to which the person whom we love remains a stranger, then occupy a place which, however small it may be at first, is always so much reconquered from the love that has been in unchallenged possession of our whole soul. We must seek to encourage these thoughts, to make them grow, while the sentiment which is no more now than a memory dwindles, so that the new elements introduced into our mind contest with that sentiment, wrest from it an ever increasing part of our soul, until at last the victory is complete. I decided that this was the only way in which my love could be killed, and I was still young enough, still courageous enough to undertake the attempt, to subject myself to that most cruel grief which springs from the certainty that, whatever time one may devote to the effort, it will prove successful in the end. The reason I now gave in my letters to Gilberte for refusing to see her was an allusion to some mysterious misunderstanding, wholly fictitious, which was supposed to have arisen between her and myself, and as to which I had hoped at first that Gilberte would insist upon my furnishing her with an explanation. But, as a matter of fact, never, even in the most insignificant relations in life, does a request for enlightenment come from a correspondent who knows that an obscure, untruthful, incriminating sentence has been written on purpose, so that he shall protest against it, and is only too glad to feel, when he reads it, that he possesses—and to keep in his own hands—the initiative in the coming operations. For all the more reason is this so in our more tender relations, in which love is endowed with so much eloquence, indifference with so little curiosity. Gilberte having never appeared to doubt nor sought to learn more about this misunderstanding, it became for me a real entity, to which I referred anew in every letter. And there is in these baseless situations, in the affectation of coldness, a sort of fascination which tempts one to persevere in them. By dint of writing: "Now that our hearts are sundered," so that Gilberte might answer: "But they are not. Do explain what you mean," I had gradually come to believe that they were. By constantly repeating, "Life may have changed for us, it will never destroy the feeling that we had for one another," in the hope of hearing myself, one day, say: "But there has been no change, the feeling is stronger now than ever it was," I was living with the idea that life had indeed changed, that we should keep only the memory of a feeling which no longer existed, as certain neurotics, from having at first pretended to be ill, end by becoming chronic invalids. Now, whenever I had to write to Gilberte, I brought my mind back to this imagined change, which, being now tacitly admitted by the silence which she preserved with regard to it in her replies, would in future subsist between us. Then Gilberte ceased to make a point of ignoring it. She too adopted my point of view; and, as in the speeches at official banquets, when the foreign Sovereign who is being entertained adopts practically the same expressions as have just been used by the Sovereign who is entertaining him, whenever I wrote to Gilberte: "Life may have parted us; the memory of the days when we knew one another will endure," she never failed to respond: "Life may have parted us; it cannot make us forget those happy hours which will always be dear to us both," (though we should have found it hard to say why or how 'Life' had parted us, or what change had occurred). My sufferings were no longer excessive. And yet, one day when I was telling her in a letter that I had heard of the death of our old barley-sugar woman in the Champs-Elysées, as I wrote the words: "I felt at once that this would distress you, in me it awakened a host of memories," I could not restrain myself from bursting into tears when I saw that I was speaking in the past tense, as though it were of some dead friend, now almost forgotten, of this love of which in spite of myself I had never ceased to think as of a thing still alive, or one that at least might be born again. Nothing can be more affectionate than this sort of correspondence between friends who do not wish to see one another any more. Gilberte's letters to me had all the delicate refinement of those which I used to write to people who did not matter, and shewed me the same apparent marks of affection, which it was so pleasant for me to receive from her.

But, as time went on, every refusal to see her disturbed me less. And as she became less dear to me, my painful memories were no longer strong enough to destroy by their incessant return the growing pleasure which I found in thinking of Florence, or of Venice. I regretted, at such moments, that I had abandoned the idea of diplomacy, and had condemned myself to a sedentary existence, in order not to be separated from a girl whom I should not see again and had already almost forgotten. We construct our house of life to suit another person, and when at length it is ready to receive her that person does not come; presently she is dead to us, and we live on, a prisoner within the walls which were intended only for her. If Venice seemed to my parents to be a long way off, and its climate treacherous, it was at least quite easy for me to go, without tiring myself, and settle down at Balbec. But to do that I should have had to leave Paris, to forego those visits thanks to which, infrequent as they were, I might sometimes hear Mme. Swann telling me about her daughter. Besides, I was beginning to find in them various pleasures in which Gilberte had no part.

When spring drew round, and with it the cold weather, during an icy Lent and the hailstorms of Holy Week, as Mme. Swann began to find it cold in the house, I used often to see her entertaining her guests in her furs, her shivering hands and shoulders hidden beneath the gleaming white carpet of an immense rectangular muff and a cape, both of ermine, which she had not taken off on coming in from her drive, and which suggested the last patches of the snows of winter, more persistent than the rest, which neither the heat of the fire nor the advancing season had succeeded in melting. And the whole truth about these glacial but already flowering weeks was suggested to me in this drawing-room, which soon I should be entering no more, by other more intoxicating forms of whiteness, that for example of the guelder-roses clustering, at the summits of their tall bare stalks, like the rectilinear trees in pre-Raphaelite paintings, their balls of blossom, divided yet composite, white as annunciating angels and breathing a fragrance as of lemons. For the mistress of Tansonville knew that April, even an ice-bound April, was not barren of flowers, that winter, spring, summer are not held apart by barriers as hermetic as might be supposed by the town-dweller who, until the first hot day, imagines the world as containing nothing but houses that stand naked in the rain. That Mme. Swann was content with the consignments furnished by her Combray gardener, that she did not, by the intervention of her own 'special' florist, fill up the gaps left by an insufficiently powerful magic with subsidies borrowed from a precocious Mediterranean shore, I do not for a moment suggest, nor did it worry me at the time. It was enough to fill me with longing for country scenes that, overhanging the loose snowdrifts of the muff in which Mme. Swann kept her hands, the guelder-rose snow-balls (which served very possibly in the mind of my hostess no other purpose than to compose, on the advice of Bergotte, a 'Symphony in White' with her furniture and her garments) reminded me that what the Good Friday music in *Parsifal* symbolised was a natural miracle which one could see performed every year, if one had the sense to look for it, and, assisted by the acid and heady perfume of the other kinds of blossom, which, although their names were unknown to me, had brought me so often to a standstill to gaze at them on my walks round Combray, made Mme. Swann's drawing-room as virginal, as candidly 'in bloom,' without the least vestige of greenery, as overladen with genuine scents of flowers as was the little lane by Tansonville.

But it was still more than I could endure that these memories should be recalled to me. There was a risk of their reviving what little remained of my love for Gilberte. Besides, albeit I no longer felt the least distress during these visits to Mme. Swann, I extended the intervals between them and endeavoured to see as little of her as possible. At most, since I continued not to go out of Paris, I allowed myself an occasional walk with her. Fine weather had come at last, and the sun was hot. As I knew that before luncheon Mme. Swann used to go out every day for an hour, and would stroll for a little in the Avenue du Bois, near the Etoile—a spot which, at that time, because of the people who used to collect there to gaze at the 'swells' whom they knew only by name, was known as the 'Shabby-Genteel Club'—I persuaded my parents, on Sundays (for on weekdays I was busy all morning), to let me postpone my luncheon until long after theirs, until a quarter past one, and go for a walk before it. During May, that year, I never missed a Sunday, for Gilberte had gone to stay with friends in the country. I used to reach the Arc de Triomphe about noon. I kept watch at the entrance to the Avenue, never taking my eyes off the corner of the side-street along which Mme. Swann, who had only a few yards to walk, would come from her house. As by this time many of the people who had been strolling there were going home to luncheon, those who remained were few in number and, for the most part, fashionably dressed. Suddenly, on the gravelled path, unhurrying, cool, luxuriant, Mme. Swann appeared, displaying around her a toilet which was never twice the same, but which I remember as being typically mauve; then she hoisted and unfurled at the end of its long stalk, just at the moment when her radiance was most complete, the silken banner of a wide parasol of a shade that matched the showering petals of her gown. A whole troop of people escorted her; Swann himself, four or five fellows from the Club, who had been to call upon her that morning or whom she had met in the street: and their black or grey agglomeration, obedient to her every gesture, performing the almost mechanical movements of a lifeless setting in which Odette was framed, gave to this woman, in whose eyes alone was there any intensity, the air of looking out in front of her, from among all those men, as from a window behind which she had taken her stand, and made her emerge there, frail but fearless, in the nudity of her delicate colours, like the apparition of a creature of a different species, of an unknown race, and of almost martial strength, by virtue of which she seemed by herself a match for all her multiple escort. Smiling, rejoicing in the fine weather, in the sunshine which had not yet become trying, with the air of calm assurance of a creator who has accomplished his task and takes no thought for anything besides; certain that her clothes—even though the vulgar herd should fail to appreciate them—were the smartest anywhere to be seen, she wore them for herself and for her friends, naturally, without exaggerated attention to them but also without absolute detachment; not preventing the little bows of ribbon upon her bodice and skirt from floating buoyantly upon the air before her, like separate creatures of whose presence there she was not unconscious, but was indulgent enough to let them play if they chose, keeping their own rhythm, provided that they accompanied her where she led the way; and even upon her mauve parasol, which, as often as not, she had not yet 'put up' when she appeared on the scene, she let fall now and then, as though upon a bunch of Parma violets, a gaze happy and so kindly that, when it was

fastened no longer upon her friends but on some inanimate object, her
eyes still seemed to smile. She thus kept open, she made her garments
occupy that interval of smartness, of which the men with whom she was
on the most familiar terms respected both the existence and its necessity,
not without shewing a certain deference, as of profane visitors to a shrine,
an admission of their own ignorance, an interval over which they recognised that their friend had (as we recognise that a sick man has over the
special precautions that he has to take, or a mother over her children's
education) a competent jurisdiction. No less than by the court which encircled her and seemed not to observe the passers-by, Mme. Swann by
the lateness of her appearance there at once suggested those rooms in
which she had spent so long, so leisurely a morning and to which she must
presently return for luncheon; she seemed to indicate their proximity by
the unhurrying ease of her progress, like the turn that one takes up and
down one's own garden; of those rooms one would have said that she was
carrying about her still the cool, the indoor shade. But for that very reason
the sight of her gave me only a stronger sensation of open air and warmth.
All the more because, being assured in my own mind that, in accordance
with the liturgy, with the ritual in which Mme. Swann was so profoundly
versed, her clothes were connected with the time of year and of day by
a bond both inevitable and unique, I felt that the flowers upon the stiff
straw brim of her hat, the baby-ribbons upon her dress, had been even
more naturally born of the month of May than the flowers in gardens and
in woods; and to learn what latest change there was in weather or season
I had not to raise my eyes higher than to her parasol, open and outstretched
like another, a nearer sky, round, clement, mobile, blue. For these rites,
if they were of sovereign importance, subjugated their glory (and, consequently, Mme. Swann her own) in condescending obedience to the day,
the spring, the sun, none of which struck me as being sufficiently flattered
that so elegant a woman had been graciously pleased not to ignore their
existence, and had chosen on their account a gown of a brighter, of a
thinner fabric, suggesting to me, by the opening of its collar and sleeves,
the moist warmness of the throat and wrists that they exposed,—in a word,
had taken for them all the pains that a great personage takes who, having
gaily condescended to pay a visit to common folk in the country, whom
everyone, even the most plebeian, knows, yet makes a point of donning,
for the occasion, suitable attire. On her arrival I would greet Mme. Swann,
she stop me and say (in English) 'Good morning,' and smile. We would
walk a little way together. And I learned then that these canons according
to which she dressed, it was for her own satisfaction that she obeyed
them, as though yielding to a Superior Wisdom of which she herself
was High Priestess: for if it should happen that, feeling too warm, she
threw open or even took off altogether and gave me to carry the jacket
which she had intended to keep buttoned up, I would discover in the blouse
beneath it a thousand details of execution which had had every chance of
remaining there unperceived, like those parts of an orchestral score to
which the composer has devoted infinite labour albeit they may never
reach the ears of the public: or in the sleeves of the jacket that lay

folded across my arm I would see, I would drink in slowly, for my own pleasure or from affection for its wearer, some exquisite detail, a deliciously tinted strip, a lining of mauve satinette which, ordinarily concealed from every eye, was yet just as delicately fashioned as the outer parts, like those gothic carvings on a cathedral, hidden on the inside of a balustrade eighty feet from the ground, as perfect as are the bas-reliefs over the main porch, and yet never seen by any living man until, happening to pass that way upon his travels, an artist obtains leave to climb up there among them, to stroll in the open air, sweeping the whole town with a comprehensive gaze, between the soaring towers.

What enhanced this impression that Mme. Swann was walking in the Avenue as though along the paths of her own garden, was—for people ignorant of her habit of 'taking exercise'—that she had come there on foot, without any carriage following, she whom, once May had begun, they were accustomed to see, behind the most brilliant 'turn-out,' the smartest liveries in Paris, gently and majestically seated, like a goddess, in the balmy air of an immense victoria on eight springs. On foot Mme. Swann had the appearance—especially as her pace began to slacken in the heat of the sun—of having yielded to curiosity, of committing an 'exclusive' breach of all the rules of her code, like those Crowned Heads who, without consulting anyone, accompanied by the slightly scandalised admiration of a suite which dares not venture any criticism, step out of their boxes during a gala performance and visit the lobby of the theatre, mingling for a moment or two with the rest of the audience. So between Mme. Swann and themselves the crowd felt that there existed those barriers of a certain kind of opulence which seem to them the most insurmountable that there are. The Faubourg Saint-Germain may have its barriers also, but these are less 'telling' to the eyes and imagination of the 'shabby-genteel.' These latter, when in the presence of a real personage, more simple, more easily mistaken for the wife of a small professional or business man, less remote from the people, will not feel the same sense of their own inequality, almost of their unworthiness, as dismays them when they encounter Mme. Swann. Of course women of that sort are not themselves dazzled, as the crowd are, by the brilliance of their apparel, they have ceased to pay any attention to it, but only because they have grown used to it, that is to say have come to look upon it more and more as natural and necessary, to judge their fellow creatures according as they are more or less initiated into these luxurious ways: so that (the grandeur which they allow themselves to display or discover in others being wholly material, easily verified, slowly acquired, the lack of it hard to compensate) if such women place a passer-by in the lowest rank of society, it is by the same instinctive process that has made them appear to him as in the highest, that is to say instinctively, at first sight, and without possibility of appeal. Perhaps that special class of society which included in those days women like Lady Israels, who mixed with the women of the aristocracy, and Mme. Swann, who was to get to know them later on, that intermediate class, inferior to the Faubourg Saint-Germain, since it 'ran after' the denizens of that quarter, but superior to everything that was not of the Faubourg Saint-

Germain, possessing this peculiarity that, while already detached from
the world of the merely rich, it was riches still that it represented, but
riches that had been canalised, serving a purpose, swayed by an idea that
was artistic, malleable gold, chased with a poetic design, taught to smile;
perhaps that class—in the same form, at least, and with the same charm—
exists no longer. In any event, the women who were its members would not
satisfy to-day what was the primary condition on which they reigned, since
with advancing age they have lost—almost all of them—their beauty.
Whereas it was (just as much as from the pinnacle of her noble fortune)
from the glorious zenith of her ripe and still so fragrant summer that Mme.
Swann, majestic, smiling, kind, as she advanced along the Avenue du
Bois, saw like Hypatia, beneath the slow tread of her feet, worlds revolv-
ing. Various young men as they passed looked at her anxiously, not knowing whether their vague acquaintance with her (especially since, having
been introduced only once, at the most, to Swann, they were afraid that he
might not remember them) was sufficient excuse for their venturing to
take off their hats. And they trembled to think of the consequences as they
made up their minds, asking themselves whether the gesture, so bold, so
sacrilegious a tempting of providence, would not let loose the catas-
trophic forces of nature or bring down upon them the vengeance of a
jealous god. It provoked only, like the winding of a piece of clockwork,
a series of gesticulations from little, responsive bowing figures, who were
none other than Odette's escort, beginning with Swann himself, who raised
his tall hat lined in green leather with an exquisite courtesy, which he had
acquired in the Faubourg Saint-Germain, but to which was no longer
wedded the indifference that he would at one time have shewn. Its place
was now taken (as though he had been to some extent permeated by
Odette's prejudices) at once by irritation at having to acknowledge the
salute of a person who was none too well dressed and by satisfaction at
his wife's knowing so many people, a mixed sensation to which he gave
expression by saying to the smart friends who walked by his side: "What!
another! Upon my word, I can't imagine where my wife picks all these
fellows up!" Meanwhile, having greeted with a slight movement of her
head the terrified youth, who had already passed out of sight though his
heart was still beating furiously, Mme. Swann turned to me: "Then it's
all over?" she put it to me, "You aren't ever coming to see Gilberte again?
I'm glad you make an exception of me, and are not going to 'drop' me
straight away. I like seeing you, but I used to like also the influence you
had over my daughter. I'm sure she's very sorry about it, too. However, I
mustn't bully you, or you'll make up your mind at once that you never
want to set eyes on me again." "Odette, Sagan's trying to speak to you!"
Swann called his wife's attention. And there, indeed, was the Prince, as
in some transformation scene at the close of a play, or in a circus, or an
old painting, wheeling his horse round so as to face her, in a magnificent
heroic pose, and doffing his hat with a sweeping theatrical and, so to
speak, allegorical flourish in which he displayed all the chivalrous courtesy
of a great noble bowing in token of his respect for Woman, were she incarnate in a woman whom it was impossible for his mother or his sister

to know. And at every moment, recognised in the depths of the liquid transparency and of the luminous glaze of the shadow which her parasol cast over her, Mme. Swann was receiving the salutations of the last belated horsemen, who passed as though in a cinematograph taken as they galloped in the blinding glare of the Avenue, men from the clubs, the names of whom, which meant only celebrities to the public, Antoine de Castellane, Adalbert de Montmorency and the rest—were for Mme. Swann the familiar names of friends. And as the average span of life, the relative longevity of our memories of poetical sensations is much greater than that of our memories of what the heart has suffered, long after the sorrows that I once felt on Gilberte's account have faded and vanished, there has survived them the pleasure that I still derive—whenever I close my eyes and read, as it were upon the face of a sundial, the minutes that are recorded between a quarter past twelve and one o'clock in the month of May—from seeing myself once again strolling and talking thus with Mme. Swann beneath her parasol, as though in the coloured shade of a wistaria bower.

PLACE-NAMES: THE PLACE

I HAD arrived at a state almost of complete indifference to Gilberte when, two years later, I went with my grandmother to Balbec. When I succumbed to the attraction of a strange face, when it was with the help of some other girl that I hoped to discover gothic cathedrals, the palaces and gardens of Italy, I said to myself sadly that this love of ours, in so far as it is love for one particular creature, is not perhaps a very real thing, since if the association of pleasant or unpleasant trains of thought can attach it for a time to a woman so as to make us believe that it has been inspired by her, in a necessary sequence of effect to cause, yet when we detach ourselves, deliberately or unconsciously, from those associations, this love, as though it were indeed a spontaneous thing and sprang from ourselves alone, will revive in order to bestow itself on another woman. At the time, however, of my departure for Balbec, and during the earlier part of my stay there, my indifference was still only intermittent. Often, our life being so careless of chronology, interpolating so many anachronisms in the sequence of our days, I lived still among those—far older days than yesterday or last week—in which I loved Gilberte. And at once not seeing her became as exquisite a torture to me as it had been then. The self that had loved her, which another self had already almost entirely supplanted, rose again in me, stimulated far more often by a trivial than by an important event. For instance, if I may anticipate for a moment my arrival in Normandy, I heard some one who passed me on the sea-front at Balbec refer to the 'Secretary to the Ministry of Posts and his family.' Now, seeing that as yet I knew nothing of the influence which that family was to exercise over my life, this remark ought to have passed unheeded; instead, it gave me at once an acute twinge, which a self that had for the most part long since been outgrown in me felt at being parted from Gilberte. Because I had never given another thought to a conversation which Gilberte had had with her father in my hearing, in which allusion was made to the Secretary to the Ministry of Posts and to his family. Now our love memories present no exception to the general rules of memory, which in turn are governed by the still more general rules of Habit. And as Habit weakens every impression, what a person recalls to us most vividly is precisely what we had forgotten, because it was of no importance, and had therefore left in full possession of its strength. That is why the better part of our memory exists outside ourselves, in a blatter of rain, in the smell of an unaired room or of the first crackling brushwood fire in a cold grate: wherever, in short, we happen upon what our mind, having no use for it, had rejected, the last treasure that the past has in store, the richest, that which when all our flow of tears seems to have dried at the source can make us weep again. Outside ourselves, did I say; rather

within ourselves, but hidden from our eyes in an oblivion more or less prolonged. It is thanks to this oblivion alone that we can from time to time
recover the creature that we were, range ourselves face to face with past
events as that creature had to face them, suffer afresh because we are no
longer ourselves but he, and because he loved what leaves us now indifferent. In the broad daylight of our ordinary memory the images of the past
turn gradually pale and fade out of sight, nothing remains of them, we
shall never find them again. Or rather we should never find them again
had not a few words (such as this 'Secretary to the Ministry of Posts')
been carefully locked away in oblivion, just as an author deposits in the
National Library a copy of a book which might otherwise become unob-
tainable.

But this suffering and this recrudescence of my love for Gilberte lasted
no longer than such things last in a dream, and this time, on the contrary, because at Balbec the old Habit was no longer there to keep them
alive. And if these two effects of Habit appear to be incompatible,
that is because Habit is bound by a diversity of laws. In Paris I
had grown more and more indifferent to Gilberte, thanks to Habit. The
change of habit, that is to say the temporary cessation of Habit, completed Habit's task when I started for Balbec. It weakens, but it sta-
bilises; it leads to disintegration but it makes the scattered elements last
indefinitely. Day after day, for years past, I had begun by modelling my
state of mind, more or less effectively, upon that of the day before. At
Balbec, a strange bed, to the side of which a tray was brought in the
morning that differed from my Paris breakfast tray, could not, obviously,
sustain the fancies upon which my love for Gilberte had fed: there are
cases (though not, I admit, commonly) in which, one's days being paralysed by a sedentary life, the best way to save time is to change one's
place of residence. My journey to Balbec was like the first outing of a
convalescent who needed only that to convince him that he was cured.

The journey was one that would now be made, probably, in a motor-
car, which would be supposed to render it more interesting. We shall see
too that, accomplished in such a way, it would even be in a sense more
genuine, since one would be following more nearly, in a closer intimacy,
the various contours by which the surface of the earth is wrinkled. But
after all the special attraction of the journey lies not in our being able to
alight at places on the way and to stop altogether as soon as we grow
tired, but in its making the difference between departure and arrival not
as imperceptible but as intense as possible, so that we are conscious of it
in its totality, intact, as it existed in our mind when imagination bore us
from the place in which we were living right to the very heart of a place
we longed to see, in a single sweep which seemed miraculous to us not so
much because it covered a certain distance as because it united two distinct individualities of the world, took us from one name to another
name; and this difference is accentuated (more than in a form of locomotion in which, since one can stop and alight where one chooses, there can
scarcely be said to be any point of arrival) by the mysterious operation
that is performed in those peculiar places, railway stations, which do not

constitute, so to speak, a part of the surrounding town but contain the essence of its personality just as upon their sign-boards they bear its painted name.

But in this respect as in every other, our age is infected with a mania for shewing things only in the environment that properly belongs to them, thereby suppressing the essential thing, the act of the mind which isolated them from that environment. A picture is nowadays 'presented' in the midst of furniture, ornaments, hangings of the same period, a second-hand scheme of decoration in the composition of which in the houses of to-day excels that same hostess who but yesterday was so crassly igno-rant, but now spends her time poring over records and in libraries; and among these the masterpiece at which we glance up from the table while we dine does not give us that exhilarating delight which we can expect from it only in a public gallery, which symbolises far better by its bare-ness, by the absence of all irritating detail, those innermost spaces into which the artist withdrew to create it.

Unhappily those marvellous places which are railway stations, from which one sets out for a remote destination, are tragic places also, for if in them the miracle is accomplished whereby scenes which hitherto have had no existence save in our minds are to become the scenes among which we shall be living, for that very reason we must, as we emerge from the waiting-room, abandon any thought of finding ourself once again within the familiar walls which, but a moment ago, were still enclosing us. We must lay aside all hope of going home to sleep in our own bed, once we have made up our mind to penetrate into the pestiferous cavern through which we may have access to the mystery, into one of those vast, glass-roofed sheds, like that of Saint-Lazare into which I must go to find the train for Balbec, and which extended over the rent bowels of the city one of those bleak and boundless skies, heavy with an accumulation of dramatic menaces, like certain skies painted with an almost Parisian modernity by Mantegna or Veronese, beneath which could be accom-plished only some solemn and tremendous act, such as a departure by train or the Elevation of the Cross.

So long as I had been content to look out from the warmth of my own bed in Paris at the Persian church of Balbec, shrouded in driving sleet, no sort of objection to this journey had been offered by my body. Its objec-tions began only when it had gathered that it would have itself to take part in the journey, and that on the evening of my arrival I should be shewn to 'my' room which to my body would be unknown. Its revolt was all the more deep-rooted in that on the very eve of my departure I learned that my mother would not be coming with us, my father, who would be kept busy at the Ministry until it was time for him to start for Spain with M. de Norpois, having preferred to take a house in the neighbourhood of Paris. On the other hand, the spectacle of Balbec seemed to me none the less desirable because I must purchase it at the price of a discomfort which, on the contrary, I felt to indicate and to guarantee the reality of the impression which I was going there to seek, an impression the place of which no spectacle of professedly equal value, no 'panorama' which I

might have gone to see without being thereby precluded from returning
home to sleep in my own bed, could possibly have filled. It was not for the
first time that I felt that those who love and those who find pleasure are
not always the same. I believed myself to be longing fully as much for
Balbec as the doctor who was treating me, when he said to me, surprised,
on the morning of our departure, to see me look so unhappy, "I don't
mind telling you that if I could only manage a week to go down and get a
blow by the sea, I shouldn't wait to be asked twice. You'll be having
races, regattas; you don't know what all!" But I had already learned the
lesson—long before I was taken to hear Berma—that, whatever it might
be that I loved, it would never be attained save at the end of a long and
heart-rending pursuit, in the course of which I should have first to sacrifice my own pleasure to that paramount good instead of seeking it there.

My grandmother, naturally enough, looked upon our exodus from a
somewhat different point of view, and (for she was still as anxious as
ever that the presents which were made me should take some artistic
form) had planned, so that she might be offering me, of this journey, a
'print' that was, at least, in parts 'old,' that we should repeat, partly by
rail and partly by road, the itinerary that Mme. de Sévigné followed when
she went from Paris to 'L'Orient' by way of Chaulnes and 'the Pont-
Audemer.' But my grandmother had been obliged to abandon this project,
at the instance of my father who knew, whenever she organised any expedition with a view to extracting from it the utmost intellectual benefit that
it was capable of yielding, what a tale there would be to tell of missed
trains, lost luggage, sore throats and broken rules. She was free at least
to rejoice in the thought that never, when the time came for us to sally
forth to the beach, should we be exposed to the risk of being kept indoors
by the sudden appearance of what her beloved Sévigné calls a 'beast of a
coachload,' since we should know not a soul at Balbec, Legrandin having
refrained from offering us a letter of introduction to his sister. (This abstention had not been so well appreciated by my aunts Céline and Flora,
who, having known as a child that lady, of whom they had always spoken
until then, to commemorate this early intimacy, as 'Renée de Cambremer,'
and having had from her and still possessing a number of those little
presents which continue to ornament a room or a conversation but to
which the feeling between the parties no longer corresponds, imagined that
they were avenging the insult offered to us by never uttering again, when
they called upon Mme. Legrandin, the name of her daughter, confining
themselves to a mutual congratulation, once they were safely out of the
house: "I made no reference to you know whom!" "I think that went
home!")

And so we were simply to leave Paris by that one twenty-two train
which I had too often beguiled myself by looking out in the railway time-
table, where its itinerary never failed to give me the emotion, almost the
illusion of starting by it, not to feel that I already knew it. As the delineation in our mind of the features of any form of happiness depends more
on the nature of the longings that it inspires in us than on the accuracy of
the information which we have about it, I felt that I knew this train in all its

details, nor did I doubt that I should feel, sitting in one of its compart-
ments, a special delight as the day began to cool, should be contemplating
this or that view as the train approached one or another station; so much
so that this train, which always brought to my mind's eye the images of
the same towns, which I bathed in the sunlight of those post-meridian
hours through which it sped, seemed to me to be different from every
other train; and I had ended—as we are apt to do with a person whom
we have never seen but of whom we like to believe that we have won his
friendship—by giving a distinct and unalterable cast of countenance to
the traveller, artistic, golden-haired, who would thus have taken me with
him upon his journey, and to whom I should bid farewell beneath the
Cathedral of Saint-Lô, before he hastened to overtake the setting sun.

As my grandmother could not bring herself to do anything so 'stupid'
as to go straight to Balbec, she was to break the journey half-way, staying
the night with one of her friends, from whose house I was to proceed the
same evening, so as not to be in the way there and also in order that I
might arrive by daylight and see Balbec Church, which, we had learned,
was at some distance from Balbec-Plage, so that I might not have a chance
to visit it later on, when I had begun my course of baths. And perhaps it
was less painful for me to feel that the desirable goal of my journey stood
between me and that cruel first night on which I should have to enter a
new habitation, and consent to dwell there. But I had had first to leave the
old; my mother had arranged to 'move in,' that afternoon, at Saint-Cloud,
and had made, or pretended to make, all the arrangements for going there
directly after she had seen us off at the station, without needing to call
again at our own house to which she was afraid that I might otherwise
feel impelled at the last moment, instead of going to Balbec, to return with
her. In fact, on the pretext of having so much to see to in the house which
she had just taken and of being pressed for time, but in reality so as to
spare me the cruel ordeal of a long-drawn parting, she had decided not
to wait with us until that moment of the signal to start at which, concealed hitherto among ineffective comings and goings and preparations
that lead to nothing definite, separation is made suddenly manifest, impossible to endure when it is no longer possibly to be avoided, concentrated in its entirety in one enormous instant of impotent and supreme
lucidity.

For the first time I began to feel that it was possible that my mother
might live without me, otherwise than for me, a separate life. She was
going to stay with my father, whose existence it may have seemed to her
that my feeble health, my nervous excitability complicated somewhat and
saddened. This separation made me all the more wretched because I told
myself that it probably marked for my mother an end of the successive
disappointments which I had caused her, of which she had never said a
word to me but which had made her realise the difficulty of our taking
our holidays together; and perhaps also the first trial of a form of existence to which she was beginning, now, to resign herself for the future, as
the years crept on for my father and herself, an existence in which I should
see less of her, in which (a thing that not even in my nightmares had yet

been revealed to me) she would already have become something of a stranger, a lady who might be seen going home by herself to a house in which I should not be, asking the porter whether there was not a letter for her from me.

I could scarcely answer the man in the station who offered to take my bag. My mother, to comfort me, tried the methods which seemed to her most efficacious. Thinking it to be useless to appear not to notice my unhappiness, she gently teased me about it:

"Well, and what would Balbec church say if it knew that people pulled long faces like that when they were going to see it? Surely this is not the enraptured tourist Ruskin speaks of. Besides, I shall know if you rise to the occasion, even when we are miles apart I shall still be with my little man. You shall have a letter to-morrow from Mamma."

"My dear," said my grandmother, "I picture you like Mme. de Sévigné, your eyes glued to the map, and never losing sight of us for an instant."

Then Mamma sought to distract my mind, asked me what I thought of having for dinner, drew my attention to Françoise, complimented her on a hat and cloak which she did not recognise, in spite of their having horrified her long ago when she first saw them, new, upon my great-aunt, one with an immense bird towering over it, the other decorated with a hideous pattern and jet beads. But the cloak having grown too shabby to wear, Françoise had had it turned, exposing an 'inside' of plain cloth and quite a good colour. As for the bird, it had long since come to grief and been thrown away. And just as it is disturbing, sometimes, to find the effects which the most conscious artists attain only by an effort occurring in a folk-song, on the wall of some peasant's cottage where above the door, at the precisely right spot in the composition, blooms a white or yellow rose—so the velvet band, the loop of ribbon which would have delighted one in a portrait by Chardin or Whistler, Françoise had set with a simple but unerring taste upon the hat, which was now charming.

To take a parallel from an earlier age, the modesty and integrity which often gave an air of nobility to the face of our old servant having spread also to the garments which, as a woman reserved but not humbled, who knew how to hold her own and to keep her place, she had put on for the journey so as to be fit to be seen in our company without at the same time seeming or wishing to make herself conspicuous,—Françoise in the cherry-coloured cloth, now faded, of her cloak, and the discreet nap of her fur collar, brought to mind one of those miniatures of Anne of Brittany painted in Books of Hours by an old master, in which everything is so exactly in the right place, the sense of the whole is so evenly distributed throughout the parts that the rich and obsolete singularity of the costume expresses the same pious gravity as the eyes, lips and hands.

Of thought, in relation to Françoise, one could hardly speak. She knew nothing, in that absolute sense in which to know nothing means to understand nothing, save the rare truths to which the heart is capable of directly attaining. The vast world of ideas existed not for her. But when one studied the clearness of her gaze, the lines of nose and lips, all those signs lacking from so many people of culture in whom they would else have signified a supreme distinction, the noble detachment of a chosen spirit, one was disquieted, as one is by the frank, intelligent eyes of a dog, to which, nevertheless, one knows that all our human concepts must be alien, and was led to ask oneself whether there might not be, among those other humble brethren, our peasant countrymen, creatures who were, like the great ones of the earth, of simple mind, or rather, doomed by a harsh fate to live among the simple-minded, deprived of heavenly light, were yet more naturally, more instinctively akin to the chosen spirits than most educated people, were, so to speak, all members, though scattered, straying, robbed of their heritage of reason, of the celestial family, kinsfolk, that have been lost in infancy, of the loftiest minds to whom—as is apparent from the unmistakable light in their eyes, although they can concentrate that light on nothing—there has been lacking, to endow them with talent, knowledge only.

My mother, seeing that I had difficulty in keeping back my tears, said to me: "'Regulus was in the habit, when things looked grave. . . .' Besides, it isn't nice for Mamma! What does Mme. de Sévigné say? Your grandmother will tell you: 'I shall be obliged to draw upon all the courage that you lack.'" And remembering that affection for another distracts one's selfish griefs, she endeavoured to beguile me by telling me that she expected the removal to Saint-Cloud to go without a hitch, that she liked the cab, which she had kept waiting, that the driver seemed civil and the seats comfortable. I made an effort to smile at these trifles, and bowed my head with an air of acquiescence and satisfaction. But they helped me only to depict to myself with more accuracy Mamma's imminent departure, and it was with an agonised heart that I gazed at her as though she were already torn from me, beneath that wide-brimmed straw hat which she had bought to wear in the country, in a flimsy dress which she had put on in view of the long drive through the sweltering midday heat; hat and dress making her some one else, some one who belonged already to the Villa Montretout, in which I should not see her.

To prevent the choking fits which the journey might otherwise give me the doctor had advised me to take, as we started, a good stiff dose of beer or brandy, so as to begin the journey in a state of what he called 'euphoria,' in which the nervous system is for a time less vulnerable. I had not yet made up my mind whether I should do this, but I wished at least that my grandmother should admit that, if I did so decide, I should have wisdom and authority on my side. I spoke therefore as if my hesitation were concerned only with where I should go for my drink, to the bar on the platform or to the restaurant-car on the train. But immediately, at the air of reproach which my grandmother's face assumed, an air of not wishing even to entertain such an idea for a moment, "What!" I said to myself, suddenly determining upon this action of going out to drink, the performance of which became necessary as a proof of my independence since the verbal announcement of it had not succeeded in passing unchallenged, "What! You know how ill I am, you know what the doctor ordered, and you treat me like this!"

When I had explained to my grandmother how unwell I felt, her distress, her kindness were so apparent as she replied, "Run along then, quickly; get yourself some beer or a liqueur if it will do you any good," that I flung myself upon her, almost smothering her in kisses. And if after that I went and drank a great deal too much in the restaurant-car of the train, that was because I felt that otherwise I should have a more violent attack than usual, which was just what would vex her most. When at the first stop I clambered back into our compartment I told my grandmother how pleased I was to be going to Balbec, that I felt that everything would go off splendidly, that after all I should soon grow used to being without Mamma, that the train was most comfortable, the steward and attendants in the bar so friendly that I should like to make the journey often so as to have opportunities of seeing them again. My grandmother, however, did not appear to feel the same joy as myself at all these good tidings. She answered, without looking me in the face:

"Why don't you try to get a little sleep?" and turned her gaze to the window, the blind of which, though we had drawn it, did not completely cover the glass, so that the sun could and did slip in over the polished oak of the door and the cloth of the seat (like an advertisement of a life shared with nature far more persuasive than those posted higher upon the walls of the compartment, by the railway company, representing places in the country the names of which I could not make out from where I sat) the same warm and slumberous light which lies along a forest glade.

But when my grandmother thought that my eyes were shut I could see her, now and again, from among the large black spots on her veil, steal a glance at me, then withdraw it, and steal back again, like a person trying to make himself, so as to get into the habit, perform some exercise that hurts him.

Thereupon I spoke to her, but that seemed not to please her either. And yet to myself the sound of my own voice was pleasant, as were the most imperceptible, the most internal movements of my body. And so I endeavoured to prolong it. I allowed each of my inflexions to hang lazily upon its word, I felt each glance from my eyes arrive just at the spot to which it was directed and stay there beyond the normal period. "Now, now, sit still and rest," said my grandmother. "If you can't manage to sleep, read something." And she handed me a volume of Madame de Sévigné which I opened, while she buried herself in the *Mémoires de Madame de Beausergent*. She never travelled anywhere without a volume of each. They were her two favourite authors. With no conscious movement of my head, feeling a keen pleasure in maintaining a posture after I had adopted it, I lay back holding in my hands the volume of Madame de Sévigné which I had allowed to close, without lowering my eyes to it, or indeed letting them see anything but the blue window-blind. But the contemplation of this blind appeared to me an admirable thing, and I should not have troubled to answer anyone who might have sought to distract me from contemplating it. The blue colour of this blind seemed to me, not perhaps by its beauty but by its intense vivacity, to efface so completely all the colours that had passed before my eyes from the day of my birth up to the moment in which I had gulped down the last of my drink and it had begun to take effect, that when compared with this blue they were as drab, as void as must be retrospectively the darkness in which he has lived to a man born blind whom a subsequent operation has at length enabled to see and to distinguish colours. An old ticket-collector came to ask for our tickets. The silvery gleam that shone from the metal buttons of his jacket charmed me in spite of my absorption. I wanted to ask him to sit down beside us. But he passed on to the next carriage, and I thought with longing of the life led by railwaymen for whom, since they spent all their time on the line, hardly a day could pass without their seeing this old collector. The pleasure that I found in staring at the blind, and in feeling that my mouth was half-open, began at length to diminish. I became more mobile; I even moved in my seat; I opened the book that my grandmother had given me and turned its pages casually, reading whatever caught my eye. And as I read I felt my admiration for Madame de Sévigné grow.

It is a mistake to let oneself be taken in by the purely formal details, idioms of the period or social conventions, the effect of which is that certain people believe that they have caught the Sévigné manner when they have said: "Tell me, my dear," or "That Count struck me as being a man of parts," or "Haymaking is the sweetest thing in the world." Mme. de Simiane imagines already that she is being like her grandmother because she can write: "M. de la Boulie is bearing wonderfully, Sir, and is in excellent condition to hear the news of his death," or "Oh, my dear Marquis, how your letter enchanted me! What can I do but answer it?" or "Meseems, Sir, that you owe me a letter, and I owe you some boxes of bergamot. I discharge my debt to the number of eight; others shall follow. . . . Never has the soil borne so many. Apparently for your gratification." And she writes in this style also her letter on bleeding, on lemons and so forth, supposing it to be typical of the letters of Madame de Sévigné. But my grandmother who had approached that lady from within, attracted to her by her own love of kinsfolk and of nature, had taught me to enjoy the real beauties of her correspondence, which are altogether different. They were presently to strike me all the more forcibly inasmuch as Madame de Sévigné is a great artist of the same school as a painter whom I was to meet at Balbec, where his influence on my way of seeing things was immense. I realised at Balbec that it was in the same way as he that she presented things to her readers, in the order of our perception of them, instead of first having to explain them in relation to their several causes. But already that afternoon in the railway carriage, as I read over again that letter in which the moonlight comes: "I cannot resist the temptation: I put on all my bonnets and veils, though there is no need of them, I walk along this mall, where the air is as sweet as in my chamber; I find a thousand phantasms, monks white and black, sisters grey and white, linen cast here and there on the ground, men enshrouded upright against the tree-trunks," I was enraptured by what, a little later, I should have described (for does not she draw landscapes in the same way as he draws characters?) as the Dostoievsky side of Madame de Sévigné's Letters.

When, that evening, after having accompanied my grandmother to her

destination and spent some hours in her friend's house, I had returned by
myself to the train, at any rate I found nothing to distress me in the
night which followed; this was because I had not to spend it in a room
the somnolence of which would have kept me awake; I was surrounded by
the soothing activity of all those movements of the train which kept me
company, offered to stay and converse with me if I could not sleep, lulled
me with their sounds which I wedded—as I had often wedded the chime
of the Combray bells—now to one rhythm, now to another (hearing as
the whim took me first four level and equivalent semi-quavers, then one
semi-quaver furiously dashing against a crotchet); they neutralised the
centrifugal force of my insomnia by exercising upon it a contrary pressure
which kept me in equilibrium and on which my immobility and presently
my drowsiness felt themselves to be borne with the same sense of refreshment that I should have had, had I been resting under the protecting
vigilance of powerful forces, on the breast of nature and of life, had I
been able for a moment to incarnate myself in a fish that sleeps in the
sea, driven unheeding by the currents and the tides, or in an eagle outstretched upon the air, with no support but the storm.

Sunrise is a necessary concomitant of long railway journeys, just as are
hard-boiled eggs, illustrated papers, packs of cards, rivers upon which
boats strain but make no progress. At a certain moment, when I was
counting over the thoughts that had filled my mind, in the preceding minutes, so as to discover whether I had just been asleep or not (and when
the very uncertainty which made me ask myself the question was to furnish me with an affirmative answer), in the pale square of the window,
over a small black wood I saw some ragged clouds whose fleecy edges were
of a fixed, dead pink, not liable to change, like the colour that dyes the
wing which has grown to wear it, or the sketch upon which the artist's
fancy has washed it. But I felt that, unlike them, this colour was due
neither to inertia nor to caprice but to necessity and life. Presently there
gathered behind it reserves of light. It brightened; the sky turned to a
crimson which I strove, gluing my eyes to the window, to see more
clearly, for I felt that it was related somehow to the most intimate life of
Nature, but, the course of the line altering, the train turned, the morning
scene gave place in the frame of the window to a nocturnal village, its
roofs still blue with moonlight, its pond encrusted with the opalescent nacre
of night, beneath a firmament still powdered with all its stars, and I was
lamenting the loss of my strip of pink sky when I caught sight of it afresh,
but red this time, in the opposite window which it left at a second bend in
the line, so that I spent my time running from one window to the other
to reassemble, to collect on a single canvas the intermittent, antipodean
fragments of my fine, scarlet, ever-changing morning, and to obtain a comprehensive view of it and a continuous picture.

The scenery became broken, abrupt, the train stopped at a little station
between two mountains. Far down the gorge, on the edge of a hurrying
stream, one could see only a solitary watch-house, deep-planted in the
water which ran past on a level with its windows. If a person can be the
product of a soil the peculiar charm of which one distinguishes in that

person, more even than the peasant girl whom I had so desperately longed
to see appear when I wandered by myself along the Méséglise way, in
the woods of Roussainville, such a person must be the big girl whom I
now saw emerge from the house and, climbing a path lighted by the first
slanting rays of the sun, come towards the station carrying a jar of milk.
In her valley from which its congregated summits hid the rest of the
world, she could never see anyone save in these trains which stopped for
a moment only. She passed down the line of windows, offering coffee and
milk to a few awakened passengers. Purpled with the glow of morning,
her face was rosier than the sky. I felt in her presence that desire to live
which is reborn in us whenever we become conscious anew of beauty and
of happiness. We invariably forget that these are individual qualities,
and, substituting for them in our mind a conventional type at which we
arrive by striking a sort of mean amongst the different faces that have
taken our fancy, the pleasures we have known, we are left with mere
abstract images which are lifeless and dull because they are lacking in
precisely that element of novelty, different from anything we have known,
that element which is proper to beauty and to happiness. And we deliver
on life a pessimistic judgment which we suppose to be fair, for we believed
that we were taking into account when we formed it happiness and beauty,
whereas in fact we left them out and replaced them by syntheses in which
there is not a single atom of either. So it is that a well-read man will at
once begin to yawn with boredom when anyone speaks to him of a new
'good book,' because he imagines a sort of composite of all the good books
that he has read and knows already, whereas a good book is something
special, something incalculable, and is made up not of the sum of all
previous masterpieces but of something which the most thorough assimilation of every one of them would not enable him to discover, since it
exists not in their sum but beyond it. Once he has become acquainted with
this new work, the well-read man, till then apathetic, feels his interest
awaken in the reality which it depicts. So, alien to the models of beauty
which my fancy was wont to sketch when I was by myself, this strapping
girl gave me at once the sensation of a certain happiness (the sole form,
always different, in which we may learn the sensation of happiness), of
a happiness that would be realised by my staying and living there by her
side. But in this again the temporary cessation of Habit played a great
part. I was giving the milk-girl the benefit of what was really my own
entire being, ready to taste the keenest joys, which now confronted her.
As a rule it is with our being reduced to a minimum that we live, most
of our faculties lie dormant because they can rely upon Habit, which
knows what there is to be done and has no need of their services. But on
this morning of travel, the interruption of the routine of my existence, the
change of place and time, had made their presence indispensable. My
habits, which were sedentary and not matutinal, played me false, and
all my faculties came hurrying to take their place, vying with one another in their zeal, rising, each of them, like waves in a storm, to the same
unaccustomed level, from the basest to the most exalted, from breath,
appetite, the circulation of my blood to receptivity and imagination. I

cannot say whether, so as to make me believe that this girl was unlike the rest of women, the rugged charm of these barren tracts had been added to her own, but if so she gave it back to them. Life would have seemed an exquisite thing to me if only I had been free to spend it, hour after hour, with her, to go with her to the stream, to the cow, to the train, to be always at her side, to feel that I was known to her, had my place in her thoughts. She would have initiated me 'into the delights of country life and of the first hours of the day. I signalled to her to give me some of her coffee. I felt that I must be noticed by her. She did not see me; I called to her. Above her body, which was of massive build, the complexion of her face was so burnished and so ruddy that she appeared almost as though I were looking at her through a lighted window. She had turned and was coming towards me; I could not take my eyes from her face which grew larger as she approached, like a sun which it was somehow possible to arrest in its course and draw towards one, letting itself be seen at close quarters, blinding the eyes with its blaze of red and gold. She fastened on me her penetrating stare, but while the porters ran along the platform shutting doors the train had begun to move. I saw her leave the station and go down the hill to her home; it was broad daylight now; I was speeding away from the dawn. Whether my exaltation had been produced by this girl or had on the other hand been responsible for most of the pleasure that I had found in the sight of her, in the sense of her presence, in either event she was so closely associated with it that my desire to see her again was really not so much a physical as a mental desire, not to allow this state of enthusiasm to perish utterly, not to be separated for ever from the person who, although quite unconsciously, had participated in it. It was not only because this state was a pleasant one. It was principally because (just as increased tension upon a cord or accelerated vibration of a nerve produces a different sound or colour) it gave another tonality to all that I saw, introduced me as an actor upon the stage of an unknown and infinitely more interesting universe; that handsome girl whom I still could see, while the train gathered speed, was like part of a life other than the life that I knew, separated from it by a clear boundary, in which the sensations that things produced in me were no longer the same, from which to return now to my old life would be almost suicide. To procure myself the pleasure of feeling that I had at least an attachment to this new life, it would suffice that I should live near enough to the little station to be able to come to it every morning for a cup of coffee from the girl. But alas, she must be for ever absent from the other life towards which I was being borne with ever increasing swiftness, a life to the prospect of which I resigned myself only by weaving plans that would enable me to take the same train again some day and to stop at the same station, a project which would have the further advantage of providing with subject matter the selfish, active, practical, mechanical, indolent, centrifugal tendency which is that of the human mind; for our mind turns readily aside from the effort which is required if it is to analyse in itself, in a general and disinterested manner, a pleasant impression which we have received. And as, on the other hand, we wish to continue to think of that impression, the mind prefers to imagine it in the future tense, which while it gives us no clue as to the real nature of the thing, saves us the trouble of recreating it in our own consciousness and allows us to hope that we may receive it afresh from without.

Certain names of towns, Vezelay or Chartres, Bourges or Beauvais, serve to indicate, by abbreviation, the principal church in those towns. This partial acceptation, in which we are so accustomed to take the word, comes at length—if the names in question are those of places that we do not yet know—to fashion for us a mould of the name as a solid whole, which from that time onwards, whenever we wish it to convey the idea of the town—of that town which we have never seen—will impose on it, as on a cast, the same carved outlines, in the same style of art, will make of the town a sort of vast cathedral. It was, nevertheless, in a railway-station, above the door of a refreshment-room, that I read the name—almost Persian in style—of Balbec. I strode buoyantly through the station and across the avenue that led past it, I asked my way to the beach so as to see nothing in the place but its church and the sea; people seemed not to understand what I meant. Old Balbec, Balbec-en-Terre, at which I had arrived, had neither beach nor harbour. It was, most certainly, in the sea that the fishermen had found, according to the legend, the miraculous Christ, of which a window in the church that stood a few yards from where I now was recorded the discovery; it was indeed from cliffs battered by the waves that had been quarried the stone of its nave and towers. But this sea, which for those reasons I had imagined as flowing up to die at the foot of the window, was twelve miles away and more, at Balbec-Plage, and, rising beside its cupola, that steeple, which, because I had read that it was itself a rugged Norman cliff on which seeds were blown and sprouted, round which the sea-birds wheeled, I had always pictured to myself as receiving at its base the last drying foam of the uplifted waves, stood on a Square from which two lines of tramway diverged, opposite a Café which bore, written in letters of gold, the word 'Billiards'; it stood out against a background of houses with the roofs of which no upstanding mast was blended. And the church—entering my mind with the Café, with the passing stranger of whom I had had to ask my way, with the station to which presently I should have to return—made part of the general whole, seemed an accident, a by-product of this summer afternoon, in which its mellow and distended dome against the sky was like a fruit of which the same light that bathed the chimneys of the houses was ripening the skin, pink, glowing, melting-soft. But I wished only to consider the eternal significance of the carvings when I recognised the Apostles, which I had seen in casts in the Trocadéro museum, and which on either side of the Virgin, before the deep bay of the porch, were awaiting me as though to do me reverence. With their benign, blunt, mild faces and bowed shoulders they seemed to be advancing upon me with an air of welcome, singing the Alleluia of a fine day. But it was evident that their expression was unchanging as that on a dead man's face, and could be modified only by my turning about to look at them in different aspects. I said to myself: "Here I am: this is the Church of Balbec. This square, which looks as though it were conscious of its glory, is the only place in the world that possesses Balbec Church. All that I have seen so far have been photographs of this church—and of these famous Apostles, this Virgin of the Porch, mere casts only. Now it is the church itself, the statue itself; these are they; they, the unique things—this is something far greater."

It was something less, perhaps, also. As a young man on the day of an examination or of a duel feels the question that he has been asked, the shot that he has fired, to be a very little thing when he thinks of the reserves of knowledge and of valour that he possesses and would like to have displayed, so my mind, which had exalted the Virgin of the Porch far above the reproductions that I had had before my eyes, inaccessible by the vicissitudes which had power to threaten them, intact although they were destroyed, ideal, endowed with universal value, was astonished to see the statue which it had carved a thousand times, reduced now to its own apparent form in stone, occupying, on the radius of my outstretched arm, a place in which it had for rivals an election placard and the point of my stick, fettered to the Square, inseparable from the head of the main street, powerless to hide from the gaze of the Café and of the omnibus office, receiving on its face half of that ray of the setting sun (half, presently, in a few hours' time, of the light of the street lamp) of which the Bank building received the other half, tainted simultaneously with that branch office of a money-lending establishment by the smells from the pastry-cook's oven, subjected to the tyranny of the Individual to such a point that, if I had chosen to scribble my name upon that stone, it was she, the illustrious Virgin whom until then I had endowed with a general existence and an intangible beauty, the Virgin of Balbec, the unique (which meant, alas, the only one) who, on her body coated with the same soot as defiled the neighbouring houses, would have displayed—powerless to rid herself of them—to all the admiring strangers come there to gaze upon her, the marks of my piece of chalk and the letters of my name; it was she, indeed, the immortal work of art, so long desired, whom I found, transformed, as was the church itself, into a little old woman in stone whose height I could measure and count her wrinkles. But time was passing; I must return to the station, where I was to wait for my grandmother and Françoise, so that we should all arrive at Balbec-Plage together. I reminded myself of what I had read about Balbec, of Swann's saying: "It is exquisite; as fine as Siena." And casting the blame for my disappointment upon various accidental causes, such as the state of my health, my exhaustion after the journey, my incapacity for looking at things properly, I endeavoured to console myself with the thought that other towns remained still intact for me, that I might soon, perhaps, be making my way, as into a shower of pearls, into the cool pattering sound that dripped from Quimperlé, cross that green water lit by a rosy glow in which Pont-Aven was bathed; but as for Balbec, no sooner had I set foot in it than it was as though I had broken open a name which ought to have been kept hermetically closed, and into which, seizing at once the opportunity that I had imprudently given them when I expelled all the images that had been living in it until then, a tramway, a Café, people crossing the square, the local branch of a Bank, irresistibly propelled by some external pressure, by a pneumatic force, had come crowding into the interior of those two syllables which, closing over them, let them now serve as a border to the porch of the Persian church, and would never henceforward cease to contain them.

In the little train of the local railway company which was to take us to Balbec-Plage I found my grandmother, but found her alone—for, imagining that she was sending Françoise on ahead of her, so as to have everything ready before we arrived, but having mixed up her instructions, she had succeeded only in packing off Françoise in the wrong direction, who at that moment was being carried down all unsuspectingly, at full speed, to Nantes, and would probably wake up next morning at Bordeaux. No sooner had I taken my seat in the carriage, filled with the fleeting light of sunset and with the lingering heat of the afternoon (the former enabling me, alas, to see written clearly upon my grandmother's face how much the latter had tired her), than she began: "Well, and Balbec?" with a smile so brightly illuminated by her expectation of the great pleasure which she supposed me to have been enjoying that I dared not at once confess to her my disappointment. Besides, the impression which my mind had been seeking occupied it steadily less as the place drew nearer to which my body would have to become accustomed. At the end—still more than an hour away—of this journey I was trying to form a picture of the manager of the hotel at Balbec, to whom I, at that moment, did not exist, and I should have liked to be going to present myself to him in more impressive company than that of my grandmother, who would be certain to ask for a reduction of his terms. The only thing positive about him was his haughty condescension; his lineaments were still vague.

Every few minutes the little train brought us to a standstill in one of the stations which came before Balbec-Plage, stations the mere names of which (Incarville, Marcouville, Doville, Pont-à-Couleuvre, Arambouville, Saint-Mars-le-Vieux, Hermonville, Maineville) seemed to me outlandish, whereas if I had come upon them in a book I should at once have been struck by their affinity to the names of certain places in the neighbourhood of Combray. But to the trained ear two musical airs, consisting each of so many notes, several of which are common to them both, will present no similarity whatever if they differ in the colour of their harmony and orchestration. So it was that nothing could have reminded me less than these dreary names, made up of sand, of space too airy and empty and of salt, out of which the termination 'ville' always escaped, as the 'fly' seems to spring out from the end of the word 'butterfly'—nothing could have reminded me less of those other names, Roussainville or Martinville, which, because I had heard them pronounced so often by my great-aunt at table, in the dining-room, had acquired a certain sombre charm in which were blended perhaps extracts of the flavour of 'preserves,' the smell of the fire of logs and of the pages of one of Bergotte's books, the colour of the stony front of the house opposite, all of which things still to-day when they rise like a gaseous bubble from the depths of my memory preserve their own specific virtue through all the successive layers of rival interests which must be traversed before they reach the surface.

These were—commanding the distant sea from the crests of their several dunes or folding themselves already for the night beneath hills of a crude green colour and uncomfortable shape, like that of the sofa in one's bedroom in an hotel at which one has just arrived, each composed of a cluster of villas whose line was extended to include a lawn-tennis court and now and then a casino, over which a flag would be snapping in the freshening breeze, like a hollow cough—a series of watering-places which now let me see for the first time their regular visitors, but let me see only the external features of those visitors—lawn-tennis players in white hats, the station-master spending all his life there on the spot among his tamarisks and roses, a lady in a straw 'boater' who, following the everyday routine of an existence which I should never know, was calling to her dog which had stopped to examine something in the road before going in to her bungalow where the lamp was already lighted for her return—which with these strangely usual and slightingly familiar sights stung my ungreeted eyes and stabbed my exiled heart. But how much were my sufferings increased when we had finally landed in the hall of the Grand Hotel at Balbec, and I stood there in front of the monumental staircase that looked like marble, while my grandmother, regardless of the growing hostility of the strangers among whom we should have to live, discussed 'terms' with the manager, a sort of nodding mandarin whose face and voice were alike covered with scars (left by the excision of countless pustules from one and from the other of the divers accents acquired from an alien ancestry and in a cosmopolitan upbringing) who stood there in a smart dinner-jacket, with the air of an expert psychologist, classifying, whenever the 'omnibus' discharged a fresh load, the 'nobility and gentry' as 'geesers' and the 'hotel crooks' as nobility and gentry. Forgetting, probably, that he himself was not drawing five hundred francs a month, he had a profound contempt for people to whom five hundred francs—or, as he preferred to put it, 'twenty-five louis' was 'a lot of money,' and regarded them as belonging to a race of pariahs for whom the Grand Hotel was certainly not intended. It is true that even within its walls there were people who did not pay very much and yet had not forfeited the manager's esteem, provided that he was assured that they were watching their expenditure not from poverty so much as from avarice. For this could in no way lower their standing since it is a vice and may consequently be found at every grade of social position. Social position was the one thing by which the manager was impressed, social position, or rather the signs which seemed to him to imply that it was exalted, such as not taking one's hat off when one came into the hall, wearing knickerbockers, or an overcoat with a waist, and taking a cigar with a band of purple and gold out of a crushed morocco case—to none of which advantages could I, alas, lay claim. He would also adorn his business conversation with choice expressions, to which, as a rule, he gave a wrong meaning.

While I heard my grandmother, who shewed no sign of annoyance at his listening to her with his hat on his head and whistling through his teeth at her, ask him in an artificial voice, "And what are . . . your charges? . . . Oh! far too high for my little budget," waiting upon a bench, I sought refuge in the innermost depths of my own consciousness, strove to migrate to a plane of eternal thoughts—to leave nothing of myself, nothing that lived and felt on the surface of my body, anaesthetised as are those of animals which by inhibition feign death when they are attacked—so as not to suffer too keenly in this place, with which my total unfamiliarity was made all the more evident to me when I saw the familiarity that seemed at the same moment to be enjoyed by a smartly dressed lady for whom the manager shewed his respect by taking liberties with the little dog that followed her across the hall, the young 'blood' with a feather in his hat who asked, as he came in, 'Any letters?'—all these people to whom it was an act of home-coming to mount those stairs of imitation marble. And at the same time the triple frown of Minos, Æacus and Rhadamanthus (beneath which I plunged my naked soul as into an unknown element where there was nothing now to protect it) was bent sternly upon me by a group of gentlemen who, though little versed perhaps in the art of receiving, yet bore the title 'Reception Clerks,' while beyond them again, through a closed wall of glass, were people sitting in a reading-room for the description of which I should have had to borrow from Dante alternately the colours in which he paints Paradise and Hell, according as I was thinking of the happiness of the elect who had the right to sit and read there undisturbed, or of the terror which my grandmother would have inspired in me if, in her insensibility to this sort of impression, she had asked me to go in there and wait for her by myself.

My sense of loneliness was further increased a moment later: when I had confessed to my grandmother that I did not feel well, that I thought that we should be obliged to return to Paris, she had offered no protest, saying merely that she was going out to buy a few things which would be equally useful whether we left or stayed (and which, I afterwards learned, were all for my benefit, Françoise having gone off with certain articles which I might need); while I waited for her I had taken a turn through the streets, packed with a crowd of people who imparted to them a sort of indoor warmth, streets in which were still open the hairdresser's shop and the pastry-cook's, the latter filled with customers eating ices, opposite the statue of Duguay-Trouin. This crowd gave me just about as much pleasure as a photograph of it in one of the 'illustrateds' might give a patient who was turning its pages in the surgeon's waiting-room. I was astonished to find that there were people so different from myself that this stroll through the town had actually been recommended to me by the manager as a distraction, and also that the torture chamber which a new place of residence is could appear to some people a 'continuous amusement,' to quote the hotel prospectus, which might, it was true, exaggerate, but was, for all that, addressed to a whole army of clients to whose tastes it must appeal. True, it invoked, to make them come to the Grand Hotel, Balbec, not only the 'exquisite fare' and the 'fairy-like view across the Casino gardens,' but also the 'ordinances of her Majesty Queen Fashion, which no one may break with impunity, or without being taken for a Bœotian, a charge that no well-bred man would willingly incur.' The need that I now had of my grandmother was enhanced by my fear that I had shattered another of her illusions. She must be feeling discouraged, feeling that if I could not stand the fatigue of this journey there was no hope that any change of air could ever do me good. I decided to return to the hotel and to wait for her there: the manager himself came forward and pressed a button, and a person whose acquaintance I had not yet made, labelled 'LIFT' (who at that highest point in the building, which corresponded to the lantern in a Norman church, was installed like a photographer in his darkroom or an organist in his loft) came rushing down towards me with the agility of a squirrel, tamed, active, caged. Then, sliding upwards again along a steel pillar, he bore me aloft in his train towards the dome of this temple of Mammon. On each floor, on either side of a narrow communicating stair, opened out fanwise a range of shadowy galleries, along one of which, carrying a bolster, a chambermaid came past. I lent to her face, which the gathering dusk made featureless, the mask of my most impassioned dreams of beauty, but read in her eyes as they turned towards me the horror of my own nonentity. Meanwhile, to dissi-. pate, in the course of this interminable assent, the mortal anguish which I felt in penetrating thus in silence the mystery of this chiaroscuro so devoid of poetry, lighted by a single vertical line of little windows which were those of the solitary water-closet on each landing, I addressed a few words to the young organist, artificer of my journey and my partner in captivity, who continued to manipulate the registers of his instrument and to finger the stops. I apologised for taking up so much room, for giving him so much trouble, and asked whether I was not obstructing him in the practice of an art to which, so as to flatter the performer, I did more than display curiosity, I confessed my strong attachment. But he vouchsafed no answer, whether from astonishment at my words, preoccupation with what he was doing, regard for convention, hardness of hearing, respect for holy ground, fear of danger, slowness of understanding, or by the manager's orders.

There is perhaps nothing that gives us so strong an impression of the reality of the external world as the difference in the positions, relative to ourselves, of even a quite unimportant person before we have met him and after. I was the same man who had taken, that afternoon, the little train from Balbec to the coast, I carried in my body the same consciousness But on that consciousness, in the place where, at six o'clock, there had been, with the impossibility of forming any idea of the manager, the Grand Hotel or its occupants, a vague and timorous impatience for the moment at which I should reach my destination, were to be found now the pustules excised from the face of the cosmopolitan manager (he was, as a matter of fact, a naturalised Monegasque, although—as he himself put it, for he was always using expressions which he thought distinguished without noticing that they were incorrect—'of Rumanian originality'), his action in ringing for the lift, the lift-boy himself, a whole frieze of puppet-show characters issuing from that Pandora's box which was the Grand Hotel, undeniable, irremovable, and, like everything that is realised, sterilising.

But at least this change, which I had done nothing to bring about, proved to me that something had happened which was external to myself—however devoid of interest that thing might be—and I was like a traveller who, having had the sun in his face when he started, concludes that he has been for so many hours on the road when he finds the sun behind him. I was half dead with exhaustion, I was burning with fever; I would gladly have gone to bed, but I had no night-things. I should have liked at least to lie down for a little while on the bed, but what good would that have done me, seeing that I should not have been able to find any rest there for that mass of sensations which is for each of us his sentient if not his material body, and that the unfamiliar objects which encircled that body, forcing it to set its perceptions on the permanent footing of a vigilant and defensive guard, would have kept my sight, my hearing, all my senses in a position as cramped and comfortless (even if I had stretched out my legs) as that of Cardinal La Balue in the cage in which he could neither stand nor sit. It is our noticing them that puts things in a room, our growing used to them that takes them away again and clears a space for us. Space there was none for me in my bedroom (mine in name only) at Balbec; it was full of things which did not know me, which flung back at me the distrustful look that I had cast at them, and, without taking any heed of my existence, shewed that I was interrupting the course of theirs. The clock—whereas at home I heard my clock tick only a few seconds in a week, when I was coming out of some profound meditation—continued without a moment's interruption to utter, in an unknown tongue, a series of observations which must have been most uncomplimentary to myself, for the violet curtains listened to them without replying, but in an attitude such as people adopt who shrug their shoulders to indicate that the sight of a third person irritates them. They gave to this room with its lofty ceiling a semi-historical character which might have made it a suitable place for the assassination of the Duc de Guise, and afterwards for parties of tourists personally conducted by one of Messrs. Thomas Cook and Son's guides, but for me to sleep in—no. I was tormented by the presence of some little bookcases with glass fronts which ran along the walls, but especially by a large mirror with feet which stood across one corner, for I felt that until it had left the room there would be no possibility of rest for me there. I kept raising my eyes—which the things in my room in Paris disturbed no more than did my eyelids themselves, for they were merely extensions of my organs, an enlargement of myself—towards the fantastically high ceiling of this belvedere planted upon the summit of the hotel which my grandmother had chosen for me; and in that region more intimate than those in which we see and hear, that region in which we test the quality of odours, almost in the very heart of my inmost self, the smell of flowering grasses next launched its offensive against my last feeble line of trenches, where I stood up to it, not without tiring myself still further, with the futile incessant defence of an anxious sniffing. Having no world, no room, no body now that was not menaced by the enemies thronging round me, invaded to the very bones by fever, I was utterly alone; I longed to die. Then my grandmother came in, and to the expansion of my ebbing heart there opened at once an infinity of space.

She was wearing a loose cambric gown which she put on at home whenever any of us was ill (because she felt more comfortable in it, she used to say, for she always ascribed to her actions a selfish motive), and which was, for tending us, for watching by our beds, her servant's livery, her nurse's uniform, her religious habit. But whereas the trouble that servants, nurses, religious take, their kindness to us, the merits that we discover in them and the gratitude that we owe them all go to increase the impression that we have of being, in their eyes, some one different, of feeling that we are alone, keeping in our own hands the control over our thoughts, our will to live, I knew, when I was with my grandmother, that, however great the misery that there was in me, it would be received by her with a pity still more vast; that everything that was mine, my cares, my wishes, would be, in my grandmother, supported upon a desire to save and prolong my life stronger than was my own; and my thoughts were continued in her without having to undergo any deflection, since they passed from my mind into hers without change of atmosphere or of personality. And— like a man who tries to fasten his necktie in front of a glass and forgets that the end which he sees reflected is not on the side to which he raises his hand, or like a dog that chases along the ground the dancing shadow of an insect in the air—misled by her appearance in the body as we are apt to be in this world where we have no direct perception of people's souls, I threw myself into the arms of my grandmother and clung with my lips to her face as though I had access thus to that immense heart which she opened to me. And when I felt my mouth glued to her cheeks, to her brow, I drew from them something so beneficial, so nourishing that I lay in her arms as motionless, as solemn, as calmly gluttonous as a babe at the breast.

At last I let go, and lay and gazed, and could not tire of gazing at her large face, as clear in its outline as a fine cloud, glowing and serene, behind which I could discern the radiance of her tender love. And everything that received, in however slight a degree, any share of her sensations, everything that could be said to belong in any way to her was at once so spiritualised, so sanctified, that with outstretched hands I smoothed her dear hair, still hardly grey, with as much respect, precaution, comfort as if I had actually been touching her goodness. She found a similar pleasure in taking any trouble that saved me one, and in a moment of immobility and rest for my weary limbs something so delicious that when, having seen that she wished to help me with my undressing and to take my boots off, I made as though to stop her and began to undress myself, with an imploring gaze she arrested my hands as they fumbled with the top buttons of my coat and boots.

"Oh, do let me!" she begged. "It is such a joy for your Granny. And be sure you knock on the wall if you want anything in the night. My bed is just on the other side, and the partition is quite thin. Just give a knock now, as soon as you are ready, so that we shall know where we are."

And, sure enough, that evening I gave three knocks—a signal which, the week after, when I was ill, I repeated every morning for several days, because my grandmother wanted me to have some milk early. Then, when I thought that I could hear her stirring, so that she should not be kept waiting but might, the moment she had brought me the milk, go to sleep again, I ventured on three little taps, timidly, faintly, but for all that distinctly, for if I was afraid of disturbing her, supposing that I had been mistaken and that she was still asleep, I should not have wished her either to lie awake listening for a summons which she had not at once caught and which I should not have the courage to repeat. And scarcely had I given my taps than I heard three others, in a different intonation from mine, stamped with a calm authority, repeated twice over so that there should be no mistake, and saying to me plainly: "Don't get excited; I heard you; I shall be with you in a minute!" and shortly afterwards my grandmother appeared. I explained to her that I had been afraid that she would not hear me, or might think that it was some one in the room beyond who was tapping; at which she smiled:

"Mistake my poor chick's knocking for anyone else! Why, Granny could tell it among a thousand! Do you suppose there's anyone else in the world who's such a silly-billy, with such feverish little knuckles, so afraid of waking me up and of not making me understand? Even if he just gave the least scratch, Granny could tell her mouse's sound at once, especially such a poor miserable little mouse as mine is. I could hear it just now, trying to make up its mind, and rustling the bedclothes, and going through all its tricks."

She pushed open the shutters; where a wing of the hotel jutted out at right angles to my window, the sun was already installed upon the roof, like a slater who is up betimes, and starts early and works quietly so as not to rouse the sleeping town, whose stillness seems to enhance his activity. She told me what o'clock, what sort of day it was; that it was not worth while my getting up and coming to the window, that there was a mist over the sea; if the baker's shop had opened yet; what the vehicle was that I could hear passing. All that brief, trivial curtain-raiser, that negligible *introit* of a new day, performed without any spectator, a little scrap of life which was only for our two selves, which I should have no hesitation in repeating, later on, to Françoise or even to strangers, speaking of the fog 'which you could have cut with a knife" at six o'clock that morning, with the ostentation of one who was boasting not of a piece of knowledge that he had acquired but of a mark of affection shewn to himself alone; dear morning moment, opened like a symphony by the rhythmical dialogue of my three taps, to which the thin wall of my bedroom, steeped in love and joy, grown melodious, immaterial, singing like the angelic choir, responded with three other taps, eagerly awaited, repeated once and again, in which it contrived to waft to me the soul of my grandmother, whole and perfect, and the promise of her coming, with a swiftness of annunciation and melodic accuracy. But on this first night after our arrival, when my grandmother had left me, I began again to feel as I had felt, the day before, in Paris, at the moment of leaving home. Perhaps this fear that I had—and shared with so many of my fellow-men—of sleeping in a strange room, perhaps this fear is only the most humble, obscure, organic, almost unconscious form of that great and desperate resistance set up by the things that constitute the better part of our present life towards our mentally assuming, by accepting it as true, the formula of a future in which those things are to have no part; a resistance which was at the root of the horror that I had so often been made to feel by the thought that my parents must, one day, die, that the stern necessity of life might oblige me to live remote from Gilberte, or simply to settle permanently in a place where I should never see any of my old friends; a resistance which was also at the root of the difficulty that I found in imagining my own death, or a survival such as Bergotte used to promise to mankind in his books, a survival in which I should not be allowed to take with me my memories, my frailties, my character, which did not easily resign themselves to the idea of ceasing to be, and desired for me neither annihilation nor an eternity in which they would have no part.

When Swann had said to me, in Paris one day when I felt particularly unwell: "You ought to go off to one of those glorious islands in the Pacific; you'd never come back again if you did." I should have liked to answer: "But then I shall not see your daughter any more; I shall be living among people and things she has never seen." And yet my better judgment whispered: "What difference can that make, since you are not going to be affected by it? When M. Swann tells you that you will not come back he means by that that you will not want to come back, and if you don't want to that is because you will be happier out there." For my judgment was aware that Habit—Habit which was even now setting to work to make me like this unfamiliar lodging, to change the position of the mirror, the shade of the curtains, to stop the clock—undertakes as well to make dear to us the companions whom at first we disliked, to give another appearance to their faces, to make attractive the sound of their voices, to modify the inclinations of their hearts. It is true that these new friendships for places and people are based upon forgetfulness of the old; but what my better judgment was thinking was simply that I could look without apprehension along the vista of a life in which I should be for ever separated from people all memory of whom I should lose, and it was by way of consolation that my mind was offering to my heart a promise of oblivion which succeeded only in sharpening the edge of its despair. Not that the heart also is not bound in time, when separation is complete, to feel the anodyne effect of habit; but until then it will continue to suffer. And our dread of a future in which we must forego the sight of faces, the sound of voices that we love, friends from whom we derive to-day our keenest joys, this dread, far from being dissipated, is intensified, if to the grief of such a privation we reflect that there will be added what seems to us now in anticipation an even more cruel grief; not to feel it as a grief at all—to remain indifferent; for if that should occur, our ego would have changed, it would then be not merely the attractiveness of our family, our mistress, our friends that had ceased to environ us, but our affection for them; it would have been so completely eradicated from our heart, in which to-day it is a conspicuous element, that we should be able to enjoy that life apart from them the very thought of which to-day makes us recoil in horror; so that it would be in a real sense the death of ourselves, a death followed, it is true, by resurrection but in a different ego, the life, the love of which are beyond the reach of those elements of the existing ego that are doomed to die. It is they—even the meanest of them, such as our obscure attachments to the dimensions, to the atmosphere of a bedroom—that grow stubborn and refuse, in acts of rebellion which we must recognise to be a secret, partial, tangible and true aspect of our resistance to death, of the long resistance, desperate and daily renewed, to a fragmentary and gradual death such as interpolates itself throughout the whole course of our life, tearing away from us at every moment a shred of ourselves, dead matter on which new cells will multiply, and grow. And for a neurotic nature such as mine, one that is to say in which the intermediaries, the nerves, perform their functions badly—fail to arrest on its way to the consciousness, allow indeed to penetrate there, distinct, exhausting, innumerable, agonising, the plaint of those most humble elements of the personality which are about to disappear—the anxiety and alarm which I felt as I lay outstretched beneath that strange and too lofty ceiling were but the protest of an affection that survived in me for a ceiling that was familiar and low. Doubtless this affection too would disappear, and another have taken its place (when death, and then another life, would, in the guise of Habit, have performed their double task); but until its annihilation, every night it would suffer afresh, and on this first night especially, confronted with a future already realised in which there would no longer be any place for it, it rose in revolt, it tortured me with the sharp sound of its lamentations whenever my straining eyes, powerless to turn from what was wounding them, endeavoured to fasten their gaze upon that inaccessible ceiling.

But next morning!—after a servant had come to call me, and had brought me hot water, and while I was washing and dressing myself and trying in vain to find the things that I wanted in my trunk, from which I extracted, pell-mell, only a lot of things that were of no use whatever, what a joy it was to me, thinking already of the delights of luncheon and of a walk along the shore, to see in the window, and in all the glass fronts of the bookcases as in the portholes of a ship's cabin, the open sea, naked, unshadowed, and yet with half of its expanse in shadow, bounded by a thin and fluctuant line, and to follow with my eyes the waves that came leaping towards me, one behind another, like divers along a springboard. Every other moment, holding in one hand the starched, unyielding towel, with the name of the hotel printed upon it, with which I was making futile efforts to dry myself, I returned to the window to gaze once more upon that vast amphitheatre, dazzling, mountainous, and upon the snowy crests of its emerald waves, here and there polished and translucent, which with a placid violence, a leonine bending of the brows, let their steep fronts, to which the sun now added a smile without face or features, run forward to their goal, totter and melt and be no more. Window in which I was, henceforward, to plant myself every morning, as at the pane of a mail coach in which one has slept, to see whether, in the night, a long sought

mountain-chain has come nearer or withdrawn—only here it was those
hills of the sea which, before they come dancing back towards us, are apt
to retire so far that often it was only at the end of a long and sandy plain
that I would distinguish, miles it seemed away, their first undulations
upon a background transparent, vaporous, bluish, like the glaciers that one
sees in the backgrounds of the Tuscan Primitives. On other mornings it
was quite close at hand that the sun was smiling upon those waters of a
green as tender as that preserved in Alpine pastures (among mountains on
which the sun spreads himself here and there like a lazy giant who may
at any moment come leaping gaily down their craggy sides) less by the
moisture of their soil than by the liquid mobility of their light. Anyhow,
in that breach which shore and water between them drive through all
the rest of the world, for the passage, the accumulation there of light, it is
light above all, according to the direction from which it comes and along
which our eyes follow it, it is light that shifts and fixes the undulations of
the sea. Difference of lighting modifies no less the orientation of a place,
constructs no less before our eyes new goals which it inspires in us the
yearning to attain, than would a distance in space actually traversed in
the course of a long journey. When, in the morning, the sun came from
behind the hotel, disclosing to me the sands bathed in light as far as the
first bastions of the sea, it seemed to be shewing me another side of the
picture, and to be engaging me in the pursuit, along the winding path of
its rays, of a journey motionless but ever varied amid all the fairest scenes
of the diversified landscape of the hours. And on this first morning the
sun pointed out to me far off with a jovial finger those blue peaks of
the sea, which bear no name upon any geographer's chart, until, dizzy with
its sublime excursion over the thundering and chaotic surface of their
crests and avalanches, it came back to take shelter from the wind in my
bedroom, swaggering across the unmade bed and scattering its riches over
the splashed surface of the basin-stand, and into my open trunk, where
by its very splendour and ill-matched luxury it added still further to the
general effect of disorder. Alas, that wind from the sea; an hour later, in
the great dining-room—while we were having our luncheon, and from the
leathern gourd of a lemon were sprinkling a few golden drops on to a pair of
soles which presently left on our plates the plumes of their picked skeletons,
curled like stiff feathers and resonant as citherns,—it seemed to my grandmother a cruel deprivation not to be able to feel its life-giving breath on
her cheek, on account of the window, transparent but closed, which like
the front of a glass case in a museum divided us from the beach while
allowing us to look out upon its whole extent, and into which the sky
entered so completely that its azure had the effect of being the colour of
the windows and its white clouds only so many flaws in the glass. Imagining that I was 'seated upon the mole' or at rest in the 'boudoir' of which
Baudelaire speaks I asked myself whether his 'Sun's rays upon the sea'
were not—a very different thing from the evening ray, simple and superficial as the wavering stroke of a golden pencil—just what at that moment
was scorching the sea topaz-brown, fermenting it, turning it pale and
milky like foaming beer, like milk, while now and then there hovered over

it great blue shadows which some god seemed, for his pastime, to be shifting to and fro by moving a mirror in the sky. Unfortunately, it was not only in its outlook that it differed from our room at Combray, giving upon the houses over the way, this dining-room at Balbec, bare-walled, filled with a sunlight green as the water in a marble font, while a few feet away the full tide and broad daylight erected as though before the gates of the heavenly city an indestructible and moving rampart of emerald and gold. At Combray, since we were known to everyone, I took heed of no one. In life at the seaside one knows only one's own party. I was not yet old enough, I was still too sensitive to have outgrown the desire to find favour in the sight of other people and to possess their hearts. Nor had I acquired the more noble indifference which a man of the world would have felt, with regard to the people who were eating their luncheon in the room, nor to the boys and girls who strolled past the window, with whom I was pained by the thought that I should never be allowed to go on expeditions, though not so much pained as if my grandmother, contemptuous of social formalities and concerned about nothing but my health, had gone to them with the request, humiliating for me to overhear, that they would consent to let me accompany them. Whether they were returning to some villa beyond my ken, or had emerged from it, racquet in hand, on their way to some lawn-tennis court, or were mounted on horses whose hooves trampled and tore my heart, I gazed at them with a passionate curiosity, in that blinding light of the beach by which social distinctions are altered, I followed all their movements through the transparency of that great bay of glass which allowed so much light to flood the room. But it intercepted the wind, and this seemed wrong to my grandmother, who, unable to endure the thought that I was losing the benefit of an hour in the open air, surreptitiously unlatched a pane and at once set flying, with the bills of fare, the newspapers, veils and hats of all the people at the other tables; she herself, fortified by the breath of heaven, remained calm and smiling like Saint Blandina, amid the torrent of invective which, increasing my sense of isolation and misery, those scornful, dishevelled, furious visitors combined to pour on us.

To a certain extent—and this, at Balbec, gave to the population, as a rule monotonously rich and cosmopolitan, of that sort of smart and 'exclusive' hotel, a quite distinctive local character—they were composed of eminent persons from the departmental capitals of that region of France, a chief magistrate from Caen, a leader of the Cherbourg bar, a big solicitor from Le Mans, who annually, when the holidays came round, starting from the various points over which, throughout the working year, they were scattered like snipers in a battle or draughtsmen upon a board, concentrated their forces upon this hotel. They always reserved the same rooms, and with their wives, who had pretensions to aristocracy, formed a little group, which was joined by a leading barrister and a leading doctor from Paris, who on the day of their departure would say to the others:

"Oh, yes, of course; you don't go by our train. You are fortunate, you will be home in time for luncheon."

"Fortunate, do you say? You, who live in the Capital, in 'Paris, the great town,' while I have to live in a wretched county town of a hundred thousand souls (it is true, we managed to muster a hundred and two thousand at the last census, but what is that compared to your two and a half millions?) going back, too, to asphalt streets and all the bustle and gaiety of Paris life?"

They said this with a rustic burring of their r's, but without bitterness, for they were leading lights each in his own province, who could like other people have gone to Paris had they chosen—the chief magistrate of Caen had several times been offered a judgeship in the Court of Appeal—but had preferred to stay where they were, from love of their native towns or of obscurity or of fame, or because they were reactionaries, and enjoyed being on friendly terms with the country houses of the neighbourhood. Besides several of them were not going back at once to their county towns.

For—inasmuch as the Bay of Balbec was a little world apart in the midst of a great world, a basketful of the seasons in which were clustered in a ring good days and bad, and the months in their order, so that not only, on days when one could make out Rivebelle, which was in itself a sign of coming storms, could one see the sunlight on the houses there while Balbec was plunged in darkness, but later on, when the cold weather had reached Balbec, one could be certain of finding on that opposite shore two or three supplementary months of warmth—those of the regular visitors to the Grand Hotel whose holidays began late or lasted long, gave orders, when rain and fog came and Autumn was in the air, for their boxes to be packed and embarked, and set sail across the Bay to find summer again at Rivebelle or Costedor. This little group in the Balbec hotel looked with distrust upon each new arrival, and while affecting to take not the least interest in him, hastened, all of them, to ply with questions their friend the head waiter. For it was the same head waiter—Aimé—who returned every year for the season, and kept their tables for them; and their good ladies, having heard that his wife was 'expecting,' would sit after meals working each at one of the 'little things,' stopping only to put up their glasses and stare at us, my grandmother and myself, because we were eating hard-boiled eggs in salad, which was considered common, and was, in fact, 'not done' in the best society of Alençon. They affected an attitude of contemptuous irony with regard to a Frenchman who was called 'His Majesty' and had indeed proclaimed himself King of a small island in the South Seas, inhabited by a few savages. He was staying in the hotel with his pretty mistress, whom, as she crossed the beach to bathe, the little boys would greet with "Three cheers for the Queen!" because she would reward them with a shower of small silver. The chief magistrate and the barrister went so far as to pretend not to see her, and if any of their friends happened to look at her, felt bound to warn him that she was only a little shop-girl.

"But I was told that at Ostend they used the royal bathing machine."

"Well, and why not? It's on hire for twenty francs. You can take it yourself, if you care for that sort of thing. Anyhow, I know for a fact that the fellow asked for an audience, when he was there, with the King, who sent back word that he took no cognisance of any Pantomime Princes."

"Really, that's interesting! What queer people there are in the world, to be sure!"

And I dare say it was all quite true: but it was also from resentment of the thought that, to many of their fellow-visitors, they were themselves simply respectable but rather common people who did not know this King and Queen so prodigal with their small change, that the solicitor, the magistrate, the barrister, when what they were pleased to call the 'Carnival' went by, felt so much annoyance, and expressed aloud an indignation that was quite understood by their friend the head waiter who, obliged to shew proper civility to these generous if not authentic Sovereigns, still, while he took their orders, would dart from afar at his old patrons a covert but speaking glance. Perhaps there was also something of the same resentment at being erroneously supposed to be less and unable to explain that they were more smart, underlining the 'fine specimen' with which they qualified a young 'blood,' the consumptive and dissipated son of an industrial magnate, who appeared every day in a new suit of clothes with an orchid in his buttonhole, drank champagne at luncheon, and then strolled out of the hotel, pale, impassive, a smile of complete indifference on his lips, to the casino to throw away at the baccarat table enormous sums, 'which he could ill afford to lose,' as the solicitor said with a resigned air to the chief magistrate, whose wife had it 'on good authority' that this 'detrimental' young man was bringing his parents' grey hair in sorrow to the grave.

On the other hand, the barrister and his friends could not exhaust their flow of sarcasm on the subject of a wealthy old lady of title, because she never moved anywhere without taking her whole household with her. Whenever the wives of the solicitor and the magistrate saw her in the dining-room at meal-times they put up their glasses and gave her an insolent scrutiny, as minute and distrustful as if she had been some dish with a pretentious name but a suspicious appearance which, after the negative result of a systematic study, must be sent away with a lofty wave of the hand and a grimace of disgust.

No doubt by this behaviour they meant only to shew that, if there were things in the world which they themselves lacked—in this instance, certain prerogatives which the old lady enjoyed, and the privilege of her acquaintance—it was not because they could not, but because they did not choose to acquire them. But they had succeeded in convincing themselves that this really was what they felt; and it was the suppression of all desire for, of all curiosity as to forms of life which were unfamiliar, of all hope of pleasing new people (for which, in the women, had been substituted a feigned contempt, an artificial brightness) that had the awkward result of obliging them to label their discontent satisfaction, and lie everlastingly to themselves, for which they were greatly to be pitied. But everyone else in the hotel was no doubt behaving in a similar fashion, though his behaviour might take a different form, and sacrificing, if not to self-importance, at any rate to certain inculcated principles and mental habits the thrilling delight of mixing in a strange kind of life. Of course, the atmosphere of the microcosm in which the old lady isolated herself was not poisoned with virulent bitterness, as was that of the group in which the wives of the solicitor and magistrate sat chattering with impotent rage. It was indeed embalmed with a delicate and old-world fragrance which, however, was none the less artificial. For at heart the old lady would prob- ably have found in attracting, in attaching to herself (and, with that object, recreating herself), the mysterious sympathy of new friends a charm which is altogether lacking from the pleasure that is to be derived from mixing only with the people of one's own world, and reminding oneself that, one's own being the best of all possible worlds, the ill-informed contempt of 'outsiders' may be disregarded. Perhaps she felt that—were she to arrive *incognito* at the Grand Hotel, Balbec, she would, in her black stuff gown and old-fashioned bonnet, bring a smile to the lips of some old reprobate, who from the depths of his rocking chair would glance up and murmur, "What a scarecrow!" or, still worse, to those of some man of repute who had, like the magistrate, kept between his pepper-and-salt whiskers a rosy complexion and a pair of sparkling eyes such as she liked to see, and would at once bring the magnifying lens of the conjugal glasses to bear upon so quaint a phenomenon; and perhaps it was in unconfessed dread of those first few minutes, which, though one knows that they will be but a few minutes, are none the less terrifying, like the first plunge of one's head under water, that this old lady sent down in advance a servant, who would inform the hotel of the personality and habits of his mistress, and, cutting short the manager's greetings, made, with an abruptness in which there was more timidity than pride, for her room, where her own curtains, substi- tuted for those that draped the hotel windows, her own screens and photo- graphs, set up so effectively between her and the outside world, to which otherwise she would have had to adapt herself, the barrier of her private life that it was her home (in which she had comfortably stayed) that trav- elled rather than herself.

Thenceforward, having placed between herself, on the one hand, and the staff of the hotel and its decorators on the other the servants who bore instead of her the shock of contact with all this strange humanity, and kept up around their mistress her familiar atmosphere, having set her prejudices between herself and the other visitors, indifferent whether or not she gave offence to people whom her friends would not have had in their houses, it was in her own world that she continued to live, by correspondence with her friends, by memories, by her intimate sense of and confidence in her own position, the quality of her manners, the competence of her politeness. And every day, when she came downstairs to go for a drive in her own carriage, the lady's-maid who came after her carrying her wraps, the foot- man who preceded her, seemed like sentries who, at the gate of an embassy, flying the flag of the country to which she belonged, assured to her upon foreign soil the privilege of extra-territoriality. She did not leave her room until late in the afternoon on the day following our arrival, so that we did not see her in the dining-room, into which the manager, since we were strangers there, conducted us, taking us under his wing, as a corporal takes a squad of recruits to the master-tailor, to have them fitted; we did see however, a moment later, a country gentleman and his daughter, of an obscure but very ancient Breton family, M. and Mlle. de Stermaria, whose table had been allotted to us, in the belief that they had gone out and would not be back until the evening. Having come to Balbec only .to see various country magnates whom they knew in that neighbourhood, they spent in the hotel dining-room, what with the invitations they accepted and the visits they paid, only such time as was strictly unavoidable. It was their stiffness that preserved them intact from all human sympathy, from interesting at all the strangers seated round about them, among whom M. de Stermaria kept up the glacial, preoccupied, distant, rude, punctilious and distrustful air that we assume in a railway refreshment-room, among fellow-passengers whom we have never seen before and will never see again, and with whom we can conceive of no other relations than to defend from their onslaught our 'portion' of cold chicken and our corner seat in the train. No sooner had we begun our luncheon than we were asked to leave the table, on the instructions of M. de Stermaria who had just arrived and, without the faintest attempt at an apology to us, requested the head waiter, in our hearing, to "see that such a mistake did not occur again," for it was repugnant to him that "people whom he did not know" should have taken his table.

And certainly into the feeling which impelled a young actress (better known, though, for her smart clothes, her smart sayings, her collection of German porcelain, than in the occasional parts that she had played at the Odéon), her lover, an immensely rich young man for whose sake she had acquired her culture, and two sprigs of aristocracy at that time much in the public eye to form a little band apart, to travel only together, to come down to luncheon—when at Balbec—very late, after everyone had finished; to spend the whole day in their sitting-room playing cards, there entered no sort of ill-humour against the rest of us but simply the requirements of the taste that they had formed for a certain type of conversation, for certain refinements of good living, which made them find pleasure in spending their time, in taking their meals only by themselves, and would have rendered intolerable a life in common with people who had not been initiated into those mysteries. Even at a dinner or a card table, each of them had to be certain that, in the diner or partner who sat opposite to him, there was, latent and not yet made use of, a certain brand of knowledge which would enable him to identify the rubbish with which so many houses in Paris were littered as genuine mediaeval or renaissance 'pieces' and, whatever the subject of discussion, to apply the critical standards common to all their party whereby they distinguished good work from bad. Probably it was only—at such moments—by some infrequent, amusing interruption flung into the general silence of meal or game, or by the new and charming frock which the young actress had put on for luncheon or for poker, that the special kind of existence in which these four friends desired, above all things, to remain plunged was made apparent. But by engulfing them thus in a system of habits which they knew by heart it sufficed to protect them from the mystery of the life that was going on all round them. All the long afternoon, the sea was suspended there before their eyes only as a canvas of attractive colouring might hang on the wall of a wealthy bachelor's flat and it was only in the intervals between the 'hands' that one of the players, finding nothing better to do, raised his eyes to it to seek from it some indication of the weather or the time, and to remind the others that tea was ready. And at night they did not dine in the hotel, where, hidden springs of electricity flooding the great dining-room with light, it became as it were an immense and wonderful aquarium against whose wall of glass the working population of Balbec, the fishermen and also the tradesmen's families, clustering invisibly in the outer darkness, pressed their faces to watch, gently floating upon the golden eddies within, the luxurious life of its occupants, a thing as extraordinary to the poor as the life of strange fishes or molluscs (an important social question, this: whether the wall of glass will always protect the wonderful creatures at their feasting, whether the obscure folk who watch them hungrily out of the night will not break in some day to gather them from their aquarium and devour them). Meanwhile there may have been, perhaps, among the gazing crowd, a motionless, formless mass there in the dark, some writer, some student of human ichthyology who, as he watched the jaws of old feminine monstrosities close over a mouthful of food which they proceeded then to absorb, was amusing himself by classifying them according to their race, by their innate characteristics as well as by those acquired characteristics which bring it about that an old Serbian lady whose buccal protuberance is that of a great sea-fish, because from her earliest years she has moved in the fresh waters of the Faubourg Saint-Germain, eats her salad for all the world like a La Rochefoucauld.

At that hour one could see the three young men in dinner-jackets, waiting for the young woman, who was as usual late but presently, wearing a dress that was almost always different and one of a series of scarves, chosen to gratify some special instinct in her lover, after having from her landing rung for the lift, would emerge from it like a doll coming out of its box. And then all four, because they found that the international phenomenon of the 'Palace,' planted on Balbec soil, had blossomed there in material splendour rather than in food that was fit to eat, bundled into a carriage and went to dine, a mile off, in a little restaurant that was well spoken of, where they held with the cook himself endless discussions of the composition of their meal and the cooking of its various dishes. During their drive, the road bordered with apple-trees that led out of Balbec was no more to them than the distance that must be traversed—barely distinguishable in the darkness from that which separated their homes in Paris from the Café Anglais or the Tour d'Argent—before they could arrive at the fashionable little restaurant where, while the young man's friends envied him because he had such a smartly dressed mistress, the latter's scarves were spread about the little company like a fragrant, flowing veil, but one that kept it apart from the outer world.

Alas for my peace of mind, I had none of the detachment that all these people shewed. To many of them I gave constant thought; I should have liked not to pass unobserved by a man with a receding brow and eyes that dodged between the blinkers of his prejudices and his education, the great nobleman of the district, who was none other than the brother-in-law of

Legrandin, and came every now and then to see somebody at Balbec and
on Sundays, by reason of the weekly garden-party that his wife and he
gave, robbed the hotel of a large number of its occupants, because one or
two of them were invited to these entertainments and the others, so as
not to appear to have been not invited, chose that day for an expedition
to some distant spot. He had had, as it happened, an exceedingly bad reception at the hotel on the first day of the season, when the staff, freshly
imported from the Riviera, did not yet know who or what he was. Not
only was he not wearing white flannels, but, with old-fashioned French
courtesy and in his ignorance of the ways of smart hotels, on coming into
the hall in which there were ladies sitting, he had taken off his hat at the
door, the effect of which had been that the manager did not so much as
raise a finger to his own in acknowledgment, concluding that this must be
some one of the most humble extraction, what he called 'sprung from the
ordinary.' The solicitor's wife, alone, had felt herself attracted by the
stranger, who exhaled all the starched vulgarity of the really respectable,
and had declared, with the unerring discernment and the indisputable authority of a person from whom the highest society of Le Mans held no
secrets, that one could see at a glance that one was in the presence of a
gentleman of great distinction, of perfect breeding, a striking contrast to
the sort of people one usually saw at Balbec, whom she condemned as impossible to know so long as she did not know them. This favourable judgment which she had pronounced on Legrandin's brother-in-law was based
perhaps on the spiritless appearance of a man about whom there was nothing to intimidate anyone; perhaps also she had recognised in this gentleman
farmer with the gait of a sacristan the Masonic signs of her own inveterate
clericalism.

It made no difference my knowing that the young fellows who went past
the hotel every day on horseback were the sons of the questionably solvent
proprietor of a linen-drapery to whom my father would never have dreamed
of speaking; the glamour of 'seaside life' exalted them in my eyes to eques-
trian statues of demi-gods, and the best thing that I could hope for was
that they would never allow their proud gaze to fall upon the wretched
boy who was myself, who left the hotel dining-room only to sit humbly
upon the sands. I should have been glad to arouse some response even from
the adventurer who had been king of a desert island in the South Seas,
even of the young consumptive, of whom I liked to think that he was hiding beneath his insolent exterior a shy and tender heart, which would perhaps have lavished on me, and on me alone, the treasures of its affection.
Besides (unlike what one generally says of the people one meets when
travelling) just as being seen in certain company can invest us, in a watering-place to which we shall return another year, with a coefficient that
has no equivalent in our true social life, so there is nothing—not which we
keep so resolutely at a distance, but—which we cultivate with such assiduity after our return to Paris as the friendships that we have formed by
the sea. I was anxious about the opinion that might be held of me by all
these temporary or local celebrities whom my tendency to put myself in
the place of other people and to reconstruct what was in their minds had

made me place not in their true rank, that which they would have held
in Paris, for instance, and which would have been quite low, but in that
which they must imagine to be, and which indeed was their rank at Balbec,
where the want of a common denominator gave them a sort of relative
superiority and an individual interest. Alas, none of these people's contempt
for me was so unbearable as that of M. de Stermaria.

For I had noticed his daughter, the moment she came into the room,
her pretty features, her pallid, almost blue complexion, what there was
peculiar in the carriage of her tall figure, in her gait, which suggested to
me—and rightly—her long descent, her aristocratic upbringing, all the
more vividly because I knew her name, like those expressive themes composed by musicians of genius which paint in splendid colours the glow of
fire, the rush of water, the peace of fields and woods, to audiences who,
having first let their eyes run over the programme, have their imaginations
trained in the right direction. The label 'Centuries of Breeding,' by adding
to Mlle. de Stermaria's charms the idea of their origin, made them more
desirable also, advertising their rarity as a high price enhances the value
of a thing that has already taken our fancy. And its stock of heredity gave
to her complexion, in which so many selected juices had been blended,
the savour of an exotic fruit or of a famous vintage.

And then mere chance put into our hands, my grandmother's and mine,
the means of giving ourselves an immediate distinction in the eyes of all
the other occupants of the hotel. On that first afternoon, at the moment
when the old lady came downstairs from her room, producing, thanks to
the footman who preceded her, the maid who came running after her with
a book and a rug that had been left behind, a marked effect upon all who
beheld her and arousing in each of them a curiosity from which it was evident that none was so little immune as M. de Stermaria, the manager leaned
across to my grandmother and, from pure kindness of heart (as one might
point out the Shah, or Queen Ranavalo to an obscure onlooker who could
obviously have no sort of connexion with so mighty a potentate, but might
be interested, all the same, to know that he had been standing within a
few feet of one) whispered in her ear, "The Marquise de Villeparisis!"
while at the same moment the old lady, catching sight of my grandmother,
could not repress a start of pleased surprise.

It may be imagined that the sudden appearance, in the guise of a little
old woman, of the most powerful of fairies would not have given me so
much pleasure, destitute as I was of any means of access to Mlle. de Stermaria, in a strange place where I knew no one: no one, that is to say, for
any practical purpose. Aesthetically the number of types of humanity is so
restricted that we must constantly, wherever we may be, have the pleasure
of seeing people we know, even without looking for them in the works of
the old masters, like Swann. Thus it happened that in the first few days
of our visit to Balbec I had succeeded in finding Legrandin, Swann's hall
porter and Mme. Swann herself, transformed into a waiter, a foreign visitor
whom I never saw again and a bathing superintendent. And a sort of mag-
netism attracts and retains so inseparably, one after another, certain characteristics, facial and mental, that when nature thus introduces a person

into a new body she does not mutilate him unduly. Legrandin turned waiter kept intact his stature, the outline of his nose, part of his chin; Mme. Swann, in the masculine gender and the calling of a bathing superintendent, had been accompanied not only by familiar features, but even by the way she had of speaking. Only, she could be of little if any more use to me, standing upon the beach there in the red sash of her office, and hoisting at the first gust of wind the flag which forbade us to bathe (for these superintendents are prudent men, and seldom know how to swim) than she would have been in that fresco of the *Life of Moses* in which Swann had long ago identified her in the portrait of Jethro's Daughter. Whereas this Mme. de Villeparisis was her real self, she had not been the victim of an enchantment which had deprived her of her power, but was capable, on the contrary, of putting at the service of my power an enchantment which would multiply it an hundredfold, and thanks to which, as though I had been swept through the air on the wings of a fabulous bird, I was to cross in a few moments the infinitely wide (at least, at Balbec) social gulf which separated me from Mlle. de Stermaria.

Unfortunately, if there was one person in the world who, more than anyone else, lived shut up in a little world of her own, it was my grandmother. She would not, indeed, have despised me, she would simply not have understood what I meant had she been told that I attached importance to the opinions, that I felt an interest in the persons of people the very existence of whom she had never noticed and would, when the time came to leave Balbec, retain no impression of their names. I dared not confess to her that if these same people had seen her talking to Mme. de Villeparisis, I should have been immensely gratified, because I felt that the Marquise counted for much in the hotel and that her friendship would have given us a position in the eyes of Mlle. de Stermaria. Not that my grandmother's friend represented to me, in any sense of the word, a member of the aristocracy: I was too well used to her name, which had been familiar to my ears before my mind had begun to consider it, when as a child I had heard it occur in conversation at home: while her title added to it only a touch of quaintness—as some uncommon Christian name would have done, or as in the names of streets, among which we can see nothing more noble in the Rue Lord Byron, in the plebeian and even squalid Rue Rochechouart, or in the Rue Grammont than in the Rue Léonce Reynaud or the Rue Hyppolyte Lebas. Mme. de Villeparisis no more made me think of a person who belonged to a special world than did her cousin MacMahon, whom I did not clearly distinguish from M. Carnot, likewise President of the Republic, or from Raspail, whose photograph Françoise had bought with that of Pius IX. It was one of my grandmother's principles that, when away from home, one should cease to have any social intercourse, that one did not go to the seaside to meet people, having plenty of time for that sort of thing in Paris, that they would make one waste on being merely polite, in pointless conversation, the precious time which ought all to be spent in the open air, beside the waves; and finding it convenient to assume that this view was shared by everyone else, and that it authorised, between old friends whom chance brought face to face in the same hotel, the fiction of a mutual *incognito,* on hearing her friend's name from the manager she merely looked the other way, and pretended not to see Mme. de Villeparisis, who, realising that my grandmother did not want to be recognised, looked also into the void. She went past, and I was left in my isolation like a shipwrecked mariner who has seen a vessel apparently coming towards him which has then, without lowering a boat, vanished under the horizon.

She, too, had her meals in the dining-room, but at the other end of it. She knew none of the people who were staying in the hotel, or who came there to call, not even M. de Cambremer; in fact, I noticed that he gave her no greeting, one day when, with his wife, he had accepted an invitation to take luncheon with the barrister, who drunken with the honour of having the nobleman at his table avoided his friends of every day, and confined himself to a distant twitch of the eyelid, so as to draw their attention to this historic event but so discreetly that his signal could not be interpreted by them as an invitation to join the party.

"Well, I hope you've got on your best clothes; I hope you feel smart enough," was the magistrate's wife's greeting to him that evening.

"Smart? Why should I?" asked the barrister, concealing his rapture in an exaggerated astonishment. "Because of my guests, do you mean?" he went on, feeling that it was impossible to keep up the farce any longer. "But what is there smart about having a few friends in to luncheon? After all, they must feed somewhere!"

"But it is smart! They are the *de* Cambremers, aren't they? I recognized them at once. She is a Marquise. And quite genuine, too. Not through the females."

"Oh, she's a very simple soul, she is charming, no stand-offishness about her. I thought you were coming to join us. I was making signals to you. . . I would have introduced you!" he asserted, tempering with a hint of irony the vast generosity of the offer, like Ahasuerus when he says to Esther:

Of all my Kingdom must I give you half!

"No, no, no, no! We lie hidden, like the modest violet."

"But you were quite wrong, I assure you," replied the barrister, growing bolder now that the danger point was passed. "They weren't going to eat you. I say, aren't we going to have our little game of bezique?"

"Why, of course! We were afraid to suggest it, now that you go about entertaining Marquises."

"Oh, get along with you; there's nothing so very wonderful about them. Why, I'm dining there to-morrow. Would you care to go instead of me? I mean it. Honestly, I'd just as soon stay here."

"No, no! I should be removed from the bench as a Reactionary," cried the chief magistrate, laughing till the tears stood in his eyes at his own joke. "But you go to Féterne too, don't you?" he went on, turning to the solicitor.

"Oh, I go there on Sundays—in at one door and out at the other. But I don't have them here to luncheon, like the Leader."

M. de Stermaria was not at Balbec that day, to the barrister's great regret. But he managed to say a word in season to the head waiter:

"Aimé, you can tell M. de Stermaria that he's not the only nobleman you've had in here. You saw the gentleman who was with me to-day at luncheon? Eh? A small moustache, looked like a military man. Well, that was the Marquis de Cambremer!"

"Was it indeed? I'm not surprised to hear it."

"That will shew him that he's not the only man who's got a title. That will teach him! It's not a bad thing to take 'em down a peg or two, those noblemen. I say, Aimé, don't say anything to him unless you like: I mean to say, it's no business of mine; besides, they know each other already."

And next day M. de Stermaria, who remembered that the barrister had once held a brief for one of his friends, came up and introduced himself.

"Our friends in common, the de Cambremers, were anxious that we should meet; the days didn't fit; I don't know quite what went wrong—" stammered the barrister, who, like most liars, imagined that other people do not take the trouble to investigate an unimportant detail which, for all that, may be sufficient (if chance puts you in possession of the humble facts of the case, and they contradict it) to shew the liar in his true colours and to inspire a lasting mistrust.

Then as at all times, but more easily now that her father had left her and was talking to the barrister, I was gazing at Mlle. de Stermaria. No less than the bold and always graceful originality of her attitudes, as when, leaning her elbows on the table, she raised her glass in both hands over her outstretched arms, the dry flame of a glance at once extinguished, the ingrained, congenital hardness that one could feel, ill-concealed by her own personal inflexions, in the sound of her voice, which had shocked my grand-mother; a sort of atavistic starting point to which she recoiled whenever, by glance or utterance, she had succeeded in expressing a thought of her own; all of these qualities carried the mind of him who watched her back to the line of ancestors who had bequeathed to her that inadequacy of human sympathy, those blanks in her sensibility, that short measure of humanity which was at every moment running out. But from a certain look which flooded for a moment the wells—instantly dry again—of her eyes, a look in which I could discern that almost obsequious docility which the predominance of a taste for sensual pleasures gives to the proudest of women, who will soon come to recognise but one form of personal distinction, that namely which any man enjoys who can make her feel those pleasures, an actor, an acrobat even, for whom, perhaps, she will one day leave her husband;—from a certain rosy tint, warm and sensual, which flushed her pallid cheeks, like the colour that stained the hearts of the white water-lilies in the Vivonne, I thought I could discern that she would readily have consented to my coming to seek in her the savour of that life of poetry and romance which she led in Brittany, a life to which, whether from over-familiarity or from innate superiority, or from disgust at the penury or the avarice of her family, she seemed not to attach any great value, but which, for all that, she held enclosed in her body. In the meagre stock of will-power that had been transmitted to her, and gave an element of weakness to her expression, she would not perhaps have found the strength to resist. And, crowned by a feather that was a trifle old-fashioned and pretentious, the grey felt hat which she invariably wore at meals made her all the more attractive to me, not because it was in harmony with her pearly or rosy complexion, but because, by making me suppose her to be poor, it brought her closer to myself. Obliged by her father's presence to adopt a conventional attitude, but already bringing to the perception and classification of the people who passed before her eyes other principles than his, perhaps she saw in me not my humble rank, but the right sex and age. If one day M. de Stermaria had gone out leaving her behind, if, above all, Mme. de Villeparisis, by coming to sit at our table, had given her an opinion of me which might have emboldened me to approach her, perhaps then we might have contrived to exchange a few words, to arrange a meeting, to form a closer tie. And for a whole month during which she would be left alone, without her parents, in her romantic Breton castle, we should perhaps have been able to wander by ourselves at evening, she and I together in the dusk which would shew in a softer light above the darkening water pink briar roses, beneath oak trees beaten and stunted by the hammering of the waves. Together we should have roamed that isle impregnated with so intense a charm for me because it had enclosed the everyday life of Mlle. de Stermaria and lay at rest in her remembering eyes. For it seemed to me that I should not really have possessed her save there, when I should have traversed those regions which enveloped her in so many memories—a veil which my desire sought to tear apart, one of those veils which nature interposes between woman and her pursuers (with the same intention as when, for all of us, she places the act of reproduction between ourselves and our keenest pleasure, and for insects, places before the nectar the pollen which they must carry away with them) in order that, tricked by the illusion of possessing her thus more completely, they may be forced to occupy first the scenes among which she lives, and which, of more service to their imagination than sensual pleasure can be, yet would not without that pleasure have had the power to attract them.

But I was obliged to take my eyes from Mlle. de Stermaria, for already, considering no doubt that making the acquaintance of an important person was a brief, inquisitive act which was sufficient in itself, and to bring out all the interest that was latent in it required only a handshake and a penetrating stare, without either immediate conversation or any subsequent relations, her father had taken leave of the barrister and returned to sit down facing her, rubbing his hands like a man who has just made a valuable acquisition. As for the barrister, once the first emotion of this interview had subsided, then, as on other days, he could be heard every minute addressing the head waiter:

"But I am not a king, Aimé; go and attend to the king! I say, Chief, those little trout don't look at all bad, do they? We must ask Aimé to let us have some. Aimé, that little fish you have over there looks to me highly commendable; will you bring us some, please, Aimé, and don't be sparing with it?"

He would repeat the name 'Aimé' all day long, one result of which was that when he had anyone to dinner the guest would remark "I can see, you are quite at home in this place," and would feel himself obliged to keep on saying 'Aimé' also, from that tendency, combining elements of timidity, vulgarity and silliness, which many people have, to believe that it is smart and witty to copy to the letter what is said by the company in which they may happen to be. The barrister repeated the name incessantly, but with a smile, for he felt that he was exhibiting at once the good terms on which he stood with the head waiter and his own superior station. And the head waiter, whenever he caught the sound of his own name, smiled too, as though touched and at the same time proud, shewing that he was conscious of the honour and could appreciate the pleasantry.

Terrifying as I always found these meals, in the vast restaurant, generally full, of the mammoth hotel, they became even more terrifying when there arrived for a few days the Proprietor (or he may have been only the General Manager, appointed by a board of directors) not only of this 'palace' but of seven or eight more besides, situated at all the four corners of France, in each of which, travelling continuously, he would spend a week now and again. Then, just after dinner had begun, there appeared every evening in the doorway of the dining-room this small man with white hair and a red nose, astonishingly neat and impassive, who was known, it appeared, as well in London as at Monte-Carlo, as one of the leading hotel-keepers in Europe. Once when I had gone out for a moment at the beginning of dinner, as I came in again I passed close by him, and he bowed to me, but with a coldness in which I could not distinguish whether it should be attributed to the reserve of a man who could never forget what he was, or to his contempt for a customer of so little importance. To those whose importance was considerable the Managing Director would bow, with quite as much coldness but more deeply, lowering his eyelids with a reverence that was almost offended modesty, as though he had found himself confronted, at a funeral, with the father of the deceased or with the Blessed Sacrament. Except for these icy and infrequent salutations, he made not the slightest movement, as if to show that his glittering eyes, which appeared to be starting out of his head, saw everything, controlled everything, assured to us in the 'Hotel dinner' perfection in every detail as well as a general harmony. He felt, evidently, that he was more than the producer of a play, than the conductor of an orchestra, nothing less than a general in supreme command. Having decided that a contemplation carried to its utmost intensity would suffice to assure him that everything was in readiness, that no mistake had been made which could lead to disaster,—to invest him, in a word, with full responsibility, he abstained not merely from any gesture but even from moving his eyes, which, petrified by the intensity of their gaze, took in and directed everything that was going on. I felt that even the movements of my spoon did not escape him, and were he to vanish after the soup, for the whole of dinner the review that he had held would have taken away my appetite. His own was exceedingly good, as one could see at luncheon, which he took like an ordinary guest of the hotel at a table that anyone else might have had in the public dining-room. His table had this peculiarity only, that by his side, while he was eating, the other manager, the resident one, remained standing all the time to make conversation. For being subordinate to this Managing Director he was anxious to please a man of whom he lived in constant fear. My fear of him diminished during these luncheons, for being then lost in the crowd of visitors he would exercise the discretion of a general sitting in a restaurant where there are also private soldiers, in not seeming to take any notice of them. Nevertheless when the porter, from among a cluster of pages, announced to me: "He leaves to-morrow morning for Dinard. Then he's going down to Biarritz, and after that to Cannes," I began to breathe more freely.

My life in the hotel was rendered not only dull because I had no friends there but uncomfortable because Françoise had made so many. It might be thought that they would have made things easier for us in various respects. Quite the contrary. The proletariat, if they succeeded only with great difficulty in being treated as people she knew by Françoise, and could not succeed at all unless they fulfilled the condition of shewing the utmost politeness to her, were, on the other hand, once they had reached the position, the only people who 'counted.' Her time-honoured code taught her that she was in no way bound to the friends of her employers, that she might, if she was busy, shut the door without ceremony in the face of a lady who had come to call on my grandmother. But towards her own acquaintance, that is to say, the select handful of the lower orders whom she admitted to an unconquerable intimacy, her actions were regulated by the most subtle and most stringent of protocols. Thus Françoise having made the acquaintance of the man in the coffee-shop and of a little maid who did dressmaking for a Belgian lady, no longer came upstairs immediately after luncheon to get my grandmother's things ready, but came an hour later, because the coffee man had wanted to make her a cup of coffee or a *tisane* in his shop, or the maid had invited her to go and watch her sew, and to refuse either of them would have been impossible, and one of the things that were not done. Moreover, particular attention was due to the little sewing-maid, who was an orphan and had been brought up by strangers to whom she still went occasionally for a few days' holiday. Her unusual situation aroused Françoise's pity, and also a benevolent contempt. She, who had a family, a little house that had come to her from her parents, with a field in which her brother kept his cows, how could she regard so uprooted a creature as her equal? And since this girl hoped, on Assumption Day, to be allowed to pay her benefactors a visit, Françoise kept on repeating: "She does make me laugh! She says, 'I hope to be going home for the Assumption.' 'Home!' says she! It isn't just that it's not her own place, they're people who took her in from nowhere, and the creature says 'home' just as if it really was her home. Poor girl! What a wretched state she must be in, not to know what it is to have a home." Still, if Françoise had associated only with the ladies'-maids brought to the hotel by other visitors, who fed with her in the 'service' quarters and, seeing her grand lace cap and her handsome profile, took her perhaps for some lady of noble birth, whom 'reduced circumstances,' or a personal attachment had driven to serve as companion to my grandmother, if in a word

Françoise had known only people who did not belong to the hotel, no great harm would have been done, since she could not have prevented them from doing us any service, for the simple reason that in no circumstances, even without her knowledge, would it have been possible for them to serve us at all. But she had formed connexions also with one of the wine waiters, with a man in the kitchen, and with the head chambermaid of our landing. And the result of this in our everyday life was that Françoise, who on the day of her arrival, when she still did not know anyone, would set all the bells jangling for the slightest thing, at an hour when my grandmother and I would never have dared to ring, and if we offered some gentle admonition answered: "Well, we're paying enough for it, aren't we?" as though it were she herself that would have to pay; nowadays, since she had made friends with a personage in the kitchen, which had appeared to us to augur well for our future comfort, were my grandmother or I to complain of cold feet, Françoise, even at an hour that was quite normal, dared not ring; she assured us that it would give offence because they would have to light the furnace again, or because it would interrupt the servants' dinner and they would be annoyed. And she ended with a formula that, in spite of the ambiguous way in which she uttered it, was none the less clear, and put us plainly in the wrong: "The fact is . . ." We did not insist, for fear of bringing upon ourselves another, far more serious: "It's a matter . . . !" So that it amounted to this, that we could no longer have any hot water because Françoise had become a friend of the man who would have to heat it.

In the end we too formed a connexion, in spite of but through my grandmother, for she and Mme. de Villeparisis came in collision one morning in a doorway and were obliged to accost each other, not without having first exchanged gestures of surprise and hesitation, performed movements of recoil and uncertainty, and finally uttered protestations of joy and greeting, as in some of Molière's plays, where two actors who have been delivering long soliloquies from opposite sides of the stage, a few feet apart, are supposed not to have seen each other yet, and then suddenly catch sight of each other, cannot believe their eyes, break off what they are saying and finally address each other (the chorus having meanwhile kept the dialogue going) and fall into each other's arms. Mme. de Villeparisis was tactful, and made as if to leave my grandmother to herself after the first greetings, but my grandmother insisted on her staying to talk to her until luncheon, being anxious to discover how her friend managed to get her letters sent up to her earlier than we got ours, and to get such nice grilled things (for Mme. de Villeparisis, a great epicure, had the poorest opinion of the hotel kitchen which served us with meals that my grandmother, still quoting Mme. de Sévigné, described as "of a magnificence to make you die of hunger.") And the Marquise formed the habit of coming every day, until her own meal was ready, to sit down for a moment at our table in the dining-room, insisting that we should not rise from our chairs or in any way put ourselves out. At the most we would linger, as often as not, in the room after finishing our luncheon, to talk to her, at that sordid moment when the knives are left littering the tablecloth among crumpled napkins. For my own part, so as to preserve (in order that I might be able to enjoy Balbec) the idea that I was on the uttermost promontory of the earth, I compelled myself to look farther afield, to notice only the sea, to seek in it the effects described by Baudelaire and to let my gaze fall upon our table only on days when there was set on it some gigantic fish, some marine monster, which unlike the knives and forks was contemporary with the primitive epochs in which the Ocean first began to teem with life, in the Cimmerians' time, a fish whose body with its numberless vertebrae, its blue veins and red, had been constructed by nature, but according to an architectural plan, like a polychrome cathedral of the deep.

As a barber, seeing an officer whom he is accustomed to shave with special deference and care recognise a customer who has just entered the shop and stop for a moment to talk to him, rejoices in the thought that these are two men of the same social order, and cannot help smiling as he goes to fetch the bowl of soap, for he knows that in his establishment, to the vulgar routine of a mere barber's-shop, are being added social, not to say aristocratic pleasures, so Aimé, seeing that Mme. de Villeparisis had found in us old friends, went to fetch our finger-bowls with precisely the smile, proudly modest and knowingly discreet, of a hostess who knows when to leave her guests to themselves. He suggested also a pleased and loving father who looks on, without interfering, at the happy pair who have plighted their troth at his hospitable board. Besides, it was enough merely to utter the name of a person of title for Aimé to appear pleased, unlike Françoise, before whom you could not mention Count So-and-so without her face darkening and her speech becoming dry and sharp, all of which meant that she worshipped the aristocracy not less than Aimé but far more. But then Françoise had that quality which in others she condemned as the worst possible fault; she was proud. She was not of that friendly and good-humoured race to which Aimé belonged. They feel, they exhibit an intense delight when you tell them a piece of news which may be more or less sensational but is at any rate new, and not to be found in the papers. Françoise declined to appear surprised. You might have announced in her hearing that the Archduke Rudolf—not that she had the least suspicion of his having ever existed—was not, as was generally supposed, dead, but 'alive and kicking'; she would have answered only 'Yes,' as though she had known it all the time. It may, however, have been that if even from our own lips, from us whom she so meekly called her masters, who had so nearly succeeded in taming her, she could not, without having to check an angry start, hear the name of a noble, that was because the family from which she had sprung occupied in its own village a comfortable and independent position, and was not to be threatened in the consideration which it enjoyed save by those same nobles, in whose households, meanwhile, from his boyhood, an Aimé would have been domiciled as a servant, if not actually brought up by their charity. Of Françoise, then, Mme. de Villeparisis must ask pardon, first, for her nobility. But (in France, at any rate) that is precisely the talent, in fact the sole occupation of our great gentlemen and ladies. Françoise, following the common tendency of servants, who pick up incessantly from the conversation of their masters with other people fragmentary observations from which they are apt to draw erroneous inductions, as the human race generally does with respect to the habits of animals, was constantly discovering that somebody had 'failed' us, a conclusion to which she was easily led, not so much, perhaps, by her extravagant love for us, as by the delight that she took in being disagreeable to us. But having once established, without possibility of error, the endless little attentions paid to us, and paid to herself also by Mme. de Villeparisis, Françoise forgave her for being a Marquise, and, as she had never ceased to be proud of her because she was one, preferred her thenceforward to all our other friends. It must be added that no one else took the trouble to be so continually nice to us. Whenever my grandmother remarked on a book that Mme. de Villeparisis was reading, or said she had been admiring the fruit which some one had just sent to our friend, within an hour the footman would come to our rooms with book or fruit. And the next time we saw her, in response to our thanks, she would say only, seeming to seek some excuse for the meagreness of her present in some special use to which it might be put: "It's nothing wonderful, but the newspapers come so late here, one must have something to read." Or, "It is always wiser to have fruit one can be quite certain of, at the seaside."—"But I don't believe I've ever seen you eating oysters," she said to us, increasing the sense of disgust which I felt at that moment, for the living flesh of the oyster revolted me even more than the gumminess of the stranded jellyfish defiled for me the beach at Balbec; "they are delicious down here! Oh, let me tell my maid to fetch your letters when she goes for mine. What, your daughter writes *every day*? But what on earth can you find to say to each other?" My grandmother was silent, but it may be assumed that her silence was due to scorn, in her who used to repeat, when she wrote to Mamma, the words of Mme. de Sévigné: "As soon as I have received a letter, I want another at once; I cannot breathe until it comes. There are few who are worthy to understand what I mean." And I was afraid of her applying to Mme. de Villeparisis the conclusion: "I seek out those who are of the chosen few, and I avoid the rest." She fell back upon praise of the fruit which Mme. de Villeparisis had sent us the day before. And this had been, indeed, so fine that the manager, in spite of the jealousy aroused by our neglect of his official offerings, had said to me: "I am like you; I'm madder about fruit than any other kind of dessert." My grandmother told her friend that she had enjoyed them all the more because the fruit which we got in the hotel was generally horrid. "I cannot," she went on, "say, like Mme. de Sévigné, that if we should take a sudden fancy for bad fruit we should be obliged to order it from Paris." "Oh yes, of course, you read Mme. de Sévigné. I saw you with her letters the day you came." (She forgot that she had never officially seen my grandmother in the hotel until their collision in the doorway.) "Don't you find it rather exaggerated, her constant anxiety about her daughter? She refers to it too often to be really sincere. She is not natural." My grandmother felt that any discussion would be futile, and so as not to be obliged to speak of the things she loved to a person incapable of understanding them, concealed by laying her bag upon them the *Mémoires de Mme. de Beausergent.*

Were she to encounter Françoise at the moment (which Françoise called 'the noon') when, wearing her fine cap and surrounded with every mark of respect, she was coming downstairs to 'feed with the service,' Mme. Villeparisis would stop her to ask after us. And Françoise, when transmitting to us the Marquise's message: "She said to me, 'You'll be sure and bid them good day,' she said," counterfeited the voice of Mme. de Villeparisis, whose exact words she imagined herself to be quoting textually, whereas she was really corrupting them no less than Plato corrupts the words of Socrates or Saint John the words of Jesus. Françoise, as was natural, was deeply touched by these attentions. Only she did not believe my grandmother, but supposed that she must be lying in the interest of her class (the rich always combining thus to support one another) when she assured us that Mme. de Villeparisis had been lovely as a young woman. It was true that of this loveliness only the faintest trace remained, from which no one—unless he happened to be a great deal more of an artist than Françoise—would have been able to restore her ruined beauty. For in order to understand how beautiful an elderly woman can once have been one must not only study but interpret every line of her face.

"I must remember, some time, to ask her whether I'm not right, after all, in thinking that there is some connexion with the Guermantes," said my grandmother, to my great indignation. How could I be expected to believe in a common origin uniting two names which had entered my consciousness, one through the low and shameful gate of experience, the other by the golden gate of imagination?

We had several times, in the last few days, seen driving past us in a stately equipage, tall, auburn, handsome, with a rather prominent nose, the Princesse de Luxembourg, who was staying in the neighbourhood for a few weeks. Her carriage had stopped outside the hotel, a footman had come in and spoken to the manager, had gone back to the carriage and had reappeared with the most amazing armful of fruit (which combined in a single basket, like the bay itself, different seasons) with a card: "La Princesse de Luxembourg," on which were scrawled a few words in pencil. For what princely traveller sojourning here *incognito,* could they be intended, those glaucous plums, luminous and spherical as was at that moment the circumfluent sea, transparent grapes clustering on a shrivelled stick, like a fine day in autumn, pears of a heavenly ultramarine? For it could not be on my grandmother's friend that the Princess had meant to pay a call. And yet on the following evening Mme. de Villeparisis sent us the bunch of grapes, cool, liquid, golden; plums too and pears which we remembered, though the plums had changed, like the sea at our dinner-hour, to a dull purple, and on the ultramarine surface of the pears there floated the forms of a few rosy clouds. A few days later we met Mme. de Villeparisis as we came away from the symphony concert that was given every morning on the beach. Convinced that the music to which I had been listening (the Prelude to *Lohengrin,* the Overture to *Tannhäuser* and suchlike) expressed the loftiest of truths, I was trying to elevate myself, as far as I could, so as to attain to a comprehension of them, I was extracting from myself so as to understand them, and was attributing to them, all that was best and most profound in my own nature at that time.

Well, as we came out of the concert, and, on our way back to the hotel, had stopped for a moment on the 'front,' my grandmother and I, for a few words with Mme. de Villeparisis who told us that she had ordered some *croque-monsieurs* and a dish of creamed eggs for us at the hotel, I saw, a long way away, coming in our direction, the Princesse de Luxembourg, half leaning upon a parasol in such a way as to impart to her tall and wonderful form that slight inclination, to make it trace that arabesque dear to the women who had been beautiful under the Empire, and knew how, with drooping shoulders, arched backs, concave hips and bent limbs, to make their bodies float as gently as a silken scarf about the rigidity of the invisible stem which might be supposed to have been passed diagonally through them. She went out every morning for a turn on the beach almost at the time when everyone else, after bathing, was climbing home to luncheon, and as hers was not until half past one she did not return to her villa until long after the hungry bathers had left the scorching 'front' a desert. Mme. de Villeparisis presented my grandmother and would have presented me, but had first to ask me my name, which she could not remember. She had, perhaps, never known it, or if she had must have forgotten years ago to whom my grandmother had married her daughter. My name, when she did hear it, appeared to impress Mme. de Villeparisis considerably. Meanwhile the Princesse de Luxembourg had given us her hand and, now and again, while she conversed with the Marquise, turned to bestow a kindly glance on my grandmother and myself, with that embryonic kiss which we put into our smiles when they are addressed to a baby out with its 'Nana.' Indeed, in her anxiety not to appear to be a denizen of a higher sphere than ours, she had probably miscalculated the distance there was indeed between us, for by an error in adjustment she made her eyes beam with such benevolence that I could see the moment approaching when she would put out her hand and stroke us, as if we were two nice beasts and had poked our heads out at her through the bars of our cage in the Gardens. And, immediately, as it happened, this idea of caged animals and the Bois de Boulogne received striking confirmation. It was the time of day at which the beach is crowded by itinerant and clamorous vendors, hawking cakes and sweets and biscuits. Not knowing quite what to do to shew her affection for us, the Princess hailed the next that came by; he had nothing left but one rye-cake, of the kind one throws to the ducks. The Princess took it and said to me: "For your grandmother." And yet it was to me that she held it out, saying with a friendly smile, "You shall give it to her yourself!" thinking that my pleasure would thus be more complete if there were no intermediary between myself and the animals. Other vendors came up; she stuffed my pockets with everything that they had, tied up in packets, comfits, sponge-cakes, sugar-sticks. "You will eat some yourself," she told me, "and give some to your grandmother," and she had the vendors paid by the little Negro page, dressed in red satin, who followed her everywhere and was a nine days' wonder upon the beach.

Then she said good-bye to Mme. de Villeparisis and held out her hand to us with the intention of treating us in the same way as she treated her friend, as people whom she knew, and of bringing herself within our reach. But this time she must have reckoned our level as not quite so low in the scale of creation, for her and our equality was indicated by the Princess to my grandmother by that tender and maternal smile which a woman gives a little boy when she says good-bye to him as though to a grown-up person. By a miraculous stride in evolution, my grandmother was no longer a duck or an antelope, but had already become what the anglophil Mme. Swann would have called a 'baby.' Finally, having taken leave of us all, the Princess resumed her stroll along the basking 'front,' curving her splendid shape which, like a serpent coiled about a wand, was interlaced with the white parasol patterned in blue which Mme. de Luxembourg held, unopened, in her hand. She was my first Royalty—I say my first, for strictly speaking Princesse Mathilde did not count. The second, as we shall see in due course, was to astonish me no less by her indulgence. One of the ways in which our great nobles, kindly intermediaries between commoners and kings, can befriend us was revealed to me next day when Mme. de Villeparisis reported: "She thought you quite charming. She is a woman of the soundest judgment, the warmest heart. Not like so many Queens and people! She has real merit." And Mme. de Villeparisis went on in a tone of conviction, and quite thrilled to be able to say it to us: "I am sure she would be delighted to see you again."

But on that previous morning, after we had parted from the Princesse de Luxembourg, Mme. de Villeparisis said a thing which impressed me far more and was not prompted merely by friendly feeling.

"Are you," she had asked me, "the son of the Permanent Secretary at the Ministry? Indeed! I am told your father is a most charming man. He is having a splendid holiday just now."

A few days earlier we had heard, in a letter from Mamma, that my father and his friend M. de Norpois had lost their luggage.

"It has been found; as a matter of fact, it was never really lost, I can tell you what happened," explained Mme. de Villeparisis, who, without our knowing how, seemed to be far better informed than ourselves of the course of my father's travels. "I think your father is now planning to come home earlier, next week, in fact, as he will probably give up the idea of going to Algeciras. But he is anxious to devote a day longer to Toledo; it seems, he is an admirer of a pupil of Titian,—I forget the name—whose work can only be seen properly there."

I asked myself by what strange accident, in the impartial glass through which Mme. de Villeparisis considered, from a safe distance, the bustling, tiny, purposeless agitation of the crowd of people whom she knew, there had come to be inserted at the spot through which she observed my father a fragment of prodigious magnifying power which made her see in such high relief and in the fullest detail everything that there was attractive about him, the contingencies that were obliging him to return home, his difficulties with the customs, his admiration for El Greco, and, altering the scale of her vision, shewed her this one man so large among all the rest quite small, like that Jupiter to whom Gustave Moreau gave, when he portrayed him by the side of a weak mortal, a superhuman stature.

My grandmother bade Mme. de Villeparisis good-bye, so that we might stay and imbibe the fresh air for a little while longer outside the hotel, until they signalled to us through the glazed partition that our luncheon was ready. There were sounds of tumult. The young mistress of the King of the Cannibal Island had been down to bathe and was now coming back to the hotel.

"Really and truly, it's a perfect plague: it's enough to make one decide to emigrate!" cried the barrister, who had happened to cross her path, in a towering rage.

Meanwhile the solicitor's wife was following the bogus Queen with eyes that seemed ready to start from their sockets.

"I can't tell you how angry Mme. Blandais makes me when she stares at those people like that," said the barrister to the chief magistrate, "I feel I want to slap her. That is just the way to make the wretches appear important; and of course that's the very thing they want, that people should take an interest in them. Do ask her husband to tell her what a fool she's making of herself. I swear I won't go out with them again if they stop and gape at those masqueraders."

As to the coming of the Princesse de Luxembourg, whose carriage, on the day on which she left the fruit, had drawn up outside the hotel, it had not passed unobserved by the little group of wives, the solicitor's, the barrister's and the magistrate's, who had for some time past been most concerned to know whether she was a genuine Marquise and not an adventuress, that Mme. de Villeparisis whom everyone treated with so much respect, which all these ladies were burning to hear that she did not deserve. Whenever Mme. de Villeparisis passed through the hall the chief magistrate's wife, who scented irregularities everywhere, would raise her eyes from her 'work' and stare at the intruder in a way that made her friends die of laughter.

"Oh, well, you know," she explained with lofty condescension, "I always begin by believing the worst. I will never admit that a woman is properly married until she has shewn me her birth certificate and her marriage lines. But there's no need to alarm yourselves; just wait till I've finished my little investigation."

And so, day after day the ladies would come together, and, laughingly, ask one another: "Any news?"

But on the evening after the Princesse de Luxembourg's call the magistrate's wife laid a finger on her lips.

"I've discovered something."

"Oh, isn't Mme. Poncin simply wonderful? I never saw anyone. . . . But do tell us! What has happened?"

"Just listen to this. A woman with yellow hair and six inches of paint on her face and a carriage like a—you could *smell* it a mile off; which only a creature like that would dare to have—came here to-day to call on the Marquise, by way of!"

"Oh-yow-yow! Tut-tut-tut-tut. Did you ever! Why, it must be that woman we saw—you remember, Leader,—we said at the time we didn't at all like the look of her, but we didn't know that it was the 'Marquise' she'd come to see. A woman with a nigger-boy, you mean?"

"That's the one."

"D'you mean to say so? You don't happen to know her name?"

"Yes, I made a mistake on purpose; I picked up her card; she *trades* under the name of the 'Princesse de Luxembourg!' Wasn't I right to have my doubts about her? It's a nice thing to have to mix promiscuously with a Baronne d'Ange like that?" The barrister quoted Mathurin Régnier's *Macette* to the chief magistrate.

It must not, however, be supposed that this misunderstanding was merely temporary, like those that occur in the second act of a farce to be cleared up before the final curtain. Mme. de Luxembourg, a niece of the King of England and of the Emperor of Austria, and Mme. de Villeparisis, when one called to take the other for a drive, did look like nothing but two 'old trots' of the kind one has always such difficulty in avoiding at a watering place. Nine tenths of the men of the Faubourg Saint-Germain appear to the average man of the middle class simply as alcoholic wasters (which, individually, they not infrequently are) whom, therefore, no respectable person would dream of asking to dinner. The middle class fixes its standard, in this respect, too high, for the feelings of these men would never prevent their being received with every mark of esteem in houses which it, the middle class, may never enter. And so sincerely do they believe that the middle class knows this that they affect a simplicity in speaking of their own affairs and a tone of disparagement of their friends, especially when they are 'at the coast,' which make the misunderstanding complete. If, by any chance, a man of the fashionable world is kept in touch with 'business people' because, having more money than he knows what to do with, he finds himself elected chairman of all sorts of important financial concerns, the business man who at last sees a nobleman worthy, he considers, to rank with 'big business,' would take his oath that such a man can have no dealings with the Marquis ruined by gambling whom the said business man supposes to be all the more destitute of friends the more friendly he makes himself. And he cannot get over his surprise when the Duke, Chairman of the Board of Directors of the colossal undertaking, arranges a marriage for his son with the daughter of that very Marquis, who may be a gambler but who bears the oldest name in France, just as a Sovereign would sooner see his son marry the daughter of a dethroned King than that of a President still in office. That is to say, the two worlds take as fantastic a view of one another as the inhabitants of a town situated at one end of Balbec Bay have of the town at the other end: from Rivebelle you can just see Marcouville l'Orgueilleuse; but even that is deceptive, for you imagine that you are seen from Marcouville, where, as a matter of fact, the splendours of Rivebelle are almost wholly invisible.

PART II

PLACE-NAMES: THE PLACE

THE Balbec doctor, who had been called in to cope with a sudden feverish attack, having given the opinion that I ought not to stay out all day on the beach, in the blazing sun, without shelter, and having written out various prescriptions for my use, my grandmother took his prescriptions with a show of respect in which I could at once discern her firm resolve not to have any of them 'made up,' but did pay attention to his advice on the matter of hygiene, and accepted an offer from Mme. de Villeparisis to take us for drives in her carriage. After this I would spend the mornings, until luncheon, going to and fro between my own room and my grandmother's. Hers did not look out directly upon the sea, as mine did, but was lighted from three of its four sides—with views of a strip of the 'front,' of a well inside the building, and of the country inland, and was furnished differently from mine, with armchairs upholstered in a metallic tissue with red flowers from which seemed to emanate the cool and pleasant odour that greeted me when I entered the room. And at that hour when the sun's rays, coming from different aspects and, as it were, from different hours of the day, broke the angles of the wall, thrust in a reflexion of the beach, made of the chest of drawers a festal altar, variegated as a bank of field-flowers, attached to the wall the wings, folded, quivering, warm, of a radiance that would, at any moment, resume its flight, warmed like a bath a square of provincial carpet before the window overlooking the well, which the sun festooned and patterned like a climbing vine, added to the charm and complexity of the room's furniture by seeming to pluck and scatter the petals of the silken flowers on the chairs, and to make their silver threads stand out from the fabric, this room in which I lingered for a moment before going to get ready for our drive suggested a prism in which the colours of the light that shone outside were broken up, or a hive in which the sweet juices of the day which I was about to taste were distilled, scattered, intoxicating, visible, a garden of hope which dissolved in a quivering haze of silver threads and rose leaves. But before all this I had drawn back my own curtains, impatient to know what Sea it was that was playing that morning by the shore, like a Nereid. For none of those Seas ever stayed with us longer than a day. On the morrow there would be another, which sometimes resembled its predecessor. But I never saw the same one twice.

There were some that were of so rare a beauty that my pleasure on catching sight of them was enhanced by surprise. By what privilege, on one morning rather than another, did the window on being uncurtained disclose to my wondering eyes the nymph Glauconome, whose lazy beauty, gently breathing, had the transparence of a vaporous emerald beneath whose surface I could see teeming the ponderable elements that coloured it? She made the sun join in her play, with a smile rendered languorous by an invisible haze which was nought but a space kept vacant about her translucent surface, which, thus curtailed, became more appealing, like those goddesses whom the sculptor carves in relief upon a block of marble, the rest of which he leaves unchiselled. So, in her matchless colour, she invited us out over those rough terrestrial roads, from which, seated beside Mme. de Villeparisis in her barouche, we should see, all day long and without ever reaching it, the coolness of her gentle palpitation.

Mme. de Villeparisis used to order her carriage early, so that we should have time to reach Saint-Mars le Vêtu, or the rocks of Quetteholme, or some other goal which, for a somewhat lumbering vehicle, was far enough off to require the whole day. In my joy at the long drive we were going to take I would be humming some tune that I had heard recently as I strolled up and down until Mme. de Villeparisis was ready. If it was Sunday hers would not be the only carriage drawn up outside the hotel; several hired flies would be waiting there, not only for the people who had been invited to Féterne by Mme. de Cambremer, but for those who, rather than stay at home all day, like children in disgrace, declared that Sunday was always quite impossible at Balbec and started off immediately after luncheon to hide themselves in some neighbouring watering-place or to visit one of the 'sights' of the district. And indeed whenever (which was often) anyone asked Mme. Blandais if she had been to the Cambremers', she would answer peremptorily: "No; we went to the Falls of the Bec," as though that were the sole reason for her not having spent the day at Féterne. And the barrister would be charitable, and say:

"I envy you. I wish I had gone there instead; they must be well worth seeing."

Beside the row of carriages, in front of the porch in which I stood waiting, was planted, like some shrub of a rare species, a young page who attracted the eye no less by the unusual and effective colouring of his hair than by his plant-like epidermis. Inside, in the hall, corresponding to the narthex, or Church of the Catechumens in a primitive basilica, through which persons who were not staying in the hotel were entitled to pass, the comrades of this 'outside' page did not indeed work much harder than he but did at least execute certain drilled movements. It is probable that in the early morning they helped with the cleaning. But in the afternoon they stood there only like a Chorus who, even when there is nothing for them to do, remain upon the stage in order to strengthen the cast. The General Manager, the same who had so terrified me, reckoned on increasing their number considerably next year, for he had 'big ideas.' And this prospect greatly afflicted the manager of the hotel, who found that all these boys about the place only 'created a nuisance,' by which he meant that they got in the visitors' way and were of no use to anyone. But between luncheon and dinner at least, between the exits and entrances of the visitors, they did fill an otherwise empty stage, like those pupils of Mme. de Maintenon who, in the garb of young Israelites, carry on the action whenever Esther or Joad 'goes off.' But the outside page, with his delicate tints, his tall, slender, fragile trunk, in proximity to whom I stood waiting for the Marquise to come downstairs, preserved an immobility into which a certain melancholy entered, for his elder brothers had left the hotel for more brilliant careers elsewhere, and he felt keenly his isolation upon this alien soil. At last Mme. de Villeparisis appeared. To stand by her carriage and to help her into it ought perhaps to have been part of the young page's duties. But he knew on the one hand that a person who brings her own servants to an hotel expects them to wait on her and is not as a rule lavish with her 'tips,' and that generally speaking this was true also of the nobility of the old Faubourg Saint-Germain. Mme. de Villeparisis was included in both these categories. The arborescent page concluded therefore that he need expect nothing from her, and leaving her own maid and footman to pack her and her belongings into the carriage, he continued to dream sadly of the enviable lot of his brothers and preserved his vegetable immobility.

We would start off; some time after rounding the railway station, we came into a country road which soon became as familiar to me as the roads round Combray, from the bend where, like a fish-hook, it was baited with charming orchards, to the turning at which we left it, with tilled fields upon either side. Among these we could see here and there an apple-tree, stripped it was true of its blossom, and bearing no more now than a fringe of pistils, but sufficient even so to enchant me since I could imagine, seeing those inimitable leaves, how their broad expanse, like the ceremonial carpet spread for a wedding that was now over, had been but the other day swept by the white satin train of their blushing flowers.

How often in Paris, during the May of the following year, was I to bring home a branch of apple-blossom from the florist, and to stay all night long before its flowers in which bloomed the same creamy essence that powdered besides and whitened the green unfolding leaves, flowers between whose snowy cups it seemed almost as though it had been the salesman who had, in his generosity towards myself, out of his wealth of invention too and as an effective contrast, added on either side the supplement of a becoming crimson bud: I sat gazing at them, I grouped them in the light of my lamp —for so long that I was often still there when the dawn brought to their whiteness the same flush with which it must at that moment have been tingeing their sisters on the Balbec road—and I sought to carry them back in my imagination to that roadside, to multiply them, to spread them out, so as to fill the frame prepared for them, on the canvas, all ready, of those closes the outline of which I knew by heart, which I so longed to see— which one day I must see again, at the moment when, with the exquisite fervour of genius, spring was covering their canvas with its colours.

Before getting into the carriage I had composed the seascape for which I was going to look out, which I had hoped to see with the 'sun radiant' upon it, and which at Balbec I could distinguish only in too fragmentary a form, broken by so many vulgar intromissions that had no place in my dream, bathers, dressing-boxes, pleasure yachts. But when, Mme. de Villeparisis's carriage having reached high ground, I caught a glimpse of the sea through the leafy boughs of trees, then no doubt at such a distance those temporal details which had set the sea, as it were, apart from nature

and history disappeared, and I could as I looked down towards its waves
make myself realise that they were the same which Leconte de Lisle describes for us in his *Orestie,* where "like a flight of birds of prey, before
the dawn of day" the long-haired warriors of heroic Hellas "with oars
an hundred thousand sweep the huge resounding deep." But on the other
hand I was no longer near enough to the sea which seemed to me not a
living thing now, but fixed; I no longer felt any power beneath its colours,
spread like those of a picture among the leaves, through which it appeared
as inconsistent as the sky and only of an intenser blue.

. Mme. de Villeparisis, seeing that I was fond of churches, promised me
that we should visit one one day and another another, and especially the
church at Carqueville 'quite buried in all its old ivy,' as she said with a
wave of the hand which seemed tastefully to be clothing the absent 'front'
in an invisible and delicate screen of foliage. Mme. de Villeparisis would
often, with this little descriptive gesture, find just the right word to define
the attraction and the distinctive features of an historic building, always
avoiding technical terms, but incapable of concealing her thorough understanding of the things to which she referred. She appeared to seek an excuse
for this erudition in the fact that one of her father's country houses, the
one in which she had lived as a girl, was situated in a district in which there
were churches similar in style to those round Balbec, so that it would have
been unaccountable if she had not acquired a taste for architecture, this
house being, incidentally, one of the finest examples of that of the Renaissance. But as it was also a regular museum, as moreover Chopin and
Liszt had played there, Lamartine recited poetry, all the most famous
artists for fully a century inscribed 'sentiments,' scored melodies, made
sketches in the family album, Mme. de Villeparisis ascribed, whether from
delicacy, good breeding, true modesty or want of intelligence, only this
purely material origin to her acquaintance with all the arts, and had come,
apparently, to regard painting, music, literature and philosophy as the
appanage of a young lady brought up on the most aristocratic lines in an
historic building that was catalogued and starred. You would have said,
listening to her, that she knew of no pictures that were not heirlooms. She
was pleased that my grandmother liked a necklace which she wore, and
which fell over her dress. It appeared in the portrait of an ancestress of
her own by Titian which had never left the family. So that one could be
certain of its being genuine. She would not listen to a word about pictures
bought, heaven knew where, by a Croesus, she was convinced before you
spoke that they were forgeries, and had so desire to see them. We knew
that she herself painted flowers in water-colour, and my grandmother, who
had heard these praised, spoke to her of them. Mme. de Villeparisis modestly changed the subject, but without shewing either surprise or pleasure
more than would an artist whose reputation was established and to whom
compliments meant nothing. She said merely that it was a delightful pastime
because, even if the flowers that sprang from the brush were nothing wonderful, at least the work made you live in the company of real flowers,
of the beauty of which, especially when you were obliged to study them
closely in order to draw them, you could never grow tired. But at Balbec

Mme. de Villeparisis was giving herself a holiday, so as to spare her eyes.

We were astonished, my grandmother and I, to find how much more 'Liberal' she was than even the majority of the middle class. She did not understand how anyone could be scandalised by the expulsion of the Jesuits, saying that it had always been done, even under the Monarchy, in Spain even. She took up the defence of the Republic, and against its anti-clericalism had not more to say than: "I should be equally annoyed whether they prevented me from hearing mass when I wanted to, or forced me to hear it when I didn't!" and even startled us with such utterances as: "Oh! the aristocracy in these days, what does it amount to?" "To my mind, a man who doesn't work doesn't count!"—perhaps only because she felt that they gained point and flavour, became memorable, in fact, on her lips.

When we heard these advanced opinions—though never so far advanced as to amount to Socialism, which Mme. de Villeparisis held in abhorrence —expressed so frequently and with so much frankness precisely by one of those people in consideration of whose intelligence our scrupulous and timid impartiality would refuse to condemn outright the ideas of the Conservatives, we came very near, my grandmother and I, to believing that in the pleasant companion of our drives was to be found the measure and the pattern of truth in all things. We took her word for it when she appreciated her Titians, the colonnade of her country house, the conversational talent of Louis-Philippe. But—like those mines of learning who hold us spellbound when we get them upon Egyptian paintings or Etruscan inscriptions, and yet talk so tediously about modern work that we ask ourselves whether we have not been over-estimating the interest of the sciences in which they are versed since there is not apparent in their treatment of them the mediocrity of mind which they must have brought to those studies just as much as to their fatuous essays on Baudelaire—Mme. de Villeparisis, questioned by me about Chateaubriand, about Balzac, about Victor Hugo, each of whom had in his day been the guest of her parents, and had been seen and spoken to by her, smiled at my reverence, told amusing anecdotes of them, such as she had a moment ago been telling us of dukes and statesmen, and severely criticised those writers simply because they had been lacking in that modesty, that self-effacement, that sober art which is satisfied with a single right line, and lays no stress on it, which avoids more than anything else the absurdity of grandiloquence, in that opportuneness, those qualities of moderation, of judgment and simplicity to which she had been taught that real greatness aspired and attained: it was evident that she had no hesitation in placing above them men who might after all, perhaps, by virtue of those qualities, have had the advantage of a Balzac, a Hugo, a Vigny in a drawing-room, an academy, a cabinet council, men like Molé, Fontanes, Vitroles, Bersot, Pasquier, Lebrun, Salvandy or Daru.

"Like those novels of Stendhal, which you seem to admire. You would have given him a great surprise, I assure you, if you had spoken to him in that tone. My father, who used to meet him at M. Mérimée's—now he was a man of talent, if you like—often told me that Beyle (that was his real name) was appallingly vulgar, but quite good company at dinner, and never in the least conceited about his books. Why, you can see for yourself how he just shrugged his shoulders at the absurdly extravagant compliments of M. de Balzac. There at least he shewed that he knew how to behave like a gentleman." She possessed the autographs of all these great men, and seemed, when she put forward the personal relations which her family had had with them, to assume that her judgment of them must be better founded than that of young people who, like myself, had had no opportunity of meeting them. "I'm sure I have a right to speak, for they used to come to my father's house; and as M. Sainte-Beuve, who was a most intelligent man, used to say, in forming an estimate you must take the word of people who saw them close, and were able to judge more exactly of their real worth."

Sometimes as the carriage laboured up a steep road through tilled country, making the fields more real, adding to them a mark of authenticity like the precious flower with which certain of the old masters used to sign their pictures, a few hesitating cornflowers, like the Combray cornflowers, would stream in our wake. Presently the horses outdistanced them, but a little way on we would catch sight of another which while it stayed our coming had pricked up to welcome us amid the grass its azure star; some made so bold as to come and plant themselves by the side of the road, and the impression left in my mind was a nebulous blend of distant memories and of wild flowers grown tame.

We began to go down hill; and then met, climbing on foot, on a bicycle, in a cart or carriage, one of those creatures—flowers of a fine day but unlike the flowers of the field, for each of them secretes something that is not to be found in another, with the result that we can never satisfy upon any of her fellows the desire which she has brought to birth in us—a farm-girl driving her cow or half-lying along a waggon, a shopkeeper's daughter taking the air, a fashionable young lady erect on the back seat of a landau, facing her parents. Certainly Bloch had been the means of opening a new era and had altered the value of life for me on the day when he had told me that the dreams which I had entertained on my solitary walks along the Méséglise way, when I hoped that some peasant girl might pass whom I could take in my arms, were not a mere fantasy which corresponded to nothing outside myself, but that all the girls one met, whether villagers or 'young ladies,' were alike ready and willing to give ear to such prayers. And even if I were fated, now that I was ill and did not go out by myself, never to be able to make love to them, I was happy all the same, like a child born in a prison or a hospital, who, having always supposed that the human organism was capable of digesting only dry bread and 'physic,' has learned suddenly that peaches, apricots and grapes are not simply part of the decoration of the country scene but delicious and easily assimilated food. Even if his gaoler or his nurse does not allow him to pluck those tempting fruits, still the world seems to him a better place and existence in it more clement. For a desire seems to us more attractive, we repose on it with more confidence, when we know that outside ourselves there is a reality which conforms to it, even if, for us, it is not to be realised. And we think with more joy of a life in which (on condition that we eliminate for a moment from our mind the tiny obstacle, accidental and special, which prevents us personally from doing so) we can imagine ourself to be assuaging that desire. As to the pretty girls who went past, from the day on which I had first known that their cheeks could be kissed, I had become curious about their souls. And the universe had appeared to me more interesting.

Mme. de Villeparisis's carriage moved fast. Scarcely had I time to see the girl who was coming in our direction; and yet—as the beauty of people is not like the beauty of things, as we feel that it is that of an unique creature, endowed with consciousness and free-will—as soon as her individuality, a soul still vague, a will unknown to me, presented a tiny picture of itself, enormously reduced but complete, in the depths of her indifferent eyes, at once, by a mysterious response of the pollen ready in me for the pistils that should receive it, I felt surging through me the embryo, as vague, as minute, of the desire not to let this girl pass without forcing her mind to become conscious of my person, without preventing her desires from wandering to some one else, without coming to fix myself in her dreams and to seize and occupy her heart. Meanwhile our carriage rolled away from her, the pretty girl was already left behind, and as she had—of me—none of those notions which constitute a person in one's mind, her eyes which had barely seen me had forgotten me already. Was it because I had caught but a fragmentary glimpse of her that I had found her so attractive? It may have been. In the first place, the impossibility of stopping when I came to her, the risk of not meeting her again another day, give at once to such a girl the same charm as a place derives from the illness or poverty that prevents us from visiting it, or the so unadventurous days through which we should otherwise have to live from the battle in which we shall doubtless fall. So that, if there were no such thing as habit, life must appear delightful to those of us who would at every moment be threatened with death—that is to say, to all mankind. Then, if our imagination is set going by the desire for what we may not possess, its flight is not limited by a reality completely perceived, in these casual encounters in which the charms of the passing stranger are generally in direct ratio to the swiftness of our passage. If only night is falling and the carriage is moving fast, whether in town or country, there is not a female torso, mutilated like an antique marble by the speed that tears us away and the dusk that drowns it, but aims at our heart, from every turning in the road, from the lighted interior of every shop, the arrows of Beauty, that Beauty of which we are sometimes tempted to ask ourselves whether it is, in this world, anything more than the complementary part that is added to a fragmentary and fugitive stranger by our imagination over-stimulated by regret.

Had I been free to stop, to get down from the carriage and to speak to the girl whom we were passing, should I perhaps have been disillusioned by some fault in her complexion which from the carriage I had not distinguished? (After which every effort to penetrate into her life would have seemed suddenly impossible. For beauty is a sequence of hypotheses which ugliness cuts short when it bars the way that we could already see opening into the unknown.) Perhaps a single word which she might have uttered, a smile, would have furnished me with a key, a clue that I had not expected, to read the expression of her face, to interpret her bearing, which would at once have ceased to be of any interest. It is possible, for I have never in real life met any girls so desirable as on days when I was with some serious person from whom, despite the· myriad pretexts that I invented, I could not tear myself away: some years after that in which I went for the first time to Balbec, as I was driving through Paris with a friend of my father, and had caught sight of a woman walking quickly along·the dark street, I felt that it was unreasonable to forfeit, for a purely conventional scruple, my share of happiness in what may very well be the only life there is, and jumping from the carriage without a word of apology I followed in quest of the stranger; lost her where two streets crossed; caught her up again in a third, and arrived at last, breathless, beneath a street lamp, face to face with old Mme. Verdurin whom I had been carefully avoiding for years, and who, in her delight and surprise, exclaimed: "But how very nice of you to have run all this way just to say how d'ye do to me!"

That year at Balbec, at the moments of such encounters, I would assure my grandmother and Mme. de Villeparisis that I had so severe a headache that the best thing for me would be to go home alone on foot. But they would never let me get out of the carriage. And I must add that pretty girl (far harder to find again than an historic building, for she was nameless and had the power of locomotion) to the collection of all those whom I promised myself that I would examine more closely at a later date. One of them, however, happened to pass more than once before my eyes in circumstances which allowed me to believe that I should be able to get to know her when I chose. This was a milk-girl who came from a farm with an additional supply of cream for the hotel. I fancied that she had recognised me also; and she did, in fact, look at me with an attentiveness which was perhaps due only to the surprise which my attentiveness caused her. And next day, a day on which I had been resting all morning, when Françoise came in about noon to draw my curtains, she handed me a letter which had been left for me downstairs. I knew no one at Balbec. I had no doubt that the letter was from the milk-girl. Alas, it was only from Bergotte who, as he happened to be passing, had tried to see me, but on hearing that I was asleep had scribbled a few charming lines for which the lift-boy had addressed an envelope which I had supposed to have been written by the milk-girl. I was bitterly disappointed, and the thought that it was more difficult, and more flattering to myself to get a letter from Bergotte did not in the least console me for this particular letter's not being from her. As for the girl, I never came across her again any more than I came across those whom I had seen only from Mme. de Villeparisis's carriage. Seeing and then losing them all thus increased the state of agitation in which I was living, and I found a certain wisdom in the philosophers who recommend us to set a limit to our desires (if, that is, they refer to our desire for people, for that is the only kind that ends in anxiety, having for its object a being at once unknown and unconscious. To suppose that philosophy could refer to the desire for wealth would be too silly.). At the same time I was inclined to regard this wisdom as incomplete, for I said to myself that these encounters made me find even more beautiful a world which thus caused to grow along all the country roads flowers at once rare and common, fleeting treasures of the day, windfalls of the drive, of which the contingent circumstances that would never, perhaps, recur had alone prevented me from taking advantage, and which gave a new zest to life.

But perhaps in hoping that, one day, with greater freedom, I should be able to find on other roads girls much the same, I was already beginning to falsify and corrupt what there is exclusively individual in the desire to live in the company of a woman whom one has found attractive, and by the mere fact that I admitted the possibility of making this desire grow artificially, I had implicitly acknowledged my allusion.

The day on which Mme. de Villeparisis took us to Carqueville, where there was that church, covered in ivy, of which she had spoken to us, a church that, built upon rising ground, dominated both its village and the river that flowed beneath it, and had kept its own little bridge from the middle ages, my grandmother, thinking that I would like to be left alone to study the building at my leisure, suggested to her friend that they should go on and wait for me at the pastry-cook's, in the village square which was clearly visible from where we were and, in its mellow bloom in the sunshine, seemed like another part of a whole that was all mediaeval. It was arranged that I should join them there later. In the mass of verdure before which I was left standing I was obliged, if I was to discover the church, to make a mental effort which involved my grasping more intensely the idea 'Church'; in fact, as happens to schoolboys who gather more fully the meaning of a sentence when they are made, by translating or by paraphrasing it, to divest it of the forms to which they are accustomed, this idea of 'Church,' which as a rule I scarcely needed when I stood beneath steeples that were recognisable in themselves, I was obliged perpetually to recall so as not to forget, here that the arch in this clump of ivy was that of a pointed window, there that the projection of the leaves was due to the swelling underneath of a capital. Then came a breath of wind, and sent a tremor through the mobile porch, which was overrun by eddies that shot and quivered like a flood of light; the pointed leaves opened one against another; and, shuddering, the arboreal front drew after it green pillars, undulant, caressed and fugitive.

As I came away from the church I saw by the old bridge a cluster of girls from the village who, probably because it was Sunday, were standing about in their best clothes, rallying the young men who went past. Not so well dressed as the others, but seeming to enjoy some ascendancy over them—for she scarcely answered when they spoke to her—with a more serious and a more determined air, there was a tall one who, hoisted upon the parapet of the bridge with her feet hanging down, was holding on her lap a small vessel full of fish which she had presumably just been catching. She had a tanned complexion, gentle eyes but with a look of contempt for her surroundings, a small nose, delicately and attractively modelled. My eyes rested upon her skin; and my lips, had the need arisen, might have believed that they had followed my eyes. But it was not only to her body that I should have liked to attain, there was also her person, which abode within her, and with which there is but one form of contact, namely to attract its attention, but one sort of penetration, to awaken an idea in it.

And this inner self of the charming fisher-girl seemed to be still closed to me, I was doubtful whether I had entered it, even after I had seen my own image furtively reflect itself in the twin mirrors of her gaze, following an index of refraction that was as unknown to me as if I had been placed in the field of vision of a deer. But just as it would not have sufficed that my lips should find pleasure in hers without giving pleasure to them also, so I should have wished that the idea of me which was to enter this creature, was to fasten itself in her, should attract to me not merely her attention but her admiration, her desire, and should compel her to keep me in her memory until the day when I should be able to meet her again. Meanwhile I could see, within a stone's-throw, the square in which Mme. de Villeparisis's carriage must be waiting for me. I had not a moment to lose; and already I could feel that the girls were beginning to laugh at the sight of me thus held suspended before them. I had a five-franc piece in my pocket. I drew it out, and, before explaining to the girl the errand on which I proposed to send her, so as to have a better chance of her listening to me, I held the coin for a moment before her eyes.

"Since you seem to belong to the place," I said to her, "I wonder if you would be so good as to take a message for me. I want you to go to a pastry-cook's—which is apparently in a square, but I don't know where that is—where there is a carriage waiting for me. One moment! To make quite sure, will you ask if the carriage belongs to the Marquise de Villeparisis? But you can't miss it; it's a carriage and pair."

That was what I wished her to know, so that she should regard me as someone of importance. But when I had uttered the words 'Marquise' and 'carriage and pair,' suddenly I had a great sense of calm. I felt that the fisher-girl would remember me, and I felt vanishing, with my fear of not being able to meet her again, part also of my desire to meet her. It seemed to me that I had succeeded in touching her person with invisible lips, and that I had pleased her. And this assault and capture of her mind, this immaterial possession had taken from her part of her mystery, just as physical possession does.

We came down towards Hudimesnil; suddenly I was overwhelmed with that profound happiness which I had not often felt since Combray; happiness analogous to that which had been given me by—among other things—the steeples of Martinville. But this time it remained incomplete. I had just seen, standing a little way back from the steep ridge over which we were passing, three trees, probably marking the entrance to a shady avenue, which made a pattern at which I was looking now not for the first time; I could not succeed in reconstructing the place from which they had been, as it were, detached, but I felt that it had been familiar to me once; so that my mind having wavered between some distant year and the present moment, Balbec and its surroundings began to dissolve and I asked myself whether the whole of this drive were not a make-believe, Balbec a place to which I had never gone save in imagination, Mme. de Villeparisis a character in a story and the three old trees the reality which one recaptures on raising one's eyes from the book which one has been reading and which describes an environment into which one has come to believe that one has been bodily transported.

I looked at the three trees; I could see them plainly, but my mind felt that they were concealing something which it had not grasped, as when things are placed out of our reach, so that our fingers, stretched out at arm's-length, can only touch for a moment their outer surface, and can take hold of nothing. Then we rest for a little while before thrusting out our arm with refreshed vigour, and trying to reach an inch or two farther. But if my mind was thus to collect itself, to gather strength, I should have to be alone. What would I not have given to be able to escape as I used to do on those walks along the Guermantes way, when I detached myself from my parents! It seemed indeed that I ought to do so now. I recognised that kind of pleasure which requires, it is true, a certain effort on the part of the mind, but in comparison with which the attractions of the inertia which inclines us to renounce that pleasure seem very slight. That pleasure, the object of which I could but dimly feel, that pleasure which I must create for myself, I experienced only on rare occasions, but on each of these it seemed to me that the things which had happened in the interval were of but scant importance, and that in attaching myself to the reality of that pleasure alone I could at length begin to lead a new life. I laid my hand for a moment across my eyes, so as to be able to shut them without Mme. de Villeparisis's noticing. I sat there, thinking of nothing, then with my thoughts collected, compressed and strengthened I sprang farther forward in the direction of the trees, or rather in that inverse direction at the end of which I could see them growing within myself. I felt again behind them the same object, known to me and yet vague, which I could not bring nearer. And yet all three of them, as the carriage moved on, I could see coming towards me. Where had I looked at them before? There was no place near Combray where an avenue opened off the road like that. The site which they recalled to me, there was no room for it either in the scenery of the place in Germany where I had gone one year with my grandmother to take the waters. Was I to suppose, then, that they came from years already so remote in my life that the landscape which accompanied them had been entirely obliterated from my memory, and that, like the pages which, with sudden emotion, we recognise in a book which we imagined that we had never read, they surged up by themselves out of the forgotten chapter of my earliest infancy? Were they not rather to be numbered among those dream landscapes, always the same, at least for me in whom their unfamiliar aspect was but the objectivation in my dreams of the effort that I had been making while awake either to penetrate the mystery of a place beneath the outward appearance of which I was dimly conscious of there being something more, as had so often happened to me on the Guermantes way, or to succeed in bringing mystery back to a place which I had longed to know and which, from the day on which I had come to know it, had seemed to me to be wholly superficial,

like Balbec? Or were they but an image freshly extracted from a dream
of the night before, but already so worn, so altered that it seemed to me to
come from somewhere far more distant? Or had I indeed never seen them
before; did they conceal beneath their surface, like the trees, like the tufts
of grass that I had seen beside the Guermantes way, a meaning as obscure,
as hard to grasp as is a distant past, so that, whereas they are pleading
with me that I would master a new idea, I imagined that I had to identify
something in my memory? Or again were they concealing no hidden
thought, and was it simply my strained vision that made me see them
double in time as one occasionally sees things double in space? I could not
tell. And yet all the time they were coming towards me; perhaps some
fabulous apparition, a ring of witches or of norns who would propound their
oracles to me. I chose rather to believe that they were phantoms of the
past, dear companions of my childhood, vanished friends who recalled our
common memories. Like ghosts they seemed to be appealing to me to take
them with me, to bring them back to life. In their simple, passionate ges-
ticulation I could discern the helpless anguish of a beloved person who has
lost the power of speech, and feels that he will never be able to say to us
what he wishes to say and we can never guess. Presently, at a cross-roads,
the carriage left them. It was bearing me away from what alone I believed
to be true, what would have made me truly happy; it was like my life.

I watched the trees gradually withdraw, waving their despairing arms,
seeming to say to me: "What you fail to learn from us to-day, you will
never know. If you allow us to drop back into the hollow of this road from
which we sought to raise ourselves up to you, a whole part of yourself
which we were bringing to you will fall for ever into the abyss." And
indeed if, in the course of time, I did discover the kind of pleasure and
of disturbance which I had just been feeling once again, and if one evening—too late, but then for all time—I fastened myself to it, of those trees
themselves I was never to know what they had been trying to give me
nor where else I had seen them. And when, the road having forked and
the carriage with it, I turned my back on them and ceased to see them,
with Mme. de Villeparisis asking me what I was dreaming about, I was
as wretched as though I had just lost a friend, had died myself, had broken
faith with the dead or had denied my God.

It was time to be thinking of home. Mme. de Villeparisis, who had a
certain feeling for nature, colder than that of my grandmother but capable
of recognising, even outside museums and noblemen's houses, the simple
and majestic beauty of certain old and venerable things, told her coachman to take us back by the old Balbec road, a road little used but planted
with old elm-trees which we thought quite admirable.

Once we had got to know this road, for a change we would return—that
is, if we had not taken it on the outward journey—by another which ran
through the woods of Chantereine and Canteloup. The invisibility of the
numberless birds that took up one another's song close beside us in the
trees gave me the same sense of being at rest that one has when one shuts
one's eyes. Chained to my back-seat like Prometheus on his rock I listened
to my Oceanides. And when it so happened that I caught a glimpse of one

of those birds as it passed from one leaf to another, there was so little
apparent connexion between it and the songs that I heard that I could
not believe that I was beholding their cause in that little body, fluttering,
startled and unseeing.

This road was like many others of the same kind which are to be found
in France, climbing on a fairly steep gradient to its summit and then
gradually falling for the rest of the way. At the time, I found no great
attraction in it, I was only glad to be going home. But it became for me later
on a frequent source of joy by remaining in my memory as a lodestone to
which all the similar roads that I was to take, on walks or drives or journeys,
would at once attach themselves without breach of continuity and would
be able, thanks to it, to communicate directly with my heart. For as soon
as the carriage or the motor-car turned into one of these roads that seemed
to be merely the continuation of the road along which I had driven with
Mme. de Villeparisis, the matter to which I found my consciousness
directly applying itself, as to the most recent event in my past, would be
(all the intervening years being quietly obliterated) the impressions that
I had had on those bright summer afternoons and evenings, driving round
Balbec, when the leaves smelt good, a mist rose from the ground, and beyond the village close at hand one could see through the trees the sun
setting as though it had been merely some place farther along the road,
a forest place and distant, which we should not have time to reach that
evening. Harmonised with what I was feeling now in another place, on a
similar road, surrounded by all the accessory sensations of breathing deep
draughts of air, of curiosity, indolence, appetite, lightness of heart which
were common to them both, and excluding all others, these impressions
would be reinforced, would take on the consistency of a particular type
of pleasure, and almost of a setting of life which, as it happened, I rarely
had the luck to come across, but in which these awakened memories placed,
amid the reality that my senses could perceive, no small part of a reality
suggested, dreamed, unseizable, to give me, among those regions through
which I was passing, more than an aesthetic feeling, a transient but exalted ambition to stay there and to live there always. How often since then,
simply because I could smell green leaves, has not being seated on a back-
seat opposite Mme. de Villeparisis, meeting the Princesse de Luxembourg
who waved a greeting to her from her own carriage, coming back to dinner
at the Grand Hotel appeared to me as one of those indescribable happi-
nesses which neither the present nor the future can restore to us, which
we may taste once only in a lifetime.

Often dusk would have fallen before we reached the hotel. Timidly I
would quote to Mme. de Villeparisis, pointing to the moon in the sky,
some memorable expression of Chateaubriand or Vigny or Victor Hugo:
'Shedding abroad that ancient secret of melancholy' or 'Weeping like
Diana by the brink of her streams' or 'The shadows nuptial, solemn and
august.'

"And so you think that good, do you?" she would ask, "inspired, as
you call it. I must confess that I am always surprised to see people taking
things seriously nowadays which the friends of those gentlemen, while

doing ample justice to their merits, were the first to laugh at. People weren't so free then with the word 'inspired' as they are now, when if you say to a writer that he has mere talent he thinks you're insulting him. You quote me a fine passage from M. de Chateaubriand about moonlight. You shall see that I have my own reasons for being refractory. M. de Chateaubriand used constantly to come to see my father. He was quite a pleasant person when you were alone with him, because then he was simple and amusing, but the moment he had an audience he would begin to pose, and then he became absurd; when my father was in the room, he pretended that he had flung his resignation in the King's face, and that he had controlled the voting in the Conclave, forgetting that it was my father whom he had asked to beg the King to take him back, and that my father had heard him make the most idiotic forecasts of the Papal election. You ought to have heard M. de Blacas on that famous Conclave; he was a very different kind of man from M. de Chateaubriand. As to his fine phrases about the moon, they became part of our regular programme for entertaining our guests. Whenever there was any moonlight about the house, if there was anyone staying with us for the first time he would be told to take M. de Chateaubriand for a stroll after dinner. When they came in, my father would take his guest aside and say: 'Well, and was M. de Chateaubriand very eloquent?'—'Oh, yes.' 'He's been talking about the moon?'—'Yes, how did you know?'—'One moment, didn't he say——' and then my father would quote the passage. 'He did; but how in the world . . . ?'—'And he spoke to you of the moonlight on the Roman Campagna?'—'But, my dear sir, you're a magician.' My father was no magician, but M. de Chateaubriand had the same little speech about the moon which he served up every time."

At the mention of Vigny she laughed: "The man who said: 'I am the Comte Alfred de Vigny!' One either is a Comte or one isn't; it is not of the slightest importance." And then perhaps she discovered that it was after all, of some slight importance, for she went on: "For one thing I am by no means sure that he was, and in any case he was of the humblest origin, that gentleman who speaks in his verses of his 'Esquire's crest.' In such charming taste, is it not, and so interesting to his readers! Like Musset, a plain Paris cit, who laid so much stress on 'The golden falcon that surmounts my helm.' As if you would ever hear a real gentleman say a thing like that! And yet Musset had some talent as a poet. But except *Cinq-Mars* I have never been able to read a thing by M. de Vigny. I get so bored that the book falls from my hands. M. Molé, who had all the cleverness and tact that were wanting in M. de Vigny, put him properly in his place when he welcomed him to the Academy. Do you mean to say you don't know the speech? It is a masterpiece of irony and impertinence." She found fault with Balzac, whom she was surprised to see her nephews admire, for having pretended to describe a society 'in which he was never received' and of which his descriptions were wildly improbable. As for Victor Hugo, she told us that M. de Bouillon, her father, who had friends among the young leaders of the Romantic movement, had been taken by some of them to the first performance of *Hernani,* but that he had been unable to sit through it, so ridiculous had he found the lines of that talented but extravagant writer who had acquired the title of 'Major Poet' only by virtue of having struck a bargain, and as a reward for the not disinterested indulgence that he shewed to the dangerous errors of the Socialists.

We had now come in sight of the hotel, with its lights, so hostile that first evening, on our arrival, now protecting and kind, speaking to us of home. And when the carriage drew up outside the door, the porter, the pages, the lift-boy, attentive, clumsy, vaguely uneasy at our lateness, were numbered, now that they had grown familiar, among those beings who change so many times in the course of our life, as we ourself change, but by whom, when they are for the time being the mirror of our habits, we find something attractive in the feeling that we are being faithfully reflected and in a friendly spirit. We prefer them to friends whom we have not seen for some time, for they contain more of what we actually are. Only the outside page, exposed to the sun all day, had been taken indoors for protection from the cold night air and swaddled in thick woollen garments which, combined with the orange effulgence of his locks and the curiously red bloom of his cheeks, made one, seeing him there through the glass front of the hall, think of a hot-house plant muffled up for protection from the frost. We got out of the carriage, with the help of a great many more servants than were required, but they were conscious of the importance of the scene and each felt obliged to take some part in it. I was always very hungry. And so, often, so as not to keep dinner waiting, I would not go upstairs first to the room which had succeeded in becoming so really mine that to catch sight of its long violet curtains and low bookcases was to find myself alone again with that self of which things, like people, gave me a reflected image; but we would all wait together in the hall until the head waiter came to tell us that our dinner was ready. And this gave us another opportunity of listening to Mme. de Villeparisis.

"But you must be tired of us by now," protested my grandmother.

"Not at all! Why, I am delighted, what could be nicer?" replied her friend with a winning smile, drawing out, almost intoning her words in a way that contrasted markedly with her customary simplicity of speech.

And indeed at such moments as this she was not natural, her mind reverted to her early training, to the aristocratic manner in which a great lady is supposed to shew common people that she is glad to see them, that she is not at all stiff. And her one and only failure in true politeness lay in this excess of politeness; which it was easy to identify as one of the professional 'wrinkles' of a lady of the Faubourg Saint-Germain, who, always seeing in her humbler friends the latent discontent that she must one day arouse in their bosoms, greedily seizes every opportunity on which she can possibly, in the ledger in which she keeps her social account with them, write down a credit balance which will allow her to enter presently on the opposite page the dinner or reception to which she will not invite them. And so, having long ago taken effect in her once and for all, and ignoring the fact that now both the circumstances and the people concerned were different, that in Paris she hoped to see us often come to her house, the spirit of her caste was urging Mme. de Villeparisis on with feverish ardour, and as if the time that was allowed her for being kind to us was limited, to multiply, while we were still at Balbec, her gifts of roses and melons, loans of books, drives in her carriage and verbal effusions. And for that reason, quite as much as the dazzling glories of the beach, the many-coloured flamboyance and subaqueous light of the rooms, as much even as the riding-lessons by which tradesmen's sons were deified like Alexander of Macedon, the daily kindnesses shewn us by Mme. de Villeparisis and also the unaccustomed, momentary, holiday ease with which my grandmother accepted them have remained in my memory as typical of life at a watering-place.

"Give them your cloaks to take upstairs."

My grandmother handed hers to the manager, and because he had been so nice to me I was distressed by this want of consideration, which seemed to pain him.

"I think you've hurt his feelings," said the Marquise. "He probably fancies himself too great a gentleman to carry your wraps. I remember so well the Duc de Nemours, when I was still quite little, coming to see my father who was living then on the top floor of the Bouillon house, with a fat parcel under his arm of letters and newspapers. I can see the Prince now, in his blue coat, framed in our doorway, which had such pretty wood-work round it—I think it was Bagard made it—you know those fine laths that they used to cut, so supple that the joiner would twist them sometimes into little shells and flowers, like the ribbons round a nosegay. 'Here you are, Cyrus,' he said to my father, 'look what your porter's given me to bring you. He said to me: "Since you're going up to see the Count, it's not worth my while climbing all those stairs; but take care you don't break the string." ' Now that you have got rid of your things, why don't you sit down; look, sit in this seat," she said to my grandmother, taking her by the hand.

"Oh, if you don't mind, not in that one! There is not room for two, and it's too big for me by myself; I shouldn't feel comfortable."

"You remind me, for it was exactly like this, of a seat that I had for many years until at last I couldn't keep it any longer because it had been given to my mother by the poor Duchesse de Praslin. My mother, though she was the simplest person in the world, really, had ideas that belonged to another generation, which even in those days I could scarcely under-stand; and at first she had not been at all willing to let herself be intro-duced to Mme. de Praslin, who had been plain Mlle. Sebastiani, while she, because she was a Duchess, felt that it was not for her to be intro-duced to my mother. And really, you know," Mme. de Villeparisis went on, forgetting that she herself did not understand these fine shades of dis-tinction, "even if she had just been Mme. de Choiseul, there was a good deal to be said for her claim. The Choiseuls are everything you could want; they spring from a sister of Louis the Fat; they were ruling princes down in Basigny. I admit that we beat them in marriages and in distinction, but the precedence is pretty much the same. This little difficulty gave rise to several amusing incidents, such as a luncheon party which was kept wait-ing a whole hour or more before one of these ladies could make up her mind to let herself be introduced to the other. In spite of which they became great friends, and she gave my mother a seat like that, in which people always refused to sit, just as you did, until one day my mother heard a carriage drive into the courtyard. She asked a young servant we had, who it was. 'The Duchesse de La Rochefoucauld, ma'am.' 'Very well, say that I am at home.' A quarter of an hour passed; no one came. 'What about the Duchesse de La Rochefoucauld?' my mother asked. 'Where is she?' 'She's on the stairs, ma'am, getting her breath,' said the young servant, who had not been long up from the country, where my mother had the excellent habit of getting all her servants. Often she had seen them born. That's the only way to get really good ones. And they're the rarest of luxuries. And sure enough the Duchesse de La Rochefoucauld had the greatest difficulty in getting upstairs, for she was an enormous woman, so enormous, indeed, that when she did come into the room my mother was quite at a loss for a moment to know where to put her. And then the seat that Mme. de Praslin had given her caught her eye. 'Won't you sit down?' she said, bringing it forward. And the Duchess filled it from side to side. She was quite a pleasant woman, for all her massiveness. 'She still creates an effect when she comes in,' one of our friends said once. 'She certainly creates an effect when she goes out,' said my mother, who was rather more free in her speech than would be thought proper nowadays. Even in Mme. de La Rochefoucauld's own drawing-room people weren't afraid to make fun of her to her face (at which she was always the first to laugh) over her ample proportions. 'But are you all alone?' my grandmother once asked M. de La Rochefoucauld, when she had come to pay a call on the Duchess, and being met at the door by him had not seen his wife who was at the other end of the room. 'Is Mme. de La Rochefoucauld not at home? I don't see her.'—'How charming of you!' replied the Duke, who had about the worst judgment of any man I have ever known, but was not altogether lacking in humour."

After dinner, when I had retired upstairs with my grandmother, I said to her that the qualities which attracted us in Mme. de Villeparisis, her tact, her shrewdness, her discretion, her modesty in not referring to herself, were not, perhaps, of very great value since those who possessed them in the highest degree were simply people like Molé and Loménie, and that if the want of them can make our social relations unpleasant yet it did not prevent from becoming Chateaubriand, Vigny, Hugo, Balzac, a lot of foolish fellows who had no judgment, at whom it was easy to mock, like Bloch. . . . But at the name of Bloch, my grandmother cried out in protest. And she began to praise Mme. de Villeparisis. As we are told that it is the preservation of the species which guides our individual preferences in love, and, so that the child may be constituted in the most normal fashion, sends fat men in pursuit of lean women and *vice versa*, so in some dim way it was the requirements of my happiness threatened by my disordered nerves, by my morbid tendency to melancholy, to solitude, that made her allot the highest place to the qualities of balance and judgment, peculiar not only to Mme. de Villeparisis but to a society in which our ancestors saw blossom the minds of a Doudan, a M. de Rémusat, not to mention a

Beausergent, a Joubert, a Sévigné, a type of mind that invests life with more happiness, with greater dignity than the converse refinements which brought a Baudelaire, a Poe, a Verlaine, a Rimbaud to sufferings, to a disrepute such as my grandmother did not wish for her daughter's child. I interrupted her with a kiss and asked her if she had noticed some expression which Mme. de Villeparisis had used and which seemed to point to a woman who thought more of her noble birth than she was prepared to admit. In this way I used to submit my impressions of life to my grandmother, for I was never certain what degree of respect was due to anyone until she had informed me. Every evening I would come to her with the mental sketches that I had made during the day of all those non-existent people who were not her. Once I said to her: "I shouldn't be able to live without you." "But you mustn't speak like that;" her voice was troubled. "We must harden our hearts more than that, you know. Or what would become of you if I went away on a journey? But I hope that you would be quite sensible and quite happy."

"I could manage to be sensible if you went away for a few days, but I should count the hours."

"But if I were to go away for months . . ." (at the bare suggestion of such a thing my heart was wrung) ". . . for years . . . for . . ."

We both remained silent. We dared not look one another in the face. And yet I was suffering more keenly from her anguish than from my own. And so I walked across to the window, and said to her, with a studied clearness of tone but with averted eyes:

"You know what a creature of habit I am. For the first few days after I have been parted from the people I love best, I am wretched. But though I go on loving them just as much, I grow used to their absence; life becomes calm, bearable, pleasant; I could stand being parted from them for months, for years . . ."

I was obliged to stop, and looked straight out of the window. My grandmother went out of the room for something. But next day I began to talk to her about philosophy, and, speaking in a tone of complete indifference, but at the same time taking care that my grandmother should pay attention to what I was saying, I remarked what a curious thing it was that, according to the latest scientific discoveries, the materialist position appeared to be crumbling, and the most likely thing to be, once again, the survival of the soul and reunion in a life everlasting.

Mme. de Villeparisis gave us warning that presently she would not be able to see so much of us. A young nephew who was preparing for Saumur, and was meanwhile stationed in the neighbourhood, at Doncières, was coming to spend a few weeks' furlough with her, and she would be devoting most of her time to him. In the course of our drives together she had boasted to us of his extreme cleverness, and above all of his goodness of heart; already I was imagining that he would have an instinctive feeling for me, that I was to be his best friend; and when, before his arrival, his aunt gave my grandmother to understand that he had unfortunately fallen into the clutches of an appalling woman with whom he was quite infatuated and who would never let him go, since I believed that that sort of love was doomed to end in mental aberration, crime and suicide, thinking how short the time was that was set apart for our friendship, already so great in my heart, although I had not yet set eyes on him, I wept for that friendship and for the misfortunes that were in store for it, as we weep for a person whom we love when some one has just told us that he is seriously ill and that his days are numbered.

One afternoon of scorching heat I was in the dining-room of the hotel, which they had plunged in semi-darkness, to shield it from the glare, by drawing the curtains which the sun gilded, while through the gaps between them I caught flashing blue glimpses of the sea, when along the central gangway leading inland from the beach to the high road I saw, tall, slender, his head held proudly erect upon a springing neck, a young man go past with searching eyes, whose skin was as fair and whose hair as golden as if they had absorbed all the rays of the sun. Dressed in a clinging, almost white material such as I could never have believed that any man would have the audacity to wear, the thinness of which suggested no less vividly than the coolness of the dining-room the heat and brightness of the glorious day outside, he was walking fast. His eyes, from one of which a monocle kept dropping, were of the colour of the sea. Everyone looked at him with interest as he passed, knowing that this young Marquis de Saint-Loup-en-Bray was famed for the smartness of his clothes. All the newspapers had described the suit in which he had recently acted as second to the young Duc d'Uzès in a duel. One felt that this so special quality of his hair, his eyes, his skin, his figure, which would have marked him out in a crowd like a precious vein of opal, azure-shot and luminous, embedded in a mass of coarser substance, must correspond to a life different from that led by other men. So that when, before the attachment which Mme. de Villeparisis had been deploring, the prettiest women in society had disputed the possession of him, his presence, at a watering-place for instance, in the company of the beauty of the season to whom he was paying court, not only made her conspicuous, but attracted every eye fully as much to himself. Because of his 'tone,' of his impertinence befitting a young 'lion,' and especially of his astonishing good looks, some people even thought him effeminate, though without attaching any stigma, for everyone knew how manly he was and that he was a passionate 'womaniser.' This was Mme. de Villeparisis's nephew of whom she had spoken to us. I was overcome with joy at the thought that I was going to know him and to see him for several weeks on end, and confident that he would bestow on me all his affection. He strode rapidly across the hotel, seeming to be in pursuit of his monocle, which kept darting away in front of him like a butterfly. He was coming from the beach, and the sea which filled the lower half of the glass front of the hall gave him a background against which he was drawn at full length, as in certain portraits whose painters attempt, without in anyway falsifying the most accurate observation of contemporary life, but by choosing for their sitter appropriate surroundings, a polo ground, golf links, a racecourse, the bridge of a yacht, to furnish a modern equivalent of those canvases on which the old masters used to present the human figure in the foreground of a landscape. A carriage and pair was waiting for him at the door; and, while his monocle resumed its gambollings in the air of the sunlit street, with the elegance and mastery which a great pianist contrives to display in the simplest piece of execution, where it has not appeared possible that he could shew himself superior to a performer of the second class, Mme. de Villeparisis's nephew, taking the reins that were handed him by the groom, jumped on to the box seat by his side and, while he opened a letter which the manager of the hotel sent out after him, made his horses start.

What a disappointment was mine on the days that followed, when, each time that I met him outside or in the hotel—his head erect, perpetually balancing the movements of his limbs round the fugitive and dancing monocle which seemed to be their centre of gravity—I was forced to admit that he had evidently no desire to make our acquaintance, and saw that he did not bow to us although he must have known that we were friends of his aunt. And calling to mind the friendliness that Mme. de Villeparisis, and before her M. de Norpois, had shewn me, I thought that perhaps they were only of a bogus nobility, and that there might be a secret section in the laws that govern the aristocracy which allowed women, perhaps, and certain diplomats to discard, in their relations with plebeians, for a reason which was beyond me, the stiffness which must, on the other hand, be piti-lessly maintained by a young Marquis. My intelligence might have told me the opposite. But the characteristic feature of the silly phase through which I was passing—a phase by no means irresponsive, indeed highly fertile—is that we do not consult our intelligence and that the most trivial attributes of other people seem to us then to form an inseparable part of their personality. In a world thronged with monsters and with gods, we are barely conscious of tranquillity. There is hardly one of the actions which we performed in that phase which we would not give anything, in later life, to be able to erase from our memory. Whereas what we ought to regret is that we no longer possess the spontaneity which made us perform them. In later life we look at things in a more practical way, in full con-formity with the rest of society, but youth was the only time in which we learned anything.

This insolence which I surmised in M. de Saint-Loup, and all that it implied of ingrained severity, received confirmation from his attitude whenever he passed us, his body as inflexibly erect, his head always held as high, his gaze as impassive, or rather, I should say, as implacable, de-void of that vague respect which one has for the rights of other people, even if they do not know one's aunt, one example of which was that I did not look in quite the same way at an old lady as at a gas lamp. These frigid manners were as far removed from the charming letters which, but a few days since, I had still been imagining him as writing to tell me of his regard for myself, as is removed from the enthusiasm of the Chamber and of the populace which he has been picturing himself as rousing by an imperishable speech, the humble, dull, obscure position of the dreamer who, after pondering it thus by himself, for himself, aloud, finds himself, once the imaginary applause has died away, just the same Tom, Dick or Harry as before. When Mme. de Villeparisis, doubtless in an attempt to counteract the bad impression that had been made on us by an exterior indicative of an arrogant and evil nature, spoke to us again of the inexhaustible goodness of her great-nephew (he was the son of one of her nieces, and a little older than myself), I marvelled how the world, with an utter disregard of truth, ascribes tenderness of heart to people whose hearts are in reality so hard and dry, provided only that they behave with common courtesy to the brilliant members of their own sets. Mme. de Villeparisis herself confirmed, though indirectly, my diagnosis, which was already a conviction, of the essential points of her nephew's character one day when I met them both coming along a path so narrow that there was nothing for it but to introduce me to him. He seemed not to hear that a person's name was being repeated to him, not a muscle of his face moved; his eyes, in which there shone not the faintest gleam of human sympathy, shewed merely in the insensibility, in the inanity of their gaze an exaggeration failing which there would have been nothing to distinguish them from lifeless mirrors. Then fastening on me those hard eyes, as though he wished to make sure of me before returning my salute, by an abrupt release which seemed to be due rather to a reflex action of his muscles than to an exercise of will, keeping between himself and me the greatest possible interval, he stretched his arm out to its full extension and, at the end of it, offered me his hand. I supposed that it must mean, at the very least, a duel when, next day, he sent me his card. But he spoke to me only of literature, declared after a long talk that he would like immensely to spend several hours with me every day. He had not only, in this encounter, given proof of an ardent zest for the things of the spirit, he had shewn a regard for myself which was little in keeping with his greeting of me the day before. After I had seen him repeat the same process whenever anyone was introduced to him, I realised that it was simply a social usage peculiar to his branch of the family, to which his mother, who had seen to it that he should be perfectly brought up, had moulded his limbs; he went through those motions without thinking, any more than he thought about his beautiful clothes or hair; they were a thing devoid of the moral significance which I had at first ascribed to them, a thing purely acquired like that other habit that he had of at once demanding an introduction to the family of anyone whom he knew, which had become so instinctive in him that, seeing me again the day after our talk, he fell upon me and without asking how I did begged me to make him known to my grandmother, who was with me, with the same feverish haste as if the request had been due to some instinct of self-preservation, like the act of warding off a blow, or of shutting one's eyes to avoid a stream of boiling water, without which precautions it would have been dangerous to stay where one was a moment longer.

The first rites of exorcism once performed, as a wicked fairy discards her outer form and endures all the most enchanting graces, I saw this disdainful creature become the most friendly, the most considerate young man that I had ever met. "Good," I said to myself, "I've been mistaken about him once already; I was taken in by a mirage; but I have corrected the first only to fall into a second, for he must be a great gentleman who has grown sick of his nobility and is trying to hide it." As a matter of fact it was not long before all the exquisite breeding, all the friendliness of Saint-Loup were indeed to let me see another creature but one very different from what I had suspected.

This young man who had the air of a scornful, sporting aristocrat had in fact no respect, no interest save for and in the things of the spirit, and especially those modern manifestations of literature and art which seemed so ridiculous to his aunt; he was imbued, moreover, with what she called 'Socialistic spoutings,' was filled with the most profound contempt for his caste and spent long hours in the study of Nietzsche and Proudhon. He was one of those intellectuals, quick to admire what is good, who shut themselves up in a book, and are interested only in pure thought. Indeed in Saint-Loup the expression of this highly abstract tendency, which removed him so far from my customary preoccupations, while it seemed to me touching, also annoyed me not a little. I may say that when I realised properly who had been his father, on days when I had been reading memoirs rich in anecdotes of that famous Comte de Marsantes, in whom were embodied the special graces of a generation already remote, the mind full of speculation—anxious to obtain fuller details of the life that M. de Marsantes had led, it used to infuriate me that Robert de Saint-Loup, instead of being content to be the son of his father, instead of being able to guide me through the old-fashioned romance of what had been that father's existence, had trained himself to enjoy Nietzsche and Proudhon. His father would not have shared my regret. He had been himself a man of brains, who had transcended the narrow confines of his life as a man of the world. He had hardly had time to know his son, but had hoped that his son would prove a better man than himself. And I really believe that, unlike the rest of the family, he would have admired his son, would have rejoiced at his abandoning what had been his own small diversions for austere meditations, and without saying a word, in his modesty as a great gentleman endowed with brains, he would have read in secret his son's favourite authors in order to appreciate how far Robert was superior to himself.

There was, however, this rather painful consideration: that if M. de Marsantes, with his extremely open mind, would have appreciated a son so different from himself, Robert de Saint-Loup, because he was one of those who believe that merit is attached only to certain forms of art and life, had an affectionate but slightly contemptuous memory of a father who had spent all his time hunting and racing, who yawned at Wagner and raved over Offenbach. Saint-Loup had not the intelligence to see that intellectual worth has nothing to do with adhesion to any one aesthetic formula, and had for the intellectuality of M. de Marsantes much the same sort of scorn as might have been felt for Boieldieu or Labiche by a son of Boieldieu or Labiche who had become adepts in the most symbolic literature and the most complex music. "I scarcely knew my father," he used to say. "He seems to have been a charming person. His tragedy was the deplorable age in which he lived. To have been born in the Faubourg Saint-Germain and to have to live in the days of La Belle Hélène would be enough to wreck any existence. Perhaps if he'd been some little shopkeeper mad about the Ring he'd have turned out quite different. Indeed they tell me that he was fond of literature. But that can never be proved, because literature to him meant such utterly god-forsaken books." And in my own case, if I found Saint-Loup a trifle earnest, he could not understand why I was not more earnest still. Never judging anything except by the weight of the intelligence that it contained, never perceiving the magic appeal to the imagination that I found in things which he condemned as frivolous, he was astonished that I—I, to whom he imagined himself to be so utterly inferior—could take any interest in them.

From the first Saint-Loup made a conquest of my grandmother, not only by the incessant acts of kindness which he went out of his way to shew to us both, but by the naturalness which he put into them as into everything. For naturalness—doubtless because through the artifice of man it allows a feeling of nature to permeate—was the quality which my grandmother preferred to all others, whether in gardens, where she did not like there to be, as there had been in our Combray garden, too formal borders, or at table, where she detested those dressed-up dishes in which you could hardly detect the foodstuffs that had gone to make them, or in piano-playing, which she did not like to be too finicking, too laboured, having indeed had a special weakness for the discords, the wrong notes of Rubinstein. This naturalness she found and enjoyed even in the clothes that Saint-Loup wore, of a pliant elegance, with nothing swagger, nothing formal about them, no stiffness or starch. She appreciated this rich young man still more highly for the free and careless way that he had of living in luxury without 'smelling of money,' without giving himself airs; she even discovered the charm of this naturalness in the incapacity which Saint-Loup had kept, though as a rule it is outgrown with childhood, at the same time as certain physiological peculiarities of that period, for preventing his face from at once reflecting every emotion. Something, for instance, that he wanted to have but had not expected, were it no more than a compliment, reacted in him in a burst of pleasure so quick, so burning, so volatile, so expansive that it was impossible for him to contain and to conceal it; a grin of delight seized irresistible hold of his face; the too delicate skin of his cheeks allowed a vivid glow to shine through them, his eyes sparkled with confusion and joy; and my grandmother was infinitely touched by this charming show of innocence and frankness, which, incidentally, in Saint-Loup—at any rate at the period of our first friendship—was not misleading. But I have known another person, and there are many such, in whom the physiological sincerity of that fleeting blush in no way excluded moral duplicity; as often as not it proves nothing more than the vivacity with which pleasure is felt—so that it disarms them and they are forced publicly to confess it—by natures capable of the vilest treachery. But where my grandmother did really adore Saint-Loup's naturalness was in his way of admitting, without any evasion, his affection for me, to give expression to which he found words than which she herself, she told me, could not have thought of any more appropriate, more truly loving, words to which 'Sévigné and Beausergent' might have set their signatures. He was

not afraid to make fun of my weaknesses—which he had discerned with
an acuteness that made her smile—but as she herself would have done,
lovingly, at the same time extolling my good qualities with a warmth, an
impulsive freedom that shewed no sign of the reserve, the coldness by
means of which young men of his age are apt to suppose that they give
themselves importance. And he shewed in forestalling every discomfort,
however slight, in covering my legs if the day had turned cold without my
noticing it, in arranging (without telling me) to stay later with me in the
evening if he thought that I was depressed or felt unwell, a vigilance
which, from the point of view of my health, for which a more hardening
discipline would perhaps have been better, my grandmother found almost
excessive, though as a proof of his affection for myself she was deeply
touched by it.

It was promptly settled between us that he and I were to be great friends
for ever, and he would say 'our friendship' as though he were speaking of
some important and delightful thing which had an existence independent
of ourselves, and which he soon called—not counting his love for his mistress—the great joy of his life. These words made me rather uncomfortable and I was at a loss for an answer, for I did not feel when I was
with him and talked to him—and no doubt it would have been the same
with everyone else—any of that happiness which it was, on the other hand,
possible for me to experience when I was by myself. For alone, at times,
I felt surging from the depths of my being one or other of those impressions which gave me a delicious sense of comfort. But as soon as I was with
some one else, when I began to talk to a friend, my mind at once 'turned
about,' it was towards the listener and not myself that it directed its
thoughts, and when they followed this outward course they brought me no
pleasure. Once I had left Saint-Loup, I managed, with the help of words,
to put more or less in order the confused minutes that I had spent with
him; I told myself that I had a good friend, that a good friend was a rare
thing, and I tasted, when I felt myself surrounded by 'goods' that were
difficult to acquire, what was precisely the opposite of the pleasure that
was natural to me, the opposite of the pleasure of having extracted from
myself and brought to light something that was hidden in my inner darkness. If I had spent two or three hours in conversation with Saint-Loup,
and he had expressed his admiration of what I had said to him, I felt a sort
of remorse, or regret, or weariness at not having been left alone and ready,
at last, to begin my work. But I told myself that one is not given intelligence for one's own benefit only, that the greatest of men have longed for
appreciation, that I could not regard as wasted hours in which I had built
up an exalted idea of myself in the mind of my friend; I had no difficulty
in persuading myself that I ought to be happy in consequence, and I hoped
all the more anxiously that this happiness might never be taken from me
simply because I had not yet been conscious of it. We fear more than the
loss of everything else the disappearance of the 'goods' that have remained
beyond our reach, because our heart has not taken possession of them. I
felt that I was capable of exemplifying the virtues of friendship better
than most people (because I should always place the good of my friends

before those personal interests to which other people were devoted but which did not count for me), but not of finding happiness in a feeling which, instead of multiplying the differences that there were between my nature and those of other people—as there are among all of us—would cancel them. At the same time my mind was distinguishing in Saint-Loup a personality more collective than his own, that of the 'noble'; which like an indwelling spirit moved his limbs, ordered his gestures and his actions; then, at such moments, although in his company, I was as much alone as I should have been gazing at a landscape the harmony of which I could understand. He was no more then than an object the properties of which, in my musing contemplations, I sought to explore. The perpetual discovery in him of this pre-existent, this aeonial creature, this aristocrat who was just what Robert aspired not to be, gave me a keen delight, but one that was intellectual and not social. In the moral and physical agility which gave so much grace to his kindnesses, in the ease with which he offered my grandmother his carriage and made her get into it, in the alacrity with which he sprang from the box, when he was afraid that I might be cold, to spread his own cloak over my shoulders, I felt not only the inherited litheness of the mighty hunters who had been for generations the ancestors of this young man who made no pretence save to intellectuality, their scorn of wealth which, subsisting in him side by side with his enjoyment of it simply because it enabled him to entertain his friends more lavishly, made him so carelessly shower his riches at their feet; I felt in him especially the certainty or the illusion in the minds of those great lords of being 'better than other people,' thanks to which they had not been able to hand down to Saint-Loup that anxiety to shew that one is 'just as good,' that dread of seeming inferior, of which he was indeed wholly unconscious, but which mars with so much ugliness, so much awkwardness, the most sincere overtures of a plebeian. Sometimes I found fault with myself for thus taking pleasure in my friend as in a work of art, that is to say in regarding the play of all the parts of his being as harmoniously ordered by a general idea from which they depended but which he did not know, so that it added nothing to his own good qualities, to that personal value, intellectual and moral, to which he attached so high a price.

And yet that idea was to a certain extent their determining cause. It was because he was a gentleman that that mental activity, those socialist aspirations, which made him seek the company of young students, arrogant and ill-dressed, connoted in him something really pure and disinterested which was not to be found in them. Looking upon himself as the heir of an ignorant and selfish caste, he was sincerely anxious that they should forgive in him that aristocratic origin which they, on the contrary, found irresistibly attractive and on account of which they sought to know him, though with a show of coldness and indeed of insolence towards him. He was thus led to make advances to people from whom my parents, faithful to the sociological theories of Combray, would have been stupefied at his not turning away in disgust. One day when we were sitting on the sands, Saint-Loup and I, we heard issuing from a canvas tent against which we were leaning a torrent of imprecation against the swarm of Israelites

that infested Balbec. "You can't go a yard without meeting them," said the
voice. "I am not in principle irremediably hostile to the Jewish nation, but
here there is a plethora of them. You hear nothing but, 'I thay, Apraham,
I've chust theen Chacop.' You would think you were in the Rue d'Abou-
kir." The man who thus inveighed against Israel emerged at last from
the tent; we raised our eyes to behold this anti-Semite. It was my old friend
Bloch. Saint-Loup at once begged me to remind him that they had met
before the Board of Examiners, when Bloch had carried off the prize of
honour, and since then at a popular university course.

At the most I may have smiled now and then, to discover in Robert the
marks of his Jesuit schooling, in the awkwardness which the fear of hurting people's feelings at once created in him whenever one of his intellectual friends made a social error, did something silly to which Saint-Loup
himself attached no importance but felt that the other would have blushed
if anybody had noticed it. And it was Robert who used to blush as though
it had been he that was to blame, for instance on the day when Bloch,
after promising to come and see him at the hotel, went on:

"As I cannot endure to be kept waiting among all the false splendour of
these great caravanserais, and the Hungarian band would make me ill, you
must tell the 'lighft-boy' to make them shut up, and to let you know at
once."

Personally, I was not particularly anxious that Bloch should come to
the hotel. He was at Balbec not by himself, unfortunately, but with his
sisters, and they in turn had innumerable relatives and friends staying
there. Now this Jewish colony was more picturesque than pleasant. Balbec
was in this respect like such countries as Russia or Rumania, where the
geography books teach us that the Israelite population does not enjoy
anything approaching the same esteem and has not reached the same
stage of assimilation as, for instance, in Paris. Always together, with no
blend of any other element, when the cousins and uncles of Bloch or their
coreligionists male or female repaired to the Casino, the ladies to dance,
the gentlemen branching off towards the baccarat-tables, they formed a
solid troop, homogeneous within itself, and utterly dissimilar to the people
who watched them go past and found them there again every year without
ever exchanging a word or a sign with them, whether these were on the
Cambremers' list, or the presiding magistrate's little group, professional
or 'business' people, or even simple corn-chandlers from Paris, whose
daughters, handsome, proud, derisive and French as the statues at Rheims,
would not care to mix with that horde of ill-bred tomboys, who carried
their zeal for 'seaside fashions' so far as to be always apparently on their
way home from shrimping or out to dance the tango. As for the men,
despite the brilliance of their dinner-jackets and patent-leather shoes, the
exaggeration of their type made one think of what people call the 'intelligent research' of painters who, having to illustrate the Gospels or the Arabian Nights, consider the country in which the scenes are laid, and give
to Saint Peter or to Ali-Baba the identical features of the heaviest 'punter'
at the Balbec tables. Bloch introduced his sisters, who, though he silenced
their chatter with the utmost rudeness, screamed with laughter at the

mildest sallies of this brother, their blindly worshipped idol. So that it is probable that this set of people contained, like every other, perhaps more than any other, plenty of attractions, merits and virtues. But in order to experience these, one had first to penetrate its enclosure. Now it was not popular; it could feel this; it saw in its unpopularity the mark of an anti-semitism to which it presented a bold front in a compact and closed phalanx into which, as it happened, no one ever dreamed of trying to make his way.

At his use of the word 'lighft' I had all the less reason to be surprised in that, a few days before, Bloch having asked me why I had come to Balbec (although it seemed to him perfectly natural that he himself should be there) and whether it had been "in the hope of making grand friends," when I had explained to him that this visit was a fulfilment of one of my earliest longings, though one not so deep as my longing to see Venice, he had replied: "Yes, of course, to sip iced drinks with the pretty ladies, while you pretend to be reading the *Stones of Venighce,* by Lord John Ruskin, a dreary shaver, in fact one of the most garrulous old barbers that you could find." So that Bloch evidently thought that in England not only were all the inhabitants of the male sex called 'Lord,' but the letter 'i' was invariably pronounced 'igh.' As for Saint-Loup, this mistake in pronunciation seemed to him all the less serious inasmuch as he saw in it pre-eminently a want of those almost 'society' notions which my new friend despised as fully as he was versed in them. But the fear lest Bloch, discovering one day that one says 'Venice' and that Ruskin was not a lord, should retro-spectively imagine that Robert had been laughing at him, made the latter feel as guilty as if he had been found wanting in the indulgence with which, as we have seen, he overflowed, so that the blush which would no doubt one day dye the cheek of Bloch on the discovery of his error, Robert al-ready, by anticipation and reflex action, could feel mounting to his own. For he fully believed that Bloch attached more importance than he to this mistake. Which Bloch proved to be true some time later, when he heard me pronounce the word 'lift,' by breaking in with:

"Oh, you say 'lift,' do you?" And then, in a dry and lofty tone: "Not that it is of the slightest importance." A phrase that is like a reflex action of the body, the same in all men whose self-esteem is great, in the gravest circumstances as well as in the most trivial, betraying there as clearly as on this occasion how important the thing in question seems to him who declares that it is of no importance; a tragic phrase at times, the first to escape (and then how heart-breaking) the lips of every man at all proud from whom we have just taken the last hope to which he still clung by refusing to do him a service. "Oh, well, it's not of the slightest importance; I shall make some other arrangement:" the other arrangement which it is not of the slightest importance that he should be driven to adopt being often suicide.

Apart from this, Bloch made me the prettiest speeches. He was cer-tainly anxious to be on the best of terms with me. And yet he asked me: "Is it because you've taken a fancy to raise yourself to the peerage that you run after de Saint-Loup-en-Bray? You must be going through a fine

crisis of snobbery. Tell me, are you a snob? I think so, what?" Not that
his desire to be friendly had suddenly changed. But what is called, in not
too correct language, 'ill breeding', was his defect, and therefore the defect
which he was bound to overlook, all the more that by which he did not
believe that other people could be shocked. In the human race the fre-
quency of the virtues that are identical in us all is not more wonderful than
the multiplicity of the defects that are peculiar to each one of us. Undoubtedly, it is not common sense that is "the commonest thing in the
world"; but human kindness. In the most distant, the most desolate ends
of the earth, we marvel to see it blossom of its own accord, as in a remote
valley a poppy like the poppies in the world beyond, poppies which it has
never seen as it has never known aught but the wind that, now and again,
stirring the folds of its scarlet cloak, disturbs its solitude. Even if this
human kindness, paralysed by self-interest, is not exercised, it exists none
the less, and whenever any inconstant egoist does not restrain its action,
when, for example, he is reading a novel or a newspaper, it will bud, blossom, grow, even in the heart of him who, cold-blooded in real life, has
retained a tender heart, as a lover of fiction, for the weak, the righteous
and the persecuted. But the variety of our defects is no less remarkable
than the similarity of our virtues. Each of us has his own, so much so that
to continue loving him we are obliged not to take them into account but
to ignore them and look only to the rest of his character. The most perfect
person in the world has a certain defect which shocks us or makes us angry.
One man is of rare intelligence, sees everything from an exalted angle,
never speaks evil of anyone, but will pocket and forget letters of supreme
importance which it was he himself who asked you to let him post for you,
and will then miss a vital engagement without offering you any excuse,
with a smile, because he prides himself upon never knowing the time.
Another is so refined, so gentle, so delicate in his conduct that he never
says anything about you before your face except what you are glad to
hear; but you feel that he refrains from uttering, that he keeps buried in
his heart, where they grow bitter, very different opinions, and the pleasure
that he derives from seeing you is so dear to him that he will let you faint
with exhaustion sooner than leave you to yourself. A third has more sincerity, but carries it so far that he feels bound to let you know, when you
have pleaded the state of your health as an excuse for not having been to
see him, that you were seen going to the theatre and were reported to be
looking well, or else that he has not been able to profit entirely by the
action which you have taken on his behalf, which, by the way, three other
of his friends had already offered to take, so that he is only moderately indebted to you. In similar circumstances the previous friend would have
pretended not to know that you had gone to the theatre, or that other people could have done him the same service. But this last friend feels himself
obliged to repeat or to reveal to somebody the very thing that is most
likely to give offence; is delighted with his own frankness and tells you,
emphatically: "I am like that." While others infuriate you by their exaggerated curiosity, or by a want of curiosity so absolute that you can speak
to them of the most sensational happenings without their grasping what

it is all about; and others again take months to answer you if your letter has been about something that concerns yourself and not them, or else, if they write that they are coming to ask you for something and you dare not leave the house for fear of missing them, do not appear, but leave you in suspense for weeks because, not having received from you the answer which their letter did not in the least 'expect,' they have concluded that you must be cross with them. And others, considering their own wishes and not yours, talk to you without letting you get a word in if they are in good spirits and want to see you, however urgent the work you may have in hand, but if they feel exhausted by the weather or out of humour, you cannot get a word out of them, they meet your efforts with an inert languor and no more take the trouble to reply, even in monosyllables, to what you say to them than if they had not heard you. Each of our friends has his defects so markedly that to continue to love him we are obliged to seek consolation for those defects—in the thought of his talent, his goodness, his affection for ourself—or rather to leave them out of account, and for that we need to display all our good will. Unfortunately our obliging obstinacy in refusing to see the defect in our friend is surpassed by the obstinacy with which he persists in that defect, from his own blindness to it or the blindness that he attributes to other people. For he does not notice it himself, or imagines that it is not noticed. Since the risk of giving offence arises principally from the difficulty of appreciating what does and what does not pass unperceived, we ought, at least, from prudence, never to speak of ourselves, because that is a subject on which we may be sure that other people's views are never in accordance with our own. If we find as many surprises as on visiting a house of plain exterior which inside is full of hidden treasures, torture-chambers, skeletons, when we discover the true lives of other people, the real beneath the apparent universe, we are no less surprised if, in place of the image that we have made of ourself with the help of all the things that people have said to us, we learn from the terms in which they speak of us in our absence what an entirely different image they have been carrying in their own minds of us and of our life. So that whenever we have spoken about ourselves, we may be sure that our inoffensive and prudent words, listened to with apparent politeness and hypocritical approbation, have given rise afterwards to the most exasperated or the most mirthful, but in either case the least favourable, criticism. The least risk that we run is that of irritating people by the disproportion that there is between our idea of ourselves and the words that we use, a disproportion which as a rule makes people's talk about themselves as ludicrous as the performances of those self-styled music-lovers who when they feel the need to hum a favourite melody compensate for the inadequacy of their inarticulate murmurings by a strenuous mimicry and a look of admiration which is hardly justified by all that they let us hear. And to the bad habit of speaking about oneself and one's defects there must be added, as part of the same thing, that habit of denouncing in other people defects precisely analogous to one's own. For it is always of those defects that people speak, as though it were a way of speaking about oneself, indirectly, which added to the pleasure of absolution that of confession. Besides it seems that our attention, always attracted by what is characteristic of ourselves, notices that more than anything else in other people. One short-sighted man says of another: "But he can scarcely open his eyes!"; a consumptive has his doubts as to the pulmonary integrity of the most robust; an unwashed man speaks only of the baths that other people do not take; an evil-smelling man insists that other people smell; a cuckold sees cuckolds everywhere, a light woman light women, a snob snobs. Then, too, every vice, like every profession, requires and trains a special knowledge which we are never loath to display. The invert detects and denounces inverts; the tailor asked out to dine, before he has begun to talk to you, has passed judgment on the cloth of your coat, which his fingers are itching to feel, and if after a few words of conversation you were to ask a dentist what he really thought of you, he would tell you how many of your teeth wanted filling. To him nothing appears more important, nor more absurd to you who have noticed his own. And it is not only when we speak of ourselves that we imagine other people to be blind; we behave as though they were. On every one of us there is a special god in attendance who hides from him or promises him the concealment from other people of his defect, just as he stops the eyes and nostrils of people who do not wash to the streaks of dirt which they carry in their ears and the smell of sweat which emanates from their armpits, and assures them that they can with impunity carry both of these about a world that will notice nothing. And those who wear artificial pearls, or give them as presents, imagine that people will take them to be genuine. Bloch was ill-bred, neurotic, a snob, and, since he belonged to a family of little repute, had to support, as on the floor of ocean, the incalculable pressure that was imposed on him not only by the Christians upon the surface but by all the intervening layers of Jewish castes superior to his own, each of them crushing with its contempt the one that was immediately beneath it. To carve his way through to the open air by raising himself from Jewish family to Jewish family would have taken Bloch many thousands of years. It was better worth his while to seek an outlet in another direction.

When Bloch spoke to me of the crisis of snobbery through which I must be passing, and bade me confess that I was a snob, I might well have replied: "If I were, I should not be going about with you." I said merely that he was not being very polite. Then he tried to apologise, but in the way that is typical of the ill-bred man who is only too glad to hark back to whatever it was if he can find an opportunity to aggravate his offence. "Forgive me," he used now to plead, whenever we met, "I have vexed you, tormented you; I have been wantonly mischievous. And yet—man in general and your friend in particular is so singular an animal—you cannot imagine the affection that I, I who tease you so cruelly, have for you. It carries me often, when I think of you, to tears." And he gave an audible sob.

What astonished me more in Bloch than his bad manners was to find how the quality of his conversation varied. This youth, so hard to please that of authors who were at the height of their fame he would say: "He's a gloomy idiot; he's a sheer imbecile," would every now and then tell, with immense gusto, stories that were simply not funny or would instance as a 'really remarkable person' some man who was completely insignificant. This double scale of measuring the wit, the worth, the interest of people continued to puzzle me until I was introduced to M. Bloch, senior.

I had not supposed that we should ever be allowed to know him, for Bloch junior had spoken ill of me to Saint-Loup and of Saint-Loup to me. In particular, he had said to Robert that I was (always) a frightful snob. "Yes, really, he is overjoyed at knowing M. LLLLegrandin." This trick of isolating a word, was, in Bloch, a sign at once of irony and of learning. Saint-Loup, who had never heard the name of Legrandin, was bewildered. "But who is he?" "Oh, he's a bit of all right, he is!" Bloch laughed, thrusting his hands into his pockets as though for warmth, convinced that he was at that moment engaged in contemplation of the picturesque aspect of an extraordinary country gentleman compared to whom those of Barbey d'Aurevilly were as nothing. He consoled himself for his inability to portray M. Legrandin by giving him a string of capital L's, smacking his lips over the name as over a wine from the farthest bin. But these subjective enjoyments remained hidden from other people. If he spoke ill of me to Saint-Loup he made up for it by speaking no less ill of Saint-Loup to me. We had each of us learned these slanders in detail, the next day, not that we repeated them to each other, a thing which would have seemed to us very wrong, but to Bloch appeared so natural and almost inevitable that in his natural anxiety, in the certainty moreover that he would be telling us only what each of us was bound sooner or later to know, he preferred to anticipate the disclosure and, taking Saint-Loup aside, admitted that he had spoken ill of him, on purpose, so that it might be repeated to him, swore to him "by Zeus Kronion, binder of oaths" that he loved him dearly, that he would lay down his life for him; and wiped away a tear. The same day, he contrived to see me alone, made his confession, declared that he had acted in my interest, because he felt that a certain kind of social intercourse was fatal to me and that I was 'worthy of better things.' Then, clasping me by the hand, with the sentimentality of a drunkard, albeit his drunkenness was purely nervous: "Believe me," he said, "and may the black Ker seize me this instant and bear me across the portals of Hades, hateful to men, if yesterday, when I thought of you, of Combray, of my boundless affection for you, of afternoon hours in class which you do not even remember, I did not lie awake weeping all night long. Yes, all night long, I swear it, and alas, I know—for I know the human soul—you will not believe me." I did indeed 'not believe' him, and to his words which, I felt, he was making up on the spur of the moment, and expanding as he went on, his swearing 'by Ker' added no great weight, the Hellenic cult being in Bloch purely literary. Besides, whenever he began to grow sentimental and wished his hearer to grow sentimental over a falsehood, he would say: "I swear it," more for the hysterical satisfaction of lying than to make people think that he was speaking the truth. I did not believe what he was saying, but I bore him no ill-will for that, for I had inherited from my mother and grandmother their incapacity for resentment even of far worse offenders, and their habit of never condemning anyone.

Besides, he was not altogether a bad youth, this Bloch; he could be, and was at times quite charming. And now that the race of Combray, the race from which sprang creatures absolutely unspoiled like my grandmother and mother, seems almost extinct, as I have hardly any choice now save between honest brutes—insensible and loyal, in whom the mere sound of their voices shews at once that they take absolutely no interest in one's life—and another kind of men who so long as they are with one understand one, cherish one, grow sentimental even to tears, take their revenge a few hours later by making some cruel joke at one's expense, but return to one, always just as comprehending, as charming, as closely assimilated, for the moment, to oneself, I think that it is of this latter sort that I prefer if not the moral worth at any rate the society.

"You cannot imagine my grief when I think of you," Bloch went on. "When you come to think of it, it is a rather Jewish side of my nature," he added ironically, contracting his pupils as though he had to prepare for the microscope an infinitesimal quantity of 'Jewish blood,' and as might (but never would) have said a great French noble who among his ancestors, all Christian, might nevertheless have included Samuel Bernard, or further still, the Blessed Virgin from whom, it is said, the Lévy family claim descent, "coming out. I rather like," he continued, "to find room among my feelings for the share (not that it is more than a very tiny share) which may be ascribed to my Jewish origin." He made this statement because it seemed to him at once clever and courageous to speak the truth about his race, a truth which at the same time he managed to water down to a remarkable extent, like misers who decide to pay their debts but have not the courage to pay more than half. This kind of deceit which consists in having the boldness to proclaim the truth, but only after mixing with it an ample measure of lies which falsify it, is commoner than people think, and even among those who do not habitually practise it certain crises in life, especially those in which love is at stake, give them an opportunity of taking to it.

All these confidential diatribes by Bloch to Saint-Loup against me and to me against Saint-Loup ended in an invitation to dinner. I am by no means sure that he did not first make an attempt to secure Saint-Loup by himself. It would have been so like Bloch to do so that probably he did; but if so success did not crown his effort, for it was to myself and Saint-Loup that Bloch said one day: "Dear master, and you, O horseman beloved of Ares, de Saint-Loup-en-Bray, tamer of horses, since I have encountered you by the shore of Amphitrite, resounding with foam, hard by the tents of the swift-shipped Méniers, will both of you come to dinner any day this week with my illustrious sire, of blameless heart?" He proffered this invitation because he desired to attach himself more closely to Saint-Loup who would, he hoped, secure him the right of entry into aristocratic circles. Formed by me for myself, this ambition would have seemed to Bloch the mark of the most hideous snobbishness, quite in keeping with the opinion that he already held of a whole side of my nature which he did not regard —or at least had not hitherto regarded—as its most important side; but the same ambition in himself seemed to him the proof of a finely developed curiosity in a mind anxious to carry out certain social explorations from which he might perhaps glean some literary benefit. M. Bloch senior, when his son had told him that he was going to bring one of his friends in to dinner, and had in a sarcastic but satisfied tone enunciated the name and title of that friend: "The Marquis de Saint-Loup-en-Bray," had been thrown into great commotion. "The Marquis de Saint-Loup-en-Bray! I'll be jiggered!" he had exclaimed, using the oath which was with him the strongest indication of social deference. And he cast at a son capable of having formed such an acquaintance an admiring glance which seemed to say: "Really, it is astounding. Can this prodigy be indeed a child of mine?" which gave my friend as much pleasure as if his monthly allowance had been increased by fifty francs. For Bloch was not in his element at home and felt that his father treated him like a lost sheep because of his lifelong admiration for Leconte de Lisle, Heredia and other 'Bohemians.' But to have got to know Saint-Loup-en-Bray, whose father had been chairman of the Suez Canal board ('I'll be jiggered!') was an indisputable 'score.' What a pity, indeed, that they had left in Paris, for fear of its being broken on the journey, the stereoscope. Alone among men, M. Bloch senior had the art, or at least the right to exhibit it. He did this, moreover, on rare occasions only, and then to good purpose, on evenings when there was a full-dress affair, with hired waiters. So that from these exhibitions of the stereoscope there emanated, for those who were present, as it were a special distinction, a privileged position, and for the master of the house who gave them a reputation such as talent confers on a man—which could not have been greater had the photographs been taken by M. Bloch himself and the machine his own invention. "You weren't invited to Solomon's yesterday?" one of the family would ask another. "No! I was not one of the elect. What was on?" "Oh, a great how-d'ye-do, the stereoscope, the whole box of tricks!" "Indeed! If they had the stereoscope I'm sorry I wasn't there; they say Solomon is quite amazing when he works it."— "It can't be helped;" said M. Bloch now to his son, "it's a mistake to let him have everything at once; that would leave him nothing to look forward to." He had actually thought, in his paternal affection and in the hope of touching his son's heart, of sending for the instrument. But there was not time, or rather they had thought there would not be; for we were obliged to put off the dinner because Saint-Loup could not leave the hotel, where he was waiting for an uncle who was coming to spend a few days with Mme. de Villeparisis. Since—for he was greatly addicted to physical culture, and especially to long walks—it was largely on foot, spending the night in wayside farms, that this uncle was to make the journey from the country house in which he was staying, the precise date of his arrival at Balbec was by no means certain. And Saint-Loup, afraid to stir out of doors, even entrusted me with the duty of taking to Incauville, where the nearest telegraph-office was, the messages that he sent every day to his mistress. The uncle for whom we were waiting was called Palamède, a name that had come down to him from his ancestors, the Princes of Sicily. And later on when I found, as I read history, belonging to this or that Podestà or Prince of the Church, the same Christian name, a fine renaissance medal—some said, a genuine antique—that had always remained in the family, having passed from generation to generation, from the Vatican cabinet to the uncle of my friend, I felt the pleasure that is reserved for those who, unable from lack of means to start a case of medals, or a picture gallery, look out for old names (names of localities, instructive and picturesque as an old map, a bird's-eye view, a sign-board or a return of customs; baptismal names, in which rings out and is plainly heard, in their fine French endings, the defect of speech, the intonation of a racial vulgarity, the vicious pronunciation by which our ancestors made Latin and Saxon words undergo lasting mutilations which in due course became the august law-givers of our grammar books) and, in short, by drawing upon their collections of ancient and sonorous words, give themselves concerts like the people who acquire viols da gamba and viols d'amour so as to perform the music of days gone by upon old-fashioned instruments. Saint-Loup told me that even in the most exclusive aristocratic society his uncle Palamède had the further distinction of being particularly difficult to approach, contemptuous, double-dyed in his nobility, forming with his brother's wife and a few other chosen spirits what was known as the Phoenix Club. There even his insolence was so much dreaded that it had happened more than once that people of good position who had been anxious to meet him and had applied to his own brother for an introduction had met with a refusal: "Really, you mustn't ask me to introduce you to my brother Palamède. My wife and I, we would all of us do our best for you, but it would be no good. Besides, there's always the danger of his being rude to you, and I shouldn't like that." At the Jockey Club he had, with a few of his friends, marked a list of two hundred members whom they would never allow to be introduced to them. And in the Comte de Paris's circle he was known by the nickname of 'The Prince' because of his distinction and his pride.

Saint-Loup told me about his uncle's early life, now a long time ago. Every day he used to take women to a bachelor establishment which he shared with two of his friends, as good-looking as himself, on account of which they were known as 'The Three Graces.'

"One day, a man who just now is very much in the eye, as Balzac would say, of the Faubourg Saint-Germain, but who at a rather awkward period of his early life displayed odd tastes, asked my uncle to let him come to this place. But no sooner had he arrived than it was not to the ladies but to my uncle Palamède that he began to make overtures. My uncle pretended not to understand, made an excuse to send for his two friends; they appeared on the scene, seized the offender, stripped him, thrashed him till he bled, and then with twenty degrees of frost outside kicked him into the street where he was found more dead than alive; so much so that the police started an inquiry which the poor devil had the greatest difficulty in getting them to abandon. My uncle would never go in for such drastic methods now, in fact you can't conceive the number of men of humble position that he, who is so haughty with people in society, has shewn his affection, taken under his wing, even if he is paid for it with ingratitude. It may be a servant who has looked after him in a hotel, for whom he will find a place in Paris, or a farm-labourer whom he will pay to have taught a trade. That is really the rather nice side of his character, in contrast to his social side." Saint-Loup indeed belonged to that type of young men of fashion, situated at an altitude at which it has been possible to cultivate such expressions as: "What is really rather nice about him," "His rather nice side," precious seeds which produce very rapidly a way of looking at things in which one counts oneself as nothing and the 'people' as everything; the exact opposite, in a word, of plebeian pride. "It seems, it is quite impossible to imagine how he set the tone, how he laid down the law for the whole of society when he was a young man. He acted entirely for himself; in any circumstances he did what seemed pleasing to himself, what was most convenient, but at once the snobs would start copying him. If he felt thirsty at the play, and sent out from his box for a drink, the little sitting-rooms behind all the boxes would be filled, a week later, with refreshments. One wet summer, when he had a touch of rheumatism, he ordered an ulster of a loose but warm vicuna wool, which is used only for travelling rugs, and kept the blue and orange stripes shewing. The big tailors at once received orders from all their customers for blue and orange ulsters of rough wool. If he had some reason for wishing to keep every trace of ceremony out of a dinner in a country house where he was spending the day, and to point the distinction had come without evening clothes and sat down to table in the suit he had been wearing that afternoon, it became the fashion, when you were dining in the country, not to dress. If he was eating some special sweet and instead of taking his spoon used a knife, or a special implement of his own invention which he had had made for him by a silversmith, or his fingers, it at once became wrong to eat it in any other way. He wanted once to hear some Beethoven quartets again (for with all his preposterous ideas he is no fool, mind, he has great gifts) and arranged for some musicians to come and play them to him and a few friends once a week. The ultra-fashionable thing that season was to give quite small parties, with chamber music. I should say he's not done at all badly out of life. With his looks, he must have had any number of women! I can't tell you exactly whom, for he is very discreet. But I do know that he was thoroughly unfaithful to my poor aunt. Not that that prevented his being always perfectly charming to her, and her adoring him; he was in mourning for her for years. When he is in Paris, he still goes to the cemetery nearly every day."

The morning after Robert had told me all these things about his uncle, while he waited for him (and waited, as it happened, in vain), as I was coming by myself past the Casino on my way back to the hotel, I had the sensation of being watched by somebody who was not far off. I turned my head and saw a man of about forty, very tall and rather stout, with a very dark moustache, who, nervously slapping the leg of his trousers with a switch, kept fastened upon me a pair of eyes dilated with observation. Every now and then those eyes were shot through by a look of intense activity such as the sight of a person whom they do not know excites only in men to whom, for whatever reason, it suggests thoughts that would not occur to anyone else—madmen, for instance, or spies. He trained upon me a supreme stare at once bold, prudent, rapid and profound, like a last shot which one fires at an enemy at the moment when one turns to flee, and, after first looking all round him, suddenly adopting an absent and lofty air, by an abrupt revolution of his whole body turned to examine a playbill on the wall in the reading of which he became absorbed, while he hummed a tune and fingered the moss-rose in his buttonhole. He drew from his pocket a note-book in which he appeared to be taking down the title of the performance that was announced, looked two or three times at his watch, pulled down over his eyes a black straw hat the brim of which he extended with his hand held out over it like a visor, as though to see whether some one were at last coming, made the perfunctory gesture of annoyance by which people mean to shew that they have waited long enough, although they never make it when they are really waiting, then pushing back his hat and exposing a scalp cropped close except at the sides where he allowed a pair of waved 'pigeon's-wings' to grow quite long, he emitted the loud panting breath that people give who are not feeling too hot but would like it to be thought that they were. He gave me the impression of a 'hotel crook' who had been watching my grandmother and myself for some days, and while he was planning to rob us had just discovered that I had surprised him in the act of spying; to put me off the scent, perhaps he was seeking only, by his new attitude, to express boredom and detachment, but it was with an exaggeration so aggressive that his object appeared to be—at least as much as the dissipating of the suspicions that I must have had of him—to avenge a humiliation which quite unconsciously I must have inflicted on him, to give me the idea not so much that he had not seen me as that I was an object of too little importance to attract his attention. He threw back his shoulders with an air of bravado, bit his lips, pushed up his moustache, and in the lens of his eyes made an adjustment of something that was indifferent, harsh, almost insulting. So effectively that the singularity of his expression made me take him at one moment for a thief and at another for a lunatic. And yet his scrupulously ordered attire was far more sober and far more simple than that of any of the summer visitors I saw at Balbec, and gave a reassurance to my own suit, so often humiliated by the dazzling and commonplace whiteness of their holiday garb. But my grandmother was coming towards me, we took a turn together, and I was waiting for her, an hour later, outside the hotel into which she had gone for a moment, when I saw emerge from it Mme. de Villeparisis with Robert de Saint-Loup and the stranger who had stared at me so intently outside the Casino. Swift as a lightning-flash his look shot through me, just as at the moment when I first noticed him, and returned, as though he had not seen me, to hover, slightly lowered, before his eyes, dulled, like the neutral look which feigns to see nothing without and is incapable of reporting anything to the mind within, the look which expresses merely the satisfaction of feeling round it the eyelids which it cleaves apart with its sanctimonious roundness, the devout, the steeped look that we see on the faces of certain hypocrites, the smug look on those of certain fools. I saw that he had changed his clothes. The suit he was wearing was darker even than the other; and no doubt this was because the true distinction in dress lies nearer to simplicity than the false; but there was something more; when one came near him one felt that if colour was almost entirely absent from these garments it was not because he who had banished it from them was indifferent to it but rather because for some reason he forbade himself the enjoyment of it. And the sobriety which they displayed seemed to be of the kind that comes from obedience to a rule of diet rather than from want of appetite. A dark green thread harmonised, in the stuff of his trousers, with the clock on his socks, with a refinement which betrayed the vivacity of a taste that was everywhere else conquered, to which this single concession had been made out of tolerance for such a weakness, while a spot of red on his necktie was imperceptible, like a liberty which one dares not take.

"How are you? Let me introduce my nephew, the Baron de Guermantes," Mme. de Villeparisis greeted me, while the stranger without looking at me, muttering a vague "Charmed!" which he followed with a "H'm, h'm, h'm" to give his affability an air of having been forced, and doubling back his little finger, forefinger and thumb, held out to me his middle and ring fingers, the latter bare of any ring, which I clasped through his suede glove; then, without lifting his eyes to my face, he turned towards Mme. de Villeparisis.

"Good gracious; I shall be forgetting my own name next!" she exclaimed. "Here am I calling you Baron de Guermantes. Let me introduce the Baron de Charlus. After all, it's not a very serious mistake," she went on, "for you're a thorough Guermantes whatever else you are."

By this time my grandmother had reappeared, and we all set out together. Saint-Loup's uncle declined to honour me not only with a word, with so much as a look, even, in my direction. If he stared strangers out of countenance (and during this short excursion he two or three times hurled his terrible and searching scrutiny like a sounding lead at insignificant people of obviously humble extraction who happened to pass), to make up for that he never for a moment, if I was to judge by myself, looked at the people whom he did know, just as a detective on special duty might except his personal friends from his professional vigilance. Leaving them—my grandmother, Mme. de Villeparisis and him—to talk to one another, I fell behind with Saint-Loup.

"Tell me, am I right in thinking I heard Mme. de Villeparisis say just now to your uncle that he was a Guermantes?"

"Of course he is; Palamède de Guermantes."

"Not the same Guermantes who have a place near Combray, and claim descent from Geneviève de Brabant?"

"Most certainly: my uncle, who is the very last word in heraldry and all that sort of thing, would tell you that our 'cry,' our war-cry, that is to say, which was changed afterwards to 'Passavant' was originally 'Combraysis,' " he said, smiling so as not to appear to be priding himself on this prerogative of a 'cry,' which only the semi-royal houses, the great chiefs of feudal bands enjoyed. "It's his brother who has the place now."

And so she was indeed related, and quite closely, to the Guermantes, this Mme. de Villeparisis who had so long been for me the lady who had given me a duck filled with chocolates, when I was little, more remote then from the Guermantes way than if she had been shut up somewhere on the Méséglise, less brilliant, less highly placed by me than was the Combray optician, and who now suddenly went through one of those fantastic rises in value, parallel to the depreciations, no less unforeseen, of other objects in our possession, which—rise and fall alike—introduce in our youth and in those periods of our life in which a trace of youth persists changes as numerous as the Metamorphoses of Ovid.

"Haven't they got, down there, the busts of all the old lords of Guermantes?"

"Yes; and a lovely sight they are!" Saint-Loup was ironical. "Between you and me, I look on all that sort of thing as rather a joke. But they have got at Guermantes, what is a little more interesting, and that is quite a touching portrait of my aunt by Carrière. It's as fine as Whistler or Velasquez," went on Saint-Loup, who in his neophyte zeal was not always very exact about degrees of greatness. "There are also some moving pictures by Gustave Moreau. My aunt is the niece of your friend Mme. de Villeparisis; she was brought up by her, and married her cousin, who was a nephew, too, of my aunt Villeparisis, the present Duc de Guermantes."

"Then who is this uncle?"

"He bears the title of Baron de Charlus. Properly speaking, when my great-uncle died, my uncle Palamède ought to have taken the title of Prince des Laumes, which his brother used before he became Duc de Guermantes, for in that family they change their names as you'd change your shirt. But my uncle has peculiar ideas about all that sort of thing. And as he feels that people are rather apt to overdo the Italian Prince and Grandee of Spain business nowadays, though he had half-a-dozen titles of 'Prince' to choose from, he has remained Baron de Charlus, as a protest, and with an apparent simplicity which really covers a good deal of pride. 'In these days,' he says, 'everybody is Prince something-or-other; one really must have a title that will distinguish one; I shall call myself Prince when I wish to travel incognito.' According to him there is no older title than the Charlus barony; to prove to you that it is earlier than the Montmorency title, though they used to claim, quite wrongly, to be the premier barons of France when they were only premier in the Ile de France, where their fief was, my uncle will explain to you for hours on end and enjoy doing it, because, although he's a most intelligent man, really gifted, he regards that sort of thing as quite a live topic of conversation," Saint-Loup smiled again. "But as I am not like him, you mustn't ask me to talk pedigrees; I know nothing more deadly, more perishing; really, life is not long enough."

I now recognised in the hard look which had made me turn round that morning outside the Casino the same that I had seen fixed on me at Tansonville, at the moment when Mme. Swann called Gilberte away.

"But, I say, all those mistresses that, you told me, your uncle M. de Charlus had had, wasn't Mme. Swann one of them?"

"Good lord, no! That is to say, my uncle's a great friend of Swann, and has always stood up for him. But no one has ever suggested that he was his wife's lover. You would make a great sensation in Paris society if people thought you believed that."

I dared not reply that it would have caused an even greater sensation in Combray society if people had thought that I did not believe it.

My grandmother was delighted with M. de Charlus. No doubt he attached an extreme importance to all questions of birth and social position, and my grandmother had remarked this, but without any trace of that severity which as a rule embodies a secret envy and the annoyance of seeing some one else enjoy an advantage which one would like but cannot oneself possess. As on the other hand my grandmother, content with her lot and never for a moment regretting that she did not move in a more brilliant sphere, employed only her intellect in observing the eccentricities of M. de Charlus, she spoke of Saint-Loup's uncle with that detached, smiling, almost affectionate kindness with which we reward the object of our disinterested study for the pleasure that it has given us, all the more that this time the object was a person with regard to whom she found that his if not legitimate, at any rate picturesque pretensions shewed him in vivid contrast to the people whom she generally had occasion to see. But it was especially in consideration of his intelligence and sensibility, qualities which it was easy to see that M. de Charlus, unlike so many of the people in society whom Saint-Loup derided, possessed in a marked degree, that my grandmother had so readily forgiven him his aristocratic prejudice. And yet this had not been sacrificed by the uncle, as it was by the nephew, to higher qualities. Rather, M. de Charlus had reconciled it with them. Possessing, by virtue of his descent from the Ducs de Nemours and Princes de Lamballe, documents, furniture, tapestries, portraits painted for his ancestors by Raphael, Velasquez, Boucher, justified in saying that he was visiting a museum and a matchless library when he was merely turning over his family relics at home, he placed in the rank from which his nephew had degraded it the whole heritage of the aristocracy. Perhaps also, being less metaphysical than Saint-Loup, less satisfied with words, more of a realist in his study of men, he did not care to neglect a factor that was essential to his prestige in their eyes and, if it gave certain disinterested pleasures to his imagination, could often be a powerfully effective aid to his utilitarian activities. No agreement can ever be reached between men of his sort and those who obey the ideal within them which urges them to strip themselves bare of such advantages so that they may seek only to realise that ideal, similar in that respect to the painters, the writers who renounce their virtuosity, the artistic peoples who modernise themselves, warrior peoples who take the initiative in a move for universal disarmament, absolute governments which turn democratic and repeal their harsh laws, though as often as not the sequel fails to reward their noble effort; for the men lose their talent, the nations their secular predominance; 'pacificism' often multiplies wars and indulgence criminality. If Saint-Loup's efforts towards sincerity and emancipation were only to be commended as most noble, to judge by their visible result, one could still be thankful that they had failed to bear fruit in M. de Charlus, who had transferred to his own home much of the admirable panelling from the

Guermantes house, instead of substituting, like his nephew, a 'modern style' of decoration, employing Lebourg or Guillaumin. It was none the less true that M. de Charlus's ideal was highly artificial, and, if the epithet can be applied to the word ideal, as much social as artistic. In certain women of great beauty and rare culture whose ancestresses, two centuries earlier, had shared in all the glory and grace of the old order, he found a distinction which made him take pleasure only in their society, and no doubt the admiration for them which he had protested was sincere, but countless reminiscences, historical and artistic, called forth by their names, entered into and formed a great part of it, just as suggestions of classical antiquity are one of the reasons for the pleasure which a booklover finds in reading an Ode of Horace that is perhaps inferior to poems of our own day which would leave the same booklover cold. Any of these women by the side of a pretty commoner was for him what are, hanging beside a contemporary canvas representing a procession or a wedding, those old pictures the history of which we know, from the Pope or King who ordered them, through the hands of people whose acquisition of them, by gift, purchase, conquest or inheritance, recalls to us some event or at least some alliance of historic interest, and consequently some knowledge that we ourselves have acquired, gives it a fresh utility, increases our sense of the richness of the possessions of our memory or of our erudition. M. de Charlus might be thankful that a prejudice similar to his own, by preventing these several great ladies from mixing with women whose blood was less pure, presented them for his veneration unspoiled, in their unaltered nobility, like an eighteenth-century house-front supported on its flat columns of pink marble, in which the passage of time has wrought no change.

M. de Charlus praised the true 'nobility' of mind and heart which characterised these women, playing upon the word in a double sense by which he himself was taken in, and in which lay the falsehood of this bastard conception, of this medley of aristocracy, generosity and art, but also its seductiveness, dangerous to people like my grandmother, to whom the less refined but more innocent prejudice of a nobleman who cared only about quarterings and took no thought for anything besides would have appeared too silly for words, whereas she was defenceless as soon as a thing presented itself under the externals of a mental superiority, so much so, indeed, that she regarded Princes as enviable above all other men because they were able to have a Labruyère, a Fénelon as their tutors. Outside the Grand Hotel the three Guermantes left us; they were going to luncheon with the Princesse de Luxembourg. While my grandmother was saying good-bye to Mme. de Villeparisis and Saint-Loup to my grandmother, M. de Charlus who, so far, had not uttered a word to me, drew back a little way from the group and, when he reached my side, said: "I shall be taking tea this evening after dinner in my aunt Villeparisis's room; I hope that you will give me the pleasure of seeing you there, and your grandmother." With which he rejoined the Marquise.

Although it was Sunday there were no more carriages waiting outside the hotel now than at the beginning of the season. The solicitor's wife, in particular, had decided that it was not worth the expense of hiring one every time simply because she was not going to the Cambremers', and contented herself with staying in her room.

"Is Mme. Blandais not well?" her husband was asked. "We haven't seen her all day."

"She has a slight headache; it's the heat, there's thunder coming. The least thing upsets her; but I expect you will see her this evening; I've told her she ought to come down. It can't do her any harm."

I had supposed that in thus inviting us to take tea with his aunt, whom I never doubted that he would have warned that we were coming, M. de Charlus wished to make amends for the impoliteness which he had shewn me during our walk that morning. But when, on our entering Mme. de Villeparisis's room, I attempted to greet her nephew, even although I walked right round him, while in shrill accents he was telling a somewhat spiteful story about one of his relatives, I did not succeed in catching his eye; I decided to say "Good evening" to him, and fairly loud, to warn him of my presence; but I realised that he had observed it, for before ever a word had passed my lips, just as I began to bow to him, I saw his two fingers stretched out for me to shake without his having turned to look at me or paused in his story. He had evidently seen me, without letting it appear that he had, and I noticed then that his eyes, which were never fixed on the person to whom he was speaking, strayed perpetually in all directions, like those of certain animals when they are frightened, or those of street hawkers who, while they are bawling their patter and displaying their illicit merchandise, keep a sharp look-out, though without turning their heads, on the different points of the horizon from any of which may appear, suddenly, the police. At the same time I was a little surprised to find that Mme. de Villeparisis, while glad to see us, did not seem to have been expecting us, and I was still more surprised to hear M. de Charlus say to my grandmother: "Ah! that was a capital idea of yours to come and pay us a visit; charming of them, is it not, my dear aunt?" No doubt he had noticed his aunt's surprise at our entry and thought, as a man accustomed to set the tone, to strike the right note, that it would be enough to transform that surprise into joy were he to shew that he himself felt it, that it was indeed the feeling which our arrival there ought to have prompted. In which he calculated wisely; for Mme. de Villeparisis, who had a high opinion of her nephew and knew how difficult it was to please him, appeared suddenly to have found new attractions in my grandmother and continued to make much of her. But I failed to understand how M. de Charlus could, in the space of a few hours, have forgotten the invitation— so curt but apparently so intentional, so premeditated—which he had addressed to me that same morning, or why he called a 'capital idea' on my grandmother's part an idea that had been entirely his own. With a scruple of accuracy which I retained until I had reached the age at which I realised that it is not by asking him questions that one learns the truth of what another man has had in his mind, and that the risk of a misunderstanding which will probably pass unobserved is less than that which may come from a purblind insistence: "But, sir," I reminded him, "you remember, surely, that it was you who asked me if we would come in this evening?" Not a sound, not a movement betrayed that M. de Charlus had so much as heard my question. Seeing which I repeated it, like a diplomat, or like young men after a misunderstanding who endeavour, with untiring and unrewarded zeal, to obtain an explanation which their adversary is determined not to give them. Still M. de Charlus answered me not a word. I seemed to see hovering upon his lips the smile of those who from a great height pass judgment on the characters and breeding of their inferiors.

Since he refused to give any explanation, I tried to provide one for myself, but succeeded only in hesitating between several, none of which could be the right one. Perhaps he did not remember, or perhaps it was I who had failed to understand what he had said to me that morning. . . . More probably, in his pride, he did not wish to appear to have sought to attract people whom he despised, and preferred to cast upon them the responsibility for their intrusion. But then, if he despised us, why had he been so anxious that we should come, or rather that my grandmother should come, for of the two of us it was to her alone that he spoke that evening, and never once to me. Talking with the utmost animation to her, as also to Mme. de Villeparisis, hiding, so to speak, behind them, as though he were seated at the back of a theatre-box, he contented himself, turning from them every now and then the exploring gaze of his penetrating eyes, with fastening it on my face, with the same gravity, the same air of preoccupation as if my face had been a manuscript difficult to decipher.

No doubt, if he had not had those eyes, the face of M. de Charlus would have been similar to the faces of many good-looking men. And when Saint-Loup, speaking to me of various other Guermantes, on a later occasion, said: "Gad, they've not got that thoroughbred air, of being gentlemen to their finger-tips, that uncle Palamède has!" confirming my suspicion that a thoroughbred air and aristocratic distinction were not anything mysterious and new but consisted in elements which I had recognised without difficulty and without receiving any particular impression from them, I was to feel that another of my illusions had been shattered. But that face, to which a faint layer of powder gave almost the appearance of a face on the stage, in vain might M. de Charlus hermetically seal its expression; his eyes were like two crevices, two loopholes which alone he had failed to stop, and through which, according to where one stood or sat in relation to him, one felt suddenly flash across one the glow of some internal engine which seemed to offer no reassurance even to him who without being altogether master of it must carry it inside him, at an unstable equilibrium and always on the point of explosion; and the circumspect and unceasingly restless expression of those eyes, with all the signs of exhaustion which, extending from them to a pair of dark rings quite low down upon his cheeks, were stamped on his face, however carefully he might compose and regulate it, made one think of some *incognito*, some disguise assumed by a powerful man in danger, or merely by a dangerous —but tragic—person. I should have liked to divine what was this secret which other men did not carry in their breasts and which had already made

M. de Charlus's gaze so enigmatic to me when I had seen him that morning outside the Casino. But with what I now knew of his family I could no longer believe that they were the eyes of a thief, nor, after what I had heard of his conversation, could I say that they were those of a madman. If he was cold with me, while making himself agreeable to my grandmother, that arose perhaps not from a personal antipathy for, generally speaking, just as he was kindly disposed towards women, of whose faults he used to speak without, as a rule, any narrowing of the broadest tolerance, so he shewed with regard to men, and especially young men, a hatred so violent as to suggest that of certain extreme misogynists for women. Two or three 'carpet-knights,' relatives or intimate friends of Saint-Loup who happened to mention their names, M. de Charlus, with an almost ferocious expression, in sharp contrast to his usual coldness, called: "Little cads!" I gathered that the particular fault which he found in the young men of the period was their extreme effeminacy. "They're absolute women," he said with scorn. But what life would not have appeared effeminate beside that which he expected a man to lead, and never found energetic or virile enough? (He himself, when he walked across country, after long hours on the road would plunge his heated body into frozen streams.) He would not even allow a man to wear a single ring. But this profession of virility did not prevent his having also the most delicate sensibilities. When Mme. de Villeparisis asked him to describe to my grandmother some country house in which Mme. de Sévigné had stayed, adding that she could not help feeling that there was something rather 'literary' about that lady's distress at being parted from "that tiresome Mme. de Grignan":

"On the contrary," he retorted, "I can think of nothing more true. Besides, it was a time in which feelings of that sort were thoroughly understood. The inhabitant of Lafontaine's Monomotapa, running to see his friend who had appeared to him in a dream, and had looked sad, the pigeon finding that the greatest of evils is the absence of the other pigeon, seem to you perhaps, my dear aunt, as exaggerated as Mme. de Sévigné's impatience for the moment when she will be alone with her daughter. It is so fine what she says when she leaves her: 'This parting gives a pain to my soul which I feel like an ache in my body. In absence one is liberal with the hours. One anticipates a time for which one is longing.'" My grandmother was in ecstasies at hearing the Letters thus spoken of, exactly as she would have spoken of them herself. She was astonished that a man could understand them so thoroughly. She found in M. de Charlus a delicacy, a sensibility that were quite feminine. We said to each other afterwards, when we were by ourselves and began to discuss him together, that he must have come under the strong influence of a woman, his mother, or in later life his daughter if he had any children. "A mistress, perhaps," I thought to myself, remembering the influence that Saint-Loup's seemed to have had over him, which enabled me to realise the point to which men can be refined by the women with whom they live.

"Once she was with her daughter, she had probably nothing to say to her," put in Mme. de Villeparisis.

"Most certainly she had: if it was only what she calls 'things so slight that nobody else would notice them but you and me.' And anyhow she was with her. And Labruyère tells us that that is everything. 'To be with the people one loves, to speak to them, not to speak to them, it is all the same.' He is right; that is the only form of happiness," added M. de Charlus in a mournful voice, "and that happiness—alas, life is so ill arranged that one very rarely tastes it; Mme. de Sévigné was after all less to be pitied than most of us. She spent a great part of her life with the person whom she loved."

"You forget that it was not 'love' in her case; the person was her daughter."

"But what matters in life is not whom or what one loves," he went on, in a judicial, peremptory, almost a cutting tone; "it is the fact of loving. What Mme. de Sévigné felt for her daughter has a far better claim to rank with the passion that Racine described in *Andromaque* or *Phèdre* than the commonplace relations young Sévigné had with his mistresses. It's the same with a mystic's love for his God. The hard and fast lines with which we circumscribe love arise solely from our complete ignorance of life."

"You think all that of *Andromaque* and *Phèdre*, do you?" Saint-Loup asked his uncle in a faintly contemptuous tone. "There is more truth in a single tragedy of Racine than in all the dramatic works of Monsieur Victor Hugo," replied M. de Charlus. "People really are overwhelming," Saint-Loup murmured in my ear. "Preferring Racine to Victor, you may say what you like, it's epoch-making!" He was genuinely distressed by his uncle's words, but the satisfaction of saying "you may say what you like" and, better still, "epoch-making" consoled him.

In these reflexions upon the sadness of having to live apart from the person whom one loves (which were to lead my grandmother to say to me that Mme. de Villeparisis's nephew understood certain things quite as well as his aunt, but in a different way, and moreover had something about him that set him far above the average clubman) M. de Charlus not only allowed a refinement of feeling to appear such as men rarely shew; his voice itself, like certain contralto voices which have not been properly trained to the right pitch, so that when they sing it sounds like a duet between a young man and a woman, singing alternately, mounted, when he expressed these delicate sentiments, to its higher notes, took on an unexpected sweetness and seemed to be embodying choirs of betrothed maidens, of sisters, who poured out the treasures of their love. But the bevy of young girls, whom M. de Charlus in his horror of every kind of effeminacy would have been so distressed to learn that he gave the impression of sheltering thus within his voice, did not confine themselves to the interpretation, the modulation of scraps of sentiment. Often while M. de Charlus was talking one could hear their laughter, shrill, fresh laughter of school-girls or coquettes quizzing their partners with all the archness of clever tongues and pretty wits.

He told us how a house that had belonged to his family, in which Marie Antoinette had slept, with a park laid out by Lenôtre, was now in the hands of the Israels, the wealthy financiers, who had bought it. "Israel—

at least that is the name these people go by, which seems to me a generic, a racial term rather than a proper name. One cannot tell; possibly people of that sort do not have names, and are designated only by the collective title of the tribe to which they belong. It is of no importance! But fancy, after being a home of the Guermantes, to belong to Israels!!!" His voice rose. "It reminds me of a room in the Château of Blois where the caretaker who was shewing me over said: 'This is where Mary Stuart used to say her prayers; I use it to keep my brooms in.' Naturally I wish to know nothing more of this house that has let itself be dishonoured, any more than of my cousin Clara de Chimay after she left her husband. But I keep a photograph of the house, when it was still unspoiled, just as I keep one of the Princess before her large eyes had learned to gaze on anyone but my cousin. A photograph acquires something of the dignity which it ordinarily lacks when it ceases to be a reproduction of reality and shews us things that no longer exist. I could give you a copy, since you are interested in that style of architecture," he said to my grandmother. At that moment, noticing that the embroidered handkerchief which he had in his pocket was shewing some coloured threads, he thrust it sharply down out of sight with the scandalised air of a prudish but far from innocent lady concealing attractions which, by an excess of scrupulosity, she regards as indecent. "Would you believe," he went on, "that the first thing the creatures did was to destroy Lenôtre's park, which is as bad as slashing a picture by Poussin? For that alone, these Israels ought to be in prison. It is true," he added with a smile, after a moment's silence, "that there are probably plenty of other reasons why they should be there! In any case, you can imagine the effect, with that architecture behind it, of an English garden."

"But the house is in the same style as the Petit Trianon," said Mme. de Villeparisis, "and Marie-Antoinette had an English garden laid out there."

"Which, all the same, ruins Gabriel's front," replied M. de Charlus. "Obviously, it would be an act of vandalism now to destroy the Hameau. But whatever may be the spirit of the age, I doubt, all the same, whether, in that respect, a whim of Mme. Israel has the same importance as the memory of the Queen."

Meanwhile my grandmother had been making signs to me to go up to bed, in spite of the urgent appeals of Saint-Loup who, to my utter confusion, had alluded in front of M. de Charlus to the depression that used often to come upon me at night before I went to sleep, which his uncle must regard as betokening a sad want of virility. I lingered a few moments still, then went upstairs, and was greatly surprised when, a little later, having heard a knock at my bedroom door and asked who was there, I heard the voice of M. de Charlus saying dryly:

"It is Charlus. May I come in, sir? Sir," he began again in the same tone as soon as he had shut the door, "my nephew was saying just now that you were apt to be worried at night before going to sleep, and also that you were an admirer of Bergotte's books. As I had one here in my luggage which you probably do not know, I have brought it to help you to while away these moments in which you are not comfortable."

I thanked M. de Charlus with some warmth and told him that, on the contrary, I had been afraid that what Saint-Loup had said to him about my discomfort when night came would have made me appear in his eyes more stupid even than I was.

"No; why?" he answered, in a gentler voice. "You have not, perhaps, any personal merit; so few of us have! But for a time at least you have youth, and that is always a charm. Besides, sir, the greatest folly of all is to laugh at or to condemn in others what one does not happen oneself to feel. I love the night, and you tell me that you are afraid of it. I love the scent of roses, and I have a friend whom it throws into a fever. Do you suppose that I think, for that reason, that he is inferior to me? I try to understand everything and I take care to condemn nothing. After all, you must not be too sorry for yourself; I do not say that these moods of depression are not painful, I know that one can be made to suffer by things which the world would not understand. But at least you have placed your affection wisely, in your grandmother. You see a great deal of her. And besides, that is a legitimate affection, I mean one that is repaid. There are so many of which one cannot say that."

He began walking up and down the room, looking at one thing, taking up another. I had the impression that he had something to tell me, and could not find the right words to express it.

"I have another volume of Bergotte here; I will fetch it for you," he went on, and rang the bell. Presently a page came. "Go and find me your head waiter. He is the only person here who is capable of obeying an order intelligently," said M. de Charlus stiffly. "Monsieur Aimé, sir?" asked the page. "I cannot tell you his name; yes, I remember now, I did hear him called Aimé. Run along, I am in a hurry." "He won't be a minute, sir, I saw him downstairs just now," said the page, anxious to appear efficient. There was an interval of silence. The page returned. "Sir, M. Aimé has gone to bed. But I can take your message." "No, you have only to get him out of bed." "But I can't do that, sir; he doesn't sleep here." "Then you can leave us alone." "But, sir," I said when the page had gone, "you are too kind; one volume of Bergotte will be quite enough." "That is just what I was thinking." M. de Charlus walked up and down the room. Several minutes passed in this way, then after a prolonged hesitation, and several false starts, he swung sharply round and, his voice once more stinging, flung at me: "Good night, sir!" and left the room. After all the lofty sentiments which I had heard him express that evening, next day, which was the day of his departure, on the beach, before noon, when I was on my way down to bathe, and M. de Charlus had come across to tell me that my grandmother was waiting for me to join her as soon as I left the water, I was greatly surprised to hear him say, pinching my neck as he spoke, with a familiarity and a laugh that were frankly vulgar:

"But he doesn't give a damn for his old grandmother, does he, eh? Little rascal!"

"What, sir! I adore her!"

"Sir," he said, stepping back a pace, and with a glacial air, "you are still young; you should profit by your youth to learn two things; first, to refrain from expressing sentiments that are too natural not to be taken for granted; and secondly not to dash into speech to reply to things that are said to you before you have penetrated their meaning. If you had taken this precaution a moment ago you would have saved yourself the appearance of speaking at cross-purposes like a deaf man, thereby adding a second absurdity to that of having anchors embroidered on your bathing-dress. I have lent you a book by Bergotte which I require. See that it is brought to me within the next hour by that head waiter with the silly and inappropriate name, who, I suppose, is not in bed at this time of day. You make me see that I was premature in speaking to you last night of the charms of youth; I should have done you a better service had I pointed out to you its thoughtlessness, its inconsequence, and its want of comprehension. I hope, sir, that this little douche will be no less salutary to you than your bathe. But don't let me keep you standing: you may catch cold. Good day, sir."

No doubt he was sorry afterwards for this speech, for some time later I received—in a morocco binding on the front of which was inlaid a panel of tooled leather representing in demi-relief a spray of forget-me-nots—the book which he had lent me, and I had sent back to him, not by Aimé who was apparently 'off duty,' but by the lift-boy.

M. de Charlus having gone, Robert and I were free at last to dine with Bloch. And I realised during this little party that the stories too readily admitted by our friend as funny were favourite stories of M. Bloch senior, and that the son's 'really remarkable person' was always one of his father's friends whom he had so classified. There are a certain number of people whom we admire in our boyhood, a father with better brains than the rest of the family, a teacher who acquires credit in our eyes from the philosophy he reveals to us, a schoolfellow more advanced than we are (which was what Bloch had been to me), who despises the Musset of the *Espoir en Dieu* when we still admire it, and when we have reached Leconte or Claudel will be in ecstasies only over:

> A Saint-Blaise, à la Zuecca
> Vous étiez, vous étiez bien aise:

with which he will include:

> Padoue est un fort bel endroit
> Où de très grands docteurs en droit. . . .
> Mais j'aime mieux la polenta. . . .
> Passe dans mon domino noir
> La Toppatelle

and of all the *Nuits* will remember only:

> Au Havre, devant l'Atlantique
> A Venise, à l'affreux Lido,
> Où vient sur l'herbe d'un tombeau
> Mourir la pâle Adriatique.

So, whenever we confidently admire anyone, we collect from him, we quote with admiration sayings vastly inferior to the sort which, left to our own judgment, we would sternly reject, just as the writer of a novel puts into it, on the pretext that they are true, things which people have actually said, which in the living context are like a dead weight, form the dull part of the work. Saint-Simon's portraits composed by himself (and very likely without his admiring them himself) are admirable, whereas what he cites as the charming wit of his clever friends is frankly dull where it has not become meaningless. He would have scorned to invent what he reports as so pointed or so coloured when said by Mme. Cornuel or Louis XIV, a point which is to be remarked also in many other writers, and is capable of various interpretations, of which it is enough to note but one for the present: namely, that in the state of mind in which we 'observe' we are a long way below the level to which we rise when we create.

There was, then, embedded in my friend Bloch a father Bloch who lagged forty years behind his son, told impossible stories and laughed as loudly at them from the heart of my friend as did the separate, visible and authentic father Bloch, since to the laugh which the latter emitted, not without several times repeating the last word so that his public might taste the full flavour of the story, was added the braying laugh with which the son never failed, at table, to greet his father's anecdotes. Thus it came about that after saying the most intelligent things young Bloch, to indicate the portion that he had inherited from his family, would tell us for the thirtieth time some of the gems which father Bloch brought out only (with his swallow-tail coat) on the solemn occasions on which young Bloch brought someone to the house on whom it was worth while making an impression; one of his masters, a 'chum' who had taken all the prizes, or, this evening, Saint-Loup and myself. For instance: "A military critic of great insight, who had brilliantly worked out, supporting them with proofs, the reasons for which, in the Russo-Japanese war, the Japanese must inevitably be beaten and the Russians victorious," or else: "He is an eminent gentleman who passes for a great financier in political circles and for a great politician among financiers." These stories were interchangeable with one about Baron de Rothschild and one about Sir Rufus Israels, who were brought into the conversation in an equivocal manner which might let it be supposed that M. Bloch knew them personally.

I was myself taken in, and from the way in which M. Bloch spoke of Bergotte I assumed that he too was an old friend. But with him as with all famous people, M. Bloch knew them only 'without actually knowing them,' from having seen them at a distance in the theatre or in the street. He imagined, moreover, that his appearance, his name, his personality were not unknown to them, and that when they caught sight of him they had often to repress a stealthy inclination to bow. People in society, because they know men of talent, original characters, and have them to dine in their houses, do not on that account understand them any better. But when one has lived to some extent in society, the silliness of its inhabitants makes one too anxious to live, suppose too high a standard of intelligence in the obscure circles in which people know only 'without actually knowing.' I was to discover this when I introduced the topic of Bergotte. M. Bloch was not the only one who was a social success at home. My friend was even more so with his sisters, whom he continually questioned in a hectoring tone, burying his face in his plate, all of which made them laugh until they cried. They had adopted their brother's language, and spoke it fluently, as if it had been obligatory and the only form of speech that people of intelligence might use. When we arrived, the eldest sister said to one of the younger ones: "Go, tell our sage father and our venerable mother!" "Puppies," said Bloch, "I present to you the cavalier Saint-Loup, hurler of javelins, who is come for a few days from Doncières to the dwellings of polished stone, fruitful in horses." And, since he was as vulgar as he was literary, his speech ended as a rule in some pleasantry of a less Homeric kind: "See, draw closer your pepla with fair clasps, what is all that that I see? Does your mother know you're out?" And the Misses Bloch subsided in a tempest of laughter. I told their brother how much pleasure he had given me by recommending me to read Bergotte, whose books I had loved.

M. Bloch senior, who knew Bergotte only by sight, and Bergotte's life only from what was common gossip, had a manner quite as indirect of making the acquaintance of his books, by the help of criticisms that were apparently literary. He lived in the world of 'very nearlies,' where people salute the empty air and arrive at wrong judgments. Inexactitude, incompetence do not modify their assurance; quite the contrary. It is the propitious miracle of self-esteem that, since few of us are in a position to enjoy the society of distinguished people, or to form intellectual friendships, those to whom they are denied still believe themselves to be the best endowed of men, because the optics of our social perspective make every grade of society seem the best to him who occupies it, and beholds as less favoured than himself, less fortunate and therefore to be pitied, the greater men whom he names and calumniates without knowing, judges and despises without understanding them. Even in cases where the multiplication of his modest personal advantages by his self-esteem would not suffice to assure a man the dose of happiness, superior to that accorded to others, which is essential to him, envy is always there to make up the balance. It is true that if envy finds expression in scornful phrases, we must translate 'I have no wish to know him' by 'I have no means of knowing him.' That is the intellectual sense. But the emotional sense is indeed, 'I have no wish to know him.' The speaker knows that it is not true, but he does not, all the same, say it simply to deceive; he says it because it is what he feels, and that is sufficient to bridge the gulf between them, that is to say to make him happy.

Self-centredness thus enabling every human being to see the universe spread out in a descending scale beneath himself who is its lord, M. Bloch afforded himself the luxury of being pitiless when in the morning, as he drank his chocolate, seeing Bergotte's signature at the foot of an article in the newspaper which he had scarcely opened, he disdainfully granted the writer an audience soon cut short, pronounced sentence upon him, and gave himself the comforting pleasure of repeating after every mouthful of the scalding brew: "That fellow Bergotte has become unreadable. My word, what a bore the creature can be. I really must stop my subscription. How involved it all is, bread and butter nonsense!" And he helped himself to another slice.

This illusory importance of M. Bloch senior did, moreover, extend some little way beyond the radius of his own perceptions. In the first place his children regarded him as a superior person. Children have always a tendency either to depreciate or to exalt their parents, and to a good son his father is always the best of fathers, quite apart from any objective reason there may be for admiring him. Now, such reasons were not altogether lacking in the case of M. Bloch, who was an educated man, shrewd, affectionate towards his family. In his most intimate circle they were all the more proud of him because, if, in 'society,' people are judged by a standard (which is incidentally absurd) and according to false but fixed rules, by comparison with the aggregate of all the other fashionable people, in the subdivisions of middle-class life, on the other hand, the dinners, the family parties all turn upon certain people who are pronounced good company, amusing, and who in 'society' would not survive a second evening. Moreover in such an environment where the artificial values of the aristocracy do not exist, their place is taken by distinctions even more stupid. Thus it was that in his family circle, and even among the remotest branches of the tree, an alleged similarity in his way of wearing his moustache and in the bridge of his nose led to M. Bloch's being called "the Duc d'Aumale's double." (In the world of club pages, the one who wears his cap on one side and his jacket tightly buttoned, so as to give himself the appearance, he imagines, of a foreign officer, is he not also a personage of a sort to his comrades?)

The resemblance was the faintest, but you would have said that it conferred a title. When he was mentioned, it would always be: "Bloch? Which one? The Duc d'Aumale?" as people say "Princesse Murat? Which one? The Queen (of Naples)?" And there were certain other minute marks which combined to give him, in the eyes of the cousinhood, an acknowledged claim to distinction. Not going the length of having a carriage of his own, M. Bloch used on special occasions to hire an open victoria with a pair of horses from the Company, and would drive through the Bois de Boulogne, his body sprawling limply from side to side, two fingers pressed to his brow, other two supporting his chin, and if people who did not know him concluded that he was an 'old nuisance,' they were all convinced, in the family, that for smartness Uncle Solomon could have taught Gramont-Caderousse a thing or two. He was one of those people who when they die, because for years they have shared a table in a restaurant on the boulevard with its news-editor, are described as "well known Paris figures" in the social column of the *Radical*. M. Bloch told Saint-Loup and me that Bergotte knew so well why he, M. Bloch, always cut him that as soon as he caught sight of him, at the theatre or in the club, he avoided his eye. Saint-Loup blushed, for it had occurred to him that this club could not be the Jockey, of which his father had been chairman. On the other hand it must be a fairly exclusive club, for M. Bloch had said that Bergotte would never have got into it if he had come up now. So it was not without the fear that he might be 'underrating his adversary' that Saint-Loup asked whether the club in question were the Rue Royale, which was considered 'lowering' by his own family, and to which he knew that certain Israelites had been admitted. "No," replied M. Bloch in a tone at once careless, proud and ashamed, "it is a small club, but far more pleasant than a big one, the Ganaches. We're very strict there, don't you know." "Isn't Sir Rufus Israels the chairman?" Bloch junior asked his father, so as to give him the opportunity for a glorious lie, never suspecting that the financier had not the same eminence in Saint-Loup's eyes as in his. The fact of the matter was that the Ganaches club boasted not Sir Rufus Israels but one of his staff. But as this man was on the best of terms with his employer, he had at his disposal a stock of the financier's cards, and would give one to M. Bloch whenever he wished to travel on a line of which Sir Rufus was a director, the result of which was that old Bloch would say: "I'm just going round to the Club to ask Sir Rufus for a line to the Company." And the card enabled him to dazzle the guards on the trains. The Misses Bloch were more interested in Bergotte and, reverting to him rather than pursue the subject of the Ganaches, the youngest asked her brother, in the most serious tone imaginable, for she believed that there existed in the world, for the designation of men of talent, no other terms than those which he was in the habit of using: "Is he really an amazing good egg, this Bergotte? Is he in the category of the great lads, good eggs like Villiers and Catullus?" "I've met him several times at dress rehearsals," said M. Nissim Bernard. "He is an uncouth creature, a sort of Schlemihl." There was nothing very serious in this allusion to Chamisso's story but the epithet 'Schlemihl' formed part of that dialect, half-German, half-Jewish, the use of which delighted M. Bloch in the family circle, but struck him as vulgar and out of place before strangers. And so he cast a reproving glance at his uncle. "He has talent," said Bloch. "Ah!" His sister sighed gravely, as though to imply that in that case there was some excuse for me. "All writers have talent," said M. Bloch scornfully. "In fact it appears," went on his son, raising his fork, and screwing up his eyes with an air of impish irony, "that he is going to put up for the Academy." "Go on. He hasn't enough to shew them," replied his father, who seemed not to have for the Academy the same contempt as his son and daughters. "He's not big enough." "Besides, the Academy is a salon, and Bergotte has no polish," declared the uncle (whose heiress Mme. Bloch was), a mild and inoffensive person whose surname, Bernard, might perhaps by itself have quickened my grandfather's powers of diagnosis, but would have appeared too little in harmony with a face which looked as if it had been brought back from Darius's palace and restored by Mme. Dieulafoy, had not (chosen by some collector desirous of giving a crowning touch of orientalism to this figure from Susa) his first name, Nissim, stretched out above it the pinions of an androcephalous bull from Khorsabad. But M. Bloch never stopped insulting his uncle, whether it was that he was excited by the unresisting good-humour of his butt, or that the rent of the villa being paid by M. Nissim Bernard, the beneficiary wished to shew that he kept his independence, and, more important still, that he was not seeking by flattery to make sure of the rich inheritance to come. What most hurt the old man was being treated so rudely in front of the manservant. He murmured an unintelligible sentence of which all that could be made out was: "when the meschores are in the room." 'Meschores,' in the Bible, means 'the servant of God.' In the family circle the Blochs used the word when they referred to their own servants, and were always exhilarated by it, because their certainty of not being understood either by Christians or by the servants themselves enhanced in M. Nissim Bernard and M. Bloch their twofold distinction of being 'masters' and at the same time 'Jews.' But this latter source of satisfaction became a source of displeasure when there was 'company.' At such times M. Bloch, hearing his uncle say 'meschores,' felt that he was making his oriental side too prominent, just as a light-of-love who has invited some of her sisters to meet her respectable friends is annoyed if they allude to their profession or use words that do not sound quite nice. Therefore, so far from his uncle's request's producing any effect on M. Bloch, he, beside himself with rage, could contain himself no longer. He let no opportunity pass of scarifying his wretched uncle. "Of course, when there is a chance of saying anything stupid, one can be quite certain that you won't miss it. You would be the first to lick his boots if he were in the room!" shouted M. Bloch, while M. Nissim Bernard in sorrow lowered over his plate the ringleted beard of King Sargon. My friend, when he began to grow his beard, which also was blue-black and crimped, became very like his great-uncle.

"What! Are you the son of the Marquis de Marsantes? Why, I knew him very well," said M. Nissim Bernard to Saint-Loup. I supposed that he meant the word 'knew' in the sense in which Bloch's father had said that he knew Bergotte, namely by sight. But he went on: "Your father was one of my best friends." Meanwhile Bloch had turned very red, his father was looking intensely cross, the Misses Bloch were choking with suppressed laughter. The fact was that in M. Nissim Bernard the love of ostentation which in M. Bloch and his children was held in cheek, had engendered the habit of perpetual lying. For instance, if he was staying in an hotel, M. Nissim Bernard, as M. Bloch equally might have done, would have his newspapers brought to him always by his valet in the dining-room, in the middle of luncheon, when everybody was there, so that they should see that he travelled with a valet. But to the people with whom he made friends in the hotel the uncle used to say what the nephew would never have said, that he was a Senator. He might know quite well that they would sooner or later discover that the title was usurped; he could not, at the critical moment, resist the temptation to assume it. M. Bloch suffered acutely from his uncle's lies and from all the embarrassments that they led to. "Don't pay any attention to him, he talks a great deal of nonsense," he whispered to Saint-Loup, whose interest was all the more whetted, for he was curious to explore the psychology of liars. "A greater liar even than the Ithacan Odysseus, albeit Athene called him the greatest liar among mortals," his son completed the indictment. "Well, upon my word!" cried M. Nissim Bernard, "If I'd only known that I was going to sit down to dinner with my old friend's son! Why, I have a photograph still of your father at home, in Paris, and any number of letters from him. He used always to call me 'uncle,' nobody ever knew why. He was a charming man, sparkling. I remember so well a dinner I gave at Nice; there were Sardou, Labiche, Augier," "Molière, Racine, Corneille," M. Bloch added with sarcasm, while his son completed the tale of guests with "Plautus, Menander, Kalidasa." M. Nissim Bernard, cut to the quick, stopped short in his reminiscence, and, ascetically depriving himself of a great pleasure, remained silent until the end of dinner.

"Saint-Loup with helm of bronze," said Bloch, "have a piece more of this duck with thighs heavy with fat, over which the illustrious sacrificer of birds has spilled numerous libations of red wine."

As a rule, after bringing out from his store for the entertainment of a distinguished guest his anecdotes of Sir Rufus Israels and others, M. Bloch, feeling that he had succeeded in touching and melting his son's heart, would withdraw, so as not to spoil his effect in the eyes of the 'big pot.' If, however, there was an absolutely compelling reason, as for instance on the night when his son won his fellowship, M. Bloch would add to the usual string of anecdotes the following ironical reflexion which he ordinarily reserved for his own personal friends, so that young Bloch was extremely proud to see it produced for his: "The Government have acted unpardonably. They have forgotten to consult M. Coquelin! M. Coquelin has let it be known that he is displeased." (M. Bloch prided himself on being a reactionary, with a contempt for theatrical people.)

But the Misses Bloch and their brother reddened to the tips of their ears, so much impressed were they when Bloch senior, to shew that he could be regal to the last in his entertainment of his son's two 'chums,' gave the order for champagne to be served, and announced casually that, as a treat for us, he had taken three stalls for the performance which a company from the Opéra-Comique was giving that evening at the Casino. He was sorry that he had not been able to get a box. They had all been taken. However, he had often been in the boxes, and really one saw and heard better down by the orchestra. All very well, only, if the defect of his son, that is to say the defect which his son believed to be invisible to other people, was coarseness, the father's was avarice. And so it was in a decanter that we were served with, under the name of champagne, a light sparkling wine, while under that of orchestra stalls he had taken three in the pit, which cost half as much, miraculously persuaded by the divine intervention of his defect that neither at table nor in the theatre (where the boxes were all empty) would the defect be noticed. When M. Bloch had let us moisten our lips in the flat glasses which his son dignified with the style and title of 'craters with deeply hollowed flanks,' he made us admire a picture to which he was so much attached that he had brought it with him to Balbec. He told us that it was a Rubens. Saint-Loup asked innocently if it was signed. M. Bloch replied, blushing, that he had had the signature cut off to make it fit the frame, but that it made no difference, as he had no intention of selling the picture. Then he hurriedly bade us good-night, in order to bury himself in the *Journal Officiel,* back numbers of which lit-

tered the house, and which, he informed us, he was obliged to read carefully on account of his 'parliamentary position' as to the precise nature
of which, however, he gave us no enlightenment. "I shall take a muffler,"
said Bloch, "for Zephyrus and Boreas are disputing to which of them shall
belong the fish-teeming sea, and should we but tarry a little after the
show is over, we shall not be home before the first flush of Eos, the rosy-
fingered. By the way," he asked Saint-Loup when we were outside, and
I trembled, for I realised at once that it was of M. de Charlus that Bloch
was speaking in that tone of irony, "who was that excellent old card
dressed in black that I saw you walking with, the day before yesterday,
on the beach?" "That was my uncle." Saint-Loup was ruffled. Unfortunately, a 'floater' was far from seeming to Bloch a thing to be avoided. He
shook with laughter. "Heartiest congratulations; I ought to have guessed;
he has an excellent style, the most priceless dial of an old 'gaga' of the
highest lineage." "You are absolutely mistaken; he is an extremely clever
man," retorted Saint-Loup, now furious. "I am sorry about that; it makes
him less complete. All the same, I should like very much to know him, for
I flatter myself I could write some highly adequate pieces about old buffers
like that. Just to see him go by, he's killing. But I should leave out of
account the caricaturable side, which really is hardly worthy of an artist
enamoured of the plastic beauty of phrases, of his mug, which (you'll forgive me) doubled me up for a moment with joyous laughter, and I should
bring into prominence the aristocratic side of your uncle, who after all
has a distinct bovine effect, and when one has finished laughing does
impress one by his great air of style. But," he went on, addressing myself
this time, "there is also a matter of a very different order about which I
have been meaning to question you, and every time we are together, some
god, blessed denizen of Olympus, makes me completely forget to ask for
a piece of information which might before now have been and is sure
some day to be of the greatest use to me. Tell me, who was the lovely lady
I saw you with in the Jardin d'Acclimatation accompanied by a gentleman
whom I seem to know by sight and a little girl with long hair?" It had
been quite plain to me at the time that Mme. Swann did not remember
Bloch's name, since she had spoken of him by another, and had described
my friend as being on the staff of some Ministry, as to which I had never
since then thought of finding out whether he had joined it. But how came
it that Bloch, who, according to what she then told me, had got himself
introduced to her, was ignorant of her name? I was so much surprised that
I stopped for a moment before answering. "Whoever she is," he went on,
"hearty congratulations; you can't have been bored with her. I picked
her up a few days before that on the Zone railway, where, speaking of
zones, she was so kind as to undo hers for the benefit of your humble
servant; I have never had such a time in my life, and we were just going
to make arrangements to meet again when somebody she knew had the
bad taste to get in at the last station but one." My continued silence did
not appear to please Bloch. "I was hoping," he said, "thanks to you, to
learn her address, so as to go there several times a week to taste in her
arms the delights of Eros, dear to the gods; but I do not insist since you seem

pledged to discretion with respect to a professional who gave herself to me three times running, and in the most refined manner, between Paris and the Point-du-Jour. I am bound to see her again, some night."

I called upon Bloch after this dinner; he returned my call, but I was out and he was seen asking for me by Françoise, who, as it happened, albeit he had visited us at Combray, had never set eyes on him until then. So that she knew only that one of 'the gentlemen' who were friends of mine had looked in to see me, she did not know 'with what object,' dressed in a nondescript way, which had not made any particular impression upon her. Now though I knew quite well that certain of Françoise's social ideas must for ever remain impenetrable by me, ideas based, perhaps, partly upon confusions between words, between names which she had once and for all time mistaken for one another, I could not restrain myself, who had long since abandoned the quest for enlightenment in such cases, from seeking—and seeking, moreover, in vain—to discover what could be the immense significance that the name of Bloch had for Françoise. For no sooner had I mentioned to her that the young man whom she had seen was M. Bloch than she recoiled several paces, so great were her stupor and disappointment. "What! Is that M. Bloch?" she cried, thunder-struck, as if so portentous a personage ought to have been endowed with an appearance which 'made you know' as soon as you saw him that you were in the presence of one of the great ones of the earth; and, like some one who has discovered that an historical character is not 'up to' the level of his reputation, she repeated in an impressed tone, in which I could detect latent, for future growth, the seeds of a universal scepticism: "What! Is that M. Bloch? Well, really, you would never think it, to look at him." She seemed also to bear me a grudge, as if I had always 'overdone' the praise of Bloch to her. At the same time she was kind enough to add: "Well, he may be M. Bloch, and all that. I'm sure Master can say he's every bit as good."

She had presently, with respect to Saint-Loup, whom she worshipped, a disillusionment of a different kind and of less severity: she discovered that he was a Republican. Now for all that, when speaking, for instance, of the Queen of Portugal, she would say with that disrespect which is, among the people, the supreme form of respect: "Amélie, Philippe's sister," Françoise was a Royalist. But when it came to a Marquis; a Marquis who had dazzled her at first sight, and who was for the Republic, seemed no longer real. And she shewed the same ill-humour as if I had given her a box which she had believed to be made of gold, and had thanked me for it effusively, and then a jeweller had revealed to her that it was only plated. She at once withdrew her esteem from Saint-Loup, but soon afterwards restored it to him, having reflected that he could not, being the Marquis de Saint-Loup, be a Republican, that he was just pretending, in his own in-terest, for with such a Government as we had it might be a great advantage to him. From that moment her coldness towards him, her resentment towards myself ceased. And when she spoke of Saint-Loup she said: "He is a hypocrite," with a broad and friendly smile which made it clear that

she 'considered' him again just as much as when she first knew him, and
that she had forgiven him.

As a matter of fact, Saint-Loup was absolutely sincere and disinterested, and it was this intense moral purity which, not being able to find
entire satisfaction in a selfish sentiment such as love, nor on the other
hand meeting in him the impossibility (which existed in me, for instance)
of finding its spiritual nourishment elsewhere than in himself, rendered
him truly capable (just as I was incapable) of friendship.

Françoise was no less mistaken about Saint-Loup when she complained
that he had 'that sort of' air, as if he did not look down upon the people,
but that it was all just a pretence, and you had only to see him when he
was in a temper with his groom. It had indeed sometimes happened that
Robert would scold his groom with a certain amount of brutality, which
proved that he had the sense not so much of the difference as of the
equality between classes and masses. "But," he said in answer to my
rebuke of his having treated the man rather harshly, "why should I go
out of my way to speak politely to him? Isn't he my equal? Isn't he just
as near to me as any of my uncles and cousins? You seem to think that I
ought to treat him with respect, as an inferior. You talk like an aristocrat!"
he added scornfully.

And indeed if there was a class to which he shewed himself prejudiced
and hostile, it was the aristocracy, so much so that he found it as hard to
believe in the superior qualities of a man in society as he found it easy to
believe in those of a man of the people. When I mentioned the Princesse
de Luxembourg, whom I had met with his aunt:

"An old trout," was his comment. "Like all that lot. She's a sort of
cousin of mine, by the way."

Having a strong prejudice against the people who frequented it, he went
rarely into 'Society,' and the contemptuous or hostile attitude which he
adopted towards it served to increase, among all his near relatives, the
painful impression made by his intimacy with a woman on the stage, a
connexion which, they declared, would be his ruin, blaming it specially for
having bred in him that spirit of denigration, that bad spirit, and for having led him astray, after which it was only a matter of time before he
would have dropped out altogether. And so, many easy-going men of the
Faubourg Saint-Germain were without compunction when they spoke of
Robert's mistress. "Those girls do their job," they would say, "they are as
good as anybody else. But that one; no, thank you! We cannot forgive her.
She has done too much harm to a fellow we were fond of." Of course, he
was not the first to be caught in that snare. But the others amused themselves like men of the world, continued to think like men of the world
about politics, about everything. As for him, his family found him 'soured.'
They did not bear in mind that, for many young men of fashion who would
otherwise remain uncultivated mentally, rough in their friendships, without gentleness or taste—it is very often their mistress who is their real
master, and connexions of this sort the only school of morals in which they
are initiated into a superior culture, and learn the value of disinterested
relations. Even among the lower orders (who, when it comes to coarseness,

so often remind us of the world of fashion) the woman, more sensitive, finer, more leisured, is driven by curiosity to adopt certain refinements, respects certain beauties of sentiment and of art which, though she may fail to understand them, she nevertheless places above what has seemed most desirable to the man, above money or position. Now whether the mistress be a young blood's (such as Saint-Loup) or a young workman's (electricians, for instance, must now be included in our truest order of Chivalry) her lover has too much admiration and respect for her not to extend them also to what she herself respects and admires; and for him the scale of values is thereby reversed. Her sex alone makes her weak; she suffers from nervous troubles, inexplicable things which in a man, or even in another woman—a woman whose nephew or cousin he was—would bring a smile to the lips of this stalwart young man. But he cannot bear to see her suffer whom he loves. The young nobleman who, like Saint-Loup, has a mistress acquires the habit, when he takes her out to dine, of carrying in his pocket the valerian 'drops' which she may need, of ordering the waiter, firmly and with no hint of sarcasm, to see that he shuts the doors quietly and not to put any damp moss on the table, so as to spare his companion those discomforts which himself he has never felt, which compose for him an occult world in whose reality she has taught him to believe, discomforts for which he now feels pity without in the least needing to understand them, for which he will still feel pity when other women than she shall be the sufferers. Saint-Loup's mistress—as the first monks of the middle ages taught Christendom—had taught him to be kind to animals, for which she had a passion, never moving without her dog, her canaries, her love-birds; Saint-Loup looked after them with motherly devotion and treated as brutes the people who were not good to dumb creatures. On the other hand, an actress, or so-called actress, like this one who was living with him,—whether she were intelligent or not, and as to that I had no knowledge—by making him find the society of fashionable women boring, and look upon having to go out to a party as a painful duty, had saved him from snobbishness and cured him of frivolity. If, thanks to her, his social engagements filled a smaller place in the life of her young lover, at the same time, whereas if he had been simply a drawing-room man, vanity or self-interest would have dictated his choice of friends as rudeness would have characterised his treatment of them, his mistress had taught him to bring nobility and refinement into his friendship. With her feminine instinct, with a keener appreciation in men of certain qualities of sensibility which her lover might perhaps, without her guidance, have misunderstood and laughed at, she had always been swift to distinguish from among the rest of Saint-Loup's friends, the one who had a real affection for him, and to make that one her favourite. She knew how to make him feel grateful to such a friend, shew his gratitude, notice what things gave his friend pleasure and what pain. And presently Saint-Loup, without any more need of her to prompt him, began to think of all these things by himself, and at Balbec, where she was not with him, for me whom she had never seen, whom he had perhaps not yet so much as mentioned in his letters to her, of his own accord would pull up the window of a carriage in which I was sitting, take out of the room the flowers that made me feel unwell, and when he had to say good-bye to several people at once manage to do so before it was actually time for him to go, so as to be left alone and last with me, to make that distinction between them and me, to treat me differently from the rest. His mistress had opened his mind to the invisible, had brought a serious element into his life, delicacy into his heart, but all this escaped his sorrowing family who repeated: "That creature will be the death of him; meanwhile she's doing what she can to disgrace him." It is true that he had succeeded in getting out of her all the good that she was capable of doing him; and that she now caused him only incessant suffering, for she had taken an intense dislike to him and tormented him in every possible way. She had begun, one fine day, to look upon him as stupid and absurd because the friends that she had among the younger writers and actors had assured her that he was, and she duly repeated what they had said with that passion, that want of reserve which we shew whenever we receive from without and adopt as our own opinions or customs of which we previously knew nothing. She readily professed, like her actor friends, that between Saint-Loup and herself there was a great gulf fixed, and not to be crossed, because they were of different races, because she was an intellectual and he, whatever he might pretend, the born enemy of the intellect. This view of him seemed to her profound, and she sought confirmation of it in the most insignificant words, the most trivial actions of her lover. But when the same friends had further convinced her that she was destroying, in company so ill-suited to her, the great hopes which she had, they said, aroused in them, that her lover would leave a mark on her, that by living with him she was spoiling her future as an artist; to her contempt for Saint-Loup was added the same hatred that she would have felt for him if he had insisted upon inoculating her with a deadly germ. She saw him as seldom as possible, at the same time postponing the hour of a definite rupture, which seemed to me a highly improbable event. Saint-Loup made such sacrifices for her that unless she was ravishingly beautiful (but he had always refused to shew me her photograph, saying: "For one thing, she's not a beauty, and besides she always takes badly. These are only some snapshots that I took myself with my kodak; they would give you a wrong idea of her.") it would surely be difficult for her to find another man who would consent to anything of the sort. I never reflected that a certain obsession to make a name for oneself, even when one has no talent, that the admiration, no more than the privately expressed admiration of people who are imposing on one, can (although it may not perhaps have been the case with Saint-Loup's mistress) be, even for a little prostitute, motives more determining than the pleasure of making money. Saint-Loup who, without quite understanding what was going on in the mind of his mistress, did not believe her to be completely sincere either in her unfair reproaches or in her promises of undying love, had all the same at certain moments the feeling that she would break with him whenever she could, and accordingly, impelled no doubt by the instinct of self-preservation which was part of his love, a love more clear-sighted, possibly, than Saint-Loup himself, making use, too, of a practical capacity for business which was compatible in him with the loftiest and blindest flights of the heart, had refused to settle upon her any capital, had borrowed an enormous sum so that she should want nothing, but made it over to her only from day to day. And no doubt, assuming that she really thought of leaving him, she was calmly waiting until she had feathered her nest, a process which, with the money given her by Saint-Loup, would not perhaps take very long, but would all the same require a time which must be conceded to prolong the happiness of my new friend—or his misery.

This dramatic period of their connexion, which had now reached its most acute stage, the most cruel for Saint-Loup, for she had forbidden him to remain in Paris, where his presence exasperated her, and had forced him to spend his leave at Balbec, within easy reach of his regiment—had begun one evening at the house of one of Saint-Loup's aunts, on whom he had prevailed to allow his friend to come there, before a large party, to recite some of the speeches from a symbolical play in which she had once appeared in an 'advanced' theatre, and for which she had made him share the admiration that she herself professed.

But when she appeared in the room, with a large lily in her hand, and wearing a costume copied from the *Ancilla Domini*, which she had persuaded Saint-Loup was an absolute 'vision of beauty,' her entrance had been greeted, in that assemblage of clubmen and duchesses, with smiles which the monotonous tone of her chantings, the oddity of certain words and their frequent recurrence had changed into fits of laughter, stifled at first but presently so uncontrollable that the wretched reciter had been unable to go on. Next day Saint-Loup's aunt had been universally censured for having allowed so grotesque an actress to appear in her drawing-room. A well-known duke made no bones about telling her that she had only herself to blame if she found herself criticised. "Damn it all, people really don't come to see 'turns' like that! If the woman had talent, even; but she has none and never will have any. 'Pon my soul, Paris is not such a fool as people make out. Society does not consist exclusively of imbeciles. This little lady evidently believed that she was going to take Paris by surprise. But Paris is not so easily surprised as all that, and there are still some things that they can't make us swallow."

As for the actress, she left the house with Saint-Loup, exclaiming:

"What do you mean by letting me in for those geese, those uneducated bitches, those dirty corner-boys? I don't mind telling you, there wasn't a man in the room who didn't make eyes at me or squeeze my foot, and it was because I wouldn't look at them that they were out for revenge."

Words which had changed Robert's antipathy for people in society into a horror that was at once deep and distressing, and was provoked in him most of all by those who least deserved it, devoted kinsmen who, on behalf of the family, had sought to persuade Saint-Loup's lady to break with him, a move which she represented to him as inspired by their passion for her. Robert, although he had at once ceased to see them, used to imagine when he was parted from his mistress as he was now, that they or others like them were profiting by his absence to return to the charge and had possibly prevailed over her. And when he spoke of the sensualists who were disloyal to their friends, who sought to seduce their friends' wives, tried to make them come to houses of assignation, his whole face would glow with suffering and hatred.

"I would kill them with less compunction than I would kill a dog, which is at least a well-behaved beast, and loyal and faithful. There are men who deserve the guillotine if you like, far more than poor wretches who have been led into crime by poverty and by the cruelty of the rich."

He spent the greater part of his time in sending letters and telegrams to his mistress. Every time that, while still preventing him from returning to Paris, she found an excuse to quarrel with him by post, I read the news at once in his evident discomposure. Inasmuch as his mistress never told him what fault she found with him, suspecting that possibly if she did not tell him it was because she did not know herself, and simply had had enough of him, he would still have liked an explanation and used to write to her: "Tell me what I have done wrong. I am quite ready to acknowledge my faults," the grief that overpowered him having the effect of persuading him that he had behaved badly.

But she kept him waiting indefinitely for her answers which, when they did come, were meaningless. And so it was almost always with a furrowed brow, and often with empty hands that I would see Saint-Loup returning from the post office, where, alone in all the hotel, he and Françoise went to fetch or to hand in letters, he from a lover's impatience, she with a servant's mistrust of others. (His telegrams obliged him to take a much longer journey.)

When, some days after our dinner with the Blochs, my grandmother told me with a joyful air that Saint-Loup had just been asking her whether, before he left Balbec, she would not like him to take a photograph of her, and when I saw that she had put on her nicest dress on purpose, and was hesitating between several of her best hats, I felt a little annoyed by this childishness, which surprised me coming from her. I even went the length of asking myself whether I had not been mistaken in my grandmother, whether I did not esteem her too highly, whether she was as unconcerned as I had always supposed in the adornment of her person, whether she had not indeed the very weakness that I believed most alien to her temperament, namely coquetry.

Unfortunately, this displeasure that I derived from the prospect of a photographic 'sitting,' and more particularly from the satisfaction with which my grandmother appeared to be looking forward to it, I made so apparent that Françoise remarked it and did her best, unintentionally, to increase it by making me a sentimental, gushing speech, by which I refused to appear moved.

"Oh, Master; my poor Madame will be so pleased at having her likeness taken, she is going to wear the hat that her old Françoise has trimmed for her, you must allow her, Master."

I acquired the conviction that I was not cruel in laughing at Françoise's sensibility, by reminding myself that my mother and grandmother, my models in all things, often did the same. But my grandmother, noticing that I seemed cross, said that if this plan of her sitting for her photograph offended me in any way she would give it up. I would not let her; I assured her that I saw no harm in it, and left her to adorn herself, but, thinking that I shewed my penetration and strength of mind, I added a few stinging words of sarcasm, intended to neutralize the pleasure which she seemed to find in being photographed, so that if I was obliged to see my grandmother's magnificent hat, I succeeded at least in driving from her face that joyful expression which ought to have made me glad; but alas, it too often happens, while the people we love best are still alive, that such expressions appear to us as the exasperating manifestation of some unworthy freak of fancy rather than as the precious form of the happiness which we should dearly like to procure for them. My ill-humour arose more particularly from the fact that, during the last week, my grandmother had appeared to be avoiding me, and I had not been able to have her to myself for a moment, either by night or day. When I came back in the afternoon to be alone with her for a little I was told that she was not in the hotel; or else she would shut herself up with Françoise for endless confabulations which I was not permitted to interrupt. And when, after being out all evening with Saint-Loup, I had been thinking on the way home of the moment at which I should be able to go to my grandmother and to kiss her, in vain might I wait for her to knock on the partition between us the three little taps which would tell me to go in and say good night to her; I heard nothing; at length I would go to bed, a little resentful of her for depriving me, with an indifference so new and strange in her, of a joy on which I had so much counted, I would lie still for a while, my heart throbbing as in my childhood, listening to the wall which remained silent, until I cried myself to sleep.

SEASCAPE, WITH FRIEZE OF GIRLS

THAT day, as for some days past, Saint-Loup had been obliged to go to Doncières, where, until his leave finally expired, he would be on duty now until late every afternoon. I was sorry that he was not at Balbec. I had seen alight from carriages and pass, some into the ball-room of the Casino, others into the ice-cream shop, young women who at a distance had seemed to me lovely. I was passing through one of those periods of our youth, unprovided with any one definite love, vacant, in which at all times and in all places—as a lover the woman by whose charms he is smitten—we desire, we seek, we see Beauty. Let but a single real feature—the little that one distinguishes of a woman seen from afar or from behind—enable us to project the form of beauty before our eyes, we imagine that we have seen her before, our heart beats, we hasten in pursuit, and will always remain half-persuaded that it was she, provided that the woman has vanished: it is only if we manage to overtake her that we realise our mistake.

Besides, as I grew more and more delicate, I was inclined to overrate the simplest pleasures because of the difficulties that sprang up in the way of my attaining them. Charming women I seemed to see all round me, because I was too tired, if it was on the beach, too shy if it was in the Casino or at a pastry-cook's, to go anywhere near them. And yet if I was soon to die I should have liked first to know the appearance at close quarters, in reality of the prettiest girls that life had to offer, even although it should be another than myself or no one at all who was to take advantage of the offer. (I did not, in fact, appreciate the desire for possession that underlay my curiosity.) I should have had the courage to enter the ball-room if Saint-Loup had been with me. Left by myself, I was simply hanging about in front of the Grand Hotel until it was time for me to join my grandmother, when, still almost at the far end of the paved 'front' along which they projected in a discordant spot of colour, I saw coming towards me five or six young girls, as different in appearance and manner from all the people whom one was accustomed to see at Balbec as could have been, landed there none knew whence, a flight of gulls which performed with measured steps upon the sands—the dawdlers using their wings to overtake the rest—a movement the purpose of which seems as obscure to the human bathers, whom they do not appear to see, as it is clearly determined in their own birdish minds.

One of these strangers was pushing as she came, with one hand, her bicycle; two others carried golf-clubs; and their attire generally was in contrast to that of the other girls at Balbec, some of whom, it was true, went in for games, but without adopting any special outfit.

It was the hour at which ladies and gentlemen came out every day for a turn on the 'front,' exposed to the merciless fire of the long glasses fastened upon them, as if they had each borne some disfigurement which she felt it her duty to inspect in its minutest details, by the chief magistrate's wife, proudly seated there with her back to the band-stand, in the middle of that dread line of chairs on which presently they too, actors turned critics, would come and establish themselves, to scrutinise in their turn those others who would then be filing past them. All these people who paced up and down the 'front,' tacking as violently as if it had been the deck of a ship (for they could not lift a leg without at the same time waving their arms, turning their heads and eyes, settling their shoulders, compensating by a balancing movement on one side for the movement they had just made on the other, and puffing out their faces), and who, pretending not to see so as to let it be thought that they were not interested, but covertly watching, for fear of running against the people who were walking beside or coming towards them, did, in fact, butt into them, became entangled with them, because each was mutually the object of the same secret attention veiled beneath the same apparent disdain; their love—and consequently their fear—of the crowd being one of the most powerful motives in all men, whether they seek to please other people or to astonish them, or to shew them that they despise them. In the case of the solitary, his seclusion, even when it is absolute and ends only with life itself, has often as its primary cause a disordered love of the crowd, which so far overrules every other feeling that, not being able to win, when he goes out, the admiration of his hall-porter, of the passers-by, of the cabman whom he hails, he prefers not to be seen by them at all, and with that object abandons every activity that would oblige him to go out of doors.

Among all these people, some of whom were pursuing a train of thought, but if so betrayed its instability by spasmodic gestures, a roving gaze as little in keeping as the circumspect titubation of their neighbours, the girls whom I had noticed, with that mastery over their limbs which comes from perfect bodily condition and a sincere contempt for the rest of humanity, were advancing straight ahead, without hesitation or stiffness, performing exactly the movements that they wished to perform, each of their members in full independence of all the rest, the greater part of their bodies preserving that immobility which is so noticeable in a good waltzer. They were now quite near me. Although each was a type absolutely different from the others, they all had beauty; but to tell the truth I had seen them for so short a time, and without venturing to look them straight in the face, that I had not yet individualised any of them. Save one, whom her straight nose, her dark complexion pointed in contrast among the rest, like (in a renaissance picture of the Epiphany) a king of Arab cast, they were known to me only, one by a pair of eyes, hard, set and mocking; another by cheeks in which the pink had that coppery tint which makes one think of geraniums; and even of these points I had not yet indissolubly attached any one to one of these girls rather than to another; and when (according to the order in which their series met the eye, marvellous because the most different aspects came next one another, because all scales of colours were combined in it, but confused as a piece of music in which I should not have been able to isolate and identify at the moment of their passage the suc-

cessive phrases, no sooner distinguished than forgotten) I saw emerge a
pallid oval, black eyes, green eyes, I knew not if these were the same that
had already charmed me a moment ago, I could not bring them home to
any one girl whom I might thereby have set apart from the rest and so
identified. And this want, in my vision, of the demarcations which I should
presently establish between them sent flooding over the group a wave of
harmony, the continuous transfusion of a beauty fluid, collective and
mobile.

It was not perhaps, in this life of ours, mere chance that had, in forming
this group of friends, chosen them all of such beauty; perhaps these girls
(whose attitude was enough to reveal their nature, bold, frivolous and
hard), extremely sensitive to everything that was ludicrous or ugly, incapable of yielding to an intellectual or moral attraction, had naturally
felt themselves, among companions of their own age, repelled by all those
in whom a pensive or sensitive disposition was betrayed by shyness, awkwardness, constraint, by what, they would say, 'didn't appeal' to them,
and from such had held aloof; while they attached themselves, on the
other hand, to others to whom they were drawn by a certain blend of grace,
suppleness, and physical neatness, the only form in which they were able
to picture the frankness of a seductive character and the promise of pleasant hours in one another's company. Perhaps, too, the class to which they
belonged, a class which I should not have found it easy to define, was at
that point in its evolution at which, whether thanks to its growing wealth
and leisure, or thanks to new athletic habits, extended now even to certain
plebeian elements, and a habit of physical culture to which had not yet
been added the culture of the mind, a social atmosphere, comparable to
that of smooth and prolific schools of sculpture, which have not yet gone
in for tortured expressions, produces naturally and in abundance fine bodies
with fine legs, fine hips, wholesome and reposeful faces, with an air of
agility and guile. And were they not noble and calm models of human
beauty that I beheld there, outlined against the sea, like statues exposed to
the sunlight upon a Grecian shore?

Just as if, in the heart of their band, which progressed along the 'front'
like a luminous comet, they had decided that the surrounding crowd was
composed of creatures of another race whose sufferings even could not
awaken in them any sense of fellowship, they appeared not to see them,
forced those who had stopped to talk to step aside, as though from the
path of a machine that had been set going by itself, so that it was no good
waiting for it to get out of their way, their utmost sign of consciousness
being when, if some old gentleman of whom they did not admit the existence
and thrust from them the contact, had fled with a frightened or furious,
but a headlong or ludicrous motion, they looked at one another and smiled.
They had, for whatever did not form part of their group, no affectation
of contempt; their genuine contempt was sufficient. But they could not set
eyes on an obstacle without amusing themselves by crossing it, either in a
running jump or with both feet together, because they were all filled to
the brim, exuberant with that youth which we need so urgently to spend
that even when we are unhappy or unwell, obedient rather to the necessities

of our age than to the mood of the day, we can never pass anything that
can be jumped over or slid down without indulging ourselves conscien-
tiously, interrupting, interspersing our slow progress—as Chopin his most
melancholy phrase—with graceful deviations in which caprice is blended
with virtuosity. The wife of an elderly banker, after hesitating between
various possible exposures for her husband, had settled him on a folding
chair, facing the 'front,' sheltered from wind and sun by the band-stand.
Having seen him comfortably installed there, she had gone to buy a newspaper which she would read aloud to him, to distract him—one of her little
absences which she never prolonged for more than five minutes, which
seemed long enough to him but which she repeated at frequent intervals
so that this old husband on whom she lavished an attention that she took
care to conceal, should have the impression that he was still quite alive
and like other people and was in no need of protection. The platform of
the band-stand provided, above his head, a natural and tempting springboard, across which, without a moment's hesitation, the eldest of the little
band began to run; she jumped over the terrified old man, whose yachting
cap was brushed by the nimble feet, to the great delight of the other girls,
especially of a pair of green eyes in a 'dashing' face, which expressed, for
that bold act, an admiration and a merriment in which I seemed to discern
a trace of timidity, a shamefaced and blustering timidity which did not
exist in the others. "Oh, the poor old man; he makes me sick; he looks
half dead;" said a girl with a croaking voice, but with more sarcasm than
sympathy. They walked on a little way, then stopped for a moment in the
middle of the road, with no thought whether they were impeding the passage of other people, and held a council, a solid body of irregular shape,
compact, unusual and shrill, like birds that gather on the ground at the
moment of flight; then they resumed their leisurely stroll along the 'front,'
against a background of sea.

By this time their charming features had ceased to be indistinct and
impersonal. I had dealt them like cards into so many heaps to compose
(failing their names, of which I was still ignorant) the big one who had
jumped over the old banker; the little one who stood out against the horizon
of sea with her plump and rosy cheeks, her green eyes; the one with the
straight nose and dark complexion, in such contrast to all the rest; another,
with a white face like an egg on which a tiny nose described an arc of a
circle like a chicken's beak; yet another, wearing a hooded cape (which
gave her so poverty-stricken an appearance, and so contradicted the smartness of the figure beneath that the explanation which suggested itself was
that this girl must have parents of high position who valued their self-
esteem so far above the visitors to Balbec and the sartorial elegance of
their own children that it was a matter of the utmost indifference to them
that their daughter should stroll on the 'front' dressed in a way which
humbler people would have considered too modest); a girl with brilliant,
laughing eyes and plump, colourless cheeks, a black polo-cap pulled down
over her face, who was pushing a bicycle with so exaggerated a movement
of her hips, with an air borne out by her language, which was so typically
of the gutter and was being shouted so loud, when I passed her (although

among her expressions I caught that irritating 'live my own life') that, abandoning the hypothesis which her friend's hooded cape had made me construct, I concluded instead that all these girls belonged to the population which frequents the racing-tracks, and must be the very juvenile mistresses of professional bicyclists. In any event, in none of my suppositions was there any possibility of their being virtuous. At first sight—in the way in which they looked at one another and smiled, in the insistent stare of the one with the dull cheeks—I had grasped that they were not. Besides, my grandmother had always watched over me with a delicacy too timorous for me not to believe that the sum total of the things one ought not to do was indivisible or that girls who were lacking in respect for their elders would suddenly be stopped short by scruples when there were pleasures at stake more tempting than that of jumping over an octogenarian.

Though they were now separately identifiable, still the mutual response which they gave one another with eyes animated by self-sufficiency and the spirit of comradeship, in which were kindled at every moment now the interest now the insolent indifference with which each of them sparkled according as her glance fell on one of her friends or on passing strangers, that consciousness, moreover, of knowing one another intimately enough always to go about together, by making them a 'band apart' established between their independent and separate bodies, as slowly they advanced, a bond invisible but harmonious, like a single warm shadow, a single atmosphere making of them a whole as homogeneous in its parts as it was different from the crowd through which their procession gradually wound.

For an instant, as I passed the dark one with the fat cheeks who was wheeling a bicycle, I caught her smiling, sidelong glance, aimed from the centre of that inhuman world which enclosed the life of this little tribe, an inaccessible, unknown world to which the idea of what I was could certainly never attain nor find a place in it. Wholly occupied with what her companions were saying, this young girl in her polo-cap, pulled down very low over her brow, had she seen me at the moment in which the dark ray emanating from her eyes had fallen on me? In the heart of what universe did she distinguish me? It would have been as hard for me to say as, when certain peculiarities are made visible, thanks to the telescope, in a neighbouring planet, it is difficult to arrive at the conclusion that human beings inhabit it, that they can see us, or to say what ideas the sight of us can have aroused in their minds.

If we thought that the eyes of a girl like that were merely two glittering sequins of mica, we should not be athirst to know her and to unite her life to ours. But we feel that what shines in those reflecting discs is not due solely to their material composition; that it is, unknown to us, the dark shadows of the ideas that the creature is conceiving, relative to the people and places that she knows—the turf of racecourses, the sand of cycling tracks over which, pedalling on past fields and woods, she would have drawn me after her, that little peri, more seductive to me than she of the Persian paradise—the shadows, too, of the home to which she will presently return, of the plans that she is forming or that others have formed for her;

and above all that it is she, with her desires, her sympathies, her revulsions, her obscure and incessant will. I knew that I should never possess this young cyclist if I did not possess also what there was in her eyes. And it was consequently her whole life that filled me with desire; a sorrowful desire because I felt that it was not to be realised, but exhilarating, because what had hitherto been my life, having ceased of a sudden to be my whole life, being no more now than a little part of the space stretching out before me, which I was burning to cover and which was composed of the lives of these girls, offered me that prolongation, that possible multiplication of oneself which is happiness. And no doubt the fact that we had, these girls and I, not one habit—as we had not one idea—in common, was to make it more difficult for me to make friends with them and to please them. But perhaps, also, it was thanks to those differences, to my consciousness that there did not enter into the composition of the nature and actions of these girls a single element that I knew or possessed, that there came in place of my satiety a thirst—like that with which a dry land burns—for a life which my soul, because it had never until now received one drop of it, would absorb all the more greedily in long draughts, with a more perfect imbibition.

I had looked so closely at the dark cyclist with the bright eyes that she seemed to notice my attention, and said to the biggest of the girls something that I could not hear. To be honest, this dark one was not the one that pleased me most, simply because she was dark and because (since the day on which, from the little path by Tansonville, I had seen Gilberte) a girl with reddish hair and a golden skin had remained for me the inaccessible ideal. But Gilberte herself, had I not loved her principally because she had appeared to me haloed with that aureole of being the friend of Bergotte, of going with him to look at old cathedrals? And in the same way could I not rejoice at having seen this dark girl look at me (which made me hope that it would be easier for me to get to know her first), for she would introduce me to the others, to the pitiless one who had jumped over the old man's head, to the cruel one who had said "He makes me sick, poor old man!"—to all of them in turn, among whom, moreover, she had the distinction of being their inseparable companion? And yet the supposition that I might some day be the friend of one or other of these girls, that their eyes, whose incomprehensible gaze struck me now and again, playing upon me unawares, like the play of sunlight upon a wall, might ever, by a miraculous alchemy, allow to interpenetrate among their ineffable particles the idea of my existence, some affection for my person, that I myself might some day take my place among them in the evolution of their course by the sea's edge—that supposition appeared to me to contain within it a contradiction as insoluble as if, standing before some classical frieze or a fresco representing a procession, I had believed it possible for me, the spectator, to take my place, beloved of them, among the godlike hierophants.

The happiness of knowing these girls was, then, not to be realised. Certainly it would not have been the first of its kind that I had renounced. I had only to recall the numberless strangers whom, even at Balbec, the car-

riage bowling away from them at full speed had forced me for ever to abandon. And indeed the pleasure that was given me by the little band, as
noble as if it had been composed of Hellenic virgins, came from some suggestion that there was in it of the flight of passing figures along a road.
This fleetingness of persons who are not known to us, who force us to put
out from the harbour of life, in which the women whose society we frequent have all, in course of time, laid bare their blemishes, urges us into
that state of pursuit in which there is no longer anything to arrest the
imagination. But to strip our pleasures of imagination is to reduce them
to their own dimensions, that is to say to nothing. Offered me by one of
those procuresses (whose good offices, all the same, the reader has seen
that I by no means scorned), withdrawn from the element which gave them
so many fine shades and such vagueness, these girls would have enchanted
me less. We must have imagination, awakened by the uncertainty of being
able to attain our object, to create a goal which hides our other goal from
us, and by substituting for sensual pleasures the idea of penetrating into
a life prevents us from recognising that pleasure, from tasting its true
savour, from restricting it to its own range.

There must be, between us and the fish which, if we saw it for the first
time cooked and served on a table, would not appear worth the endless
trouble, craft and stratagem that are necessary if we are to catch it, interposed, during our afternoons with the rod, the ripple to whose surface come
wavering, without our quite knowing what we intend to do with them, the
burnished gleam of flesh, the indefiniteness of a form, in the fluidity of a
transparent and flowing azure.

These girls benefited also by that alteration of social values characteristic of seaside life. All the advantages which, in our ordinary environment,
extend and magnify our importance, we there find to have become invisible,
in fact to be eliminated; while on the other hand the people whom we
suppose, without reason, to enjoy similar advantages appear to us amplified to artificial dimensions. This made it easy for strange women generally, and to-day for these girls in particular, to acquire an enormous
importance in my eyes, and impossible to make them aware of such importance as I might myself possess.

But if there was this to be said for the excursion of the little band, that
it was but an excerpt from the innumerable flight of passing women, which
had always disturbed me, their flight was here reduced to a movement so
slow as to approach immobility. Now, precisely because, in a phase so far
from rapid, faces no longer swept past me in a whirlwind, but calm and
distinct still appeared beautiful, I was prevented from thinking as I had
so often thought when Mme. de Villeparisis's carriage bore me away that,
at closer quarters, if I had stopped for a moment, certain details, a pitted
skin, drooping nostrils, a silly gape, a grimace of a smile, an ugly figure
might have been substituted, in the face and body of the woman, for
those that I had doubtless imagined; for there had sufficed a pretty outline, a glimpse of a fresh complexion, for me to add, in entire good faith,
a fascinating shoulder, a delicious glance of which I carried in my mind
for ever a memory or a preconceived idea, these rapid decipherings of a

person whom we see in motion exposing us thus to the same errors as those too rapid readings in which, on a single syllable and without waiting to identify the rest, we base instead of the word that is in the text a wholly different word with which our memory supplies us. It could not be so with me now. I had looked well at them all; each of them I had seen, not from every angle and rarely in full face, but all the same in two or three aspects different enough to enable me to make either the correction or the verification, to take a 'proof' of the different possibilities of line and colour that are hazarded at first sight, and to see persist in them, through a series of expressions, something unalterably material. I could say to myself with conviction that neither in Paris nor at Balbec, in the most favourable hypotheses of what might have happened, even if I had been able to stop and talk to them, the passing women who had caught my eye, had there ever been one whose appearance, followed by her disappearance without my having managed to know her, had left me with more regret than would these, had given me the idea that her friendship might be a thing so intoxicating. Never, among actresses nor among peasants nor among girls from a convent school had I beheld anything so beautiful, impregnated with so much that was unknown, so inestimably precious, so apparently inaccessible. They were, of the unknown and potential happiness of life, an illustration so delicious and in so perfect a state that it was almost for intellectual reasons that I was desperate with the fear that I might not be able to make, in unique conditions which left no room for any possibility of error, proper trial of what is the most mysterious thing that is offered to us by the beauty which we desire and console ourselves for never possessing, by demanding pleasure—as Swann had always refused to do before Odette's day—from women whom we have not desired, so that, indeed, we die without having ever known what that other pleasure was. No doubt it was possible that it was not in reality an unknown pleasure, that on a close inspection its mystery would dissipate and vanish, that it was no more than a projection, a mirage of desire. But in that case I could blame only the compulsion of a law of nature—which if it applied to these girls would apply to all—and not the imperfection of the object. For it was that which I should have chosen above all others, feeling quite certain, with a botanist's satisfaction, that it was not possible to find collected anywhere rarer specimens than these young flowers who were interrupting at this moment before my eyes the line of the sea with their slender hedge, like a bower of Pennsylvania roses adorning a garden on the brink of a cliff, between which is contained the whole tract of ocean crossed by some steamer, so slow in gliding along the blue and horizontal line that stretches from one stem to the next that an idle butterfly, dawdling in the cup of a flower which the moving hull has long since passed, can, if it is to fly and be sure of arriving before the vessel, wait until nothing but the tiniest slice of blue still separates the questing prow from the first petal of the flower towards which it is steering.

I went indoors because I was to dine at Rivebelle with Robert, and my grandmother insisted that on those evenings, before going out, I must lie down for an hour on my bed, a rest which the Balbec doctor presently ordered me to extend to the other evenings also.

However, there was no need, when one went indoors, to leave the 'front' and to enter the hotel by the hall, that is to say from behind. By virtue of an alteration of the clock which reminded me of those Saturdays when, at Combray, we used to have luncheon an hour earlier, now with summer at the full the days had become so long that the sun was still high in the heavens, as though it were only tea-time, when the tables were being laid for dinner in the Grand Hotel. And so the great sliding windows were kept open from the ground. I had but to step across a low wooden sill to find myself in the dining-room, through which I walked and straight across to the lift.

As I passed the office I addressed a smile to the manager, and with no shudder of disgust gathered one for myself from his face which, since I had been at Balbec, my comprehensive study of it was injecting and transforming, little by little, like a natural history preparation. His features had become familiar to me, charged with a meaning that was of no importance but still intelligible, like a script which one can read, and had ceased in any way to resemble these queer, intolerable characters which his face had presented to me on that first day, when I had seen before me a personage now forgotten, or, if I succeeded in recalling him, unrecognisable, difficult to identify with this insignificant and polite personality of which the other was but a caricature, a hideous and rapid sketch. Without either the shyness or the sadness of the evening of my arrival I rang for the attendant, who no longer stood in silence while I rose by his side in the lift as in a mobile thoracic cage propelled upwards along its ascending pillar, but repeated:

"There aren't the people now there were a month back. They're beginning to go now; the days are drawing in." He said this not because there was any truth in it but because, having an engagement, presently, for a warmer part of the coast, he would have liked us all to leave, so that the hotel could be shut up and he have a few days to himself before 'rejoining' in his new place. 'Rejoin' and 'new' were not, by the way, incompatible terms, since, for the lift-boy, 'rejoin' was the usual form of the verb 'to join.' The only thing that surprised me was that he condescended to say 'place,' for he belonged to that modern proletariat which seeks to efface from our language every trace of the rule of domesticity. A moment later, however, he informed me that in the 'situation' which he was about to 'rejoin,' he would have a smarter 'tunic' and a better 'salary,' the words 'livery' and 'wages' sounding to him obsolete and unseemly. And as, by an absurd contradiction, the vocabulary has, through thick and thin, among us 'masters,' survived the conception of inequality, I was always failing to understand what the lift-boy said. For instance, the only thing that interested me was to know whether my grandmother was in the hotel. Now, forestalling my questions, the lift-boy would say to me: "That lady has just gone out from your rooms." I was invariably taken in; I supposed that he meant my grandmother. "No, that lady; I think she's an employee of yours." As in the old speech of the middle classes, which ought really to be done away with, a cook is not called an employee, I thought for a moment: "But he must be mistaken. We don't own a factory; we haven't any employees." Suddenly I remembered that the title of 'employee' is, like the wearing of a moustache among waiters, a sop to their self-esteem given to servants, and realised that this lady who had just gone out must be Françoise (probably on a visit to the coffee-maker, or to watch the Belgian lady's little maid at her sewing), though even this sop did not satisfy the lift-boy, for he would say quite naturally, speaking pityingly of his own class, 'with the working man' or 'the small person,' using the same singular form as Racine when he speaks of 'the poor.' But as a rule, for my zeal and timidity of the first evening were now things of the past, I no longer spoke to the lift-boy. It was he now who stood there and received no answer during the short journey on which he threaded his way through the hotel, hollowed out inside like a toy, which extended round about us, floor by floor, the ramifications of its corridors in the depths of which the light grew velvety, lost its tone, diminished the communicating doors, the steps of the service stairs which it transformed into that amber haze, unsubstantial and mysterious as a twilight, in which Rembrandt picks out here and there a window-sill or a well-head. And on each landing a golden light reflected from the carpet indicated the setting sun and the lavatory window.

I asked myself whether the girls I had just seen lived at Balbec, and who they could be. When our desire is thus concentrated upon a little tribe of humanity which it singles out from the rest, everything that can be associated with that tribe becomes a spring of emotion and then of reflexion. I had heard a lady say on the 'front': "She is a friend of the little Simonet girl" with that self-important air of inside knowledge, as who should say: "He is the inseparable companion of young La Rochefoucauld." And immediately she had detected on the face of the person to whom she gave this information a curiosity to see more of the favoured person who was 'a friend of the little Simonet.' A privilege, obviously, that did not appear to be granted to all the world. For aristocracy is a relative state. And there are plenty of inexpensive little holes and corners where the son of an upholsterer is the arbiter of fashion and reigns over a court like any young Prince of Wales. I have often since then sought to recall how it first sounded for me there on the beach, that name of Simonet, still quite indefinite as to its form, which I had failed to distinguish, and also as to its significance, to the designation by it of such and such a person, or perhaps of some one else; imprinted, in fact, with that vagueness, that novelty which we find so moving in the sequel, when the name whose letters are every moment engraved more deeply on our hearts by our incessant thought of them has become (though this was not to happen to me with the name of the 'little Simonet' until several years had passed) the first coherent sound that comes to our lips, whether on waking from sleep or on recovering from a swoon, even before the idea of what o'clock it is or of where we are, almost before the word 'I,' as though the person whom it names were more 'we' even than we ourselves, and as though after a brief spell of unconsciousness the phase that is the first of all to dissolve is that in which we were not thinking of her. I do not know why I said to myself from the first that the name Simonet must be that of one of the band of girls; from that moment I never ceased to ask myself how I could get to know the Simonet family, get to know them, moreover, through people whom they considered superior to themselves (which ought not to be diffi-cult if the girls were only common little 'bounders') so that they might not form a disdainful idea of me. For one cannot have a perfect knowledge, one cannot effect the complete absorption of a person who disdains one, so long as one has not overcome her disdain. And since, whenever the idea of women who are so different from us penetrates our senses, unless we are able to forget it or the competition of other ideas eliminates it, we know no rest until we have converted those aliens into something that is com-patible with ourself, our heart being in this respect endowed with the same kind of reaction and activity as our physical organism, which cannot abide the infusion of any foreign body into its veins without at once striving to digest and assimilate it: the little Simonet must be the prettiest of them all—she who, I felt moreover, might yet become my mistress, for she was the only one who, two or three times half-turning her head, had appeared to take cognisance of my fixed stare. I asked the lift-boy whether he knew of any people at Balbec called Simonet. Not liking to admit that there was anything which he did not know, he replied that he seemed to have heard the name somewhere. As we reached the highest landing I told him to have the latest lists of visitors sent up to me.

I stepped out of the lift, but instead of going to my room I made my way farther along the corridor, for before my arrival the valet in charge of the landing, despite his horror of draughts, had opened the window at the end, which instead of looking out to the sea faced the hill and valley inland, but never allowed them to be seen, for its panes, which were made of clouded glass, were generally closed. I made a short 'station' in front of it, time enough just to pay my devotions to the view which for once it revealed over the hill against which the back of the hotel rested, a view that contained but a solitary house, planted in the middle distance, though the perspective and the evening light in which I saw it, while preserving its mass, gave it a sculptural beauty and a velvet background, as though to one of those architectural works in miniature, tiny temples or chapels wrought in gold and enamels, which serve as reliquaries and are exposed only on rare and solemn days for the veneration of the faithful. But this moment of adoration had already lasted too long, for the valet, who carried in one hand a bunch of keys and with the other saluted me by touching his verger's skull-cap, though without raising it, on account of the pure, cool evening air, came and drew together, like those of a shrine, the two sides of the window, and so shut off the minute edifice, the glistening relic from my adoring gaze. I went into my room. Regularly, as the season advanced, the picture that I found there in my window changed. At first it was broad daylight, and dark only if the weather was bad: and then, in the greenish glass which it distended with the curve of its round waves, the sea, set among the iron uprights of my window like a piece of stained glass in its leads, ravelled out over all the deep rocky border of the bay little plumed triangles of an unmoving spray delineated with the delicacy of a feather or a downy breast from Pisanello's pencil, and fixed in that white, unalterable, creamy enamel which is used to depict fallen snow in Gallé's glass.

Presently the days grew shorter and at the moment when I entered my room the violet sky seemed branded with the stiff, geometrical, travelling, effulgent figure of the sun (like the representation of some miraculous sign, of some mystical apparition) leaning over the sea from the hinge of the horizon as a sacred picture leans over a high altar, while the different parts of the western sky exposed in the glass fronts of the low mahogany bookcases that ran along the walls, which I carried back in my mind to the marvellous painting from which they had been detached, seemed like those different scenes which some old master executed long ago for a confraternity upon a shrine, whose separate panels are now exhibited side by side upon the wall of a museum gallery, so that the visitor's imagination alone can restore them to their place on the predella of the reredos. A few weeks later, when I went upstairs, the sun had already set. Like the one that I used to see at Combray, behind the Calvary, when I was coming home from a walk and looking forward to going down to the kitchen before dinner, a band of red sky over the sea, compact and clear-cut as a layer of aspic over meat, then, a little later, over a sea already cold and blue like a grey mullet, a sky of the same pink as the salmon that we should presently be ordering at Rivebelle reawakened the pleasure which I was to derive from the act of dressing to go out to dinner. Over the sea, quite near the shore, were trying to rise, one beyond another, at wider and wider intervals, vapours of a pitchy blackness but also of the polish and consistency of agate, of a visible weight, so much so that the highest among them, poised at the end of their contorted stem and overreaching the centre of gravity of the pile that had hitherto supported them, seemed on the point of bringing down in ruin this lofty structure already half the height of the sky, and of precipitating it into the sea. The sight of a ship that was moving away like a nocturnal traveller gave me the same impression that I had had in the train of being set free from the necessity of sleep and from confinement in a bedroom. Not that I felt myself a prisoner in the room in which I now was, since in another hour I should have left it and be getting into the carriage. I threw myself down on the bed; and, just as if I had been lying in a berth on board one of those steamers which I could see quite near to me and which, when night came, it would be strange to see stealing slowly out into the darkness, like shadowy and silent but unsleeping swans, I was on all sides surrounded by pictures of the sea.

But as often as not they were, indeed, only pictures; I forgot that below their coloured expanse was hollowed the sad desolation of the beach, travelled by the restless evening breeze whose breath I had so anxiously felt on my arrival at Balbec; besides, even in my room, being wholly taken up with thoughts of the girls whom I had seen go past, I was no longer in a state of mind calm or disinterested enough to allow the formation of any really deep impression of beauty. The anticipation of dinner at Rivebelle made my mood more frivolous still, and my mind, dwelling at such moments upon the surface of the body which I was going to dress up so as to try to appear as pleasing as possible in the feminine eyes which would be scrutinising me in the brilliantly lighted restaurant, was incapable of putting any depth behind the colour of things. And if, beneath my window, the unwearying, gentle flight of sea-martins and swallows had not arisen like a playing fountain, like living fireworks, joining the intervals between their soaring rockets with the motionless white streaming lines of long horizontal wakes of foam, without the charming miracle of this natural and local phenomenon, which brought into touch with reality the scenes that I had before my eyes, I might easily have believed that they were no more than a selection, made afresh every day, of paintings which were shewn quite arbitrarily in the place in which I happened to be and without having any necessary connexion with that place. At one time it was an exhibition of Japanese colour-prints: beside the neat disc of sun, red and round as the moon, a yellow cloud seemed a lake against which black swords were outlined like the trees upon its shore; a bar of a tender pink which I had never seen again after my first paint-box swelled out into a river on either bank of which boats seemed to be waiting high and dry for some one to push them down and set them afloat. And with the contemptuous, bored, frivolous glance of an amateur or a woman hurrying through a picture gallery between two social engagements, I would say to myself: "Curious sunset, this; it's different from what they usually are but after all I've seen them just as fine, just as remarkable as this." I had more pleasure on evenings when a ship, absorbed and liquefied by the horizon so much the same in colour as herself (an Impressionist exhibition this time) that it seemed to be also of the same matter, appeared as if some one had simply cut out with a pair of scissors her bows and the rigging in which she tapered into a slender filigree from the vaporous blue of the sky. Sometimes the ocean filled almost the whole of my window, when it was enlarged and prolonged by a band of sky edged at the top only by a line that was of the same blue as the sea, so that I supposed it all to be still sea, and the change in colour due only to some effect of light and shade. Another day the sea was painted only in the lower part of the window, all the rest of which was so filled with innumerable clouds, packed one against another in horizontal bands, that its panes seemed to be intended, for some special purpose or to illustrate a special talent of the artist, to present a 'Cloud Study,' while the fronts of the various bookcases shewing similar clouds but in another part of the horizon and differently coloured by the light, appeared to be offering as it were the repetition—of which certain of our contemporaries are so fond—of one and the same effect always observed at different hours but able now in the immobility of art to be seen all together in a single room, drawn in pastel and mounted under glass. And sometimes to a sky and sea uniformly grey a rosy touch would be added with an exquisite delicacy, while a little butterfly that had gone to sleep at the foot of the window seemed to be attaching with its wings at the corner of this 'Harmony in Grey and Pink' in the Whistler manner the favourite signature of the Chelsea master. The pink vanished; there was nothing now left to look at. I rose for a moment and before lying down again drew close the inner curtains. Above them I could see from my bed the ray of light that still remained, growing steadily fainter and thinner, but it was without any feeling of sadness, without any regret for its passing that I thus allowed to die above the curtains the hour at which, as a rule, I was seated at table, for I knew that this day was of another kind than ordinary days, longer, like those arctic days which night interrupts for a few minutes only; I knew that from the chrysalis of the dusk was preparing to emerge, by a radiant metamorphosis, the dazzling light of the Rivebelle restaurant. I said to myself: "It is time"; I stretched myself on the bed, and rose, and finished dressing; and I found a charm in these idle moments, lightened of every material burden, in which while down below the others were dining I was employing the forces accumulated during the inactivity of this last hour of the day only in drying my washed body, in putting on a dinner jacket, in tying my tie, in making all those gestures which were already dictated by the anticipated pleasure of seeing again some woman whom I had noticed, last time, at Rivebelle, who had seemed to be watching me, had perhaps left the table for a moment only in the hope that I would follow her; it was with joy that I enriched myself with all these attractions so as to give myself, whole, alert, willing, to a new life, free, without cares, in which I would lean my hesitations upon the calm strength of Saint-Loup, and would choose from among the different species of animated nature and the produce of every land those which, composing the unfamiliar dishes that my companion would at once order, might have tempted my appetite or my imagination. And then at the end of the season came the days when I could no longer pass indoors from the 'front' through the dining-room; its windows stood open no more, for it was night now outside and the swarm of poor folk and curious idlers, attracted by the blaze of light which they might not reach, hung in black clusters chilled by the north wind to the luminous sliding walls of that buzzing hive of glass.

There was a knock at my door; it was Aimé who had come upstairs in person with the latest lists of visitors.

Aimé could not go away without telling me that Dreyfus was guilty a thousand times over. "It will all come out," he assured me, "not this year, but next. It was a gentleman who's very thick with the General Staff, told me. I asked him if they wouldn't decide to bring it all to light at once, before the year is out. He laid down his cigarette," Aimé went on, acting the scene for my benefit, and, shaking his head and his forefinger as his informant had done, as much as to say: "We mustn't expect too much!"— " 'Not this year, Aimé,' those were his very words, putting his hand on my shoulder, 'It isn't possible. But next Easter, yes!' " And Aimé tapped me gently on my shoulder, saying, "You see, I'm letting you have it exactly as he told me," whether because he was flattered at this act of familiarity by a distinguished person or so that I might better appreciate, with a full knowledge of the facts, the worth of the arguments and our grounds for hope.

It was not without a slight throb of the heart that on the first page of the list I caught sight of the words 'Simonet and family.' I had in me a store of old dream-memories which dated from my childhood, and in which all the tenderness (tenderness that existed in my heart, but, when my heart felt it, was not distinguishable from anything else) was wafted to me by a person as different as possible from myself. This person, once again I fashioned her, utilising for the purpose the name Simonet and the memory of the harmony that had reigned between the young bodies which I had seen displaying themselves on the beach, in a sportive procession worthy of Greek art or of Giotto. I knew not which of these girls was Mlle. Simonet, if indeed any of them were so named, but I did know that I was loved by Mlle. Simonet and that I was going, with Saint-Loup's help, to attempt to know her. Unfortunately, having on that condition only obtained an extension of his leave, he was obliged to report for duty every day at Doncières: but to make him forsake his military duty I had felt that I might count, more even than on his friendship for myself, on that same curiosity, as a human naturalist, which I myself had so often felt—even without having seen the person mentioned, and simply on hearing some one say that there was a pretty cashier at a fruiterer's—to acquaint myself with a new variety of feminine beauty. But that curiosity I had been wrong in hoping to excite in Saint-Loup by speaking to him of my band of girls. For it had been and would long remain paralysed in him by his love for that actress whose lover he was. And even if he had felt it lightly stirring him he would have repressed it, from an almost superstitious belief that on his own fidelity might depend that of his mistress. And so it was without any promise from him that he would take an active interest in my girls that we started out to dine at Rivebelle.

At first, when we arrived there, the sun used just to have set, but it was light still; in the garden outside the restaurant, where the lamps had not yet been lighted, the heat of the day fell and settled, as though in a vase along the sides of which the transparent, dusky jelly of the air seemed of such consistency that a tall rose-tree fastened against the dim wall which it streaked with pink veins, looked like the arborescence that one sees at the heart of an onyx. Presently night had always fallen when we left the carriage, often indeed before we started from Balbec if the evening was wet and we had put off sending for the carriage in the hope of the weather's improving. But on those days it was without any sadness that I listened to the wind howling, I knew that it did not mean the abandonment of my plans, imprisonment in my bedroom; I knew that in the great dining-room of the restaurant, which we would enter to the sound of the music of the gypsy band, the innumerable lamps would triumph easily over darkness and chill, by applying to them their broad cauteries of molten gold, and I jumped light-heartedly after Saint-Loup into the closed carriage which stood waiting for us in the rain. For some time past the words of Bergotte, when he pronounced himself positive that, in spite of all I might say, I had been created to enjoy, pre-eminently, the pleasures of the mind, had restored to me, with regard to what I might succeed in achieving later on, a hope that was disappointed afresh every day by the boredom that I felt on setting myself down before a writing-table to start work on a critical essay or a novel. "After all," I said to myself, "possibly the pleasure that its author has found in writing it is not the infallible test of the literary value of a page; it may be only an accessory, one that is often to be found superadded to that value, but the want of which can have no prejudicial effect on it. Perhaps some of the greatest masterpieces were written yawning." My grandmother set my doubts at rest by telling me that I should be able to work and should enjoy working as soon as my health improved. And, our doctor having thought it only prudent to warn me of the grave risks to which my state of health might expose me, and having outlined all the hygienic precaution that I ought to take to avoid any accident—I subordinated all my pleasures to an object which I judged to be infinitely more important than them, that of becoming strong enough to be able to bring into being the work which I had, possibly, within me; I had been exercising over myself, ever since I had come to Balbec, a scrupulous and constant control. Nothing would have induced me, there, to touch the cup of coffee which would have robbed me of the night's sleep that was necessary if I was not to be tired next day. But as soon as we reached Rivebelle, immediately, what with the excitement of a new pleasure, and finding myself in that different zone into which the exception to our rule of life takes us after it has cut the thread, patiently spun throughout so many days, that was guiding us towards wisdom—as though there were never to be any such thing as to-morrow, nor any lofty aims to be realised, vanished all that exact machinery of prudent hygienic measures which had been working to safeguard them. A waiter was offering to take my coat, whereupon Saint-Loup asked: "You're sure you won't be cold? Perhaps you'd better keep it: it's not very warm in here."

"No, no," I assured him; and perhaps I did not feel the cold; but however that might be, I no longer knew the fear of falling ill, the necessity of not dying, the importance of work. I gave up my coat; we entered the dining-room to the sound of some warlike march played by the gipsies, we advanced between two rows of tables laid for dinner as along an easy path of glory, and, feeling a happy glow imparted to our bodies by the rhythms of the orchestra which rendered us its military honours, gave us this unmerited triumph, we concealed it beneath a grave and frozen mien, beneath a languid, casual gait, so as not to be like those music-hall 'mashers' who, having wedded a ribald verse to a patriotic air, come running on to the stage with the martial countenance of a victorious general.

From that moment I was a new man, who was no longer my grandmother's grandson and would remember her only when it was time to get up and go, but the brother, for the time being, of the waiters who were going to bring us our dinner.

The dose of beer—all the more, that of champagne—which at Balbec I should not have ventured to take in a week, albeit to my calm and lucid consciousness the flavour of those beverages represented a pleasure clearly appreciable, since it was also one that could easily be sacrificed, I now imbibed at a sitting, adding to it a few drops of port wine, too much distracted to be able to taste it, and I gave the violinist who had just been playing the two louis which I had been saving up for the last month with a view to buying something, I could not remember what. Several of the waiters, set going among the tables, were flying along at full speed, each carrying on his outstretched palms a dish which it seemed to be the object of this kind of race not to let fall. And in fact the chocolate *soufflés* arrived at their destination unspilled, the potatoes *à l'anglaise,* in spite of the pace which ought to have sent them flying, came arranged as at the start round the Pauilhac lamb. I noticed one of these servants, very tall, plumed with superb black locks, his face dyed in a tint that suggested rather certain species of rare birds than a human being, who, running without pause (and, one would have said, without purpose) from one end of the room to the other, made me think of one of those macaws which fill the big aviaries in zoological gardens with their gorgeous colouring and incomprehensible agitation. Presently the spectacle assumed an order, in my eyes at least, growing at once more noble and more calm. All this dizzy activity became fixed in a quiet harmony. I looked at the round tables whose innumerable assemblage filled the restaurant like so many planets as planets are represented in old allegorical pictures. Moreover, there seemed to be some irresistibly attractive force at work among these divers stars, and at each table the diners had eyes only for the tables at which they were not sitting, except perhaps some wealthy amphitryon who, having managed to secure a famous author, was endeavouring to extract from him, thanks to the magic properties of the turning table, a few unimportant remarks at which the ladies marvelled. The harmony of these astral tables did not prevent the incessant revolution of the countless servants who, because instead of being seated like the diners they were on their feet, performed their evolutions in a more exalted sphere. No doubt they were running, one to fetch the *hors d'œuvres,* another to change the wine or with clean glasses. But despite these special reasons, their perpetual course among the round tables yielded, after a time, to the observer the law of its dizzy but ordered circulation. Seated behind a bank of flowers, two horrible cashiers, busy with endless calculations, seemed two witches occupied in forecasting by astrological signs the disasters that might from time to time occur in this celestial vault fashioned according to the scientific conceptions of the middle ages.

And I rather pitied all the diners because I felt that for them the round tables were not planets and that they had not cut through the scheme of things one of those sections which deliver us from the bondage of appearances and enable us to perceive analogies. They thought that they were dining with this or that person, that the dinner would cost roughly so much, and that to-morrow they would begin all over again. And they appeared absolutely unmoved by the progress through their midst of a train of young assistants who, having probably at that moment no urgent duty, advanced processionally bearing rolls of bread in baskets. Some of them, the youngest, stunned by the cuffs which the head waiters administered to them as they passed, fixed melancholy eyes upon a distant dream and were consoled only if some visitor from the Balbec hotel in which they had once been employed, recognising them, said a few words to them, telling them in person to take away the champagne which was not fit to drink, an order that filled them with pride.

I could hear the twinging of my nerves, in which there was a sense of comfort independent of the external objects that might have produced it, a comfort which the least shifting of my body or of my attention was enough to make me feel, just as to a shut eye a slight pressure gives the sensation of colour. I had already drunk a good deal of port wine, and if I now asked for more it was not so much with a view to the comfort which the additional glasses would bring me as an effect of the comfort produced by the glasses that had gone before. I allowed the music itself to guide to each of its notes my pleasure which, meekly following, rested on each in turn. If, like one of those chemical industries by means of which are prepared in large quantities bodies which in a state of nature come together only by accident and very rarely, this restaurant at Rivebelle united at one and the same moment more women to tempt me with beckoning vistas of happiness than the hazard of walks and drives would have made me encounter in a year; on the other hand, this music that greeted our ears,—arrangements of waltzes, of German operettas, of music-hall songs, all of them quite new to me—was itself like an ethereal resort of pleasure superimposed upon the other and more intoxicating still. For these tunes, each as individual as a woman, were not keeping, as she would have kept, for some privileged person, the voluptuous secret which they contained: they offered me their secrets, ogled me, came up to me with affected or vulgar movements, accosted me, caressed me as if I had suddenly become more seductive, more powerful and more rich; I indeed found in these tunes an element of cruelty; because any such thing as a disinterested feeling for beauty, a gleam of intelligence was unknown to them; for them physical pleasures alone existed. And they are the most merciless of hells, the most gateless and imprisoning for the jealous wretch to whom they present that pleasure—that pleasure which the woman he loves is enjoying with another—as the only thing that exists in the world for her who is all the world to him. But while I was humming softly to myself the notes of this tune, and returning its kiss, the pleasure peculiar to itself which it made me feel became so dear to me that I would have left my father and mother, to follow it through the singular world which it constructed in the invisible, in lines instinct with alternate languor and vivacity. Although such a pleasure as this is not calculated to enhance the value of the person to whom it comes, for it is perceived by him alone, and although whenever, in the course of our life, we have failed to attract a woman who has caught sight of us, she could not tell whether at that moment we possessed this inward and subjective felicity which, consequently, could in no way have altered the judgment that she passed on us, I felt myself more powerful, almost irresistible. It seemed to me that my love was no longer something unattractive, at which people might smile, but had precisely the touching beauty, the seductiveness of this music, itself comparable to a friendly atmosphere in which she whom I loved and I were to meet, suddenly grown intimate.

This restaurant was the resort not only of light women; it was frequented also by people in the very best society, who came there for afternoon tea or gave big dinner-parties. The tea-parties were held in a long gallery, glazed and narrow, shaped like a funnel, which led from the entrance hall to the dining-room and was bounded on one side by the garden, from which it was separated (save for a few stone pillars) only by its wall of glass, in which panes would be opened here and there. The result of which, apart from ubiquitous draughts, was sudden and intermittent bursts of sunshine, a dazzling light that made it almost impossible to see the tea-drinkers, so that when they were installed there, at tables crowded pair after pair the whole way along the narrow gully, as they were shot with colours at every movement they made in drinking their tea or in greeting one another, you would have called it a reservoir, a stewpond in which the fisherman has collected all his glittering catch, and the fish, half out of water and bathed in sunlight, dazzle the eye as they mirror an ever-changing iridescence.

A few hours later, during dinner, which, naturally, was served in the dining-room, the lights would be turned on, although it was still quite light out of doors, so that one saw before one's eyes, in the garden, among summer-houses glimmering in the twilight, like pale spectres of evening, alleys whose greyish verdure was pierced by the last rays of the setting sun and, from the lamp-lit room in which we were dining, appeared through the glass —no longer, as one would have said of the ladies who had been drinking tea there in the afternoon, along the blue and gold corridor, caught in a glittering and dripping net—but like the vegetation of a pale and green aquarium of gigantic size seen by a supernatural light. People began to rise from table; and if each party while their dinner lasted, albeit they spent the whole time examining, recognising, naming the party at the next table, had been held in perfect cohesion about their own, the attractive force that had kept them gravitating round their host of the evening lost its power at the moment when, for coffee, they repaired to the same corridor that had been used for the tea-parties; it often happened that in its passage from place to place some party on the march dropped one or more of its human corpuscles who, having come under the irresistible attraction of the rival party, detached themselves for a moment from their own, in which their places were taken by ladies or gentlemen who had come across to speak to friends before hurrying off with an "I really must fly: I'm dining with M. So-and-So." And for the moment you would have been reminded, looking at them, of two separate nosegays that had exchanged a few of their flowers. Then the corridor too began to empty. Often, since even after dinner there was still a little light left outside, they left this long corridor unlighted, and, skirted by the trees that overhung it on the other side of the glass, it suggested a pleached alley in a wooded and shady garden. Here and there, in the gloom, a fair diner lingered. As I passed through this corridor one evening on my way out I saw, sitting among a group of strangers, the beautiful Princesse de Luxembourg. I raised my hat without stopping. She remembered me, and bowed her head with a smile; in the air, far above her bowed head, but emanating from the movement, rose melodiously a few words addressed to myself, which must have been a somewhat amplified good-evening, intended not to stop me but simply to complete the gesture, to make it a spoken greeting. But her words remained so indistinct and the sound which was all that I caught was prolonged so sweetly and seemed to me so musical that it seemed as if among the dim branches of the trees a nightingale had begun to sing. If it so happened that, to finish the evening with a party of his friends whom we had met, Saint-Loup decided to go on to the Casino of a neighbouring village, and, taking them with him, put me in a carriage by myself, I would urge the driver to go as fast as he possibly could, so that the minutes might pass less slowly which I must spend without having anyone at hand to dispense me from the obligation myself to provide my sensibility—reversing the engine, so to speak, and emerging from the passivity in which I was caught and held as in the teeth of a machine—with those modifications which, since my arrival at Rivebelle, I had been receiving from other people. The risk of collision with a carriage coming the other way along those lanes where there was barely room for one and it was dark as pitch, the insecurity of the soil, crumbling in many places, at the cliff's edge, the proximity of its vertical drop to the sea, none of these things exerted on me the slight stimulus that would have been required to bring the vision and the fear of danger within the scope of my reasoning. For just as it is not the desire to become famous but the habit of being laborious that enables us to produce a finished work, so it is not the activity of the present moment but wise reflexions from the past that help us to safeguard the future. But if already, before this point, on my arrival at Rivebelle, I had flung irretrievably away from me those crutches of reason and self-control which help our infirmity to follow the right road, if I now found myself the victim of a sort of moral ataxy, the alcohol that I had drunk, by unduly straining my nerves, gave to the minutes as they came a quality, a charm which did not have the result of leaving me more ready, or indeed more resolute to inhibit them, prevent their coming; for while it made me prefer them a thousand times to anything else in my life, my exaltation made me isolate them from everything else; I was confined to the present, as heroes are or drunkards; eclipsed for the moment, my past no longer projected before me that shadow of itself which we call our future; placing the goal of my life no longer in the realisation of the dreams of that past, but in the felicity of the present moment, I could see nothing now of what lay beyond it. So that, by a contradiction which, however, was only apparent, it was at the very moment in which I was tasting an unfamiliar pleasure, feeling that my life might yet be happy, in which it should have become more precious in my sight; it was at this very moment that, delivered from the anxieties which my life had hitherto contrived to suggest to me, I unhesitatingly abandoned it to the chance of an accident. After all, I was doing no more than concentrate in a single evening the carelessness that, for most men, is diluted throughout their whole existence, in which every day they face, unnecessarily, the dangers of a sea-voyage, of a trip in an aeroplane or motor-car, when there is waiting for them at home the creature whose life their death would shatter, or when there is still stored in the fragile receptacle of their brain that book the approaching publication of which is their one object, now, in life. And so too in the Rivebelle restaurant, on evenings when we just stayed there after dinner, if anyone had come in with the

intention of killing me, as I no longer saw, save in a distant prospect too
remote to have any reality, my grandmother, my life to come, the books
that I was going to write, as I clung now, body and mind, wholly to the
scent of the lady at the next table, the politeness of the waiters, the outline
of the waltz that the band was playing, as I was glued to my immediate
sensation, with no extension beyond its limits, nor any object other than
not to be separated from it, I should have died in and with that sensation,
I should have let myself be strangled without offering any resistance, without a movement, a bee drugged with tobacco smoke that had ceased to
take any thought for preserving the accumulation of its labours and the
hopes of its hive.

I ought here to add that this insignificance into which the most serious
matters subsided, by contrast with the violence of my exaltation, came in
the end to include Mlle. Simonet and her friends. The enterprise of knowing them seemed to me easy now but hardly worth the trouble, for my
immediate sensation alone, thanks to its extraordinary intensity, to the
joy that its slightest modifications, its mere continuity provoked, had any
importance for me; all the rest—parents, work, pleasures, girls at Balbec
weighed with me no more than does a flake of foam in a strong wind that
will not let it find a resting place, existed no longer save in relation to this
internal power: intoxication makes real for an hour or two a subjective
idealism, pure phenomenism; nothing is left now but appearances, nothing
exists save as a function of our sublime self. This is not to say that a
genuine love, if we have one, cannot survive in such conditions. But we
feel so unmistakably, as though in a new atmosphere, that unknown pressures have altered the dimensions of that sentiment that we can no longer
consider it in the old way. It is indeed still there and we shall find it, but
in a different place, no longer weighing upon us, satisfied by the sensation
which the present affords it, a sensation that is sufficient for us, since for
what is not actually present we take no thought. Unfortunately the coefficient which thus alters our values alters them only in the hour of intoxication. The people who had lost all their importance, whom we scattered
with our breath like soap-bubbles, will to-morrow resume their density;
we shall have to try afresh to settle down to work which this evening had
ceased to have any significance. A more serious matter still, these mathe-
matics of the morrow, the same as those of yesterday, in whose problems
we shall find ourselves inexorably involved, it is they that govern us even
in these hours, and we alone are unconscious of their rule. If there should
happen to be, near us, a woman, virtuous or inimical, that question so
difficult an hour ago—to know whether we should succeed in finding favour
with her—seems to us now a million times easier of solution without having
become easier in any respect, for it is only in our own sight, in our own
inward sight, that we have altered. And she is as much annoyed with us
at this moment as we shall be next day at the thought of our having given
a hundred francs to the messenger, and for the same reason which in our
case has merely been delayed in its operation, namely the absence of
intoxication.

I knew none of the women who were at Rivebelle and, because they formed a part of my intoxication just as its reflexions form part of a mirror, appeared to me now a thousand times more to be desired than the less and less existent Mlle. Simonet. One of them, young, fair, by herself, with a sad expression on a face framed in a straw hat trimmed with field-flowers, gazed at me for a moment with a dreamy air and struck me as being attractive. Then it was the turn of another, and of a third; finally of a dark one with glowing cheeks. Almost all of them were known, if not to myself, to Saint-Loup.

He had, in fact, before he made the acquaintance of his present mistress, lived so much in the restricted world of amorous adventure that all the women who would be dining on these evenings at Rivebelle, where many of them had appeared quite by chance, having come to the coast some to join their lovers, others in the hope of finding fresh lovers there, there was scarcely one that he did not know from having spent—or if not he, one or other of his friends—at least one night in their company. He did not bow to them if they were with men, and they, albeit they looked more at him than at anyone else, for the indifference which he was known to feel towards every woman who was not his mistress gave him in their eyes an exceptional interest, appeared not to know him. But you could hear them whispering: "That's young Saint-Loup. It seems he's still quite gone on that girl of his. Got it bad, he has. What a dear boy! I think he's just wonderful; and what style! Some girls do have all the luck, don't they? And he's so nice in every way. I saw a lot of him when I was with d'Orléans. They were quite inseparable, those two. He was going the pace, that time. But he's given it all up now, she can't complain. She's had a good run of luck, that she can say. And I ask you, what in the world can he see in her? He must be a bit of a chump, when all's said and done. She's got feet like boats, whiskers like an American, and her undies are filthy. I can tell you, a little shop girl would be ashamed to be seen in her knickers. Do just look at his eyes a moment; you would jump into the fire for a man like that. Hush, don't say a word; he's seen me; look, he's smiling. Oh, he remembers me all right. Just you mention my name to him, and see what he says!" Between these girls and him I surprised a glance of mutual understanding. I should have liked him to introduce me to them, so that I might ask them for assignations and they give them to me, even if I had been unable to keep them. For otherwise their appearance would remain for all time devoid, in my memory, of that part of itself—just as though it had been hidden by a veil—which varies in every woman, which we cannot imagine in any woman until we have actually seen it in her, and which is apparent only in the glance that she directs at us, that acquiesces in our desire and promises that it shall be satisfied. And yet, even when thus reduced, their aspect was for me far more than that of women whom I should have known to be virtuous, and it seemed to me not to be, like theirs, flat, with nothing behind it, fashioned in one piece with no solidity. It was not, of course, for me what it must be for Saint-Loup who, by an act of memory, beneath the indifference, transparent to him, of the motionless features which affected not to know him, or beneath the dull formality of the greeting that might equally well have been addressed to anyone else, could recall, could see, through dishevelled locks, a swooning mouth, a pair of half-closed eyes, a whole silent picture like those that painters, to cheat their visitors' senses, drape with a decent covering. Undoubtedly, for me who felt that nothing of my personality had penetrated the surface of this woman or that, or would be borne by her upon the unknown ways which she would tread through life, those faces remained sealed. But it was quite enough to know that they did open, for them to seem to me of a price which I should not have set on them had they been but precious medals, instead of lockets within which were hidden memories of love. As for Robert, scarcely able to keep in his place at table, concealing beneath a courtier's smile his warrior's thirst for action—when I examined him I could see how closely the vigorous structure of his triangular face must have been modelled on that of his ancestors' faces, a face devised rather for an ardent bowman than for a delicate student. Beneath his fine skin the bold construction, the feudal architecture were apparent. His head made one think of those old dungeon keeps on which the disused battlements are still to be seen, although inside they have been converted into libraries.

On our way back to Balbec, of those of the fair strangers to whom he had introduced me I would repeat to myself without a moment's interruption, and yet almost unconsciously: "What a delightful woman!" as one chimes in with the refrain of a song. I admit that these words were prompted rather by the state of my nerves than by any lasting judgment. It was nevertheless true that if I had had a thousand francs on me and if there had still been a jeweller's shop open at that hour, I should have bought the lady a ring. When the successive hours of our life are thus displayed against too widely dissimilar backgrounds, we find that we give away too much of ourselves to all sorts of people who next day will not interest us in the least. But we feel that we are still responsible for what we said to them overnight, and that we must honour our promises.

As on these evenings I came back later than usual to the hotel, it was with joy that I recognised, in a room no longer hostile, the bed on which, on the day of my arrival, I had supposed that it would always be impossible for me to find any rest, whereas now my weary limbs turned to it for support; so that, in turn, thighs, hips, shoulders burrowed into, trying to adhere at every angle to, the sheets that covered its mattress, as if my fatigue, like a sculptor, had wished to take a cast of an entire human body. But I could not go to sleep; I felt the approach of morning; peace of mind, health of body, were no longer mine. In my distress it seemed that never should I recapture them. I should have had to sleep for a long time if I were to overtake them. But then, had I begun to doze, I must in any event be awakened in a couple of hours by the symphonic concert on the beach. Suddenly I was asleep, I had fallen into that deep slumber in which are opened to us a return to childhood, the recapture of past years, of lost feelings, the disincarnation, the transmigration of the soul, the evoking of the dead, the illusions of madness, retrogression towards the most elementary of the natural kingdoms (for we say that we often see animals in our dreams, but we forget almost always that we are ourself then an animal deprived of that reasoning power which projects upon things the light of certainty; we present on the contrary to the spectacle of life only a dubious vision, destroyed afresh every moment by oblivion, the former reality fading before that which follows it as one projection of a magic lantern fades before the next as we change the slide), all those mysteries which we imagine ourselves not to know and into which we are in reality initiated almost every night, as we are into the other great mystery of annihilation and resurrection. Rendered more vagabond by the difficulty of digesting my Rivebelle dinner, the successive and flickering illumination of shadowy zones of my past made of me a being whose supreme happiness would have been that of meeting Legrandin, with whom I had just been talking in my dream.

And then, even my own life was entirely hidden from me by a new setting, like the 'drop' lowered right at the front of the stage before which, while the scene shifters are busy behind, actors appear in a fresh 'turn.' The turn in which I was now cast for a part was in the manner of an Oriental fairy-tale; I retained no knowledge of my past or of myself, on account of the intense proximity of this interpolated scenery; I was merely a person who received the bastinado and underwent various punishments for a crime the nature of which I could not distinguish, though it was actually that of having taken too much port wine. Suddenly I awoke and discovered that, thanks to a long sleep, I had not heard a note of the concert. It was already afternoon; I verified this by my watch after several efforts to sit up in bed, efforts fruitless at first and interrupted by backward falls on to my pillow, but those short falls which are a sequel of sleep as of other forms of intoxication, whether due to wine or to convalescence; besides, before I had so much as looked at the time, I was certain that it was past midday. Last night I had been nothing more than an empty vessel, without weight, and (since I must first have gone to bed to be able to keep still, and have been asleep to be able to keep silent) had been unable to refrain from moving about and talking; I had no longer any stability, any centre of gravity, I was set in motion and it seemed that I might have continued on my dreary course until I reached the moon. But if, while I slept, my eyes had not seen the time, my body had nevertheless contrived to calculate it, had measured the hours; not on a dial superficially marked and figured, but by the steadily growing weight of all my replenished forces which, like a powerful clockwork, it had allowed, notch by notch, to descend from my brain into the rest of my body in which there had risen now to above my knees the unbroken abundance of their store. If it is true that the sea was once upon a time our native element, into which we must plunge our cooling blood if we are to recover our strength, it is the same with the oblivion, the mental non-existence of sleep; we seem then to absent ourselves for a few hours from Time, but the forces which we have gathered in that interval without expending them, measure it by their quantity as accurately as the pendulum of the clock or the crumbling pyramid of the sandglass. Nor does one emerge more easily from such sleep than from a prolonged spell of wakefulness, so strongly does everything tend to persist; and if it is true that certain narcotics make us sleep, to have slept for any time is an even stronger narcotic, after which we have great difficulty in making ourselves wake up. Like a sailor who sees plainly the harbour in which he can moor his vessel, still tossed by the waves, I had a quite definite idea of looking at the time and of getting up, but my body was at every moment cast back upon the tide of sleep; the landing was difficult, and before I attained a position in which I could reach my watch and confront with its time that indicated by the wealth of accumulated material which my stiffened limbs had at their disposal, I fell back two or three times more upon my pillow.

At length I could reach and read it: "Two o'clock in the afternoon!" I rang; but at once I returned to a slumber which, this time, must have lasted infinitely longer, if I was to judge by the refreshment, the vision of an immense night overpassed, which I found on awakening. And yet as my awakening was caused by the entry of Françoise, and as her entry had been prompted by my ringing the bell, this second sleep which, it seemed to me, must have been longer than the other, and had brought me so much comfort and forgetfulness, could not have lasted for more than half a minute.

My grandmother opened the door of my bedroom; I asked her various questions about the Legrandin family.

It is not enough to say that I had returned to tranquillity and health, for it was more than a mere interval of space that had divided them from me yesterday, I had had all night long to struggle against a contrary tide, and now I not only found myself again in their presence, they had once more entered into me. At certain definite and still somewhat painful points beneath the surface of my empty head which would 'one day be broken, letting my ideas escape for all time, those ideas had once again taken their proper places and resumed that existence by which hitherto, alas, they had failed to profit.

Once again I had escaped from the impossibility of sleeping, from the deluge, the shipwreck of my nervous storms. I feared now not at all the menaces that had loomed over me the evening before, when I was dismantled of repose. A new life was opening before me; without making a single movement, for I was still shattered, although quite alert and well, I savoured my weariness with a light heart; it had isolated and broken asunder the bones of my legs and arms, which I could feel assembled before me, ready to cleave together, and which I was to raise to life merely by singing, like the builder in the fable.

Suddenly I thought of the fair girl with the sad expression whom I had seen at Rivebelle, where she had looked at me for a moment. Many others, in the course of the evening, had seemed to me attractive; now she alone arose from the dark places of my memory. I had felt that she noticed me, had expected one of the waiters to come to me with a whispered message from her. Saint-Loup did not know her and fancied that she was respectable. It would be very difficult to see her, to see her constantly. But I was prepared to make any sacrifice, I thought now only of her. Philosophy distinguishes often between free and necessary acts. Perhaps there is none to the necessity of which we are more completely subjected than that which, by virtue of an ascending power held in check during the act itself, makes so unfailingly (once our mind is at rest) spring up a memory that was levelled with other memories by the distributed pressure of our indifference, and rush to the surface, because unknown to us it contained, more than any of the others, a charm of which we do not become aware until the following day. And perhaps there is not, either, any act so free, for it is still unprompted by habit, by that sort of mental hallucination which, when we are in love, facilitates the invariable reappearance of the image of one particular person.

This was the day immediately following that on which I had seen file past me against a background of sea the beautiful procession of young girls. I put questions about them to a number of the visitors in the hotel, people who came almost every year to Balbec. They could tell me nothing. Later on, a photograph shewed me why. Who could ever recognise now in them, scarcely and yet quite definitely beyond an age in which one changes so utterly, that amorphous, delicious mass, still wholly infantine, of little girls who, only a few years back, might have been seen sitting in a ring on the sand round a tent; a sort of white and vague constellation in which one would have distinguished a pair of eyes that sparkled more than the rest, a mischievous face, flaxen hair, only to lose them again and to confound them almost at once in the indistinct and milky nebula.

No doubt, in those earlier years that were still so recent, it was not, as it had been yesterday when they appeared for the first time before me, one's impression of the group, but the group itself that had been lacking in clearness. Then those children, mere babies, had been still at that elementary stage in their formation when personality has not set its seal on every face. Like those primitive organisms in which the individual barely exists by itself, consists in the reef rather than in the coral insects that compose it, they were still pressed one against another. Sometimes one pushed her neighbour over, and then a wild laugh, which seemed the sole manifestation of their personal life, convulsed them all at once, obliterating, confounding those indefinite, grinning faces in the congealment of a single cluster, scintillating and tremulous. In an old photograph of themselves, which they were one day to give me, and which I have kept ever since, their infantile troop already presents the same number of participants as, later, their feminine procession; one can see from it that their presence must, even then, have made on the beach an unusual mark which forced itself on the attention; but one cannot recognise them individually in it save by a process of reasoning, leaving a clear field to all the transformations possible during girlhood, up to the point at which one reconstructed form would begin to encroach upon another individuality, which must be identified also, and whose handsome face, owing to the accessories of a large build and curly hair, may quite possibly have been, once, that wizened and impish little grin which the photograph album presents to us; and the distance traversed in a short interval of time by the physical characteristics of each of these girls making of them a criterion too vague to be of any use, whereas what they had in common and, so to speak, collectively, had at that early date been strongly marked, it sometimes happened that even their most intimate friends mistook one for another in this photograph, so much so that the question could in the last resort be settled only by some detail of costume which one of them could be certain that she herself, and not any of the others, had worn. Since those days, so different from the day on which I had just seen them strolling along the 'front,' so different and yet so close in time, they still gave way to fits of laughter, as I had observed that afternoon, but to laughter of a kind that was no longer the intermittent and almost automatic laughter of child-hood, a spasmodic discharge which, in those days, had continually sent their heads dipping out of the circle, as the clusters of minnows in the Vivonne used to scatter and vanish only to gather again a moment later; each countenance was now mistress of itself, their eyes were fixed on the goal towards which they were marching; and it had taken, yesterday, the indecision and tremulousness of my first impression to make me confuse vaguely (as their childish hilarity and the old photograph had confused) the spores now individualised and disjoined of the pale madrepore.

Repeatedly, I dare say, when pretty girls went by, I had promised myself that I would see them again. As a rule, people do not appear a second time; moreover our memory, which speedily forgets their existence, would find it difficult to recall their appearance; our eyes would not recognise them, perhaps, and in the meantime we have seen new girls go by, whom we shall not see again either. But at other times, and this was what was to happen with the pert little band at Balbec, chance brings them back in-sistently before our eyes. Chance seems to us then a good and useful thing, for we discern in it as it were rudiments of organisation, of an attempt to arrange our life; and it makes easy to us, inevitable, and sometimes—after interruptions that have made us hope that we may cease to remember—cruel, the retention in our minds of images to the possession of which we shall come in time to believe that we were predestined, and which but for chance we should from the very first have managed to forget, like so many others, with so little difficulty.

Presently Saint-Loup's visit drew to an end. I had not seen that party of girls again on the beach. He was too little at Balbec in the afternoons to have time to bother about them, or to attempt, in my interest, to make their acquaintance. In the evenings he was more free, and continued to take me constantly to Rivebelle. There are, in those restaurants, as there are in public gardens and railway trains, people embodied in a quite ordi-nary appearance, whose name astonishes us when, having happened to ask it, we discover that this is not the mere inoffensive stranger whom we sup-posed but nothing less than the Minister or Duke of whom we have so often heard. Two or three times already, in the Rivebelle restaurant, we had—Saint-Loup and I—seen come in and sit down at a table when every-one else was getting ready to go, a man of large stature, very muscular, with regular features and a grizzled beard, gazing, with concentrated atten-tion, into the empty air. One evening, on our asking the landlord who was this obscure, solitary and belated diner, "What!" he exclaimed, "do you mean to say you don't know the famous painter Elstir?" Swann had once mentioned his name to me, I had entirely forgotten in what connexion; but the omission of a particular memory, like that of part of a sentence when we are reading, leads sometimes not to uncertainty but to a birth of certainty that is premature. "He is a friend of Swann, a very well known artist, extremely good," I told Saint-Loup. Whereupon there passed over us both, like a wave of emotion, the thought that Elstir was a great artist, a celebrated man, and that, confounding us with the rest of the diners, he had no suspicion of the ecstasy into which we were thrown by the idea of his talent. Doubtless, his unconsciousness of our admiration and of our acquaintance with Swann would not have troubled us had we not been at the seaside. But since we were still at an age when enthusiasm cannot keep silence, and had been transported into a life in which not to be known is unendurable, we wrote a letter, signed with both our names, in which we revealed to Elstir in the two diners seated within a few feet of him two passionate admirers of his talent, two friends of his great friend Swann, and asked to be allowed to pay our homage to him in person. A waiter undertook to convey this missive to the celebrity.

A celebrity Elstir was, perhaps, not yet at this period quite to the extent claimed by the landlord, though he was to reach the height of his fame within a very few years. But he had been one of the first to frequent this restaurant when it was still only a sort of farmhouse, and had brought to it a whole colony of artists (who had all, as it happened, migrated else-where as soon as the farm-yard in which they used to feed in the open air, under a lean-to roof, had become a fashionable centre); Elstir himself had returned to Rivebelle this evening only on account of a temporary absence of his wife, from the house which he had taken in the neighbour-hood. But great talent, even when its existence is not yet recognised, will inevitably provoke certain phenomena of admiration, such as the landlord had managed to detect in the questions asked by more than one English lady visitor, athirst for information as to the life led by Elstir, or in the number of letters that he received from abroad. Then the landlord had further remarked that Elstir did not like to be disturbed when he was working, that he would rise in the middle of the night and take a little model down to the water's edge to pose for him, nude, if the moon was shining; and had told himself that so much labour was not in vain, nor the admiration of the tourists unjustified when he had, in one of Elstir's pictures, recognised a wooden cross which stood by the roadside as you came into Rivebelle.

"It's all right!" he would repeat with stupefaction, "there are all the four beams! Oh, he does take a lot of trouble!"

And he did not know whether a little *Sunrise Over the Sea* which Elstir had given him might not be worth a fortune.

We watched him read our letter, put it in his pocket, finish his dinner, begin to ask for his things, get up to go; and we were so convinced that we had shocked him by our overture that we would now have hoped (as keenly as at first we had dreaded) to make our escape without his noticing us. We did not bear in mind for a single instant a consideration which should, nevertheless, have seemed to us most important, namely that our enthusiasm for Elstir, on the sincerity of which we should not have allowed the least doubt to be cast, which we could indeed have supported with the evidence of our breathing arrested by expectancy, our desire to do no matter what that was difficult or heroic for the great man, was not, as we imagined it to be, admiration, since neither of us had ever seen anything that he had painted; our feeling might have as its object the hollow idea of a 'great artist,' but not a body of work which was unknown to us. It was, at the most, admiration in the abstract, the nervous envelope, the sentimental structure of an admiration without content, that is to say a thing as indissolubly attached to boyhood as are certain organs which have ceased to exist in the adult man; we were still boys. Elstir meanwhile was reaching the door when suddenly he turned and came towards us. I was transported by a delicious thrill of terror such as I could not have felt a few years later, because, while age diminishes our capacity, familiarity with the world has meanwhile destroyed in us any inclination to provoke such strange encounters, to feel that kind of emotion.

In the course of the few words that Elstir had come back to say to us, sitting down at our table, he never gave any answer on the several occasions on which I spoke to him of Swann. I began to think that he did not know him. He asked me, nevertheless, to come and see him at his Balbec studio, an invitation which he did not extend to Saint-Loup, and which I had earned (as I might not, perhaps, from Swann's recommendation, had Elstir been intimate with him, for the part played by disinterested motives is greater than we are inclined to think in people's lives) by a few words which made him think that I was devoted to the arts. He lavished on me a friendliness which was as far above that of Saint-Loup as that was above the affability of a mere tradesman. Compared with that of a great artist, the friendliness of a great gentleman, charming as it may be, has the effect of an actor's playing a part, of being feigned. Saint-Loup sought to please; Elstir loved to give, to give himself. Everything that he possessed, ideas, work, and the rest which he counted for far less, he would have given gladly to anyone who could understand him. But, failing society that was endurable, he lived in an isolation, with a savagery which fashionable people called pose and ill-breeding, public authorities a recalcitrant spirit, his neighbours madness, his family selfishness and pride.

And no doubt at first he had thought, even in his solitude, with enjoyment that, thanks to his work, he was addressing, in spite of distance, he was giving a loftier idea of himself, to those who had misunderstood or hurt him. Perhaps, in those days, he lived alone not from indifference but from love of his fellows, and, just as I had renounced Gilberte to appear to her again one day in more attractive colours, dedicated his work to certain people as a way of approaching them again, by which without actually seeing him they would be made to love him, admire him, talk about him; a renunciation is not always complete from the start, when we decide upon it in our original frame of mind and before it has reacted upon us, whether it be the renunciation of an invalid, a monk, an artist or a hero. But if he had wished to produce with certain people in his mind, in producing he had lived for himself, remote from the society to which he had become indifferent; the practice of solitude had given him a love for it, as happens with every big thing which we have begun by fearing, because we knew it to be incompatible with smaller things to which we clung, and of which it does not so much deprive us as it detaches us from them. Before we experience it, our whole preoccupation is to know to what extent we can reconcile it with certain pleasures which cease to be pleasures as soon as we have experienced it.

Elstir did not stay long talking to us. I made up my mind that I would go to his studio during the next few days, but on the following afternoon, when I had accompanied my grandmother right to the point at which the 'front' ended, near the cliffs of Canapville, on our way back, at the foot of one of the little streets which ran down at right angles to the beach, we came upon a girl who, with lowered head like an animal that is being driven reluctant to its stall, and carrying golf-clubs, was walking in front of a person in authority, in all probability her or her friends' 'Miss,' who suggested a portrait of Jeffreys by Hogarth, with a face as red as if her favourite beverage were gin rather than tea, on which a dried smear of tobacco at the corner of her mouth prolonged the curve of a moustache that was grizzled but abundant. The girl who preceded her was like that one of the little band who, beneath a black polo-cap, had shewn in an inexpressive chubby face a pair of laughing eyes. Now, the girl who was now passing me had also a black polo-cap, but she struck me as being even prettier than the other, the line of her nose was straighter, the curve of nostril at its base fuller and more fleshy. Besides, the other had seemed a proud, pale girl, this one a child well-disciplined and of rosy complexion. And yet, as she was pushing a bicycle just like the other's, and was wearing the same reindeer gloves, I concluded that the differences arose perhaps from the angle and circumstances in which I now saw her, for it was hardly likely that there could be at Balbec a second girl, with a face that, when all was said, was so similar and with the same details in her accoutrements. She cast a rapid glance in my direction; for the next few days, when I saw the little band again on the beach, and indeed long afterwards when I knew all the girls who composed it, I could never be absolutely certain that any of them—even she who among them all was most like her, the girl with the bicycle—was indeed the one that I had seen that evening at the end of the 'front,' where a street ran down to the beach, a girl who differed hardly at all, but was still just perceptibly different from her whom I had noticed in the procession.

From that moment, whereas for the last few days my mind had been occupied chiefly by the tall one, it was the one with the golf-clubs, presumed to be Mlle. Simonet, who began once more to absorb my attention. When walking with the others she would often stop, forcing her friends, who seemed greatly to respect her, to stop also. Thus it is, calling a halt, her eyes sparkling beneath her polo-cap, that I see her again to-day, outlined against the screen which the sea spreads out behind her, and separated from me by a transparent, azure space, the interval of time that has elapsed since then, a first impression, faint and fine in my memory, desired, pursued, then forgotten, then found again, of a face which I have many times since projected upon the cloud of the past to be able to say to myself, of a girl who was actually in my room: "It is she!"

But it was perhaps yet another, the one with geranium cheeks and green eyes, whom I should have liked most to know. And yet, whichever of them it might be, on any given day, that I preferred to see, the others, without her, were sufficient to excite my desire which, concentrated now chiefly on one, now on another, continued—as, on the first day, my confused vision—to combine and blend them, to make of them the little world apart, animated by a life in common, which for that matter they doubtless imagined themselves to form; and I should have penetrated, in becoming a friend of one of them—like a cultivated pagan or a meticulous Christian going among barbarians—into a rejuvenating society in which reigned health, unconsciousness of others, sensual pleasures, cruelty, unintellectuality and joy.

My grandmother, who had been told of my meeting with Elstir, and rejoiced at the thought of all the intellectual profit that I might derive from his friendship, considered it absurd and none too polite of me not to have gone yet to pay him a visit. But I could think only of the little band, and being uncertain of the hour at which the girls would be passing along the front, I dared not absent myself. My grandmother was astonished, too, at the smartness of my attire, for I had suddenly remembered suits which had been lying all this time at the bottom of my trunk. I put on a different one every day, and had even written to Paris ordering new hats and neckties.

It adds a great charm to life in a watering-place like Balbec if the face of a pretty girl, a vendor of shells, cakes or flowers, painted in vivid colours in our mind, is regularly, from early morning, the purpose of each of those leisured, luminous days which we spend upon the beach. They become then, and for that reason, albeit unoccupied by any business, as alert as working-days, pointed, magnetised, raised slightly to meet an approaching moment, that in which, while we purchase sand-cakes, roses, ammonites, we will delight in seeing upon a feminine face its colours displayed as purely as on a flower. But at least, with these little traffickers, first of all we can speak to them, which saves us from having to construct with our imagination their aspects other than those with which the mere visual perception of them furnishes us, and to recreate their life, magnifying its charm, as when we stand before a portrait; moreover, just because we speak to them, we can learn where and at what time it will be possible to see them again. Now I had none of these advantages with respect to the little band. Their habits were unknown to me; when on certain days I failed to catch a glimpse of them, not knowing the cause of their absence I sought to discover whether it was something fixed and regular, if they were to be seen only every other day, or in certain states of the weather, or if there were days on which no one ever saw them. I imagined myself already friends with them, and saying: "But you weren't there the other day?" "Weren't we? Oh, no, of course not; that was because it was a Saturday. On Saturdays we don't ever come, because . . ." If it were only as simple as that, to know that on black Saturday it was useless to torment oneself, that one might range the beach from end to end, sit down outside the pastry-cook's and pretend to be nibbling an *éclair*, poke into the curiosity shop, wait for bathing time, the concert, high tide, sunset, night, all without seeing the longed-for little band. But the fatal day did not, perhaps, come once a week. It did not, perhaps, of necessity fall on Saturdays. Perhaps certain atmospheric conditions influenced it or were entirely unconnected with it. How many observations, patient but not at all serene, must one accumulate of the movements, to all appearance irregular, of those unknown worlds before being able to be sure that one has not allowed oneself to be led astray by mere coincidence, that one's forecasts will not be proved wrong, before one elucidates the certain laws, acquired at the cost of so much painful experience, of that passionate astronomy. Remembering that I had not yet seen them on some particular day of the week, I assured myself that they would not be coming, that it was useless to wait any longer on the beach. And at that very moment I caught sight of them. And yet on another day which, so far as I could suppose that there were laws that guided the return of those constellations, must, I had calculated, prove an auspicious day, they did not come. But to this primary uncertainty whether I should see them or not that day, there was added another, more disquieting: whether I should ever set eyes on them again, for I had no reason, after all, to know that they were not about to sail for America, or to return to Paris. This was enough to make me begin to love them. One can feel an attraction towards a particular person. But to release that fount of sorrow, that sense of the irreparable, those agonies which prepare the way for love, there must be—and this is, perhaps, more than any person can be, the actual object which our passion seeks so anxiously to embrace—the risk of an impossibility. Thus there were acting upon me already those influences which recur in the course of our successive love-affairs, which can, for that matter, be provoked (but then rather in the life of cities) by the thought of little working girls whose half-holiday is we know not on what day, and whom we are afraid of having missed as they came out of the factory; or which at least have recurred in mine. Perhaps they are inseparable from love; perhaps everything that formed a distinctive feature of our first love attaches itself to those that come after, by recollection, suggestion, habit, and through the successive periods of our life gives to its different aspects a general character.

I seized every pretext for going down to the beach at the hours when I hoped to succeed in finding them there. Having caught sight of them once while we were at luncheon, I now invariably came in late for it, waiting interminably upon the 'front' for them to pass; devoting all the short time that I did spend in the dining-room to interrogating with my eyes its azure wall of glass; rising long before the dessert, so as not to miss them should they have gone out at a different hour, and chafing with irritation at my grandmother, when, with unwitting malevolence, she made me stay with her past the hour that seemed to me propitious. I tried to prolong the horizon by setting my chair aslant; if, by chance, I did catch sight of no matter which of the girls, since they all partook of the same special essence, it was as if I had seen projected before my face in a shifting, diabolical hallucination, a little of the unfriendly and yet passionately coveted dream which, but a moment ago, had existed only—where it lay stagnant for all time—in my brain.

I was in love with none of them, loving them all, and yet the possibility of meeting them was in my daily life the sole element of delight, alone made to burgeon in me those high hopes by which every obstacle is surmounted, hopes ending often in fury if I had not seen them. For the moment, these girls eclipsed my grandmother in my affection; the longest journey would at once have seemed attractive to me had it been to a place in which they might be found. It was to them that my thoughts comfortably clung when I supposed myself to be thinking of something else or of nothing. But when, even without knowing it, I thought of them, they, more unconsciously still, were for me the mountainous blue undulations of the sea, a troop seen passing in outline against the waves. Our most intensive love for a person is always the love, really, of something else as well.

Meanwhile my grandmother was shewing, because now I was keenly interested in golf and lawn-tennis and was letting slip an opportunity of seeing at work and hearing talk an artist whom she knew to be one of the greatest of his time, a disapproval which seemed to me to be based on somewhat narrow views. I had guessed long ago in the Champs-Elysées, and had since established to my own satisfaction, that when we are in love with a woman we simply project into her a state of our own soul, that the important thing is, therefore, not the worth of the woman but the depth of the state; and that the emotions which a young girl of no kind of distinction arouses in us can enable us to bring to the surface of our consciousness some of the most intimate parts of our being, more personal, more remote, more essential than would be reached by the pleasure that we derive from the conversation of a great man or even from the admiring contemplation of his work.

I was to end by complying with my grandmother's wishes, all the more reluctantly in that Elstir lived at some distance from the 'front' in one of the newest of Balbec's avenues. The heat of the day obliged me to take the tramway which passed along the Rue de la Plage, and I made an effort (so as still to believe that I was in the ancient realm of the Cimmerians, in the country it might be, of King Mark, or upon the site of the Forest of Broceliande) not to see the gimcrack splendour of the buildings that extended on either hand, among which Elstir's villa was perhaps the most sumptuously hideous, in spite of which he had taken it, because, of all that there were to be had at Balbec, it was the only one that provided him with a really big studio.

It was also with averted eyes that I crossed the garden, which had a lawn—in miniature, like any little suburban villa round Paris—a statuette of an amorous gardener, glass balls in which one saw one's distorted reflexion, beds of begonias and a little arbour, beneath which rocking chairs were drawn up round an iron table. But after all these preliminaries hall-marked with philistine ugliness, I took no notice of the chocolate mouldings on the plinths once I was in the studio; I felt perfectly happy, for, with the help of all the sketches and studies that surrounded me, I foresaw the possibility of raising myself to a poetical understanding, rich in delights, of many forms which I had not, hitherto, isolated from the general spectacle of reality. And Elstir's studio appeared to me as the laboratory of a sort of new creation of the world in which, from the chaos that is all the things we see, he had extracted, by painting them on various rectangles of canvas that were hung everywhere about the room, here a wave of the sea crushing angrily on the sand its lilac foam, there a young man in a suit of white linen, leaning upon the rail of a vessel. His jacket and the spattering wave had acquired fresh dignity from the fact that they continued to exist, even although they were deprived of those qualities in which they might be supposed to consist, the wave being no longer able to splash nor the jacket to clothe anyone.

At the moment at which I entered, the creator was just finishing, with the brush which he had in his hand, the form of the sun at its setting.

The shutters were closed almost everywhere round the studio, which was fairly cool and, except in one place where daylight laid against the wall its brilliant but fleeting decoration, dark; there was open only one little rectangular window embowered in honeysuckle, which, over a strip of garden, gave on an avenue; so that the atmosphere of the greater part of the studio was dusky, transparent and compact in the mass, but liquid and sparkling at the rifts where the golden clasp of sunlight banded it, like a lump of rock crystal of which one surface, already cut and polished, here and there, gleams like a mirror with iridescent rays. While Elstir, at my request, went on painting, I wandered about in the half-light, stopping to examine first one picture, then another.

Most of those that covered the walls were not what I should chiefly have liked to see of his work, paintings in what an English art journal which lay about on the reading-room table in the Grand Hotel called his first and second manners, the mythological manner and the manner in which he shewed signs of Japanese influence, both admirably exemplified, the article said, in the collection of Mme. de Guermantes. Naturally enough, what he had in his studio were almost all seascapes done here, at Balbec. But I was able to discern from these that the charm of each of them lay in a sort of metamorphosis of the things represented in it, analogous to what in poetry we call metaphor, and that, if God the Father had created things by naming them, it was by taking away their names or giving them other names that Elstir created them anew. The names which denote things correspond invariably to an intellectual notion, alien to our true impressions, and compelling us to eliminate from them everything that is not in keeping with itself.

Sometimes in my window in the hotel at Balbec, in the morning when Françoise undid the fastenings of the curtains that shut out the light, in the evening when I was waiting until it should be time to go out with Saint-Loup, I had been led by some effect of sunlight to mistake what was only a darker stretch of sea for a distant coastline, or to gaze at a belt of liquid azure without knowing whether it belonged to sea or sky. But presently my reason would re-establish between the elements that distinction which in my first impression I had overlooked. In the same way I used, in Paris, in my bedroom, to hear a dispute, almost a riot, in the street below, until I had referred back to its cause—a carriage for instance that was rattling towards me—this noise, from which I now eliminated the shrill and discordant vociferations which my ear had really heard but which my reason knew that wheels did not produce. But the rare moments in which we see nature as she is, with poetic vision, it was from those that Elstir's work was taken. One of his metaphors that occurred most commonly in the seascapes which he had round him was precisely that which, comparing land with sea, suppressed every line of demarcation between them. It was this comparison, tacitly and untiringly repeated on a single canvas, which gave it that multiform and powerful unity, the cause (not always clearly perceived by themselves) of the enthusiasm which Elstir's work aroused in certain collectors.

It was, for instance, for a metaphor of this sort—in a picture of the harbour of Carquethuit, a picture which he had finished a few days earlier and at which I now stood gazing my fill—that Elstir had prepared the mind of the spectator by employing, for the little town, only marine terms, and urban terms for the sea. Whether its houses concealed a part of the harbour, a dry dock, or perhaps the sea itself came cranking in among the land, as constantly happened on the Balbec coast, on the other side of the promontory on which the town was built the roofs were overtopped (as it had been by mill-chimneys or church-steeples) by masts which had the effect of making the vessels to which they belonged appear town-bred, built on land, an impression which was strengthened by the sight of other boats, moored along the jetty but in such serried ranks that you could see men talking across from one deck to another without being able to distinguish the dividing line, the chink of water between them, so that this fishing fleet seemed less to belong to the water than, for instance, the churches of Criquebec which, in the far distance, surrounded by water on every side because you saw them without seeing the town, in a powdery haze of sunlight and crumbling waves, seemed to be emerging from the waters, blown in alabaster or in sea-foam, and, enclosed in the band of a particoloured rainbow, to form an unreal, a mystical picture. On the beach in the foreground the painter had arranged that the eye should discover no fixed boundary, no absolute line of demarcation between earth and ocean. The men who were pushing down their boats into the sea were running as much through the waves as along the sand, which, being wet, reflected their hulls as if they were already in the water. The sea itself did not come up in an even line but followed the irregularities of the shore, which the perspective of the picture increased still further, so that a ship actually at sea, half-hidden by the projecting works of the arsenal, seemed to be sailing across the middle of the town; women who were gathering shrimps among the rocks had the appearance, because they were surrounded by water and because of the depression which, after the ringlike barrier of rocks, brought the beach (on the side nearest the land) down to sea-level, of being in a marine grotto overhung by ships and waves, open yet unharmed in the path of a miraculously averted tide. If the whole picture gave this impression of harbours in which the sea entered into the land, in which the land was already subaqueous and the population amphibian, the strength of the marine element was everywhere apparent; and round about the rocks, at the mouth of the harbour, where the sea was rough, you felt from the muscular efforts of the fishermen and the obliquity of the boats leaning over at an acute angle, compared with the calm erectness of the warehouse on the harbour, the church, the houses of the town to which some of the figures were returning while others were coming out to fish, that they were riding bareback on the water, as it might be a swift and fiery animal whose rearing, but for their skill, must have unseated them. A party of holiday makers were putting gaily out to sea in a boat that tossed like a jaunting-car on a rough road; their boatman, blithe but attentive, also, to what he was doing, trimmed the bellying sail, every one kept in his place, so that the weight should not be all on one side of the boat, which might capsize, and so they went racing over sunlit fields into shadowy places, dashing down into the troughs of waves. It was a fine morning in spite of the recent storm. Indeed, one could still feel the powerful activities that must first be neutralized in order to attain the easy balance of the boats that lay motionless, enjoying sunshine and breeze, in parts where the sea was so calm that its reflexions had almost more solidity and reality than the floating hulls, vaporised by an effect of the sunlight, parts which the perspective of the picture dovetailed in among others. Or rather you would not have called them other parts of the sea. For between those parts there was as much difference as there was between one of them and the church rising from the water, or the ships behind the town. Your reason then set to work and made a single element of what was here black beneath a gathering storm, a little farther all of one colour with the sky and as brightly burnished, and elsewhere so bleached by sunshine, haze and foam, so compact, so terrestrial, so circumscribed with houses that you thought of some white stone causeway or of a field of snow, up the surface of which it was quite frightening to see a ship go climbing high and dry, as a carriage climbs dripping from a ford, but which a moment later, when you saw on the raised and broken surface of the solid plain boats drunkenly heaving, you understood, identical in all these different aspects, to be still the sea.

Although we are justified in saying that there can be no progress, no discovery in art, but only in the sciences, and that the artist who begins afresh upon his own account an individual effort cannot be either helped or hindered by the efforts of all the others, we must nevertheless admit that, in so far as art brings into prominence certain laws, once an industry has taken those laws and vulgarised them, the art that was first in the field loses, in retrospect, a little of its originality. Since Elstir began to paint, we have grown familiar with what are called 'admirable' photographs of scenery and towns. If we press for a definition of what their admirers mean by the epithet, we shall find that it is generally applied to some unusual picture of a familiar object, a picture different from those that we are accustomed to see, unusual and yet true to nature, and for that reason doubly impressive to us because it startles us, makes us emerge from our habits and at the same time brings us back to ourselves by recalling to us an earlier impression. For instance, one of these 'magnificent' photographs

will illustrate a law of perspective, will shew us some cathedral which we
are accustomed to see in the middle of a town, taken instead from a selected
point of view from which it will appear to be thirty times the height of
the houses and to be thrusting a spur out from the bank of the river, from
which it is actually a long way off. Now the effort made by Elstir to reproduce things not as he knew them to be but according to the optical illusions
of which our first sight of them is composed, had led him exactly to this
point; he gave special emphasis to certain of these laws of perspective,
which were thus all the more striking, since his art had been their first in-
terpreter. A river, because of the windings of its course, a bay because of
the apparent contact of the cliffs on either side of it, would look as though
there had been hollowed out in the heart of the plain or of the mountains
a lake absolutely landlocked on every side. In a picture of a view from
Balbec painted upon a scorching day in summer an inlet of the sea appeared to be enclosed in walls of pink granite, not to be the sea, which
began farther out. The continuity of the ocean was suggested only by the
gulls which, wheeling over what, when one looked at the picture, seemed
to be solid rock, were as a matter of fact inhaling the moist vapour of the
shifting tide. Other laws were discernible in the same canvas, as, at the
foot of immense cliffs, the lilliputian grace of white sails on the blue mirror
on whose surface they looked like butterflies asleep, and certain contrasts
between the depth of the shadows and the pallidity of the light. This play
of light and shade, which also photography has rendered commonplace,
had interested Elstir so much that at one time he had painted what were
almost mirages, in which a castle crowned with a tower appeared as a perfect circle of castle prolonged by a tower at its summit, and at its foot by
an inverted tower, whether because the exceptional purity of the atmosphere on a fine day gave the shadow reflected in the water the hardness and
brightness of the stone, or because the morning mists rendered the stone
as vaporous as the shadow. And similarly, beyond the sea, behind a line
of woods, began another sea roseate with the light of the setting sun, which
was, in fact, the sky. The light, as it were precipitating new solids, thrust
back the hull of the boat on which it fell behind the other hull that was
still in shadow, and rearranged like the steps of a crystal staircase what
was materially a plane surface, but was broken up by the play of light and
shade upon the morning sea. A river running beneath the bridges of a town
was caught from a certain point of view so that it appeared entirely dis-
located, now broadened into a lake, now narrowed into a rivulet, broken
elsewhere by the interruption of a hill crowned with trees among which the
burgher would repair at evening to taste the refreshing breeze; and the
rhythm of this disintegrated town was assured only by the inflexible up-
rightness of the steeples which did not rise but rather, following the plumb
line of the pendulum marking its cadence as in a triumphal march, seemed
to hold in suspense beneath them all the confused mass of houses that
rose vaguely in the mist along the banks of the crushed, disjointed stream.
And (since Elstir's earliest work belonged to the time in which a painter
would make his landscape attractive by inserting a human figure), on the
cliff's edge or among the mountains, the road, that half human part of

nature, underwent, like river or ocean, the eclipses of perspective. And whether a sheer wall of mountain, or the mist blown from a torrent, or the sea prevented the eye from following the continuity of the path, visible to the traveller but not to us, the little human personage in old-fashioned attire seemed often to be stopped short on the edge of an abyss, the path which he had been following ending there, while, a thousand feet above him in those pine-forests, it was with a melting eye and comforted heart that we saw reappear the threadlike whiteness of its dusty surface, hospitable to the wayfaring foot, whereas from us the side of the mountain had hidden, where it turned to avoid waterfall or gully, the intervening bends.

The effort made by Elstir to strip himself, when face to face with reality, of every intellectual concept, was all the more admirable in that this man who, before sitting down to paint, made himself deliberately ignorant, forgot, in his honesty of purpose, everything that he knew, since what one knows ceases to exist by itself, had in reality an exceptionally cultivated mind. When I confessed to him the disappointment that I had felt upon seeing the porch at Balbec: "What!" he had exclaimed, "you were disappointed by the porch! Why, it's the finest illustrated Bible that the people have ever had. That Virgin, and all the bas-reliefs telling the story of her life, they are the most loving, the most inspired expression of that endless poem of adoration and praise in which the middle ages extolled the glory of the Madonna. If you only knew, side by side with the most scrupulous accuracy in rendering the sacred text, what exquisite ideas the old carver had, what profound thoughts, what delicious poetry!

"A wonderful idea, that great sheet in which the angels are carrying the body of the Virgin, too sacred for them to venture to touch it with their hands"; (I mentioned to him that this theme had been treated also at Saint-André-des-Champs; he had seen photographs of the porch there, and agreed, but pointed out that the bustling activity of those little peasant figures, all hurrying at once towards the Virgin, was not the same thing as the gravity of those two great angels, almost Italian, so springing, so gentle) "the angel who is carrying the Virgin's soul, to reunite it with her body; in the meeting of the Virgin with Elizabeth, Elizabeth's gesture when she touches the Virgin's Womb and marvels to feel that it is great with child; and the bandaged arm of the midwife who had refused, unless she touched, to believe the Immaculate Conception; and the linen cloth thrown by the Virgin to Saint Thomas to give him a proof of the Resurrection; that veil, too, which the Virgin tears from her own bosom to cover the nakedness of her Son, from Whose Side the Church receives in a chalice the Wine of the Sacrament, while, on His other side the Synagogue, whose kingdom is at an end, has its eyes bandaged, holds a half-broken sceptre and lets fall, with the crown that is slipping from its head, the tables of the old law; and the husband who, on the Day of Judgment, as he helps his young wife to rise from her grave, lays her hand against his own heart to reassure her, to prove to her that it is indeed beating, is that such a trumpery idea, do you think, so stale and commonplace? And the angel who is taking away the sun and the moon, henceforth useless, since it is written that the Light of the Cross shall be seven times brighter than the light of the firmament; and the one who is dipping his hand in the water of the Child's bath, to see whether it is warm enough; and the one emerging from the clouds to place the crown upon the Virgin's brow, and all the angels who are leaning from the vault of heaven, between the balusters of the New Jerusalem, and throwing up their arms with terror or joy at the sight of the torments of the wicked or the bliss of the elect! For it is all the circles of heaven, a whole gigantic poem full of theology and symbolism that you have before you there. It is fantastic, mad, divine, a thousand times better than anything you will see in Italy, where for that matter this very tympanum has been carefully copied by sculptors with far less genius. There never was a time when genius was universal; that is all nonsense; it would be going beyond the age of gold. The fellow who carved that front, you may make up your mind that he was every bit as great, that he had just as profound ideas as the men you admire most at the present day. I could shew you what I mean if we went there together. There are certain passages from the Office of the Assumption which have been rendered with a subtilty of expression that Redon himself has never equalled."

This vast celestial vision of which he spoke to me, this gigantic theological poem which, I understood, had been inscribed there in stone, yet when my eyes, big with desire, had opened to gaze upon the front of Balbec church, it was not these things that I had seen. I spoke to him of those great statues of saints, which, mounted on scaffolds, formed a sort of avenue on either side.

"It starts from the mists of antiquity to end in Jesus Christ," he explained. "You see on one side His ancestors after the spirit, on the other the Kings of Judah, His ancestors after the flesh. All the ages are there. And if you had looked more closely at what you took for scaffolds you would have been able to give names to the figures standing on them. At the feet of Moses you would have recognised the calf of gold, at Abraham's the ram and at Joseph's the demon counselling Potiphar's wife."

I told him also that I had gone there expecting to find an almost Persian building, and that this had doubtless been one of the chief factors in my disappointment. "Indeed, no," he assured me, "it is perfectly true. Some parts of it are quite oriental; one of the capitals reproduces so exactly a Persian subject that you cannot account for it by the persistence of Oriental traditions. The carver must have copied some casket brought from the East by explorers." And he did indeed shew me, later on, the photograph of a capital on which I saw dragons that were almost Chinese devouring one another, but at Balbec this little piece of carving had passed unnoticed by me in the general effect of the building which did not conform to the pattern traced in my mind by the words, 'an almost Persian church.'

The intellectual pleasures which I enjoyed in this studio did not in the least prevent me from feeling, although they enveloped us as it were in spite of ourselves, the warm polish, the sparkling gloom of the place itself and, through the little window framed in honeysuckle, in the avenue that was quite rustic, the resisting dryness of the sun-parched earth, screened only by the diaphanous gauze woven of distance and of a tree-cast shade.

Perhaps the unaccountable feeling of comfort which this summer day was giving me came like a tributary to swell the flood of joy that had surged in me at the sight of Elstir's *Carquethuit Harbour*.

I had supposed Elstir to be a modest man, but I realised my mistake on seeing his face cloud with melancholy when, in a little speech of thanks, I uttered the word 'fame.' Men who believe that their work will last—as was the case with Elstir—form the habit of placing that work in a period when they themselves will have crumbled into dust. And thus, by obliging them to reflect on their own extinction, the thought of fame saddens them because it is inseparable from the thought of death. I changed the conversation in the hope of driving away the cloud of ambitious melancholy with which unwittingly I had loaded Elstir's brow. "Some one advised me once," I began, thinking of the conversation we had had with Legrandin at Combray, as to which I was glad of an opportunity of learning Elstir's views, "not to visit Brittany, because it would not be wholesome for a mind with a natural tendency to dream." "Not at all;" he replied. "When the mind has a tendency to dream, it is a mistake to keep dreams away from it, to ration its dreams. So long as you distract your mind from its dreams, it will not know them for what they are; you will always be being taken in by the appearance of things, because you will not have grasped their true nature. If a little dreaming is dangerous, the cure for it is not to dream less but to dream more, to dream all the time. One must have a thorough understanding of one's dreams if one is not to be troubled by them; there is a way of separating one's dreams from one's life which so often produces good results that I ask myself whether one ought not, at all costs, to try it, simply as a preventive, just as certain surgeons make out that we ought, to avoid the risk of appendicitis later on, to have all our appendices taken out when we are children."

Elstir and I had meanwhile been walking about the studio, and had reached the window that looked across the garden on to a narrow avenue, a side-street that was almost a country lane. We had gone there to breathe the cooler air of the late afternoon. I supposed myself to be nowhere near the girls of the little band, and it was only by sacrificing for once the hope of seeing them that I had yielded to my grandmother's prayers and had gone to see Elstir. For where the thing is to be found that we are seeking we never know, and often we steadily, for a long time, avoid the place to which, for quite different reasons, everyone has been asking us to go. But we never suspect that we shall there see the very person of whom we are thinking. I looked out vaguely over the country road which, outside the studio, passed quite close to it but did not belong to Elstir. Suddenly there appeared on it, coming along it at a rapid pace, the young bicyclist of the little band, with, over her dark hair, her polo-cap pulled down towards her plump cheeks, her eyes merry and almost importunate; and on that auspicious path, miraculously filled with promise of delights, I saw her beneath the trees throw to Elstir the smiling greeting of a friend, a rainbow that bridged the gulf for me between our terraqueous world and regions which I had hitherto regarded as inaccessible. She even came up to give her hand to the painter, though without stopping, and I could see that she had a tiny beauty spot on her chin. "Do you know that girl, sir?" I asked Elstir, realising that he could if he chose make me known to her, could invite us both to the house. And this peaceful studio with its rural horizon was at once filled with a surfeit of delight such as a child might feel in a house where he was already happily playing when he learned that, in addition, out of that bounteousness which enables lovely things and noble hosts to increase their gifts beyond all measure, there was being prepared for him a sumptuous repast. Elstir told me that she was called Albertine Simonet, and gave me the names also of her friends, whom I described to him with sufficient accuracy for him to identify them almost without hesitation. I had, with regard to their social position, made a mistake, but not the mistake that I usually made at Balbec. I was always ready to take for princes the sons of shopkeepers when they appeared on horseback. This time I had placed in an interloping class the daughters of a set of respectable people, extremely rich, belonging to the world of industry and business. It was the class which, on first thoughts, interested me least, since it held for me neither the mystery of the lower orders nor that of a society such as the Guermantes frequented. And no doubt if an inherent quality, a rank which they could never forfeit, had not been conferred on them, in my dazzled eyes, by the glaring vacuity of the seaside life all round them, I should perhaps not have succeeded in resisting and overcoming the idea that they were the daughters of prosperous merchants. I could not help marvelling to see how the French middle class was a wonderful studio full of sculpture of the noblest and most varied kind. What unimagined types, what richness of invention in the character of their faces, what firmness, what freshness, what simplicity in their features. The shrewd old money-changers from whose loins these Dianas and these nymphs had sprung seemed to me to have been the greatest of statuaries. Before I had time to register the social metamorphosis of these girls—so are these discoveries of a mistake, these modifications of the notion one has of a person instantaneous as a chemical combination—there was already installed behind their faces, so street-arab in type that I had taken them for the mistresses of racing bicyclists, of boxing champions, the idea that they might easily be connected with the family of some lawyer or other whom we knew. I was barely conscious of what was meant by Albertine Simonet; she had certainly no conception of what she was one day to mean to me. Even the name, Simonet, which I had already heard spoken on the beach, if I had been asked to write it down I should have spelt with a double 'n,' never dreaming of the importance which this family attached to there being but one in their name. In proportion as we descend the social scale our snobbishness fastens on to mere nothings which are perhaps no more null than the distinctions observed by the aristocracy, but, being more obscure, more peculiar to the individual, take us more by surprise. Possibly there had been Simonnets who had done badly in business, or something worse still even. The fact remains that the Simonets never failed, it appeared, to be annoyed if anyone doubled their 'n.' They wore the air of being the only Simonets in the world with one 'n' instead of two, and were as proud of it, perhaps, as the Montmorency family were of being the premier barons of

France. I asked Elstir whether these girls lived at Balbec; yes, he told me, some of them at any rate. The villa in which one of them lived was at that very spot, right at the end of the beach, where the cliffs of Canapville began. As this girl was a great friend of Albertine Simonet, this was another reason for me to believe that it was indeed the latter whom I had met that day when I was with my grandmother. There were of course so many of those little streets running down to the beach, and all at the same angle, that I could not have pointed out exactly which of them it had been. One would like always to remember a thing accurately, but at the time one's vision was clouded. And yet that Albertine and the girl whom I had seen going to her friend's house were one and the same person was a practical certainty. In spite of which, whereas the countless images that have since been furnished me by the dark young golfer, however different they may have been from one another, have overlaid one another (because I now know that they all belong to her), and if I retrace the thread of my memories I can, under cover of that identity, and as though along a tunnelled passage, pass through all those images in turn without losing my consciousness of the same person behind them all, if, on the other hand, I wish to revert to the girl whom I passed that day when I was with my grandmother, I must escape first into freer air. I am convinced that it is Albertine whom I find there, the same girl as her who would often stop dead among her moving comrades, in her walk along the foreground of the sea; but all those more recent images remain separate from that earlier one because I am unable to confer on her retrospectively an identity which she had not for me at the moment in which she caught my eye; whatever assurance I may derive from the law of probabilities, that girl with plump cheeks who stared at me so boldly from the angle of the little street and the beach, and by whom I believe that I might have been loved, I have never, in the strict sense of the words, seen again.

My hesitation between the different girls of the little band, all of whom retained something of the collective charm which had at first disturbed me, combined with the reasons already given to allow me later on, even at the time of my greater—my second—passion for Albertine, a sort of intermittent and very brief liberty to abstain from loving her. From having strayed among all her friends before it finally concentrated itself on her, my love kept, now and then, between itself and the image of Albertine a certain 'play' of light and shade which enabled it, like a badly fitted lamp, to flit over the surface of each of the others before settling its focus upon her; the connexion between the pain which I felt in my heart and the memory of Albertine did not seem to me necessary; I might perhaps have managed to co-ordinate it with the image of another person. Which enabled me, in a momentary flash, to banish reality altogether, not only external reality, as in my love for Gilberte (which I had recognised to be an internal state in which I drew from myself alone the particular quality, the special character of the person whom I loved, everything that rendered her indispensable to my happiness), but even the other reality, internal and purely subjective.

"Not a day passes but one or the other of them comes by here, and looks

in for a minute or two," Elstir told me, plunging me in despair when I
thought that if I had gone to see him at once, when my grandmother had
begged me to do so, I should, in all probability, long since have made Albertine's acquaintance.

She had passed on; from the studio she was no longer in sight. I supposed that she had gone to join her friends on the 'front.' Could I have
appeared there suddenly with Elstir, I should have got to know them all.
I thought of endless pretexts for inducing him to take a turn with me on
the beach. I had no longer the same peace of mind as before the apparition
of the girl in the frame of the little window; so charming until then in its
fringe of honeysuckle, and now so drearily empty. Elstir caused me a joy
that was tormenting also when he said that he would go a little way with
me, but that he must first finish the piece of work on which he was engaged.
It was a flower study but not one of any of the flowers, portraits of which
I would rather have commissioned him to paint than the portrait of a
person, so that I might learn from the revelation of his genius what I had
so often sought in vain from the flowers themselves—hawthorn white and
pink, cornflowers, apple-blossom. Elstir as he worked talked botany to me,
but I scarcely listened; he was no longer sufficient in himself, he was now
only the necessary intermediary between these girls and me; the distinction
which, only a few moments ago, his talent had still given him in my eyes
was now worthless save in so far as it might confer a little on me also in
the eyes of the little band to whom I should be presented by him.

I paced up and down the room, impatient for him to finish what he
was doing; I picked up and examined various sketches, any number of
which were stacked against the walls. In this way I happened to bring to
light a water-colour which evidently belonged to a much earlier period in
Elstir's life, and gave me that particular kind of enchantment which is
diffused by works of art not only deliciously executed but representing a
subject so singular and so seductive that it is to it that we attribute a great
deal of their charm, as if the charm were something that the painter had
merely to uncover, to observe, realised already in a material form by
nature, and to reproduce in art. That such objects can exist, beautiful quite
apart from the painter's interpretation of them, satisfies a sort of innate
materialism in us, against which our reason contends and acts as a coun-
terpoise to the abstractions of aesthetics. It was—this water-colour—the
portrait of a young woman, by no means beautiful but of a curious type,
in a close-fitting mob-cap not unlike a 'billy-cock' hat, trimmed with a
ribbon of cherry-coloured silk; in one of her mittened hands was a lighted
cigarette, while the other held, level with her knee, a sort of broad-brimmed
garden hat, nothing more than a fire screen of plaited straw to keep off
the sun. On a table by her side, a tall vase filled with pink carnations. Often
(and it was the case here) the singularity of such works is due principally
to their having been executed in special conditions for which we do not
at first sight make proper allowance, if, for instance, the strange attire of
a feminine model is her costume for a masked ball, or conversely the scarlet
cloak which an elderly man looks as though he had put on to humour some
whim in the painter is his gown as a professor or alderman or his cardinal's

cassock. The ambiguous character of the person whose portrait now confronted me arose, without my understanding it, from the fact that she
was a young actress of an earlier generation half dressed for a part. But
the cap or hat, beneath which the hair stuck out but was cut short, the
velvet coat opening without lapels over a white shirt-front, made me hesitate as to the period of the clothes and the sex of the model, so that I did
not know what it was exactly that I was holding before my eyes, unless
simply the brightest coloured of these scraps of painting. And the pleasure
which it afforded me was disturbed only by the fear that Elstir, by delay-
ing further, would make me miss the girls, for the sun was now declining
and hung low in the little window. Nothing in this water-colour was merely
stated there as a fact and painted because of its utility to the composition,
the costume because the young woman must be wearing something, the
vase to hold the flowers. The glass of the vase, cherished for its own sake,
seemed to be holding the water in which the stems of the carnations were
dipped in something as limpid, almost as liquid as itself; the woman's
dress encompassed her in a manner that had an independent, a brotherly
charm, and, if the works of man can compete in charm with the wonders
of nature, as delicate, as pleasing to the touch of the eye, as freshly painted
as the fur of a cat, the petals of a flower, the feathers of a dove. The whiteness of the shirt-front, fine as driven rain, with its gay pleats gathered
into little bells like lilies of the valley, was starred with bright gleams of
light from the room, as sharply edged and as finely shaded as though they
had been posies of flowers stitched on the woven lawn. And the velvet of
the coat, brilliant with a milky sheen, had here and there a roughness, a
scoring, a shagginess on its surface which made one think of the crumpled
brightness of the carnations in the vase. But above all one felt that Elstir,
sublimely indifferent to whatever immoral suggestion there might be in
this disguise of a young actress for whom the talent with which she would
play her part on the stage was doubtless of less importance than the irri-
tant attraction which she would offer to the jaded or depraved senses of
some of her audience, had on the contrary fastened upon those ambiguous
points as on an aesthetic element which deserved to be brought into prominence, and which he had done everything in his power to emphasise. Along
the lines of the face, the latent sex seemed to be on the point of confessing
itself to be that of a somewhat boyish girl, then vanished and farther on
reappeared with a suggestion rather of an effeminate youth, vicious and
pensive, then fled once more to remain uncapturable. The dreamy sadness
in the expression of her eyes, by the mere fact of its contrast with the
accessories belonging to the world of love-making and play-acting, was
not the least disturbing element in the picture. One imagined moreover
that it must be feigned, and that the young person who seemed ready to
submit to caresses in this provoking costume had probably thought it
effective to enhance the provocation with this romantic expression of a
secret longing, an unspoken grief. At the foot of the picture was inscribed
"Miss Sacripant: October, 1872." I could not contain my admiration. "Oh,
it's nothing, only a rough sketch I did when I was young; it was a costume
for a variety show. It's all ages ago now." "And what has become of the

model?" A bewilderment provoked by my words preceded on Elstir's face the indifferent, absent-minded air which, a moment later, he displayed there. "Quick, give it to me!" he cried, "I hear Madame Elstir coming, and, though, I assure you, the young person in the billy-cock hat never played any part in my life, still there's no point in my wife's coming in and finding it staring her in the face. I have kept it only as an amusing sidelight on the theatre of those days." And, before putting it away behind the pile, Elstir, who perhaps had not set eyes on the sketch for years, gave it his careful scrutiny. "I must keep just the head," he murmured, "the lower part is really too shockingly bad, the hands are a beginner's work." I was miserable at the arrival of Mme. Elstir, who could only delay us still further. The window sill was already aglow. Our excursion would be a pure waste of time. There was no longer the slightest chance of our seeing the girls, consequently it mattered now not at all how soon Mme. Elstir left us or how long she stayed. Not that she did stay for any length of time. I found her most tedious; she might have been beautiful, once, at twenty, driving an ox in the Roman Campagna, but her dark hair was streaked with grey and she was common without being simple, because she believed that a pompous manner and majestic attitudes were required by her statuesque beauty, which, however, advancing age had robbed of all its charm. She was dressed with the utmost simplicity. And it was touching, but at the same time surprising to hear Elstir, whenever he opened his mouth, and with a respectful gentleness, as if merely uttering the words moved him to tenderness and veneration, repeat: "My beautiful Gabrielle!" Later on, when I had become familiar with Elstir's mythological paintings, Mme. Elstir acquired beauty in my eyes also. I understood then that to a certain ideal type illustrated by certain lines, certain arabesques which reappeared incessantly throughout his work, to a certain canon of art he had attributed a character that was almost divine, since the whole of his time, all the mental effort of which he was capable, in a word his whole life he had consecrated to the task of distinguishing those lines as clearly and of reproducing them as faithfully as possible. What such an ideal inspired in Elstir was indeed a cult so solemn, so exacting that it never allowed him to be satisfied with what he had achieved; was the most intimate part of himself, and so he had never been able to look at it from a detached standpoint, to extract emotion from it, until the day on which he encountered it realised outside, apart from himself, in the body of a woman, the body of her who in due course became Mme. Elstir and in whom he had been able (as one is able only with something that is not oneself) to find it meritorious, moving, god-like. How comforting, moreover, to let his lips rest upon that Beauty which hitherto he had been obliged with so great labour to extract from within himself, whereas now, mysteriously incarnate, it offered itself to him in a series of communions, filled with saving grace. Elstir at this period was no longer in that early youth in which we look only to the power of our own mind for the realisation of our ideal. He was nearing the age at which we count on bodily satisfactions to stimulate the forces of the brain, at which the exhaustion of the brain inclining us to materialism and the diminution of our activity to the possibility of influences passively received, begin to make us admit that there may indeed be certain bodies, certain callings, certain rhythms that are privileged, realising so naturally our ideal that even without genius, merely by copying the movement of a shoulder, the tension of a throat, we can achieve a masterpiece, it is the age at which we like to caress Beauty with our eyes objectively, outside ourselves, to have it near us, in a tapestry, in a lovely sketch by Titian picked up in a second-hand shop, in a mistress as lovely as Titian's sketch. When I understood this I could no longer look without pleasure at Mme. Elstir, and her body began to lose its heaviness, for I filled it with an idea, the idea that she was an immaterial creature, a portrait by Elstir. She was one for me, and for him also I dare say. The facts of life have no meaning for the artist, they are to him merely an opportunity for exposing the naked blaze of his genius. One feels unmistakably, when one sees side by side ten portraits of different people painted by Elstir, that they are all, first and foremost, Elstirs. Only, after this rising tide of genius, which sweeps over and submerges a man's life, when the brain begins to tire, gradually the balance is upset and, like a river that resumes its course after the counter-flow of a spring tide, it is life that once more takes the upper hand. While the first period lasted, the artist has gradually evolved the law, the formula of his unconscious gift. He knows what situations, should he be a novelist— if a painter, what scenes—furnish him with the subject matter, which may be anything in the world but, whatever it is, is essential to his researches as a laboratory might be of a workshop. He knows that he has created his masterpieces out of effects of attenuated light, the action of remorse upon consciousness of guilt, out of women posed beneath trees or half-immersed in water, like statues. A day will come when, owing to the exhaustion of his brain, he will no longer have the strength, when provided with those materials which his genius was wont to use, to make the intellectual effort which alone can produce his work, and will yet continue to seek them out, happy when he finds himself in their presence, because of the spiritual pleasure, the allurement to work that they arouse in him; and, surrounding them besides with a kind of hedge of superstition as if they were superior to all things else, as if in them already dwelt a great part of the work of art which they might be said to carry within them ready made, he will confine himself to the company, to the adoration of his models. He will hold endless conversations with the repentant criminals whose remorse, whose regeneration formed, when he still wrote, the subject of his novels; he will buy a country house in a district where mists attenuate the light, he will spend long hours gazing at the limbs of bathing women; will collect sumptu-ous stuffs. And thus the beauty of life, a phase that has to some extent lost its meaning, a stage beyond the boundaries of art at which I had already seen Swann come to rest, was that also which, by a slackening of the creative ardour, idolatry of the forms which had inspired it, desire to avoid effort, must ultimately arrest an Elstir's progress.

At last he had applied the final brush-stroke to his flowers; I sacrificed a minute to look at them; I acquired no merit by the act, for I knew that there was no chance now of our finding the girls on the beach; and yet, had I believed them to be still there, and that these wasted moments would make me miss them, I should have stopped to look none the less, for I should have told myself that Elstir was more interested in his flowers than in my meeting with the girls. My grandmother's nature, a nature that was the exact counterpart of my complete egoism, was nevertheless reflected in certain aspects of my own. In circumstances in which someone to whom I was indifferent, for whom I had always made a show of affection or respect, ran the risk merely of some unpleasantness whereas I was in real danger, I could not have done otherwise than commiserate with him on his annoyance as though it had been something important, and treat my own danger as nothing, because I would feel that these were the proportions in which he must see things. To be quite accurate, I would go even further, and not only not complain of the danger in which I myself stood but go half-way to meet it, and with that which involved other people try, on the contrary, were I to increase the risk of my being caught myself, to avert it from them. The reasons for this are several, none of which does me the slightest credit. One is that if, while only my reason was employed, I have always believed in self-preservation, whenever in the course of my existence I have found myself obsessed by moral anxieties, or merely by nervous scruples, so puerile often that I dare not enumerate them here, if an unforeseen circumstance then arose, involving for me the risk of being killed, this new preoccupation was so trivial in comparison with the others that I welcomed it with a sense of relief, almost of hilarity. Thus I find myself, albeit the least courageous of men, to have known that feeling which has always seemed to me, in my reasoning moods, so foreign to my nature, so inconceivable, the intoxication of danger. But even although I were, when any, even a deadly peril threatened me, passing through an entirely calm and happy phase, I could not, were I with another person, refrain from sheltering him behind me and choosing for myself the post of danger. When a sufficient store of experience had taught me that I invariably acted, and enjoyed acting, thus, I discovered—and was deeply ashamed by the discovery—that it was because, in contradiction of what I had always believed and asserted, I was extremely sensitive to the opinions of others. Not that this kind of unconfessed self-esteem is in any sense vanity or conceit. For what might satisfy one or other of those failings would give me no pleasure, and I have always refrained from indulging them. But with the people in whose company I have succeeded in concealing most effectively the slight advantages a knowledge of which might have given them a less derogatory idea of myself, I have never been able to deny myself the pleasure of shewing them that I take more trouble to avert the risk of death from their path than from my own. As my motive is then self-esteem and not valour, I find it quite natural that in any crisis they should act differently. I am far from blaming them for it, as I should perhaps if I had been moved by a sense of duty, a duty which would seem to me, in that case, to be as incumbent upon them as upon myself. On the contrary, I feel that it is eminently sensible of them to safeguard their lives, though at the same time I cannot prevent my own safety from receding into the background, which is particularly silly and culpable of me since I have come to realise that the lives of many of the people in front of whom I plant myself when

a bomb bursts are more valueless even than my own. However, on the day
of this first visit to Elstir, the time was still distant at which I was to become conscious of this difference in value, and there was no question of
danger, but simply—a harbinger this of that pernicious self-esteem—the
question of my not appearing to attach to the pleasure which I so ardently
desired more importance than to the work which the painter had still to
finish. It was finished at last. And, once we were out of doors, I discovered
that—so long were the days still at this season—it was not so late as I
had supposed; we strolled down to the 'front.' What stratagems I employed
to keep Elstir standing at the spot where I thought that the girls might
still come past. Pointing to the cliffs that towered beside us, I kept on
asking him to tell me about them, so as to make him forget the time and
stay there a little longer. I felt that we had a better chance of waylaying
the little band if we moved towards the end of the beach. "I should like
to look at those cliffs with you from a little nearer," I said to him, having
noticed that one of the girls was in the habit of going in that direction.
"And as we go, do tell me about Carquethuit. I should so like to see Carquethuit," I went on, without thinking that the so novel character which
manifested itself with such force in Elstir's *Carquethuit Harbour,* might
belong perhaps rather to the painter's vision than to any special quality
in the place itself. "Since I've seen your picture, I think that is where I
should most like to go, there and to the Pointe du Raz, but of course that
would be quite a journey from here." "Yes, and besides, even if it weren't
nearer, I should advise you perhaps all the same to visit Carquethuit,"
he replied. "The Pointe du Raz is magnificent, but after all it is simply the
high cliff of Normandy or Brittany which you know already. Carquethuit
is quite different, with those rocks bursting from a level shore. I know
nothing in France like it, it reminds me rather of what one sees in some
parts of Florida. It is most interesting, and for that matter extremely wild
too. It is between Clitourps and Nehomme; you know how desolate those
parts are; the sweep of the coast-line is delicious. Here, the coast-line is
like anywhere else; but along there I can't tell you what charm it has, what
softness."

Night was falling; it was time to be turning homewards; I was escorting
Elstir in the direction of his villa when suddenly, as it were Mephistopheles
springing up before Faust, there appeared at the end of the avenue—like
simply an objectification, unreal, diabolical, of the temperament diametrically opposed to my own, of the semi-barbarous and cruel vitality of which
I, in my weakness, my excess of tortured sensibility and intellectuality was
so destitute—a few spots of the essence impossible to mistake for anything
else in the world, a few spores of the zoophytic band of girls, who wore an
air of not having seen me but were unquestionably, for all that, proceeding
as they advanced to pass judgment on me in their ironic vein. Feeling
that a collision between them and us was now inevitable, and that Elstir
would be certain to call me, I turned my back, like a bather preparing to
meet the shock of a wave; I stopped dead and, leaving my eminent companion to pursue his way, remained where I was, stooping, as if I had
suddenly become engrossed in it, towards the window of the curiosity

shop which we happened to be passing at the moment. I was not sorry to
give the appearance of being able to think of something other than these
girls, and I was already dimly aware that when Elstir did call me up to
introduce me to them I should wear that sort of challenging expression
which betokens not surprise but the wish to appear as though one were
surprised—so far is every one of us a bad actor, or everyone else a good
thought-reader;—that I should even go so far as to point a finger to my
breast, as who should ask "It is me, really, that you want?" and then run
to join him, my head lowered in compliance and docility and my face coldly
masking my annoyance at being torn from the study of old pottery in order
to be introduced to people whom I had no wish to know. Meanwhile I
explored the window and waited for the moment in which my name, shouted
by Elstir, would come to strike me like an expected and innocuous bullet.
The certainty of being introduced to these girls had had the result of making me not only feign complete indifference to them, but actually to feel
it. Inevitable from this point, the pleasure of knowing them began at once
to shrink, became less to me than the pleasure of talking to Saint-Loup,
of dining with my grandmother, of making, in the neighbourhood of Balbec,
excursions which I would regret the probability, in consequence of my
having to associate with people who could scarcely be much interested
in old buildings, of my being forced to abandon. Moreover, what diminished the pleasure which I was about to feel was not merely the imminence
but the incoherence of its realisation. Laws as precise as those of hydro-
statics maintain the relative position of the images which we form in a
fixed order, which the coming event at once upsets. Elstir was just about
to call me. This was not at all the fashion in which I had so often, on the
beach, in my bedroom, imagined myself making these girls' acquaintance.
What was about to happen was a different event, for which I was not prepared. I recognised neither my desire nor its object; I regretted almost
that I had come out with Elstir. But, above all, the shrinking of the pleasure that I expected to feel was due to the certainty that nothing, now,
could take that pleasure from me. And it resumed, as though by some
latent elasticity in itself, its whole extent when it ceased to be subjected
to the pressure of that certainty, at the moment when, having decided to
turn my head, I saw Elstir, standing where he had stopped a few feet
away with the girls, bidding them good-bye. The face of the girl who stood
nearest to him, round and plump and glittering with the light in her eyes,
reminded me of a cake on the top of which a place has been kept for a
morsel of blue sky. Her eyes, even when fixed on an object, gave one the
impression of motion, just as on days of high wind the air, although invisible, lets us perceive the speed with which it courses between us and the
unchanging azure. For a moment her gaze intersected mine, like those
travelling skies on stormy days which hurry after a rain-cloud that moves
less rapidly than they, overtake, touch, cover, pass it and are gone; but
they do not know one another, and are soon driven far apart. So our eyes
were for a moment confronted, neither pair knowing what the celestial
continent that lay before their gaze held of future blessing or disaster.
Only at the moment when her gaze was directly coincident with mine,

without slackening its movement it grew perceptibly duller. So on a starry night the wind-swept moon passes behind a cloud and veils her brightness for a moment, but soon will shine again. But Elstir had already said good-bye to the girls, and had never summoned me. They disappeared down a cross street; he came towards me. My whole plan was spoiled.

I have said that Albertine had not seemed to me that day to be the same as on previous days and that afterwards, each time I saw her, she was to appear different. But I felt at that moment that certain modifications in the appearance, the importance, the stature of a person may also be due to the variability of certain states of consciousness interposed between that person and us. One of those that play an important part in such trans-formations is belief; that evening my belief, then the vanishing of my belief, that I was about to know Albertine had, with a few seconds' interval only, rendered her almost insignificant, then infinitely precious in my sight; some years later, the belief, then the disappearance of the belief, that Albertine was faithful to me brought about similar changes.

Of course, long ago, at Combray, I had seen shrink or stretch, according to the time of day, according as I was entering one or the other of the two dominant moods that governed my sensibility in turn, my grief at not having my mother with me, as imperceptible all afternoon as is the moon's light when the sun is shining, and then, when night had come, reigning alone in my anxious heart in the place of recent memories now obliterated. But on that day at Balbec, when I saw that Elstir was leaving the girls and had not called me, I learned for the first time that the variations in the importance which a pleasure or a pain has in our eyes may depend not merely on this alternation of two moods, but on the displacement of in-visible beliefs, such, for example, as make death seem to us of no account because they bathe it in a glow of unreality, and thus enable us to attach importance to our attending an evening party, which would lose much of its charm for if, on the announcement that we were sentenced to die by the guillotine, the belief that had bathed the party in its warm glow was instantly shattered; and this part that belief plays, it is true that some-thing in me was aware of it; this was my will; but its knowledge is vain if the mind, the heart continue in ignorance; these last act in good faith when they believe that we are anxious to forsake a mistress to whom our will alone knows that we are still attached. This is because they are clouded by the belief that we shall see her again at any moment. But let this belief be shattered, let them suddenly become aware that this mistress is gone from us for ever, then the mind and heart, having lost their focus, are driven like mad things, the meanest pleasure becomes infinitely great.

Variance of a belief, annulment also of love, which, pre-existent and mobile, comes to rest at the image of any one woman simply because that woman will be almost impossible of attainment. Thenceforward we think not so much of the woman of whom we find difficult in forming an exact picture, as of the means of getting to know her. A whole series of agonies develops and is sufficient to fix our love definitely upon her who is its al-most unknown object. Our love becomes immense; we never dream how small a place in it the real woman occupies. And if suddenly, as at the moment when I had seen Elstir stop to talk to the girls, we cease to be uneasy, to suffer pain, since it is this pain that is the whole of our love, it seems to us as though love had abruptly vanished at the moment when at length we grasp the prey to whose value we had not given enough thought before. What did I know of Albertine? One or two glimpses of a profile against the sea, less beautiful, assuredly, than those of Veronese's women whom I ought, had I been guided by purely aesthetic reasons, to have preferred to her. By what other reasons could I be guided, since, my anxiety having subsided, I could recapture only those mute profiles; I possessed nothing of her besides. Since my first sight of Albertine I had meditated upon her daily, a thousandfold, I had carried on with what I called by her name an interminable unspoken dialogue in which I made her question me, answer me, think and act, and in the infinite series of imaginary Albertines who followed one after the other in my fancy, hour after hour, the real Albertine, a glimpse caught on the beach, figured only at the head, just as the actress who creates a part, the star, appears, out of a long series of performances, in the few first alone. That Albertine was scarcely more than a silhouette, all that was superimposed being of my own growth, so far when we are in love does the contribution that we ourself make outweigh—even if we consider quantity only—those that come to us from the beloved object. And the same is true of love that is given its full effect. There are loves that manage not only to be formed but to subsist around a very little core—even among those whose prayer has been answered after the flesh. An old drawing-master who had taught my grandmother had been presented by some obscure mistress with a daughter. The mother died shortly after the birth of her child, and the drawing-master was so broken-hearted that he did not long survive her. In the last months of his life my grandmother and some of the Combray ladies, who had never liked to make any allusion in the drawing-master's presence to the woman, with whom, for that matter, he had not officially 'lived' and had had comparatively slight relations, took it into their heads to ensure the little girl's future by combining to purchase an annuity for her. It was my grandmother who suggested this; several of her friends made difficulties; after all was the child really such a very interesting case, was she even the child of her reputed father; with women like that, it was never safe to say. Finally, everything was settled. The child came to thank the ladies. She was plain, and so absurdly like the old drawing-master as to remove every shadow of doubt; her hair being the only nice thing about her, one of the ladies said to her father, who had come with her: "What pretty hair she has." And thinking that now, the woman who had sinned being dead and the old man only half alive, a discreet allusion to that past of which they had always pretended to know nothing could do no harm, my grandmother added: "It runs in families. Did her mother have pretty hair like that?" "I don't know," was the old man's quaint answer. "I never saw her except with a hat on."

But I must not keep Elstir waiting. I caught sight of myself in a glass. To add to the disaster of my not having been introduced to the girls, I noticed that my necktie was all crooked, my hat left long wisps of hair shewing, which did not become me; but it was a piece of luck, all the same, that they should have seen me, even thus attired, in Elstir's company and so could not forget me; also that I should have put on, that morning, at my grandmother's suggestion, my smart waistcoat, when I might so easily have been wearing one that was simply hideous, and be carrying my best stick. For while an event for which we are longing never happens quite in the way we have been expecting, failing the advantages on which we supposed that we might count, others present themselves for which we never hoped, and make up for our disappointment; and we have been so dreading the worst that in the end we are inclined to feel that, taking one thing with another, chance has, on the whole, been rather kind to us.

"I did so much want to know them," I said as I reached Elstir. "Then why did you stand a mile away?" These were his actual words, not that they expressed what was in his mind, since, if his desire had been to grant mine, to call me up to him would have been quite easy, but perhaps because he had heard phrases of this sort, in familiar use among common people when they are in the wrong, and because even great men are in certain respects much the same as common people, take their everyday excuses from the same common stock just as they get their daily bread from the same baker; or it may be that such expressions (which ought, one might almost say, to be read 'backwards,' since their literal interpretation is the opposite of the truth) are the instantaneous effect, the negative exposure of a reflex action. "They were in a hurry." It struck me that of course they must have stopped him from summoning a person who did not greatly attract them; otherwise he would not have failed, after all the questions that I had put to him about them, and the interest which he must have seen that I took in them, to call me. "We were speaking just now of Carquethuit," he began, as we walked towards his villa. "I have done a little sketch, in which you can see much better how the beach curves. The painting is not bad, but it is different. If you will allow me, just to cement our friendship, I would like to give you the sketch," he went on, for the people who refuse us the objects of our desire are always ready to offer us something else.

"I should very much like, if you have such a thing, a photograph of the little picture of Miss Sacripant. 'Sacripant'—that's not a real name, surely?" "It is the name of a character the sitter played in a stupid little musical comedy." "But, I assure you, sir, I have never set eyes on her; you look as though you thought that I knew her." Elstir was silent. "It isn't Mme. Swann, before she was married?" I hazarded, in one of those sudden fortuitous stumblings upon the truth, which are rare enough in all conscience, and yet give, in the long run, a certain cumulative support to the theory of presentiments, provided that one takes care to forget all the wrong guesses that would invalidate it. Elstir did not reply. The portrait was indeed that of Odette de Crécy. She had preferred not to keep it for many reasons, some of them obvious. But there were others less apparent. The portrait dated from before the point at which Odette, disciplining her features, had made of her face and figure that creation the broad outlines of which her hairdressers, her dressmakers, she herself—in her way of standing, of speaking, of smiling, of moving her hands, her eyes, of thinking—were to respect throughout the years to come. It required the vitiated tastes of a surfeited lover to make Swann prefer to all the countless photographs of the 'sealed pattern' Odette which was his charming wife the little photographs which he kept in his room and in which, beneath a straw hat trimmed with pansies, you saw a thin young woman, not even good-looking, with bunched-out hair and drawn features.

But apart from this, had the portrait been not anterior like Swann's favourite photograph, to the systematisation of Odette's features in a fresh type, majestic and charming, but subsequent to it, Elstir's vision would alone have sufficed to disorganise that type. Artistic genius in its reactions is like those extremely high temperatures which have the power to disintegrate combinations of atoms which they proceed to combine afresh in a diametrically opposite order, following another type. All that artificially harmonious whole into which a woman has succeeded in bringing her limbs and features, the persistence of which every day, before going out, she studies in her glass, changing the angle of her hat, smoothing her hair, exercising the sprightliness in her eyes, so as to ensure its continuity, that harmony the keen eye of the great painter instantly destroys, substituting for it a rearrangement of the woman's features such as will satisfy a certain pictorial ideal of femininity which he carries in his head. Similarly it often happens that, after a certain age, the eye of a great seeker after truth will find everywhere the elements necessary to establish those relations which alone are of interest to him. Like those craftsmen, those players who, instead of making a fuss and asking for what they cannot have, content themselves with the instrument that comes to their hand, the artist might say of anything, no matter what, that it would serve his purpose. Thus a cousin of the Princesse de Luxembourg, a beauty of the most queenly type, having succumbed to a form of art which was new at that time, had asked the leading painter of the naturalist school to do her portrait. At once the artist's eye had found what he sought everywhere in life. And on his canvas there appeared, in place of the proud lady, a street-boy, and behind him a vast, sloping, purple background which made one think of the Place Pigalle. But even without going so far as that, not only will the portrait of a woman by a great artist not seek in the least to give satisfaction to various demands on the woman's part—such as for instance, when she begins to age, make her have herself photographed in dresses that are almost those of a young girl, which bring out her still youthful figure and make her appear like the sister, or even the daughter of her own daughter, who, if need be, is tricked out for the occasion as a 'perfect fright' by her side—it will, on the contrary, emphasise those very drawbacks which she seeks to hide, and which (as for instance a feverish, that is to say a livid complexion) are all the more tempting to him since they give his picture 'character'; they are quite enough, however, to destroy all the illusions of the ordinary man who, when he sees the picture, sees crumble into dust the ideal which the woman herself has so proudly sustained for him, which has placed her in her unique, her unalterable form so far apart, so far above the rest of humanity. Fallen now, represented otherwise than in her own type in which she sat unassailably enthroned, she is become nothing more than just an ordinary woman, in the legend of whose superiority we have lost all faith. In this type we are so accustomed to regard as included not only the beauty of an Odette but her personality, her identity, that standing before the portrait which has thus transposed her from it we are inclined to protest not simply "How plain he has made her!" but "Why, it isn't the least bit like her!" We find it hard to believe that it can be she. We do not recognise her. And yet there is a person there on the canvas whom we are quite conscious of having seen before. But that person is not Odette; the face of the person, her body, her general appearance seem familiar. They recall to us not this particular woman who never held herself like that, whose natural pose had no suggestion of any such strange and teasing arabesque in its outlines, but other women, all the women whom Elstir has ever painted, women whom invariably, however they may differ from one another, he has chosen to plant thus on his canvas facing you, with an arched foot thrust out from under the skirt, a large round hat in one hand, symmetrically corresponding at the level of the knee which it hides to what also appears as a disc, higher up in the picture: the face. And further-more, not only does a portrait by the hand of genius disintegrate and destroy a woman's type, as it has been defined by her coquetry and her selfish conception of beauty, but if it is also old, it is not content with ageing the original in the same way as a photograph ages its sitter, by shewing her dressed in the fashions of long ago. In a portrait, it is not only the manner the woman then had of dressing that dates it, there is also the manner the artist had of painting. And this, Elstir's earliest manner, was the most damaging of birth certificates for Odette because it not only established her, as did her photographs of the same period, as the younger sister of various time-honoured courtesans, but made her portrait con-temporary with the countless portraits that Manet or Whistler had painted of all those vanished models, models who already belonged to oblivion or to history.

It was along this train of thought, meditated in silence by the side of Elstir as I accompanied him to his door, that I was being led by the dis-covery that I had just made of the identity of his model, when this original discovery caused me to make a second, more disturbing still, involving the identity of the artist. He had painted the portrait of Odette de Crécy. Could it possibly be that this man of genius, this sage, this eremite, this philosopher with his marvellous flow of conversation, who towered over everyone and everything, was the foolish, corrupt little painter who had at one time been 'taken up' by the Verdurins? I asked him if he had known them, whether by any chance it was he that they used to call M. Biche. He answered me in the affirmative, with no trace of embarrassment, as if my question referred to a period in his life that was ended and already somewhat remote, with no suspicion of what a cherished illusion his words were shattering in me, until looking up he read my disappointment upon my face. His own assumed an expression of annoyance. And, as we were now almost at the gate of his house, a man of less outstanding eminence, in heart and brain, might simply have said 'good-bye' to me, a trifle dryly, and taken care to avoid seeing me again. This however was not Elstir's way with me; like the master that he was—and this was, perhaps, from the point of view of sheer creative genius, his one fault, that he was a master in that sense of the word, for an artist if he is to live the true life of the spirit in its full extent, must be alone and not bestow himself with profusion, even upon disciples—from every circumstance, whether involving himself or other people, he sought to extract, for the better edification of the young, the element of truth that it contained. He chose therefore, rather than say anything that might have avenged the injury to his pride, to say what he thought would prove instructive to me. "There is no man," he began, "however wise, who has not at some period of his youth said things, or lived in a way the consciousness of which is so unpleasant to him in later life that he would gladly, if he could, expunge it from his memory. And yet he ought not entirely to regret it, because he cannot be certain that he has indeed become a wise man—so far as it is possible for any of us to be wise—unless he has passed through all the fatuous or unwholesome incarnations by which that ultimate stage must be preceded. I know that there are young fellows, the sons and grandsons of famous men, whose masters have instilled into them nobility of mind and moral refinement in their schooldays. They have, perhaps, when they look back upon their past lives, nothing to retract; they can, if they choose, publish a signed account of everything they have ever said or done; but they are poor creatures, feeble descendants of doctrinaires, and their wisdom is negative and sterile. We are not provided with wisdom, we must discover it for ourselves, after a journey through the wilderness which no one else can take for us, an effort which no one can spare us, for our wisdom is the point of view from which we come at last to regard the world. The lives that you admire, the attitudes that seem noble to you are not the result of training at home, by a father, or by masters at school, they have sprung from beginnings of a very different order, by reaction from the influence of everything evil or commonplace that prevailed round about them. They represent a struggle and a victory. I can see that the picture of what we once were, in early youth, may not be recognisable and cannot, certainly, be pleasing to contemplate in later life. But we must not deny the truth of it, for it is evidence that we have really lived, that it is in accordance with the laws of life and of the mind that we have, from the common elements of life, of the life of studios, of artistic groups—assuming that one is a painter—extracted something that goes beyond them." Meanwhile we had reached his door. I was disappointed at not having met the girls. But after all there was now the possibility of meeting them again later on; they had ceased to do no more than pass beyond a horizon on which I had been ready to suppose that I should never see them reappear. Around them no longer swirled that sort of great eddy which had separated me from them, which had been merely the expression of the perpetually active desire, mobile, compelling, fed ever on fresh anxieties, which was aroused in me by their inaccessibility, their flight from me, possibly for ever. My desire for them, I could now set it at rest, hold it in reserve, among all those other desires the realisation of which, as soon as I knew it to be possible, I would cheerfully postpone. I took leave of Elstir; I was alone once again. Then all of a sudden, despite my recent disappointment, I saw in my mind's eye all that chain of coincidence which I had not supposed could possibly come about, that Elstir should be a friend of those very girls, that they who only that morning had been to me merely figures in a picture with the sea for background had seen me, had seen me walking in friendly intimacy with a great painter, who was now informed of my secret longing and would no doubt do what he could to assuage it. All this had been a source of pleasure to me, but that pleasure had remained hidden; it was one of those visitors who wait before letting us know that they are in the room until all the rest have gone and we are by ourselves. Then only do we catch sight of them, and can say to them, "I am at your service," and listen to what they have to tell us. Sometimes between the moment at which these pleasures have entered our consciousness and the moment at which we are free to entertain them, so many hours have passed, we have in the interval seen so many people that we are afraid lest they should have grown tired of waiting. But they are patient, they do not grow tired, and as soon as the crowd has gone we find them there ready for us. Sometimes it is then we who are so exhausted that it seems as though our weary mind will not have the strength left to seize and retain those memories, those impressions for which our frail self is the one habitable place, the sole means of realisation. And we should regret that failure, for existence to us is hardly interesting save on the days on which the dust of realities is shot with magic sand, on which some trivial incident of life becomes a spring of romance. Then a whole promontory of the inaccessible world rises clear in the light of our dream, and enters into our life, our life in which, like the sleeper awakened, we actually see the people of whom we have been so ardently dreaming that we came to believe that we should never behold them save in our dreams.

The sense of comfort that I drew from the probability of my now being able to meet the little band whenever I chose was all the more precious to me because I should not have been able to keep watch for them during the next few days, which would be taken up with preparations for Saint-Loup's departure. My grandmother was anxious to offer my friend some proof of her gratitude for all the kindnesses that he had shewn to her and myself. I told her that he was a great admirer of Proudhon, and this put it into her head to send for a collection of autograph letters by that philosopher which she had once bought; Saint-Loup came to her room to look at them on the day of their arrival, which was also his last day at Balbec. He read them eagerly, fingering each page with reverence, trying to get the sentences by heart; and then, rising from the table, was beginning to apologise to my grandmother for having stayed so long, when he heard her say: "No, no; take them with you; they are for you to keep; that was why I sent for them, to give them to you."

He was overpowered by a joy which he could no more control than we can a physical condition that arises without the intervention of our will. He blushed scarlet as a child who has just been whipped, and my grandmother was a great deal more touched to see all the efforts that he was making (without success) to control the joy that convulsed him than she would have been to hear any words of thanks that he could have uttered. But he, fearing that he had failed to shew his gratitude properly, begged me to make his excuses to her again, next day, leaning from the window of the little train of the local railway company which was to take him back to his regiment. The distance was, as a matter of fact, nothing. He had thought of going, as he had frequently done that summer, when he was to return the same evening and was not encumbered with luggage, by road. But this time he would have had, anyhow, to put all his heavy luggage in the train. And he found it simpler to take the train himself also, following the advice of the manager who, on being consulted, replied that "Carriage or train, it was more or less equivocal." He meant us to understand that they were equivalent (in fact, very much what Françoise would have expressed as "coming to as near as made no difference"). "Very well," Saint-Loup had decided, "I will take the 'little crawler.' " I should have taken it too, had I not been tired, and gone with my friend to Doncières; failing this I kept on promising, all the time that we waited in the Balbec station—the time, that is to say, which the driver of the little train spent in waiting for unpunctual friends, without whom he refused to start, and also in seeking some refreshment for himself—to go over there and see him several times a week. As Bloch had come to the station also—much to Saint-Loup's disgust—the latter, seeing that our companion could hear him begging me to come to luncheon, to dinner, to stay altogether at Doncières, finally turned to him and, in the most forbidding tone, intended to counteract the forced civility of the invitation and to prevent Bloch from taking it seriously: "If you ever happen to be passing through Doncières any afternoon when I am off duty, you might ask for me at the barracks; but I hardly ever am off duty." Perhaps, also, Robert feared lest, if left to myself, I might not come, and, thinking that I was more intimate with Bloch than I made out, was providing me in this way with a travelling companion, one who would urge me on.

I was afraid that this tone, this way of inviting a person while warning him not to come, might have wounded Bloch, and felt that Saint-Loup would have done better, saying nothing. But I was mistaken, for after the train had gone, while we were walking back together as far as the crossroads at which we should have to part, one road going to the hotel, the other to the Blochs' villa, he never ceased from asking me on what day we should go to Doncières, for after "all the civilities that Saint-Loup had shewn" him, it would be 'too unmannerly' on his part not to accept the invitation. I was glad that he had not noticed, or was so little displeased as to wish to let it be thought that he had not noticed on how far from pressing, how barely polite a note the invitation had been sounded. At the same time I should have liked Bloch, for his own sake, to refrain from making a fool of himself by going over at once to Doncières. But I dared not offer a piece of advice which could only have offended him by hinting that Saint-Loup had been less pressing than himself impressed. He was a great deal too ready to respond, and even if all his faults of this nature were atoned for by remarkable qualities which others, with more reserve than he, would not possess, he carried indiscretion to a pitch that was almost maddening. The week must not, to hear him speak, pass without our going to Doncières (he said 'our' for I think that he counted to some extent on my presence there as an excuse for his own). All the way home, opposite the gymnasium, in its grove of trees, opposite the lawn-tennis courts, the mayor's office, the shell-fish stall, he stopped me, imploring me to fix a day, and, as I did not, left me in a towering rage, saying: "As your lordship pleases. For my part, I'm obliged to go since he has invited me."

Saint-Loup was still so much afraid of not having thanked my grandmother properly that he charged me once again to express his gratitude to her a day or two later in a letter I received from him from the town in which he was quartered, a town which seemed, on the envelope where the post-mark had stamped its name, to be hastening to me across country, to tell me that within its walls, in the Louis XVI cavalry barracks, he was thinking of me. The paper was embossed with the arms of Marsantes, in which I could make out a lion, surmounted by a coronet formed by the cap of a Peer of France.

"After a journey which," he wrote, "passed pleasantly enough, with a book I bought at the station, by Arvède Barine (a Russian author, I fancy; it seemed to me remarkably well written for a foreigner, but you shall give me your critical opinion, you are bound to know all about it, you fount of knowledge who have read everything), here I am again in the thick of this debased existence, where, alas, I feel a sad exile, not having here what I had to leave at Balbec; this life in which I cannot discover one affectionate memory, any intellectual attraction; an environment on which you would probably look with contempt—and yet it has a certain charm. Everything seems to have changed since I was last here, for in the interval one of the most important periods in my life, that from which our friendship dates, has begun. I hope that it may never come to an end. I have spoken of our friendship, of you, to one person only, to the friend I told you of, who has just paid me a surprise visit here. She would like immensely to know you, and I feel that you would get on well together, for she too is extremely literary. I, on the other hand, to go over in my mind all our talk, to live over again those hours which I never shall forget, have shut myself off from my comrades, excellent fellows, but altogether incapable of understanding that sort of thing. This remembrance of moments spent with you I should almost have preferred, on my first day here, to call up for my own solitary enjoyment, without writing. But I was afraid lest you, with your subtle mind and ultra-sensitive heart, might, if you did not hear from me, needlessly torment yourself, if, that is to say, you still condescend to occupy your thoughts with this blunt trooper whom you will have a hard task to polish and refine, and make a little more subtle and worthier of your company."

On the whole this letter, in its affectionate spirit, was not at all unlike those which, when I did not yet know Saint-Loup, I had imagined that he would write to me, in those daydreams from which the coldness of his first greeting had shaken me by bringing me face to face with an icy reality which was not, however, to endure. Once I had received this letter, whenever, at luncheon-time, the post was brought in, I could tell at once when it was from him that a letter came, for it had always that second face which a person assumes when he is absent, in the features of which (the characters of his script) there is no reason why we should not suppose that we are tracing an individual soul just as much as in the line of a nose or the inflexions of a voice.

I would now gladly remain at the table while it was being cleared, and, if it was not a moment at which the girls of the little band might be passing, it was no longer solely towards the sea that I would turn my eyes. Since I had seen such things depicted in water-colours by Elstir, I sought to find again in reality, I cherished, as though for their poetic beauty, the broken gestures of the knives still lying across one another, the swollen convexity of a discarded napkin upon which the sun would patch a scrap of yellow velvet, the half-empty glass which thus shewed to greater advantage the noble sweep of its curved sides, and, in the heart of its translucent crystal, clear as frozen daylight, a dreg of wine, dusky but sparkling with reflected lights, the displacement of solid objects, the transmutation of liquids by the effect of light and shade, the shifting colour of the plums which passed from green to blue and from blue to golden yellow in the half-plundered dish, the chairs, like a group of old ladies, that came twice daily to take their places round the white cloth spread on the table as on an altar at which were celebrated the rites of the palate, where in the hollows of oyster-shells a few drops of lustral water had gathered as in tiny holy water stoups of stone; I tried to find beauty there where I had never imagined before that it could exist, in the most ordinary things, in the profundities of 'still life.'

When, some days after Saint-Loup's departure, I had succeeded in persuading Elstir to give a small tea-party, at which I was to meet Albertine, that freshness of appearance, that smartness of attire, both (alas) fleeting, which were to be observed in me at the moment of my starting out from the Grand Hotel, and were due respectively to a longer rest than usual and to special pains over my toilet, I regretted my inability to reserve them (and also the credit accruing from Elstir's friendship) for the captivation of some other, more interesting person; I regretted having to use them all up on the simple pleasure of making Albertine's acquaintance. My brain assessed this pleasure at a very low value now that it was assured me. But, inside, my will did not for a moment share this illusion, that will which is the persevering and unalterable servant of our successive personalities; hiding itself in secret places, despised, downtrodden, untiringly faithful, toiling without intermission and with no thought for the variability of the self, its master, if only that master may never lack what he requires. Whereas at the moment when we are just about to start on a long-planned and eagerly awaited holiday, our brain, our nerves begin to ask themselves whether it is really worth all the trouble involved, the will, knowing that those lazy masters would at once begin to consider their journey the most wonderful experience, if it became impossible for them to take it, the will leaves them explaining their difficulties outside the station, multiplying their hesitations; but busies itself with taking the

tickets and putting us into the carriage before the train starts. It is as invariable as brain and nerves are fickle, but as it is silent, gives no account
of its actions, it seems almost non-existent; it is by its dogged determination that the other constituent parts of our personality are led, but without
seeing it, while they distinguish clearly all their own uncertainties. My
nerves and brain then started a discussion as to the real value of the pleasure that there would be in knowing Albertine, while I studied in the glass
vain and perishable attractions which nerves and brain would have preserved intact for use on some other occasion. But my will would not let the
hour pass at which I must start, and 'it was Elstir's address that it called
out to the driver. Brain and nerves were at liberty, now that the die was
cast, to think this 'a pity.' If my will had given the man a different address,
they would have been finely 'sold.'

When I arrived at Elstir's, a few minutes later, my first impression was
that Mlle. Simonet was not in the studio. There was certainly a girl sitting
there in a silk frock, bareheaded, but one whose marvellous hair, whose nose,
meant nothing to me, in whom I did not recognise the human entity that I
had formed out of a young cyclist strolling past, in a polo-cap, between
myself and the sea. It was Albertine, nevertheless. But even when I knew
it to be she, I gave her no thought. On entering any social gathering, when
we are young, we lose consciousness of our old self, we become a different
man, every drawing-room being a fresh universe, in which, coming under
the sway of a new moral perspective, we fasten our attention, as if they
were to matter to us for all time, on people, dances, card-tables, all of
which we shall have forgotten by the morning. Obliged to follow, if I was
to arrive at the goal of conversation with Albertine, a road in no way of
my own planning, which first brought me to a halt at Elstir, passed by
other groups of guests to whom I was presented, then along the table, at
which I was offered, and ate, a strawberry tart or two, while I listened,
motionless, to the music that was beginning in another part of the room,
I found myself giving to these various incidents the same importance as
to my introduction to Mlle. Simonet, an introduction which was now nothing more than one among several such incidents, having entirely forgotten
that it had been, but a few minutes since, my sole object in coming there
that day. But is it not ever thus in the bustle of daily life, with every
true happiness, every great sorrow? In a room full of other people we receive from her whom we love the answer, propitious or fatal, which we
have been awaiting for the last year. But we must go on talking, ideas come,
one after another, forming a smooth surface which is pricked, at the very
most, now and then by a dull throb from within of the memory, deep-
rooted enough but of very slender growth, that misfortune has come upon
us. If, instead of misfortune, it is happiness, it may be that not until many
years have elapsed will we recall that the most important event in our
sentimental life occurred without our having time to give it any prolonged attention, or even to become aware of it almost, at a social gathering, it may have been, to which we had gone solely in expectation of that
event.

When Elstir asked me to come with him so that he might introduce me to Albertine, who was sitting a little farther down the room, I first of all finished eating a coffee *éclair* and, with a show of keen interest, asked an old gentleman whose acquaintance I had just made (and thought that I might, perhaps, offer him the rose in my buttonhole which he had admired) to tell me more about the old Norman fairs. This is not to say that the introduction which followed did not give me any pleasure, nor assume a definite importance in my eyes. But so far as the pleasure was concerned, I was not conscious of it, naturally, until some time later, when, once more in the hotel, and in my room alone, I had become myself again. Pleasure in this respect is like photography. What we take, in the presence of the beloved object, is merely a negative film; we develop it later, when we are at home, and have once again found at our disposal that inner dark-room, the entrance to which is barred to us so long as we are with other people.

If my consciousness of the pleasure it had brought me was thus retarded by a few hours, the importance of this introduction I felt immediately. At such moments of introduction, for all that we feel ourselves to have been suddenly enriched, to have been furnished with a pass that will admit us henceforward to pleasures which we have been pursuing for weeks past, but in vain, we realise only too clearly that this acquisition puts an end for us not merely to hours of toilsome search—a relief that could only fill us with joy—but also to the very existence of a certain person, her whom our imagination had wildly distorted, our anxious fear that we might never become known to her enlarged. At the moment when our name sounds on the lips of the person introducing us, especially if he amplifies it, as Elstir was now doing, with a flattering account of us—in that sacramental moment, as when in a fairy tale the magician commands a person suddenly to become someone else, she to whose presence we have been longing to attain vanishes; how could she remain the same when, for one thing—owing to the attention which the stranger is obliged to pay to the announcement of our name and the sight of our person—in the eyes that only yesterday were situated at an infinite distance (where we supposed that our eyes, wandering, uncontrolled, desperate, divergent, would never succeed in meeting them) the conscious gaze, the incommunicable thought which we have been seeking have been miraculously and quite simply replaced by our own image, painted in them as though behind the glass of a smiling mirror. If this incarnation of ourself in the person who seems to differ most from us is what does most to modify the appearance of the person to whom we have just been introduced, the form of that person still remains quite vague; and we are free to ask ourself whether she will turn out to be a god, a table or a basin. But, as nimble as the wax-modellers who will fashion a bust before our eyes in five minutes, the few words which the stranger is now going to say to us will substantiate her form, will give her something positive and final that will exclude all the hypotheses by which, a moment ago, our desire, our imagination were being tempted. Doubtless, even before her coming to this party, Albertine had ceased to be to me simply that sole phantom worthy to haunt our life which is what remains of a passing stranger, of whom we know nothing and have caught but the barest glimpse. Her relation to Mme. Bontemps had already restricted the scope of those marvellous hypotheses, by stopping one of the channels along which they might have spread. As I drew closer to the girl, and began to know her better, my knowledge of her underwent a process of subtraction, all the factors of imagination and desire giving place to a notion which was worth infinitely less, a notion to which, it must be admitted, there was added presently what was more or less the equivalent, in the domain of real life, of what joint stock companies give one, after paying interest on one's capital, and call a bonus. Her name, her family connexions had been the original limit set to my suppositions. Her friendly greeting while, standing close beside her, I saw once again the tiny mole on her cheek, below her eye, marked another stage; last of all, I was surprised to hear her use the adverb 'perfectly' (in place of 'quite') of two people whom she mentioned, saying of one: "She is perfectly mad, but very nice for all that," and of the other, "He is a perfectly common man, a perfect bore." However little to be commended this use of 'perfectly' may be, it indicates a degree of civilisation and culture which I could never have imagined as having been attained by the bacchante with the bicycle, the frenzied muse of the golf-course. Nor did it mean that after this first transformation Albertine was not to change again for me, many times. The good and bad qualities which a person presents to us, exposed to view on the surface of his or her face, rearrange themselves in a totally different order if we approach them from another angle—just as, in a town, buildings that appear strung irregularly along a single line, from another aspect retire into a graduated distance, and their relative heights are altered. To begin with, Albertine now struck me as not implacable so much as almost frightened; she seemed to me rather respectably than ill bred, judging by the description, 'bad style,' 'a comic manner' which she applied to each in turn of the girls of whom I spoke to her; finally, she presented as a target for my line of sight a temple that was distinctly flushed and hardly attractive to the eye, and no longer the curious gaze which I had always connected with her until then. But this was merely a second impression and there were doubtless others through which I was successively to pass. Thus it can be only after one has recognised, not without having had to feel one's way, the optical illusions of one's first impression that one can arrive at an exact knowledge of another person, supposing such knowledge to be ever possible. But it is not; for while our original impression of him undergoes correction, the person himself, not being an inanimate object, changes in himself, we think that we have caught him, he moves, and, when we imagine that at last we are seeing him clearly, it is only the old impressions which we had already formed of him that we have succeeded in making clearer, when they no longer represent him.

And yet, whatever the inevitable disappointments that it must bring in its train, this movement towards what we have only half seen, what we have been free to dwell upon and imagine at our leisure, this movement is the only one that is wholesome for the senses, that whets the appetite. How dreary a monotony must pervade those people's lives who, from indolence or timidity, drive in their carriages straight to the doors of friends whom they have got to know without having first dreamed of knowing them, without ever daring, on the way, to stop and examine what arouses their desire.

I returned home, my mind full of the party, the coffee *éclair* which I had finished eating before I let Elstir take me up to Albertine, the rose which I had given the old gentleman, all the details selected without our knowledge by the circumstances of the occasion, which compose in a special and quite fortuitous order the picture that we retain of a first meeting. But this picture, I had the impression that I was seeing it from a fresh point of view, a long way remote from myself, realising that it had not existed only for me, when some months later, to my great surprise, on my speaking to Albertine on the day on which I had first met her, she reminded me of the *éclair*, the flower that I had given away, all those things which I had supposed to have been—I will not say of importance only to myself but—perceived only by myself, and which I now found thus transcribed, in a version the existence of which I had never suspected, in the mind of Albertine. On this first day itself, when, on my return to the hotel, I was able to visualise the memory which I had brought away with me, I realised the consummate adroitness with which the sleight of hand had been performed, and how I had talked for a moment or two with a person who, thanks to the skill of the conjurer, without actually embodying anything of that other person whom I had for so long been following as she paced beside the sea, had been effectively substituted for her. I might, for that matter, have guessed as much in advance, since the girl of the beach was a fabrication invented by myself. In spite of which, as I had, in my conversations with Elstir, identified her with this other girl, I felt myself in honour bound to fulfil to the real the promises of love made to the imagined Albertine. We betroth ourselves by proxy, and think ourselves obliged, in the sequel, to marry the person who has intervened. Moreover, if there had disappeared, provisionally at any rate, from my life, an anguish that found adequate consolation in the memory of polite manners, of that expression 'perfectly common' and of the glowing temple, that memory awakened in me desire of another kind which, for all that it was placid and not at all painful, resembling rather brotherly love, might in the long run become fully as dangerous by making me feel at every moment a compelling need to kiss this new person, whose charming ways, shyness, unlooked-for accessibility, arrested the futile process of my imagination but gave birth to a sentimental gratitude. And then, since memory begins at once to record photographs independent of one another, eliminates every link, any kind of sequence from between the scenes portrayed in the collection which it exposes to our view, the most recent does not necessarily destroy or cancel those that came before. Confronted with the commonplace though appealing Albertine to whom I had spoken that afternoon, I still saw the other, mysterious Albertine outlined against the sea. These were now memories, that is to say pictures neither of which now seemed to me any more true than the other. But, to make an end of this first afternoon of my introduction to Albertine, when trying to recapture that little mole on her cheek, just under the eye, I remembered that, looking from Elstir's window, when Albertine had gone by, I had seen the mole on her chin. In fact, whenever I saw her I noticed that she had a mole, but my inaccurate memory made it wander about the face of Albertine, fixing it now in one place, now in another.

Whatever my disappointment in finding in Mlle. Simonet a girl so little different from those that I knew already, just as my rude awakening when I saw Balbec Church did not prevent me from wishing still to go to Quimperlé, Pont-Aven and Venice, I comforted myself with the thought that through Albertine at any rate, even if she herself was not all that I had hoped, I might make the acquaintance of her comrades of the little band.

I thought at first that I should fail. As she was to be staying (and I too) for a long time still at Balbec, I had decided that the best thing was not to make my efforts to meet her too apparent, but to wait for an accidental encounter. But should this occur every day, even, it was greatly to be feared that she would confine herself to acknowledging my bow from a distance, and such meetings, repeated day after day throughout the whole season, would benefit me not at all.

Shortly after this, one morning when it had been raining and was almost cold, I was accosted on the 'front' by a girl wearing a close-fitting toque and carrying a muff, so different from the girl whom I had met at Elstir's party that to recognise in her the same person seemed an operation beyond the power of the human mind; mine was, nevertheless, successful in performing it, but after a momentary surprise which did not, I think, escape Albertine's notice. On the other hand, when I instinctively recalled the good breeding which had so impressed me before, she filled me with a converse astonishment by her rude tone and manners typical of the 'little band.' Apart from these, her temple had ceased to be the optical centre, on which the eye might comfortably rest, of her face, either because I was now on her other side, or because her toque hid it, or else possibly because its inflammation was not a constant thing. "What weather!" she began. "Really the perpetual summer of Balbec is all stuff and nonsense. You don't go in for anything special here, do you? We don't ever see you playing golf, or dancing at the Casino. You don't ride, either. You must be bored stiff. You don't find it too deadly, staying about on the beach all day? I see, you just bask in the sun like a lizard; you enjoy that. You must have plenty of time on your hands. I can see you're not like me; I simply adore all sports. You weren't at the Sogne races! We went in the 'tram,' and I can quite believe you don't see the fun of going in an old 'tin-pot' like that. It took us two whole hours! I could have gone there and back three times on my bike." I, who had been lost in admiration of Saint-Loup when he, in the most natural manner in the world, called the little local train the 'crawler,' because of the ceaseless windings of its line, was positively alarmed by the glibness with which Albertine spoke of the 'tram,' and called it a 'tin-pot.' I could feel her mastery of a form of speech in which I was afraid of her detecting and scorning my inferiority. And yet the full wealth of the synonyms that the little band possessed to denote this railway had not yet been revealed to me. In speaking, Albertine kept her

head motionless, her nostrils closed, allowing only the corners of her lips
to move. The result of this was a drawling, nasal sound, into the composition of which there entered perhaps a provincial descent, a juvenile affectation of British phlegm, the teaching of a foreign governess and a con-
gestive hypertrophy of the mucus of the nose. This enunciation which, as
it happened, soon disappeared when she knew people better, giving place
to a natural girlish tone, might have been thought unpleasant. But it was
peculiar to herself, and delighted me. Whenever I had gone for several
days without seeing her, I would refresh my spirit by repeating to myself:
"We don't ever see you playing golf," with the nasal intonation in which
she had uttered the words, point blank, without moving a muscle of her
face. And I thought then that there could be no one in the world so desirable.

We formed that morning one of those couples who dotted the 'front'
here and there with their conjunction, their stopping together for time
enough just to exchange a few words before breaking apart, each to resume
separately his or her divergent stroll. I seized the opportunity, while she
stood still, to look again and discover once and for all where exactly the
little mole was placed. Then, just as a phrase of Vinteuil which had delighted me in the sonata, and which my recollection allowed to wander
from the andante to the finale, until the day when, having the score in my
hands, I was able to find it, and to fix it in my memory in its proper place,
in the scherzo, so this mole, which I had visualised now on her cheek, now
on her chin, came to rest for ever on her upper lip, just below her nose. In
the same way, too, do we come with amazement upon lines that we
know by heart in a poem in which we never dreamed that they were to be
found.

At that moment, as if in order that against the sea there might multiply
in freedom, in the variety of its forms, all the rich decorative whole which
was the lovely unfolding of the train of maidens, at once golden and rosy,
baked by sun and wind, Albertine's friends, with their shapely limbs,
their supple figures, but so different one from another, came into sight in
a cluster that expanded as it approached, advancing towards us, but keeping closer to the sea, along a parallel line. I asked Albertine's permission
to walk for a little way with her. Unfortunately, all she did was to wave
her hand to them in greeting. "But your friends will be disappointed if
you don't go with them," I hinted, hoping that we might all walk together.
A young man with regular features, carrying a bag of golf-clubs, saun-
tered up to us. It was the baccarat-player, whose fast ways so enraged the
chief magistrate's wife. In a frigid, impassive tone, which he evidently
regarded as an indication of the highest refinement, he bade Albertine good
day. "Been playing golf, Octave?" she asked. "How did the game go?
Were you in form?" "Oh, it's too sickening; I can't play for nuts," he
replied. "Was Andrée playing?" "Yes, she went round in seventy-seven."
"Why, that's a record!" "I went round in eighty-two yesterday." He was
the son of an immensely rich manufacturer who was to take an important
part in the organisation of the coming World's Fair. I was struck by the
extreme degree to which, in this young man and in the other by no means

numerous male friends of the band of girls, the knowledge of everything that pertained to clothes and how to wear them, cigars, English drinks, horses, a knowledge which he possessed in its minutest details with a haughty infallibility that approached the reticent modesty of the true expert, had been developed in complete isolation, unaccompanied by the least trace of any intellectual culture. He had no hesitation as to the right time and place for dinner-jacket or pyjamas, but neither had he any suspicion of the circumstances in which one might or might not employ this or that word, or even of the simplest rules of grammar. This disparity between the two forms of culture must have existed also in his father, the President of the Syndicate that 'ran' Balbec, for, in an open letter to the electors which he had recently had posted on all the walls, he announced: "I desired to see the Mayor, to speak to him of the matter; he would not listen to my righteous plaint." Octave, at the Casino, took prizes in all the dancing competitions, for bostons, tangos and what-not, an accomplishment that would entitle him, if he chose, to make a fine marriage in that seaside society where it is not figuratively but in sober earnest that the young women 'marry their dancing-partners.' He lighted a cigar with a "D'you mind?" to Albertine, as one who asks permission to finish, while going on talking, an urgent piece of work. For he was one of those people who can never be 'doing nothing,' although there was nothing, for that matter, that he could ever be said to do. And as complete inactivity has the same effect on us, in the end, as prolonged overwork, and on the character as much as on the life of body and muscles, the unimpaired nullity of intellect that was enshrined behind Octave's meditative brow had ended by giving him, despite his air of unruffled calm, ineffectual longings to think which kept him awake at night, for all the world like an overwrought philosopher.

Supposing that if I knew their male friends I should have more opportunities of seeing the girls, I had been on the point of asking for an introduction to Octave. I told Albertine this, as soon as he had left us, still muttering, "I couldn't play for nuts!" I thought I would thus put into her head the idea of doing it next time. "But I can't," she cried, "introduce you to a tame cat like that. This place simply swarms with them. But what on earth would they have to say to you? That one plays golf quite well, and that's all there is to it. I know what I'm talking about; you'd find he wasn't at all your sort." "Your friends will be cross with you if you desert them like this," I repeated, hoping that she would then suggest my joining the party. "Oh, no, they don't want me." We ran into Bloch, who directed at me a subtle, insinuating smile, and, embarrassed by the presence of Albertine, whom he did not know, or, rather, knew 'without knowing' her, bent his head with a stiff, almost irritated jerk. "What's he called, that Ostrogoth?" Albertine asked. "I can't think why he should bow to me; he doesn't know me. And I didn't bow to him, either." I had no time to explain to her, for, bearing straight down upon us, "Excuse me," he began, "for interrupting you, but I must tell you that I am going to Doncières to-morrow. I cannot put it off any longer without discourtesy; indeed, I ask myself, what must de Saint-Loup-en-Bray think of me. I just came to let you know that I shall take the two o'clock train. At your service." But I thought now only of seeing Albertine again, and of trying to get to know her friends, and Doncières, since they were not going there, and my going would bring me back too late to see them still on the beach, seemed to me to be situated at the other end of the world. I told Bloch that it was impossible. "Oh, very well, I shall go alone. In the fatuous words of Master Arouet, I shall say to Saint-Loup, to beguile his clericalism:

> 'My duty stands alone, by his in no way bound;
> Though he should choose to fail, yet faithful I'll be found.' "

"I admit he's not a bad looking boy," was Albertine's comment, "but he makes me feel quite sick." I had never thought that Bloch might be 'not a bad looking boy'; and yet, when one came to think of it, so he was. With his rather prominent brow, very aquiline nose, and his air of extreme cleverness and of being convinced of his cleverness, he had a pleasing face. But he could not succeed in pleasing Albertine. This was perhaps due, to some extent, to her own disadvantages, the harshness, the want of feeling of the little band, its rudeness towards everything that was not itself. And later on, when I introduced them, Albertine's antipathy for him grew no less. Bloch belonged to a section of society in which, between the free and easy customs of the 'smart set' and the regard for good manners which a man is supposed to shew who 'does not soil his hands,' a sort of special compromise has been reached which differs from the manners of the world and is nevertheless a peculiarly unpleasant form of worldliness. When he was introduced to anyone he would bow with a sceptical smile, and at the same time with an exaggerated show of respect, and, if it was to a man, would say: "Pleased to meet you, sir," in a voice which ridiculed the words that it was uttering, though with a consciousness of belonging to some one who was no fool. Having sacrificed this first moment to a custom which he at once followed and derided (just as on the first of January he would greet you with a 'Many happy!') he would adopt an air of infinite cunning, and would 'proffer subtle words' which were often true enough but 'got on' Albertine's nerves. When I told her on this first day that his name was Bloch, she exclaimed: "I would have betted anything he was a Jewboy. Trust them to put their foot in it!" Moreover, Bloch was destined to give Albertine other grounds for annoyance later on. Like many intellectuals, he was incapable of saying a simple thing in a simple way. He would find some precious qualification for every statement, and would sweep from particular to general. It vexed Albertine, who was never too well pleased at other people's shewing an interest in what she was doing, that when she had sprained her ankle and was keeping quiet, Bloch said of her: "She is outstretched on her chair, but in her ubiquity has not ceased to frequent simultaneously vague golf-courses and dubious tennis-courts." He was simply being 'literary,' of course, but this, in view of the difficulties which Albertine felt that it might create for her with friends whose invitations she had declined on the plea that she was unable to move, was quite enough to disgust her with the face, the sound of the voice, of the young man who could say such things about her. We parted, Albertine and I, after promising to take a walk together later. I had talked to her without being any more conscious of where my words were falling, of what became of them, than if I were dropping pebbles into a bottomless pit. That our words are, as a general rule, filled, by the person to whom we address them, with a meaning which that person derives from her own substance, a meaning widely different from that which we had put into the same words when we uttered them, is a fact which the daily round of life is perpetually demonstrating. But if we find ourselves as well in the company of a person whose education (as Albertine's was to me) is inconceivable, her tastes, her reading, her principles unknown, we cannot tell whether our words have aroused in her anything that resembles their meaning, any more than in an animal, although there are things that even an animal may be made to understand. So that to attempt any closer friendship with Albertine seemed to me like placing myself in contact with the unknown, if not the impossible, an occupation as arduous as breaking a horse, as reposeful as keeping bees or growing roses.

I had thought, a few hours before, that Albertine would acknowledge my bow but would not speak to me. We had now parted, after planning to make some excursion soon together. I vowed that when I next met Albertine I would treat her with greater boldness, and I had sketched out in advance a draft of all that I would say to her, and even (being now quite convinced that she was not strait-laced) of all the favours that I would demand of her. But the mind is subject to external influences, as plants are, and cells and chemical elements, and the medium in which its immersion alters it is a change of circumstances, or new surroundings. Grown different by the mere fact of her presence, when I found myself once again in Albertine's company, what I said to her was not at all what I had meant to say. Remembering her flushed temple, I asked myself whether she might not appreciate more keenly a polite attention which she knew to be disinterested. Besides, I was embarrassed by certain things in her look, in her smile. They might equally well signify a laxity of morals and the rather silly merriment of a girl who though full of spirits was at heart thoroughly respectable. A single expression, on a face as in speech, is susceptible of divers interpretations, and I stood hesitating like a schoolboy faced by the difficulties of a piece of Greek prose.

On this occasion we met almost immediately the tall one, Andrée, the one who had jumped over the old banker, and Albertine was obliged to introduce me. Her friend had a pair of eyes of extraordinary brightness, like, in a dark house, a glimpse through an open door of a room into which the sun is shining with a greenish reflexion from the glittering sea.

A party of five were passing, men whom I had come to know very well by sight during my stay at Balbec. I had often wondered who they could be. "They're nothing very wonderful," said Albertine with a sneering laugh. "The little old one with dyed hair and yellow gloves has a fine touch; he knows how to draw all right, he's the Balbec dentist; he's a good sort. The fat one is the Mayor, not the tiny little fat one, you must have seen him before, he's the dancing master; he's rather a beast, you know; he can't stand us, because we make such a row at the Casino; we smash his chairs, and want to have the carpet up when we dance; that's why he never gives us prizes, though we're the only girls there who can dance a bit. The dentist is a dear, I would have said how d'ye do to him, just to make the dancing master swear, but I couldn't because they've got M. de Sainte-Croix with them; he's on the General Council; he comes of a very good family, but he's joined the Republicans, to make more money. No nice people ever speak to him now. He knows my uncle, because they're both in the Government, but the rest of my family always cut him. The thin one in the waterproof is the bandmaster. You know him, of course. You don't? Oh, he plays divinely. You haven't been to *Cavalleria Rusticana?* I thought it too lovely! He's giving a concert this evening, but we can't go because it's to be in the town hall. In the Casino it wouldn't matter, but in the town hall, where they've taken down the crucifix. Andrée's mother would have a fit if we went there. You're going to say that my aunt's husband is in the Government. But what difference does that make? My aunt is my aunt. That's not why I'm fond of her. The only thing she has ever wanted has been to get rid of me. No, the person who has really been a mother to me, and all the more credit to her because she's no relation at all, is a friend of mine whom I love just as much as if she was my mother. I will let you see her 'photo.' " We were joined for a moment by the golf champion and baccarat plunger, Octave. I thought that I had discovered a bond between us, for I learned in the course of conversation that he was some sort of relative, and even more a friend of the Verdurins. But he spoke contemptuously of the famous Wednesdays, adding that M. Verdurin had never even heard of a dinner-jacket, which made it a horrid bore when one ran into him in a music-hall, where one would very much rather not be greeted with "Well, you young rascal," by an old fellow in a frock coat and black tie, for all the world like a village lawyer. Octave left us, and soon it was Andrée's turn, when we came to her villa, into which she vanished without having uttered a single word to me during the whole of our walk. I regretted her departure, all the more in that, while I was complaining to Albertine how chilling her friend had been with me, and was comparing in my mind this difficulty which Albertine seemed to find in making me know her friends with the hostility that Elstir, when he might have granted my desire, seemed to have encountered on that first afternoon, two girls came by to whom I lifted my hat, the young Ambresacs, whom Albertine greeted also.

I felt that, in Albertine's eyes, my position would be improved by this meeting. They were the daughters of a kinswoman of Mme. de Villeparisis, who was also a friend of Mme. de Luxembourg. M. and Mme. d'Ambresac, who had a small villa at Balbec and were immensely rich, led the simplest of lives there, and always went about dressed he in an unvarying frock coat, she in a dark gown. Both of them used to make sweeping bows to my grandmother, which never led to anything further. The daughters, who were very pretty, were dressed more fashionably, but in a fashion suited rather to Paris than to the seaside. With their long skirts and large hats, they had the look of belonging to a different race from Albertine. She, I discovered, knew all about them.

"Oh, so you know the little d'Ambresacs, do you? Dear me, you have some swagger friends. After all, they're very simple souls," she went on as though this might account for it. "They're very nice, but so well brought up that they aren't allowed near the Casino, for fear of us—we've such a bad tone. They attract you, do they? Well, it all depends on what you like. They're just little white rabbits, really. There may be something in that, of course. If little white rabbits are what appeals to you, they may supply a long-felt want. It seems, there must be some attraction, because one of them has got engaged already to the Marquis de Saint-Loup. Which is a cruel blow to the younger one, who is madly in love with that young man. I'm sure, the way they speak to you with their lips shut is quite enough for me. And then they dress in the most absurd way. Fancy going to play golf in silk frocks! At their age, they dress more showily than grown-up women who really know about clothes. Look at Mme. Elstir; there's a well dressed woman if you like." I answered that she had struck me as being dressed with the utmost simplicity. Albertine laughed. "She does put on the simplest things, I admit, but she dresses wonderfully, and to get what you call simplicity costs her a fortune." Mme. Elstir's gowns passed unnoticed by any one who had not a sober and unerring taste in matters of attire. This was lacking in me. Elstir possessed it in a supreme degree, or so Albertine told me. I had not suspected this, nor that the beautiful but quite simple objects which littered his studio were treasures long desired by him which he had followed from sale room to sale room, knowing all their history, until he had made enough money to be able to acquire them. But as to this Albertine, being as ignorant as myself, could not enlighten me. Whereas when it came to clothes, prompted by a coquettish instinct, and perhaps by the regretful longing of a penniless girl who is able to appreciate with greater disinterestedness, more delicacy of feeling, in other, richer people the things that she will never be able to afford for herself, she expressed herself admirably on the refinement of Elstir's taste, so hard to satisfy that all women appeared to him badly dressed, while, attaching infinite importance to right proportions and shades of colour, he would order to be made for his wife, at fabulous prices, the sunshades, hats and cloaks which he had learned from Albertine to regard as charming, and which a person wanting in taste would no more have noticed than myself. Apart from this, Albertine, who had done a little painting, though without, she confessed, having any 'gift' for it, felt a boundless admiration for Elstir, and, thanks to his precept and example, shewed a judgment of pictures which was in marked contrast to her enthusiasm for *Cavalleria Rusticana*. The truth was, though as yet it was hardly apparent, that she was highly intelligent, and that in the things that she said the stupidity was not her own but that of her environment and age. Elstir's had been a good but only a partial influence. All the branches of her intelligence had not reached the same stage of development. The taste for pictures had almost caught up the taste for clothes and all forms of smartness, but had not been followed by the taste for music, which was still a long way behind.

Albertine might know all about the Ambresacs; but as he who can achieve great things is not necessarily capable of small, I did not find her, after I had bowed to those young ladies, any better disposed to make me known to her friends. "It's too good of you to attach any importance to them. You shouldn't take any notice of them; they don't count. What on earth can a lot of kids like them mean to a man like you? Now Andrée, I must say, is remarkably clever. She is a good girl, that, though she is perfectly fantastic at times, but the others are really dreadfully stupid." When I had left Albertine, I felt suddenly a keen regret that Saint-Loup should have concealed his engagement from me and that he should be doing anything so improper as to choose a wife before breaking with his mistress. And then, shortly afterwards, I met Andrée, and as she went on talking to me for some time I seized the opportunity to tell her that I would very much like to see her again next day, but she replied that this was impossible, because her mother was not at all well, and she would have to stay beside her. The next day but one, when I was at Elstir's, he told me how greatly Andrée had been attracted by me; on my protesting: "But it was I who was attracted by her from the start; I asked her to meet me again yesterday, but she could not." "Yes, I know; she told me all about that," was his reply, "she was very sorry, but she had promised to go to a picnic, somewhere miles from here. They were to drive over in a break, and it was too late for her to get out of it." Albeit this falsehood (Andrée knowing me so slightly) was of no real importance, I ought not to have continued to seek the company of a person who was capable of uttering it. For what people have once done they will do again indefinitely, and if you go every year to see a friend who, the first time, was not able to meet you at the appointed place, or was in bed with a chill, you will find him in bed with another chill which he has just caught, you will miss him again at another meeting-place at which he has failed to appear, for a single and unalterable reason in place of which he supposes himself to have various reasons, drawn from the circumstances. One morning, not long after Andrée's telling me that she would be obliged to stay beside her mother, I was taking a short stroll with Albertine, whom I had found on the beach tossing up and catching again on a cord an oddly shaped implement which gave her a look of Giotto's 'Idolatry'; it was called, for that matter, 'Diabolo,' and is so fallen into disuse now that, when they come upon the picture of a girl playing with one, the critics of future generations will solemnly discuss, as it might be over one of the allegorical figures in the Arena, what it is that she is holding. A moment later their friend with the penurious and harsh appearance, the same one who on that first day had sneered so malevolently: "I do feel sorry for him, poor old man," when she saw the old gentleman's head brushed by the flying feet of Andrée, came up to Albertine with "Good morning, 'm I disturbing you?" She had taken off her hat, for comfort, and her hair, like a strange and fascinating plant, lay over her brow, displaying all the delicate tracery of its foliation. Albertine, perhaps because she resented seeing the other bare-headed, made no reply, preserved a frigid silence in spite of which the girl stayed with us, kept apart from myself by Albertine, who arranged at one moment to be alone with her, at another to walk with me leaving her to follow. I was obliged, to secure an introduction, to ask for it in the girl's hearing. Then,.

as Albertine was uttering my name, on the face and in the blue eyes of this girl, whose expression I had thought so cruel when I heard her say: "Poor old man, I do feel so sorry for him," I saw gather and gleam a cordial, friendly smile, and she held out her hand. Her hair was golden, and not her hair only; for if her cheeks were pink and her eyes blue it was like the still roseate morning sky which sparkles everywhere with dazzling points of gold.

At once kindled by her flame, I said to myself that this was a child who when in love grew shy, that it was for my sake, from love for me that she had remained with us, despite Albertine's rebuffs, and that she must have rejoiced in the opportunity to confess to me at last, by that smiling, friendly gaze, that she would be as kind to me as she was terrible to other people. Doubtless she had noticed me on the beach, when I still knew nothing of her, and had been thinking of me ever since; perhaps it had been to win my admiration that she mocked at the old gentleman, and because she had not succeeded in getting to know me that on the following days she appeared so morose. From the hotel I had often seen her, in the evenings, walking by herself on the beach. Probably in the hope of meeting me. And now, hindered as much by Albertine's presence as she would have been by that of the whole band, she had evidently attached herself to us, braving the increasing coldness of her friend's attitude, only in the hope of outstaying her, of being left alone with me, when she might make an appointment with me for some time when she would find an excuse to slip away without either her family's or her friends' knowing that she had gone, and would meet me in some safe place before church or after golf. It was all the more difficult to see her because Andrée had quarrelled with her and now detested her. "I have put up far too long with her terrible dishonesty," she explained to me, "her baseness; I can't tell you all the vile insults she has heaped on me. I have stood it all because of the others. But her latest effort was really too much!" And she told me of some foolish thing that this girl had done, which might indeed have injurious consequences to Andrée herself.

But those private words promised me by Gisèle's confiding eyes for the moment when Albertine should have left us by ourselves, were destined never to be spoken, because after Albertine, stubbornly planted between us, had answered with increasing curtness, and finally had ceased to respond at all to her friend's remarks, Gisèle at length abandoned the attempt and turned back. I found fault with Albertine for having been so disagreeable. "It will teach her to be more careful how she behaves. She's not a bad kid, but she'd talk the head off a donkey. She's no business, either, to go poking her nose into everything. Why should she fasten herself on to us without being asked? In another minute, I'd have told her to go to blazes. Besides I can't stand her going about with her hair like that; it's such bad form." I gazed at Albertine's cheeks as she spoke, and asked myself what might be the perfume, the taste of them: this time they were not cool, but glowed with a uniform pink, violet-tinted, creamy, like certain roses whose petals have a waxy gloss. I felt a passionate longing for them such as one feels sometimes for a particular flower. "I hadn't noticed it," was all that I said. "You stared at her hard enough; anyone would have said you wanted to paint her portrait," she scolded, not at all softened by the fact that it was at herself that I was now staring so fixedly. "I don't believe you would care for her, all the same. She's not in the least a flirt. You like little girls who flirt with you, I know. Anyhow, she won't have another chance of fastening on to us and being sent about her business; she's going off to-day to Paris." "Are the rest of your friends going too?" "No; only she and 'Miss,' because she's got an exam. coming; she's got to stay at home and swot for it, poor kid. It's not much fun for her, I don't mind telling you. Of course, you may be set a good subject, you never know. But it's a tremendous risk. One girl I know was asked: *Describe an accident that you have witnessed*. That was a piece of luck. But I know another girl who got: *State which you would rather have as a friend, Alceste or Philinte*. I'm sure I should have dried up altogether! Apart from everything else, it's not a question to set to girls. Girls go about with other girls; they're not supposed to have gentlemen friends." (This announcement, which shewed that I had but little chance of being admitted to the companionship of the band, froze my blood.) "But in any case, supposing it was set to boys, what on earth would you expect them to say to a question like that? Several parents wrote to the *Gaulois*, to complain of the difficult questions that were being set. The joke of it is that in a collection of prize-winning essays they gave two which treated the question in absolutely opposite ways. You see, it all depends on which examiner you get. One would like you to say that Philinte was a flatterer and a scoundrel, the other that you couldn't help admiring Alceste, but that he was too cantankerous, and that as a friend you ought to choose Philinte. How can you expect a lot of unfortunate candidates to know what to say when the professors themselves can't make up their minds. But that's nothing. They get more difficult every year. Gisèle will want all her wits about her if she's to get through." I returned to the hotel. My grandmother was not there. I waited for her for some time; when at last she appeared, I begged her to allow me, in quite unexpected circumstances, to make an expedition which might keep me away for a couple of days. I had luncheon with her, ordered a carriage and drove to the station. Gisèle would shew no surprise at seeing me there. After we had changed at Doncières, in the Paris train, there would be a carriage with a corridor, along which, while the governess dozed, I should be able to lead Gisèle into dark corners, and make an appointment to meet her on my return to Paris, which I would then try to put forward to the earliest possible date. I would travel with her as far as Caen or Evreux, whichever she preferred, and would take the next train back to Balbec. And yet, what would she have thought of me had she known that I had hesitated for a long time between her and her friends, that quite as much as with her I had contemplated falling in love with Albertine, with the bright-eyed girl, with Rosemonde. I felt a pang of remorse now that a bond of mutual affection was going to unite me with Gisèle. I could, moreover, truthfully have assured her that Albertine no longer interested me. I had seen her that morning as she swerved aside, almost turning her back on me, to speak to Gisèle. On her head, which was bent sullenly over her bosom, the hair that grew at the back, different from and darker even than the rest, shone as though she had just been bathing. "Like a dying duck in a thunderstorm!" I thought to myself, this view of her hair having let into Albertine's body a soul entirely different from that implied hitherto by her glowing complexion and mysterious gaze. That shining cataract of hair at the back of her head had been for a moment or two all that I was able to see of her, and continued to be all that I saw in retrospect. Our memory is like a shop in the window of which is exposed now one, now another photograph of the same person. And as a rule the most recent exhibit remains for some time the only one to be seen. While the coachman whipped on his horse I sat there listening to the words of gratitude and affection which Gisèle was murmuring in my ear, born, all of them, of her friendly smile and outstretched hand, the fact being that in those periods of my life in which I was not actually, but desired to be in love, I carried in my mind not only an ideal form of beauty once seen, which I recognised at a glance in every passing stranger who kept far enough from me for her confused features to resist any attempt at identification, but also the moral phantom —ever ready to be incarnate—of the woman who was going to fall in love with me, to take up her cues in the amorous comedy which I had had written out in my mind from my earliest boyhood, and in which every nice girl seemed to me to be equally desirous of playing, provided that she had also some of the physical qualifications required. In this play, whoever the new star might be whom I invited to create or to revive the leading part, the plot, the incidents, the lines themselves preserved an unalterable form.

Within the next few days, in spite of the reluctance that Albertine had shewn from introducing me to them, I knew all the little band of that first afternoon (except Gisèle, whom, owing to a prolonged delay at the level crossing by the station and a change in the time-table, I had not succeeded in meeting on the train, which had been gone some minutes before I arrived, and to whom as it happened I never gave another thought), and two or three other girls as well to whom at my request they introduced me. And thus, my expectation of the pleasure which I should find in a new girl springing from another girl through whom I had come to know her, the latest was like one of those new varieties of rose which gardeners get by using first a rose of another kind. And as I passed from blossom to blossom along this flowery chain, the pleasure of knowing one that was different would send me back to her to whom I was indebted for it, with a gratitude in which desire was mingled fully as much as in my new expectation. Presently I was spending all my time among these girls.

Alas! in the freshest flower it is possible to discern those just perceptible signs which to the instructed mind indicate already what will be, by the desiccation or fructification of the flesh that is to-day in bloom, the ultimate form, immutable and already predestinate, of the autumnal seed. The eye rapturously follows a nose like a wavelet that deliciously curls the water's face at daybreak and seems not to move, to be capturable by the pencil, because the sea is so calm then that one does not notice its tidal flow. Human faces seem not to change while we are looking at them, because the revolution which they perform is too slow for us to perceive it. But we have only to see, by the side of any of those girls, her mother or her aunt, to realise the distance over which, obeying the gravitation of a type that is, generally speaking, deplorable, her features will have travelled in less than thirty years, and must continue to travel until the sunset hour, until her face, having vanished altogether below the horizon, catches the light no more. I knew that, as deep, as ineluctable as is their Jewish patriotism or Christian atavism in those who imagine themselves to be the most emancipated of their race, there dwelt beneath the rosy inflorescence of Albertine, Rosemonde, Andrée, unknown to themselves, held in reserve until the circumstances should arise, a coarse nose, a protruding jaw, a bust that would create a sensation when it appeared, but was actually in the wings, ready to "come on," just as it might be a burst of Dreyfusism, or clericalism, sudden, unforeseen, fatal, some patriotic, some feudal form of heroism emerging suddenly when the circumstances demand it from a nature anterior to that of the man himself, by means of which he thinks, lives, evolves, gains strength himself or dies, without ever being able to distinguish that nature from the successive phases which in turn he takes for it. Even mentally, we depend a great deal more than we think upon natural laws, and our mind possesses already, like some cryptogamous plant, every little peculiarity that we imagine ourselves to be selecting. For we can see only the derived ideas, without detecting the primary cause (Jewish blood, French birth or whatever it may be) that inevitably produced them, and which at a given moment we expose. And perhaps, while the former appear to us to be the result of deliberate thought, the latter that of an imprudent disregard for our own health, we take from our family, as the papilionaceae take the form of their seed, as well the ideas by which we live as the malady from which we shall die.

As on a plant whose flowers open at different seasons, I had seen, expressed in the form of old ladies, on this Balbec shore, those shrivelled seedpods, those flabby tubers which my friends would one day be. But what matter? For the moment it was their flowering-time. And so when Mme. de Villeparisis asked me to drive with her I sought an excuse to be prevented. I never went to see Elstir unless accompanied by my new friends. I could not even spare an afternoon to go to Doncières, to pay the visit I had promised Saint-Loup. Social engagements, serious discussions, even a friendly conversation, had they usurped the place allotted to my walks with these girls, would have had the same effect on me as if, when the luncheon bell rang, I had been taken not to a table spread with food but to turn the pages of an album. The men, the youths, the women, old or mature, whose society we suppose that we shall enjoy, are borne by us only on an unsubstantial plane surface, because we are conscious of them only by visual perception restricted to its own limits; whereas it is as delegates from our other senses that our eyes dart towards young girls; the senses follow, one after another, in search of the various charms, fragrant, tactile, savoury, which they thus enjoy even without the aid of fingers and lips; and able, thanks to the art of transposition, the genius for synthesis in which desire excels, to reconstruct beneath the hue of cheeks or bosom the feel, the taste, the contact that is forbidden them, they give to these girls the same honeyed consistency as they create when they stand rifling the sweets of a rose-garden, or before a vine whose clusters their eyes alone devour.

If it rained, although the weather had no power to daunt Albertine, who was often to be seen in her waterproof spinning on her bicycle through the driving showers, we would spend the day in the Casino, where on such days it would have seemed to me impossible not to go. I had the greatest contempt for the young Ambresacs, who had never set foot in it. And I willingly joined my friends in playing tricks on the dancing master. As a rule we had to listen to admonition from the manager, or from some of his staff, usurping dictatorial powers, because my friends, even Andrée herself, whom on that account I had regarded when I first saw her as so dionysiac a creature, whereas in reality she was delicate, intellectual, and this year far from well, in spite of which her actions were controlled less by the state of her health than by the spirit of that age which overcomes every other consideration and confounds in a general gaiety the weak with the strong, could not enter the outer hall of the rooms without starting to run, jumping over all the chairs, sliding back along the floor, their balance maintained by a graceful poise of their outstretched arms, singing the while, mingling all the arts, in that first bloom of youth, in the manner of those poets of ancient days for whom the different 'kinds' were not yet separate, so that in an epic poem they would introduce rules of agriculture with theological doctrine.

This Andrée who had struck me when I first saw them as the coldest of them all, was infinitely more refined, more loving, more sensitive than Albertine, to whom she displayed the caressing, gentle affection of an elder sister. At the Casino she would come across the floor to sit down by me, and knew instinctively, unlike Albertine, to refuse my invitation to dance, or even, if I was tired, to give up the Casino and come to me instead at the hotel. She expressed her friendship for me, for Albertine, in terms which were evidence of the most exquisite understanding of the things of the heart, which may have been partly due to the state of her health. She had always a merry smile of excuse for the childish behaviour of Albertine, who expressed with a crude violence the irresistible temptation held out to her by the parties and picnics to which she had not the sense, like Andrée, resolutely to prefer staying and talking with me. When the time came for her to go off to a luncheon party at the golf-club, if we were all three together she would get ready to leave us, then, coming up to Andrée: "Well, Andrée, what are you waiting for now? You know we are lunching at the golf-club." "No; I'm going to stay and talk to him," replied Andrée, pointing to me. "But you know, Mme. Durieux invited you," cried Albertine, as if Andrée's intention to remain with me could be explained only by ignorance on her part where else and by whom she had been bidden. "Look here, my good girl, don't be such an idiot," Andrée chid her. Albertine did not insist, fearing a suggestion that she too should stay with me. She tossed her head. "Just as you like," was her answer, uttered in the tone one uses to an invalid whose self-indulgence is killing him by inches, "I must fly; I'm sure your watch is slow," and off she went. "She is a dear girl, but quite impossible," said Andrée, bathing her friend in a smile at once caressing and critical. If in this craze for amusement Albertine might be said to echo something of the old original Gilberte, that is because a certain similarity exists, although the type evolves, between all the women we love, a similarity that is due to the fixity of our own temperament, which it is that chooses them, eliminating all those who would not be at once our opposite and our complement, fitted that is to say to gratify our senses and to wring our heart. They are, these women, a product of our temperament, an image inversely projected, a negative of our sensibility. So that a novelist might, in relating the life of his hero, describe his successive love-affairs in almost exactly similar terms, and thereby give the impression not that he was repeating himself but that he was creating, since an artificial novelty is never so effective as a repetition that manages to suggest a fresh truth. He ought, moreover, to indicate in the character of the lover a variability which becomes apparent as the story moves into fresh regions, into different latitudes of life. And perhaps he would be stating yet another truth if while investing all the other persons of his story with distinct characters he refrained from giving any to the beloved. We understand the characters of people who do not interest us; how can we ever grasp that of a person who is an intimate part of our existence, whom after a little we no longer distinguish in any way from ourselves, whose motives provide us with an inexhaustible supply of anxious hypotheses which we perpetually reconstruct. Springing from somewhere beyond our understanding, our curiosity as to the woman whom we love overleaps the bounds of that woman's character, which we might if we chose but probably will not choose to stop and examine. The object of our uneasy investigation is something more essential than those details of character comparable to the tiny particles of epidermis whose varied combinations form the florid originality of human flesh. Our intuitive radiography pierces them, and the images which it photographs for us, so far from being those of any single face, present rather the joyless universality of a skeleton.

Andrée, being herself extremely rich while the other was penniless and an orphan, with real generosity lavished on Albertine the full benefit of her wealth. As for her feelings towards Gisèle, they were not quite what I had been led to suppose. News soon reached us of the young student, and when Albertine handed round the letter she had received, a letter intended by Gisèle to give an account of her journey and to report her safe arrival to the little band, pleading laziness as an excuse for not having written yet to the rest, I was surprised to hear Andrée (for I imagined an irreparable breach between them) say: "I shall write to her to-morrow, because if I wait for her to write I may have to wait for years, she's such a slacker." And, turning to myself, she added: "You saw nothing much in her, evidently; but she's a jolly nice girl, and besides I'm really very fond of her." From which I concluded that Andrée's quarrels were apt not to last very long.

Except on these rainy days, as we had always arranged to go on our bicycles along the cliffs, or on an excursion inland, an hour or so before it was time to start I would go upstairs to make myself smart and would complain if Françoise had not laid out all the things that I wanted. Now even in Paris she would proudly, angrily straighten a back which the years had begun to bend, at the first word of reproach, she so humble, she so modest and charming when her self-esteem was flattered. As this was the main-spring of her life: her satisfaction, her good humour were in direct ratio to the difficulty of the tasks imposed on her. Those which she had to perform at Balbec were so easy that she shewed almost all the time a discontent which was suddenly multiplied an hundredfold, with the addition of an ironic air of offended dignity when I complained, on my way down to join my friends, that my hat had not been brushed or my ties sorted. She who was capable of taking such endless pains, without in consequence assuming that she had done anything at all, on my simply remarking that a coat was not in its proper place, not only did she boast of the care with which she had "put it past sooner than let it go gathering the dust," but, paying a formal tribute to her own labours, lamented that it was little enough of a holiday that she was getting at Balbec, and that we would not find another person in the whole world who would consent to put up with such treatment. "I can't think how anyone can leave things lying about the way you do; you just try and get anyone else to find what you want in such a mix-up. The devil himself would give it up as a bad job." Or else she would adopt a regal mien, scorching me with her fiery glance, and preserve a silence that was broken as soon as she had fastened the door behind her and was outside in the passage, which would then reverberate with utterances which I guessed to be insulting, though they remained as indistinct as those of characters in a play whose opening lines are spoken in the wings, before they appear on the stage. And even if nothing was missing and Françoise was in a good temper, still she made herself quite intolerable when I was getting ready to go out with my friends. For, drawing upon a store of stale witti-cisms at their expense which, in my need to be talking about the girls, I had made in her hearing, she put on an air of being about to reveal to me things of which I should have known more than she had there been any truth in her statements, which there never was, Françoise having misunderstood what she had heard. She had, like most people, her own ways; a person is never like a straight highway, but surprises us with the strange, unavoid-able windings of his course through life, by which, though some people may not notice them, we find it a perpetual annoyance to be stopped and hin-dered. Whenever I arrived at the stage of "Where is my hat?" or uttered the name of Andrée or Albertine, I was forced by Françoise to stray into endless and absurd side-tracks which greatly delayed my progress. So too when I asked her to cut me the sandwiches of cheese or salad, or sent her out for the cakes which I was to eat while we rested on the cliffs, sharing them with the girls, and which the girls "might very well have taken turns to provide, if they had not been so close," declared Françoise, to whose aid there came at such moments a whole heritage of atavistic peasant rapacity and coarseness, and for whom one would have said that the soul of her late enemy Eulalie had been broken into fragments and reincarnate, more at-tractively than it had ever been in Saint-Eloi's, in the charming bodies of my friends of the little band. I listened to these accusations with a dull fury at finding myself brought to a standstill at one of those places beyond which the well-trodden country path that was Françoise's character became impassable, though fortunately never for very long. Then, my hat or coat found and the sandwiches ready, I sailed out to find Albertine, Andrée, Rosemonde, and any others there might be, and on foot or on our bicycles we would start.

In the old days I should have preferred our excursion to be made in bad weather. For then I still looked to find in Balbec the 'Cimmerians' land,' and fine days were a thing that had no right to exist there, an intrusion of the vulgar summer of seaside holiday-makers into that ancient region swathed in eternal mist. But now, everything that I had hitherto despised, shut out of my field of vision, not only effects of sunlight upon sea and shore, but even the regattas, the race-meetings, I would have sought out with ardour, for the reason for which formerly I had wanted only stormy seas, which was that these were now associated in my mind, as the others had been, with an aesthetic idea. Because I had gone several times with my new friends to visit Elstir, and, on the days when the girls were there, what he had selected to shew us were drawings of pretty women in yachting dress, or else a sketch made on a race-course near Balbec. I had at first shyly admitted to Elstir that I had not felt inclined to go to the meetings that were being held there. "You were wrong," he told me, "it is such a pretty sight, and so well worth seeing. For one thing, that peculiar animal, the jockey, on whom so many eager eyes are fastened, who in the paddock there looks so grim, a colourless face between his brilliant jacket and cap, one body and soul with the prancing horse he rides, how interesting to analyse his professional movements, the bright splash of colour he makes, with the horse's coat blending in it, as they stream down the course. What a transformation of every visible object in that luminous vastness of a racecourse where one is constantly surprised by fresh lights and shades which one sees only there. How charming the women can look there, too! The first day's racing was quite delightful, and there were women there exquisitely dressed, in the misty light of a Dutch landscape, in which one could feel rising to cloud the sun itself the penetrating coldness of the water. Never have I seen women arriving in carriages, or standing with glasses to their eyes in so extraordinary a light, which was due, I suppose, to the moisture from the sea. I should simply have loved to paint it. I came home from the races quite mad, and so keen to get to work!" After which he became more enthusiastic still over the yacht-races, and I realised that regattas, social fixtures where well-dressed women might be seen bathed in the greenish light of a marine race-course, might be for a modern artist as interesting a subject as were the revels which they so loved to depict for a Veronese or Carpaccio. When I suggested this to Elstir, "Your comparison is all the more true," he replied, "since, from the position of the city in which they painted, those revels were to a great extent aquatic. Except that the beauty of the shipping in those days lay as a rule in its solidity, in the complication of its structure. They had water-tournaments, as we have here, held generally in honour of some Embassy, such as Carpaccio shews us in his *Legend of Saint Ursula*. The vessels were massive, built up like architecture, and seemed almost amphibious, like lesser Venices set in the heart of the greater, when, moored to the banks by hanging stages decked with crimson satin and Persian carpets, they bore their freight of ladies in cherry-red brocade and green damask close under the balconies incrusted with many-coloured marbles from which other ladies leaned to gaze at them, in gowns with black sleeves slashed with white, stitched with pearls or bordered with lace. You cannot tell where the land ends and the water begins, what is still the palace or already the vessel, the caravel, the galeas, the Bucintoro." Albertine had listened with the keenest interest to these details of costume, these visions of elegance that Elstir was describing to us. "Oh, I should so like to see that lace you speak of; it's so pretty, the Venice-point," she cried. "Besides, I should love to see Venice." "You may, perhaps, before very long, be able," Elstir informed her, "to gaze upon the marvellous stuffs which they used to wear. Hitherto one has seen them only in the works of the Venetian painters, or very rarely among the treasures of old churches, except now and then when a specimen has come into the sale-room. But I hear that a Venetian artist, called Fortuny, has recovered the secret of the craft, and that before many years have passed women will be able to walk abroad, and better still to sit at home in brocades as sumptuous as those that Venice adorned, for her patrician daughters, with patterns brought from the Orient. But I don't know that I should much care for that, that it wouldn't be too much of an anachronism for the women of to-day, even when they parade at regattas, for, to return to our modern pleasure-craft, the times have completely changed since 'Venice, Queen of the Adriatic.' The great charm of a yacht, of the furnishings of a yacht, of yachting dress, is their simplicity, as just things for the sea, and I do so love the sea. I must confess to you that I prefer the fashions of to-day to those of Veronese's and even of Carpaccio's time. What there is so attractive about our yachts—and the smaller yachts especially, I don't like the huge ones, they're too much like ships; yachts are like women's hats, you must keep within certain limits—is the unbroken surface, simple, gleaming, grey, which under a cloudy, leaden sky takes on a creamy softness. The cabin in which we live ought to make us think of a little café. And women's clothes on board a yacht are the same sort of thing; what really are charming are those light garments, uniformly white, of cloth or linen or nankeen or drill, which in the sunlight and against the blue of the sea shew up with as dazzling a whiteness as a spread sail. You very seldom see a woman, for that matter, who knows how to dress, and yet some of them are quite wonderful. At the races, Mlle. Léa had a little white hat and a little white sunshade, simply enchanting. I don't know what I wouldn't give for that little sunshade." I should have liked very much to know in what respect this little sunshade differed from any other, and for other reasons, reasons of feminine vanity, Albertine was still more curious. But, just as Françoise used to explain the excellence of her *soufflés* by "It's the way you do them," so here the difference lay in the cut. "It was," Elstir explained, "quite tiny, quite round, like a Chinese umbrella." I mentioned the sunshades carried by various ladies, but it was not like any of them. Elstir found them all quite hideous. A man of exquisite taste, singularly hard to please, he would isolate some minute detail which was the whole difference between what was worn by three-quarters of the women he saw, and horrified him, and a thing which enchanted him by its prettiness; and—in contrast to its effect on myself, whose mind any display of luxury at once sterilised—stimulated his desire to paint "so as to make something as attractive." "Here you see a young lady who has guessed what the hat and sunshade were like," he said to me, pointing to Albertine whose eyes shone with envy. "How I should love to be rich, to have a yacht!" she said to the painter. "I should come to you to tell me how to run it. What lovely trips I'd take. And what fun it would be to go to Cowes for the races. And a motor-car! Tell me, do you think the ladies' fashions for motoring pretty?" "No"; replied Elstir, "but that will come in time. You see, there are very few firms at present, one or two only, Callot—although they go in rather too freely for lace— Doucet, Cheruit, Paquin sometimes. The others are all horrible." "Then, is there a vast difference between a Callot dress and one from any ordinary shop?" I asked Albertine. "Why, an enormous difference, my little man! I beg your pardon! Only, alas! what you get for three hundred francs in an ordinary shop will cost two thousand there. But there can be no comparison; they look the same only to people who know nothing at all about it." "Quite so," put in Elstir; "though I should not go so far as to say that it is as profound as the difference between a statue from Rheims Cathedral and one from Saint-Augustin. By the way, talking of cathedrals," he went on, addressing himself exclusively to me, because what he was saying had reference to an earlier conversation in which the girls had not taken part, and which for that matter would not have interested them at all, "I spoke to you the other day of Balbec Church as a great cliff, a huge breakwater built of the stone of the country; now look at this"; he handed me a water-colour. "Look at these cliffs (it's a sketch I did close to here, at the Creuniers); don't these rocks remind you of a cathedral?" And indeed one would have taken them for soaring red arches. But, painted on a roasting hot day, they seemed to have crumbled into dust, made volatile by the heat which had drunk up half the sea, distilled over the whole surface of the picture almost into a gaseous state. On this day on which the sunlight had, so to speak, destroyed reality, reality concentrated itself in certain dusky and transparent creatures which, by contrast, gave a more striking, a closer impression of life: the shadows. Ravening after coolness, most of them, deserting the scorched open spaces, had fled for shelter to the foot of the rocks, out of reach of the sun; others, swimming gently upon the tide, like dolphins, kept close under the sides of the moving vessels, whose hulls they extended upon the pale surface of the water with their glossy blue forms. It was perhaps the thirst for coolness which they conveyed that did most to give me the sensation of the heat of this day and made me exclaim how much I regretted not knowing the Creuniers. Albertine and Andrée were positive that I must have been there hundreds of times. If so I had been there without knowing it, never suspecting that one day the sight of these rocks was to inspire me with such a thirst for beauty, not perhaps exactly natural beauty such as I had been seeking hitherto among the cliffs of Balbec, but rather architectural. Above all, I who, having come here to visit the kingdom of the storm, had never found, on any of my drives with Mme. de Villeparisis, when often we saw it only from afar, painted in a gap between the trees, the ocean sufficiently real, sufficiently liquid, giving a sufficient impression that it was hurling its massed forces against the shore, and would have liked to see it lie motionless only under a wintry shroud of fog, I could never have believed that I should now be dreaming of a sea which was nothing more than a whitish vapour that had lost both consistency and colour. But of such a sea Elstir, like the people who sat musing on board those vessels drowsy with the heat, had so intensely felt the enchantment that he had succeeded in transcribing, in fixing for all time upon the painted sheet the imperceptible reflux of the tide, the throb of one happy moment; and one suddenly became so enamoured, at the sight of this magic portrait, that one could think of nothing else than to range the world over, seeking to recapture the vanished day in its instantaneous, slumbering beauty.

So that if before these visits to Elstir, before I had set eyes on one of his sea-pictures in which a young woman in a dress of white serge or linen, on the deck of a yacht flying the American flag, had duplicated a white linen dress and coloured flag in my imagination which at once bred in me an insatiable desire to visit the spot and see there with my own eyes white linen dresses and flags against the sea, as though no such experience had ever yet befallen me, always until then I had taken care when I stood by the sea to expel from my field of vision, as well as the bathers in the fore-ground, the yachts with their too dazzling sails that were like seaside cos-tumes, everything that prevented me from persuading myself that I was contemplating the immemorial flood of ocean which had been moving with the same mysterious life before the appearance of the human race; and had grudged even the days of radiant sunshine which seemed to me to invest with the trivial aspect of the world's universal summer this coast of fog and tempest, to mark simply an interruption, equivalent to what in music is known as a rest; now on the other hand it was the bad days that appeared to me to be some disastrous accident, a thing that could no longer find any place for itself in the world of beauty; I felt a keen desire to go out and recapture in reality what had so powerfully aroused my imagination, and I hoped that the weather would be propitious enough for me to see from the summit of the cliff the same blue shadows as were in Elstir's picture.

Nor, as I went along, did I still make a frame about my eyes with my hands as in the days when, conceiving nature to be animated by a life an-terior to the first appearance of man, and inconsistent with all those wearisome perfections of industrial achievement which had hitherto made me yawn with boredom at Universal Exhibitions or in the milliners' win-dows, I endeavoured to include only that section of the sea over which there was no steamer passing, so that I might picture it to myself as im-memorial, still contemporary with the ages in which it had been set apart from the land, or at least with the first dawn of life in Greece, which en-abled me to repeat in their literal meaning the lines of 'Father Leconte' of which Bloch was so fond:

'Gone are the Kings, gone are their towering prows,
Vanished upon the raging deep, alas,
The long-haired warrior heroes of Hellas.'

I could no longer despise the milliners, now that Elstir had told me that
the delicate touches by which they give a last refinement, a supreme caress
to the ribbons or feathers of a hat after it is finished, would be as interesting
to him to paint as the muscular action of the jockeys themselves (a statement which had delighted Albertine). But I must wait until I had returned
—for milliners, to Paris—for regattas and races to Balbec, where there
would be no more now until next year. Even a yacht with women in white
linen garments was not to be found.

Often we encountered Bloch's sisters, to whom I was obliged to bow
since I had dined with their father. My new friends did not know them. "I
am not allowed to play with Israelites," Albertine explained. Her way of
pronouncing the word—'Issraelites' instead of 'Izraelites'—would in itself
have sufficed to shew, even if one had not heard the rest of the sentence,
that it was no feeling of friendliness towards the chosen race that inspired
these young Frenchwomen, brought up in God-fearing homes, and quite
ready to believe that the Jews were in the habit of massacring Christian
children. "Besides, they're shocking bad form, your friends," said Andrée
with a smile which implied that she knew very well that they were no friends
of mine. "Like everything to do with the tribe," went on Albertine, in the
sententious tone of one who spoke from personal experience. To tell the
truth, Bloch's sisters, at once overdressed and half naked, with their languishing, bold, blatant, sluttish air did not create the best impression. And
one of their cousins, who was only fifteen, scandalised the Casino by her
unconcealed admiration for Mlle. Léa, whose talent as an actress M. Bloch
senior rated very high, but whose tastes were understood to lead her not
exactly in the direction of the gentlemen.

Some days we took our refreshment at one of the outlying farms which
catered to visitors. These were the farms known as Les Ecorres, Marie-
Thérèse, La Croix d'Heuland, Bagatelle, Californie and Marie-Antoinette.
It was the last that had been adopted by the little band.

But at other times, instead of going to a farm, we would climb to the highest point of the cliff, and, when we had reached it and were seated on the
grass, would undo our parcel of sandwiches and cakes. My friends preferred
the sandwiches, and were surprised to see me eat only a single chocolate
cake, sugared with gothic tracery, or an apricot tart. This was because, with
the sandwiches of cheese or of green-stuff, a form of food that was novel to
me and knew nothing of the past, I had nothing in common. But the cakes
understood, the tarts were gossips. There were in the former an insipid taste
of cream, in the latter a fresh taste of fruit which knew all about Combray,
and about Gilberte, not only the Gilberte of Combray but her too of Paris,
at whose tea-parties I had found them again. They reminded me of those
cake-plates of the Arabian Nights pattern, the subjects on which were such
a distraction to my aunt Léonie when Françoise brought her up, one day,
Aladdin or the Wonderful Lamp, another day Ali-Baba, or the Sleeper

Awakes, or Sinbad the Sailor embarking at Bassorah with all his treasure.
I should dearly have liked to see them again, but my grandmother did not
know what had become of them, and thought moreover that they were
just common plates that had been bought in the village. No matter, in that
grey, midland Combray scene they and their pictures were set like many-
coloured jewels, as in the dark church were the windows with their shifting
radiance, as in the dusk of my bedroom were the projections cast by the
magic-lantern, as in the foreground of the view of the railway-station and
the little local line the buttercups from the Indies and the Persian lilacs,
as were my great-aunt's shelves of old porcelain in the sombre dwelling of
an elderly lady in a country town.

Stretched out on the cliff I would see before me nothing but grassy
meadows and beyond them not the seven heavens of the Christian cos-
mogony but two stages only, one of a deeper blue, the sea, and over it
another more pale. We ate our food, and if I had brought with me also some
little keepsake which might appeal to one or other of my friends, joy sprang
with such sudden violence into her translucent face, flushed in an instant,
that her lips had not the strength to hold it in, and to allow it to escape
parted in a shout of laughter. They had gathered close round me, and between their faces which were almost touching one another the air that
separated them traced azure pathways such as might have been cut by a
gardener wishing to clear the ground a little so as to be able himself to move
freely through a thicket of roses.

When we had finished eating we would play games which until then I
should have thought boring, sometimes such childish games as King of the
Castle, or Who Laughs First; not for a kingdom would I have renounced
them now; the rosy dawn of adolescence, with which the faces of these
girls were still aglow, and from which I, young as I was, had already
emerged, shed its light on everything round about them and, like the fluid
painting of some of the Primitives, brought out the most insignificant details of their daily lives in relief against a golden background. Even the faces
of the girls were, for the most part, clouded with this misty effulgence of a
dawn from which their actual features had not yet emerged. One saw only
a charming sheet of colour beneath which what in a few years' time would
be a profile was not discernible. The profile of to-day had nothing definite
about it, and could be only a momentary resemblance to some deceased
member of the family to whom nature had paid this commemorative courtesy. It comes so soon, the moment when there is nothing left to wait for,
when the body is fixed in an immobility which holds no fresh surprise in
store, when one loses all hope on seeing—as on a tree in the height of summer leaves already brown—round a face still young hair that is growing
thin or turning grey; it is so short, that radiant morning time that one comes
to like only the very youngest girls, those in whom the flesh, like a precious
leaven, is still at work. They are no more yet than a stream of ductile matter, moulded ever afresh by the fleeting impression of the moment. You
would say that each of them was in turn a little statuette of childish gaiety,
of a child grown earnest, coaxing, surprised, taking its pattern from an
expression frank and complete, but fugitive. This plasticity gives a wealth

of variety and charm to the pretty attentions which a little girl pays to us. Of course, such attentions are indispensable in the woman also, and she whom we do not attract, or who fails to let us see that we have attracted her, tends to assume in our eyes a somewhat tedious uniformity. But even these pretty attentions, after a certain age, cease to send gentle ripples over a face which the struggle for existence has hardened, has rendered unalterably militant or ecstatic. One—owing to the prolonged strain of the obedience that subjects wife to husband—will seem not so much a woman's face as a soldier's; another, carved by the sacrifices which a mother has consented to make, day after day, for her children, will be the face of an apostle. A third is, after a stormy passage through the years, the face of an ancient mariner, upon a body of which its garments alone indicate the sex. Certainly the attentions that a woman pays us can still, so long as we are in love with her, scatter fresh charms over the hours that we spend in her company. But she is not then for us a series of different women. Her gaiety remains external to an unchanging face. Whereas adolescence is anterior to this complete solidification; and from this it follows that we feel, in the company of young girls, the refreshing sense that is afforded us by the spectacle of forms undergoing an incessant process of change, a play of unstable forces which makes us think of that perpetual re-creation of the primordial elements of nature which we contemplate when we stand by the sea.

It was not merely a social engagement, a drive with Mme. de Villeparisis, that I would have sacrificed to the 'Ferret' or 'Guessing Games' of my friends. More than once, Robert de Saint-Loup had sent word that, since I was not coming to see him at Doncières, he had applied for twenty-four hours' leave, which he would spend at Balbec. Each time I wrote back that he was on no account to come, offering the excuse that I should be obliged to be away myself that very day, when I had some duty call to pay with my grandmother on family friends in the neighbourhood. No doubt I fell in his estimation when he learned from his aunt in what the 'duty call' consisted, and who the persons were who combined to play the part of my grandmother. And yet I had not been wrong, perhaps, after all, in sacrificing not only the vain pleasures of the world but the real pleasure of friendship to that of spending the whole day in this green garden. People who enjoy the capacity—it is true that such people are artists, and I had long been convinced that I should never be that—are also under an obligation to live for themselves. And friendship is a dispensation from this duty, an abdication of self. Even conversation, which is the mode of expression of friendship, is a superficial digression which gives us no new acquisition. We may talk for a lifetime without doing more than indefinitely repeat the vacuity of a minute, whereas the march of thought in the solitary travail of artistic creation proceeds downwards, into the depths, in the only direction that is not closed to us, along which we are free to advance—though with more effort, it is true—towards a goal of truth. And friendship is not merely devoid of virtue, like conversation, it is fatal to us as well. For the sense of boredom which it is impossible not to feel in a friend's company (when, that is to say, we must remain exposed on the surface of our consciousness, instead of pursuing our voyage of discovery into the depths) for those of

us in whom the law of development is purely internal—that first impression
of boredom our friendship impels us to correct when we are alone again,
to recall with emotion the words uttered by our friend, to look upon them
as a valuable addition to our substance, albeit we are not like buildings to
which stones can be added from without, but like trees which draw from
their own sap the knot that duly appears on their trunks, the spreading
roof of their foliage. I was lying to myself, I was interrupting the process
of growth in that direction in which I could indeed really be enlarged and
made happy, when I congratulated myself on being liked, admired, by so
good, so clever, so rare a creature as Saint-Loup, when I focussed my mind,
not upon my own obscure impressions which duty bade me unravel, but
on the words uttered by my friend, in which, when I repeated them to
myself—when I had them repeated to me by that other self who dwells in
us and on to whom we are always so ready to transfer the burden of taking
thought,—I strove to make myself find a beauty very different from that
which I used to pursue in silence when I was really alone, but one that
would enhance the merit of Robert, of myself, of my life. In the life which
a friend like this provided for me, I seemed to myself to be comfortably
preserved from solitude, nobly desirous of sacrificing myself for him, in fact
quite incapable of realising myself. Among the girls, on the other hand, if
the pleasure which I enjoyed was selfish, at least it was not based on the
lie which seeks to make us believe that we are not irremediably alone, and
which, when we talk to another person, prevents us from admitting that
it is no longer we who speak, that we are fashioning ourselves in the likeness
of strangers and not of our own ego, which is quite different from them. The
words that passed between the girls of the little band and myself were not of
any interest; they were, moreover, but few, broken by long spells of silence
on my part. All of which did not prevent me from finding, in listening to
them when they spoke to me, as much pleasure as in gazing at them, in
discovering in the voice of each one of them a brightly coloured picture. It
was with ecstasy that I caught their pipings. Love helps us to discern things,
to discriminate. Standing in a wood, the lover of birds at once distinguishes
the notes of the different species, which to ordinary people sound the same.
The lover of girls knows that human voices vary even more. Each one
possesses more notes than the richest instrument of music. And the combinations in which the voice groups those notes are as inexhaustible as the
infinite variety of personalities. When I talked with any one of my friends
I was conscious that the original, the unique portrait of her individuality
had been skilfully traced, tyranically imposed on my mind as much by the
inflexions of her voice as by those of her face, and that these were two separate spectacles which rendered, each in its own plane, the same single
reality. No doubt the lines of the voice, like those of the face, were not yet
definitely fixed; the voice had still to break, as the face to change. Just as
children have a gland the secretion in which enables them to digest milk, a
gland which is not found in grown men and women, so there were in the
twitterings of these girls notes which women's voices no longer contain.
And on this instrument with its greater compass they played with their lips,
shewing all the application, the ardour of Bellini's little angel musicians,

qualities which also are an exclusive appanage of youth. Later on these girls would lose that note of enthusiastic conviction which gave a charm to their simplest utterances, whether it were Albertine who, in a tone of authority, repeated puns to which the younger ones listened with admiration, until that wild impulse to laugh caught them all with the irresistible violence of a sneeze, or Andrée who began to speak of their work in the schoolroom, work even more childish seemingly than the games they played, with a gravity essentially puerile; and their words changed in tone, like the lyrics of ancient times when poetry, still hardly differentiated from music, was declaimed upon the different notes of a scale. In spite of which, the girls' voices already gave a quite clear indication of the attitude that each of these little people had adopted towards life, an attitude so personal that it would be speaking in far too general terms to say of one: "She treats everything as a joke," of another: "She jumps from assertion to assertion," of a third: "She lives in a state of expectant hesitation." The features of our face are hardly more than gestures which force of habit has made permanent. Nature, like the destruction of Pompeii, like the metamorphosis of a nymph into a tree, has arrested us in an accustomed movement. Similarly, our intonations embody our philosophy of life, what a person says to himself about things at any given moment. No doubt these peculiarities were to be found not only in the girls. They were those of their parents. The individual is a part of something that is more generally diffused than himself. By this reckoning, our parents furnish us not only with those habitual gestures which are the outlines of our face and voice, but also with certain mannerisms in speech, certain favourite expressions, which, almost as unconscious as an intonation, almost as profound, indicate likewise a definite point of view towards life. It is quite true, since we are speaking of girls, that there are certain of these expressions which their parents do not hand on to them until they have reached a certain age, as a rule not before they are women. These are kept in reserve. Thus, for instance, if you were to speak of the pictures of one of Elstir's friends, Andrée, whose hair was still 'down,' could not yet make use, personally, of the expression which her mother and elder sister employed: "It appears, the man is quite charming!" But that would come in due course, when she was allowed to go to the Palais-Royal. And already, since her first communion, Albertine had begun to say, like a friend of her aunt: "I'm sure I should find that simply terrible!" She had also had given to her, as a little present, the habit of repeating whatever you had just been saying to her, so as to appear to be interested, and to be trying to form an opinion of her own. If you said that an artist's work was good, or his house nice, "Oh, his work is good, is it?" "Oh, his house is nice, is it?" Last of all, and even more general than the family heritage, was the rich layer imposed by the native province from which they derived their voices and of which indeed their intonations smacked. When Andrée sharply struck a solemn note she could not prevent the Perigordian string of her vocal instrument from giving back a resonant sound quite in harmony, moreover, with the Meridional purity of her features; while to the incessant pranks of Rosemonde the substance of her North-Country face and voice responded, whatever her mood at the time, in the accent of their province. Between that province and the temperament of the little girl who dictated these inflexions, I caught a charming dialogue. A dialogue, not in any sense a discord. It would not have been possible to separate the girl herself and her native place. She was herself; she was still it also. Moreover this reaction of locally procured materials on the genius who utilises them and to whose work their reaction imparts an added freshness, does not make the work any less individual, and whether it be that of an architect, a cabinet-maker or a composer, it reflects no less minutely the most subtle shades of the artist's personality, because he has been compelled to work in the millstone of Senlis or the red sandstone of Strasbourg, has respected the knots peculiar to the ash-tree, has borne in mind, when writing his score, the resources, the limitations, the volume of sound, the possibilities of flute or alto voice.

All this I realised, and yet we talked so little. Whereas with Mme. de Villeparisis or Saint-Loup I should have displayed by my words a great deal more pleasure than I should actually have felt, for I used always to be worn out when I parted from them; when, on the other hand, I was lying on the grass among all these girls, the plenitude of what I was feeling infinitely outweighed the paucity, the infrequency of our speech, and brimmed over from my immobility and silence in floods of happiness, the waves of which rippled up to die at the feet of these young roses.

For a convalescent who rests all day long in a flower-garden or orchard, a scent of flowers or fruit does not more completely pervade the thousand trifles that compose his idle hours than did for me that colour, that fragrance in search of which my eyes kept straying towards the girls, and the sweetness of which finally became incorporated in me. So it is that grapes grow sugary in sunshine. And by their slow continuity these simple little games had gradually wrought in me also, as in those who do nothing else all day but lie outstretched by the sea, breathing the salt air and growing sunburned, a relaxation, a blissful smile, a vague sense of dizziness that had spread from brain to eyes.

Now and then a pretty attention from one or another of them would stir in me vibrations which dissipated for a time my desire for the rest. Thus one day Albertine had suddenly asked: "Who has a pencil?" Andrée had provided one, Rosemonde the paper; Albertine had warned them: "Now, young ladies, you are not to look at what I write." After carefully tracing each letter, supporting the paper on her knee, she had passed it to me with: "Take care no one sees." Whereupon I had unfolded it and read her message, which was: "I love you."

"But we mustn't sit here scribbling nonsense," she cried, turning impetuously, with a sudden gravity of demeanour, to Andrée and Rosemonde. "I ought to shew you the letter I got from Gisèle this morning. What an idiot I am; I've had it all this time in my pocket—and you can't think how important it may be to us." Gisèle had been moved to copy out for her friend, so that it might be passed on to the others, the essay which she had written in her certificate examination. Albertine's fears as to the difficulty of the subjects set had been more than justified by the two from which Gisèle had had to choose. The first was: "Sophocles, from the Shades, writes

to Racine to console him for the failure of *Athalie*"; the other: "Suppose
that, after the first performance of *Esther*, Mme. de Sévigné is writing to
Mme. de La Fayette to tell her how much she regretted her absence." Now
Gisèle, in an excess of zeal which ought to have touched the examiners'
hearts, had chosen the former, which was also the more difficult of the two
subjects, and had handled it with such remarkable skill that she had been
given fourteen marks, and had been congratulated by the board. She would
have received her 'mention' if she had not 'dried up' in the Spanish paper.
The essay, a copy of which Gisèle had now sent her, was immediately read
aloud to us by Albertine, for, having presently to pass the same examination,
she was anxious to have an opinion from Andrée, who was by far the
cleverest of them all and might be able to give her some good 'tips.' "She
did have a bit of luck!" was Albertine's comment. "It's the very subject her
French mistress made her swot up while she was here." The letter from
Sophocles to Racine, as drafted by Gisèle, ran as follows: "My dear friend,
You must pardon me the liberty of addressing you when I have not the
honour of your personal acquaintance, but your latest tragedy, *Athalie*,
shews, does it not, that you have made the most thorough study of my own
modest works. You have not only put poetry in the mouths of the pro-
tagonists, or principal persons of the drama, but you have written other,
and, let me tell you without flattery, charming verses for the choruses, a
feature which was not too bad, according to all one hears, in Greek Tragedy,
but is a complete novelty in France. Nay more, your talent always so
fluent, so finished, so winning, so fine, so delicate, has here acquired an
energy on which I congratulate you. Athalie, Joad—these are figures which
your rival Corneille could have wrought no better. The characters are
virile, the plot simple and strong. You have given us a tragedy in which
love is not the keynote, and on this I must offer you my sincerest compliments. The most familiar proverbs are not always the truest. I will give
you an example:

'This passion treat, which makes the poet's art
Fly, as on wings, straight to the listener's heart.'

You have shewn us that the religious sentiment in which your choruses are
steeped is no less capable of moving us. The general public may have been
puzzled at first, but those who are best qualified to judge must give you
your due. I have felt myself impelled to offer you all my congratulations,
to which I would add, my dear brother poet, an expression of my very
highest esteem." Albertine's eyes, while she was reading this to us, had not
ceased to sparkle. "Really, you'd think she must have cribbed it somewhere!" she exclaimed, as she reached the end. "I should never have believed that Gisèle could hatch out anything like as good! And the poetry
she brings in! Where on earth can she have got that from?" Albertine's
admiration, with a change, it is true, of object, but with no loss—an increase, rather—of intensity, combined with the closest attention to what
was being said, continued to make her eyes 'start from her head' all the
time that Andrée (consulted as being the biggest of the band and more
knowledgeable than the others) first of all spoke of Gisèle's essay with a

certain irony, then with a levity of tone which failed to conceal her under-lying seriousness proceeded to reconstruct the letter in her own way. "It is not badly done," she told Albertine, "but if I were you and had the same subject set me, which is quite likely, as they do very often set that, I shouldn't do it in that way. This is how I would tackle it. Well, first of all, if I had been Gisèle, I should not have let myself get tied up, I should have begun by making a rough sketch of what I was going to write on a separate piece of paper. On the top line I should state the question and give an account of the subject, then the general ideas to be worked into the de-velopment. After that, appreciation, style, conclusion. In that way, with a summary to refer to, you know where you are. But at the very start, where she begins her account of the subject, or, if you like, Titine, since it's a letter we're speaking of, where she comes to the matter, Gisèle has gone off the rails altogether. Writing to a person of the seventeenth century, Sophocles ought never to have said, 'My dear friend.' " "Why, of course, she ought to have said, 'My dear Racine,' " came impetuously from Al-bertine. "That would have been much better." "No," replied Andrée, with a trace of mockery in her tone, "she ought to have put 'Sir.' In the same way, to end up, she ought to have thought of something like, 'Suffer me, Sir,' (at the very most, 'Dear Sir') to inform you of the sense of high es-teem with which I have the honour to be your servant.' Then again, Gisèle says that the choruses in *Athalie* are a novelty. She is forgetting *Esther*, and two tragedies that are not much read now but happen to have been analysed this year by the Professor himself, so that you need only mention them, since he's got them on the brain, and you're bound to pass. I mean *Les Juives*, by Robert Garnier, and Montchrestien's *L'Aman*." Andrée quoted these titles without managing quite to conceal a secret sense of benevolent superiority, which found expression in a smile, quite a delight-ful smile, for that matter. Albertine could contain herself no longer. "Andrée, you really are a perfect marvel," she cried. "You must write down those names for me. Just fancy, what luck it would be if I got on to that, even in the oral, I should bring them in at once and make a colossal impres-sion." But in the days that followed, every time that Albertine begged Andrée just to tell her again the names of those two plays so that she might write them down, her blue-stocking friend seemed most unfortunately to have forgotten them, and left her none the wiser. "And another thing," Andrée went on with the faintest note in her voice of scorn for companions so much younger than herself, though she relished their admiration and attached to the manner in which she herself would have composed the essay a greater importance than she wanted us to think, "Sophocles in the Shades must be kept well-informed of all that goes on. He must know, therefore, that it was not before the general public but before the King's Majesty and a few privileged courtiers that *Athalie* was first played. What Gisèle says in this connexion of the esteem of qualified judges is not at all bad, but she might have gone a little further. Sophocles, now that he is im-mortal, might quite well have the gift of prophecy and announce that, according to Voltaire, *Athalie* is to be the supreme achievement not of Racine merely but of the human mind." Albertine was drinking in every word. Her eyes blazed. And it was with the utmost indignation that she rejected Rosemonde's suggestion that they should begin to play. "And so," Andrée concluded, in the same easy, detached tone, blending a faint sneer with a certain warmth of conviction, "if Gisèle had noted down properly, first of all, the general ideas that she was going to develop, it might perhaps have occurred to her to do what I myself should have done, point out what a difference there is between the religious inspiration of Sophocles's choruses and Racine's. I should have made Sophocles remark that if Racine's choruses are instinct with religious feeling like those of the Greek Trage-dians, the gods are not the same. The God of Joad has nothing in com-mon with the god of Sophocles. And that brings us quite naturally, when we have finished developing the subject, to our conclusion: What does it matter if their beliefs are different? Sophocles would hesitate to insist upon such a point. He would be afraid of wounding Racine's convic-tions, and so, slipping in a few appropriate words on his masters at Port-Royal, he prefers to congratulate his disciple on the loftiness of his poetic genius."

Admiration and attention had so heated Albertine that great drops were rolling down her cheeks. Andrée preserved the unruffled calm of a female dandy. "It would not be a bad thing either to quote some of the opinions of famous critics," she added, before they began their game. "Yes," put in Albertine, "so I've been told. The best ones to quote, on the whole, are Sainte-Beuve and Merlet, aren't they?" "Well, you're not absolutely wrong," Andrée told her, "Merlet and Sainte-Beuve are by no means bad. But you certainly ought to mention Deltour and Gascq-Desfossés." She refused, however, despite Albertine's entreaties, to write down these two unfamiliar names.

Meanwhile I had been thinking of the little page torn from a scribbling block which Albertine had handed me. "I love you," she had written. And an hour later, as I scrambled down the paths which led back, a little too vertically for my liking, to Balbec, I said to myself that it was with her that I would have my romance.

The state of being indicated by the presence of all the signs by which we are accustomed to recognise that we are in love, such as the orders which I left in the hotel not to awaken me whoever might ask to see me, unless it were one or other of the girls, the beating of my heart while I waited for her (whichever of them it might be that I was expecting) and on those mornings my fury if I had not succeeded in finding a barber to shave me, and must appear with the disfigurement of a hairy chin before Albertine, Rosemonde or Andrée, no doubt this state, recurring indifferently at the thought of one or another, was as different from what we call love as is from human life the life of the zoophytes, where an existence, an indi-viduality, if we may term it, is divided up among several organisms. But natural history teaches us that such an organization of animal life is indeed to be observed, and that our own life, provided only that we have outgrown the first phase, is no less positive as to the reality of states hitherto unsus-pected by us, through which we have to pass, and can then abandon them altogether. Such was for me this state of love divided among several girls at once. Divided—say rather undivided, for more often than not what was so delicious to me, different from the rest of the world, what was beginning to become so precious to me that the hope of finding it again on the morrow was the greatest happiness in my life, was rather the whole of the group of girls, taken as they were all together on those afternoons on the cliffs, during those lifeless hours, upon that strip of grass on which were laid those forms, so exciting to my imagination, of Albertine, Rosemonde, Andrée; and that without my being able to say which of them it was that made those scenes so precious to me, which of them I was most anxious to love. At the start of a new love as at its ending, we are not exclusively attached to the object of that love, but rather the desire to be loving from which it will presently emerge (and, later on, the memory which it leaves behind) wanders voluptuously through a zone of interchangeable charms —simply natural charms, it may be, gratification of appetite, enjoyment of one's surroundings—which are so far harmonised among themselves that it does not in the presence of any one of them feel itself out of place. Besides, as my perception of them was not yet dulled by familiarity, I had still the faculty of seeing them, that is to say of feeling a profound astonishment every time that I found myself in their presence. No doubt this astonishment is to some extent due to the fact that the other person on such occasions presents himself in a fresh aspect; but so great is the multiformity of each of us, so abundant the wealth of lines of face and body, lines so few of which leave any trace, once we have parted from the other person, on the arbitrary simplicity of our memory. As our mind has selected some peculiarity that had struck us, has isolated it, exaggerated it, making of a woman who has appeared to us tall, a sketch in which her figure is absurdly elongated, or of a woman who has seemed to be pink-cheeked and golden-haired a pure 'Harmony in pink and gold,' so, the moment that woman is once again standing before us, all the other forgotten qualities which restore the balance of that one remembered feature at once assail us, in their confused complexity, diminishing her height, paling her cheeks, and substituting for what we have come to her solely to seek other peculiarities which we remember now that we did notice the first time, and fail to understand how we can so far have forgotten to look out for again. We thought we remembered; it was a peahen, surely; we go to see it and find a peony. And this inevitable astonishment is not the only one; for, side by side with it comes another, born of the difference, not now between the stereotyped forms of memory and reality, but between the person whom we saw last time and him who appears to us to-day from another angle and shews us another aspect. The human face is indeed, like the face of the God of some Oriental theogony, a whole cluster of faces, crowded together but on different surfaces so that one does not see them all at once.

But to a great extent our astonishment springs from the other person's presenting to us also a face that is the same as before. It would require so immense an effort to reconstruct everything that has been imparted to us by things other than ourselves—were it only the taste of a fruit—that no sooner is the impression received than we begin imperceptibly to descend the slope of memory and, without noticing anything, in a very short time,

we have come a long way from what we actually felt. So that every fresh
encounter is a sort of rectification, which brings us back to what we really
did see. We have no longer any recollection of this, to such an extent does
what we call remembering a person consist really in forgetting him. But so
long as we can still see at the moment when the forgotten aspect appears,
we recognise it, we are obliged to correct the straying line; thus the perpetual and fruitful surprise which made so salutary and invigorating for me
these daily outings with the charming damsels of the sea shore, consisted
fully as much in recognition as in discovery. When there is added to this the
agitation aroused by what these girls were to me, which was never quite
what I had supposed, and meant that my expectancy of our next meeting
resembled not so much my expectancy the time before as the still throbbing
memory of our latest conversation, it will be realised that each of our excursions made a violent interruption in the course of my thoughts and moved
them clean out of the direction which, in the solitude of my own room, I had
been able to trace for them at my leisure. That plotted course was forgotten,
had ceased to exist, when I returned home buzzing like a hive of bees with
remarks which had disquieted me when I heard them and were still echoing
in my brain. The other person is destroyed when we cease to see him; after
which his next appearance means a fresh creation of him, different from
that which immediately preceded it, if not from them all. For the minimum variation that is to be found in these creations is duality. If we have
in mind a strong and searching glance, a bold manner, it is inevitably, next
time, by a half-languid profile, a sort of dreamy gentleness, overlooked by
us in our previous impression, that we shall be, on meeting him again, astonished, that is to say almost solely struck. In confronting our memory with
the new reality it is this that will mark the extent of our disappointment or
surprise, will appear to us like the revised version of an earlier reality
warning us that we had not remembered it correctly. In its turn, the facial
aspect neglected the time before, and for that very reason the most striking
this time, the most real, the most documentary, will become a matter for
dreams and memories. It is a languorous and rounded profile, a gentle,
dreamy expression which we shall now desire to see again. And then, next
time, such resolution, such strength of character as there may be in the
piercing eyes, the pointed nose, the tight lips, will come to correct the discrepancy between our desire and the object to which it has supposed itself
to correspond. It is understood, of course, that this loyalty to the first and
purely physical impressions which I formed afresh at each encounter with
my friends did not involve only their facial appearance, since the reader
has seen that I was sensible also of their voices, more disquieting still, perhaps (for not only does a voice offer the same strange and sensuous surfaces as a face, it issues from that unknown, inaccessible region the mere
thought of which sets the mind swimming with unattainable kisses), their
voices each like the unique sound of a little instrument into which the player
put all her artistry and which was found only in her possession. Traced by
a casual inflexion, a sudden deep chord in one of their voices would astonish
me when I recognised after having forgotten it. So much so that the cor-
rections which after every fresh meeting I was obliged to make so as to

ensure absolute accuracy were as much those of a tuner or singing-master
as a draughtsman's.

As for the harmonious cohesion in which had been neutralised for some
time, by the resistance that each brought to bear against the expansion of
the others, the several waves of sentiment set in motion in me by these
girls, it was broken in Albertine's favour one afternoon when we were
playing the game of 'ferret.' It was in a little wood on the cliff. Stationed
between two girls, strangers to the little band, whom the band had brought
in its train because we wanted that day to have a bigger party than usual, I
gazed enviously at Albertine's neighbour, a young man, saying to myself
that if I had been in his place I could have been touching my friend's hands
all those miraculous moments which might perhaps never recur, and that
this would have been but the first stage in a great advance. Already, by
itself, and even without the consequences which it would probably have
involved, the contact of Albertine's hands would have been delicious to me.
Not that I had never seen prettier hands than hers. Even in the group of
her friends, those of Andrée, slender hands and much more finely modelled,
had as it were a private life of their own, obedient to the commands of
their mistress, but independent, and used often to strain out before her
like a leash of thoroughbred greyhounds, with lazy pauses, long dreams,
sudden stretchings of a joint, seeing which Elstir had made a number of
studies of these hands. And in one of them, in which you saw Andrée
warming her hands at the fire, they had, with the light behind them, the
gilded transparency of two autumn leaves. But, plumper than these, the
hands of Albertine would yield for a moment, then resist the pressure of
the hand that clasped them, giving a sensation that was quite peculiar to
themselves. The act of pressing Albertine's hand had a sensual sweetness
which was in keeping somehow with the rosy, almost mauve colouring of
her skin. That pressure seemed to allow you to penetrate into the girl's
being, to plumb the depths of her senses, like the ringing sound of her
laughter, indecent as may be the cooing of doves or certain animal cries.
She was the sort of woman with whom shaking hands affords so much
pleasure that one feels grateful to civilisation for having made of the hand-
clasp a lawful act between young men and girls when they meet. If the
arbitrary code of good manners had replaced the clasp of hands by some
other gesture, I should have gazed, day after day, at the unattainable
hands of Albertine with a curiosity to know the feel of them as ardent as
was my curiosity to learn the savour of her cheeks. But in the pleasure of
holding her hand unrestrictedly in mine, had I been next to her at 'ferret'
I did not envisage that pleasure alone; what avowals, declarations silenced
hitherto by my bashfulness, I could have conveyed by certain pressures
of hand on hand; on her side, how easy it would have been for her, in
responding by other pressures, to shew me that she accepted; what com-
plicity, what a vista of happiness stood open! My love would be able to
make more advance in a few minutes spent thus by her side than it had
yet made in all the time that I had known her. Feeling that they would
last but a short time, were rapidly nearing their end, since presumably
we were not going on much longer with this game, and that once it was

over I should be too late, I could not keep in my place for another moment.
I let myself deliberately be caught with the ring, and, having gone into
the middle, when the ring passed I pretended not to see it but followed its
course with my eyes, waiting for the moment when it should come into the
hands of the young man next to Albertine, who herself, pealing with helpless laughter, and in the excitement and pleasure of the game, was blushing
like a rose. "Why, we really are in the Fairy Wood!" said Andrée to me,
pointing to the trees that grew all round, with a smile in her eyes which
was meant only for me and seemed to pass over the heads of the other
players, as though we two alone were clever enough to double our parts,
and make, in connexion with the game we were playing, a remark of a
poetic nature. She even carried the delicacy of her fancy so far as to sing
half-unconsciously: "The Ferret of the Wood has passed this way, Sweet
Ladies; he has passed by this way, the Ferret of Fairy Wood!" like those
people who cannot visit Trianon without getting up a party in Louis XVI
costume, or think in effective to have a song sung to its original setting. I
should no doubt have been sorry that I could see no charm in this piece
of mimicry, had I had time to think of it. But my thoughts were all elsewhere. The players began to shew surprise at my stupidity in never getting
the ring. I was looking at Albertine, so pretty, so indifferent, so gay, who,
though she little knew it, was to be my neighbour when at last I should
catch the ring in the right hands, thanks to a stratagem which she did not
suspect, and would certainly have resented if she had. In the heat of the
game her long hair had become loosened, and fell in curling locks over her
cheeks on which it served to intensify, by its dry brownness, the carnation
pink. "You have the tresses of Laura Dianti, of Eleanor of Guyenne, and
of her descendant so beloved of Chateaubriand. You ought always to wear
your hair half down like that," I murmured in her ear as an excuse for
drawing close to her. Suddenly the ring passed to her neighbour. I sprang
upon him at once, forced open his hands and seized it; he was obliged now
to take my place inside the circle, while I took his beside Albertine. A few
minutes earlier I had been envying this young man, when I saw that his
hands as they slipped over the cord were constantly brushing against hers.
Now that my turn was come, too shy to seek, too much moved to enjoy
this contact, I no longer felt anything save the rapid and painful beating
of my heart. At one moment Albertine leaned towards me, with an air
of connivance, her round and rosy face, making a show of having the ring,
so as to deceive the ferret, and keep him from looking in the direction in
which she was just going to pass it. I realised at once that this was the
sole object of Albertine's mysterious, confidential gaze, but I was a little
shocked to see thus kindle in her eyes the image—purely fictitious, invented to serve the needs of the game—of a secret, an understanding between her and myself which did not exist, but which from that moment
seemed to me to be possible and would have been divinely sweet. While I
was still being swept aloft by this thought, I felt a slight pressure of Albertine's hand against mine, and her caressing finger slip under my finger along
the cord, and I saw her, at the same moment, give me a wink which she
tried to make pass unperceived by the others. At once, a mass of hopes,

invisible hitherto by myself, crystallised within me. "She is taking advantage of the game to let me feel that she really does love me," I thought to myself, in an acme of joy, from which no sooner had I reached it than I fell, on hearing Albertine mutter furiously: "Why can't you take it? I've been shoving it at you for the last hour." Stunned with grief, I let go the cord, the ferret saw that ring and swooped down on it, and I had to go back into the middle, where I stood helpless, in despair, looking at the unbridled rout which continued to circle round me, stung by the jeering shouts of all the players, obliged, in reply, to laugh when I had so little mind for laughter, while Albertine kept on repeating: "People can't play if they don't pay attention, and spoil the game for the others. He shan't be asked again when we're going to play, Andrée; if he is, I don't come." Andrée, with a mind above the game, still chanting her 'Fairy Wood' which, in a spirit of imitation, Rosemonde had taken up too, but without conviction, sought to make a diversion from Albertine's reproaches by saying to me: "We're quite close to those old Creuniers you wanted so much to see. Look, I'll take you there by a dear little path, and we'll leave these silly idiots to go on playing like babies in the nursery." As Andrée was extremely nice to me, as we went along I said to her everything about Albertine that seemed calculated to make me attractive to the latter. Andrée replied that she too was very fond of Albertine, thought her charming; in spite of which the compliments that I was paying to her friend did not seem altogether to please her. Suddenly, in the little sunken path, I stopped short, touched to the heart by an exquisite memory of my childhood. I had just recognised, by the fretted and glossy leaves which it thrust out towards me, a hawthorn-bush, flowerless, alas, now that spring was over. Around me floated the atmosphere of far-off Months of Mary, of Sunday afternoons, of beliefs, or errors long ago forgotten. I wanted to stay it in its passage. I stood still for a moment, and Andrée, with a charming divination of what was in my mind, left me to converse with the leaves of the bush. I asked them for news of the flowers, those hawthorn flowers that were like merry little girls, headstrong, provocative, pious. "The young ladies have been gone from here for a long time now," the leaves told me. And perhaps they thought that, for the great friend of those young ladies that I pretended to be, I seemed to have singularly little knowledge of their habits. A great friend, but one who had never been to see them again for all these years, despite his promises. And yet, as Gilberte had been my first love among girls, so these had been my first love among flowers. "Yes, I know all that, they leave about the middle of June," I answered, "but I am so delighted to see the place where they stayed when they were here. They came to see me, too, at Combray, in my room; my mother brought them when I was ill in bed. And we used to meet on Saturday evenings, too, at the Month of Mary devotions. Can they get to them from here?" "Oh, of course! Why, they make a special point of having our young ladies at Saint-Denis du Désert, the church near here." "Then, if I want to see them now?" "Oh, not before May, next year." "But I can be sure that they will be here?" "They come regularly every year." "Only I don't know whether it will be easy to find the place." "Oh, dear, yes! They are so gay, the young ladies, they stop laughing only to sing hymns together, so that you can't possibly miss them, you can tell by the scent from the other end of the path."

I caught up Andrée, and began again to sing Albertine's praises. It was inconceivable to me that she would not repeat what I said to her friend, seeing the emphasis that I put into it. And yet I never heard that Albertine had been told. Andrée had, nevertheless, a far greater understanding of the things of the heart, a refinement of nice behaviour; finding the look, the word, the action that could most ingeniously give pleasure, keeping to herself a remark that might possibly cause pain, making a sacrifice (and making it as though it were no sacrifice at all) of an afternoon's play, or it might be an 'at home' or a garden party in order to stay beside a friend who was feeling sad, and thus shew him or her that she preferred the simple company of a friend to frivolous pleasures; these were her habitual delicacies. But when one knew her a little better one would have said that it was with her as with those heroic cravens who wish not to be afraid, and whose bravery is especially meritorious, one would have said that in her true character there was none of that generosity which she displayed at every moment out of moral distinction, or sensibility, or a noble desire to shew herself a true friend. When I listened to all the charming things she was saying to me about a possible affection between Albertine and myself it seemed as though she were bound to do everything in her power to bring it to pass. Whereas, by mere chance perhaps, not even of the least of the various minor opportunities which were at her disposal and might have proved effective in uniting me to Albertine did she ever make any use, and I would not swear that my effort to make myself loved by Albertine did not—if not provoke in her friend secret stratagems destined to bring it to nought—at any rate arouse in her an anger which however she took good care to hide and against which even, in her delicacy of feeling, she may herself have fought. Of the countless refinements of goodness which Andrée shewed Albertine would have been incapable, and yet I was not certain of the underlying goodness of the former as I was to be, later on, of the latter's. Shewing herself always tenderly indulgent to the exuberant frivolity of Albertine, Andrée would greet her with speeches, with smiles which were those of a friend, better still, she always acted towards her as a friend. I have seen her, day after day, in order to give the benefit of her own wealth, to bring some happiness to this penniless friend take, without any possibility of advantage to herself, more pains than a courtier would take who sought to win his sovereign's favour. She was charmingly gentle always, charming in her choice of sweet, pathetic expressions, when you said to her what a pity it was that Albertine was so poor, and took infinitely more trouble on her behalf than she would have taken for a wealthy friend. But if anyone were to hint that Albertine was perhaps not quite so poor as people made out, a just discernible cloud would veil the light of Andrée's eyes and brow; she seemed out of temper. And if you went on to say that after all Albertine might perhaps be less difficult to marry off than people supposed, she would vehemently contradict you, repeating almost angrily: "Oh dear, no; she will never get married! I am quite

certain of it; it is a dreadful worry to me!" In so far as I myself was concerned, Andrée was the only one of the girls who would never have repeated to me anything not very pleasant that might have been said about
me by a third person; more than that, if it were I who told her what had
been said she would make a pretence of not believing it, or would furnish
some explanation which made the remark inoffensive; it is the aggregate
of these qualities that goes by the name of tact. Tact is the attribute of
those people who, if we have called a man out in a duel, congratulate us
and add that there was no necessity, really; so as to enhance still further
in our own eyes the courage of which we have given proof without having
been forced to do so. They are the opposite of the people who, in similar
circumstances, say: "It must have been a horrid nuisance for you, fighting
a duel, but on the other hand you couldn't possibly swallow an insult like
that, there was nothing else to be done." But as there is always something
to be said on both sides, if the pleasure, or at least the indifference shewn by
our friends in repeating something offensive that they have heard said
about us, proves that they do not exactly put themselves in our skin at the
moment of speaking, but thrust in the pin-point, turn the knife-blade as
though it were gold-beater's skin and not human, the art of always keeping
hidden from us what might be disagreeable to us in what they have heard
said about our actions, or in the opinion which those actions have led the
speakers themselves to form of us, proves that there is in the other kind of
friends, in the friends who are so full of tact, a strong vein of dissimulation.
It does no harm if indeed they are incapable of thinking evil, and if what
is said by other people only makes them suffer as it would make us. I
supposed this to be the case with Andrée, without, however, being absolutely sure.

We had left the little wood and had followed a network of overgrown
paths through which Andrée managed to find her way with great skill.
Suddenly, "Look now," she said to me, "there are your famous Creuniers,
and, I say, you are in luck, it's just the time of day, and the light is the
same as when Elstir painted them." But I was still too wretched at having
fallen, during the game of 'ferret,' from such a pinnacle of hopes. And
so it was not with the pleasure which otherwise I should doubtless have
felt that I caught sight, almost below my feet, crouching among the rocks,
where they had gone for protection from the heat, of marine goddesses for
whom Elstir had lain in wait and surprised them there, beneath a dark
glaze as lovely as Leonardo would have painted, the marvellous Shadows,
sheltered and furtive, nimble and voiceless, ready at the first glimmer of
light to slip behind the stone, to hide in a cranny, and prompt, once the
menacing ray had passed, to return to rock or seaweed beneath the sun
that crumbled the cliffs and the colourless ocean, over whose slumbers
they seemed to be watching, motionless lightfoot guardians letting appear
on the water's surface their viscous bodies and the attentive gaze of their
deep blue eyes.

We went back to the wood to pick up the other girls and go home together. I knew now that I was in love with Albertine; but, alas! I had no
thought of letting her know it. This was because, since the days of our

games in the Champs-Elysées, my conception of love had become different, even if the persons to whom my love was successively assigned remained practically the same. For one thing, the avowal, the declaration of my passion to her whom I loved no longer seemed to me one of the vital and necessary incidents of love, nor love itself an external reality, but simply a subjective pleasure. And as for this pleasure, I felt that Albertine would do everything necessary to furnish it, all the more since she would not know that I was enjoying it.

As we walked home the image of Albertine, bathed in the light that streamed from the other girls, was not the only one that existed for me. But as the moon, which is no more than a tiny white cloud of a more definite and fixed shape than other clouds during the day, assumes her full power as soon as daylight dies, so when I was once more in the hotel it was Albertine's sole image that rose from my heart and began to shine. My room seemed to me to have become suddenly a new place. Of course, for a long time past, it had not been the hostile room of my first night in it. All our lives we go on patiently modifying the surroundings in which we dwell; and gradually, as habit dispenses us from feeling them, we suppress the noxious elements of colour, shape and smell which were at the root of our discomfort. Nor was it any longer the room, still potent enough over my sensibility, not certainly to make me suffer, but to give me joy, the fount of summer days, like a marble basin in which, half way up its polished sides, they mirrored an azure surface steeped in light over which glided for an instant, impalpable and white as a wave of heat, a shadowy and fleeting cloud; not the room, wholly aesthetic, of the pictorial evening hours; it was the room in which I had been now for so many days that I no longer saw it. And now I was just beginning again to open my eyes to it, but this time from the selfish angle which is that of love. I liked to feel that the fine big mirror across one corner, the handsome bookcases with their fronts of glass would give Albertine, if she came to see me, a good impression of myself. Instead of a place of transit in which I would stay for a few minutes before escaping to the beach or to Rivebelle, my room became real and dear to me, fashioned itself anew, for I looked at and appreciated each article of its furniture with the eyes of Albertine.

A few days after the game of 'ferret,' when, having allowed ourselves to wander rather too far afield, we had been fortunate in finding at Maineville a couple of little "tubs" with two seats in each which would enable us to be back in time for dinner, the keenness, already intense, of my love for Albertine, had the following effect, first of all, that it was Rosemonde and Andrée in turn that I invited to be my companion, and never once Albertine, after which, in spite of my manifest preference for Andrée or Rosemonde, I led everybody, by secondary considerations of time and distance, cloaks and so forth, to decide, as though against my wishes, that the most practical policy was that I should take Albertine, to whose company I pretended to resign myself for good or ill. Unfortunately, since love tends to the complete assimilation of another person, while other people are not comestible by way of conversation alone, Albertine might be (and indeed was) as friendly as possible to me on our way home; when I had deposited her at her own door she left me happy but more famished for her even than I had been at the start, and reckoning the moments that we had spent together as only a prelude, of little importance in itself, to those that were still to come. And yet this prelude had that initial charm which is not to be found again. I had not yet asked anything of Albertine. She could imagine what I wanted, but, not being certain of it, would suppose that I was tending only towards relations without any definite purpose, in which my friend would find that delicious vagueness, rich in surprising fulfilments of expectations, which is true romance.

In the week that followed I scarcely attempted to see Albertine. I made a show of preferring Andrée. Love is born; one would like to remain, for her whom one loves, the unknown whom she may love in turn, but one has need of her, one requires contact not so much with her body as with her attention, her heart. One slips into a letter some spiteful expression which will force the indifferent reader to ask for some little kindness in compensation, and love, following an unvarying procedure, sets going with an alternating movement the machinery in which one can no longer either refrain from loving or be loved. I gave to Andrée the hours spent by the others at a party which I knew that she would sacrifice for my sake, with pleasure, and would have sacrificed even with reluctance, from a moral nicety, so as not to let either the others or herself think that she attached any importance to a relatively frivolous amusement. I arranged in this way to have her entirely to myself every evening, meaning not to make Albertine jealous, but to improve my position in her eyes, or at any rate not to imperil it by letting Albertine know that it was herself and not Andrée that I loved. Nor did I confide this to Andrée either, lest she should repeat it to her friend. When I spoke of Albertine to Andrée I affected a coldness by which she was perhaps less deceived that I by her apparent credulity. She made a show of believing in my indifference to Albertine, of desiring the closest possible union between Albertine and myself. It is probable that, on the contrary, she neither believed in the one nor wished for the other. While I was saying to her that I did not care very greatly for her friend, I was thinking of one thing only, how to become acquainted with Mme. Bontemps, who was staying for a few days near Balbec, and to whom Albertine was going presently on a short visit. Naturally I did not let Andrée become aware of this desire, and when I spoke to her of Albertine's people, it was in the most careless manner possible. Andrée's direct answers did not appear to throw any doubt on my sincerity. Why then did she blurt out suddenly, about that time: "Oh, guess who' I've just seen—Albertine's aunt!" It is true that she had not said in so many words: "I could see through your casual remarks all right that the one thing you were really thinking of was how you could make friends with Albertine's aunt." But it was clearly to the presence in Andrée's mind of some such idea which she felt it more becoming to keep from me that the word 'just' seemed to point. It was of a kind with certain glances, certain gestures which, for all that they have not a form that is logical, rational, deliberately calculated to match the listener's intelligence, reach him nevertheless in their true significance, just as human speech, converted into

electricity in the telephone, is turned into speech again when it strikes the
ear. In order to remove from Andrée's mind the idea that I was interested
in Mme. Bontemps, I spoke of her from that time onwards not only carelessly but with downright malice, saying that I had once met that idiot of
a woman, and trusted I should never have that experience again. Whereas
I was seeking by every means in my power to meet her.

I tried to induce Elstir (but without mentioning to anyone else that I
had asked him) to speak to her about me and to bring us together. He
promised to introduce me to her, though he seemed greatly surprised at
my wishing it, for he regarded her as a contemptible woman, a born in-
triguer, as little interesting as she was disinterested. Reflecting that if I
did see Mme. Bontemps, Andrée would be sure to hear of it sooner or later,
I thought it best to warn her in advance. "The things one tries hardest to
avoid are what one finds one cannot escape," I told her. "Nothing in the
world could bore me so much as meeting Mme. Bontemps again, and yet I
can't get out of it, Elstir has arranged to invite us together." "I have never
doubted it for a single instant," exclaimed Andrée in a bitter tone, while
her eyes, enlarged and altered by her annoyance, focussed themselves
upon some invisible object. These words of Andrée's were not the most
recent statement of a thought which might be expressed thus: "I know that
you are in love with Albertine, and that you are working day and night to
get in touch with her people." But they were the shapeless fragments,
easily pieced together again by me, of some such thought which I had
exploded by striking it, through the shield of Andrée's self-control. Like
her 'just,' these words had no meaning save in the second degree, that is to
say they were words of the sort which (rather than direct affirmatives)
inspires in us respect or distrust for another person, and leads to a rupture.

If Andrée had not believed me when I told her that Albertine's relatives
left me indifferent, that was because she thought that I was in love with
Albertine. And probably she was none too happy in the thought.

She was generally present as a third party at my meetings with her
friend. And yet there were days when I was to see Albertine by herself, days
to which I looked forward with feverish impatience, which passed without
bringing me any decisive result, without having, any of them, been that
cardinal day whose part I immediately entrusted to the day that was to
follow, which would prove no more apt to play it; thus there crumbled
and collapsed, one after another, like waves of the sea, those peaks at once
replaced by others.

About a month after the day on which we had played 'ferret' together,
I learned that Albertine was going away next morning to spend a couple of
days with Mme. Bontemps, and, since she would have to start early, was
coming to sleep that night at the Grand Hotel, from which, by taking the
omnibus, she would be able, without disturbing the friends with whom she
was staying, to catch the first train in the morning. I mentioned this to
Andrée. "I don't believe a word of it," she replied, with a look of annoyance. "Anyhow it won't help you at all, for I'm quite sure Albertine won't
want to see you if she goes to the hotel by herself. It wouldn't be 'regu-
lation,' " she added, employing an epithet which had recently come into

favour with her, in the sense of 'what is done.' "I tell you this because I understand Albertine. What difference do you suppose it makes to me, whether you see her or not? Not the slightest, I can assure you!"

We were joined by Octave who had no hesitation in telling Andrée the number of strokes he had gone round in, the day before, at golf, then by Albertine, counting her diabolo as she walked along, like a nun telling her beads. Thanks to this pastime she could be left alone for hours on end without growing bored. As soon as she joined us I became conscious of the obstinate tip of her nose, which I had omitted from my mental pictures of her during the last few days; beneath her dark hair the vertical front of her brow controverted—and not for the first time—the indefinite image that I had preserved of her, while its whiteness made a vivid splash in my field of vision; emerging from the dust of memory, Albertine was built up afresh before my eyes. Golf gives one a taste for solitary pleasures. The pleasure to be derived from diabolo is undoubtedly one of these. And yet, after she had joined us, Albertine continued to toss up and catch her missile, just as a lady on whom friends have come to call does not on their account stop working at her crochet. "I hear that Mme. de Villeparisis," she remarked to Octave, "has been complaining to your father." I could hear, underlying the word, one of those notes that were peculiar to Albertine; always, just as I had made certain that I had forgotten them, I would be reminded of a glimpse caught through them before of Albertine's determined and typically Gallic mien. I might have been blind, and yet have detected certain of her qualities, alert and slightly provincial, from those notes, just as plainly as from the tip of her nose. These were equivalent and might have been substituted for one another, and her voice was like what we are promised in the photo-telephone of the future; the visual image was clearly outlined in the sound. "She's not written only to your father, either, she wrote to the Mayor of Balbec at the same time, to say that we must stop playing diabolo on the 'front' as somebody hit her in the face with one." "Yes, I was hearing about that. It's too silly. There's little enough to do here as it is." Andrée did not join in the conversation; she was not acquainted, any more than was Albertine or Octave, with Mme. de Villeparisis. She did, however, remark: "I can't think why this lady should make such a song about it. Old Mme. de Cambremer got hit in the face, and she never complained." "I will explain the difference," replied Octave gravely, striking a match as he spoke. "It's my belief that Mme. de Cambremer is a woman of the world, and Mme. de Villeparisis is just an upstart. Are you playing golf this afternoon?" And he left us, followed by Andrée. I was alone now with Albertine. "Do you see," she began, "I'm wearing my hair now the way you like—look at my ringlet. They all laugh at me and nobody knows who' I'm doing it for. My aunt will laugh at me too. But I shan't tell her why, either." I had a sidelong view of Albertine's cheeks, which often appeared pale, but, seen thus, were flushed with a coursing stream of blood which lighted them up, gave them that dazzling clearness which certain winter mornings have when the stones sparkling in the sun seem blocks of pink granite and radiate joy. The joy that I was drawing at this moment from the sight of Albertine's cheeks was equally keen, but led to another desire on my part, which was not to walk with her but to take her in my arms. I asked her if the report of her plans which I had heard were correct. "Yes," she told me, "I shall be sleeping at your hotel to-night, and in fact as I've got rather a chill, I shall be going to bed before dinner. You can come and sit by my bed and watch me eat, if you like, and afterwards we'll play at anything you choose. I should have liked you to come to the station to-morrow morning, but I'm afraid it might look rather odd, I don't say to Andrée, who is a sensible person, but to the others who will be there; if my aunt got to know, I should never hear the last of it. But we can spend the evening together, at any rate. My aunt will know nothing about that. I must go and say good-bye to Andrée, So long, then. Come early, so that we can have a nice long time together," she added, smiling. At these words I was swept back past the days in which I loved Gilberte to those in which love seemed to me not only an external entity but one that could be realised as a whole. Whereas the Gilberte whom I used to see in the Champs-Elysées was a different Gilberte from the one whom I found waiting inside myself when I was alone again, suddenly in the real Albertine, her whom I saw every day, whom I supposed to be stuffed with middle-class prejudices and entirely open with her aunt, there was incarnate the imaginary Albertine, she whom, when I still did not know her, I had suspected of casting furtive glances at myself on the 'front,' she who had worn an air of being reluctant to go indoors when she saw me making off in the other direction.

I went in to dinner with my grandmother. I felt within me a secret which she could never guess. Similarly with Albertine; to-morrow her friends would be with her, not knowing what novel experience she and I had in common; and when she kissed her niece on the brow Mme. Bontemps would never imagine that I stood between them, in that arrangement of Albertine's hair which had for its object, concealed from all the world, to give me pleasure, me who had until then so greatly envied Mme. Bontemps because, being related to the same people as her niece, she had the same occasions to don mourning, the same family visits to pay; and now I found myself meaning more to Albertine than did the aunt herself. When she was with her aunt, it was of me that she would be thinking. What was going to happen that evening, I scarcely knew. In any event, the Grand Hotel, the evening, would no longer seem empty to me; they contained my happiness. I rang for the lift-boy to take me up to the room which Albertine had engaged, a room that looked over the valley. The slightest movements, such as that of sitting down on the bench in the lift, were satisfying, because they were in direct relation to my heart; I saw in the ropes that drew the cage upwards, in the few steps that I had still to climb, only a materialisation of the machinery, the stages of my joy. I had only two or three steps to take now along the corridor before coming to that room in which was enshrined the precious substance of that rosy form—that room which, even if there were to be done in it delicious things, would keep that air of permanence, of being, to a chance visitor who knew nothing of its history, just like any other room, which makes of inanimate things the obstinately mute witnesses, the scrupulous confidants, the inviolable depositaries of our pleasure. Those few steps from the landing to Albertine's door, those few steps which no one now could prevent my taking, I took with delight, with prudence, as though plunged into a new and strange element, as if in going forward I had been gently displacing the liquid stream of happiness, and at the same time with a strange feeling of absolute power, and of entering at length into an inheritance which had belonged to me from all time. Then suddenly I reflected that it was wrong to be in any doubt; she had told me to come when she was in bed. It was as clear as daylight; I pranced for joy, I nearly knocked over Françoise who was standing in my way, I ran, with glowing eyes, towards my friend's room. I found Albertine in bed. Leaving her throat bare, her white nightgown altered the proportions of her face, which, flushed by being in bed or by her cold or by dinner, seemed pinker than before; I thought of the colours which I had had, a few hours earlier, displayed beside me, on the 'front,' the savour of which I was now at last to taste; her cheek was crossed obliquely by one of those long, dark, curling tresses, which, to please me, she had undone altogether. She looked at me and smiled. Beyond her, through the window, the valley lay bright beneath the moon. The sight of Albertine's bare throat, of those strangely vivid cheeks, had so intoxi-cated me (that is to say had placed the reality of the world for me no longer in nature, but in the torrent of my sensations which it was all I could do to keep within bounds), as to have destroyed the balance be-tween the life, immense and indestructible, which circulated in my being, and the life of the universe, so puny in comparison. The sea, which was visible through the window as well as the valley, the swelling breasts of the first of the Maineville cliffs, the sky in which the moon had not yet climbed to the zenith, all of these seemed less than a featherweight on my eyeballs, which between their lids I could feel dilated, resisting, ready to bear very different burdens, all the mountains of the world upon their fragile sur-face. Their orbit no longer found even the sphere of the horizon adequate to fill it. And everything that nature could have brought me of life would have seemed wretchedly meagre, the sigh of the waves far too short a sound to express the enormous aspiration that was surging in my breast. I bent over Albertine to kiss her. Death might have struck me down in that mo-ment; it would have seemed to me a trivial, or rather an impossible thing, for life was not outside, it was in me; I should have smiled pityingly had a philosopher then expressed the idea that some day, even some distant day, I should have to die, that the external forces of nature would survive me, the forces of that nature beneath whose godlike feet I was no more than a grain of dust; that, after me, there would still remain those rounded, swelling cliffs, that sea, that moonlight and that sky! How was that pos-sible; how could the world last longer than myself, since it was it that was enclosed in me, in me whom it went a long way short of filling, in me, where, feeling that there was room to store so many other treasures, I flung contemptuously into a corner sky, sea and cliffs. "Stop that, or I'll ring the bell!" cried Albertine, seeing that I was flinging myself upon her to kiss her. But I reminded myself that it was not for no purpose that a girl made a young man come to her room in secret, arranging that her aunt should not know—that boldness, moreover, rewards those who know how to seize their opportunities; in the state of exaltation in which I was, the round face of Albertine, lighted by an inner flame, like the glass bowl of a lamp, started into such prominence that, copying the rotation of a burning sphere, it seemed to me to be turning, like those faces of Michelangelo which are being swept past in the arrested headlong flight of a whirlwind. I was going to learn the fragrance, the flavour which this strange pink fruit concealed. I heard a sound, precipitous, prolonged, shrill. Albertine had pulled the bell with all her might.

❧

I had supposed that the love which I felt for Albertine was not based on the hope of carnal possession. And yet, when the lesson to be drawn from my experience that evening was, apparently, that such possession was impossible; when, after having had not the least doubt, that first day, on the beach, of Albertine's being unchaste, and having then passed through various intermediate assumptions, I seemed to have quite definitely reached the conclusion that she was absolutely virtuous; when, on her return from her aunt's, a week later, she greeted me coldly with: "I forgive you; in fact I'm sorry to have upset you, but you must never do it again,"—then, in contrast to what I had felt on learning from Bloch that one could always have all the women one liked, and as if, in place of a real girl, I had known a wax doll, it came to pass that gradually there detached itself from her my desire to penetrate into her life, to follow her through the places in which she had spent her childhood, to be initiated by her into the athletic life; my intellectual curiosity to know what were her thoughts on this subject or that did not survive my belief that I might take her in my arms if I chose. My dreams abandoned her, once they had ceased to be nourished by the hope of a possession of which I had supposed them to be independent. Thenceforward they found themselves once more at liberty to transmit themselves, according to the attraction that I had found in her on any particular day, above all according to the chances that I seemed to detect of my being, possibly, one day, loved by her—to one or another of Albertine's friends, and to Andrée first of all. And yet, if Albertine had not existed, perhaps I should not have had the pleasure which I began to feel more and more strongly during the days that followed in the kindness that was shewn me by Andrée. Albertine told no one of the check which I had received at her hands. She was one of those pretty girls who, from their earliest youth, by their beauty, but especially by an attraction, a charm which remains somewhat mysterious and has its source perhaps in reserves of vitality to which others less favoured by nature come to quench their thirst, have always—in their home circle, among their friends, in society—proved more attractive than other more beautiful and richer girls; she was one of those people from whom, before the age of love and ever so much more after it is reached, one asks more than they ask in return, more even than they are able to give. From her childhood Albertine had always had round her in an adoring circle four or five little girl friends, among them Andrée who was so far her superior and knew it (and perhaps this attraction which Albertine exerted quite involuntarily had been the origin, had laid the foundations of the little band). This attraction was still potent even at a great social distance, in circles quite brilliant in comparison, where if there was a pavane to be danced, they would send for Albertine rather than have it danced by another girl of better family. The consequence was that, not having a penny to her name, living a hard enough life, moreover, on the hands of M. Bontemps, who was said to be 'on the rocks,' and was anyhow anxious to be rid of her, she was nevertheless invited, not only to dine but to stay, by people who, in Saint-Loup's sight, might not have had any distinction, but to Rosemonde's mother or Andrée's, women who though very rich themselves did not know these other and richer people, represented something quite incalculable. Thus Albertine spent a few weeks every year with the family of one of the Governors of the Bank of France, who was also Chairman of the Board of Directors of a great Railway Company. The wife of this financier entertained people of importance, and had never mentioned her 'day' to Andrée's mother, who thought her wanting in politeness, but was nevertheless prodigiously interested in everything that went on in her house. Accordingly she encouraged Andrée every year to invite Albertine down to their villa, because, as she said, it was a real charity to offer a holiday by the sea to a girl who had not herself the means to travel and whose aunt did so little for her; Andrée's mother was probably not prompted by the thought that the banker and his wife, learning that Albertine was made much of by her and her daughter, would form a high opinion of them both; still less did she hope that Albertine, good and clever as she was, would manage to get her invited, or at least to get Andrée invited, to the financier's garden-parties. But every evening at the dinner-table, while she assumed an air of indifference slightly tinged with contempt, she was fascinated by Albertine's accounts of everything that had happened at the big house while she was staying there, and the names of the other guests, almost all of them people whom she knew by sight or by name. True, the thought that she knew them only in this indirect fashion, that is to say did not know them at all (she called this kind of acquaintance knowing people 'all my life'), gave Andrée's mother a touch of melancholy while she plied Albertine with questions about them in a lofty and distant tone, speaking with closed lips, and might have left her doubtful and uneasy as to the importance of her own social position had she not been able to reassure herself, to return safely to the 'realities of life,' by saying to the butler: "Please tell the chef that he has not made the peas soft enough." She then recovered her serenity. And she was quite determined that Andrée was to marry nobody but a man—of the best family, of course—rich enough for her too to be able to keep a chef and a couple of coachmen. This was the proof positive, the practical indication of 'position.' But the fact that Albertine had dined at the banker's house in the country with this or that great lady, and that the said great lady had invited the girl to stay with her next winter, did not invalidate a sort of special consideration which Albertine shewed towards Andrée's mother, which went very well with the pity, and even repulsion, excited by the tale of her misfortunes, a repulsion increased by the fact that M. Bontemps had proved a traitor to the cause (he was even, people said, vaguely Panamist) and had rallied to the Government. Not that this deterred Andrée's mother, in her passion for abstract truth, from withering with her scorn the people who appeared to believe that Albertine was of humble origin. "What's that you say? Why, they're one of the best families in the country. Simonet with a single 'n,' you know!" Certainly, in view of the class of society in which all this went on, in which money plays so important a part, and mere charm makes people ask you out but not marry you, a 'comfortable' marriage did not appear to be for Albertine a practical outcome of the so distinguished patronage which she enjoyed but which would not have been held to compensate for her poverty. But even by themselves, and with no prospect of any matrimonial consequence, Albertine's 'successes' in society excited the envy of certain spiteful mothers, furious at seeing her received like one of the family by the banker's wife, even by Andrée's mother, neither of whom they themselves really knew. They therefore went about telling common friends of those ladies and their own that both ladies would be very angry if they knew the facts, which were that Albertine repeated to each of them everything that the intimacy to which she was rashly admitted enabled her to spy out in the household of the other, a thousand little secrets which it must be infinitely unpleasant to the interested party to have made public. These envious women said this so that it might be repeated and might get Albertine into trouble with her patrons. But, as often happens, their machinations met with no success. The spite that prompted them was too apparent, and their only result was to make the women who had planned them appear rather more contemptible than before. Andrée's mother was too firm in her opinion of Albertine to change her mind about her now. She looked upon her as a 'poor wretch,' but the best-natured girl living, and one who would do anything in the world to give pleasure.

If this sort of select popularity to which Albertine had attained did not seem likely to lead to any practical result, it had stamped Andrée's friend with the distinctive marks of people who, being always sought after, have never any need to offer themselves, marks (to be found also, and for analogous reasons, at the other end of the social scale among the leaders of fashion) which consist in their not making any display of the successes they have scored, but rather keeping them to themselves. She would never say to anyone: "So-and-so is anxious to meet me," would speak of everyone with the greatest good nature, and as if it had been she who ran after, who sought to know other people, and not they. If you spoke of a young man who, a few minutes earlier, had been, in private conversation with her, heaping the bitterest reproaches upon her because she had refused him an assignation, so far from proclaiming this in public, or betraying any resentment she would stand up for him: "He is such a nice boy!" Indeed it quite annoyed her when she attracted people, because that compelled her to disappoint them, whereas her natural instinct was always to give pleasure. So much did she enjoy giving pleasure that she had come to employ a particular kind of falsehood, found among utilitarians and men who have 'arrived.' Existing besides in an embryonic state in a vast number of people, this form of insincerity consists in not being able to confine the pleasure arising out of a single act of politeness to a single person. For instance, if Albertine's aunt wished her niece to accompany her to a party which was not very lively, Albertine might have found it sufficient to extract from the incident the moral profit of having given pleasure to her aunt. But being courteously welcomed by her host and hostess, she thought it better to say to them that she had been wanting to see them for so long that she had finally seized this opportunity and begged her aunt to take her to their party. Even this was not enough: at the same party there happened to be one of Albertine's friends who was in great distress. "I did not like the idea of your being here by yourself. I thought it might do you good to have me with you. If you would rather come away from here, go somewhere else, I am ready to do anything you like; all I want is to see you look not so sad."—Which, as it happened, was true also. Sometimes it happened however that the fictitious object destroyed the real. Thus, Albertine, having a favour to ask on behalf of one of her friends, went on purpose to see a certain lady who could help her. But on arriving at the house of this lady—a kind and sympathetic soul—the girl, unconsciously following the principle of utilising a single action in a number of ways, felt it to be more ingratiating to appear to have come there solely on account of the pleasure she knew she would derive from seeing the lady again. The lady was deeply touched that Albertine should have taken a long journey purely out of friendship for herself. Seeing her almost overcome by emotion, Albertine began to like the lady still better. Only, there was this awkward consequence: she now felt so keenly the pleasure of friendship which she pretended to have been her motive in coming, that she was afraid of making the lady suspect the genuineness of sentiments which were actually quite sincere if she now asked her to do the favour, whatever it may have been, for her friend. The lady would think that Albertine had come for that purpose, which was true, but would conclude also that Albertine had no disinterested pleasure in seeing her, which was not. With the result that she came away without having asked the favour, like a man sometimes who has been so good to a woman, in the hope of winning her, that he refrains from declaring his passion in order to preserve for his goodness an air of nobility. In other instances it would be wrong to say that the true object was sacrificed to the subordinate and subsequently conceived idea, but the two were so far incompatible that if the person to whom Albertine endeared herself by stating the second had known of the existence of the first, his pleasure would at once have been turned into the deepest annoyance. At a much later point in this story, we shall have occasion to see this kind of incompatibility expressed in clearer terms. Let us say for the present, borrowing an example of a completely different order, that they occur very frequently in the most divergent situations that life has to offer. A husband has established his mistress in the town where he is quartered with his regiment. His wife, left by herself in Paris, and with an inkling of the truth, grows more and more miserable, and writes her husband letters embittered by jealousy. Very well; the mistress is obliged to go up to Paris for the day. The husband cannot resist her entreaties that he will go with her, and applies for short leave, which is granted. But as he is a good-natured fellow, and hates to make his wife unhappy, he goes to her and tells her, shedding a few quite genuine tears, that, driven to desperation by her letters, he has found the means of getting away from his duties to come to her, to console her in his arms. He has thus contrived by a single journey to furnish wife and mistress alike with proofs of his affection. But if the wife were to learn the reason for which he has come to Paris, her joy would doubtless be turned into grief, unless her pleasure in seeing the faithless wretch outweighed, in spite of everything, the pain that his infidelities had caused her. Among the men who have struck me as practising with most perseverance this system of what might be called killing any number of birds with one stone, must be included M. de Norpois. He would now and then agree to act as intermediary between two of his friends who had quarrelled, which led to his being called the most obliging of men. But it was not sufficient for him to appear to be doing a service to the friend who had come to him to demand it; he would represent to the other the steps which he was taking to effect a reconciliation as undertaken not at the request of the first friend but in the interest of the second, an attitude of the sincerity of which he had never any difficulty in convincing a listener already influenced by the idea that he saw before him the 'most serviceable of men.' In this fashion, playing in two scenes turn about, what in stage parlance is called 'doubling' two parts, he never allowed his influence to be in the slightest degree imperilled, and the services which he rendered constituted not an expenditure of capital but a dividend upon some part of his credit. At the same time every service, seemingly rendered twice over, correspondingly enhanced his reputation as an obliging friend, and, better still, a friend whose interventions were efficacious, one who did not draw bows at a venture, whose efforts were always justified by success, as was shewn by the gratitude of both parties. This duplicity in rendering services was—allowing for disappointments such as are the lot of every human being—an important element of M. de Norpois's character. And often at the Ministry he would make use of my father, who was a simple soul, while making him believe that it was he, M. de Norpois, who was being useful to my father.

Attracting people more easily than she wished, and having no need to proclaim her conquests abroad, Albertine kept silence with regard to the scene with myself by her bedside, which a plain girl would have wished the whole world to know. And yet of her attitude during that scene I could not arrive at any satisfactory explanation. Taking first of all the supposition that she was absolutely chaste (a supposition with which I had originally accounted for the violence with which Albertine had refused to let herself be taken in my arms and kissed, though it was by no means essential to my conception of the goodness, the fundamentally honourable character of my friend), I could not accept it without a copious revision of its terms. It ran so entirely counter to the hypothesis which I had constructed that day when I saw Albertine for the first time. Then ever so many different acts, all acts of kindness towards myself (a kindness that was caressing, at times uneasy, alarmed, jealous of my predilection for Andrée) came up on all sides to challenge the brutal gesture with which, to escape from me, she had pulled the bell. Why then had she invited me to come and spend the evening by her bedside? Why had she spoken all the time in the language of affection? What object is there in your desire to see a friend, in your fear that he is fonder of another of your friends than of you; why seek to give him pleasure, why tell him, so romantically, that the others will never know that he has spent the evening in your room, if you refuse him so simple a pleasure and if to you it is no pleasure at all? I could not believe, all the same, that Albertine's chastity was carried to such a pitch as that, and I had begun to ask myself whether her violence might not have been due to some reason of coquetry, a disagreeable odour, for instance, which she suspected of lingering about her person, and by which she was afraid that I might be disgusted, or else of cowardice, if for instance she imagined, in her ignorance of the facts of love, that my state of nervous exhaustion was due to something contagious, communicable to her in a kiss.

She was genuinely distressed by her failure to afford me pleasure, and gave me a little gold pencil-case, with that virtuous perversity which people shew who, moved by your supplications and yet not consenting to grant you what those supplications demand, are anxious all the same to bestow on you some mark of their affection; the critic, an article from whose pen would so gratify the novelist, asks him instead to dinner; the duchess does not take the snob with her to the theatre but lends him her box on an evening when she will not be using it herself. So far are those who do least for us, and might easily do nothing, driven by conscience to do something. I told Albertine that in giving me this pencil-case she was affording me great pleasure, and yet not so great as I should have felt if, on the night she had spent at the hotel, she had permitted me to embrace her. "It would have made me so happy; what possible harm could it have done you? I was simply astounded at your refusing to let me do it." "What astounds me," she retorted, "is that you should have thought it astounding. Funny sort of girls you must know if my behaviour surprises you." "I am extremely sorry if I annoyed you, but even now I cannot say that I think I was in the wrong. What I feel is that all that sort of thing is of no importance, really, and I can't understand a girl who could so easily give pleasure not consenting to do so. Let us be quite clear about it," I went on, throwing a sop of sorts to her moral scruples, as I recalled how she and her friends had scarified the girl who went about with the actress Léa. "I don't mean to say for a moment that a girl can behave exactly as she likes, or that there's no such thing as immorality. Take, let me see now, yes, what you were saying the other day about a girl who is staying at Balbec and her relations with an actress; I call that degrading, so degrading that I feel sure it must all have been made up by the girl's enemies, and that there can't be any truth in the story. It strikes me as improbable, impossible. But to let a friend kiss you, and go farther than that even— since you say that I am your friend . . ." "So you are, but I have had friends before now, I have known lots of young men who were every bit as friendly, I can assure you. There wasn't one of them would ever have dared to do a thing like that. They knew they'd get their ears boxed if they tried it on. Besides, they never dreamed of trying, we would shake hands in an open, friendly sort of way, like good pals, but there was never a word said about kissing, and yet we weren't any the less friends for that. Why, if it's my friendship you are after, you've nothing to complain of; I must be jolly fond of you to forgive you. But I'm sure you don't care two straws about me, really. Own up now, it's Andrée you're in love with. After all, you're quite right; she is ever so much prettier than I am, and perfectly charming! Oh! You men!" Despite my recent disappointment, these words so frankly uttered, by giving me a great respect for Albertine, made a very pleasant impression on me. And perhaps this impression was to have serious and vexatious consequences for me later on, for it was round it that there began to form that feeling almost of brotherly intimacy, that moral core which was always to remain at the heart of my love for Albertine. A feeling of this sort may be the cause of the keenest pain. For in order really to suffer at the hands of a woman one must have believed in her completely. For the moment, that embryo of moral esteem, of friendship, was left embedded in me like a stepping-stone in a stream. It could have availed nothing, by itself, against my happiness if it had remained there without growing, in an inertia which it was to retain the following year, and still more during the final weeks of this first visit to Balbec. It dwelt in me like one of those foreign bodies which it would be wiser when all is said to expel, but which we leave where they are without disturbing them, so harmless for the present does their weakness, their isolation amid a strange environment render them.

My dreams were now once more at liberty to concentrate on one or another of Albertine's friends, and returned first of all to Andrée, whose kindnesses might perhaps have appealed to me less strongly had I not been certain that they would come to Albertine's ears. Undoubtedly the preference that I had long been pretending to feel for Andrée had furnished me—in the habit of conversation with her, of declaring my affection—with, so to speak, the material, prepared and ready, for a love of her which had hitherto lacked only the complement of a genuine sentiment, and this my heart being once more free was now in a position to supply. But for me really to love Andrée, she was too intellectual, too neurotic, too sickly, too much like myself. If Albertine now seemed to me to be void of substance, Andrée was filled with something which I knew only too well. I had thought, that first day, that what I saw on the beach there was the mistress of some racing cyclist, passionately athletic; and now Andrée told me that if she had taken up athletic pastimes, it was under orders from her doctor, to cure her neurasthenia, her digestive troubles, but that her happiest hours were those which she spent in translating one of George Eliot's novels. The misunderstanding, due to an initial mistake as to what Andrée was, had not, as a matter of fact, the slightest importance. But my mistake was one of the kind which, if they allow love to be born, and are not recognised as mistakes until it has ceased to be under control, become a cause of suffering. Such mistakes—which may be quite different from mine with regard to Andrée, and even its exact opposite,—are frequently due (and this was especially the case here) to our paying too much attention to the aspect, the manners of what a person is not but would like to be, in forming our first impression of that person. To the outward appearance affectation, imitation, the longing to be admired, whether by the good or by the wicked, add misleading similarities of speech and gesture. These are cynicisms and cruelties which, when put to the test, prove no more genuine than certain apparent virtues and generosities. Just as we often discover a vain miser beneath the cloak of a man famed for his bountiful charity, so her flaunting of vice leads us to suppose a Messalina a respectable girl with middle-class prejudices. I had thought to find in Andrée a healthy, primitive creature, whereas she was merely a person in search of health, as were doubtless many of those in whom she herself had thought to find it, and who were in reality no more healthy than a burly arthritic with a red face and in white flannels is necessarily a Hercules. Now there are circumstances in which it is not immaterial to our happiness that the person whom we have loved because of what appeared to be so healthy about her is in reality only one of those invalids who receive such health as they possess from others, as the planets borrow their light, as certain bodies are only conductors of electricity.

No matter, Andrée, like Rosemonde and Gisèle, indeed more than they, was, when all was said, a friend of Albertine, sharing her life, imitating her conduct, so closely that, the first day, I had not at once distinguished them one from another. Over these girls, flowering sprays of roses whose principal charm was that they outlined themselves against the sea, the same undivided partnership prevailed as at the time when I did not know them, when the appearance of no matter which of them had caused me such violent emotion by its announcement that the little band was not far off. And even now the sight of one of them filled me with a pleasure into which there entered, to an extent which I should not have found it easy to define, the thought of seeing the others follow her in due course, and even if they did not come that day, speaking about them, and knowing that they would be told that I had been on the beach.

It was no longer simply the attraction of those first days, it was a regular love-longing which hesitated among them all, so far was each the natural substitute for the others. My bitterest grief would not have been to be thrown over by whichever of the girls I liked best, but I should at once have liked best, because I should have fastened on to her the whole of the melancholy dream which had been floating vaguely among them all, her who had thrown me over. It would, moreover, in that event, be the loss of all her friends, in whose eyes I should speedily have forfeited whatever advantage I might possess, that I should, in losing her, have unconsciously regretted, having vowed to them that sort of collective love which the politician and the actor feel for the public for whose desertion of them after they have enjoyed all its favours they can never be consoled. Even those favours which I had failed to win from Albertine I would hope suddenly to receive from one or other who had parted from me in the evening with a word or glance of ambiguous meaning, thanks to which it was to her that, for the next day or so, my desire would turn.

It strayed among them all the more voluptuously in that upon those volatile faces a comparative fixation of features had now begun, and had been carried far enough for the eye to distinguish—even if it were to change yet further—each malleable and floating effigy. To the differences that existed among them there was doubtless very little that corresponded in the no less marked differences in the length and breadth of those features, any of which might, perhaps, dissimilar as the girls appeared, almost have been lifted bodily from one face and imposed at random upon any other. But our knowledge of faces is not mathematical. In the first place, it does not begin with the measurement of the parts, it takes as its starting point an expression, a combination of the whole. In Andrée, for instance, the fineness of her gentle eyes seemed to go with the thinness of her nose, as slender as a mere curve which one could imagine as having been traced in order to produce along a single line the idea of delicacy divided higher up between the dual smile of her twin gaze. A line equally fine was engraved in her hair, pliant and deep as the line with which the wind furrows the sand. And in her it must have been hereditary; for the snow-white hair of Andrée's mother was driven in the same way, forming here a swelling, there a depression, like a snowdrift that rises or sinks according to the irregularities of the soil. Certainly, when compared with the fine delineation of Andrée's, Rosemonde's nose seemed to present broad surfaces, like a high tower raised upon massive foundations. Albeit expression suffices to make us believe in enormous differences between things that are separated by infinitely little—albeit that infinitely little may by itself create an expression that is absolutely unique, an individuality—it was not only the infinitely little of its lines and the originality of its expression that made each of these faces appear irreducible to terms of any other. Between my friends' faces their colouring established a separation wider still, not so much by the varied beauty of the tones with which it provided them, so contrasted that I felt when I looked at Rosemonde—flooded with a sulphurous rose colour, with the further contrast of the greenish light in her eyes—and then at Andrée—whose white cheeks received such an austere distinction from her black hair—the same kind of pleasure as if I had been looking alternately at a geranium growing by a sunlit sea and a camellia in the night; but principally because the infinitely little differences of their lines were enlarged out of all proportion, the relations between one and another surface entirely changed by this new element of colour which, in addition to being a dispenser of tints, is great at restoring, or rather at altering, dimensions. So that faces which were perhaps constructed on not dissimilar lines, according as they were lighted by the flaming torch of an auburn poll or high complexion, or by the white glimmer of a dull pallor, grew sharper or broader, became something else, like those properties used in the Russian ballet, consisting sometimes, when they are seen in the light of day, of a mere disc of paper, out of which the genius of a Bakst, according to the blood-red or moonlit effect in which he plunges his stage, makes a hard incrustation, like a turquoise on a palace well, or a swooning softness, as of a Bengal rose in an eastern garden. And so when acquiring a knowledge of faces we take careful measurements, but as painters, not as surveyors.

So it was with Albertine as with her friends. On certain days, slim, with grey cheeks, a sullen air, a violet transparency falling obliquely from her such as we notice sometimes on the sea, she seemed to be feeling the sorrows of exile. On other days her face, more sleek, caught and glued my desires to its varnished surface and prevented them from going any farther; unless I caught a sudden glimpse of her from the side, for her dull cheeks, like white wax on the surface, were visibly pink beneath, which made me anxious to kiss them, to reach that different tint which thus avoided my touch. At other times happiness bathed her cheeks with a clarity so mobile that the skin, grown fluid and vague, gave passage to a sort of stealthy and sub-cutaneous gaze, which made it appear to be of another colour but not of another substance than her eyes; sometimes, instinctively, when one looked at her face punctuated with tiny brown marks among which floated what were simply two larger, bluer stains, it was like looking at the egg of a goldfinch—or often like an opalescent agate cut and polished in two places only, where, from the heart of the brown stone, shone like the transparent wings of a sky-blue butterfly her eyes, those features in which the flesh becomes a mirror and gives us the illusion that it allows us, more than through the other parts of the body, to approach the soul. But most often of all she shewed more colour, and was then more animated; sometimes the only pink thing in her white face was the tip of her nose, as finely pointed as that of a mischievous kitten with which one would have liked to stop and play; sometimes her cheeks were so glossy that one's glance slipped, as over the surface of a miniature, over their pink enamel, which was made to appear still more delicate, more private, by the enclosing though half-opened case of her black hair; or it might happen that the tint of her cheeks had deepened to the violet shade of the red cyclamen, and, at times, even, when she was flushed or feverish, with a suggestion of un-healthiness which lowered my desire to something more sensual and made her glance expressive of something more perverse and unwholesome, to the deep purple of certain roses, a red that was almost black; and each of these Albertines was different, as in every fresh appearance of the dancer whose colours, form, character, are transmuted according to the innumer-ably varied play of a projected limelight. It was perhaps because they were so different, the persons whom I used to contemplate in her at this period, that later on I became myself a different person, corresponding to the par-ticular Albertine to whom my thoughts had turned; a jealous, an indif-ferent, a voluptuous, a melancholy, a frenzied person, created anew not merely by the accident of what memory had risen to the surface, but in proportion also to the strength of the belief that was lent to the support of one and the same memory by the varying manner in which I appreciated it. For this is the point to which we must always return, to these beliefs with which most of the time we are quite unconsciously filled, but which for all that are of more importance to our happiness than is the average person whom we see, for it is through them that we see him, it is they that impart his momentary greatness to the person seen. To be quite accurate I ought to give a different name to each of the 'me's' who were to think about Albertine in time to come; I ought still more to give a different name

to each of the Albertines who appeared before me, never the same, like—
called by me simply and for the sake of convenience 'the sea'—those seas
that succeeded one another on the beach, in front of which, a nymph likewise, she stood apart. But above all, in the same way as, in telling a story
(though to far greater purpose here), one mentions what the weather was
like on such and such a day, I ought always to give its name to the belief
that, on any given day on which I saw Albertine, was reigning in my soul,
creating its atmosphere, the appearance of people like that of seas being
dependent on those clouds, themselves barely visible, which change the
colour of everything by their concentration, their mobility, their dissemination, their flight—like that cloud which Elstir had rent one evening by
not introducing me to these girls, with whom he had stopped to talk, whereupon their forms, as they moved away, had suddenly increased in beauty
—a cloud that had formed again a few days later when I did get to know
the girls, veiling their brightness, interposing itself frequently between my
eyes and them, opaque and soft, like Virgil's Leucothea.

No doubt, all their faces had assumed quite new meanings for me since
the manner in which they were to be read had been to some extent indicated
to me by their talk, talk to which I could ascribe a value all the greater in
that, by questioning them, I could prompt it whenever I chose, could vary
it like an experimenter who seeks by corroborative proofs to establish the
truth of his theory. And it is, after all, as good a way as any of solving the
problem of existence to approach near enough to the things that have appeared to us from a distance to be beautiful and mysterious, to be able to
satisfy ourselves that they have neither mystery nor beauty. It is one of
the systems of hygiene among which we are at liberty to choose our own,
a system which is perhaps not to be recommended too strongly, but it gives
us a certain tranquillity with which to spend what remains of life, and also
—since it enables us to regret nothing, by assuring us that we have attained
to the best, and that the best was nothing out of the common—with which
to resign ourselves to death.

I had now substituted, in the brains of these girls, for their supposed
contempt for chastity, their memories of daily 'incidents,' honest principles,
liable, it might be, to relaxation, but principles which had hitherto kept
unscathed the children who had acquired them in their own respectable
homes. And yet, when one has been mistaken from the start, even in trifling
details, when an error of assumption or recollection makes one seek for the
author of a malicious slander, or for the place where one has lost something, in the wrong direction, it frequently happens that one discovers one's
error only to substitute for it not the truth but a fresh error. I drew, so
far as their manner of life and the proper way to behave with them went,
all the possible conclusions from the word 'Innocence' which I had read,
in talking familiarly with them, upon their faces. But perhaps I had been
reading carelessly, with the inaccuracy born of a too rapid deciphering,
and it was no more written there than was the name of Jules Ferry on the
programme of the performance at which I had heard Berma for the first
time, an omission which had not prevented me from maintaining to M. de

Norpois that Jules Ferry, beyond any possibility of doubt, was a person who wrote curtain-raisers.

No matter which it might be of my friends of the little band, was not inevitably the face that I had last seen the only face that I could recall, since, of our memories with respect to a person, the mind eliminates everything that does not agree with our immediate purpose of our daily relations (especially if those relations are quickened with an element of love which, ever unsatisfied, lives always in the moment that is about to come)? That purpose allows the chain of spent days to slip away, holding on only to the very end of it, often of a quite different metal from the links that have vanished in the night, and in the journey which we make through life, counts as real only in the place in which we at any given moment are. But all those earliest impressions, already so remote, could not find, against the blunting process that assailed them day after day, any remedy in my memory; during the long hours which I spent in talking, eating, playing with these girls, I did not remember even that they were the same ruthless, sensual virgins whom I had seen, as in a fresco, file past between me and the sea.

Geographers, archaeologists may conduct us over Calypso's island, may excavate the Palace of Minos. Only Calypso becomes then nothing more than a woman, Minos than a king with no semblance of divinity. Even the good and bad qualities which history teaches us to have been the attributes of those quite real personages, often differ widely from those which we had ascribed to the fabulous beings who bore the same names as they. Thus had there faded and vanished all the lovely mythology of Ocean which I had composed in those first days. But it is not altogether immaterial that we do succeed, at any rate now and then, in spending our time in familiar intercourse with what we have thought to be unattainable and have longed to possess. In our later dealings with people whom at first we found disagreeable there persists always, even among the artificial pleasure which we have come at length to enjoy in their society, the lingering taint of the defects which they have succeeded in hiding. But, in relations such as I was now having with Albertine and her friends, the genuine pleasure which was there at the start leaves that fragrance which no amount of skill can impart to hot-house fruits, to grapes that have not ripened in the sun. The supernatural creatures which for a little time they had been to me still introduced, even without any intention on my part, a miraculous element into the most commonplace dealings that I might have with them, or rather prevented such dealings from ever becoming commonplace at all. My desire had sought so ardently to learn the significance of the eyes which now knew and smiled to see me, but whose glances on the first day had crossed mine like rays from another universe; it had distributed so generously, so carefully, so minutely, colour and fragrance over the carnation surfaces of these girls who now, outstretched on the cliff-top, were simply offering me sandwiches or guessing riddles, that often, in the afternoon, while I lay there among them, like those painters who seek to match the grandeurs of antiquity in modern life, give to a woman cutting her toe-nail the nobility of the *Spinario,* or, like Rubens, make goddesses out of women whom they know, to people some mythological scene; at those lovely forms, dark and fair, so dissimilar in type, scattered around me in the grass, I would gaze without emptying them, perhaps, of all the mediocre contents with which my everyday experience had filled them, and at the same time without expressly recalling their heavenly origin, as if, like young Hercules or young Telemachus, I had been set to play amid a band of nymphs.

Then the concerts ended, the bad weather began, my friends left Balbec; not all at once, like the swallows, but all in the same week. Albertine was the first to go, abruptly, without any of her friends understanding, then or afterwards, why she had returned suddenly to Paris whither neither her work nor any amusement summoned her. "She said neither why nor wherefore, and with that she left!" muttered Françoise, who, for that matter, would have liked us to leave as well. We were, she thought, inconsiderate towards the staff, now greatly reduced in number, but retained on account of the few visitors who were still staying on, and towards the manager who was 'just eating up money.' It was true that the hotel, which would very soon be closed for the winter, had long since seen most of its patrons depart, but never had it been so attractive. This view was not shared by the manager; from end to end of the rooms in which we sat shivering, and and at the doors of which no page now stood on guard, he paced the corridors, wearing a new frock coat, so well tended by the hairdresser that his insipid face appeared to be made of some composition in which, for one part of flesh, there were three of cosmetics, incessantly changing his neckties. (These refinements cost less than having the place heated and keeping on the staff, just as a man who is no longer able to subscribe ten thousand francs to a charity can still parade his generosity without inconvenience to himself by tipping the boy who brings him a telegram with five.) He appeared to be inspecting the empty air, to be seeking to give, by the smartness of his personal appearance, a provisional splendour to the desolation that could now be felt in this hotel where the season had not been good, and walked like the ghost of a monarch who returns to haunt the ruins of what was once his palace. He was particularly annoyed when the little local railway company, finding the supply of passengers inadequate, discontinued its trains until the following spring. "What is lacking here," said the manager, "is the means of commotion." In spite of the deficit which his books shewed, he was making plans for the future on a lavish scale. And as he was, after all, capable of retaining an exact memory of fine language when it was directly applicable to the hotel-keeping industry and had the effect of enhancing its importance: "I was not adequately supported, although in the dining room I had an efficient squad," he explained; "but the pages left something to be desired. You will see, next year, what a phalanx I shall collect." In the meantime the suspension of the services of the B. C. B. obliged him to send for letters and occasionally to dispatch visitors in a light cart. I would often ask leave to sit by the driver, and in this way I managed to be out in all weathers, as in the winter that I had spent at Combray.

Sometimes, however, the driving rain kept my grandmother and me, the Casino being closed, in rooms almost completely deserted, as in the lowest hold of a ship when a storm is raging; and there, day by day, as in the course of a sea-voyage, a new person from among those in whose company we had spent three months without getting to know them, the chief magistrate from Caen, the leader of the Cherbourg bar, an American lady and her daughters, came up to us, started conversation, discovered some way of making the time pass less slowly, revealed some social accomplishment, taught us a new game, invited us to drink tea or to listen to music, to meet them at a certain hour, to plan together some of those diversions which contain the true secret of pleasure-giving, which is to aim not at giving pleasure but simply at helping us to pass the time of our boredom, in a word, formed with us, at the end of our stay at Balbec, ties of friendship which, in a day or two, their successive departures from the place would sever. I even made the acquaintance of the rich young man, of one of his pair of aristocratic friends and of the actress, who had reappeared for a few days; but their little society was composed now of three persons only, the other friend having returned to Paris. They asked me to come out to dinner with them at their restaurant. I think, they were just as well pleased that I did not accept. But they had given the invitation in the most friendly way imaginable, and albeit it came actually from the rich young man, since the others were only his guests, as the friend who was staying with him, the Marquis Maurice de Vaudémont, came of a very good family indeed, instinctively the actress, in asking me whether I would not come, said, to flatter my vanity: "Maurice will be so pleased."

And when in the hall of the hotel I met them all three together, it was M. de Vaudémont (the rich young man effacing himself) who said to me: "Won't you give us the pleasure of dining with us?"

On the whole I had derived very little benefit from Balbec, but this only strengthened my desire to return there. It seemed to me that I had not stayed there long enough. This was not what my friends at home were thinking, who wrote to ask whether I meant to stay there for the rest of my life. And when I saw that it was the name 'Balbec' which they were obliged to put on the envelope—just as my window looked out not over a landscape or a street but on to the plains of the sea, as I heard through the night its murmur to which I had before going to sleep entrusted my ship of dreams, I had the illusion that this life of promiscuity with the waves must effectively, without my knowledge, pervade me with the notion of their charm, like those lessons which one learns by heart while one is asleep.

The manager offered to reserve better rooms for me next year, but I had now become attached to mine, into which I went without ever noticing the scent of flowering grasses, while my mind, which had once found such difficulty in rising to fill its space had come now to take its measurements so exactly that I was obliged to submit it to a reverse process when I had to sleep in Paris, in my own room, the ceiling of which was low.

It was high time, indeed, to leave Balbec, for the cold and damp had become too penetrating for us to stay any longer in a hotel which had neither fireplaces in the rooms nor a central furnace. Moreover, I forgot almost immediately these last weeks of our stay. What my mind's eye did almost invariably see when I thought of Balbec were the hours which, every morning during the fine weather, as I was going out in the afternoon with Albertine and her friends, my grandmother, following the doctor's orders, insisted on my spending lying down, with the room darkened. The manager gave instructions that no noise was to be made on my landing, and came up himself to see that they were obeyed. Because the light outside was so strong, I kept drawn for as long as possible the big violet curtains which had adopted so hostile an attitude towards me the first evening. But as, in spite of the pins with which, so that the light should not enter, Françoise fastened them every night, pins which she alone knew how to unfasten; as in spite of the rugs, the red cretonne table-cover, the various fabrics collected here and there which she fitted in to her defensive scheme, she never succeeded in making them meet exactly, the darkness was not complete, and they allowed to spill over the carpet as it were a scarlet shower of anemone-petals, among which I could not resist the temptation to plunge my bare feet for a moment. And on the wall which faced the window and so was partially lighted, a cylinder of gold with no visible support was placed vertically and moved slowly along like the pillar of fire which went before the Hebrews in the desert. I went back to bed; obliged to taste without moving, in imagination only, and all at once, the pleasures of games, bathing, walks which the morning prompted, joy made my heart beat thunderingly like a machine set going at full speed but fixed to the ground, which can spend its energy only by turning upon its own axis.

I knew that my friends were on the 'front,' but I did not see them as they passed before the links of the sea's uneven chain, far at the back of which, and nestling amid its bluish peaks like an Italian citadel, one could occasionally, in a clear moment, make out the little town of Rivebelle, drawn in minutest detail by the sun. I did not see my friends, but (while there mounted to my belvedere the shout of the newsboy, the 'journalists' as Françoise used to call them, the shouts of the bathers and of children at play, punctuating like the cries of sea-birds the sound of the gently breaking waves) I guessed their presence, I heard their laughter enveloped like the laughter of the Nereids in the smooth tide of sound that rose to my ears. "We looked up," said Albertine in the evening, "to see if you were coming down. But your shutters were still closed when the concert began." At ten o'clock, sure enough, it broke out beneath my windows. In the intervals in the blare of the instruments, if the tide were high, would begin again, slurred and continuous, the gliding surge of a wave which seemed to enfold the notes of the violin in its crystal spirals and to be spraying its foam over echoes of a submarine music. I grew impatient because no one had yet come with my things, so that I might rise and dress. Twelve o'clock struck, Françoise arrived at last. And for months on end, in this Balbec to which I had so looked forward because I imagined it only as battered by the storm and buried in fogs, the weather had been so dazzling and so unchanging that when she came to open the window I could always, without once being wrong, expect to see the same patch of sunlight folded in the corner of the outer wall, of an unalterable colour which was less moving as a sign of summer than depressing as the colour of a lifeless and composed enamel. And after Françoise had removed her pins from the mouldings of the window-frame, taken down her various cloths, and drawn back the curtains, the summer day which she disclosed seemed as dead, as immemorially ancient as would have been a sumptuously attired dynastic mummy from which our old sérvant had done no more than precautionally unwind the linen wrappings before displaying it to my gaze, embalmed in its vesture of gold.

MARCEL PROUST (1871–1922) was born and died in Paris. Educated at the Lycée Condorcet, he did one year's military service and briefly studied law and political science. Proust's charm and ambition gained him entrance to the *salons* of Parisian society—the setting that provides the background for *A la recherche du temps perdu.* After his mother's death in 1905 Proust, suffering from asthma, retreated from active social life and secluded himself in a cork-lined room in his Paris apartment. From 1910 on he was at work on *A la recherche du temps perdu*, publishing the first volume at his own expense in 1913. In 1920 the second volume won him the Prix Goncourt. Until his death in 1922 he continued writing and rewriting his monumental work.

VINTAGE FICTION, POETRY, AND PLAYS

V-814   **ABE, KOBO** / The Woman in the Dunes
V-2014   **AUDEN, W. H.** / Collected Longer Poems
V-2015   **AUDEN, W. H.** / Collected Shorter Poems 1927-1957
V-102   **AUDEN, W. H.** / Selected Poetry of W. H. Auden
V-601   **AUDEN, W. H. AND PAUL B. TAYLOR (trans.)** / The Elder Edda
V-20   **BABIN, MARIA-THERESA AND STAN STEINER (eds.)** / Borinquen: An Anthology of Puerto-Rican Literature
V-271   **BEDIER, JOSEPH** / Tristan and Iseult
V-523   **BELLAMY, JOE DAVID (ed.)** / Superfiction or The American Story Transformed: An Anthology
V-72   **BERNIKOW, LOUISE (ed.)** / The World Split Open: Four Centuries of Women Poets in England and America 1552-1950
V-321   **BOLT, ROBERT** / A Man for All Seasons
V-21   **BOWEN, ELIZABETH** / The Death of the Heart
V-294   **BRADBURY, RAY** / The Vintage Bradbury
V-670   **BRECHT, BERTOLT (ed. by Ralph Manheim and John Willett)** / Collected Plays, Vol. 1
V-759   **BRECHT, BERTOLT (ed. by Ralph Manheim and John Willett)** / Collected Plays, Vol. 5
V-216   **BRECHT, BERTOLT (ed. by Ralph Manheim and John Willett)** / Collected Plays, Vol. 7
V-819   **BRECHT, BERTOLT (ed. by Ralph Manheim and John Willett)** / Collected Plays, Vol. 9
V-841   **BYNNER, WITTER AND KIANG KANG-HU (eds.)** / The Jade Mountain: A Chinese Anthology
V-207   **CAMUS, ALBERT** / Caligula & Three Other Plays
V-281   **CAMUS, ALBERT** / Exile and the Kingdom
V-223   **CAMUS, ALBERT** / The Fall
V-865   **CAMUS, ALBERT** / A Happy Death: A Novel
V-626   **CAMUS, ALBERT** / Lyrical and Critical Essays
V-75   **CAMUS, ALBERT** / The Myth of Sisyphus and Other Essays
V-258   **CAMUS, ALBERT** / The Plague
V-245   **CAMUS, ALBERT** / The Possessed
V-30   **CAMUS, ALBERT** / The Rebel
V-2   **CAMUS, ALBERT** / The Stranger
V-28   **CATHER, WILLA** / Five Stories
V-705   **CATHER, WILLA** / A Lost Lady
V-200   **CATHER, WILLA** / My Mortal Enemy
V-179   **CATHER, WILLA** / Obscure Destinies
V-252   **CATHER, WILLA** / One of Ours
V-913   **CATHER, WILLA** / The Professor's House
V-434   **CATHER, WILLA** / Sapphira and the Slave Girl
V-680   **CATHER, WILLA** / Shadows on the Rock
V-684   **CATHER, WILLA** / Youth and the Bright Medusa
V-140   **CERF, BENNETT (ed.)** / Famous Ghost Stories
V-203   **CERF, BENNETT (ed.)** / Four Contemporary American Plays
V-127   **CERF, BENNETT (ed.)** / Great Modern Short Stories
V-326   **CERF, CHRISTOPHER (ed.)** / The Vintage Anthology of Science Fantasy
V-293   **CHAUCER, GEOFFREY** / The Canterbury Tales (a prose version in Modern English)
V-142   **CHAUCER, GEOFFREY** / Troilus and Cressida
V-723   **CHERNYSHEVSKY, N. G.** / What Is to Be Done?
V-173   **CONFUCIUS (trans. by Arthur Waley)** / Analects
V-155   **CONRAD, JOSEPH** / Three Great Tales: The Nigger of the Narcissus, Heart of Darkness, Youth
V-10   **CRANE, STEPHEN** / Stories and Tales
V-126   **DANTE, ALIGHIERI** / The Divine Comedy
V-177   **DINESEN, ISAK** / Anecdotes of Destiny

VINTAGE POLITICAL SCIENCE AND SOCIAL CRITICISM

V-568 **ALINSKY, SAUL D.** / Reveille for Radicals
V-736 **ALINSKY, SAUL D.** / Rules for Radicals
V-726 **ALLENDE, PRESIDENT SALVADOR AND REGIS DEBRAY** / The Chilean Revolution
V-286 **ARIES, PHILIPPE** / Centuries of Childhood
V-604 **BAILYN, BERNARD** / Origins of American Politics
V-334 **BALTZELL, E. DIGBY** / The Protestant Establishment
V-571 **BARTH, ALAN** / Prophets With Honor: Great Dissents & Great Dissenters in the Supreme Court
V-791 **BAXANDALL, LEE (ed.) AND WILHELM REICH** / Sex-Pol.: Essays 1929-1934
V-60 **BECKER, CARL L.** / The Declaration of Independence
V-563 **BEER, SAMUEL H.** / British Politics in the Collectivist Age
V-994 **BERGER, PETER & BRIGITTE AND HANSFRIED KELLNER** / The Homeless Mind: Modernization and Consciousness
V-77 **BINZEN, PETER** / Whitetown, USA
V-513 **BOORSTIN, DANIEL J.** / The Americans: The Colonial Experience
V-11 **BOORSTIN, DANIEL J.** / The Americans: The Democratic Experience
V-358 **BOORSTIN, DANIEL J.** / The Americans: The National Experience
V-501 **BOORSTIN, DANIEL J.** / Democracy and Its Discontents: Reflections on Everyday America
V-414 **BOTTOMORE, T. B.** / Classes in Modern Society
V-742 **BOTTOMORE, T. B.** / Sociology: A Guide to Problems & Literature
V-305 **BREINES, SIMON AND WILLIAM J. DEAN** / The Pedestrian Revolution: Streets Without Cars
V-44 **BRINTON, CRANE** / The Anatomy of Revolution
V-30 **CAMUS, ALBERT** / The Rebel
V-966 **CAMUS, ALBERT** / Resistance, Rebellion & Death
V-33 **CARMICHAEL, STOKELY AND CHARLES HAMILTON** / Black Power
V-2024 **CARO, ROBERT A.** / The Power Broker: Robert Moses and The Fall of New York
V-862 **CASE, JOHN AND GERRY HUNNIUS AND DAVID G. CARSON** / Workers Control: A Reader on Labor and Social Change
V-98 **CASH, W. J.** / The Mind of the South
V-555 **CHOMSKY, NOAM** / American Power and the New Mandarins
V-248 **CHOMSKY, NOAM** / Peace in the Middle East? Reflections on Justice and Nationhood
V-815 **CHOMSKY, NOAM** / Problems of Knowledge and Freedom
V-788 **CIRINO, ROBERT** / Don't Blame the People
V-17 **CLARKE, TED AND DENNIS JAFFE (eds.)** / Worlds Apart: Young People and The Drug Problems
V-383 **CLOWARD, RICHARD AND FRANCES FOX PIVEN** / The Politics of Turmoil: Essays on Poverty, Race and The Urban Crisis
V-743 **CLOWARD, RICHARD AND FRANCES FOX PIVEN** / Regulating the Poor: The Functions of Public Welfare
V-940 **COBB, JONATHAN AND RICHARD SENNETT** / Hidden Injuries of Class
V-311 **CREMIN, LAWRENCE A.** / The Genius of American Education
V-519 **CREMIN, LAWRENCE A.** / The Transformation of the School
V-808 **CUMMING, ROBERT D. (ed.)** / The Philosophy of Jean-Paul Sartre
V-2019 **CUOMO, MARIO** / Forest Hills Diary: The Crisis of Low-Income Housing
V-305 **DEAN, WILLIAM J. AND SIMON BREINES** / The Pedestrian Revolution: Streets Without Cars
V-726 **DEBRAY, REGIS AND PRESIDENT SALVADOR ALLENDE** / The Chilean Revolution
V-638 **DENNISON, GEORGE** / The Lives of Children
V-746 **DEUTSCHER, ISAAC** / The Prophet Armed
V-748 **DEUTSCHER, ISAAC** / The Prophet Outcast
V-617 **DEVLIN, BERNADETTE** / The Price of My Soul

VINTAGE BELLES—LETTRES

V-418   **AUDEN, W. H.** / The Dyer's Hand
V-887   **AUDEN, W. H.** / Forewords and Afterwords
V-271   **BEDIER, JOSEPH** / Tristan and Iseult
V-512   **BLOCH, MARC** / The Historian's Craft
V-572   **BRIDGE HAMPTON** / Bridge Hampton Works & Days
V-161   **BROWN, NORMAN O.** / Closing Time
V-544   **BROWN, NORMAN O.** / Hermes the Thief
V-419   **BROWN, NORMAN O.** / Love's Body
V-75   **CAMUS, ALBERT** / The Myth of Sisyphus and Other Essays
V-30   **CAMUS, ALBERT** / The Rebel
V-608   **CARR, JOHN DICKSON** / The Life of Sir Arthur Conan Doyle: The Man Who Was Sherlock Holmes
V-407   **HARDWICK, ELIZABETH** / Seduction and Betrayal: Women and Literature
V-244   **HERRIGEL, EUGEN** / The Method of Zen
V-663   **HERRIGEL, EUGEN** / Zen in the Art of Archery
V-201   **HUGHES, H. STUART** / Consciousness & Society
V-235   **KAPLAN, ABRAHAM** / New World of Philosophy
V-337   **KAUFMANN, WALTER (trans.) AND FRIEDRICH NIETZSCHE** / Beyond Good and Evil
V-369   **KAUFMANN, WALTER (trans.) AND FRIEDRICH NIETZSCHE** / The Birth of Tragedy and the Case of Wagner
V-985   **KAUFMANN, WALTER (trans.) AND FRIEDRICH NIETZSCHE** / The Gay Science
V-401   **KAUFMANN, WALTER (trans.) AND FRIEDRICH NIETZSCHE** / On the Genealogy of Morals and Ecce Homo
V-437   **KAUFMANN, WALTER (trans.) AND FRIEDRICH NIETZSCHE** / The Will to Power
V-995   **KOTT, JAN** / The Eating of the Gods: An Interpretation of Greek Tragedy
V-685   **LESSING, DORIS** / A Small Personal Voice: Essays, Reviews, Interviews
V-329   **LINDBERGH, ANNE MORROW** / Gift from the Sea
V-479   **MALRAUX, ANDRE** / Man's Fate
V-406   **MARCUS, STEVEN** / Engels, Manchester and the Working Class
V-58   **MENCKEN, H. L.** / Prejudices (Selected by James T. Farrell)
V-25   **MENCKEN, H. L.** / The Vintage Mencken (Gathered by Alistair Cooke)
V-151   **MOFFAT, MARY JANE AND CHARLOTTE PAINTER (eds.)** / Revelations: Diaries of Women
V-926   **MUSTARD, HELEN (trans.)** / Heinrich Heine: Selected Works
V-337   **NIETZSCHE, FRIEDRICH AND WALTER KAUFMANN (trans.)** / Beyond Good and Evil
V-369   **NIETZSCHE, FRIEDRICH AND WALTER KAUFMANN (trans.)** / The Birth of Tragedy and the Case of Wagner
V-985   **NIETZSCHE, FRIEDRICH AND WALTER KAUFMANN (trans.)** / The Gay Science
V-401   **NIETZSCHE, FRIEDRICH AND WALTER KAUFMANN (trans.)** / On the Genealogy of Morals and Ecce Homo
V-437   **NIETZSCHE, FRIEDRICH AND WALTER KAUFMANN (trans.)** / The Will to Power
V-672   **OUSPENSKY, P. D.** / The Fourth Way
V-524   **OUSPENSKY, P. D.** / A New Model of the Universe
V-943   **OUSPENSKY, P. D.** / The Psychology of Man's Possible Evolution
V-639   **OUSPENSKY, P. D.** / Tertium Organum
V-151   **PAINTER, CHARLOTTE AND MARY JANE MOFFAT (eds.)** / Revelations: Diaries of Women
V-986   **PAUL, DAVID (trans.)** / Poison & Vision: Poems & Prose of Baudelaire, Mallarme and Rimbaud
V-598   **PROUST, MARCEL** / The Captive
V-597   **PROUST, MARCEL** / Cities of the Plain
V-596   **PROUST, MARCEL** / The Guermantes Way

VINTAGE HISTORY—AMERICAN

VINTAGE BIOGRAPHY AND AUTOBIOGRAPHY

VINTAGE WOMEN'S STUDIES

V-72   **BERNIKOW, LOUISE (ed.)** / The World Split Open: Four Centuries of Women Poets in England and America, 1552-1950

V-227   **DE BEAUVOIR, SIMONE** / The Second Sex

V-359   **DeCROW, KAREN** / Sexist Justice

V-642   **GLUCK, SHERNA (ed.)** / From Parlor to Prison: Five American Suffragists Talk About Their Lives

V-407   **HARDWICK, ELIZABETH** / Seduction and Betrayal: Women and Literature

V-896   **HATCH, JAMES AND VICTORIA SULLIVAN (eds.)** / Plays By and About Women

V-880   **LERNER, GERDA** / Black Women in White America: A Documentary History

V-685   **LESSING, DORIS** / A Small Personal Voice: Essays, Reviews, Interviews

V-422   **MITCHELL, JULIET** / Psychoanalysis and Feminism

V-905   **MITCHELL, JULIET** / Woman's Estate

V-851   **MORGAN, ROBIN** / Monster

V-539   **MORGAN, ROBIN (ed.)** / Sisterhood is Powerful: An Anthology of Writings from the Women's Liberation Movement

V-151   **MOFFAT, MARY JANE AND CHARLOTTE PAINTER (eds.)** / Revelations: Diaries of Women

V-960   **OAKLEY, ANN** / Woman's Work: The Housewife, Past and Present

V-151   **PAINTER, CHARLOTTE AND MARY JANE MOFFAT (eds.)** / Revelations: Diaries of Women

V-621   **ROWBOTHAM, SHEILA** / Hidden From History: Rediscovering Women in History from the 17th Century to the Present

V-954   **ROWBOTHAM, SHEILA** / Women, Resistance and Revolution: A History of Women and Revolution in the Modern World

V-41   **SARGENT, PAMELA (ed.)** / Women of Wonder: Science Fiction Stories by Women about Women

V-738   **SCHNEIR, MIRIAM (ed.)** / Feminism

V-806   **SHERFEY, MARY JANE** / The Nature and Evolution of Female Sexuality

V-896   **SULLIVAN, VICTORIA AND JAMES HATCH (eds.)** / Plays By and About Women

VINTAGE CRITICISM: LITERATURE, MUSIC, AND ART

V-570 **ANDREWS, WAYNE** / American Gothic
V-418 **AUDEN, W. H.** / The Dyer's Hand
V-887 **AUDEN, W. H.** / Forewords and Afterwords
V-161 **BROWN, NORMAN O.** / Closing Time
V-75 **CAMUS, ALBERT** / The Myth of Sisyphus and Other Essays
V-626 **CAMUS, ALBERT** / Lyrical and Critical Essays
V-535 **EISEN, JONATHAN** / The Age of Rock: Sounds of the American Cultural Revolution
V-4 **EINSTEIN, ALFRED** / A Short History of Music
V-13 **GILBERT, STUART** / James Joyce's Ulysses
V-407 **HARDWICK, ELIZABETH** / Seduction and Betrayal: Women and Literature
V-114 **HAUSER, ARNOLD** / Social History of Art, Vol. I
V-115 **HAUSER, ARNOLD** / Social History of Art, Vol. II
V-116 **HAUSER, ARNOLD** / Social History of Art, Vol. III
V-117 **HAUSER, ARNOLD** / Social History of Art, Vol. IV
V-610 **HSU, KAI-YU** / The Chinese Literary Scene
V-201 **HUGHES, H. STUART** / Consciousness and Society
V-88 **KERMAN, JOSEPH** / Opera as Drama
V-995 **KOTT, JAN** / The Eating of the Gods: An Interpretation of Greek Tragedy
V-685 **LESSING, DORIS** / A Small Personal Voice: Essays, Reviews, Interviews
V-677 **LESTER, JULIUS** / The Seventh Son, Vol. I
V-678 **LESTER, JULIUS** / The Seventh Son, Vol. II
V-720 **MIRSKY, D. S.** / A History of Russian Literature
V-118 **NEWMAN, ERNEST** / Great Operas, Vol. I
V-119 **NEWMAN, ERNEST** / Great Operas, Vol. II
V-976 **QUASHA, GEORGE AND JEROME ROTHENBERG (eds.)** / America A Prophecy: A New Reading of American Poetry from Pre-Columbian Times to the Present
V-976 **ROTHENBERG, JEROME AND GEORGE QUASHA (eds.)** / America A Prophecy: A New Reading of American Poetry from Pre-Columbian Times to the Present
V-415 **SHATTUCK, ROGER** / The Banquet Years, Revised
V-435 **SPENDER, STEPHEN** / Love-Hate Relations: English and American Sensibilities
V-278 **STEVENS, WALLACE** / The Necessary Angel
V-100 **SULLIVAN, J. W. N.** / Beethoven: His Spiritual Development
V-166 **SZE, MAI-MAI** / The Way of Chinese Painting
V-162 **TILLYARD, E. M. W.** / The Elizabethan World Picture